Hope Springs

Books 7-9

Not Until Someday

Not Until Now

Not Until Then

Valerie M. Bodden

Hope Springs Books 7-9 © 2023 by Valerie M. Bodden.

NOT UNTIL SOMEDAY

NOT UNTIL NOW

NOT UNTIL THEN

Not Until Someday Copyright © 2020 by Valerie M. Bodden. All Rights Reserved.

Not Until Now Copyright © 2021 by Valerie M. Bodden. All Rights Reserved.

Not Until Then Copyright © 2022 by Valerie M. Bodden. All Rights Reserved.

Scriptures taken from the Holy Bible, New International Version®, NIV®. Copyright © 1973, 1978, 1984, 2011 by Biblica, Inc.™ Used by permission of Zondervan. All rights reserved worldwide. www.zondervan.com The "NIV" and "New International Version" are trademarks registered in the United States Patent and Trademark Office by Biblica, Inc.™

All rights reserved. No portion of this book may be reproduced in any form without permission from the publisher, except as permitted by U.S. copyright law.

This is a work of fiction. Names, characters, places, and incidents either are products of the author's imagination or used in a fictitious manner. Any resemblance to any person, living or dead, is coincidental.

Valerie M. Bodden

Visit me at www.valeriembodden.com

Hope Springs Series

Not Until Forever
Not Until This Moment
Not Until You
Not Until Us
Not Until Christmas Morning
Not Until This Day
Not Until Someday
Not Until Now
Not Until Then
Not Until The End

River Falls Series

Pieces of Forever
Songs of Home
Memories of the Heart
Whispers of Truth
Promises of Mercy
Hearts of Hope

River Falls Christmas Romances

Christmas of Joy

Love on Sanctuary Shores

Trusting His Promise

A Hope Springs Gift for You

Members of my Reader's Club get a FREE book, available exclusively to my subscribers. When you sign up, you'll also be the first to know about new releases, book deals, and giveaways.
Visit www.valeriembodden.com/gift to join!

Need a refresher of who's who in the Hope Springs series?

If you love the whole gang in Hope Springs but need a refresher of who's who and how everyone is connected, check out the handy character map at https://www.valeriembodden.com/hscharacters

Not Until Someday

A Hope Springs Novel

Valerie M. Bodden

Not as I will, but as you will.

Matthew 26:39

Chapter 1

"Hey, aren't you Levi Donovan?"

Levi grabbed the bottled water out of the rest stop vending machine and turned toward the kid standing behind him.

"Sure am." His eyes tracked from the freckle-faced boy—maybe twelve years old, if Levi had to guess—to the attractive woman standing with her hand on the kid's shoulder. A hand that didn't sport a wedding ring. "I see you're a Titans fan." He gestured to the boy's cap. "You want me to autograph that?" He directed the question to the kid but kept his eyes on the mom.

The kid shrugged and passed his cap to Levi.

Levi patted the pocket of his leather riding jacket. Time was, he'd never left home without a pen for just such an occasion.

"You used to be pretty good," the kid said. "You ever going to play again?"

Pretty good? Levi resisted the urge to correct the kid. His rookie season, he'd set a new passing yards record. A record he'd then beaten three years in a row, until he'd been sidelined by an ACL injury.

"Nah. I'm retired now." At twenty-nine. Not that he'd had much of a choice. His comeback attempt had been less than stellar, with a broken thumb and a stress fracture in his foot.

Anyway, he'd been released, no teams had picked him up, and now here he was, getting a rush from signing some kid's cap in a rest stop.

Or not signing it. He gave his pocket another pat. "Sorry, Sport. I don't have a pen. Maybe your mom does?" He returned his gaze to the woman.

"I'm sure I do." She rummaged in her purse, retrieving a pen with a smile and passing it to Levi. He let his fingertips subtly brush hers as he took it, then signed his name across the cap with a flourish.

"Where you folks headed?" He passed the cap back to the kid.

"Disney World." The kid bounced on his toes. "Where are you going?"

"Nowhere as exciting as that." Actually, every time Levi thought about where he was going, he considered turning his Harley right back around.

"Thank you." The mom smiled at him. "This was sweet of you."

He tipped his chin and headed for the parking lot. "Have a good trip."

When he reached the Harley he'd purchased the moment he was no longer under a contract that prohibited riding, he tucked his water into the saddlebag and pulled on his helmet. He had hundreds of miles of open road ahead of him before he arrived in Hope Springs.

And he was going to enjoy them.

Because goodness knew he wasn't planning to enjoy his time there.

Grace dipped her head to pull in a deep breath of the mixed bouquet—asters, roses, tulips, some sort of lilies, and tiny white flowers she couldn't identify but that gave the whole arrangement a heavenly scent.

This was it. The perfect bouquet.

She meandered toward the flower shop's counter, smiling at the high school student working the register.

"These are pretty." The girl wrapped the flowers in paper. "Who are they for?"

"Myself. A birthday indulgence."

"You're buying yourself birthday flowers? That's so sad." The girl gave her a pitying look, eyeing her as if she were an old maid, and Grace bit her tongue against the urge to say she was only twenty-nine. She supposed that would seem like an old maid to a sixteen-year-old.

"Don't feel bad for me." Grace was careful not to let her smile slip. "I happen to love buying myself flowers. I always get the ones I want that way."

Actually, the last few years, a guy *had* bought her birthday flowers—but not the way the employee meant it. It had been her grandfather. This was her first birthday without him, and she'd found herself missing him so much that she'd decided to come out and buy herself a bouquet.

She took her credit card back, tucked it into her purse, and scooped up the flowers, keeping her chin up as she made her way to the door.

In the car, she nestled the flowers into the passenger seat, then leaned back against the headrest and blew out a long breath. It wasn't that she minded buying flowers for herself—or even that she minded being alone. It was just that she was so tired of everyone assuming that because she didn't have a boyfriend, her life was empty.

She wouldn't mind having someone someday—but only if it was the right someone. She'd learned the hard way that it was better to have no one than the wrong one.

It was why she kept a checklist in her head: loves and serves the Lord, good with kids, sensitive enough to show emotion, kind to others, and drives a sensible car.

If she could find a man who checked all those boxes, she'd be happy to settle down. But until then, she was perfectly content on her own.

She slid the key into the ignition, but before she could start the car, her phone rang. She dug it out of her purse, suppressing a groan as Mama's picture flashed on the screen. Speaking of people who assumed she needed a man—not to mention, a passel of kids.

Maybe she should let it go to voicemail. But Mama would know Grace was ignoring her call. And she was probably only calling to wish Grace a happy birthday—maybe as a gift, she'd avoid mentioning Grace's lack of a boyfriend.

Here was hoping. "Hi, Mama."

"Happy birthday, Grace." Mama's Southern accent was soft but slightly more pronounced than Grace's. "How's your special day going?"

"Great." Grace made sure to fill her voice with cheer. "I just came from working on a fundraiser at church." She left out the part about buying flowers for herself. Mama would certainly take the flower shop cashier's view of things. "Now I'm headed home to make sure everything is ready to start the renovation on Grandfather's place next week."

A flutter of excitement went through her as she backed out of her parking space. She still couldn't believe Grandfather had left her the house that had been in the family for four generations. She'd spoken to him so many times about what a beautiful bed-and-breakfast it would make, but never had she imagined he would leave her the home—and the money to make her dream possible.

"I still don't understand why you feel the need to do this." Mama put on the voice she always assumed for guilt trips.

"I know you don't, Mama." Even though Grace had tried to explain it to her about a million times. "It's just something I need to do." She didn't add that it felt like a calling—like she'd at last found her purpose in life.

As far as Mama was concerned, she should only have one purpose. Babies.

"You're not getting any younger, you know."

"Yes, Mama, I know that." Mama had only reminded her every birthday for the past five years.

"By the time I was twenty-nine," Mama kept going, "I'd been married eight years and had five children."

"Four children, Mama. I'm number four."

"Whatever." Impatience shortened the word. "The point is, that's a lot more children than you currently have."

"Yes, Mama." That was a tension headache starting behind her eyes.

"Isn't it time to sell that old house and come home? Get married. Settle down. Give me some grandbabies."

"Mama, I told you, I don't—" Grace glanced down as the car's gas light dinged on.

"Before you tell me you're not interested in coming home, I've got some news that will change your mind," Mama chirped.

Grace shifted her phone to her other hand as she turned onto Hope Street and followed it past the fudge shop and the bakery and the antique store toward the edge of town.

"What are you talking about, Mama?"

"Remember Aaron Cooper? He just moved back to River Falls. He's our new youth pastor."

Grace could almost picture Mama waving pom-poms on the other end of the line.

"Of course I remember Aaron Cooper." His daddy and hers had served together at the Bible camp her daddy had run when Grace was younger. Aaron had practically been a part of her family, until the camp had closed when she was in middle school. Last she'd heard, his family had been in the mission field.

"Well, he's all grown up now. Very good-looking too. And single."

"That's nice, Mama."

"You know, I always thought he'd be a good match for you."

Grace snorted. "Mama, we were eleven when he moved away."

"I know, but if he had stayed, maybe everything with Hunter wouldn't have happened."

"But it did happen." She didn't exactly want to spend her birthday dwelling on the biggest mistake of her life.

She slowed and pulled into the gas station.

"Well, he's back now," Mama repeated. "And I still think you two would be perfect together."

"We haven't seen each other in nearly twenty years."

"Yes, but when I showed him your picture and told him you were single, he—"

"Mama!" Grace yanked the steering wheel toward a gas pump.

"What?" Mama's voice was all calm innocence. "He happens to be looking for a wife. It's perfect."

Grace shook her head violently enough that she'd be surprised if Mama didn't get dizzy through the phone. "Mama, it's not perfect." Heavens to Betsy, she couldn't believe they were having this conversation. "I don't even know Aaron Cooper anymore. And he's in River Falls, and I'm in Hope Springs."

"That's easy enough to fix."

"And I'm seeing someone." The words popped out of Grace's mouth before the thought had fully formed in her mind.

"You are?" Mama's voice rang with surprise. "Why didn't you say so?"

Grace rubbed at her temple. She couldn't very well say it was because she'd just thought of it.

"It's new, Mama." She opened her car door and stood waiting at the pump. There had to be a way to wrap up this conversation before she said anything even stupider.

"Well, who is he? What's his name? You're sure he's a good one? You know your judgment can be . . ."

A motorcycle roared up to the other side of Grace's gas pump.

Thank you, Lord.

"Sorry, Mama," she shouted to be heard over the motorcycle's engine. "I can't hear you. We'll talk more later." She hung up and tossed the phone into the car just as the motorcycle's engine cut off.

She lifted the gas pump, trying to figure out what she'd been thinking, telling Mama she was seeing someone when she hadn't been on a date in years.

She'd just have to pray that Mama would forget she'd said anything.

Sure. Mama was about as likely to forget as the right guy was to materialize right here at the gas station.

"Long day?"

The deep voice made her jump, and Grace spun around. "Excuse me?"

The motorcyclist on the other side of the pump had pulled his helmet off to reveal mussed dark hair and a charming smile, complete with dimple.

"Sorry, you looked like you were having one of those days. Can I get you a coffee? Cheer you up?"

"Ah, no. I'm fine, thanks." Grace gave him a tight smile. Though she usually enjoyed meeting new people, she was very much not in the mood for small talk right now.

"Do you have a piece of paper and a pen I could borrow?" the stranger asked.

"Uh. Sure." Ducking her head back into the car, Grace rummaged in her purse until she'd found the requested items, then passed them to the guy and busied herself washing the car windows.

When she was done, he was leaning against the gas pump, waiting. He passed her the pen, then the paper. "For you."

"What's this?" She glanced at the handwriting scrawled on the paper. A name and a phone number.

"My number. In case you decide you want that coffee after all. I'd love to take you out."

Grace stared at him. How could he know he'd love to take her out? Until two minutes ago, he'd never seen her before in his life.

"Thanks." She forced a smile as she passed the paper back to him. As certain as she was of what she wanted in a man, she was equally sure of what she *didn't* want. And a motorcycle-riding bad boy topped that list. She'd been down that road once before, and it had almost cost her everything.

"I'm actually seeing someone." Well, why not? If her imaginary boyfriend could get her out of a conversation with Mama, why not use him to make this guy back off too?

"Oh." He looked mildly surprised, as if no one had ever turned him down before. "Sorry. I should have realized." He gestured toward her car. "He must be a good one if he got you flowers."

"Yeah." Grace flipped the gas pump off though her tank wasn't full yet. "It was nice to meet you."

She jumped into her car and sped away before she had to tell any more lies about Mr. Invisible.

Chapter 2

Oh well.

There'd be others.

Levi shrugged as he watched the woman drive off, then got on his bike and pulled away from the gas station.

It was her mocha eyes. That was what had made him ask her out in the first place. He'd always been a sucker for dark eyes.

That and the way she'd stood at the gas pump, looking so forlorn.

He'd been so sure she would be an easy yes that he hadn't even taken a moment to consider that she might turn him down.

It didn't matter. It wasn't like he'd been interested in anything more serious than a single date, maybe two.

Never more than that.

Levi leaned into a turn, the town feeling strangely familiar and yet new at the same time. He hadn't been home in over two years, and he suddenly couldn't remember if the awning over the antique store had always been blue and white or whether the sign at the marina had always been so big.

Too soon, he was slowing for the turn into his parents' driveway. As he parked and took off his helmet, the house too felt strangely new and old all at once. He would have sworn on his Super Bowl ring that the home he'd grown up in was yellow, but the siding was now taupe, with blue shutters. And the plum tree that he'd climbed as a kid was missing from the front yard. He double-checked the address.

Yep. This was the right place.

Modest. That was the word to describe this house.

Not bad. But nothing compared to what he could have bought his parents if they'd let him.

But every time he'd offered, he'd received the same answer—they were comfortable here.

So he'd stopped offering.

Hanging his helmet from the bike's handlebars, Levi grabbed his pack from the luggage rack, then made his way up the porch steps to the front door. It all felt a little surreal, as if maybe this was one of those dreams where everything was the same as in real life but different.

Until the front door sprang open and Mom was launching herself at him, pulling him into a ferocious hug. "I wasn't sure you'd come."

Levi squeezed her tight, her comforting citrus scent making him aware of how much he'd missed her. "I wasn't either."

He still wasn't sure why he was here. Only that Mom's message that Dad needed his help had touched something in him. After two years of refusing to speak to Levi, the fact that Dad would ask for his help felt like a big step.

When Mom finally let go, Levi took a step back, examining her. She had maybe one or two extra lines around her eyes now, but other than that, she looked as young and strong as ever.

"Hey, is that my brother?" The voice from behind Mom was deeper than Levi remembered but as cheerful as ever.

"Come see," Mom said over her shoulder, moving aside and gesturing for Levi to enter the house.

But he froze in the doorway, his chest tightening as his eyes fell on the cane in Luke's hand. Since the day his brother had been diagnosed with Becker muscular dystrophy eleven years ago, they'd all known there might come a time when Luke would need help getting around—when he might even need a wheelchair. But Levi had assumed that day would be far in the future.

Luke was only twenty-five. He should be out running and throwing footballs. Not limping around with a cane.

"Hey, brother." Luke's grin swept from his mouth all the way to his eyes as he made his way to the door. "Long time no see."

"Yeah." Levi swallowed, painfully aware of his own smooth steps as he walked toward his brother and held out a hand, realizing too late that Luke held the cane in his right hand. Instead of taking his hand, Luke shifted his cane to the side and wrapped his other arm around Levi's back.

Levi gingerly put an arm around his brother.

"Dude, I'm not going to break." Luke tightened his grip on Levi until Levi lifted his other arm and pulled Luke in closer, still not one hundred percent sure he wouldn't hurt him.

When Luke finally let go, Levi looked around.

Though the outside of the house had changed, everything in here was identical to what he remembered. Pictures of Luke and Levi still decorated the walls. The big beige couch they'd piled on for family movie nights still took up one side of the living room. And Dad's old recliner was still tucked into the corner, his worn Bible perched on the table next to it.

"Where's Dad?" Might as well acknowledge the elephant in the room—or not in the room.

"At work." Mom gestured him toward the couch. "Come on, let's sit down."

"Maybe I should go over to the shop. Find out what he needs help with."

Mom and Luke exchanged a look.

"What?" Levi's head swiveled between them. Luke stared at the floor, and Mom busied herself rearranging throw pillows. "He didn't want me to come, did he?"

"It's not that." Mom gave up on the pillows.

"This is more of an intervention," Luke cut in. "Before he works himself to death."

"I'm sure there are plenty of people he could hire." Actually, this was good. It meant Levi didn't have to stay.

"Probably." But Mom's eyes filled, and Levi had to look away. He'd only seen his mom cry twice in his life—the day Luke was diagnosed, and the day Levi left for college—and he'd been shaken both times.

"But we wanted to see you." Luke had always been good at coming out and saying what he meant, whether or not it came across as sappy. "We've missed you."

Levi softened. "I've missed you guys too. But we all know Dad isn't going to be happy to see me here. I think it's best if I go now, before he gets home." He stood.

But the sound of the door from the garage to the kitchen pulled their attention toward the next room.

"Sandra, whose Harley is that blocking the garage?" Dad's voice boomed as loud as Levi remembered.

"Come and see." Mom pushed to her feet and moved toward the kitchen, throwing a pleading look at Levi over her shoulder.

He shook his head but dropped back onto the couch. It wasn't like he had much of a choice. He wasn't going to go sneaking out of here like some coward. He'd stay and face Dad.

Then he'd leave.

The murmur of Mom's low voice carried from the kitchen, followed by Dad's more explosive one.

"So how've you been?" Luke leaned forward, clearly trying to distract Levi.

"Bored." The word came out before Levi could think it through.

Funny. He hadn't been able to put his finger on the feeling before today. But that was it. He was bored.

He'd kept up with his training for the first year or so after he'd retired, until he'd realized there was no point. Mostly, he spent his days playing video games and his nights going out with friends.

It wasn't such a bad life, he supposed. But it lacked the thrill of getting onto the field, the satisfaction of a game well-played, the purpose of striving to be the best he could be.

"What about you?" Levi asked, but Dad burst into the room, followed by Mom.

"What are you doing here, Levi?" Dad's voice was flat. "You need money or something? Blow through your riches already?"

Seriously?

"No, Dad, I don't need money." He knew plenty of guys who blew through their salaries in record time, but he was smarter than that. He'd made enough on his investments that he'd probably never have to work another day in his life if he didn't want to.

"Well, I didn't know." Dad unbuttoned the Donovan Construction shirt he always wore over a white t-shirt. "All those pictures of you with all those women. Figured it must get expensive."

"Whatever, Dad." Judgment was the one thing Dad had always been good at. "I didn't come here so you could stand over me and judge me."

"What *did* you come for? To make a mockery of your family again?"

"A mockery?" Levi turned helplessly from Dad to Mom and Luke, who offered him a sympathetic look that was no help at all. "When did I ever—"

"That interview, Levi. Your whole lifestyle. Different woman every night."

"Hold on. I'm not with a different woman every night. And I didn't say anything against my family in that interview. All I said was—"

Mom stood, holding out a hand toward each of them. "Stop. Please."

Levi fell silent.

"I asked Levi to come." Mom's voice was firm as she turned to Dad. "You need help on your crews. You've had three guys quit in the last two weeks, and you're working yourself to death. And," she continued as Dad opened his mouth, "I need to see my son."

"She's right, Dad," Luke piped from his spot next to Levi. "We've got half a dozen jobs lined up for the next month alone. There's no way we're going to get them all done without help. And Levi knows what he's doing already. He doesn't need any training. He can step in and lead a crew."

That was true enough. From the time he could swing a hammer, Levi had been helping Dad on the various renovation projects he took on. During college, he'd spent summers managing the company's top crew. Before he'd been drafted into the NFL, he and Dad had talked about the possibility of partnering and expanding the company.

But none of that changed the fact that Dad no longer wanted anything to do with Levi. The feeling was mutual.

"And you want to work for me?" Dad's cloudy blue eyes met Levi's.

The answer to that was an unequivocal no. But his gaze flicked to Mom, then to Luke. Both looked so hopeful.

He nodded once, painfully.

"Fine." Dad marched toward the kitchen. "Luke, get him up to speed on the Calvano project."

"Thank you." Mom squeezed his shoulder as she followed Dad out of the room.

Levi tried to muster a smile. It was only for the summer, he reminded himself. And if nothing else, at least he shouldn't be bored anymore.

Chapter 3

Grace held the two paint samples against the dining room wall for the twentieth time.

She usually wasn't this indecisive, but she wanted everything in the house to be perfect by the time she had guests. She had to make a success of this, as much for Grandfather's sake as to prove to Mama that she wasn't wasting her time.

She stepped to the window, her eyes going from the vase of flowers she'd placed on the sill to the soft purple of the heather blanketing the hill that sloped down to the beach. That settled it. She'd go with a light lilac in here.

Grace watched the low waves chasing the seagulls along the shore. She may only have lived in Hope Springs for five years, but in that time it had become home. More than home, it was like this little town was a part of her, and the people here had become a second family.

Her phone dinged with a text, but Grace ignored it. Mama had been messaging all morning, asking for details about her mystery man, sending her all kinds of warnings about being careful what kind of man she dated, reminding her that Aaron Cooper was a pastor—exactly the right kind of man.

Grace knew she was going to have to fess up about her fib at some point, but for now she was still holding out hope that God might see fit to drop Mr. Right on her doorstep.

A loud knock from the front of the house made her jump.

"That was quick, Lord." She giggled to herself as she considered how ironic it would be if God had indeed brought Mr. Right to her doorstep. Then again, more miraculous things had happened. If Jesus could walk on water, surely he could deliver her the right man, right here and now.

Smoothing a hand over her unruly hair, she forced herself to wipe the silly smile off her face before opening the heavy wooden door.

"You?"

This was definitely not Mr. Right.

She'd known that the moment she'd laid eyes on him yesterday. From the motorcycle to the slick leather jacket to the arrogant way he'd asked her out, as if he couldn't fathom her saying no—everything about him had screamed that he was the kind of guy Mama had warned her to run far, far away from.

Just like Hunter.

She hadn't listened the first time.

But she'd learned her lesson.

"What are you doing here?" Was he stalking her or something? Grace gripped the front door, ready to slam it if he took so much as a step closer.

"I'm looking for Grace Calvano."

"That's me." How had he learned her name? This was getting creepier by the moment.

"You own this place?"

"Yes." Her knuckles tightened on the door.

"Wonderful." Was that sarcasm in his voice? "Can I come in?"

"No. I don't think so." She stepped back to swing the door closed. Hospitality was one thing. Stupidity was quite another. And she was pretty sure letting this guy in would be the height of stupidity.

He held out a hand to keep the door from latching, and Grace's heart just about stopped.

"What are you doing?"

"I need to take some measurements."

"Measurements?" She tried to nudge the door again, but his grip was firm.

"For your renovation." He spoke slowly, as if she were a child having a hard time grasping a new concept.

"I've already lined up the reno. With Donovan Construction."

"Right. And I'm Levi Donovan." He said it as if she should already know that.

What did he think? That she'd memorized the name on the piece of paper he'd tried to give her yesterday?

She peered over his shoulder, catching a glimpse of the Donovan Construction work truck in the driveway. "I thought I was working with Harold Donovan." She knew Harold and his family from church. This guy she'd never seen before yesterday.

"Well now you're working with me. I'm Harold's son. Are you going to let me in or what?"

She hesitated a moment longer. But she had to admit that his story seemed to check out. She let go of her grip on the door and stepped aside slowly.

"Thank you." He didn't sound particularly thankful.

"Where do you need to measure?" She brushed aside her annoyance as she led him toward the stairs. He may not be Mr. Right, but he was here to help her make her dreams of turning this place into a bed-and-breakfast a reality. The least she could do was be civil.

He smirked at her. "I can find my own way around, thanks."

Yeah, like she was going to let this stranger roam her house by himself. She spun toward the stairs. "Let me give you the tour."

He followed her, as she'd known he would. So much for Mr. I-Can-Find-My-Own-Way-Around.

She flipped on the light switch as she started up the staircase. Weak yellow light barely brightened the steps. "I need a bigger fixture here. Something to make it bright and cheerful."

"You're from the South, aren't you? I can hear it in the way you say 'I.'"

Grace stared at him. Was he paying attention to a word she was saying? "Yeah." She led the way to the first of six bedrooms.

"What brings you to Hope Springs?"

"I moved here to take care of my grandfather, if you must know. Anyway, up here I need the carpet ripped out of all the bedrooms." She bent to lift a corner of the carpet. "Grandfather never understood why his parents covered the hardwood floors."

"Your grandfather lives here too?" Levi peered over his shoulder, as if expecting Grandfather to appear out of the woodwork. "Maybe I should talk to him."

"Grandfather is happily in heaven right now, so I don't think he's going to have time to come by for a chat."

"Oh, I—" Levi pushed a hand through his hair, making a tuft stand up right in the middle of his head. "I'm sorry. I didn't mean—"

"It's fine." Grace slid easily past him. "I miss him, but I rejoice for him too."

Levi gave her an odd look but followed her as she led the way toward the bathrooms. "So where are you from then?"

"Tennessee." She flipped the light switch in the bathroom. "There are two bathrooms right now. Obviously, they need to be completely redone."

"Oh yeah? I played football in Tennessee."

Football. Add that to the strikes against him. Hunter had been a football player too.

Grace steered the conversation back to the topic at hand. "Actually, I'd really love to incorporate a bathroom into each of the guest rooms, if we can make it fit in the budget, which Luke seemed to think would be possible."

"Of course he did," Levi muttered. "He's not the one who has to put them in." He made a note in the tiny notebook he carried. "What else?"

Grace led him on a tour of the rest of the house, skipping over the small suite at the back of the first floor, which she used as her personal quarters, and pointing out the wall she wanted to take down between the living room and the dining room as well as the octagonal sitting room she wanted to transform into a library complete with floor-to-ceiling built-in bookshelves.

They ended the tour in the front parlor, which she hoped to turn into a comfy reception area for guests.

A thrill went up her spine at the word. Ever since she was a little girl, pretending to work at her own hotel, she'd dreamed of the day when she'd see to the needs of guests in her own establishment. And now it was really happening.

Levi finished scribbling something in his notebook, then looked up to study the large fireplace.

"It's beautiful, isn't it?" The stone-covered chimney was her favorite feature of the entire house.

Levi pursed his lips, and a low whistle slipped from between his teeth. "You can put one huge TV on that thing. Of course, you'll have to take the rock off. It's too uneven. But you could drywall it, or maybe cover it with tile or brick."

"A TV?" Grace shook her head until her hair flew into her face. "Absolutely not."

"You're not going to have a TV out here either?"

"Nope." She'd already told him there wouldn't be televisions in the guest rooms. Her bed-and-breakfast was a place for people to come to reconnect—with each other, with nature, and with God—not a place for them to rot their brains in front of a screen.

"You're going to seriously cut down on your business if you don't have a single TV on the property. No guy is going to go somewhere they can't catch the game."

"What game?"

He threw his arms up. "I don't know. Any game. Football. Don't you watch football?"

"Not really." With six brothers, she'd sat through enough football games to last a lifetime, though of course she enjoyed cheering them on.

Levi muttered something under his breath, making the pages of his notebook flap.

"Sorry, I didn't catch that."

"Nothing." Levi bounced his pencil against the notebook. "I need to get some measurements upstairs, so we can figure out the bathroom situation."

The grandfather clock in the corner of the room chimed five times. "Actually, I have plans tonight. Could we finish this another time?"

Levi waved her off. "Go do whatever you have to do. I can find my own way. I'll lock up on my way out."

"The plans are here."

Levi shrugged. "That works too." He strode toward the stairs, not bothering to wait for her approval.

Grace watched him climb the steps, thinking again of her earlier hope that God had delivered Mr. Right to her door.

Very funny, Lord. Apparently, she and God had gotten their signals crossed somewhere along the line.

She moved toward the kitchen, ignoring the sound of footsteps upstairs.

Like it or not, it looked like Levi Donovan was going to be spending a lot of time at her house.

Chapter 4

What was that delicious smell?

Levi retracted his tape measure and lifted his nose into the air, inhaling deeply. Something garlicky, but he couldn't place what it was.

He worked out a knot in his back, then bent his head to write the measurements he'd just taken. He hadn't seen Grace in the past hour, and that was fine with him.

The way she'd looked at him when she'd opened the door to find him standing there—like he'd gone out of his way to track her down.

Don't flatter yourself.

Not that she wasn't pretty. She was.

But her no-makeup-messy-hair-t-shirt-athletic-shorts look wasn't really his thing.

Those eyes though.

Man alive. They'd almost pulled him in again today.

It wasn't the color so much as the warmth, he decided. That was what made them so enchanting.

And then there was her smell—sort of sweet and fruity, though he couldn't place it.

He shook himself out of it as he tucked his notebook into his pocket. She'd made it abundantly clear that she had no interest in him.

The sound of voices carried up the staircase as he traipsed down it. A lilting laugh, followed by a deeper voice.

Ah, the flower-buying boyfriend. He should have realized her plans were a date.

He wondered what the guy was like.

Probably scrawny and geeky—the kind of guy who needed to buy flowers to keep a girl.

At the bottom of the stairs, Levi froze.

It wasn't just one guy but a whole group of people.

Grace glanced toward him, and he thought for a second that she was going to ignore him.

But then she stepped forward. "Everyone—" She sounded less than enthusiastic. "This is—"

"Levi Donovan," a chorus of both male and female voices broke in.

Levi grinned, soaking up the surge that always went through him at being recognized. He shot a quick look at Grace to see if she'd noticed.

The surprise on her face was so worth it. "Y'all know him?"

"Not personally." A guy who looked close to Levi's own age stepped forward and held out a hand to Levi. "But he's a Hope Springs legend. Broke about every football record in the school. Played in the NFL. Nice to meet you, man. I'm Dan. This is my wife Jade and my daughter Hope." He gestured to a blond woman with a little girl on her lap and a very pregnant belly. "Heard you retired. Helping out your dad?" He gestured to the tape measure in Levi's hand.

"Just for the summer." Or less, if Levi could find someone to take over for him. Surely, one of the guys here would fit the bill.

"Anyway—" He turned to Grace. "I've got everything I need, so I'll be back bright and early Monday."

"You should stay for dinner." Dan looked to Grace. "Grace's baked ziti is the best. And we always have more than enough food. Right Grace?"

That was a forced smile if he'd ever seen one. But Grace's voice was cheerful as she said, "Of course you should stay. Let me introduce you to everyone else."

She kept that fake smile plastered on her face as she led him around the room. Levi tried to focus as she listed off names: Emma, Nate and Violet, Jared and Peyton, Ethan and Ariana and a little girl named Joy, Dan's sister Leah with her husband Austin and their teenage son Jackson, Sophie and Spencer and their twins Rylan and Aubrey. But mostly he concentrated on not being distracted by Grace's scent.

"Should we wait for Isabel and Tyler to eat?" Grace asked the woman she'd introduced as Sophie.

"Oh. I almost forgot. They decided to take a few extra days on their honeymoon. The kids were enjoying the beach so much."

"Why anyone would bring their kids on their honeymoon," Sophie's husband muttered, and she hit his shoulder playfully.

"You know they wanted the kids to have time to get used to their new family dynamic."

"Those kids couldn't be more family if they'd been raised together." Spencer stood, then helped his wife up, and they disappeared into the kitchen, the others trailing behind them.

"After you." Grace gestured Levi forward.

"We need the birthday girl," someone called from the kitchen. "Get in here, Grace."

"It's your birthday?" Nice. He'd crashed her birthday party.

"Yesterday."

"Ah, that explains the flowers. Where is your boyfriend anyway?" All the men she'd just introduced him to were married.

Pink tickled Grace's cheekbones. "Out of town."

"Oh. Well, happy birthday."

"Thanks." The mumbled word was barely out before Grace turned and practically sprinted to the kitchen.

The house was quiet at last.

Too quiet.

Grace settled onto the love seat in her small sitting room, a cup of hot cocoa curled in her hands despite the fact that it was the first day of June. Growing up, Mama had insisted cocoa was only for Christmastime, but Grandfather had been a year-round cocoa believer, and he'd easily converted Grace.

Sighing, Grace attempted to figure out what it was about tonight's birthday dinner that had fallen flat for her. She'd always loved meals like this, with all her friends, and she treasured them even more now as everyone's busy lives with marriage and kids had made them less frequent.

Her thoughts landed on Levi. The way he'd fit right in with everyone, as if he'd always been a part of the group. She supposed it helped that he'd grown up here—and that he was famous, apparently.

That was it. It was Levi being here that had ruined the night for her, though she couldn't put her finger on why.

Or she could, but she didn't want to admit it.

She was disappointed.

Disappointed that at the very moment she'd asked God to send Mr. Right, he'd sent Levi Donovan—who checked just about every box on the Mr. Wrong list—instead.

She supposed it served her right. She should know better than to tell God when and where to answer her prayers.

If only Dan hadn't invited him to stay for dinner, her evening might have been salvaged.

And the irony that when she'd first moved to Hope Springs she'd been convinced Dan would be her Mr. Right hadn't escaped her either. It had seemed to make so much sense at the time—why would God bring her right to a single, young pastor if she weren't intended to marry him? After all, she was a pastor's daughter, raised by Mama to be a pastor's wife. Now that she looked back on it, she could admit that she'd been more attracted to Dan's role as a pastor than to the man himself. Not that there was anything wrong with Dan—he was a wonderful man—but there was no spark between them, at least not beyond friendship. That, and Dan was still in love with his high school sweetheart—which Grace had helped them both see.

Anyway, that was five years ago, and Grace couldn't be happier for Dan and Jade, who'd quickly become her best friend.

It would just be nice to know that God had something like that planned for her.

It didn't have to be now.

She could be patient.

But someday. Someday she'd like to have a relationship like that. A family like that.

All she had to do was find another single, young pastor near Hope Springs. Which kind of limited her options.

Levi crossed her thoughts again.

No. Levi Donovan definitely wasn't an option.

She pulled out her phone. She'd felt at a disadvantage tonight, since everyone else seemed to know more about this guy who was working on her house than she did.

"Okay, Levi Donovan," she muttered to herself. "Let's see who you are."

Pictures of Levi in the light blue of the Titans popped onto her screen, interspersed with images of him dressed in suits and tuxes, a different woman at his side in each one.

Yep.

Levi Donovan was exactly the kind of guy she'd figured he was.

The kind of guy you ran away from as fast as you could.

As she scrolled, her eyes caught on the title of a video: "Levi Donovan Renounces Faith of His Family, Says God Is Irrelevant." It was dated two years ago.

Grace bit her lip. Did she really want to see this?

Her finger hovered over the video. After a second, she tapped it.

The Levi on her screen came to life, laughing at something the interviewer had said. His dimple was on full display, and he gave the camera a confident smile. The guy definitely had presence on the screen.

"But in all seriousness, Levi," a female voice said from off camera. "Fans have noticed that you used to give thanks to God after a win. You stopped doing that a few games before your big injury, and you haven't mentioned God since. Is there a reason for that?"

Levi's expression had sobered as the interviewer spoke, and he shifted in his seat. "I guess I hadn't noticed," he said at last.

"You were brought up in a fairly religious home?" the interviewer pushed.

"You could say that, yeah."

"Went to church every week?"

Levi nodded. "My dad didn't give us much of a choice." His voice became gruffer. "'As long as you live under my roof, you'll go to church.'"

"And now that you don't live under your father's roof, do you still go to church?"

"Nah." Levi shook his head. "Haven't in a while."

"Do you still believe in God?" The interviewer's voice was quiet, serious.

Levi's gaze slid to something offscreen, then back to the camera. "I don't know."

It was the most heartbreakingly honest answer Grace had ever heard, and she pressed her fingers to her mouth.

"What changed?" the interviewer asked.

Levi's sigh was deep enough that Grace could almost feel it through the screen. "I guess I started asking the hard questions."

"And you didn't like the answers?"

Levi's headshake was subtle. "More like I realized it didn't matter what the answers were. They wouldn't change anything. I guess I just realized that God is irrelevant."

Grace's finger tapped the screen to stop the video.

That confirmed that Levi definitely wasn't the man for her.

But it also meant she had her work cut out for her. Clearly God hadn't sent Levi here to be her Mr. Right. He'd sent Levi here so she could show him God was far from irrelevant.

He was the One thing Levi needed. Whether he knew it or not.

Chapter 5

Levi downed the last of his coffee as he turned into the driveway of the Calvano house Monday morning. The Victorian-style home was certainly grand, with its tall windows, wraparound porch, and octagonal tower. Thankfully, the exterior was in good shape, though a contrasting color on the door and shutters would add to the appeal.

Maybe he'd suggest it to Grace. Though he had a feeling she wouldn't listen—he got the distinct impression she didn't like him, bolstered by the look of relief on her face when he'd left the other night.

He hadn't expected to have a good time—honestly, he'd only stayed for the food—but Grace's friends turned out to be nice. Though they'd certainly shown an interest in his career, they also seemed to see him as more than a football player. He'd nearly forgotten what that was like, and it made for a nice change.

He parked the truck alongside the massive dumpster he'd ordered over the weekend and hopped out, jumping into the bed of the pickup to collect the tools he'd need for today's task: demo.

"What can I do to help?" Grace's voice came out of nowhere, and he lifted his head in surprise, smacking it on the ladder rack above him.

"Ouch. That looked like it hurt."

"It did. Thanks." He rubbed the tender spot on top of his head. "And as far as helping, the most helpful thing you can do is stay out of the way."

"I hope you're kidding." Grace reached up to tug the sledgehammer from his hands, then almost dropped it on her toes.

"Careful. And no, I'm not kidding." He'd learned early on that the last thing he needed was a homeowner hanging over his shoulder.

"I already told your father that I'm helping with this reno as much as possible. I want to put a part of myself into this house." Grace's look challenged him to defy her. "If you have a problem with that, maybe we need to call your dad and get this squared away."

Oh, she wanted to play hardball, did she? "If you're not careful with that sledgehammer, the only part of you you're going to be putting into this house is a broken foot. And if you want to help, fine. Be my guest. But don't complain to me when everything takes three times as long as it would without you." He vaulted down from the pickup bed and wrapped his tool belt around his waist, fumbling with the buckle.

"No offense, but you're sure you know what you're doing, right?"

A rough laugh burst out of him before he could stuff it down. This woman definitely said what was on her mind. "What part of that wasn't supposed to be offensive?"

She didn't smile. "Look, I'm sure you're a great football player and everything, but I don't see how that qualifies you to renovate my house."

"Believe it or not, I'm not just a dumb jock."

Her question had been fair enough. But the way she'd asked it made her disdain for his career plenty obvious.

"I managed my dad's top crew in college. And I have a degree in construction management. I know what I can do and what I can't do—and whatever I can't do, I know how to supervise the people who can do. That good enough for you?"

"That will do." Grace took a step toward the house, lugging the sledgehammer with her. "Where do we start?"

It was going to be a long morning.

"Where do we start?" Grace asked again as she followed Levi into the house, careful to keep the sledgehammer above the ground though it pulled at her muscles to hold it up.

"We'll take down this wall first." Levi strode through the living room to the far wall that blocked off the dining room. He set down the toolbox and drill case he'd been carrying and held out a hand, gesturing to the sledgehammer. "I'll need that."

She moved it out of his reach. "I think you mean I'll need it."

He smirked. "Sure. Take the first hit. You know how to use that?"

She shrugged. You swung and hit. Couldn't be that hard.

She hoisted the sledgehammer behind her head, not letting him see how it strained her triceps.

"Whoa. Whoa. Whoa. Not like that." Levi snatched it out of her hands, handling it as if it weighed no more than a regular hammer.

He held it parallel with the ground, one hand near the head, the other at the back of the handle, and pantomimed driving the sledgehammer forward to hit the wall head-on.

Then he held it out to her.

All right then. She'd do it that way.

Drawing the sledgehammer back, she paused for a moment, then rammed it forward with all her strength.

The shock of the blow traveled up her arms and into her shoulders as a small hole opened in the drywall.

She let out a cheer of triumph and glanced at Levi.

He was grinning too, though he wiped it away the moment he noticed her watching him.

Her smile grew.

See? She could do this.

"All right. My turn." Levi held out his hand again.

"Uh uh. That was too fun."

Levi crossed his arms in front of his chest, making his biceps bulge under his t-shirt. Grace looked away, concentrating on the wall as she lined up her next blow.

"And what am I going to do?" he asked. "Stand here and watch you?"

She couldn't quite tell if he was amused or annoyed, and she didn't really care. She took another hit at the wall, opening another small hole a few feet from the first.

Levi leaned against the wall, arms still crossed. "Maybe I'll take a nap. You're going to be at this all day at this rate."

"And I suppose you think you could do it faster?" Dumb question. With those arms, he'd probably have the wall down in two strikes.

But that wasn't the point.

Grace wanted to have a part in bringing out all the potential she saw in this place.

"I know I can." Levi pulled a regular hammer from his tool belt. "Ready?" He raised an eyebrow. "Set. Go."

He slammed his hammer into the wall before Grace realized it was supposed to be a race. In only two blows, he held a large chunk of drywall in his hands.

Well. Grace didn't have six brothers for nothing. She was as competitive as the rest of them.

She heaved the sledgehammer at the wall, this time creating a good-sized dent.

For the next ten minutes, the smack of their hammers against the drywall was the only sound in the room.

Finally, as she pulled the last piece of drywall off, Levi turned to her with a half-grin. "You're not too bad at that. What do you think?"

"Thanks." Grace was still panting slightly. "And I think I totally smoked you."

Levi laughed. "That's wishful thinking. But I meant what do you think about the room? With the wall down?"

Grace stood back to look. Light flooded from the back of the house to the front, and she could now see straight out to the lake from the front door. "I love it."

"Good. Because if you didn't, you'd be on your own." Levi winked, but Grace was pretty sure he was serious.

"What's next?"

"Normally, I'd do the kitchen right away, but since you're still going to be living here, we'll leave that for now. Let's go demo some bathrooms."

Grace gave a satisfied nod and followed him toward the stairs. At least it didn't look like she'd have to fight him on helping out with the reno anymore.

Maybe she'd even earned a little bit of his respect.

Not that she needed it.

Four hours later, Grace brushed her hair out of her eyes and examined the demolished bathroom. "I don't know about you, but I'm ready for some lunch. Would you like something?"

"Nah. I'm good."

"Come on. I have some leftover ziti." She hadn't failed to notice the three helpings he'd had the other night.

He set down the pry bar he'd been using to pull up the flooring. "I guess I can take a break for some ziti."

"Good." She led the way down the stairs and through the newly opened dining room.

"Looks like we got some dust on your flowers." Levi pointed to the vase on the dining room windowsill. "Sorry about that."

Grace brushed the drywall dust off the petals. "It's fine."

"So did your boyfriend make it back from his trip okay?"

Grace froze, concentrating on the flower petal in her hand. "Why are you so interested in my boyfriend?"

Levi watched her. "There is no boyfriend, is there?" He didn't sound mocking or accusatory. Just curious.

"What?"

"You made him up, right? To let me down easy."

"I didn't—"

"It's okay. I'm a big boy. I can handle it."

Grace dropped the act. There was no point in keeping up the ruse. "There is no boyfriend. I bought the flowers for myself." The pitying look of the cashier crossed her mind again—as if she were the most pathetic woman in the world.

"My grandfather used to buy me flowers for my birthday every year." Yeah, because that made her sound like less of a loser. "I bought them the other day because I was missing him."

"Good idea."

She turned in surprise. Levi wasn't looking at her with pity.

"And for the record," he added, "next time you don't want to go out with me, you can tell me. I can take it."

Grace laughed, even as those two words repeated in her head.
Next time?
There was so not going to be a next time he asked her out.
Right?

Chapter 6

Levi finished sweeping the last of the debris into the garbage bag Grace held.

A week into this reno and he had to admit he was impressed. She'd worked alongside him every day, not exactly cutting the demo time in half but still contributing. And she hadn't complained once. Not even when she smashed her finger with the hammer.

"I need to run to the hardware store to grab a few things." He brushed his hands on his dusty jeans. "See you Monday?"

"Actually, I need to pick up some stuff for a fundraiser at church, so maybe I'll ride with you." Grace shoved a stray curl off her face. "If you don't mind."

Levi shrugged. "Why not?" Other than the fact that she'd made up a boyfriend to avoid going out with him, he had to admit she was pretty okay.

She was down-to-earth, funny, and easy to talk to. Plus, the fact that she had no interest in dating him took off all the pressure. He didn't have to be Levi Donovan, star quarterback, or Levi Donovan, ladies' man, or Levi Donovan, celebrity.

He could just be Levi Donovan, guy-who-was-renovating-her-house.

It was refreshing, actually.

Though he wouldn't have minded knowing why exactly she'd been so desperate to avoid a date with him. But so far he hadn't worked up the courage to ask. Some things a person was better off not knowing.

"Let me go change really quick." Grace rubbed at the streak of dirt on her shirt.

"You look fine." Levi snapped his tape measure onto his jeans pocket. "Everyone at the hardware store is a mess."

"Thanks." Grace made a face at him but followed him to the front door. "I think that's the nicest compliment I've gotten today."

Levi held the door for her. "Just call me Prince Charming."

They continued to banter as Levi steered the Donovan Construction truck toward the hardware store.

It was strange how comfortable Levi felt with her already. It reminded him of how things had been with Rayna.

Maybe it was a good thing Grace had said no when he'd asked her out. Because he had a feeling if he went out with her once, he'd want to go out with her again. And again.

And he'd promised himself the day Rayna had walked out that he'd never get involved in a serious relationship again.

He pulled into the parking lot of the hardware store and jumped out of the truck, waiting in front of it for Grace. Instinct told him to open her door for her. But that was what he did on a date—and this was anything but a date.

"So what do you need?" Grace came up beside him, and he was careful not to walk too close to her as they made their way inside.

Levi took out his phone and scrolled to his list. "A lot. Why don't you go find what you need, and I'll meet you outside when I'm done?"

"That sounds good." Grace disappeared down an aisle, and Levi let out a long breath.

Man alive, what was going on with him?

He'd been perfectly comfortable with Grace ten minutes ago—and nothing had changed between them since then.

It must have been the unexpected thoughts of Rayna in the car. That always threw him.

He scrolled through his list again.

What he needed was to focus on finding his supplies.

"Excuse me." A woman with blond highlights and a skirt that didn't leave much to the imagination stopped in front of Levi. "Do you know where I can find a staple gun?"

Levi looked at the display in front of him. "Right here."

The woman giggled and dropped a hand onto Levi's forearm. "I swear, I can be so dense sometimes." She lowered her eyelids, peering at him through her lashes. "You're Levi Donovan, right?"

The familiar surge went through him.

"In the flesh." He offered her his most inviting smile.

"Oh my goodness. I knew it. I'm Madeline Avery. I was a year younger than you in high school, but I was always too shy to say hi."

"You seem to have gotten over your shyness." He winked at her.

"That I have." She curled a piece of hair around her finger. Always a good sign. "In fact, I never would have done this when I was younger, but can I have your autograph?" She dug into her purse, pulling out a piece of paper and a pen and passing them to him. "And maybe your number?"

Grace checked blue paint off her list. Now she needed to find an inflatable swimming pool that was at least a few feet deep for the ink pool game they'd planned for the fundraiser.

She pushed her cart toward the pool displays she'd seen at the front of the store. The boxes were stacked pretty high, but if nothing else, she could always find Levi and ask him to help her reach one.

Much as she hated to admit it, working with him was growing on her. He was hardworking and dedicated—qualities that came from his athletic training, no doubt—but every once in a while he could be a goofball too, and he'd gotten her laughing for minutes at a time.

Not that she wanted to date him or anything. He was still the totally wrong kind of guy for that. But she was grateful that they'd managed to work together without any lingering awkwardness over the fact that he'd asked her out—and that she'd pretended to have a boyfriend to avoid it.

She turned her cart out of the aisle and toward the front of the store, then froze, glancing down at her stained clothes.

Really, Levi? Everyone goes to the hardware store a mess?

Tell that to the woman he was talking to, whose hair was perfect, face fully made up, clothes out of a designer store.

As Grace watched, Levi passed the woman a piece of paper and a pen.

"I'll call you." The woman winked and tucked the paper into her shirt, then sashayed toward the door.

"Wait," Levi called after her. "You forgot this." He held out what looked like a staple gun.

"Oh." The woman's laugh was flirtatious. "Confession: that was just a pretext."

Levi's laugh joined the woman's, and Grace rolled her eyes.

She waited until the woman had disappeared through the exit doors, then approached Levi.

"Looks like that's one thing you can cross off your list."

"What?"

But she stalked past him to the pool display. If he wanted to pick up women at the hardware store, that was his choice. It didn't matter one iota to her.

Fortunately, the pool she needed was on the lowest shelf.

She turned to tell Levi she'd be waiting for him at the truck. But he was nowhere in sight.

All the better.

She'd pay for her purchases and wait for him outside. And while she waited, she'd use the time to concentrate on not thinking about him.

"Thank you." Levi took the last bag from the cashier and tossed it into the cart, then hustled for the exit.

It hadn't taken Madeline long to call—and they'd arranged to meet for drinks and dinner in an hour. Which should give him just enough time to drop Grace off and run home to shower.

Outside, he nearly sprinted for the truck. But it was empty. He tossed his purchases into the back, then scanned the area for Grace. There was a grocery store next door. Maybe she'd run in there?

He tapped the tailgate impatiently, turning the other direction to see where else she might have gone. His eyes caught on a petite form with dark hair across the street. She was facing away from him, watching a group of kids toss a football around, but even from here he could tell it was Grace. He jogged through the parking lot and across the street.

"Sorry to keep you waiting. Ready to go?" The shouts of the kids on the field carried to them, and Levi couldn't help looking over. This very field was where he'd fallen in love with football.

Seemed like a lifetime ago.

"In a couple minutes." Grace didn't take her eyes off the boys on the field.

"I thought you didn't like football." Levi pulled out his phone to check the time. He now had forty-five minutes before he had to pick Madeline up.

"That's Leah and Austin's son over there." She pointed to a tall kid. "Jackson. He's pretty good, right?"

Levi watched for a moment as the kid faked a handoff, then threw a long spiral toward a receiver. The ball went long.

"Needs better control," he muttered. "It's not always about power. Now can we go?"

"What's the rush?" Grace turned to him, a teasing note in her voice. "Do you have a—" The teasing melted away as understanding dawned on her face. "You have a date," she said flatly.

"Actually, yeah, I do . . ." No reason to deny it.

She'd had her chance. And she'd turned him down.

"Hey, Mr. Donovan," a kid shouted from the field. "Want to come throw a few with us?"

Grace tilted her head, giving him a questioning look. She clearly thought he'd say no.

He checked his phone again.

He didn't want to give her the satisfaction of being right. And yet, he really didn't have time to play football with a bunch of kids.

"Not today," he called. "Maybe next time." He mostly succeeded in ignoring the disappointment on the kid's face.

The look on Grace's face, however—that was harder to ignore.

But he ignored it anyway.

Chapter 7

Levi pulled his pillow over his head as a sharp knock sounded on his bedroom door.

"It's Sunday." His father's voice was loud through the closed door.

"I know. That's why I'm sleeping in," he called back.

"Get up and get ready for church." The command was clear, and Levi pushed the pillow off his head.

Last week, he'd managed to be out of the house well before his family got up for church to avoid exactly this scenario. But this weekend, he'd decided to take his chances. He'd thought he'd be safe since Dad hadn't brought up church once since Levi had been home.

Apparently, Dad had been biding his time.

Levi grumbled out of the same bed he'd slept in as a teenager. It had been too small for him then and was like a baby bed for him now.

He yanked the bedroom door open, shoving a hand through his hair. "I'm not going to church."

"Yes, you are." Dad buttoned the collar of his dress shirt and wrapped a tie around his neck. "Put some clothes on. We leave in twenty minutes."

"You're not hearing me, Dad. I'm not going."

"As long as you're living under my roof, you'll go to church with your family."

Oh, that was nice.

"The only reason I'm living under your roof is because *you* needed help. You don't want me here, I can leave. You want me here, it's on *my* terms. And those terms are no church."

Dad pointed a finger at Levi's chest. "Someday, you're going to wake up and realize there's only one God. And it's not you."

The door next to Levi's room opened, and Luke poked his head out. "Lay off, Dad. You raised him to know the Lord, but you can't force him to believe."

Dad looked from Luke to Levi. "I swear, Levi, I don't know where we went wrong with you. We raised you the same as we raised your brother. So why did you turn out so different?"

"I don't know, Dad. Sorry to be such a *disappointment*." Wouldn't most fathers be proud their sons had made it to the NFL? But not his dad.

Dad jerked the knot of his tie tight. "Don't give me that hurt puppy dog look. If you want me to be proud of you, then be someone I can be proud of."

"If throwing four thousand yards my rookie season didn't make you proud . . ."

But Dad lifted a hand. "I'm proud of what you've accomplished." Dad didn't sound terribly proud. "But I want to be proud of *who* you are too. Understand?"

Levi stepped backward, rubbing at his chest as if he'd just taken a helmet to the solar plexus. Dad wasn't proud of *who Levi was*?

"Yeah. I got it." Levi backed into his room as Dad marched away.

"He didn't mean it the way it sounded." Luke took Dad's spot in the hallway.

"Not many other ways to mean it."

"That interview you did really hurt him. He's having a hard time getting over it."

Levi scrubbed his scratchy cheeks. "For the last time, that interview had nothing to do with my family. I didn't say a single word against any of you."

"Maybe not directly." Luke moved his cane to take a step closer. "But I think Dad takes you falling away as a personal affront. It was his job to raise you to know Jesus, and he feels like he failed."

"That's ridiculous." Levi crossed his arms, leaning on his door frame. "Like you said, he can't make me believe."

"But he would if he could. Because he loves you."

Levi snorted. "Funny way of showing it."

"Yeah, well, for the record, I'm still praying for you, that you'll see God's love for you. I'm not giving up on you. And neither is God."

"Whatever." Levi closed his door. "I'm going back to bed."

But there was no point. Dad's words kept colliding in his brain.

Be someone I can be proud of.

As if that wasn't what Levi had worked his whole life to be. As if that wasn't why he'd gotten up at five in the morning to work out from the time he was fourteen years old. As if that wasn't why he'd spent more time on the practice field than he'd spent in his own bed. As if that wasn't why he was here now.

He pushed out of bed the moment the sounds of his family faded.

Dad wanted to be proud of him?

Fine. Let him be proud of the way Levi got the bed-and-breakfast done in record time—and then left town for good.

Grace was still humming the last hymn as she walked out of church. As always, Dan's sermon had been challenging and uplifting and soul-filling all at once. It made her want to go out into the world and proclaim Christ's love from the rooftop of the bed-and-breakfast.

Or maybe inside its walls.

To Levi, the next time she saw him.

Not that she ever hid her faith from him—he'd seen her pray before their shared lunches, and he knew she was working on a fundraiser for church. But so far, she hadn't found a way to begin an actual discussion about God.

Mostly because every time she thought she'd worked up the nerve to do it, she pictured the video she'd watched. The one where he'd called God irrelevant. How was she supposed to overcome that?

But she wasn't the one who had to overcome it, she reminded herself yet again. Her job was simply to faithfully share God's Word—and trust the Holy Spirit to work in Levi's heart.

Please guide me in that, Lord, she prayed as she waved goodbye to her friends and emerged from the new, larger lobby that had been added onto the church after the tornado two summers ago.

"Grace."

She turned at the sound of her name and smiled as she spotted Harold Donovan, standing with his wife Sandra, Luke, and Luke's girlfriend May.

"Hello, Donovan family. How are y'all today?"

"We're well, dear." Sandra was soft-spoken, but Grace got the impression she could be ferocious when needed—when it came to protecting her sons.

"Levi said you've been right in the thick of things with the reno." Luke grinned at her. She'd only met him a few months ago, when they'd started attending the same Bible study, but already he had become a good friend. "Said you're tougher than you look."

A flush crept up Grace's neck. She hadn't been sure that she wasn't slowing the whole reno down, so the unexpected compliment boosted her confidence.

But Harold frowned at her. "He's making you do his job? He shouldn't—"

"Oh no, no," Grace jumped in. "Levi didn't want me to help, but I insisted. I want to make this place as much my own as possible. Put my blood, sweat, and tears into it."

Harold eyed her. "If you want to help, that's fine. But don't let him slack on you."

Slack? Grace was pretty sure Levi didn't know the meaning of the word.

"He's not." She didn't know why she kept feeling the need to jump in and defend him. "He's been busier than a moth in a mitten. We're ahead of schedule on most everything."

Apparently satisfied, Harold nodded.

"So what are y'all up to today?" Grace turned to Luke and May, smiling at their interlocked hands.

"We're going to a movie, if you want to join us," May offered.

From what she knew of May, the younger woman was quiet but sweet. And she'd love to get to know the couple better. But she didn't exactly feel like being a third wheel today.

"That's kind, thanks. But I have some things to get done at home. Y'all should come by for a tour sometime." She said goodbye to the Donovans and strolled to her car.

Though no one had said anything, the tension of Levi's absence from church had hung over them. She didn't have to imagine their heartache over Levi's turn from the faith. In college, her brother Judah had renounced his faith—and he still hadn't come back.

On the drive home, Grace prayed for her brother and for Levi—that God would open their hearts and call them back to him.

As she pulled into the driveway, her eyes tracked to the building's facade. Levi had suggested painting the doors and shutters a bright teal blue to contrast the white siding. Although she'd at first dismissed the suggestion, she could picture it now. It would certainly make a statement. She'd have to discuss it with him more tomorrow.

Grace steered around the dumpster to park in the shaded area off to the side of the driveway. It wasn't until she stepped around the dumpster that she spotted the motorcycle tucked next to it.

She only knew one person who drove a motorcycle—but what was he doing here?

Clearly not working, since he hadn't brought the truck.

Her stomach did a strange little dip.

He wasn't here to ask her out again, was he? Because she'd already made her feelings about that clear.

But then she remembered that he'd just asked that woman at the hardware store out two days ago.

She had nothing to worry about.

Chapter 8

With a hard shove, Levi rolled up the last remnants of the carpet in the largest bedroom. He'd already managed to pull up the carpet in the other five rooms. Which put him at least two full days ahead of schedule.

He wrapped his arms around the carpet roll in a bear hug and lugged it toward the stairs. The house had become familiar enough now that he could trundle down the stairs even with the massive carpet obstructing his view.

"Hey! Whoa!"

It took him a moment to register that the voice was Grace's. And that he'd nearly plowed her down the stairs.

He put on the brakes just in time, leaning back as the carpet's momentum tried to propel him forward.

He maneuvered the carpet so he could see around it. Grace stood two steps below, blinking up at him. In place of her usual athletic shorts and t-shirt, she wore a white and coral colored dress that set off her dark hair and eyes.

"Hey. You look nice." Oops. That was not supposed to come out. "I mean, are you okay?"

"What are you doing here?" Direct and to the point as always.

"Figured I might as well get a jump on the week." He shifted the weight of the rug.

"It's Sunday. Your father said Donovan doesn't work on Sundays."

"Well, I'm not my father. You weren't home, so I used the extra key you gave me."

"I was at church." She studied him, as if testing what his reaction would be. "Your family was there."

"Yeah." Not a conversation he was interested in having. "Would you mind moving out of the way? This thing isn't exactly getting lighter."

"Oh, sorry." Grace bounced down the steps ahead of him. "I'm going to get changed and make some lunch."

Levi's ears perked at the word. He was starving.

"I thought I'd make some pancakes. You want some?"

He should say no. She really didn't have to go to that trouble. But pancakes were his absolute favorite. "That'd be great."

He wrangled the carpet out the front door and tossed it into the dumpster.

By the time he got back inside, Grace was already pulling out mixing bowls and baking ingredients. She'd changed out of her dress and into her usual athletic gear.

She looked like a different person. And yet . . . not so different.

She was still beautiful in an entirely natural and unaffected kind of way.

"What?" Grace paused with her hand in the flour.

Levi shook himself. Had he been staring? "Nothing. You want some help?"

Her look screamed skepticism.

"What? You don't think I know how to make pancakes?"

"Do you?" She raised a challenging eyebrow.

"As a matter of fact, I make the best pancakes this side of the Mississippi. You sit down. I'll prove it."

He washed his hands, then took the measuring cup from her and nudged her aside.

"Levi, you don't have to—"

"You're never going to believe me unless I show you, right?"

"Well . . ."

"Okay. Then I'll show you." He started measuring flour into the bowl. Then the baking soda and baking powder.

He hadn't made pancakes since Rayna left, but as he fell into the rhythm, there was something soothing about it.

Or maybe it was this place. He was starting to feel at peace whenever he came here.

Or it could be Grace.

He turned the thought over. Was it her company he enjoyed?

"So how was your date the other night?" Her question pulled him out of his musing—probably for the best.

"It was fine."

"What did you do?"

He shrugged. "Dinner, a drink, a walk along the lake." Completely casual and uncomplicated. No commitment.

Exactly the way he liked it.

"Are you going out with her again?"

He stopped whisking. Since when was she so interested in his love life? "I don't know. Maybe. Why, you jealous?"

Grace's eye roll was more exaggerated than necessary, although he could have sworn there was a hint of pink in her cheeks. "You wish. How are those pancakes coming?"

"Patience. You can't rush perfection."

She watched him in silence as he separated the eggs and added the milk and butter. He was so used to her constant chatter as they worked that it was slightly unnerving that she wasn't talking now. But for some reason, he couldn't gather the nerve to ask her what she was thinking.

Finally, he flipped the first golden pancake onto her plate and passed her the syrup. He waited impatiently as she bowed her head and closed her eyes. The expression on her face as she prayed was so earnest that he was almost tempted to ask her what she was praying for.

When she at last looked up, she gave him a smile that he couldn't read and picked up her fork.

The moment she popped the pancake into her mouth, he could tell he'd convinced her.

"Told you. Best pancakes this side of the Mississippi."

She pointed her fork at him. "I need this recipe. This is going to be my Saturday breakfast for guests for sure."

He piled a stack of pancakes onto his own plate and crossed to the other side of the island to sit next to her. "You're going to do the full breakfast and everything, huh?"

"Of course." Grace's eyes went dreamy. "I've been practicing new recipes. But I hadn't found the perfect pancake recipe. Until now."

"It's not the recipe." Levi shoved a forkful into his mouth. "It's the chef."

"In that case, you're hired."

Levi laughed. "Sorry. That would require me to stay in Hope Springs."

"Isn't that what you're planning to do?" Grace paused with her next bite halfway to her mouth. "Stay here and work with your dad?"

"That is a definite no." Levi got up and moved to the refrigerator to get out the pitcher of orange juice he knew she always had in there, then grabbed two glasses. "I only came to help out for the summer. The sooner I can get out of here, the better. My dad and I don't exactly see eye-to-eye on a lot of things."

"Like religion?"

Levi set his fork down, his last bite still on it. "Yeah, among other things."

"I saw the interview you did with Sports World." Grace's comment was hesitant, and Levi tensed.

"Already got the lecture on that from my dad this morning, thanks."

Grace had just come from church. She'd obviously see things the same way as Dad. She didn't take her eyes off him, but he couldn't find the condemnation in them.

"I thought it was really honest," she said at last.

Levi didn't know how to react to that. "My dad thought it was a personal attack. Sees me as a big disappointment."

"I'm sure he doesn't—"

"He told me as much just this morning, so . . ." He picked up his plate, scraping the last uneaten bite into the garbage.

"I'm sure he didn't mean it." But Grace's words rang hollow.

"Whatever. I'm sure your parents have never said anything like that to you."

Grace's face whitened, and she took a long drink of her juice. "Once." She said it more to her plate than to him. "But they had a good reason."

"I doubt that." Levi leaned on the counter. "You don't strike me as the kind of person who disappoints people often."

Grace stepped past him to put her plate and glass in the sink. "Looks can be deceiving. I let them down big time. Anyway, they'd be proud if I moved home, married a man I haven't seen since I was eleven, and had a passel of babies."

"And you don't want to do that? Get married and have babies?" Levi definitely would have pegged her as the family type—the very opposite of his type.

"Someday, yes. When I meet the right man."

"And what will the right man be like? You have a list, right?"

She was definitely the list-making type.

She busied herself putting away the baking ingredients. "Maybe."

He barely heard her mumble, but he grinned. "I knew it. What's on this list?"

"Nothing. Don't you have work to do?"

"Nope." He tipped his head at her. "It's Sunday, remember? Think I'll take Gloria out for a spin."

Grace gave him a blank look. "Gloria?"

"My Harley." He hesitated. "Want to come?"

Grace's reaction was instantaneous. She backed away from him, holding out her hands and shaking her head as if afraid he was going to physically abduct her and force her onto the bike.

"Your loss." He strode toward the front door, telling himself it wasn't his loss too.

Chapter 9

"How about Grandpa's Place?" Grace asked.

All week they'd been throwing around potential names for the bed-and-breakfast. Coming up with a name that conveyed exactly the homey feeling she wanted to portray was turning out to be a lot harder than she'd expected.

Levi groaned. "That's the worst one yet. Sounds like a bar. Or a bait stand."

She threw the sandpaper she'd been using on the dining room windowsill at him, but it went wide by a good three feet.

"Nice throw." He smirked.

"I don't hear you suggesting anything better." She retrieved the sandpaper and started working again, the sound mixing with that of the hammers and nail guns from the crew framing out the new bathrooms upstairs.

"It'd be tough to come up with anything worse," Levi teased, filling a nail hole.

Grace nearly threw the sandpaper again, then realized she'd only end up chasing it across the room again.

Levi lowered his putty knife and tapped his chin as if deep in thought, then pointed his finger into the air.

"How about Grace's Place?"

Grace wrinkled her nose. "It rhymes."

"I know. Think of the jingles. 'Grace's place. Where we have the space. So you can race. Don't forget—" Levi hesitated, looking skyward, obviously trying to come up with a rhyme. "Your mace," he finished.

A giggle escaped Grace. She had to admit that she quite liked it when Levi let his playful side escape.

But she tried to put on a stern look. "Didn't you learn that the customer is always right?"

Levi set down the putty and picked up a piece of sandpaper, joining her at the window. "Not when the customer is so obviously wrong."

Grace swatted at his arm before she could find the common sense to resist. Her hand met firm muscle, and she quickly pulled it back.

His cool, masculine scent—a mix of cedar and sandalwood—drifted to her, and she took a step sideways.

"Speaking of being wrong—" Levi spoke as he scrubbed the sandpaper against the window frame, taking off more paint in five seconds than she had in the past five minutes. "Are you still set on purple in here?"

"Nice." She almost swatted at him again but resisted this time. "You know I could fire you, right?"

"Dare you."

He had her there. She needed him if she had any prayer of getting this place done.

"To answer your question, no, I'm not still set on the *lilac*." She emphasized the word. Levi didn't seem to understand that there were hundreds of shades of every color. "You've made me second-guess. I hope you're happy."

"I aim to please. But you do have to make a decision by Monday so we can keep things moving."

Grace nodded, and they fell silent as they finished sanding the windows. She was about to suggest a break when there was a knock from the front door.

"I need a doorbell too." She brushed the dust off her hands and headed for the front of the house.

"Yes, ma'am," Levi called behind her. "Your wish is my command."

Ha. Yeah right. More like her wish was his to argue with. But she appreciated his honesty. She hadn't anticipated all the tiny decisions that went into a reno, from the shape of the drawer pulls in the bathrooms to whether she wanted dimmable lights in the guest rooms, not to mention the big decisions, like what to call the place.

"Grandpa's Place," she whispered to herself.

Yeah, now that she heard it out loud, she realized it wasn't going to work.

Too bad she had no idea what would.

She opened the front door, still pondering.

"Luke. May. I'm so glad y'all dropped by."

"Thanks for inviting us." May stepped forward to give Grace a quick hug, which she happily returned. Mama had raised her to be a hugger, and she didn't get enough opportunities for hugs these days.

"Come on in." She opened the door wider so Luke could get through with his cane. "Levi's in the dining room. We were just arguing about paint colors. Maybe y'all can help me decide."

She led the way to the dining room.

"Who was—" Levi froze as he turned, his eyes going straight to Luke's and May's joined hands.

"Hey, brother," Luke said.

Grace had never heard the man sound anything less than cheerful.

"Hey." Levi, on the other hand, was glowering.

Grace peered back and forth between the brothers.

From the way they both talked, she'd assumed they got along well. But that was not the impression she was getting right now—at least not from Levi.

"I want you to meet May. My girlfriend." If a man's chest could have burst with pride, Grace was pretty sure Luke's would have. "May, this is my brother. Levi."

May let go of Luke's hand and stepped forward, holding her hand out to Levi.

He stared at it, and for a moment Grace was sure he would refuse to shake it.

Finally, he reached out, pumped May's hand once, then turned back to the windowsill, working his sandpaper harder than before.

"So—" Grace sent Levi a daggers-to-the-eyeballs look, but he didn't so much as glance at her. "Y'all want a tour?"

"We'd love one." May's voice was warm and cheerful, though the hurt expression from Levi's snub hadn't yet disappeared. Luke, too, was looking at Levi as if he'd been betrayed.

Levi kept his focus on the window, but his voice reached them. "There are a lot of stairs."

Oh.

How could she have been so inconsiderate?

"I'm sorry. I wasn't thinking . . ." She turned to Luke.

"Nothing to apologize for. I'll be fine."

Her eyes shifted back to Levi, who dropped the sandpaper, shoulders stiff. "It's too much. I've seen the way you struggle on the little porch steps at home."

"He can do it." May's voice was quiet but certain, and Luke shot her a grateful look.

"Whatever." Levi threw his hands in the air. "But don't ask me for help when he falls."

Grace led them away. "So, this is going to be the library." She kept her voice low, walking into the octagonal room.

"I don't know what right he thinks—" Luke burst out as soon as they were out of earshot of Levi.

May laid a hand on his arm. "He's just worried about you." She leaned to kiss Luke's cheek and slipped her hand into his.

Luke drew in a short breath. "I guess. Sorry, Grace. Tell us more about this room."

When Grace had finished the tour of the first floor, she eyed the stairway.

Was Levi right? Was it too much for Luke?

But surely Luke was the best judge of that.

As if reading her mind, Luke stepped closer. "I'll be fine."

She nodded and started slowly up the stairs, glancing over her shoulder to watch as May helped him navigate the space.

Behind May, Levi appeared at the foot of the staircase. He didn't say a word, just watched as Luke made his way up one step at a time. The concentration on Levi's face said he was there out of more than curiosity. Despite what he'd said, Levi was there to make sure his brother didn't get hurt.

A shot of something unfamiliar went through Grace's chest.

For all his faults, it was just possible that Levi Donovan had a heart after all.

Chapter 10

Levi stepped out of the steaming bathroom, fastening the last button on his shirt. He'd needed that hot shower to pound away the tension in his shoulders before his date tonight.

Madeline had called after work to ask if he'd like to go to a movie, and he'd figured he might as well, even if he knew this would be their last date.

Two dates maximum. That was his rule.

From the hallway, he could hear the sound of Luke's forced cough, stimulated by the cough assist machine that helped keep his lungs clear. The sound had always bothered Levi, a constant reminder of his brother's illness.

In his own room, Levi tucked his wallet and keys into his pocket, then grabbed his cologne, trying to work up some enthusiasm for this date.

But instead of Madeline, he kept picturing Grace. The disapproving look she'd stuck him with when he didn't welcome May with open arms. The way she'd gone all quiet and distant after Luke and May had left.

She didn't understand. Not the way he did.

Having a girlfriend meant Luke was opening himself up to heartache. What happened when May got tired of Luke's illness? When she decided he wasn't what she wanted anymore?

Levi forced his thoughts off Grace. It didn't matter what she thought.

He stepped out of his room, checking the time. He'd spent longer in the shower than he'd meant to. He'd have to get a move on if he didn't want to be late.

As he reached Luke's room, the door opened, and Luke stepped out in front of him. Levi dodged to the side to scoot past his brother, but Luke widened his stance and planted his hands on either side of the hallway.

"What are you doing?" Levi took a step back. "Let me through."

"What was that all about today?" Luke didn't move a single muscle, aside from his jaw.

"What was what about? Look, come on, move. I have a date."

"Funny. I did too. And you were a jerk to her. You owe both of us an apology."

"I don't think so, man. Come on. Move." He feinted to the right, then moved to the left, but Luke didn't fall for it.

"You know I could easily make you move, right?" Not that he wanted to have to resort to force.

"Try it." Luke's lip curled.

"Seriously, Luke—"

"Oh, seriously?" Luke stepped forward and shoved Levi in the chest. "Seriously, you owe May an apology. She was in tears when we left."

Levi had made sure to be out of sight when they left, so he wouldn't know, but he sincerely doubted May had shed any tears over him.

"What's your problem with her?" Luke didn't shove him this time, but he didn't back off either. "Or is your problem with me? You're jealous I have a girl and you don't, is that it?"

"Don't be a moron. I'm going on a date right now, aren't I? So no, I'm not jealous that you have a girl. I can have any girl I want." Except maybe Grace. But he didn't want her anyway.

"Maybe." Luke pressed a finger to Levi's chest. "But you don't have love. And I do. And you can't stand that."

"Love?" Levi scoffed. "You think I want that? Love doesn't mean anything. Soon as things get hard, you think *love* is going to help? You think May's going to stick around when you're in the hospital? You think she's going to push you around when you're in a wheelchair?"

Levi never saw the punch coming.

One second, he was sneering at his brother, thinking how naive Luke was to believe love was real; the next, his hand was on his cheek, covering the throbbing spot on his jaw where Luke's fist had connected.

Levi straightened. If Luke had been anyone else, he'd already have a fist through his nose. Instead, Levi stood there, opening and closing his mouth a few times. Painful but not broken.

"Just because you didn't stick around—" Luke's voice shook. "Doesn't mean she won't." He took two halting steps into his room. "Some people actually know the meaning of love." His door slammed.

Levi stared at it for a moment, still rubbing his jaw. Then he spun on his heel and left for his date.

Luke thought he didn't know the meaning of love?

He did.

And he knew it always ended up with someone getting hurt.

Chapter 11

"Your jaw is looking better." Grace dipped her roller into the paint tray. When Levi had shown up last Monday with a black and blue jaw, she'd assumed he'd been in a bar fight or something. Even when he'd told her it was Luke, she'd had a hard time believing him. Until he'd given her the look that said he didn't want to talk about it.

And she hadn't brought it up. For two weeks.

But now that the bruise was nearly gone, she figured maybe it was time to talk.

"Yeah."

Then again, maybe not.

"I'm getting hungry. Want to get some lunch?"

"I'd rather finish up in here first." He gestured at the guest room walls they'd been painting a soft gray. "You go ahead though. I'll take care of it."

Grace crossed her arms in front of her, careful to adjust the roller so she wouldn't get paint on herself. "You think I'm slowing you down, don't you?"

Levi continued to roll paint onto the far wall, which he'd almost completed in the time it'd taken her to paint a quarter of hers. "You're not exactly setting any speed records."

"Just for that, I'm staying. And I bet I can finish this wall before you do that one." She pointed to the wall between them, which hadn't been touched yet.

"You want me to finish this wall and paint another whole wall before you finish the half a wall you have left?"

"It's three-quarters of a wall. And what's the matter? Afraid you can't do it?"

"Nope." Levi offered her the first true grin she'd seen from him in two weeks. "Just wanted to be certain of the terms of our bet. What are the stakes?"

"Lunch." Grace pressed a hand to her hungry stomach. "Loser buys lunch at the Hidden Cafe."

"You're on." Levi's roller took two long swipes down his wall. "Oh, and just so you know, I'm starved today. So I hope you have plenty of money for lunch."

"Little overconfident, aren't you? Don't forget you have another whole wall to do." But she filled her roller with paint and fell silent as she concentrated on rolling the wall as quickly as she could, trying to imitate Levi's long, smooth strokes.

After half an hour, her arm was burning. But she kept pushing, trying to ignore the fact that Levi was getting awfully close to done with his walls.

"Be right back." Levi set his roller down. "I need some water. You want anything?"

She shook her head. "I'm not stopping, you know."

"I wouldn't expect you to. I'm not worried." He sent her a smug smile. "I'll still beat you."

Grace put on a burst of speed as Levi's footsteps receded down the stairs. Ignoring the pain in her shoulders and neck, she sped toward the last section of the wall.

When she heard Levi's feet on the stairs ten minutes later, she was ready. She planted herself in the middle of the room, a smirk all set on her lips.

Levi stepped into the room, swigging from a water bottle. He lowered it as his eyes fell on her, and he looked from her to the wall.

"That's what you get for underestimating—" But something about his expression stopped her.

He didn't look surprised; he looked pleased with himself.

"You did that on purpose, didn't you?" Her hand went to her hip, tracking a line of paint onto her shorts.

"I don't know what you're talking about." Levi took another long drink.

"It didn't take you fifteen minutes to get water. You let me win."

Levi pointed at his chest. "Are you accusing me of throwing the game?" His look of feigned innocence clinched it.

"You're going to regret this." She waved her roller at him. "It just so happens that I'm starved today too."

So he'd thrown the paint race. Which was so not like him. He'd once made a bet with a kid on a plane ride that he could win a staring contest. And when he'd won, he'd happily taken the kid's airplane peanuts.

But for some reason he couldn't pinpoint, he really wanted to take Grace to lunch today.

Maybe it was because she'd somehow known that today's little race was exactly what he'd needed to get himself out of the funk he'd been in for the past two weeks. He and Luke had barely said a word to one another in that entire time, and much as he hated to admit it, it was wearing on him.

Part of the reason he'd agreed to come home for the summer was because he'd hoped he could make up for lost time with his brother. Instead, they were further apart than ever.

"Ready?" Grace emerged from her suite, looking fresh in a pair of denim shorts and a sleeveless shirt that accented her delicate shoulders.

"Yep. We'll have to take my Harley though."

"What?" Grace halted halfway through the kitchen. "Why?"

"It's what I drove this morning. My dad's Donovan truck is in the shop, so he needed mine."

"I can drive."

Levi shook his head. "I'm supposed to be taking you to lunch, if you remember."

"Then you can drive my car." Grace snatched her keys off the kitchen counter. "Please?"

He studied her. "There's nothing to be scared of, you know. The bike is quite safe. I even have an extra helmet."

"I'm not scared." Grace gave him a defiant look. "I just don't want to mess up my hair."

Levi snickered.

"What?"

"Nothing." He crossed the room to stand in front of her and lifted a strand of her hair. "You might want to get the paint out of your hair first."

Grace's eyes widened, and she snagged the strand from him. "One second."

"Yeah." But suddenly all he could think about was the feel of her hair in his fingers. And how he wanted to touch it again.

He jammed his hands into his pockets as she grabbed a paper towel and wet it, then rubbed it down her hair.

"There. Now am I presentable?"

Levi eyed her. She was more than presentable. She was beautiful. "You'll do."

"So you'll drive my car?" She held out her keys.

He considered pushing for her to ride the bike with him. But maybe it was best if they took a vehicle that didn't require them to sit so close together. Because this new awareness of her beauty was getting to him.

He took the keys and led her outside. He almost opened the car door for her but veered at the last second to go straight to the driver's side.

They spent the drive to the Hidden Cafe discussing what they'd already accomplished on the bed-and-breakfast and what they had left to do.

It was a big job, and with his crew shorthanded, it would likely be another few months before they finished.

The thought should have bothered him—but it didn't. Despite the tension at home with Dad and Luke, he was mostly enjoying his time in Hope Springs. It felt good to have a reason to get up and go to work every day. Maybe once he left Hope Springs, he'd have to look into getting a job—or starting his own company. Maybe he could specialize in bed-and-breakfast renovations.

Though he had a feeling he wouldn't enjoy them half as much if Grace wasn't there.

Uh uh. That was a dangerous thing to think. None of that.

Grace was a client and maybe a friend. Nothing more.

He pulled into a parking spot at the Hidden Cafe, then walked with her to the door, careful not to get too close to her. Even so, her sweet scent wafted toward him, teasing his senses. He held his breath as he opened the building's door. He didn't need that mystery fragrance to confuse him more than he already was.

Grace struck up a conversation with the hostess as she led them to a table, and Levi hung back a little, both to give himself some air and to watch Grace.

She was asking about the hostess's grandchildren, but the way she did it, it wasn't like other people. She really cared about the hostess's answer—really listened.

"A view of the lake is what you two lovebirds need." The older woman stopped at a table along the giant picture windows that overlooked the lake.

"Oh, we're not—" Grace started, but the woman pulled out a pad of paper.

"Can I start you with something to drink?"

Grace shot Levi a helpless look. He shrugged and sat down. He supposed it was harmless enough if this woman thought he and Grace were together.

They each requested a glass of water, and the woman swept toward the kitchen, promising to give them plenty of privacy.

"I wonder what she thinks we're going to do?" Levi peered around at the half dozen other customers in the restaurant.

"Levi!" But Grace giggled. "Mrs. Hurston is a hopeless romantic. Always trying to set people up."

"Ah, that explains it." Levi settled back in his seat, letting his gaze travel out the window. "The view is good."

"Yep." Grace was watching him thoughtfully. "Can I ask you a question?"

Levi blew out a long breath. He should have seen this coming. "Look, Grace, you're sweet and all, but—"

"What?" That was genuine confusion on her face.

"Nothing. Go ahead." Boy, Levi sure could use that water he'd ordered right about now.

"It's about Luke." Grace smoothed her hand across the table.

"Oh." That wasn't a topic he wanted to get into either. But he didn't see a way out of it. "What about him?"

"It's hard for you to see him like this, isn't it?"

A young waiter stopped at the table to drop off their waters, and Levi took a long drink as Grace placed her order for a cheeseburger and fries. He ordered the same.

When the waiter had left, Grace sat just looking at him. He took another long drink. At this rate, he was going to need more water before their food arrived.

"We don't have to talk about it if you don't want to," she said.

Levi played with the wrapper from his straw. "He wasn't using a cane the last time I saw him. That was a couple years ago, but I guess it feels like he's deteriorated really fast."

"When was he diagnosed?"

"My senior year of high school." Levi did the math in his head. "So eleven years ago."

He steepled his fingers under his chin. "He was never the fastest kid, but he wanted to play football."

"Like you." Grace lowered her hand to the table, letting it come to rest halfway between them. He studied her delicate fingers, covered with cuts and scratches from the work she'd been helping him with over the past few weeks.

"Yeah. Like me. By then, I was starting to hear talk of scouts, and I was training pretty hard. Anyway, I tried to train with him, but he couldn't keep up. I got so frustrated. I told him he should quit because there was no way he'd make the team." Regret burned hot and sharp in his chest. "He started training harder than ever. But the harder he trained, the more it seemed like he struggled. He started falling down when he'd go out running. Got skinned up pretty badly one time. Twisted an ankle another time."

He could still picture the look on his parents' faces when they'd come home from that doctor appointment. They'd anticipated a sprained ankle. Not a diagnosis that would change their lives.

"The doctors figured out it was Becker muscular dystrophy pretty quickly." He didn't add that the disease was genetic. That the chance his mother's sons would get it was fifty percent. That if his brother hadn't gotten it, he likely would have.

"That must have been hard." Grace's eyes on him were too intense, too sympathetic. He shifted to watch the white caps of the waves roll toward shore.

"Yeah." But not for the reason she thought. Levi had been a dumb kid then, with no awareness of how serious Luke's condition was. All he noticed was that because of Luke, his parents missed nearly all of his final season of high school football, including the game when six college scouts had come to see him play.

"And the bruise on your jaw?" Grace tapped her own face in the exact spot where his bruise from Luke's punch had mostly faded.

He shrugged. "He was upset because he thought I was rude to May."

"And did you apologize?"

He should have known she'd take Luke's side. "I was only trying to protect him."

"By being rude to his girlfriend?" She didn't say it ironically or like an accusation. More like she really didn't understand.

"By warning him that she won't stick around when things get hard. When he's not who she expects him to be."

"How can you know that? May is a sweet girl."

"Yeah. Well." Levi slid his empty water glass to the edge of the table. "Let's just say I know." Rayna had made sure of that. The moment he wasn't the NFL star she'd been after, she'd found herself a new star: his replacement on the field—and off.

"What—" But the waiter stopped at their table with a tray of food and piled it in front of them.

Grace bowed her head, and by the time she'd finished praying, he had half his burger gone.

Her eyes widened. "I guess you weren't kidding about being starved."

"Told you." He took another big bite.

Thankfully, she got the hint that he was done talking and bit into her own burger. For the rest of the meal, they resumed their argument about whether she should have at least one TV in the bed-and-breakfast.

When they were back in the car, Grace turned to him. "Can I ask you one more question?"

He shifted into drive without answering, which she apparently took as an invitation.

"Is that why you said you weren't sure if you believed in God anymore in that interview? Because of everything that happened to Luke?"

Levi turned onto Hope Street, keeping his eyes on the road and off of her. "Partly, yeah."

He waited for her to tell him that everything happened for a reason. That God had a plan in everything. That all he had to do was believe hard enough and everything would be fine.

But she was silent so long that he finally glanced over at her.

She turned to meet his gaze. "Thanks for telling me. All of it."

He nodded. He wasn't sure why he had. He'd never really talked to anyone about Luke. Not his teammates. Not his coaches. Not even his dates.

But talking to Grace had been surprisingly easy. And comforting.

He let himself relax into the seat just a little.

So long as he didn't get used to it.

Chapter 12

"Could you pass me the drill?"

Today's job was starting to build the shelves for the library, and Grace felt mostly useless, aside from holding up boards and passing Levi tools and screws.

She should really go finalize her plans for furniture. But she couldn't quite bring herself to leave the room.

She had been working a little too hard to convince herself it was because she wanted to be able to honestly say she'd had a hand in every part of the renovation.

But she couldn't deny that there was also something new in the air between her and Levi today. Maybe it was because of how they'd talked about Luke at lunch yesterday. Or maybe it was something in their coffee. Either way, he seemed friendlier and more open than usual, and she didn't want to jeopardize that.

She passed him the drill, and he gave her that same smile he'd been giving her all day. It was different than his usual smile—mostly in that it caused the slightest flutter in her belly.

Which she was studiously ignoring.

So he had a cute smile. That didn't mean she was attracted to him. More importantly, it didn't mean he was anywhere near the right kind of guy for her.

Which was why she wasn't in any danger from spending time with him now, flutters or no flutters.

From across the room, Grace's phone rang, and she wound around their pile of boards to dig through the various supplies that had accumulated on the floor.

"Where is it?" she muttered, picking up Levi's sweatshirt.

There.

She concentrated on not noticing the enticing sandalwood scent of the shirt as she answered the phone.

"Hey, Leah. What's up? Need me to pick up something for tomorrow?" It was hard to believe the fundraiser they'd spent months planning was finally here.

"Nope. Just calling to let you know I'm an aunt again. Jade had a baby boy this morning. Matthias Paul. He and Jade are healthy and happy. And Dan's over the moon, of course."

"That's wonderful. Tell them I say congratulations. I'll stop by the hospital to visit on my way to set up for the Messtival."

"If you can recruit anyone else to help tonight, that'd be awesome," Leah said. "We're obviously going to be short one pastor and his wife."

"I'll see what I can do." Grace sized up Levi as she hung up.

He finished screwing in a shelf and took a step back from it. "Good news?"

"Dan and Jade had their baby this morning. A boy."

"That's great." He picked up another board.

"Yeah."

Levi set the board back down, leaning it against the wall. "But . . ."

"How did you know there was a but?"

"I could see it in your face."

Oh. Did he know her that well? Warmth filled her, but she pushed it aside. Likely, anyone would have seen it.

She'd never had a good poker face.

"The Messtival is tomorrow, and without Dan and Jade, we're down two key team members. I'm not quite sure how we're going to pull it off."

Levi gave her a blank look. "Messtival?"

She rolled her eyes. So much for thinking he really knew her. "The fundraiser I've been talking about for the past month."

"Oh. That." He nodded, as if he had a clue.

"Whatever. You have no idea what I'm talking about."

"The fundraiser to raise money for the youth mission trip. The one where every activity is messy."

Grace felt her mouth open a crack. It seemed he did listen when she talked. There went that shot of warmth again.

She ignored it again.

"Anyway, we have a ton of stuff to set up tonight. And it's going to take a lot longer without them." She checked the time. "Actually, I might head over there now to get started." She hesitated, then decided to go for it. What did she have to lose? "You could come too, if you wanted. We could use the help."

"Sorry." Levi picked up the board again. "I'd love to help, but I have a date tonight."

"Oh." That was *not* disappointment Grace felt. Or, well, it was. But not over Levi having a date. It was only disappointment that she hadn't been able to recruit another helper. "Things with Madeline must be going well."

"I'm not going out with Madeline."

"Oh, that's too bad. What happened?"

Levi fit the board into place. "Nothing."

"But you're going out with someone else?"

"Yeah. Gina." He said it flippantly, as if it were completely normal to be going out with a different woman already. Then again, from what she'd seen when she Googled him, she supposed it *was* normal for him.

"All right, then. See you Monday." As she stepped out the door, she breathed a sigh of relief. At least now those little flutters she'd felt for Levi today would beat it.

He'd confirmed once again that he was the very opposite of her Mr. Right.

She thought of Jade and Dan, celebrating the birth of their new baby.

I do want that, Lord, she prayed as she got into her car. *And if you want to bring Mr. Right-for-Real into my life sooner rather than later, I won't complain. But if not, I'll keep waiting for someday.*

With one last glance in the mirror, Levi grabbed the keys to his Harley off his dresser and exited his room. He'd met Gina when he'd ridden his bike to the marina last weekend, and she'd been fascinated with it.

Unlike Grace, who looked freaked out at the mere mention of the bike, Gina had asked for a ride then and there. And he'd been happy to oblige. When he'd asked her out for tonight, she'd insisted he bring the bike.

Actually, Levi thought she might like the bike more than she liked him. But that was fine. He wasn't looking to fall in love. Just have a nice time and then go their own ways.

Voices carried down the hallway from the kitchen, and Levi hesitated.

Mom and Luke.

Maybe he should go out the front door. But his bike was in the garage—through the kitchen.

The moment he stepped into the room, Luke fell silent, shot him a glare, and got up from his seat at the table.

"I'm just passing through." Levi gestured for Luke to keep his seat.

But his brother retreated into the hallway.

"Suit yourself," Levi muttered.

"I don't understand what's going on with you two." Mom's brow creased. "But can't you make up?"

"Ask him that."

"I have." Mom's sigh ran deep. "He says he's waiting for you to apologize."

Levi snorted. "That's nice. He punches me in the jaw, and he wants me to apologize?"

"Can't you?" Mom turned pleading eyes on him. "I can't stand to see you two like this. You used to be so close. Until . . ."

"I didn't abandon him, Mom." A headache sprouted in Levi's temple as he struggled to believe his own words.

"I never thought you did." Mom offered a more than convincing look of shock. "I only wish your father and I had handled everything better. We were just so overwhelmed at first, and you were doing so well with everything, that I think we lost sight of the fact that you still needed us too. I hope you don't resent your brother for that." Mom blinked, but not before Levi spotted the glisten in her eyes.

"You did what you had to do, Mom. And I don't resent him. If anything, he resents me."

"Are you kidding me?" Mom sniffed and straightened her back. "He idolizes you."

"Right. That's why he punched me." Levi massaged his jaw, though it didn't hurt anymore. "I have to get going. Don't wait up for me. I'll see you tomorrow." He dropped a quick kiss on Mom's cheek.

"Another date with Madeline?" Mom sounded hopeful.

"No, actually. Gina."

The frown Mom directed at him could have rivaled some of Dad's best.

"What?" Not that he supposed he wanted to hear it.

"I know Rayna hurt you, but do you think this is the best way to deal with it? Going out with a different woman every week?"

"This has nothing to do with Rayna." Levi moved to the door.

"Just because she left you doesn't mean every woman will." Mom stared him down. For such a small woman, she could still intimidate him.

"I know." They wouldn't leave him because he wouldn't give them a chance.

"You can't go through life alone, Levi, just because one woman hurt you. That'd be like never throwing another pass because of one sack. Don't you want to get married, have a family?"

"Not really, Mom." He opened the door to the garage. "I don't think I'm the family type. I gotta go. Love you."

"Someday you're going to change your mind about that," Mom called behind him.

But he closed the door and jumped on his Harley.

Mom might think he'd want a family someday.

But he knew better.

Chapter 13

Seven.

Levi was awake at seven o'clock on a Saturday morning.

And he had nothing to do with his day.

It didn't pay to go back to bed, since he'd gotten plenty of sleep, given that he'd been home from last night's date by ten o'clock. It wasn't that it'd been a bad date or that Gina hadn't been fun.

But somehow, the evening had been rather . . . blah.

After riding his Harley up and down the shoreline, they'd had a nice dinner, Gina asking the whole meal about what it was like to be in the NFL. Usually, he ate that up—dates who wanted to talk about his rise to stardom.

But for some reason, he couldn't stop thinking about the conversation he and Grace had had over lunch the day before.

It had been so . . . real.

Like Grace saw past the football player and had discovered the real person he was now. It was unnerving in some ways—but it also felt nice to really be seen. Understood.

And then there'd been his mom's words ringing in his head the entire date. *Don't you want to get married, have a family?*

He had wanted that once with Rayna.

He'd wanted it so much that he'd had the ring in his pocket the night she broke up with him.

Much as that had hurt, he would forever be grateful that something had held him back from proposing that night.

He'd learned an important lesson that night too: The moment you stopped being who people expected you to be, they walked away.

Even though he was sure Mom's prediction that he'd change his mind about marriage someday was wrong, it hadn't helped his date. Every time he'd looked at Gina, all he could think was, *This definitely is not the woman I'd choose to spend the rest of my life with.*

Finally, he'd given in, pleaded a headache, and dropped her off at home. The best he could do when she told him to call her sometime was offer a slight grunt that he hoped she'd taken as a gentle let down.

Kind of like Grace telling him she had a boyfriend.

He rolled out of bed. As long as he was awake, maybe he'd go make some progress on the bed-and-breakfast. Grace had her Messtival thing today, so he'd have the place all to himself.

Except the thought of working there without Grace fell flat for him.

Well then, what if he went over to the Messtival?

It sounded like they could use the help—and he could only imagine the look of surprise on Grace's face when he showed up.

That was enough motivation for him. He got up and got ready.

They were never going to get this all done.

Grace reviewed her checklist.

Over half the items had yet to be completed, and the Messtival opened in under two hours.

"Has anyone seen the squid?" a teenager called from the grassy area in front of the church where they'd set up the ink pool.

"The what now?" The deep, laughing voice behind Grace pulled her head in that direction.

She was sure she recognized it, but that couldn't be. He would never . . .

But there he was, striding toward her in khaki cargo shorts and a navy polo shirt.

"Levi." His name came out sounding more delighted than surprised, and she worked to rein that in. The only reason she was happy was that she might be able to rope him into helping. "What are you doing here?"

"Thought I'd check out this Messtival you keep talking about." He stopped a couple feet in front of her, hands in his pockets. "What's this about a squid?"

"Oh, yes." She turned toward the teen at the ink pool, who was still awaiting her instructions. "Did someone already put it in the pool?" she called across the lawn.

"Maybe," the girl called back, shrugging.

Grace exhaled, checking her clipboard again. "This day is not going as planned."

"What can I do to help?"

She could feel Levi reading over her shoulder.

"Seriously? You want to help? Actually, never mind." She seized his wrist and pulled him toward the far end of the parking lot. "You already offered. I'm not going to give you a chance to back out."

She pointed to the pile of ropes, plastic sheeting, and buckets of goop the teens had mixed up using water, paint, and food thickener. "Can you turn this into a tug-of-war pit? The plastic sheet goes on the ground, the goop on top of it, then the ropes—"

"Yeah. I've seen tug-of-war before. I've got this." He nudged her toward the teen who'd been calling for her. "Go take care of your squid emergency." He grinned. "There's a sentence I bet no one's ever said before."

"Thank you." Grace didn't have time to argue or to ask if he was sure he knew what he was doing. She jogged to the ink pool.

Fortunately, by the time she got there, another teen had found the missing squid. Grace watched as they threw it into the dark blue goop they'd filled the two-foot-deep pool with. Barely bigger than a quarter, the squid sank and disappeared from sight.

She hoped at least a few people would find it. It'd be disappointing if no one won the game.

"Grace, we need you over here."

She took off for the next emergency, spending the next hour locating a missing pinata, filling water balloons with paint, and lining up eggs for the egg toss.

Every once in a while, she peeked up to check on Levi's progress.

He'd finished the tug-of-war, and last she'd seen, he'd been surrounded by a group of teen boys, including Jackson, and was helping them set up the paint dodgeball course. He'd had the biggest smile on his face as he'd listened to one of the boys.

Grace had been tempted to pull out her phone and snap a picture, but then she'd been called away to sort out an issue with the prizes for the shaving cream slip-n-slide obstacle course.

By the time she had that all figured out, cars had started to fill the parking lot. Grace checked the time. Ten o'clock on the dot.

Then she checked her list. Every last item was done.

"Thank you, Lord," she breathed. "Please bless everyone who comes with a fun day."

"Now what?"

She jumped as Levi popped up next to her.

"Now I say thank you for helping. I don't think we'd have gotten it done without you."

"You're welcome." He stepped closer, watching families pour toward the ticket booth. "And now that you've thanked me, what's next?"

"Next?" Did he mean between them, or . . .

"Do you need help overseeing the games or anything?"

"Oh." She turned her back to him so she could survey the various activities—and so he wouldn't see the blush she could feel rising to her cheeks. "Nope. The teens should have that all covered."

"Good. Then let's go."

"Go? Levi, I can't go. I have to stay in case—"

But he grabbed her hand, tugging her toward the line that had formed at the ink pool. "I need to see what this squid thing is all about. Let's go play."

"Oh no, I really can't. I have to walk around and make sure there aren't any problems. Make sure everyone's having fun."

"Sure." Levi didn't let go of her. "But first *you* need to have some fun. You did all this hard work. Now you have to enjoy it."

"I *am* enjoying it." But she let him pull her into the line. She had to admit that for all the years she'd helped with this event, she'd never once played any of the games. And based on the shrieks coming from all around them, it was fun.

They ended up in line for the ink pool behind Tyler and Isabel, who were patiently answering the questions Isabel's daughter Gabby was tossing at them, while Tyler's twin boys threw a squishy ball back and forth. All five of them were covered with paint and goop already.

"Hey. I've barely seen y'all since you got back from your honeymoon." Grace pulled them each into a hug.

When she stepped back from Gabby's full-body launch, Isabel frowned. "We got you all covered in goop."

"No worries. Levi says I have to try the ink pool, so I guess I'm about to get messier."

"That's why they call it the Messtival." One of the twins grinned at her—Jeremiah she was pretty sure, though even after knowing them for five years, she still sometimes had a hard time telling them apart.

"And you must be Levi." Isabel stepped around Grace to hold out a hand to him.

"Oh, sorry. Levi, this is Isabel and her husband Tyler. And their kids—Gabby, Jonah, and Jeremiah. Y'all, this is Levi Donovan."

"Nice to meet you." Tyler held out a hand too. "Your name's pretty well known in these parts." He turned to his boys. "Levi used to play in the NFL. Isn't that cool?"

Instead of the overconfident smile he usually wore when someone recognized him, Levi looked a little bit . . . humble as Jonah and Jeremiah exclaimed over how awesome that was.

"We need a new coach for the boys' team," Tyler said to Levi. "If you're going to be around in fall."

"Oh. Uh—"

"Levi's only home for the summer," Grace jumped in. No point in letting the twins get their hopes up when Levi wouldn't be around by fall.

Levi gave her a strange look but nodded. "Sorry."

"All right, Weston family, you're up," the teen running the booth called.

Isabel smiled. "I love being called that." She turned and climbed into the goop-filled kiddie pool with the rest of her family.

"So what's the object of this game?" Levi's voice came from right behind her, and she jumped, moving forward a few steps to fill in the space vacated by the Westons.

"Basically, you get in the pool and try to be the first one to find the squid. You have three minutes."

"And if you find it?"

"You get to choose a prize, of course." She gestured to the display of prizes various shops around town had donated.

"Sounds easy enough. Prepare to be smoked by me. Again."

She shook her head. "If you recall, I won our last race."

He smirked. "Only because I let—" He broke off, eyes widening.

She poked an accusatory finger at his chest. "I knew you let me win."

"Busted." He chuckled, and she realized her finger was still pressed against him.

She pulled her hand back. "You should know I hate when people let me win. My brother Zeb did that once, and I punched him in the gut."

A loud, clear laugh burst from Levi. "You did not."

"Honest to goodness. I did. So you'd better not let me win this time."

Levi schooled his face into a mock serious expression and raised one hand, as if he were taking an oath. "I solemnly swear."

"Good." They watched as Isabel, Tyler, and the kids finished out their turn in the pool, giggling and shrieking but coming up empty-handed.

As they climbed out, the teen gestured for Levi and Grace to get into the pool.

The goop came up to Grace's knees as she stepped in. It was warmer than she'd expected it to be—and slimier. She slid her feet across the bottom of the pool to make room for Levi. He made a face as he got in.

"Kind of squeamish for a football player, aren't you?" She lifted a handful of the goop and lobbed it at him. It hit him square in the chest. "Kind of slow too."

"You think so, huh?" He picked up a much bigger handful of goop, chucking it at her.

But she managed to dodge out of the way before it could land on her cheek.

She reached for another scoop of the goop, as did Levi, but just then the teen called, "Ready. Go!"

They both dropped the goop from their hands and started feeling around under the opaque surface. Grace dropped to her knees, letting the goop cover her thighs.

She was going to win this one fair and square.

"What do you say? Winner gets to dunk the other person?" Levi's tongue poked out of the corner of his mouth as he slid his arms through the goop.

Grace spun to search the section behind her. "Hope you brought your nose plugs."

"I don't think I'll be needing them." Levi lifted his arm triumphantly from the goop and held it over his head. "Because I win."

"What?" Grace stood, examining his hand, which was dripping with goop but which also undoubtedly held the squid.

"You already had that when you made the bet, didn't you?"

He shot her a sneaky, boyish grin. "You told me not to let you win."

"I didn't tell you to cheat!"

"I wasn't cheating." Levi took a step closer to her. "I was being clever." He reached for her.

"You wouldn't!" Grace tried to back away from him. But the pool was too slippery. Before she could react, her feet had shot out from under her, and she was on her back, head submerged in the goop.

A flash of real panic shot through her. Was it possible to drown in two feet of goop? Was she going to be the first person to ever find out?

Something solid wrapped around her arms, and before she could figure out what it was, she was being hoisted into the air. Fresh air rushed into her nostrils, and she sputtered, trying to lift a hand to get the goop out of her eyes.

But her arms were still in that grip.

"For the record—" The pressure on Grace's arms eased, and something soft rubbed against her face, wiping the goop from her eyes. She opened them to find Levi lowering his goop-covered shirt. "I wasn't really going to dunk you."

He took her hand and led her to the side of the pool.

"So you say." But she squeezed his hand. "Thanks for saving me."

"Anytime you fall into goop, you know who to call." He supported her elbow as she stepped out of the pool, then followed her out.

They toweled off, then made their way to the prize booth, where Levi tried to make her choose the prize, even though he'd technically been the one to win it. When she refused, he picked a giant plush flamingo.

"That's not tacky at all." She wrinkled her nose as the teen handed it to him. "You should give that to your next date. She'll love it."

"I'm glad you feel that way." Levi grinned at her. "Because I got it for you."

"Um, no." Why was her heart hammering like that? It wasn't like Levi had meant that the way it'd sounded. He just wanted to offload the tacky stuffed toy on her.

Levi raised an eyebrow. "No to the flamingo, or no to the date?"

Or he did mean it the way it'd sounded.

She wiped a hand over a stray blob of goop that had fallen from her hair to her shoulder. "Both."

Right?

Yes. She definitely meant both. She didn't want some pink monstrosity of a bird in her house. And she definitely didn't want to date Levi.

"Fair enough." Levi tucked the bird under his arm. "Up for some tug-of-war? I hear it was set up by an expert."

"Is that so?" She followed him toward the rope, trying to figure out what the sudden tug-of-war in her heart was all about.

Chapter 14

"Where've you been hiding?" Levi looked up as Grace came into the bedroom where he'd been laying hardwood flooring. His crew had finished installing all the upstairs bathrooms, so things were moving along well.

"Why? Did you miss me?" Grace teased. She'd been doing that more this past week. Acting less guarded with him. More open.

He supposed that was what happened when you swam in goop together.

Levi made a face at her. So what if he had?

He was getting used to working side-by-side with her. "No. Just wondered how long you were going to slack off while I did all the work."

"For your information—" Grace passed him a steaming cup of coffee and a donut from the bakery. "I was getting fitted for my bridesmaid's dress for my brother's wedding. Trust me, I would have rather been here."

"Hey, if you're going to make a run to the bakery every morning, feel free to slack as much as you want." Levi shifted his weight to sit on the half-finished floor, and Grace plopped down across from him.

"So your brother's getting married? The one you punched in the gut for letting you win?"

"No. Zeb's already married. It's my oldest brother, Simeon, who's getting married this time."

"How many siblings do you have?" He wasn't sure why he was asking. Only that his donut was almost gone, and he didn't want her to disappear on him again.

"Six. All brothers."

He whistled. "That explains it."

"Explains what?" She tore off a piece of donut and popped it into her mouth, but her eyes challenged him.

"Your competitiveness. Your toughness. Your propensity to speak your mind."

"My—" But she laughed. "You make me sound like a rather unlikable person."

"Nope." He took a sip of his coffee, studying her over the rim. "Those are all likable qualities."

"If you say so." She brushed the powdered sugar from her hands. "So what are we doing today?"

Levi watched her. She didn't like receiving compliments, that much he'd learned. Then again, he supposed it had been a rather backhanded compliment.

Maybe he should be more direct. Come out and tell her she was stunning even in her faded purple t-shirt and running shorts.

Nope.

That would definitely not be a good idea.

He drained the rest of his coffee, then pushed to his feet. "Today you get to learn how to lay a hardwood floor."

Fortunately, she was a quick learner, and by late afternoon they had the floor finished.

Grace straightened her legs with a groan once the last board was in place. "No one told me you were going to work me this hard, Levi Donovan."

"You said you wanted to put a piece of yourself into this place. I'm just trying to help."

"Thanks for that." But the smile she gave him said she was sincere in spite of the sarcastic tone. "Be honest. This is harder than the NFL, isn't it?"

He laughed. "Ask me that after you've been tackled by a three-hundred-pound defensive end."

"Do you miss it?" Her question was quiet, no trace of teasing or sarcasm left.

He thought for a moment. "Sometimes, yeah. I miss the fields and the lights and the sound of the crowds. The smell of the turf. I especially loved the stadiums with natural grass. Always reminded me of the first time I played, in middle school."

"Have you thought at all about what Tyler said? About coaching here?"

He shook his head. "Like you said, I won't be here by fall."

"Right." She turned away, picking up the tools they'd left scattered on the floor. "It's Friday. If you want to quit early, it's fine."

"Why would I want to quit early?"

She lifted one shoulder.

"I don't have a date every Friday night, if that's what you were thinking."

"I wasn't thinking anything." But he could have sworn that was relief in her eyes. "You've just been working really hard here, and we got the room done, so I figured you deserved a break."

"How about this? We'll call it a day. But we go to the hardware store to get some more nails for the nail gun."

"You need me to come along for that?"

"No. I don't *need* you to." Though he did *want* her to. Which should probably concern him. "Just figured you might like to come. I could show you what I had in mind for the kitchen cabinets. But we can always do it another time."

"No. I'll come along." Grace's smile landed on him, making his insides do a weird sort of half-jump. He ordered them to settle down. It was a ride to the hardware store for business. Nothing to get all excited about.

"Let me go change," Grace added. "Last time you told me everyone goes to the hardware store a mess, I discovered what a liar you are."

"Oh come on, you were the prettiest one in there." The words came out of their own volition.

Grace blinked at him, then turned and fled for the door. "I'll be ready in two minutes. Meet you in the car."

Great.

Hopefully those two minutes would give Levi enough time to relocate his common sense.

Because if he kept saying things like that, he had a feeling both he and Grace were going to regret it.

Chapter 15

"What do you think of these?" Grace pointed to a set of Shaker-style cabinet doors, glancing at Levi out of the corner of her eye. They'd been at the hardware store for an hour already, but he didn't show any signs of being in a hurry to leave.

"I like those. Maybe in white."

She turned to full-out stare at him.

"What?" His stubbly jaw line lifted in a smile.

"I think that might be the first time we've agreed on anything about this project."

"That's not true." Levi's eyes took on a playful glint, and he tugged on a strand of her hair that had escaped from her ponytail. "We also agreed that you were wrong about the dining room paint color and the showerheads and the whole TV situation."

Grace shoved him. "We did not agree about that last one." Though she had to admit she was glad she'd gone with his suggestions for the dining room and the showerheads. He had surprisingly good taste.

"I'll convince you yet." His wink was completely friendly, and yet it made Grace's heart quiver just a little.

"Excuse me?" A woman approached them, her gaze clearly on Levi alone. She looked a year or two younger than Grace but supremely more confident. "Do you happen to know where the faucets are?"

Grace ducked her head so neither of them would see her eye roll. Did women really think asking where to find things in the hardware store was a good way to pick up a man? Then again, judging by Levi's reaction last time, it apparently was.

"Over there." Levi pointed toward the far side of the store. "So I was thinking maybe we skip door pulls with these cabinets. Keep the lines clean and simple."

It took Grace a moment to realize he was talking to her. "What? Oh. Yeah. I mean, I agree."

The woman looked at Levi again, then at Grace, then walked off in the direction Levi had pointed. Grace swallowed a smile as she turned back to the cabinets.

She did *not* feel gratified that Levi had ignored another woman for her sake. Besides, it wasn't like he'd done it for her sake at all. The woman probably just wasn't his type.

And even if he had done it for her sake, he needn't have bothered. She had absolutely no interest in who Levi Donovan did or did not ignore.

"So I'll order these then?" Levi opened and closed the cabinet again.

"Yeah. That'd be great. What about the countertops?"

"You up for picking that out yet today? Otherwise we can come back next week."

"I'm game if you are. This is fun." The vision she'd had for the bed-and-breakfast was really coming together.

"All right." He grinned at her. "Don't want to stop your fun." If he thought she was lame for finding spending her Friday evening at the hardware store fun, he didn't let on.

For the next hour, he patiently led her through the options. After they'd agreed on a gray-black quartz, Levi led the way to the checkout, stopping at a small freezer and digging out two wrapped ice cream bars.

He paid for them, then passed one to her. "I ate two of these a day every day growing up. You have to try one."

She relented, unwrapping her bar as he held the exit door open for her.

Outside, Grace examined the streaks of orange and peach ribboning across the sky. "How long were we in there?" Somehow, the sun was nearly on the horizon. "Sorry to take up your whole night."

"The night is young yet." Levi pointed to her ice cream bar. "Now stop stalling and try that."

He watched as she took a bite. "How good is that?"

In truth, it tasted the same as every other ice cream bar Grace had ever eaten. But somehow, Levi's enthusiasm gave it a little extra something.

She smiled and took another bite. "Delicious."

"Good." Levi looked happy with himself as they walked to the truck, where he stashed the bags in the back. He lifted a hand to shield his eyes and peer toward the football field across the street, where a group of high school boys was playing.

"Is that tall one Jackson?"

Grace squinted. "Hard to tell from here. But I think so."

"He seems like a good kid."

"He is. Came from a rough background. Mom overdosed when he was little, and he was in and out of foster care for years before Leah adopted him. He's become a very thoughtful young man."

Levi watched the boys another minute. "You in a hurry?"

"No." She answered slowly, slightly apprehensively. What if he was about to ask her to dinner? "Why?"

"Come on." He took her hand and dragged her toward the road, not letting go even when she fell into step beside him.

She gently pulled her hand back, though he didn't seem to notice.

Good.

That meant the handholding hadn't meant anything to him. Nor had it to her.

"Hey, guys," Levi called as they reached the field. "Got room for one more?"

Would wonders never cease? She turned to Levi, and he laughed.

"Don't look so surprised. I can actually be a pretty nice guy."

Yeah.

She'd been starting to notice that.

Levi jogged toward the boys, who had stopped playing to wait for him, their faces lit with the excitement of meeting a hero.

Grace settled onto the grass, telling herself it didn't make a hill of beans of difference to her if Levi was a nice guy. He might be kind and he might show the occasional emotion and he might even prove to be good with kids. But that didn't change the fact that he was the wrong man for her. If his overactive dating life wasn't enough to prove that, his attitude toward God was.

Not only was he not a pastor, but he had admitted to not being sure if he believed anymore. And while she was committed to sharing Christ's love with him in any way she could, dating him was out of the question.

Not that he was asking.

Still, as she watched him play, Grace couldn't help but appreciate the way he offered the boys encouragement and gentle correction without crushing their confidence. Tyler had been right—Levi would make a good coach.

If he were staying in Hope Springs.

Which he wasn't. And that was one more reason he could never be Mr. Right.

Levi and the boys played ball until the sun had fully set and dark started to creep over the field.

"All right, guys. I have to call it a night. I've kept my friend waiting too long already." Levi waved to the boys and jogged toward Grace.

Friend. She had to admit she liked the idea of being friends with Levi.

As long as that was what it remained.

They trooped across the street and into the truck.

"That was nice of you. Playing with those kids. Imagine the stories they'll be able to tell their kids someday."

Levi shrugged, looking uncharacteristically modest. "I had fun."

"I could tell."

"Yeah?" Levi sent her a questioning look. "How?"

"I don't know." Actually, she did know, but she didn't want to tell him that she'd watched him closely. That she knew the difference between his fake smile and his real smile. That when he was enjoying himself, his dimple just barely showed. "You just seemed to have a natural way with those kids."

They fell silent, though Levi still sported that happy look.

She was glad. He wore it much better than his usual surly expression.

He pulled into the driveway of the bed-and-breakfast and stopped the truck near the front porch, then cut the engine.

A ripple went through Grace's tummy. "You don't need to walk me to the door or anything."

"I know." But Levi pushed his door open. "I'm going to carry in the stuff we bought."

Oh yeah. A wave of foolishness washed over her. Why would she have thought Levi wanted to walk her to the door?

All these signs of interest she thought she was seeing in him were a figment of her imagination.

Levi lifted the bags out of the back of the truck as she scurried up the steps to unlock the front door. She waited in the entryway as Levi set the packages on the floor.

"I'll sort through everything on Monday." He straightened, meeting her eyes. "Thanks for coming with me. It was fun."

She nodded, and he shifted, then gave a self-conscious laugh and grabbed the door. "See you Monday then."

"Yep."

She watched as he bounded down the porch steps toward the truck.

"Levi?" Heavens to Betsy, what had made her call out like that?

"Yeah?" He took a step in her direction.

"A bunch of us are having dinner at Sophie and Spencer's tomorrow night. I'm sure they'd love it if you came too."

Levi ran a hand through his hair, looking uncertain. "Maybe I will. Thanks."

"Goodnight." Grace ducked into the house, closing the door behind her before she could say something else stupid.

Chapter 16

Levi raised a hand to knock on the door of the ranch-style house, glancing around him at the acres of cherry orchards surrounding the property.

He had gone back and forth a hundred times today about whether or not to come to the dinner at Sophie and Spencer's, which was unlike him—he was usually a decisive man. But when it came to Grace, he'd felt more and more like he was playing on a new field for the first time. Except she was a lot harder to figure out than football.

On the one hand, she was so not his type. Not to mention that she'd made it abundantly clear he was the furthest thing from her type.

But on the other hand, he couldn't deny that he enjoyed spending time with her. Or that, on occasion, she seemed to like being with him too.

The door opened to reveal Grace, her usual casual attire replaced by a simple yellow sundress. "I figured it had to be you. No one else knocks." She closed the door behind him. "I'm glad you came."

"Me too." He planted his hands in his pockets before he could brush away the piece of hair that had fallen across her forehead. "Where is everyone?"

"Out back." She pointed toward a patio door at the other end of the house.

He stepped that direction, but a hand on his arm stopped him.

Grace was biting her lip and studying the floor. "There's something I should probably tell you."

He eyed her. "Something I'm not going to like?"

"I don't know. Maybe." She drew up her shoulders as if preparing to do battle with him. "I invited Luke and May too."

"You— Why?" It was bad enough that Luke still wouldn't talk to him at home. He didn't need his brother to ruin his time here too.

"They're my friends." She gave him a defiant look. "And I think if you get to know May you'll like her. She's kind and sweet and—"

"That's not the point." Levi ran a hand through his hair. Why couldn't anyone else see it? "Luke has BMD."

Grace's eyes sparked. "Is that all you see when you look at your brother? His disability?" She crossed her arms in front of her. "Has it ever occurred to you that your brother is sweet and charming and kind and . . ."

Yeah. He got it. All the things he wasn't.

"That may be. But it doesn't change the fact that he's likely going to end up an invalid someday. Does May know what that's going to be like? Is she going to stick by his side through that? In my experience, people don't hang around when things don't turn out the way they expected. I don't want my brother to have to go through that."

"May's not like that." Grace seemed so earnest. "Just give her a chance. Please."

Levi shook his head. "Why does it matter so much to you?"

Grace chewed her lip again. "I don't like to see families torn apart," she said at last. "And I know how much it bothers you that you and Luke aren't speaking right now."

She couldn't know that. Because it didn't bother him one bit.

"I'm speaking to him. And he can speak to me anytime he wants."

The sound of voices approaching the front door drew their attention to the window. Great.

"Please, Levi," Grace pleaded. "Just be nice. Give her a chance."

He sighed. He didn't see how he had much of a choice. His desire to stay and spend the evening with Grace—and her friends, of course—just slightly outweighed his desire to avoid his brother.

"Thank you," Grace said before he could respond. She scooted past him to open the door, and he took the opportunity to escape to the backyard. Just because he'd said he'd stay didn't mean he had to hang out and talk to Luke and May.

Grace's friends greeted him as he stepped outside onto the deck. To his surprise, he remembered most everyone's names from the last time they'd met.

Most of the group was gathered around Dan and Jade and their new baby, but Austin broke away to shake Levi's hand.

"Thanks for playing ball with Jackson and his friends last night. He hasn't stopped talking about it all day. When he wasn't in the yard lobbing passes at the tree."

"It was my pleasure," Levi said honestly. "Kid's got a good arm."

"You ever think about coaching? I know our high school program could use someone of your caliber."

What was it with everyone asking him about coaching? "Yeah. Maybe."

Wait.

Where had that answer come from? He didn't have any intention of coaching. Or of sticking around Hope Springs.

But before he could correct himself, Grace was emerging from the house with Luke and May. Her eyes zeroed in on him, and even from this distance he could read the disapproval in them. He didn't doubt she'd bring Luke and May straight to him, just to spite him.

But after letting her glare burn through him for a few more seconds, she led Luke and May toward the others gathered around Dan and Jade.

"Everyone." Grace's voice cut over the chatter. "I think most of y'all know these guys from church, but in case you don't, this is Luke Donovan. Levi's brother. And May. Luke's girlfriend." Grace directed a pointed look at Levi as a chorus of hellos and welcomes filled the evening.

"Luke Donovan. You were a baseball star at the high school, weren't you?" Ethan asked.

Luke ducked his head, but that didn't keep Levi from noticing his pleased expression.

"Levi is the star," Luke said. "But yeah, I played baseball."

"You were good," Ethan insisted. "I heard you almost made the All-State team your senior year."

He had? Levi stared at his brother. He'd known Luke liked baseball, but he'd assumed his brother's disease meant that he'd spent his seasons riding the bench.

"It was no big deal," Luke mumbled. "Not like it was the Super Bowl or anything." His eyes cut to Levi.

But what was he supposed to say to that?

"You still play?" someone asked.

"Once in a while. Getting a little tougher now, but I get in a game when I can."

"How about right now?" Grace asked. "The backyard is plenty big enough. We could get in a quick game before dinner."

"That's not a good—" Levi stepped forward. What was Grace thinking? Couldn't she see that Luke couldn't even *walk*? How was he supposed to play baseball?

"That sounds fun, actually." Luke glanced at May, who offered an encouraging nod.

Everyone except Jade, who was holding her baby, filed into the yard.

"Levi?" Grace called, the expectation in her voice clear.

"I'm good, thanks." He searched out a place to sit.

But Grace marched toward him. "You said you'd try," she hissed. "It's a game of baseball. You don't even have to talk."

"Fine." It was totally unfair that this woman could get him to do things he had no intention of doing. "But put us on different teams."

Grace rolled her eyes, but as they joined the others, she made sure both she and Levi were on the opposite team to Luke and May, who had taken up positions in the outfield.

Spencer batted first, hitting a line drive that got him onto first. Then Sophie was up, managing a pop fly that got her husband to third. Levi let himself relax. It didn't look like anyone here was going to knock one toward Luke.

Grace was up next, with a respectable hit down center field, but Tyler was quick on his feet and threw her out. She gave a good-natured shrug as she returned to the lineup.

71

"You're up, Levi," Spencer called from third base. "How about a homer?"

Levi grimaced. Baseball had never been his sport. But he'd never yet backed down from a challenge. He kept his eyes on the ball as Jared wound up, then released his pitch. It was low and to the outside, but Levi swung.

The bat connected with the ball, sending it up and over the heads of the infielders, directly toward Luke's position.

Instinct told Levi to run out there, put himself between Luke and the ball. But logic told him he'd never make it in time. He could only stand and watch, ignoring his teammates' shouts to run.

The ball reached the top of its arc and rocketed toward Luke, who let his cane fall to the ground and shifted two steps to the right, his eyes never leaving the sky.

He raised his gloved hand into the air, and the ball dropped into it with a perfect thud.

His team erupted into cheers, and Levi had to grin, even as a pang went through him. He should have been around more when Luke was in high school. His schedule with college ball and then the NFL had kept him too busy.

But that was mostly an excuse. In all honesty, he hadn't wanted to come back. Hadn't wanted to see Luke deteriorate. But maybe he'd missed out on the best years they could have spent together.

Levi forced his attention back to the game. Emma was up to bat next but struck out. As the teams switched positions, Levi moved to congratulate Luke on his catch.

But May ran to Luke's side and pressed a kiss to his cheek. "Nice catch."

Levi veered away, marching toward first base.

Why did it bother him so much, he wondered, Luke and May's relationship?

Grace had asked if the only thing he saw when he looked at Luke was his disability.

If he was honest, the answer was probably yes. But only because he *had* to see Luke that way. It was the only way to protect him.

Levi was so caught up in his thoughts that he missed an easy catch, allowing Tyler to get on first.

"You're up next, Luke," someone called.

"All right." Luke stood to make his way slowly to home plate. "I'm going to need a designated runner though. Legs aren't quite what they used to be."

"I'll run for you." May popped up next to him.

From across the field, Grace shot Levi a look that screamed "told you so."

Luke was almost at home plate when he went down.

It took Levi a moment to register that his brother was on the ground. But the moment he did, he sprinted for Luke's crumpled form.

He'd known baseball was a bad idea. But would anyone listen to him?

When he reached Luke, May was already crouching at his side, holding his cane out to him.

"What happened?" Levi scanned his brother for signs of injury.

The others began to reach them as well.

"Is he all right?" someone asked from the back of the group.

May stood, looking from Luke to the others. "Nothing to worry about. He just likes to practice his stunt double moves sometimes. He's expecting a call from James Bond any day."

Luke gave her a pained smile, but Levi glowered over May. "This is a joke to you?"

"No, of course not. I was only—"

"Get out of the way." Crouching behind Luke, Levi wrapped his hands under his brother's armpits.

"Oh, he can—" May started.

But Levi cut her off with a look, then hoisted Luke to his feet, waiting until he'd taken the cane and was steady on his feet to let go.

Luke gave him a long look, then shuffled away without a word.

"You're welcome," Levi muttered.

Grace appeared at his side. "That was kind of scary. You okay?"

Levi gave a terse nod, though it was a lie.

How could he be okay when his baby brother so clearly wasn't?

Chapter 17

"I think I'm going to take off." Levi leaned toward Grace, who'd been sitting next to him as they ate, lifting his empty plate off his lap. He'd managed to clear it, despite the fact that everything tasted like cardboard. Not that it wasn't perfectly good food—based on the last time he'd eaten with this group, he was sure it was all delicious. But his heart wasn't in food right now.

No matter what he did or how many times Grace tried to strike up a conversation, he couldn't get the image of Luke splayed on the ground out of his head. Or the way May had laughed at Luke. Or the way everyone was acting as if nothing had happened.

"Don't go." Grace set a hand on his arm, and the warmth of her fingers went through him.

But he pushed to his feet. "I'm not much fun right now."

Grace stood too. "It's going to be fine, you know. He's going to be fine." She looked so sincere and so concerned all at once that he had a sudden urge to step into her arms for a good old-fashioned hug. How long had it been since anyone had given him one of those?

"Yeah." He massaged a knot at the back of his neck. "I'll see you Monday, okay?"

She set those worried eyes on him again but nodded.

Levi brought his plate into the house, then made his way toward the front door, pausing at a family picture of Sophie and Spencer with their twins. Instead of looking at the camera, they were all looking at Rylan, who appeared to be reaching for something in the grass. Levi peered closer.

A frog.

They looked like a happy family. A normal family. The kind of family he'd had until Luke had been diagnosed and they'd fallen apart.

"Levi?"

Though the voice was quiet, he jumped. He hadn't heard anyone else come into the house. He glanced over his shoulder.

"I was just leaving." He kept his tone short. He didn't have any desire to talk to May.

"I know." She looked tentative, as if one word from him might send her scurrying out the door. Definitely not the type of woman who was strong enough to stand up to the kinds of challenges Luke would face.

"I just wanted to say, I know it's hard for you to see Luke like this. But he's okay."

Levi ground his teeth. She had no idea what it was like for him.

This was the baby brother he'd grown up with. Played and climbed trees with. Run with. Thrown a ball with.

And now look at him. Luke very much was *not* okay.

He took a step toward her. "Is that why you laughed at him? Mocked him right in front of everyone else? Because he's okay?"

"What?" May's eyes widened, and she stepped back. "I didn't laugh—"

"You think he hasn't gone through enough in his life? The mocking, the bullying. You think he needs you to point out that he's no James Bond?"

"I wasn't trying to—"

But Levi didn't want to stand here and listen to her excuses. "Like I said, I have to go." He strode toward the front door.

"Levi, wait."

He yanked the door open, staring into the fading light for a moment, then faced her. "What do you want with Luke anyway? We both know you're going to stick around until he gets too sick and then you'll get tired of him and be off, chasing after someone who's whole and complete and healthy. So why don't you save everyone involved some heartache and be on your way now?"

He lurched out the door and pulled it shut behind him, breathing heavily.

That had been completely unfair, and he knew it.

Because though he did worry that May would eventually desert his brother, those words had been directed not at her but at Rayna.

He huffed out a breath and jogged to his Harley. He'd have to apologize at some point, he supposed. But right now, all he wanted to do was put as much distance as possible between himself and other people.

"You okay?" Grace set the load of dishes she'd collected from outside on the counter, then moved toward the kitchen stool where May was sitting. The younger woman looked all trembly and shaken.

May sent her a weak smile that barely lifted her lips. "Can I ask you something?"

"Of course." Grace pulled out a stool and sat next to her. "What's up?"

"Do you think family is the most important thing?"

Grace frowned. "Most important for what?"

"I don't know. To keep together? Have a good relationship?"

"I do." Grace bit her lip. "Though we can't always please them." She thought of Mama, probably sitting at home right now scheming ways to get her to come home and marry Aaron.

"Do you have siblings?" May asked.

Grace laughed. "Yeah. Six brothers. Why?"

"I'm an only child, so I've always wished I could have had a brother or sister. Are you and your brothers close?"

The question brought the familiar ache to her soul. "Mostly. I'm in my brother Simeon's wedding in three weeks. But my brother Judah is estranged from the family. None of us have even seen him in six years."

"That's so sad." May set a hand on hers.

"It's hard. I don't think any of us realized how much we needed each other until he was gone." Grace patted May's hand. "But I pray for him every day. And I trust that God will bring him back to us—and back to the Lord—one day."

"I'll pray that too." May slid her chair back. "Thanks for the talk. I feel much better."

"Good." Grace waved her toward the backyard. "Now you'd better get out there. I'm sure there's one young man who's getting impatient to see you again."

"Yeah." A look of sadness flickered in May's eyes, but then she was gone out the door.

Grace moved into the kitchen and started putting food away. By the time everyone left, Sophie and Spencer would be exhausted and want to get the twins to bed.

She was almost done when Jade slipped into the room, a sleeping baby Matthias cradled in her arms.

Grace smiled at her, whispering, "You two look so happy."

"Which two?" Jade rubbed her baby's cheek. "Me and Dan? Or me and Matthias?"

"Both. All of you. I'm so happy for you."

"Thanks." Jade shifted Matthias to her shoulder, and he wiggled, scrunching his legs up under him. "I have to say, you've been looking pretty happy yourself."

"Me?" Grace grabbed a dishrag to wipe down the counter. "I'm excited with the progress on the bed-and-breakfast. I still can't believe it's really happening sometimes."

She felt Jade's eyes on her, and she scrubbed harder at a drip from the strawberry pie Peyton had brought.

When she couldn't scrub anymore, she looked up. "What?"

"Nothing." But Jade's knowing smile belied the word.

"Seriously, what?" Grace set the rag down and dried her hands.

"All right." Jade's smile grew. "I was just wondering if you're sure the renovation is the only thing making you so happy."

"I have a lot of things to be happy about. God's love. Singing in choir. How successful the Messtival was. Did you know we raised—"

"Levi Donovan," Jade cut in.

"What?"

"Levi Donovan is one of the things making you happy."

"Uh, no." But she could feel every drop of blood in her body rushing to her cheeks. "Levi makes me a lot of things—annoyed, irritated, frustrated—but not happy."

Jade only laughed.

"What?"

"Methinks the lady doth protest too much."

"Seriously, I don't—" But she made herself stop. No use solidifying Jade's opinion by protesting more. "He's become a friend. But I have zero interest in him in any other way. He's the complete opposite of my type."

"If you say so." Jade patted baby Matthias on the back as he started to fuss. "Just remember, Dan and I were the complete opposite of each other's type too." She made quiet shushing sounds to Matthias and glided out of the room.

Grace didn't need to be reminded of how different Dan and Jade had been. But now that she knew them, she couldn't imagine either of them with anyone else.

But that was Dan and Jade.

She and Levi were an entirely different story.

Levi had spent the night zoning in and out in front of a baseball game on television. But he had no idea what was happening or who was winning. He couldn't stop stewing over Luke's fall, Grace's compassion, May's hurt—and for good measure, he kept remembering the look of indifference on Rayna's face when she'd walked out on him.

He clicked the TV off and sat staring at the blank screen.

He had no idea how much time had passed when he heard the front door open. Luke's shuffling steps paused in the doorway.

"What are you doing?" Luke's voice was strained as he looked from Levi to the TV.

Levi shoved himself off the couch and moved toward his brother. "Waiting for you. About May . . ." He could at least apologize to Luke now, and maybe Luke could pass his apology on to May.

"You don't have to lecture me about her anymore." Luke pressed his fingers to his eyelids. "You were right." As Luke dropped his hand, Levi looked closer. His brother's eyes were red-rimmed and bloodshot.

"Right about what?" A sick feeling flooded Levi's stomach.

"That she wouldn't stick around." Luke's voice was hoarse. "She just broke up with me. Said she couldn't see us working out long term."

A brief flare of guilt rose in Levi's chest, but he squashed it down. If May couldn't handle a few honest questions about her relationship with Luke, then Levi had obviously been right in his assessment of her. She wouldn't stick around for the tough parts. And with Luke's condition, there were bound to be a lot tougher moments than this.

"Look, man." Levi clapped a hand to Luke's shoulder. "I know you don't want to hear this right now, but I really do think you're better off this way."

Luke rubbed at his eyes. "How can I be better off when I'm missing a part of myself?"

"Trust me." Levi patted Luke's shoulder again. "We'll be bachelor brothers. The Donovan boys. We can go out whenever we want, come in whenever we want, watch sports whenever we want." He thought of Grace's silly no-TVs- in-the-bed-and-breakfast rule.

"I'm going to bed." Luke shuffled toward the hallway, head down, shoulders slumped.

"Luke, wait," Levi called.

Luke turned.

"It'll be great." Levi had to work to sound enthusiastic.

But it *would* be great. Wouldn't it?

He'd been a bachelor for the past two years, and he'd never felt freer.

Sure, it was lonely sometimes.

As it had the habit of doing at the most inconvenient times, an image of Grace popped into his head. He was never lonely when he was with her.

But loneliness was a small price to pay to guarantee he'd never be hurt again.

Chapter 18

"This is all my fault." Grace sipped at her too-hot coffee, pulling it away from her mouth as it burned her tongue. She had to take off in a minute for her final dress fitting, but she couldn't leave until she'd drilled Levi on what he knew about Luke and May's breakup. When she'd noticed them sitting separately at church yesterday, she'd been concerned. But when she'd tried to ask each of them what had happened, both had politely said they didn't want to talk about it.

"Careful." Levi blew across his own mug. "And it's not your fault. It's May's. She's the one who decided to walk away from him."

"She was acting strange the other night. Asking all kinds of weird questions about family and stuff. I should have pressed harder to find out what it was all about. Maybe I could have changed her mind. They seemed so in love."

Levi shrugged. "Things aren't always what they seem."

Grace stared at him. How could he be so callous? "I suppose you're happy about this?"

"No." Was that hurt in his eyes? "Believe it or not, I don't want my brother to be unhappy. But I do think he's better off this way. Better that she leave him now than in another couple of months or years."

Grace picked up her keys. "Why were you so sure she'd leave?" Not that he'd been wrong.

"Experience," Levi said simply.

"Right. Because you get rejected by women so often."

"You rejected me," he pointed out.

She nearly choked on her coffee. "That's different. You're not—"

"Your type. I know." Levi set his coffee down. "So what is your type then, if you don't like the strong, handsome, athletic type?"

Grace rolled her eyes. "I'll be back in a little while."

"I see how it is," Levi's tone turned teasing. "Weaseling out of work again."

"Trust me, I'd rather stay here and work. But unless you want to go get fitted for a dress for me . . ."

Levi struck a ridiculous pose that Grace guessed was supposed to be modeling a dress. "I could pull it off."

"And you'd have to face my mama too."

"I bet I could take her."

Grace snorted. "You obviously haven't met my mama."

But forty-five minutes later, as she modeled her dress over a video call for Mama to see, she wished she'd taken Levi up on the offer to try on the dress—and deal with Mama—for her.

"There's plenty of time, Mama," she said into the phone. "This should be the last of the alterations, and the wedding isn't for three weeks yet."

"You sound like Abigail. 'Stop worrying, Mrs. Calvano. Everything is under control, Mrs. Calvano. I don't want a big fuss, Mrs. Calvano.'" Mama huffed. "As if any bride doesn't want a big fuss."

Grace lifted her arms so Harper could tack a pin into the seam of the empire waistline. "How's Simeon doing? Is he nervous?"

Grace already knew the answer to that question, since she'd been texting with her brother yesterday. Simeon had always been the most laid-back of her brothers, so she hadn't been surprised that he was taking it all in stride. His biggest worry was dealing with Mama. Grace had reassured him that in three weeks it'd be all over and Mama would stop meddling in his wedding—and start meddling in his marriage instead.

"You know your brother." She could picture Mama's embroidery needle flying through the pattern as she talked. "Won't say a word about how he's feeling. But he's nervous. Can't hide that from his mama."

Grace bit her tongue so that she wouldn't tell Mama the thing he was most nervous about was that his mother would drive his bride away before the wedding day.

"I wish you'd consider coming home earlier for the wedding. We have plenty of room for you. And we never get to see you anymore."

Grace let Harper spin her one hundred eighty degrees and switched her phone to her other hand.

"I know, Mama. But I have too much going on here. The renovation on the bed-and-breakfast is really coming along, and I can't afford to lose any momentum on it."

"I thought we raised you to appreciate your family." The comment was a perfectly crafted guilt trip, and Grace knew it.

But that didn't make it any less effective.

She dropped her arm, nearly getting stuck by a pin before quickly raising it again.

"Sorry," Harper whispered.

Grace shook her head. "I'll see what I can do, Mama. Maybe I can come a couple days early."

"Oh good," Mama's voice sparkled with triumph. "That will give you and Aaron more time to spend together. He's been asking after you. I'll make reservations for y'all. How about The Shed?"

Grace almost fell off the small platform she was standing on. Harper reached up to steady her.

"I'm not going to go on a date with Aaron, Mama."

"Why ever not?" Mama's voice was all innocence. "He's a wonderful man, loves the Lord, looking for a wife. I know God brought him here for you."

Why ever not? Grace raised her free hand to her forehead. She could not have this conversation with Mama one more time.

"Because I'm bringing someone," she blurted.

Silence crackled from the other end of the line, and Grace congratulated herself. It'd been a long time since she'd shocked Mama into speechlessness.

It only lasted a moment. "Is it that fellow you started seeing?"

Grace angled the phone away from her face. What fellow was Mama talking about?

And then she remembered the conversation she'd had with Mama on her birthday. The one where she'd made up a boyfriend to get Mama to stop talking about Aaron.

Well, it had worked then. She supposed it could work now.

"Yes, Mama. That's who I'm bringing."

"Are you sure that's a good idea, Grace? You haven't told me anything about him. And if you're too ashamed to tell your mama about him, he can't be good for you."

"I'm not ashamed to tell you about him, Mama." It was pretty hard to be ashamed of someone who didn't exist. "But I have to run for now. I'll see you soon."

She hung up before Mama could start demanding actual details, then stood there, staring at her phone.

Now all she had to do was find a man who was willing to come to her brother's wedding with her—and pretend to be her date.

No problem.

Chapter 19

"Got a minute?" Levi wiped a bead of sweat off his forehead and peered into the dining room, where Grace was seated at a makeshift table, her laptop open in front of her.

She smiled. "Yes, please. I'm going crazy trying to pick out table settings."

He waited for her to shut down her computer and stand up.

"Close your eyes."

"Why?" But she closed them. "This isn't some sort of prank, is it?"

"Nope." He wrapped an arm around her back to steer her. "A surprise."

"Oh, I like surprises." She let him pull her in closer, and he took the opportunity to draw in a breath of that sweet scent he could never place.

"I know." He felt like there were a lot of things he knew about her now. And it'd grown harder every day to convince himself that knowing her better didn't make him like her more.

Not that it mattered if it did. Like he'd told Luke, he was a bachelor, and he liked it that way.

Of course, that had been two weeks ago. Since then, his belief in his own statement had been sorely tested by his days with Grace.

He led her out the front door and down the porch steps, adding his other hand to her elbow to keep her from falling.

"Where are we going?" She giggled as he led her down the driveway.

Finally he stopped. He wanted her to get the full effect.

"Ready?" He leaned closer.

"Yes." Her voice brimmed with the excitement of a kid on Christmas morning.

"Open your eyes."

"Wow. Levi." She took in a deep breath. "I don't know how to say this, but . . . you were right."

Pleasure shot through his chest. "Saying it just like that works. So you like it?"

She took a few steps closer to the building. "I love it. That teal really pops on the shutters and the door. I guess I should trust you more often."

"That's what I'm saying." He pulled out his phone to check the time. "Oh man. I have to get going." He'd been so busy trying to get this done for Grace that he'd completely lost track of the time.

"Got a date?" Grace teased.

He hesitated. But there was no reason he shouldn't tell her. "Yeah."

"Oh." Her expression didn't change, but she started walking toward the house.

"How about you? What are you doing tonight?" He jogged to catch up with her.

"Me? I think I'll stay home and have a good cry."

"What?" He grabbed her elbow and pulled her to a stop. "What's wrong?" She wasn't really going to cry over him, was she? He'd cancel the date if it meant that much to her. Honestly, the only reason he'd made it was to fight off this growing desire he had to spend all his time with Grace.

"Nothing's wrong." Grace's face was completely serene, and he relaxed a little. "I just thought I'd watch *Marley and Me*. That movie wrecks me every time."

"I've never understood that." Levi scratched his head. "Why would a person choose to watch a movie they know is going to make them sad?"

Grace looked thoughtful. "Sometimes you just need a good cry."

"If you say so." He fished the truck keys out of his pocket. "Have fun, I guess."

"I will. You too." Grace ran up the porch steps and disappeared into the house without looking back.

Levi sat in his truck, uncertainty creeping over him. Was this what his life was always going to be like? Going on one or two dates with a woman, then moving on to the next? Never getting close to anyone because he didn't want to end up feeling like a fool again?

So far, it'd been easy. He hadn't met a woman he really wanted to get close to.

Until Grace.

He pulled his phone out of his pocket and dialed the number the woman from the grocery store had given him. When she didn't answer, he frowned. He'd much rather not do this over voicemail. But now that he'd made the decision, he couldn't imagine spending his night any other way.

He left a brief message, apologizing but being careful not to imply that he'd like to reschedule.

Then he hopped out of the truck and took the porch steps two at a time. Faced with the new teal door, he hesitated. On a normal workday, he'd use his key and walk right in.

But this wasn't a normal workday. He'd already said goodbye to Grace. If he walked in now, he might frighten her.

He lifted his hand to knock on the door frame, careful not to hit the wet paint on the door. As he waited for Grace to answer, he pulled out his phone and jotted a reminder to have her choose a doorbell.

He was still typing when Grace opened the door.

"Levi. Did you forget something?"

He put his phone away, meeting her slightly surprised expression. "Yeah. I mean no. I mean, I was wondering if you wanted some company while you cry your eyes out." The idea of anything making Grace sad fired a strange protective instinct in him. Maybe that was why he found himself standing here, watching her expression go from surprised to perplexed.

"I thought you had a date."

"Fell through. So what do you say? Can I tag along and watch—what was it again?"

"*Marley and Me*."

"Yeah. Can I watch it with you? I've never seen it."

"There's probably going to be some ugly crying."

He doubted anything she did could be ugly. "I don't mind."

"All right then. I'll make some popcorn." She moved to let him in, and an inexplicable sense of peace came over him. Like this was where he was meant to be right now.

Ten minutes later, with popcorn bowls in hand, they entered the sitting room at the back of the house that made up part of her private quarters. He'd only been in this area once before, since she wasn't planning to remodel it.

The room was small, with mismatched furniture, but it looked out on the backyard and an incredible view of the lake below.

"Best view in the house." Levi moved to the window, not sure whether to sit on the love seat where Grace had settled or the room's lone chair, which was at a weird angle to the TV.

Outside, the sun had dropped behind the trees on the far shore, leaving deep shadows on the lake.

"It's starting." Grace kicked her feet up on the oversized ottoman and gestured for him to take a seat next to her.

He practically tiptoed across the room and eased himself onto the love seat, careful not to encroach on Grace's cushion by even a centimeter.

She sent him a quick smile, apparently completely unaware of how her sweet perfume toyed with his senses.

He stuffed a handful of popcorn into his mouth. At least if he was chewing, he should be able to resist the impulse to lean closer.

Chapter 20

Grace fought to get the quaking in her lip under control.

This part of the movie always did her in. But much as she'd warned Levi about the ugly crying, she really didn't want to do it in front of him. She felt him look at her, and she blinked hard.

But then his hand landed on hers, and there was nothing she could do to prevent it any longer. The sob hiccupped out of her.

Instead of recoiling, Levi slid closer, and his fingers curled around hers.

"You weren't kidding about this movie." His voice was raspy, and out of her peripheral vision, she caught his other hand rubbing his eyes. It was there and gone in less than a second.

But it was enough to confirm what she'd begun to suspect: under his football-tough exterior, Levi Donovan was a softy.

She sniffed loudly. "It gets worse."

Levi's exclamation of disbelief tugged a laugh out of her even as the tears rained faster. "We can turn it off," she said.

He shook his head, tightening his grip on her hand. "I can handle it if you can."

She nodded, resisting the urge to burrow her face into his shoulder, mostly so she wouldn't have to see what was coming next, but partly because she wondered what it would feel like to have his arms around her.

She was suddenly way too aware of how close he was sitting. She extracted her hand from his, leaning forward to pick up her water bottle. After she'd guzzled a long drink, she set it down, then settled back into the love seat, pressing her body against the armrest, as far from Levi as she could physically get on the too-small piece of furniture.

She'd forgotten herself for a moment. It was the emotion of the movie, that was all. And maybe the fact that Levi had asked to watch it with her.

She reminded herself that it wasn't like he'd gone out of his way to spend time with her. She was only a backup plan because his date had fallen through.

She directed her gaze to the screen, forcing herself to give all her attention to the movie. Every once in a while, Levi's head swiveled toward her. But she refused to let herself look back.

An hour later, she was wrung out but satisfied. She sighed as she wiped at her eyes. "What'd you think?"

Levi stared at her. If she wasn't mistaken, his eyes were a little red. "I think I'm glad I didn't watch that with the guys."

She clicked the TV off, leaving them in the near dark, the only light coming from a small floor lamp on the other side of the room. "I've never let anyone watch that movie with me before. I'm too much of a mess afterward." She scrubbed at her still-wet cheeks.

"You don't look like a mess." Levi's eyes met hers, and there was something in them she'd never seen before.

His hand lifted toward her cheek, and she was next to certain he was going to tuck her hair behind her ear.

She froze for half a second before her good sense kicked in, propelling her to her feet. She scooped up the popcorn bowls, trying to ignore the feel of Levi's eyes on her.

Thankfully, her phone rang, breaking the growing silence. She shifted the bowls to one hand and pulled out her phone with the other.

But the name on her screen made her groan.

"Is that your reaction whenever I call?" Levi asked.

Grace laughed. That was better. More like the Levi who loved to antagonize her. Less like the one who'd held her hand.

"It's my mama." She tucked the phone back into her pocket.

"I can go if you want to talk to her."

Grace shook her head. She'd hear it from Mama tomorrow. But she didn't have the energy to deal with Mama's hundred questions about her fellow tonight.

A fellow she still hadn't found. And she had exactly five days left before she had to get on a plane—with or without her imaginary boyfriend.

"She's just calling about Simeon's wedding."

"That's next week, right?"

"Yeah. I leave Wednesday. You sure you've got everything under control while I'm gone?"

He gave her a look, and she lifted her hands. She may have already asked that—more than once. "Sorry."

"Your mom still planning on setting you up with that guy you haven't seen since you were kids?"

Oh, why had she ever told him about that? "I don't think so."

"Yeah?" Levi's face brightened. "She came to her senses?"

"Not exactly. I told her I was bringing someone." The words spilled out like grape juice on white carpeting.

"You did? Who?" Surprise mingled in Levi's voice with something she couldn't identify.

"I don't know," she wailed. "There *is* no one. I just wanted her to stop hounding me."

"So find someone."

Grace looked at the floor. She was pretty sure no one in the history of the world had ever been as humiliated as she was right now. "There is no one. I haven't been on a date in years. All of my guy friends are married. Where am I supposed to find a single man who happens to be free to travel to Tennessee with me on less than a week's notice?"

"I'll do it." He said it simply, as if he were offering to run to the hardware store for her.

"You'll do what?"

"I'll come to Tennessee with you."

Whoa, Levi. What are you doing?

Had he just offered to go to Tennessee with Grace? More importantly, *why* had he just offered to go to Tennessee with Grace?

"You'll come to Tennessee with me?" She sounded as shocked as he felt.

"Sure. I mean, if it will help you out."

Grace bit her lip. "I don't know. I should probably call and tell my mama the truth. I don't want to deceive my family."

"You won't be deceiving them. You said you were bringing someone. And I'm someone." Why was he working so hard to convince her?

But now that he'd offered, he couldn't deny that he really wanted to spend some time with her away from work.

"I implied I was *dating* this person I'm bringing."

Levi rubbed his chin. "That *does* make it more complicated. I suppose we could go on a date first, so technically you'd be bringing someone you were dating."

"I— Wait. Are you asking me on a date?"

A strange sort of nervousness went through him.

What if she said no?

Well, then she said no. It wouldn't be the first time. And it wasn't like he was asking her on a real date this time. "Just for appearance's sake."

"I don't know." Grace set down the popcorn bowls she'd been holding and plopped back onto the love seat.

"I'm a good actor." Levi stepped in front of her. "Watch. Happy." He smiled and threw his head back as if someone had just told a joke. "Angry." He shook a fist in the air. "In love." He batted his eyelashes.

A laugh poured out of her, silky and light as air. It filled him.

"Is that a yes?"

"Okay." She slapped her palms against her legs. "Yes."

"Great." The grin that took control of his mouth was no act. "What time should I pick you up tomorrow night?"

"Tomorrow night?"

"We fly out Wednesday, right? That doesn't give us much time."

"True. How about seven? What should we do?"

"Leave that to me."

She eyed him. "Let's keep it simple though. And not romantic."

"Of course." He headed for the door. "Goodnight, Grace."

Her lilting goodnight followed him out the door and stuck with him all the way home.

Chapter 21

Grace rummaged through her closet—again. She'd already changed six times.

But it wasn't her fault.

First of all, she had no idea what a person was supposed to wear on a date that wasn't really a date.

And second of all, Levi had texted to say she probably didn't want to wear a dress. Which left her worried about what he could possibly have planned.

She pulled out a peasant blouse and wrinkled her nose at it. It had to be at least a decade old.

A knock at the front door made her jump. Nerves zipped from her spine out to her limbs.

Only because she wasn't ready.

She glanced in the mirror. Her white capris and soft gray top would have to do.

She slipped on a pair of flats, grabbed her purse, and moved toward the door. She could see Levi through the window, though his back was to her. Good. That gave her a second to push aside the unexpected surge of attraction.

Levi Donovan was a handsome man, she'd never deny that.

But that didn't mean she needed to go getting all gaga over him. And it certainly didn't mean he was the right kind of man for her. All it meant was that she needed to be more on her guard.

Because Hunter had been an attractive man too. That was part of the problem.

With a quick inhale, she opened the door.

When Levi turned toward her, the first thing she noticed was his smile—wide and open and maybe a little nervous—and then the flowers he held out to her. Purple tulips.

"Oh." She took them awkwardly. Why was this feeling more and more like a date by the moment? "You didn't have to. It's not like this is a real date."

Levi shrugged. "You don't want to deceive your parents, right? So I thought it should be as much like a real date as possible."

Grace swallowed. As long as he didn't think a real date included any kissing.

Because that was so not happening.

"I'll put these in some water." She escaped to the kitchen, rummaging to find the vase that had held the flowers she'd bought for her birthday.

She wouldn't have expected then that only a month and a half later, a man would be buying her flowers.

He didn't buy you flowers, she reminded herself. *He got them as part of the act.*

"Allow me." Levi took the vase from her and filled it with water, then held the stems of the flowers under the faucet as he cut the bottoms off.

"Wow. You're an expert. You must buy a lot of flowers."

Levi cut the last stem and lowered the flowers into the vase. "Not really. My mom taught me when I was young, and I guess it stuck with me. I think the last time I bought flowers was three years ago. For my mom."

"Oh." Grace searched for a response to that, working not to feel special that he hadn't bought his other dates flowers. "That's sweet."

"There." Levi set the vase in the middle of the kitchen counter. "Ready to go?"

"I don't know. Am I dressed appropriately for whatever we're doing? I didn't wear a dress, as instructed."

"You look perfect." Levi's eyes landed on hers, then zipped away. "I mean, that's perfect for what we're doing."

"Which is?" Grace followed Levi to the front door and stepped through when he held it open for her. Her eyes stopped on the van in the driveway.

"I hope you don't mind. I borrowed my mom's van." He sounded strangely self-conscious. "I've been thinking about buying a car, but I haven't gotten around to it yet."

"I don't mind." Actually, it was kind of cute that he was driving his mom's van. Made him seem more like a normal guy.

"Good." He opened the door for her. "I didn't think you'd like to take the bike. Some women don't like to get their hair messed up on a date."

She touched a hand to her head. She wasn't sure which bothered her more—the fact that he kept acting like this was an actual date or the fact that he knew what "some women" liked on dates. She thought of the number of dates he'd been on just since she'd known him. Likely, he knew what a lot more women than "some" liked.

"You're not afraid of heights are you?" Levi asked as he pulled out of the driveway.

"Depends. What are we doing?"

Levi shook his head. "Nice try."

"No, I'm not afraid of heights," she admitted. "One time my brothers dared me to climb the town water tower, and I started to, but my daddy caught us before I got halfway up." She'd gotten quite the lecture that night—about how she'd face temptation in life, sometimes from people she loved, and she had to learn to say no to it.

They'd given her the same lecture the night they'd caught her with Hunter. Only stricter. And with more disappointment woven through it.

"What about water?"

She reeled her thoughts back to the present. To the man sitting next to her, who was a little too much like Hunter for her comfort. "What about water, what?"

"You're not scared of it, are you?"

"I live on the lake." What could they possibly be doing that involved both heights and water? Not cliff jumping. They were headed the wrong direction for that.

And then she knew. "Oh. *That's* what we're doing."

"What?" Levi's eyes darted to her. "You don't know what we're doing."

"Do too." She couldn't help the teasing note.

"Do not."

She just smiled at him. Let him have a taste of his own medicine.

"Prove it." He shot her a challenging look, before driving right past the road to the marina.

"I think you missed your turn."

He chuckled as he made a quick U-turn. "You *do* know what we're doing. Have you ever been?"

She shook her head. "I've always wanted to try it though."

"Good." He seemed genuinely pleased to have chosen something she would enjoy. "I thought it'd be pretty to watch the sunset from up there."

Grace stuffed down the flutter that trickled up from her belly. How many times had she seen couples riding together in the parasails at sunset and thought how romantic it would be to do that with her own special someone?

Oh well.

Levi might not be her special someone, but it should still be fun.

Levi parked the car, and she reached for the door handle.

"Freeze." His voice startled her into pulling her hand back.

"If this is a date, then I need to open your door for you." He ducked out of the vehicle before she could remind him yet again that this wasn't a date.

When he opened the door, she took her chance. "Levi, this isn't a—"

He held up a finger. "I don't want to hear that for the rest of the night. You want to be able to honestly tell your parents we're dating, then this is a date."

"But—"

Levi ignored her. "Let's see. The guy said to meet him at . . ." He squinted toward the docks, where rows of sailboats, yachts, and motorboats rocked in the gentle waves. "There he is."

He planted his hand on her lower back to steer her toward the white-haired man waving to them from the docks.

With a reminder to herself that the touch was only to keep up appearances, she took off faster than necessary. When she dared a glance at Levi, his hands were in his pockets, and he looked completely at ease.

As was she.

Why wouldn't she be?

Chapter 22

The higher the parasail got, the less tethered Levi felt to the world below. Up here there was no wondering if his dad would ever be proud of him. No worrying about Luke. No trying to figure out what he was going to do with the rest of his life. Up here there were no expectations.

There was only Grace.

Far from being afraid of heights, she was leaning forward, exclaiming at every new sight, from the lighthouse on the edge of the cliff to the pelicans flying alongside them to the small group of islands in the distance.

Sometimes Levi forgot how beautiful this place where he'd grown up really was. He had a brief flash of what his life could be like if he stayed here, but he dismissed it as quickly—Hope Springs might be beautiful, but it didn't hold anything else for him.

Except this woman next to you.

He dismissed that thought even faster.

Or at least he tried to. But the more he worked at it, the more he realized—he liked her.

He could tell himself all he wanted that he'd only offered to do this to help her out. But the truth was, pretending to date her gave him a chance to spend time with her without the risk.

She'd already rejected him once, and he was quite sure that if he asked her out for real again, she'd say no.

But a fake date?

There was no risk in that. And maybe if they spent enough time together, she'd realize that he wasn't so wrong for her after all.

"This was such a great idea." Grace's cheeks were bright, her eyes brighter.

He'd taken women to world-renowned restaurants, ushered them down the red carpet at awards shows, even flown them on private planes to house parties hosted by celebrities—but not one of them had ever looked at him like this.

Like they really appreciated the thought he'd put into the evening.

Then again, he wasn't sure he'd ever put as much thought into a date as this one.

"Oh look." Grace pointed toward the horizon. "The color in those clouds. It's like . . ." She closed her eyes as if searching for the perfect description.

Levi forced his eyes off her animated face to look toward the clouds sitting low in the western sky. They seemed to glow from the inside out with a color somewhere between red and orange.

"Tangerine," he said.

She opened her eyes, staring at him in wonder. "That's the word I just thought of."

"My mom used to take Luke and me outside to lay on a blanket and find shapes in the clouds." He'd forgotten about that until he said it, and nostalgia tightened his chest. That had been before they knew about Luke's diagnosis. Before his family's whole existence had shifted.

"Look. That one's a dragon." He pointed toward a cloud off to his side.

She squinted and leaned to look around him. "I don't see any cloud that looks remotely like a dragon."

"Right there." He pointed again. "See, there's the eyes. And the snout. And the puff of smoke from his fire. He even has wings." She had to see it. It was the biggest cloud in the sky.

But she shook her head. "Not seeing it."

"Here." He reached an arm around her and pulled her closer, then used his hand to turn her head ever so slightly. With his other arm, he pointed so that her line of sight would have to travel right past his finger.

Grace repositioned, bringing her head closer. "Oh that? That's not a dragon. It's a castle."

"What?" There was no way they were looking at the same thing. "That cloud. With the two giant wings sticking up from the back."

"Those are towers," Grace said patiently. "And that over there isn't a dragon snout. It's a princess waving to her subjects."

A laugh burst out of him, shaking his whole body.

The movement seemed to remind them both that his arm was still around her. He pulled away at the same time that she sat up.

They fell silent, watching the play of light on the clouds as it deepened from orange and red to pink and purple and finally to a deep blue that teetered on the brink of black.

"That was amazing," Grace said as the boat's captain began to reel in the parasail's rope.

Levi watched the water grow closer, trying not to feel the world closing back in.

Grace tried to reorient herself.

Her feet were firmly planted on the dock, and yet she still felt like she was flying.

She'd always figured she'd enjoy parasailing, but that had been beyond enjoyable. It had been . . . exhilarating.

She let herself watch Levi as he climbed off the boat behind her. Would she have enjoyed the ride as much if he hadn't been along? If she'd gone by herself? Or with another man? Someone more suited to her?

Somehow, she couldn't imagine it.

"Ready for some dinner?" Levi turned to walk up the dock.

"Oh, you don't have to take me out for dinner. This was more than enough." Grace tried to fall into step beside him. But she really did feel like everything was still swaying, and she stumbled.

Levi's hand landed on her elbow, and he kept it there even after she was steady on her feet.

She supposed she should pull away, but she had no desire to end up in the water tonight.

"What kind of date would this be if I sent you home hungry? Plus, I'm starving. We have reservations at Alessandro's."

"Alessandro's? Levi, that's too much."

The only restaurant on the peninsula with a Michelin star, Alessandro's was expensive. And romantic. Not exactly suited to fake dates.

"Come on." Levi steered her toward the van.

Soft music played in the vehicle, and Grace let herself relax into the seat.

"Can I ask you something?" Levi interrupted her silent musing on how she'd ended up here, going on a fake date with a man who was so totally wrong for her—and enjoying herself.

"Sure. As long as it's not what I'm going to order. I've heard everything at Alessandro's is delicious."

"You've never been there either?"

"A night of firsts for me, I guess." Including first fake date. "What'd you want to ask?"

"Why don't you date?"

Grace sat up straighter, suddenly on alert. "Who says I don't date?"

"You did. Last night. You said you haven't been on a date in years."

Grace didn't say anything. It wasn't like there was any reason to deny it.

"So why not?" Levi glanced sideways at her. "It's obviously not for lack of opportunity."

She spluttered. He was going to talk to her about opportunity—when he'd had more than his share of *opportunities* to date? "What is that supposed to mean?"

Levi lifted his hands off the wheel. "Nothing. Just that you're a beautiful woman, so I assume you get asked out all the time."

"I— Oh." How was she supposed to respond to that?

"I don't get asked out all that often," she confessed. "And when I do get asked, I guess I just don't . . . None of them have been the right kind of man."

"Ah." Levi nodded, as if he had her all figured out. "None of them checked all the boxes on your list."

She shrugged. "Maybe." That was nothing to be ashamed of. She'd made that list for a reason, and as long as she stuck to it, she wouldn't find herself in a compromising situation again.

"Fair enough." Levi pulled into the driveway at Alessandro's, and Grace glanced down at her casual outfit.

"Uh, Levi?"

"Yeah?" He pulled into a parking spot and shut off the van.

"I think this may be a bad idea."

Chapter 23

Levi sat with his hand still on the car keys. "Look, Grace. I know I probably don't meet half the qualifications on your checklist. But it's just a fake date. Surely I'll do for that."

"What?" She turned puzzled eyes on him.

"You said this was a bad idea. And I'm just saying—"

"Not that—" She gestured to her lap. "This. I think we're a little underdressed for Alessandro's."

"Oh." He looked from her capris to his own khaki shorts. "Does it matter?"

"I'll feel self-conscious."

"Okay then." He started the van back up. "How about ice cream for dinner?"

"Really?" Grace's eyes lit up but then fell. "Wait. You don't mean those hardware store ice cream bars, do you?"

"Ouch. Don't hate on my ice cream bars. But no. I was thinking the Chocolate Chicken."

"It's like you read my mind." She rested her hand on the console between the seats—only inches from his.

He swallowed, wishing he could read her mind about more than just ice cream. Like what did she really think of him? How far short of her list did he fall? And would he ever be able to convince her otherwise?

She looked peaceful and content, sitting here with him—and he took that as something. Maybe there was hope yet.

Levi pulled the van up to one of the last empty parking spots in front of the Chocolate Chicken. As they waited in line, they debated favorite ice cream flavors. She was a die-hard chocolate fan, while he preferred butter pecan.

Just one more thing about them that was different. But Levi didn't mind—it made life more interesting that she didn't simply agree with him on everything, like so many of his dates in the past had.

She challenged him in a way that he hadn't been challenged in a long time.

"Eat these in the park?" he asked as they walked out of the crowded building.

"Read my mind again."

They turned their steps toward the public gardens on the hill above the marina, settling in the large gazebo that overlooked the water below.

"This is one of my favorite spots in Hope Springs." Grace's sigh spoke contentment as she licked at a drip of ice cream. "I couldn't even tell you how many hours I've spent in here, praying."

"We toilet papered it once when I was in middle school. Some buddies and I."

Grace eyed him, as if she weren't sure whether to believe him. "You did not."

"We did. Got caught too. Got a nice ride home in a police cruiser."

Grace snickered. "I wouldn't lead with that when you meet my parents."

"Thanks for the tip." Levi finished off his ice cream. "What are your parents like?"

"Protective."

"Ah." In Levi's experience, protective meant intrusive. Maybe that was why Grace was so hesitant to date.

"Ah, what?"

"Nothing." Levi held up his hands. He had no desire to get into a fight with her about her parents.

"It's not like it sounds." Grace looked thoughtful as she stared over the water. "They just want what's best for me."

"It means a lot to you—what they think—doesn't it?"

She looked at him in surprise.

"I know you better than you think, Grace. Though I'm not quite sure *why* their opinion means so much to you." Like he was one to talk, working here all summer just to prove something to his dad.

Grace took a big bite of her cone, and he turned to watch the light at the end of the breakwater as it swiveled over the waves in the dark. It was none of his business, her relationship with her family.

"My senior year of high school—" Grace's voice was strained. "There was this guy who I was— Well, I thought I was in love with him. My parents saw right away that he wasn't the right kind of guy for me. But I didn't listen. And—"

His eyes followed her as she moved to the trash can to throw away her napkin.

And? He wanted to ask. But he held his tongue. If she wanted to tell him, she would. And if not, he wouldn't press her.

"And it turned out they were right," she said finally.

"So you made a list." It was all starting to make sense. "So you wouldn't end up with that kind of guy again. So you'd end up with the kind of guy your parents would approve of."

"Pretty much." Grace ran a finger over her lips, as if checking to make sure she didn't have any ice cream on them.

"You missed a little bit. Right there." He pointed to the corner of her lip, the part that turned up just so when she smiled.

"Thanks." She scrubbed her fingers at it. "Better?"

"Perfect." He worked to pull his eyes off her mouth. "Now what?"

"Now it's my turn to ask you a question."

He spread his arms wide. "Shoot. I'm an open book."

"Why do you date so many women?"

Grace watched as Levi shifted from one foot to the other. Her question had clearly made him uncomfortable. But he had asked about her dating life—it was only fair that she got to ask about his.

"Because it's fun, I guess." He took a step, as if to leave the gazebo.

"Levi." She wasn't buying it.

He sighed, brushing a hand over his hair. "I'm not some playboy or something."

"Okay." Grace waited. That hadn't really answered her question, had it?

Levi's cheeks puffed out as he exhaled. "You're not going to let me off the hook here, are you?"

She shook her head.

"Believe it or not, I had a long-term girlfriend. Someone I thought I was in love with. Someone I thought was in love with me."

Grace tried to picture Levi in love, taking his girlfriend on dates, curling up with his girlfriend to watch a movie, tucking his girlfriend's hair behind her ear.

Oddly, it didn't feel like that much of a stretch.

"What happened?"

He gave an ironic laugh. "Turns out she wasn't so much in love with me as with the idea of me. She walked the day I was cut." He turned his gaze away from Grace. "The day I was planning to propose."

"Oh." Grace had a distinct urge to knock that woman over the head. Levi might not be the right man for Grace, but that didn't mean he deserved to be treated like that. "I'm sorry."

He shrugged. "Anyway, I guess it's just easier not to let anyone else get too close. You know?"

She gave a slow nod. She supposed she did know, in a way. In the end, his dating a lot of women and her dating no one came from the same place—fear.

"On that note—" Levi seemed to snap out of his reverie. "I suppose we should call it a night."

"Probably." Grace tried to ignore the swoop of disappointment. It was only because it was such a beautiful night that she didn't want to go home yet. "I have to sing at church tomorrow, so I should get a good night's sleep."

"You sing?" Levi swiveled to look at her as they walked toward the van. "Why have I not heard you? We have the radio on every day."

Grace rubbed her arms, nerves she'd managed to push aside all week suddenly taking over. "I don't really like to sing in front of people."

"But you're singing for church?"

Grace pressed a fist to her stomach. "A solo. Don't ask me how they talked me into that. Do you think it's too late to back out?"

Levi chuckled as he opened the van door for her. "Probably. But I'm sure you'll be great."

Grace couldn't help the groan that escaped as she fastened her seatbelt. Now that she'd started thinking about it, the nerves were multiplying exponentially, as if they'd decided to host a party in her stomach.

Levi jumped into the driver's side. "What are you singing?"

"Great Is Thy Faithfulness."

He frowned. "Sounds familiar, but I can't think of how it goes. Sing it for me?"

"Uh, no." Grace blew out a breath. If just thinking about it was nearly making her sick, how would she get through singing it at church tomorrow?

"Please." Levi folded his hands on the steering wheel, as if begging.

But she shook her head. "If you want to hear it, you'll have to come to church. Assuming I don't die the minute I get up in front of all those people."

"You're that scared?"

Petrified was more like it. "I have no idea how you managed to play football in front of millions of people every week."

"I tried to remember why people were there. To watch a good game of football."

She made a face. "That doesn't help me."

"Well, why are people at church?"

"To hear God's Word." That one was pretty obvious.

"Okay then. Is that what you're going to do? Share God's Word?"

She nodded.

"There you go." He tapped her arm as if he'd just solved her problem.

"I'm still nervous, you know."

"I know." Levi smiled at her. "I'd be worried if you weren't. But you're going to have to trust me. You'll be great."

Grace leaned back in her seat. Easy for him to say.

He wasn't the one who was going to have hundreds of eyeballs on him tomorrow.

By the time Levi pulled up to her door, Grace was so worked up that she almost forgot her plan for the end of the evening. Although she was close to one hundred percent certain Levi wouldn't attempt to kiss her, she wasn't taking any chances.

"Well, goodnight." She sprang out of the van before he could put it in park.

But before she'd rounded the vehicle, he'd cut the ignition and was getting out.

"I'm fine." She kept plenty of space between them as she strode toward the house. "You don't have to walk me to the door."

He ignored the comment, his long legs keeping pace with her as if she had the stride of a child.

When they reached the door, she pulled out her keys and turned them in the lock, then allowed herself to tilt her head ever so slightly, so she could just see his face.

The moonlight hit it, illuminating the way his smile ended in a dimple.

"Thanks. This was nice." Nice? The guy had taken her on the best date of her life, and all she had to say was that it was nice?

"I thought so too." Levi took a step closer, and she got ready to duck into the house.

They were *not* going to kiss.

But instead of lowering his head, he raised a hand, squeezed her arm gently, then turned and jogged down the steps.

"Goodnight, Grace," he called over his shoulder. "See you tomorrow."

"Goodnight, Levi." She was too busy noticing the tingle that lingered where his fingers had met her skin to ask what he meant about seeing her tomorrow. And by the time she thought to ask, he was already driving away.

Chapter 24

Levi held up two ties, debating. He didn't know when he'd decided that he'd go to church today. Only that Grace had looked so vulnerable when she'd confessed to being nervous about singing. And he'd thought that if he could be there for her, maybe somehow that would help. Which sounded crazy now. But he'd already told her he'd be there. And he had no desire to let her down.

Their date last night had been . . . He didn't know how to describe it.

Fun. Playful. But also honest. Open. Unguarded.

All those things he never allowed himself to be around other women.

He picked up the ties again, then tossed them both on his bed. No need to go overboard.

All activity in the kitchen stopped the moment he walked in. You'd think he was some kind of exotic zoo creature, the way every member of his family was staring at him. Even Luke, who'd been entirely oblivious to the world around him since he and May had broken up. Although the lovesick expression he'd worn for two weeks didn't change, his eyes did flick to Levi's dress clothes with a hint of interest.

Mom recovered first. "Breakfast? I made eggs."

"That'd be great, Mom. Thanks." Levi took the plate she passed him.

"We leave in five minutes." Dad's voice was gruff, but under it, Levi could hear the hope.

He wanted to tell him not to get his hopes up. This didn't mean he was going to become a choirboy or something. It simply meant that for this one day he was going to give church a chance.

Four minutes later—Levi checked the clock—Dad was ushering them all to the van. Levi shoveled in a last bite of eggs on the way to the door.

In the van, Mom and Dad struck up their own conversation, and Levi turned to glance at Luke. A fresh wave of nostalgia rippled through him. It wouldn't take much to imagine they'd traveled back in time twenty years. All Levi had to do was reach out and act like he was going to poke Luke, then Luke would complain to Mom and Dad that Levi was touching him, then Levi would point out that he wasn't, then Mom would tell them to stop, then, when they didn't, Dad would yell and threaten to pull over.

Levi turned away from Luke to gaze out his window.

Those days when their biggest problem was who was touching whom were long past.

Mom turned in her seat to look at him, as if she was afraid he might have jumped out while the car was moving. "You know that Pastor Zellner's son Dan is pastor now?"

He nodded. "Grace introduced us. Seems like a decent guy."

"Oh that's right, he's friends with Grace." The way Mom said it, Levi knew she hadn't forgotten that for one second. It was simply a way for her to "subtly" sneak in her next question. Which should be arriving in five, four, three, two—

"What did you and Grace end up doing last night?"

Levi held in his groan. His mom was only curious—his parents had never been stifling the way it sounded like Grace's had been.

"I took her parasailing."

Mom gasped. "What if she was scared of heights?"

"She loved it."

Mom shook her head. "Why anyone would attach themselves to that contraption and let themselves be suspended over the lake like that . . ." She shuddered and looked at Dad. "Don't *ever* ask me to do that."

"Wasn't going to," Dad replied.

Levi's gaze slipped to his father's profile as Mom faced forward again. His parents loved each other, he'd never doubted that. But it'd always seemed to him more like a workman type of love—more like a partnership than a romantic whirlwind. He had no idea when the last time his parents had been on a date was.

He wondered what that would be like—not worrying about wining and dining a woman. Just putting your head down and doing the work together—going through life together. Facing the hard times together.

An image of working side-by-side with Grace sprang into his head.

That kind of life might not be so bad.

As Dad pulled into the parking lot of Hope Church, Levi leaned forward. "It looks different."

"We had to rebuild after the tornado," Mom said. "I called and left you a message about it."

Now that she mentioned it, Levi did vaguely remember a message about a storm, but he hadn't paid too much attention to it, other than registering the fact that his family was safe.

"It looks bigger."

"Yeah. Hope Springs has been growing, and so has the church. We added some new meeting rooms and classrooms. Plus a much bigger lobby." Dad parked the car, and Levi tugged at his open collar. What was he doing here? He didn't belong among all these people who went to church every week. Who hadn't spent the last few years questioning whether God really mattered. Sometimes wondering if he even existed.

"Come on." Dad gestured for him to hurry. "Service will be starting in a minute." Same old Dad. Considered five minutes early to be late.

Inside the lobby, Levi was greeted by several of Grace's friends as he followed his family into the sanctuary. He smirked as Dad led them to the exact spot his family had always sat when Levi was growing up: right side of the church, third row from the front.

He took the seat on the aisle, sitting with his hands on his knees as the rest of his family bent their heads to pray. Levi stared straight ahead. It'd been so long since he'd prayed, he was pretty sure God wouldn't remember who he was. Besides, he wasn't convinced that the various prayers he'd sent up over the years—prayers for victory, prayers for his career, prayers for Luke—weren't just floating somewhere in space, unheard and unheeded by this so-called God who was supposed to love him.

Levi might not be an expert in love, but even he knew that if you claimed to love someone, you listened to them.

Music started from the far side of the sanctuary, and Levi turned to see a band warming up. Nate sat at the piano bench, smiling like there was nothing he'd rather be doing.

A moment later, a line of people wearing black pants and maroon shirts filed in behind the band.

The choir?

Levi had been expecting them to be wearing robes. He searched the faces a little too eagerly until his eyes picked out Grace. Though she was dressed the same as everyone else and was shorter than the women on either side of her, still she managed to stand out.

Maybe it was the joy that always radiated from her, highlighted by the shaft of sunlight that fell on her face from the large windows at the side of the church. Or maybe it was the fact that she kept pushing her hair behind her ear, then pulling it in front of her again, then pushing it back again. She was nervous.

And that made him nervous.

An overwhelming desire to run over there and give her a pep talk came over him. But that wouldn't exactly be a churchy thing to do.

Instead, he kept his eyes on her, willing her to look his way. All he wanted was a chance to smile at her, to let her know he was here for her.

She scanned the crowd, like she was looking for someone.

Him?

But her eyes were far from him when the smile broke across her face. Levi followed her gaze, a tiny hit of jealousy taking him down a notch. Had she been lying about there being no one she wanted to date? Maybe she'd been trying to work up the nerve to ask someone else when he'd stepped in and volunteered himself.

There.

His eyes landed on the row she was focused on. Jade's little girl, Hope, was waving at her like crazy.

Levi turned back to Grace, who grinned at Hope, sent her a small wave, and then resumed her search of the sanctuary.

"Good morning." Dan's welcome from the front of the church pulled Levi's attention off of Grace, only for a second. But it was long enough for her to pick up her choir binder. He guessed he'd never know if her eyes had been on their way to him next.

She was going to vomit.

Right here and now, in front of the whole church.

Why had she ever agreed to do this? Just because the choir director had been begging her for years to do it and just because everyone in the choir had urged her to do it and just because she hated to disappoint people, that didn't mean she should have accepted.

She'd had stage fright since she'd run off the stage in tears at her first piano recital in second grade.

Put her in a group, put her behind the scenes, and she was fine.

But put her in front of people, and she froze up like a pig on an ice pond.

And it didn't help that she'd been on edge all morning wondering if Levi would be here. That had to have been what he'd meant when he'd said "See you tomorrow," didn't it? The thought had made her half-giddy—Levi was going to hear God's Word—and half-petrified—Levi was going to hear her sing.

But it turned out it didn't matter. She'd searched nearly the entire sanctuary before Dan had started the service, and she hadn't seen a sign of him.

"Our opening hymn this morning will be sung by our choir, accompanied by the worship band," Dan was saying now.

Grace tried to swallow, though her mouth had turned into a cotton field. She couldn't worry about Levi now. She had to focus.

Which would be a whole lot easier to do if the words on the page weren't blurring in front of her.

This was it. She was going to pass out. Topple over and knock the rest of the choir down with her, like dominoes.

The director gave her the cue to come forward to the microphone they'd adjusted to her height before church. She stepped forward, her eyes scanning wildly over the packed seats in front of her.

There were so many people. Too many people.

She couldn't do—

Her eyes fell on him.

Levi.

He was watching her, and the moment her eyes locked on his, he sent her a confident smile.

You can do it, he mouthed.

What had he said last night? To remember what all these people were here for.

They were here to listen to God's Word. And she was here to share it in the form of song.

She sucked in what may have been the deepest breath of her life and closed her eyes.

Her stomach was still flopping around like a fish on a riverbank, but the words came out clear and true: "Great is thy faithfulness, O God my Father."

She risked opening her eyes, letting them travel to Levi. He wasn't smiling anymore—he looked serious. Thoughtful.

Please let your Word touch him, Lord. Show him your love. Grace sent up the prayer even as she continued to sing, and somehow she wasn't afraid anymore. She let her eyes scan the rest of the sanctuary.

Some people were watching her and smiling, some had their eyes closed and were swaying to the music. Little kids were coloring or munching on snacks, and Jade and Dan's daughter Hope was clapping along to the music.

A swell of joy rolled through her as she took a step back from the microphone to join the choir in the refrain. This was her church family. None of these people were perfect. They were all sinners. But they were all people Christ had died for. People God had shown his faithfulness.

Her voice was stronger on the second verse, and so strong on the third verse that she wondered if it was even her singing anymore. As she sang, the words hit her as if she were hearing them for the first time:

"Pardon for sin and a peace that endureth,

Thine own dear presence to cheer and to guide,

Strength for today and bright hope for tomorrow—

Blessings all mine, with ten thousand beside!"

As the last words faded, Grace switched off the microphone and ducked her head, stepping back to follow the choir to their designated seats on the left side of the church. They'd be singing another song later in the service—one she didn't have a solo in, thankfully. Because now that the song was done, she had no idea how she'd gotten through it. The nerves came back in fresh, rolling waves.

She'd managed not to get sick in front of the church, but she wasn't sure how much longer that would last.

As the people around her whispered that she'd done a good job, she mumbled an apology and rushed for the nearest exit.

Chapter 25

As a kid, Levi had been yelled at for fidgeting in church more times than he could count. But Grace's singing had stunned him into stillness.

It wasn't just her voice—though that was amazing. And it wasn't just the expression of joy on her face—also incredible. It was the depth she put into the words—like she really believed them. Like they were really true and she had experienced them.

Some small part of Levi wanted to know what that was like.

As Dan called for the congregation to stand, Levi realized he was still staring at the now-empty microphone. His gaze skipped to the rows where the choir members had settled, but he couldn't pick out Grace. A flash of movement behind them caught his eye as someone slipped out the sanctuary door into the lobby. He didn't know why, but he was sure it was Grace.

"I'll be right back," he leaned over to whisper to Mom.

She shot him a concerned look, but he offered a reassuring hand pat before striding down the aisle toward the back of the church. A couple of people smiled at him, but most didn't even seem to notice him.

When he reached the lobby, he stopped, scanning the area. Other than Jade, who was swaying with a crying Matthias in her arms, he didn't see a sign of anyone.

"Looking for Grace?" Jade shifted the baby to her shoulder, and he stopped crying for a moment to stare at Levi.

"Hey there." He made a funny face, and Matthias's wails started in again, more intense than ever.

"Sorry." He took a step back. "I didn't mean to scare him."

Jade shook her head, rubbing the baby's back. "He's tired. Decided to stay up and party all night. Grace went in the women's room."

Ah. Well, that made sense. And there was no point in him standing out here to wait for her. How clingy would that seem?

"Actually, she was looking kind of peaked. I was going to go check on her, but Matthias wasn't having it. If you want to hold him for a second, I'll go." She held Matthias out toward him, as if she were handing off a football.

Levi lifted his hands to his sides, a clear signal that he did *not* want to hold the child.

"It's all right. He doesn't bite." Jade bounced the baby a little. "And I know you won't drop him. You always hold onto the ball."

Yeah. The ball. Not a *kid*.

But Levi's hands came together, and Jade placed the baby into them.

The child was heavier than a football. Definitely squirmier. And louder.

But somehow holding him didn't feel weird.

"I'll be right back." Jade hurried toward the far side of the lobby, and Levi stood there, staring down at the baby.

The volume of the kid's cries lowered a little, and Levi bent his knees, then straightened, bouncing gently the way Jade had been doing.

After a couple of seconds, the cries lowered to a soft whimper.

"See, it's okay, buddy. I've got you."

The baby made a strange noise, one like Levi had never heard before. If he had to describe it, he'd say the baby had cooed, kind of like a pigeon.

"You like that?" He bounced some more, eliciting more coos.

"How did you get him to stop crying?"

Levi startled as Jade came up beside him, looking like she was about to hug him. Behind her, Grace was watching him, her lips curved up slightly.

He passed the baby back. "Honestly? I have no idea."

"Well, thank you. Now I can sit down again." Jade gathered the baby to her shoulder, then slipped through the doors back into the sanctuary.

"You're good at that," Grace whispered, stepping into the spot Jade had vacated.

"What are you doing here?"

"Oh, I—" Did she mean "here" at church or "here" in the lobby? Either way, the answer was the same.

Looking for her.

"You sounded amazing. From now on, I'm going to have to insist that you sing along with the radio."

"Thanks." She ducked her head, letting her hair cover her face.

Over the speaker that piped the service into the lobby, he heard Dan begin another Bible reading.

"I should get back in there," Grace whispered.

"Yeah."

"I'm over on that side."

"Okay." Great time to lose the ability to string together a sentence of more than one word.

She offered him one more quick smile, then crossed in front of him to pass through the door to the sanctuary. He almost called out to her to wait. Almost asked her to lunch after the service. But he stopped himself. That felt a little too much like opening himself up to rejection.

Besides, he'd be spending the next week with her. He could go one afternoon without her.

In fact, he probably *should* go one afternoon without her.

Levi waited a few seconds after Grace had gone back into the sanctuary to reenter through the doors at the other side.

As he slipped into his seat, Dan stepped to the podium at the front of the church. Ah, time for the sermon. Never his favorite part of the service.

He sat back in his seat, kicking his legs out under the row in front of him, and started counting the number of tiles on the floor.

"Let me ask you something." Dan sounded like he was talking to an old friend instead of an entire church full of people. In spite of himself, Levi looked up from his counting. Dan stepped out from behind the podium, bringing himself closer to the congregation. "What are you doing here?"

Levi snorted to himself. Seemed to be a popular question today.

One he couldn't answer.

"I don't mean here, as in at church this morning," Dan continued. "Although I suppose plenty of people would ask us that. But why are you *here* here? On this earth. Right now, at this specific time, in this specific place."

Levi gave up counting the floor tiles and leaned forward in spite of himself. The truth was, he had no idea what the answer to that question was. Ever since he'd lost the ability to play football, it was like he'd lost his whole reason for being. He was floating around like some useless piece of space debris.

Or at least he had been, until he'd started working on Grace's renovation.

His eyes traveled the sanctuary, settling again on the spot where she sat with the rest of the choir members. The look of intense concentration on her face said she was one hundred percent interested in Dan's sermon.

Definitely not thinking about Levi.

"I guess what I'm really asking is—" Dan was still talking, and Levi picked up on the thread of the sermon. "What is your purpose?"

Purpose.

Something about that word struck a chord with Levi. Was that what he was looking for? Purpose? If Dan could tell him how to find that, maybe he was worth listening to.

"So many people are looking for purpose in so many places. In success. In money. In meditation. In being a good person. But there is only one purpose."

Levi glanced around the church. Was anyone buying this? Dan wanted them to believe that every single person in the world had the same purpose? There was no way. Obviously they weren't all going to be pro athletes or brain surgeons or even parents.

"I can hear you now," Dan said. "You're telling me to get on with it and tell you this purpose already." There were a few chuckles across the congregation. "I'll do you one better," Dan continued. "I'll let *God* tell you what your purpose is." He lifted a Bible off the podium behind him and opened it, letting his finger scan down the page.

"Listen to the purpose God calls you to. In John chapter eight, Jesus tells us: 'If you hold to my teaching, you are really my disciples. Then you will know the truth, and the truth will set you free.'" Dan closed the Bible, keeping his finger in the pages. "Do you see your purpose there?"

Levi almost shook his head. How on earth was that verse supposed to show him his purpose? What did it even have to do with anything?

"Your purpose," Dan announced, "is to hold to God's Word."

Levi sat back, disappointment pulling his shoulders down. He should have known he wouldn't find any useful advice here. Just a bunch of platitudes about how everything would be fine if he simply read the Bible and prayed. Well, he'd tried that, and it hadn't worked.

"But why?" Dan asked. "Why does Jesus tell us to hold onto—to remain in—his Word? To boost his own ego? To show us everything we're doing wrong? To make life easier for ourselves?"

He scanned the entire congregation before continuing. "No, no, and no." He counted off on his fingers. "He tells us why we need to remain in him—so we will know the Truth."

Right. Truth. Who even knew what the truth was anymore?

Dan paused. "That's a slippery word these days, isn't it? Truth? People will tell you it's relative. They'll say that just because something is true for you doesn't mean it's true for them."

Dan hung his head a moment before lifting his chin. "They're wrong. They're so, so wrong. There is only One Truth. And he doesn't want anyone to die without knowing him. Jesus is that Truth. He tells us that himself: 'I am the way and the truth and the life.'"

Dan paced toward Levi's side of the church. "Knowing that is the only thing that matters. Nothing else we do, nothing else we learn or achieve means anything without the Truth."

"When you don't know that Truth, when it eludes you and you're searching for your purpose in all the wrong places—searching in your job or in your money or even in your family—you're never going to know true peace. Something will always be missing."

Those words. They caught at Levi.

Something missing.

As much as he tried to deny it, even to himself, there had been plenty of days when he'd felt like something was missing.

"God's purpose for you is right here." Dan picked up his Bible, holding it over his head. "It's the purpose of knowing the Truth that you are saved in Christ. That Jesus went to the cross for you. That he suffered the punishment for your sins. That he rose from the dead to give you the promise of eternal life."

Dan's smile traveled across the room. "That purpose has nothing to do with who you are or what you've done. It's all about the One who is 'the way and the truth and the life.' And it's an *eternal* purpose."

Levi shifted, sure the sermon was over, but Dan spoke again. "Maybe you're thinking that's all well and good, but what you really need is a purpose for *right now*. For while you're here on earth. Before you die."

Yeah. That would be nice. But as far as he knew, the Bible didn't deal with the here and now, except to make rules.

"All right, then," Dan said. "That can be summed up in one word: glorify. Our purpose in this world is to hear God's Word, worship him, and share his glory with the whole world. I don't know about you, but that's bigger than any other purpose I could ever come up with. In fact, it feels too big sometimes, doesn't it?" His smile said he had an answer for that too. "God tells us how to do that too, and it's actually quite simple: 'Whatever you do, do it all for the glory of God.' Share his Word. Shine the light of his love to others. That's it. Plain and simple."

As Dan finished the sermon, Levi stood with the rest of the congregation. The word *purpose* was still echoing in his head.

Maybe purpose was what he needed.

But was that purpose really Jesus?

He'd been so sure for so many years that it wasn't.

But now—now he wasn't quite so certain.

Chapter 26

Grace watched out of the corner of her eye as Levi grabbed a bottle of water out of the fridge while she boxed up dishes in preparation for the kitchen demo when they got back from Tennessee.

She'd asked him yesterday what he'd thought of church, and he'd said it was fine. Not a word more. And she hadn't yet figured out how to bring it up again.

"What?" Levi raised an eyebrow.

Great. He'd caught her staring at him.

"Nothing. We should prob—" A lilting chime dinged from above them, and she swiveled, searching for the source. "What was that?"

Levi grinned. "Your new doorbell. Like it?"

She actually did. Very much. But— "I thought I was going to pick one out?"

"I know." Levi capped his water bottle. "But I knew you'd like this one, so I thought I'd surprise you. Worked, didn't it?"

"Yes, but—"

"Come on. That's probably Tori at the door. Don't want to give her a bad impression by making her wait all day."

Grace pressed down a fresh onslaught of nerves. No big deal. It was only a chat between two women. Even if one of them did have a national travel blog.

Levi reached the door before she did and gave her a thumbs-up before opening it.

Grace's mouth dropped as the woman outside the door stepped into Levi's open arms for a bear hug. There was no way to describe the woman other than gorgeous.

Grace had dressed with care this morning, putting on a flowing skirt and a sleeveless blouse and even a subtle layer of makeup.

But next to the woman in Levi's arms, who wore a fitted black dress, perfect hair, and long legs, she looked like a ragamuffin.

Well, that was fine. It wasn't like anyone would see her.

She cleared her throat and stepped forward as Levi released the woman. "I'm Grace Calvano. You must be Tori." She held out a hand, and the woman shook it with a gracious smile.

"It's so nice to meet you." Tori glanced around the unfinished space. "Looks like a beautiful place you have here."

"Thank you. Please come this way. We're in the middle of the remodel, so I thought we could enjoy the view in the backyard."

She led the way to the back patio.

"This is quite a view." Tori sat in the lounge chair Grace indicated. She pulled out her phone and tapped the screen. "You don't mind if I video record our interview, do you? I like to include a couple of brief clips with each post."

"Oh. Uh—" Blind panic. That's what this feeling must be.

"It's fine," Levi cut in, smiling at Tori.

"And I assume you'll be joining us for the interview?" Her comment was directed to Levi.

"Sure. Why not?" Levi settled into the chair between Grace and Tori.

"Great." Tori pulled an expandable tripod out of her bag and attached her phone to it, setting it up so that it would have a clear shot of all three of them.

"So—" Tori leaned back in her chair, seeming to be completely at ease in front of the camera. "How did you manage to snag Levi Donovan to renovate your bed-and-breakfast?"

"Um." Grace licked her lips. She'd thought this interview was supposed to be about why she wanted to open the bed-and-breakfast, the kind of experience she wanted to create for guests, that sort of thing. But she supposed the renovation was part of it. "He kind of just showed up at my door one day, saying he worked for the construction company I'd hired."

Tori laughed. "Your lucky day, I guess."

Levi flashed a self-confident smile at the camera.

"I guess." Grace crossed her legs in front of her in a vain attempt to appear as confident as Tori and Levi. "Actually, I—"

"And Levi, what brought you to work for this construction company? I'm guessing you don't need the money."

"Nah." Levi shrugged, and Grace recognized the false humility in his smile. It wasn't nearly as attractive as the real humility he could show on occasion. "It's my dad's company. I came home to help out for the summer."

"That's sweet." Tori jotted something on her paper. "So what kind of work are you doing here?"

Levi settled back into his chair. "Let's see, I took out a wall between the living room and dining room, put bathrooms in all the guest rooms, refinished the floors throughout the house, painted, built a library . . . You name it, I pretty much did it to this place. Oh, and I just put in a new doorbell."

Grace gaped at him. *He* had taken out a wall? *He* had added bathrooms? *He* had refinished the floors and painted and built the library? What about her? She'd been part of every single one of those projects. She'd poured her blood, sweat, and tears into this place. Not to mention all the work his crew had done.

"Actually, we did a lot of that together. I really thought it was important that I—"

"Oh yeah." Levi's smile felt condescending. "Grace has been a great helper."

Helper? This was her home. Her bed-and-breakfast. If anyone was the helper here, it was him.

"So what next? After this is done?" Tori's question was directed to Levi. "Will you stay in construction? Stay in Hope Springs?"

"I'm not sure what I'll do." Levi leaned forward. "Right now I'm weighing my options"

Options? She'd give him options.

Right now, he had the option to leave voluntarily or risk her throwing him out. On camera.

"Is there any chance—"

"Would you like a tour?" Grace interrupted Tori's next question to Levi.

Tori looked surprised. "I was under the impression that the place wasn't ready for tours yet."

"It's not." Grace fumbled. "But—"

"The library is almost done," Levi cut in smoothly. "You'll love it." He sent Grace a look that said *you're welcome*.

She barely resisted kicking him in the shin.

In the library, Levi pointed out the shelves *he* had built, the floor *he* had finished, the window seat *he* had designed. Okay, Grace would give him that one. But she'd added the cushions and pillows to make it cozy.

"It's nice." Tori panned the space with her camera. "But where are all the books?"

"That's Grace's department." Levi waved at her.

Oh, was she really going to get a chance to talk at her own interview?

Tori turned the camera on her, and Grace's tongue latched to the roof of her mouth.

"What kinds of books will you have in here?" Tori prompted. "Will guests be able to check them out?"

Grace managed a mute nod.

"Let me ask you something." Levi stepped in front of the camera, blocking Grace's view of Tori.

At last, she managed to pull in a breath. "Yes, guests will be able to check out books," she blurted from behind Levi.

Tori stepped around Levi, who turned to peer at Grace too.

"That's good." Tori pointed her camera back to Levi.

"And if they're in the middle of a book when their stay is done—" Grace rushed on, causing Tori's camera to swing back to her. "They can bring it home."

"That's great." Tori's smile was patronizing as she turned away from Grace to talk to Levi again. "You wanted to ask something."

Levi leaned against an empty shelf, looking totally at ease, totally photogenic. "Do most places like this have TVs?"

Grace shook her head. Not this old argument again.

"Some do. Some don't," Tori answered.

Grace threw a triumphant look at Levi. So there. She wasn't crazy not to want a TV.

But Levi was still looking at Tori. "And which do people like better, the ones with or without TVs?"

"I suppose it depends on what people are looking for," Tori said. "But I'd say the ones with TVs are more common."

"Thank you." Levi turned to Grace. "I rest my case."

"I take it this is an ongoing argument?" Tori watched them with an amused smile.

Levi laughed. "You could say that. Grace wants people to come here to connect. I say you can connect over TV. Like while watching a sad movie together." Levi's eyes darted her way.

Grace froze. That was so not what had happened while they were watching the movie the other night. They hadn't made a connection.

"Let me show you the fireplace. It's original to the house." She left the room without checking that Tori and Levi were following her.

"It's the perfect place to put a TV too," she heard Levi mutter behind her.

She chose to ignore him. She didn't want to be seen yelling on video.

"I think that went well." Levi closed the door behind Tori. "Should drum up plenty of business for this place."

Grace spun away from the door and marched to the kitchen, the clattering of dishes soon carrying through the house.

She'd seemed off all afternoon, but he'd chalked it up to stage fright. She definitely hadn't been comfortable in front of the camera. He probably should have warned her about that.

Fortunately, he'd done a pretty good job of covering for her.

He winced at the sound of shattering glass and sprinted for the kitchen.

"You okay?" He found Grace standing barefoot in a minefield of glass.

"Stay put. I'll go get a broom."

"I got it." Grace picked her way through the shards.

"Seriously Grace. You're going to get cut. Stay there. I got it."

"Just like you do everything else around here too?" Grace pelted the question at him.

"What?"

She winced and pulled her foot back from the spot she'd been about to step.

"For crying out loud. You're so stubborn." In three quick strides he'd crossed to the closet that held the broom and pulled it out.

When he reached Grace, he started to sweep the glass, but the broom was yanked unceremoniously from his hands.

"What on—" He looked up to find Grace sweeping glass with a vengeance.

"I said I've got it." Her voice was hard, and she didn't look at him.

"Grace? What's going on? Are you upset that I didn't warn you Tori was going to film? Because I'm sorry. I should have known—" He fumbled as her incredulous stare landed on him.

"You really don't know why I'm upset? Are you that self-involved?"

Levi took an involuntary step backwards. "Self-involved?"

"I was under the impression that the interview was supposed to be about the bed-and-breakfast. Not the Levi Donovan show."

"What are you talking about?" He gripped the back of his neck. She was crazy. "All we talked about was the bed-and-breakfast."

"Yeah. And all the work the wonderful and famous Levi Donovan is doing on it. Oh, Levi—" She put on the false, high-pitched voice of a belle. "Whatever would I do without you?"

"What did you want me to do? Say I wasn't working on it?"

"You called me your little helper, Levi." Her voice was dangerously quiet.

Levi held up his hands. "I never said little."

"You might as well have."

"Look, I don't know what you're complaining about. If I hadn't called in a favor with Tori, you wouldn't have had the interview in the first place."

"Yeah. It looked like a real hardship for you to ask for that favor from Tori."

"What's that supposed to mean?"

Grace glared at him a moment, then looked away. "Nothing. Never mind."

Levi grasped for a way to turn this conversation around. "It will be good for business. People will want to come to the bed-and-breakfast Levi Donovan decorated. It's a selling point."

That was obviously not the right thing to say.

Grace drew in a long breath, then exhaled all at once. "I think you should leave now."

"Look—" Was it possible he *had* taken over the interview? He was so used to being the star that it hadn't occurred to him that he was hogging the limelight. "I'm sorry, okay? I wasn't trying to steal your show. All I wanted to do was help."

"Yeah. I know." But her tone said she didn't know. And she didn't forgive him.

"I have to finish packing." She rubbed at her temples. "I'll see you tomorrow, okay? Our flight leaves at nine, so if you want to be here at six, that should be plenty of time to get to the airport and get checked in."

"Will do." At least she still wanted him to go to Tennessee with her. "And I really am sorry. I didn't mean—"

"Okay." Her voice was tired, like she couldn't deal with him anymore today.

He watched her a moment longer. He'd screwed up, and he had no idea how to fix it.

With Rayna, jewelry had always worked. But he had a feeling that wouldn't cut it with Grace. Not to mention they weren't really in the type of relationship where it would be appropriate for him to buy her jewelry.

Not yet, anyway.

Not ever, probably, if he couldn't fix this.

"I'll see you tomorrow." He grabbed his keys. "Have a good night."

Chapter 27

"Here."

Grace eyed the steaming cup of coffee Levi held out to her—a peace offering, she supposed.

She'd hardly gotten a wink of sleep last night, thinking about that interview. And though Levi had apologized again this morning when he'd pulled up to her house ten minutes early, the drive to the airport had been nearly silent.

"Try it. I got you hazelnut."

She made a face. He knew she drank her coffee unflavored and black. But the caffeine called to her, and she brought it to her lips, taking a cautious sip.

The warm liquid swirled on her tongue, a hint of bitter mixed with the slightest taste of sweetness.

Oh, that was good.

She lowered the cup, trying for an indifferent expression.

"So?"

She shrugged. "It's fine. Thanks."

"Come on, admit it. You love it. You just don't want to forgive me."

She grabbed the handle of her carry-on and dragged it behind her toward their gate. So what if he was right? She knew she had to forgive him—eventually. But she wasn't quite ready for that yet.

"The problem is—" Levi easily kept pace with her, though he had his carry-on duffel draped over his shoulder. "You can't stay mad at me. It's physically impossible."

She snorted. Watch her.

"All right. Just remember that you brought this on yourself."

"Brought what on—" But she cut off as Levi stopped dead in the middle of the path, forcing the people who had been following them to veer off to the sides.

He dropped his bag, then flung his arms wide and . . . sang.

"I'm sorry. So sorry . . ."

Or at least she thought that was supposed to be singing.

The words were scratchy and off-pitch and oh-so-loud. The man couldn't carry a tune in a bucket with a lid, bless him.

She lifted a hand to hide her eyes and ducked her head, slinking a step farther away from him. But a firm hand gripped hers and drew her closer. His other arm wrapped around her back, snugging her right up to him.

And still he was singing.

She took a quick, wild glance around her, searching for an escape route, but a crowd had started to gather around them.

"Levi, stop," she hissed.

But he shook his head, laughing, as the song continued to pour out of him.

Someone in the crowd whistled, and Levi waved with one hand, his other still firmly planted on her back. She ducked her head farther, burying it in his sweatshirt. This was mortifying. But also kind of . . . *No, it was not kind of sweet. It was mortifying. Period.*

At long last, the song ended. A smattering of applause broke out around them.

Fire licked up Grace's cheeks, and yet, they also felt a little bit strange. As if she was . . . Yes, she was smiling.

Why was she smiling?

"What'd you do?" a voice from the crowd called.

"I was an idiot." Levi's whole chest moved as he responded, and Grace suddenly realized her face was still pressed against him.

She took one very large step backward, keeping her head down so she wouldn't have to see the people gathered around them.

"Do you forgive him?" that same voice called.

Grace raised her eyes to Levi's. He was watching her with a goofy yet pleading look. He folded his hands in front of him, angelic style, and mouthed, "Please."

Grace gave one quick nod.

Forgiving him was better than standing here with all these people staring at her.

"Kiss her." That ever-so-helpful spectator again.

Grace balked.

Of course Levi wasn't going to kiss her.

And she wasn't going to kiss him.

But he looked at her, raising both eyebrows. She gave an emphatic shake of her head. No way.

She was not kissing Levi Donovan in front of all these people.

She was not kissing Levi Donovan. Ever. Period. End of story.

Levi was still watching her, and for half a second, she was sure he was going to do it anyway. Her blood thundered in her ears, drowning out the voice that was repeating the request.

But then Levi stooped to pick up their bags. "She's shy."

He winked at her, then turned and started walking toward their gate again.

She scurried after him, unwilling to be left alone with the crowd. When she reached his side, he still sported an overly large grin.

"I can't believe you did that."

"I told you, you brought it on yourself. Oh, and just so you know, Tori and I never dated. That wasn't why I called in a favor. I helped her get an interview with Lawrence Brooks—who she ended up marrying."

"I— Oh." Why he thought she would care about his connection to Tori was beyond her. "That's . . . interesting."

"Is it?" He lifted a shoulder. "Come on, we don't want to miss our flight."

"So are we friends again?" Levi didn't dare lean closer to Grace, though he kept his voice low. She'd been acting weird since the moment they'd gotten on the plane. And he'd seen the look on her face when that guy in the airport had said he should kiss her—pure terror.

Did she really find him that repulsive? That undesirable?

"Yeah." Her sigh said she'd given the answer against her better judgment. "We're friends."

"Friends who pretend to be more?"

"I guess. Wouldn't be much point in dragging you along otherwise."

"Speaking of, we should probably practice."

Grace gave him a blank look. "Practice?"

"Acting like a couple. You know, holding hands. Talking. Hugging." He raised an eyebrow. He really shouldn't push it right now, but he had to see how she'd react. "Kissing."

Alarm lit her eyes. "We are not kissing. If you think—"

He laughed. "Relax. I was kidding. I know I'm not your type. Here." He held out his hand, palm up, fingers splayed.

Grace stared at it, and he nodded his chin at her hand.

Slowly, she lifted it and let her palm come to a rest against his.

He folded his fingers around hers. "There. That's not so bad, is it?"

She didn't reply.

"Now, what's our story?" He tightened his grip on her hand, feeling the scrapes and callouses from the weeks of hard work at his side. Though nearly every woman's hand he'd ever held had been soft and smooth, he preferred Grace's without question.

"Our story?"

"You know, how did we meet? What do we enjoy doing together? That sort of thing."

A flitter of panic crossed Grace's face. "Maybe this was a mistake. I don't want to make up a whole lie to tell my family."

"Okay. We'll tell them the truth."

"But—"

"We met when I started working on the bed-and-breakfast. And we like to work together, eat ice cream, and parasail. See?" He turned to her. "None of that is a lie, right? Unless you don't like doing those things with me?"

"No. I do. But . . ."

"Good. Now how about pet names? Pookey, Snookums, Honey Bear? Which do you want to be?"

Grace laughed, and the anxiety slipped from her face. "Who have you ever heard call someone Pookey? Let's stick with Grace and Levi."

"Fair enough. Now for the important part."

Grace gave him a wary look.

"I need a primer on your family. I aim to make a good impression."

For the next hour, Grace told him all about her family, her hand planted firmly in his the whole while. By the time the plane landed, Levi knew that Grace was closest to her brother Zeb, who was only a year older than her and a cop. He knew that Simeon had met his bride on a mission trip, that Judah was a doctor and likely wouldn't be at the wedding, since he had cut himself off from the family, that Asher was a park ranger, Joseph was studying to be a vet, and Benjamin played football, had just graduated from high school, and wanted to become a chef.

He also got the impression that all six of them were fiercely protective of their sister.

As they filed off the plane, Grace slid her hand into his. He looked down at her with a smile, his heart making a short, quick trip to his throat until he reminded himself that she was just doing what they'd practiced.

"Last chance. You sure you want to do this?" She sounded adorably nervous.

But he wasn't sure if it was because she was afraid he'd say no—or afraid he'd say yes.

"I'm sure." He leaned over to take her bag from her. "Let's do this, Pookey."

She swatted at his arm, but the smile that lit her face made it so worth it.

Chapter 28

"Benjamin!" Grace shrieked as she threw herself into her baby brother's arms. He had to have grown at least three inches since she'd seen him at Christmas. The worst thing about being the only girl in a family of boys was that everyone was taller than her. Well, that and the perpetual mess in the bathroom.

"Hey, sis." Benjamin's long arms squeezed her tight, and he ducked his head, whispering, "You could have mentioned that the someone you were bringing was Levi Donovan."

She supposed she could have, but it hadn't occurred to her. Somehow, she usually forgot that Levi was a big football star everyone knew. To her, he was simply the guy renovating her house. And pretending to be her boyfriend.

She let go of her brother. "Sorry. Benjamin, this is Levi. Levi, my youngest brother Benjamin."

"Ah." Levi shook Benjamin's hand. "The football star."

Benjamin's cheeks colored, and Grace turned to look at Levi. He'd remembered what she'd told him on the plane?

"I'm not a star," Benjamin mumbled.

"You are too." Grace slugged him. "You don't take your team to state three years in a row without being a star."

"She's right, man." Levi slung an arm over Grace's shoulders.

She stiffened but didn't move away.

He's supposed to be your boyfriend, she reminded herself. *That's what boyfriends do.*

"Maybe we can get in a game while we're here. If your sister doesn't mind." He leaned over and brushed the lightest kiss onto Grace's hair.

Pulling away slightly, she shot him a look. Hadn't she said no kissing? And she'd meant it.

Even if his gesture had felt sweet and friendly more than passionate or romantic.

"Come on. I'd better get y'all home." Benjamin opened the passenger door of his ridiculously tiny Gremlin. "Mama's been in a tizzy all day long, waiting to meet Grace's special fellow. Wait till she finds out it's Levi Donovan. I can't believe you didn't tell us."

Actually, now that he said it, Grace couldn't believe it either. What *would* her family think when they learned she was dating Levi Donovan?

She moved to climb into the car's tiny backseat, but Levi pulled her back. "You take shotgun. Catch up with your brother."

She eyed Levi's long legs. "There's no way you're going to fit back there."

Without waiting for him to argue, she climbed in. Once she was settled, Levi crammed himself into the seat in front of her.

"You sure you're okay back there?" He craned his neck to check on her.

"Positive." If okay meant having some sort of spring sticking out of the seat into her back, then she was great.

"Sorry." Benjamin crammed the luggage onto the seat next to her, then climbed into the driver's seat. "She needs a little work, but I'm going to fix her up." He pulled into traffic. "Levi Donovan," he muttered. "Unbelievable. How did you two even meet?"

Levi launched into the story of how he was helping with the bed-and-breakfast. Every once in a while, he sought her confirmation, and she nodded absently. She was too busy worrying to jump in. What if Mama and Daddy didn't like Levi? Didn't approve of him?

She studied what she could see of his profile from back here. He was good-looking, that was for sure. But her parents wouldn't care a lick about that.

And he was a nice enough guy, charming when he wanted to be. Which seemed to be a lot more often lately.

She told herself it didn't matter what her parents thought of him. It wasn't like he was really her boyfriend. Just a convenient stand-in to keep them off her back while she was home. Even so, she really wanted them to like him.

To approve of her choice.

Even if he wasn't really her choice.

Ugh. Her head spun.

Levi and Benjamin's conversation moved from how Levi and Grace had met to football, then to Benjamin's plans for next year.

"Grace says you want to go to culinary school?"

Grace's eyes about dropped out of her head. It wasn't only football that he'd been paying attention to on the plane.

"Yeah. It's not exactly the NFL, but . . ."

"It's a good choice," Levi interrupted. "Women love a man who can cook. Just ask your sister. I made her pancakes, and that was the moment she knew she was in love with me."

Grace choked on her own spit, gasping for air around her coughs.

Levi turned to peer at her. "You okay, Honey Bear?"

The most Grace could do was curl a lip at him, and he laughed.

"If cooking is your passion," he said to Benjamin, "that's what you should do."

"Thanks, man. You're pretty cool."

Levi swiveled to look at Grace again. "You hear that? I'm pretty cool."

She smirked. "Don't let it go to your head."

But yeah, he actually was pretty cool. The way he was encouraging her brother, who as the baby of the family had always been a little less sure of himself, was more than pretty cool.

Not that he needed to know she thought that.

"I think we're off to a good start," Levi whispered to Grace as he held out a hand to help pry her out of the backseat of Benjamin's Gremlin. "Your family likes me."

"Benjamin's the easiest one," Grace whispered back. "Especially since he apparently idolizes you." But she was happy about that, he could tell. "Mama's going to be the tough nut."

"There y'all are." A woman who looked strikingly like Grace, only older, stepped onto the wide front porch of the spacious Revival-style home.

Grace shot him a deer-in-the-headlights look.

"Relax. It's going to be great. She'll like me, you'll see."

Grace gripped his forearm. "Whatever you do, don't mention your Harley."

"I don't see how it would come up. Why?"

But Grace's mother had descended the porch stairs and was beelining for them.

"Mama." Grace left his side and wrapped her mother in a hug.

When the two women pulled apart Levi held out a hand. "I'm Levi Donovan. It's so nice to meet you."

Mrs. Calvano gave him a long, appraising look before shaking his hand. "Heather Calvano."

"That's a lovely name."

"Hmm." Mrs. Calvano turned to Grace. "Abigail and Carly are bunking with you in your old room." Levi made a mental checklist—Abigail was the bride, Carly was Zeb's wife.

"I put Levi in with the boys." She turned to him. "I hope you don't mind sleeping on the floor. We don't have enough beds."

"Mama, can't Benjamin—"

"Of course I don't mind," Levi cut in. "I'm just grateful for the invitation to come. I don't know how I'd handle five days without my girl."

Mrs. Calvano scrutinized him, and Grace frowned. Okay, maybe that had been a tad over the top.

But her mother seemed like the kind of person it would take over the top to impress.

"Well, I hope you weren't planning on spending too much time with her while you're here." Mrs. Calvano shepherded them toward the house. "As a bridesmaid, Grace is going to be plenty busy with wedding activities."

"Oh. I'm sure I won't be *that* busy. Levi and I will still have time to spend together."

"Maybe." Mrs. Calvano gave a polite nod. "Come on. Everyone's out back."

As they followed Mrs. Calvano, Grace sent him her best told-you-so look.

Fine. He could admit he had his work cut out for him, getting her mother to like him. But he was up for the challenge.

Chapter 29

"What are you doing out here?" Grace closed the French doors that led to the back patio Mama and Daddy had put in last summer. The morning was warm and sticky, the sun just starting to burn off the dew sparkling in the grass all the way down to the river.

Levi was sprawled on a chaise lounge, and she padded closer, cup of coffee in hand. She'd planned to sneak out here for some quiet time in prayer before the rest of the family woke and chaos took over. She'd assumed Levi was still sleeping.

"Your brothers sound like they're sawing down a forest in there. I couldn't sleep." He eyed her coffee.

"Here." She passed the mug to him. "You look like you need this more than I do."

"Thank you. Have a seat." He moved his legs to make room for her at the foot of the chair. After taking a sip of the coffee, he held the mug out to her. She gave it a dubious look.

"What? I promise I don't have cooties."

No, maybe not. But sharing a cup of coffee felt a little too intimate.

She set the mug on the arm of the chair, and he shrugged, then took another sip.

"So this is where you grew up?"

She nodded, taking in the sweeping view of the backyard that ran right down to the banks of the Serenity River. "From sixth grade on, yes. Before that, my dad helped run a Bible camp nearby, so we lived in a cabin at the camp."

"That explains a lot."

"What does that mean?"

Levi took a slow drink of coffee, obviously enjoying making her wait for an explanation.

"Levi."

He laughed, holding up a protective hand. "Nothing. Just that you're a hard worker, not afraid to get dirty or break a nail. Not a girly girl."

"Oh." Was that supposed to be a compliment or an insult?

"That's a good thing, by the way." Levi's smile was too warm—or rather, it made her too warm.

"So what are we doing today?" He was apparently oblivious to the effect of his smile on her—as he should be.

"I'm not sure what Mama has planned."

Levi's smile transformed to a grimace. "Whatever it is, I'm sure it doesn't involve me. She was pretty clear that she didn't plan to give us much time together."

"She's just a little wound up about the wedding. Mama's the kind of person who wants everything to be perfect."

"Hmm. I wonder if I know anyone else like that," Levi teased.

She swatted at him, making him slosh coffee onto his arm.

"Hey." Levi wiped at the coffee with his other hand. "Here's a thought—you could try doing what you want to do today, instead of letting your mom tell you what to do."

"And what do I want to do today?"

"You'll think of something."

They both turned at the sound of someone stepping onto the patio.

"Speak of the—" Levi muttered, but Grace shot him a quelling look.

"What?" His expression was all innocence. "I was going to say 'mother.'"

Right.

"Good morning, Mama."

Mama's eyes traveled from her to Levi. "Did y'all sleep out here all night?" It was subtle, but Grace heard the suspicion—the unspoken accusation—in the question.

If Levi noticed, he didn't give any indication. "No, ma'am. Just stepped out this morning to watch the glorious sunrise. This is a beautiful view you have." He gave her mother an angelic smile that somehow didn't look the least forced or fake.

Grace could have hugged him. He was trying so hard to get Mama to like him. Daddy and the boys had been a shoo-in—they'd even asked him to golf with them tomorrow. But like she'd warned Levi, Mama would be a tougher nut. Maybe impossible.

Not that it mattered too much what Mama thought about Levi—as long as she was convinced enough that they were dating that she didn't try to meddle and set Grace up with Aaron.

Ignoring Levi, Mama turned to Grace. "I need to go over to the church this morning to finalize some things with Pastor Cooper. I thought you could come with me. Might be nice to catch up."

Grace stared at Mama. Why would she want to catch up with Daddy's old associate? And then it hit her—Pastor Cooper was Aaron's name now too.

Her mouth opened. Here she was, with her *boyfriend*, as far as Mama knew, and still Mama wanted to set her up with Aaron. Mama would never be satisfied with anyone Grace chose for herself. Grace had shown her lack of judgment once, and Mama was forever going to hold it over her head.

She turned to Levi, who watched her, a question in his eyes. Was she going to do what Mama told her to? Or was she going to make her own decision?

Her gaze snapped back to Mama. "Actually, Mama, I promised Levi I'd take him on a tour of River Falls today. Since I'll be doing bridesmaid stuff all day tomorrow and Saturday."

Mama waved off her protest. "That won't take long. Y'all can do it later."

"Sorry, Mama." Grace called on all her gumption. "We wanted to get an early start. Tell Pastor Cooper I say hi, though."

Mama's eyes grew three times bigger, and her mouth opened, but she spun and disappeared into the house without a word.

Grace blew out a long breath.

"So," Levi piped from beside her. "I guess we're touring River Falls today?" There was a chuckle in his voice but also maybe a bit of admiration.

Grace nodded, but inside a new worry was working its way up. Now she had to spend the entire day with Levi.

And she was looking forward to it way more than she should.

Chapter 30

"Pull over here."

Levi obeyed Grace's directions, pulling into a scenic overlook on the hilly road they'd been navigating in the Gremlin Benjamin had lent them for the day. He turned off the car, and Grace opened her door, bouncing out. She seemed to be full of a strange sort of energy today that had propelled them through downtown River Falls, to the banks of the river, and now up onto a high mountain overview.

And he wouldn't change it for the world. This time alone with her—time when they weren't working but simply being—was turning out to be pretty incredible.

Grace walked to the edge of the overlook, which sloped gently down the tree-covered mountainside to a valley below, where he could make out a few of the buildings Grace had taken him to earlier.

Grace pointed to an arc in the river that threaded between the buildings. "See how the town's right in the middle of that heart-shaped curve in the river?"

Levi squinted. "Looks more like a kidney bean to me."

Grace smacked his arm, and Levi grinned. He would never admit it to her, but he'd been saying things to provoke her all morning, just so she'd do that. He couldn't get enough of that contact with her. But even though they'd practiced holding hands so diligently on the plane, Grace hadn't once taken his hand since the moment her mom had come out of the house to greet them yesterday.

Levi's stomach rumbled, and he glanced at the time. Two o'clock. No wonder he was starved. "As usual, you worked me right through lunch. Want to grab a bite?"

"Pie." Grace's eyes gleamed. "I'm craving some pie from Daisy's."

"Pie for lunch?" Levi bumped his shoulder against hers. "I had no idea you were so rebellious."

They stuffed themselves into the Gremlin, and Grace directed him back into town. He tried to imagine her growing up here, riding through these streets on her bicycle, meeting up with friends, maybe a boyfriend.

No. That he didn't want to imagine.

Anyway, it was difficult to picture Grace living anywhere aside from Hope Springs. She was so woven into the fabric of that community.

As they walked into the pie shop, he let himself wonder, not for the first time in the last few weeks, what it would be like if he did that too—wove himself into the community of Hope Springs. He wasn't sure yet that he was ready to take such a drastic step. But each time he thought about it, it became just a little more appealing. Maybe because each time he thought about it, his thoughts lingered just a little longer on Grace.

"Levi?"

"What? Sorry." Levi shook himself out of his nonsensical thoughts, focusing on the woman behind the counter, who was apparently waiting to get his pie order.

"I'll go with . . ." He scanned the rows and rows of pies in the display case. "A slice of cherry and a slice of apple."

Grace raised her eyebrows.

"What? If you want me to have pie for lunch, I need one for my meal and one for dessert."

Grace unzipped her purse and pulled out a credit card, but he already had his ready. "I got this."

But she shook her head and plucked his card out of his fingers, passing the cashier hers instead.

"Grace—"

Her look stopped him. "You flew all this way for me. The least I can do is buy you a piece of pie."

"Two pieces," he corrected.

"Okay, then." Her laughing eyes met his. "Two pieces."

They carried their pie to a small table near a window that overlooked the river outside.

Levi took a bite, closing his eyes as the pastry flaked on his tongue and the tart cherries popped against his taste buds.

"Good, right?"

When he opened his eyes, Grace's smile bumped right up against his heart.

"You have to taste it." He loaded his fork with a generous bite and lifted it toward her mouth.

She considered it, and for a second he was sure she was going to refuse it as she had the coffee earlier. But then she leaned forward and opened her mouth, and he gently steered the fork into it.

Her eyes closed too as she chewed. "I wonder if I can get Daisy to deliver these to Hope Springs. My guests would never want to leave then."

They dug into their pie slices in earnest, Levi easily outpacing her, finishing both his pieces before she'd gotten halfway through her one slice of French silk pie. Finally, she scooped the last bite onto her fork, then held it out to him.

His eyes met hers, and again he was drawn in by their mocha color, nearly an exact match to the chocolate of her pie.

"I couldn't. That's your last bite."

She bounced the pie lightly. "I had some of yours. It's only fair."

She moved her fork closer, almost sending the pie toppling off. Levi reached to steady her hand, wrapping his own around hers and bringing the fork to his mouth.

This time he didn't close his eyes, instead keeping them focused on her. She swallowed and ducked her head as she slid her hand out of his.

"Like it?" Her words sounded forced.

"I do."

She looked up, her eyes widening and her face growing pale.

"Sorry. I didn't mean to make you—"

But she was staring beyond him, toward the door. Levi swiveled in his seat to get a better view.

A guy in full motorcycle gear strode toward the register, pulling off a pair of aviators. He didn't glance in their direction.

Levi turned to Grace. But if anything, she'd gone even paler.

"What's wrong?"

"We have to go," she whispered, as if they were fugitives and the guy was FBI.

"Why? Who is that?"

Grace shook her head. "A mistake."

Levi peered at the counter again. The guy was talking with the cashier as she rang up his order. Didn't exactly seem like a threat.

"Okay." Levi pushed his chair back. "Let's go."

Grace stood too, just as the guy took his pie and started in their direction.

"Oh no." Grace's whisper was so quiet Levi wasn't sure that was what she'd said.

But he turned toward her, reached out his arms, and pulled her in close for a hug, tucking her face against his chest. She squirmed for a second but then reached her arms around his back. Levi let his head drop to rest on top of hers, that sweet smelling perfume doing crazy things to his imagination as he wondered what it would be like to hug her for real.

He waited for the guy to pass and take a seat at the far end of the shop.

"Okay." He spoke low and into Grace's hair. "Coast is clear. Stay in front of me."

He reluctantly let her go, steering her in front of him so that his larger form would shield her from the other guy's view, should he look over.

When they were safely outside, he pointed to the river. "Want to go for a walk? Or do you want to go back to your parents'?"

Grace looked over her shoulder at the pie shop, then toward the water.

"Walk," she finally said.

"You got it."

They'd been walking for ten minutes before Grace felt like she could breathe normally again. As far as she knew, Hunter had moved to Nashville after high school. She had been totally unprepared to see him today. But she'd acted a little bit like a lunatic, and she should probably apologize to Levi for that.

"You probably think I'm crazy."

He laughed. "Well, yes. But I've known that for a long time now."

"Funny." But his teasing took a weight off her. "Sorry I acted so weird back there. I really didn't want to run into Hunter."

"Yeah. I gathered that." Something squeezed her fingers, and she looked down. How long had they been holding hands? And why did it feel so natural?

They lapsed into silence again, though Grace threw furtive glances at Levi every few seconds.

Finally, he stopped and turned toward her. "Why do you keep looking at me like that?"

"Like what?" She looked away. "I'm not looking at you."

"Yes you are. You're wondering what I think of you. If you should explain what happened between you and Hunter or not. So I'll answer you." He tugged her back into a walk. "You don't have to tell me if you don't want to. The past is in the past. Sometimes it's best to keep it there."

Grace sighed. She didn't have to tell him. But for some reason, she wanted to.

"You remember I told you about not trusting my parents' judgment about a guy I was seeing?"

Levi nodded.

"Hunter was that guy." She pulled her hand out of his and wrapped her arms around herself. "He had been pressuring me for a long time to show him that I really loved him. So one night, he took me to this secluded little pond. I didn't realize my parents had followed us—I think one of my brothers tipped them off—and let's just say they caught us . . ." Heat and shame rushed to her cheeks, but she made herself finish the thought. "In a compromising position."

"Oh." Levi's expression didn't change.

"I promised them I'd never see him again. And I haven't."

"I don't think they meant you literally have to hide if he comes into a room."

"I know." Grace covered her face with her hands. "I don't know what came over me back there."

Though it hadn't been so bad having Levi hold her close. "Thanks for your quick thinking."

"At your service." He gave a slight bow, and they resumed walking.

Chapter 31

"Ready to go?" Grace's dad, whom Levi couldn't quite bring himself to call Abe, though he'd insisted on it three times already, closed his SUV's hatch.

"Yes, sir." Levi checked to make sure his credit card was in his pocket. A sure way to impress Grace's dad would be to pick up the tab today. "Let me run inside and say goodbye to Grace."

"Didn't you already say goodbye?" Asher called to his back.

Levi tossed a grin over his shoulder. Didn't hurt to throw in an extra goodbye for her family's benefit, just in case any of them doubted he and Grace were really in love.

Inside, Grace sat with her mother at the kitchen table, which had been transformed into a makeshift greenhouse for assembling the centerpieces.

"Those look nice."

Grace glanced up, a surprised smile lifting her lips. "What are you doing in here? Don't tell me they left without you. They did that to Judah once."

Grace's mother stiffened at the name. Grace hadn't gone into much detail about what had happened with her older brother, and Levi got the impression that the family avoided talking about it.

"No, they're waiting for me. I think." He turned to check out the window. The SUV was still there. "I didn't want to leave without saying goodbye."

Grace's eyes widened, but Levi's gaze shifted to Mrs. Calvano. She barely seemed to notice he was there. So much for impressing her with his attentiveness to her daughter.

He crossed the room and pressed a kiss onto the top of Grace's head, her sweet scent making him want to linger.

She froze, the flowers she'd been cutting floating in mid-air. He was probably going to hear about this later—he knew she'd said no kisses—but desperate times called for desperate measures.

"Those look a lot like the flowers I gave you for our first date. Remember?" He straightened, and Grace offered him a half-amused look.

"I remember." He could tell it was on the tip of her tongue to say *since it was only last week*, but she resisted. She turned to her mother. "They were beautiful, Mama. Purple tulips. You should have seen them."

"That's nice." Mrs. Calvano didn't look up from her arranging. "You'd best get going before you make the boys miss their tee time."

Well, he'd tried.

"See you later." It'd probably be pushing it to kiss Grace again, so he squeezed her shoulder.

Then he jogged out to the car and squished into the backseat with Asher and Joseph. Zeb sat in the front, and Benjamin had insisted on driving Simeon in his Gremlin.

The brothers spent most of the car ride ribbing each other in that way that showed how close they really were. A small pang went through Levi, as he wondered if he and Luke would have been closer if life had been different. If he hadn't been so busy with college and then the NFL. If Luke hadn't gotten sick.

By the time they got to the golf course, Levi's cheeks hurt from laughing so much. They piled out of the vehicle and grabbed their clubs, joining Simeon and Benjamin at the clubhouse.

A sweet scent caught Levi's attention as he was about to enter the building. He stopped abruptly.

Grace?

But there was no one around aside from her brothers. And he knew from spending the past half hour in the car with them that the sweet smell definitely wasn't them.

Next to him, a vine wound up a trellis, pink and orange flowers covering its green stem. He stepped closer to it, inhaling deeply.

This was it. This was what Grace smelled like.

"You good, man?" Zeb sounded amused to find Levi stopping to smell the flowers.

"Yeah." He stepped back and went through the door Zeb still held. "What kind of plant is that?"

"Honeysuckle, I think. Why?"

"No reason." He sped up to reach the counter, where Grace's dad was about to pay for the group.

"I've got this, sir." He pulled out his card and reached past Grace's dad to hand it to the concierge.

"That's not necessary." Grace's dad gave him a searching look, and Levi felt oddly exposed.

"Yeah, we all like you already," Joseph quipped.

"I know it's not. But I'd like to. If you don't mind. You've all been so good about welcoming me into the family."

"Thankfully, I'm not too proud to accept a gift." Grace's dad put his card away. "Thank you."

"My pleasure." Levi felt suddenly like he'd passed some sort of test.

As they moved onto the course, he settled into an easy camaraderie with the brothers. Even Grace's dad was personable and easy to get along with, which at first threw Levi for a bit of a loop. But after a while, he was joking about Pastor Calvano's slice along with the others.

At the ninth hole, as they paused for a water break, Zeb pulled Levi aside.

"Look man, I wanted to talk to you a minute." Zeb seemed to be the most serious of the brothers.

"Okay. What about?"

"Grace." Zeb folded his arms across his chest, which may have been broader than Levi's. "I like you. I can see that she likes you. You make her happy."

He did? That was good to hear. He could never tell.

"But your reputation isn't exactly as a one-woman man, if you know what I mean."

"I—"

Zeb raised a hand. "Hey, I believe people can change. I see it all the time. And I hope you really do care for her the way you seem to."

"I do." The words came out effortlessly. It wasn't his feelings for Grace he questioned. It was hers for him.

"Good. Because you may be Levi Donovan, but if you hurt her, you'll have to answer to us."

Levi swallowed. "I won't hurt her." Right? How could he hurt her if she had no real feelings for him?

Zeb slapped his shoulder. "That's good to hear."

Levi nodded, lifting his water bottle for a long swig.

"I look forward to when we can do this for your wedding," Zeb said as he walked to join the others.

Levi gasped with the water bottle still to his mouth, sucking liquid right down into his lungs.

He sputtered and coughed for a full minute before he finally had it under control.

"You okay?" Benjamin gave him a concerned look.

"I'm great." Levi picked up his clubs and followed the others. They didn't really expect him to marry Grace, did they?

When he didn't, would they make things worse for her than they'd been to begin with?

Maybe this whole thing had been a big mistake. Maybe he should have let Grace come back alone to reconnect with this Aaron guy.

The guy was a pastor, for crying out loud. He probably ticked every box on Grace's checklist.

Whereas Levi doubted he checked a single one.

Chapter 32

Levi searched the crowded backyard for the familiar tumble of dark hair.

He'd barely seen Grace since he'd left this morning. By the time they'd gotten back from golfing, she'd already left to prepare for the rehearsal. There hadn't been a moment to talk to her during the rehearsal either, since she was in the wedding party.

As he'd watched her walk down the aisle in her soft blue sundress, Zeb's comment from earlier had come back to him. After Rayna, he'd been sure he'd never consider marriage again. But maybe . . .

Levi shook himself. That was way too far in the future to think about.

Finally, he spotted her at a table for two. Nice. It would be good to have a chance to talk alone. Even if they were surrounded by people. But as he stepped closer, a guy with bleached blond hair and a smile that seemed to touch his ears slid into the seat across from her.

Levi picked up his pace, ready to tell the guy to scram—that was his girl—but Grace offered the stranger a welcoming smile and took the glass of punch he held out to her.

Levi stopped.

An elbow to the gut would have been more pleasant.

He debated. He could go over there and tell the stranger to bug off, remind Grace that she might want to put on a better show of being his girlfriend for her family. Or he could walk away.

"Hey man. Looking for somewhere to sit?" Benjamin came up next to him.

"Who's that guy sitting with Grace?"

Benjamin followed the direction of Levi's head bob. "Pastor Cooper? He's pretty cool. Got a lot of the kids involved in youth group. We're all over by that picnic table. Unless you're going to sit by Grace?"

Levi had never been one to walk away from a challenge. But he knew when to fold. Grace might think she didn't want to be set up with the man her mom wanted her to be with. But she was only fooling herself.

He wouldn't let her fool him too.

"Nah." He followed Benjamin. "I'm not going to sit by Grace."

Where was he?

Grace had been searching the guests gathered in her parents' backyard for half an hour, trying to find Levi.

It wasn't until she heard the shouts from the front yard that she realized her brothers must have gotten a game of football going. That had to be where Levi was.

She followed the sounds around the house but slowed as she spotted the group. Though dark had fallen a good hour ago, the front yard was well-lit, and she spotted Levi instantly. He was huddled with Asher and Benjamin and had an arm over each.

A tickle of joy went through her at the way he fit so easily into her family, followed by a wave of regret. Her brothers would be crushed when she and Levi "broke up."

Unless they didn't. Break up.

The thought had taken hold of her earlier today, when Levi had kissed her head again. The gesture had been so sweet and spontaneous, and she'd found herself wondering what it would be like if he did that all the time. For real.

Grace shook herself as she plopped onto the grass to watch the football game.

This was only pretend. Levi was only putting on an act for her family. Come Sunday evening, she'd have to return to reality. Better not to wander too far from it now.

Especially since, even on the off chance that Levi would be interested in making this real, it didn't change the fact that he wasn't the right man for her.

When the game finally broke up, Grace pushed to her feet. "Y'all looked like you were having fun out there."

"Yeah, your boyfriend's not too bad at football," Simeon joked.

"You guys gave me a run for my money." Levi exchanged fist bumps with them as they dissipated.

"Thanks for playing with them." Grace stepped to Levi's side.

He tossed the football from hand to hand. "They're fun guys."

"I'm sorry we haven't had a chance to see each other much today. Mama had the bridal party running all over the place."

Levi shrugged. "It was fine."

Grace set a hand on his arm, and he stopped tossing the ball. "Is something wrong?"

"Nope."

"How was golfing?"

"Good."

She crossed her arms. "If nothing's wrong, why are you being like this?"

"Being like what?"

Grace huffed. This man was maddening sometimes. "So short with me."

"Sorry. I figured you were tired of talking after your long conversation with Pastor Cooper."

"Pastor Cooper?" Was that what this was about? "We only talked for a few minutes. He had a youth group thing to get to."

"Well, maybe *y'all*"—his lips sneered around the word—"can sneak in a quick date tomorrow after the wedding."

"A date?" Wasn't that what Levi was here to prevent? "I don't want to go on a date with Aaron."

"Could have fooled me. You two looked pretty happy together. Just wish you hadn't dragged me all the way here to keep your mom off your back about him only to turn around and throw yourself at him."

Grace drew back her shoulders. "Throw myself at him?"

"Don't worry. I'm sure your mom will be happy. Just tell her we broke up. Say I realized I'd never live up to who you want me to be." Levi tossed the football over his shoulder and marched toward the house.

Chapter 33

Grace flipped onto her back. Then to her side. Then to her back again.

If she didn't get some sleep, she was going to look like a wreck for Simeon's wedding tomorrow.

But how could she sleep, after the way Levi had treated her before?

The man had dated more women than she could count. And he had the nerve to call her out for talking to a man her mother happened to want to set her up with?

She wasn't going to deny that catching up with Aaron had been nice. But that was all it had been.

She'd found herself sitting there, thinking about Levi, even telling Aaron about him.

He'd said he was happy for her, hadn't said a word about missing her or wanting to marry her.

So either Mama's reports of his interest in her had been wildly exaggerated or Aaron respected the fact that she was with someone else.

Someone who had retreated to the boys' bedroom right after their fight.

Grace turned to her side again. What she couldn't figure out was why Levi cared so much.

They were doing this whole ruse for her benefit, not his. So what did it matter to him if she talked to another man? He'd acted as if he were . . . jealous.

Grace's eyes popped open, and she rolled to stare at the ceiling.

But he couldn't have been. Right?

She thought of those moments when his acting had been so good he'd almost convinced her his feelings were real. Like when he'd kissed her head. Or held her hand. Or sent her that smile that said . . . all kinds of things she hadn't let herself think it said. She'd told herself he was just a good actor, but what if . . .

Grace sat upright.

There was no way she was going to be able to sleep now.

She tiptoed out of the room so she wouldn't wake Abigail, then crept through the hallway, pausing for a moment to listen to the honking snores coming from the boys' room. No wonder Levi hadn't been able to sleep the other night.

She opened the French doors as quietly as possible and slipped outside.

The night had grown damp, with a slight chill, but it was alive with the calls of bullfrogs and katydids.

She padded to the chaise lounge she and Levi had shared the other morning.

A soft scream escaped her at the sight of a body on it.

The eyes flew open.

"Levi." She pressed a hand to her galloping heart. "What are you doing out here?"

"Couldn't sleep." He blinked at her. "Why aren't you in bed?"

"Couldn't sleep either." She rocked from foot to foot on the cool flagstones as they looked at each other.

Levi moved his feet and gestured to the end of the chair just as he had the other morning. Hesitantly, she sat.

"Stars are beautiful tonight." Levi's voice was low, suited for the dark and the late hour.

She tilted her head back to study the sky.

"That's Venus over there," Levi said.

She followed his arm toward a bright dot straight above them. "I didn't know you liked astronomy."

"I told you. Not just a dumb jock."

"I know." She dropped her chin to look at him. "About before. I'm sorry. I wasn't trying to make you uncomfortable by talking to Aaron. You were right, I did drag you all the way down here, and I should have been more considerate instead of leaving you to fend for yourself with my family."

"About that." Levi gave her a sheepish grin. "I think I may have overreacted a little. You can talk to whoever you want. And for the record, you didn't drag me here. I volunteered."

"You did, didn't you?" Grace almost asked him why, but she wasn't sure whether he'd say it was because he wanted to spend time with her or because he needed a diversion. And she wasn't sure which she wanted it to be.

Levi tipped his head back toward the stars, and Grace followed suit. They sat like that, silent but peaceful, until the chill air started to seep through Grace's skin.

She rubbed her hands on her arms. She wasn't ready to go inside yet.

"Here." Levi slid to the side of the chair and patted the spot next to him.

Grace contemplated it. There was definitely enough room for her. But was it a good idea?

Levi waited, not pressuring her.

Another shiver went through her, and she pictured her cozy bed inside. But for some reason it didn't hold as much appeal as sitting out here with Levi.

She scooted up the seat until she was planted next to him, but his shoulders were too broad for her to sit back.

"One second." Levi repositioned himself, and she felt his arm across her shoulders. "There, now sit back."

She did, tentatively, and he adjusted his position so that his hand rested lightly on her upper arm.

"There. That's better."

She nodded, his clean sandalwood scent sneaking past her defenses.

"You smell good," Levi murmured. "Like honeysuckle."

Grace twisted her neck to look over at him. "Not many guys could pick out the smell of honeysuckle."

"It's been driving me crazy for weeks, trying to place the smell. Then I walked past these flowers at the golf course, and Zeb said they were honeysuckle."

Grace giggled at the image. "You asked my brother about flowers? You could have asked me what the smell was if you wanted to know."

Did he say he'd been thinking about her scent for weeks?

She sat back, nestling into his arm, and closed her eyes, letting the sounds of the night wash over her. The crickets had quieted now, but the bullfrogs still thumped out their rhythm, and in the distance an owl hooted. Next to her, the steady in and out of Levi's breath lulled her.

"Can I ask you something?" Levi asked after a while.

"Mmm hmm." She was feeling pleasantly warm and sleepy in his arms, but she opened her eyes.

"Dan's sermon the other day. Do you really believe that?"

Grace held her breath. She'd been praying for an opportunity like this. "Which part? I mean, I believe all of it, but which part are you wondering about?"

"About there only being one purpose." Levi said the words slowly, as if he were putting a lot of thought into them. "About holding onto God's Word and there only being one truth. About our role on earth being to glorify God." He chuckled low in his throat. "So basically, all of it."

"I do." Grace angled her head so that she was facing him, her ear pressed to his upper arm.

"So why do you bother with the bed-and-breakfast then? Or with anything that isn't reading God's Word or preaching about him? If that's supposedly our purpose."

"Those things are our purpose, yes." Grace searched for a way to explain it. "But that doesn't mean we can't carry them out in lots of ways, including running a bed-and-breakfast. Or playing football. It's more that as we do those things, we keep God first in our hearts. And we give him glory for everything he's given us, including our talents and skills."

"Hmm." Levi reached to tuck a strand of hair behind her ear, as if he'd done it a thousand times before. "You make it sound so easy."

"Easy?" Grace laughed. "It's definitely not easy. At least not all the time. But I find that the more time I spend in prayer and in God's Word, the more I want to spend time with him. It's like when you meet someone new and you want to know more and more about them."

Levi was watching her with a strange smile.

"What?"

He shook his head. "Nothing. I like how you describe that. I guess I always saw church as something I had to do because my parents made me and the Bible as just a bunch of rules. I haven't spent a lot of time reading the Bible or praying on my own."

"It's never too late to start. God's Word is . . ." She searched for an adequate description. "It's the greatest love story ever told." She bit her lip. "I suppose that sounds corny, but it's true. It's the story of a love so great God would do anything to make us his own. Even give up his Son. Reading it fills me. And it makes me want to live my life in a way that will please him. Not to follow the rules, but to show my love for him. Not that I always succeed."

Levi scoffed. "If I've ever met anyone who was in line for angel-of-the-year, it'd be you."

Grace shook her head. "First of all, people can't be angels. And second of all, you of all people should know I struggle with this."

"Why me of all people?"

"Because I had a hard time being civil to you when we first met. You managed to rile me up all the time so I couldn't control my tongue."

"Only when we first met?" Levi teased.

"Yes." She smacked his chest. "I'm much nicer now."

"Why is that?" His eyes met hers and held on.

Her mouth went completely dry. What was she supposed to say to that?

"I'm not sure," she mumbled.

Levi's eyes traveled to the dark yard.

"But I do know," she rushed to fill in, "that God loves you, Levi." She broke off. It felt suddenly like an intensely personal thing to say to someone.

"Yeah." Levi didn't sound certain, but he didn't sound hostile either. "Thanks."

She nodded, turning to face forward again.

Peace washed over her as she thanked God for giving her the opportunity to talk to Levi about him. She had no way of knowing if it had made an impact. But she trusted that the Holy Spirit could take this little seed she'd planted and grow it into something strong and beautiful.

Next to her, Levi's breaths deepened, and she let her head droop to his shoulder. Just a little longer . . . she'd let herself stay in his arms just a little longer, then go inside.

Chapter 34

Wow.

Levi had no words as he watched Grace glide down the aisle of the church.

He hadn't seen her since he'd woken on the chaise lounge at three in the morning to find her asleep on his shoulder. He'd sneaked a kiss to her forehead, then gently woken her so they could tiptoe back to their bedrooms for a few more hours of sleep.

When he'd woken, she'd already been whisked off to the salon with the rest of the wedding party.

As she reached the pew he sat in now, she slipped him a soft smile. A twinge in his chest told him what he already suspected—he had it bad for this woman.

And he had no idea what to do about it.

Usually, when he saw a woman he was interested in, he simply asked if she'd like to go out and she said yes and that was the end of the story.

But Grace had already rejected him once. And he had next to no confidence that if he asked her out again she wouldn't do the same, their talk last night notwithstanding.

That talk had been—it had probably been the deepest conversation he'd ever had with anyone in his life. Usually, he found talk of faith off-putting, but Grace's sincerity and passion for God had struck against something in him that he had been sure was hard and dried up.

She'd said learning about God was like getting to know someone new. Like wanting to know everything about that person.

There was no denying that was how he'd been feeling about her lately. So if he picked up a Bible and started reading it, would he feel that way about God too?

He wasn't sure if he was ready to find out.

He directed his focus to the front of the church, where Simeon and Abigail faced each other, tears streaming down their cheeks.

According to Grace, Simeon had been a confirmed bachelor with no intention of ever marrying before he'd met Abigail. And then he'd fallen hard and fast, proposing within three months.

Levi thought again of the ring he'd bought for Rayna. They'd been together for three years before he'd felt ready for that step. And even that hadn't been long enough to know who Rayna really was. What she really cared about.

I look forward to when we can do this for your wedding, Zeb had said yesterday.

But could Levi ever imagine himself standing up there, pledging his life to one woman?

His eyes went to Grace, who had tears on her cheeks as she watched her brother and his bride.

Maybe, if—

Nah. Levi Donovan was not the marrying type, and he knew it.

Didn't he?

Grace dropped onto a soft chair in the ballroom lobby and eased her feet out of her shoes with a groan. She wasn't sure her toes would ever be the same again.

"Better?"

She jumped but smiled involuntarily at the sound of Levi's voice behind her. She hadn't had a chance to talk to him all day, and she had missed him.

"Much. I'm not sure how I survived this long."

"Well, you look beautiful. I may have to rethink my assessment that you're not a girly girl."

"Thank you." Oddly, his compliment didn't embarrass her, though it did send a flare of warmth through her. "You look pretty spiffy yourself." The tailored suit fit his broad shoulders just right.

"You up for a dance, or are you too tired?" Levi studied his hands, looking sweetly uncertain.

"That depends. Are you asking me to dance?" Somehow, his uncertainty made her bolder.

He looked up with a grin. "As a matter of fact, I am." He held out a hand. "Grace Calvano, may I have this dance?"

She set her hand lightly in his, ignoring the trickle of joy in her fingers. "As long as you don't make me put my shoes on." She nudged them under the chair. She'd come back for them later.

Or not.

Levi led her to the dance floor and wrapped his other arm around her waist, letting his hand come to a rest on the small of her back.

She had never been a terribly skillful dancer, but he made her feel graceful as he led her naturally around the dance floor.

"You're a good dancer." She didn't mean to sound surprised. "Did you have to learn for football?" She'd heard of that—football players doing dance to improve their balance and flexibility.

Levi chuckled, pulling her closer. "Not this kind of dance, thankfully. My teammates didn't smell nearly as nice as you."

He tightened his arm, cinching her closer still, and she tentatively turned her head to rest it on his chest. The steady rhythm of his heart beat in her ear, and she closed her eyes, letting the rest of the room fade away.

They swayed silently until he leaned his lips close to her ear. "I didn't get a chance to thank you."

"For what?" She pulled back in surprise, needing to see his eyes.

"For last night. For talking to me. I had— It was . . ."

"I know," she whispered.

His throat bobbed, and with his eyes still locked on hers, he lifted one hand to her cheek.

He was going to kiss her. She could feel it.

And she wanted him to. She raised onto her toes.

Their lips touched for only the sweetest, briefest moment before Levi pulled back.

"Sorry," he whispered. "I just realized your whole family is watching."

"Oh." Grace swiveled to look around the room. Sure enough, three of her brothers, not to mention one very unhappy looking Mama, were staring in their direction.

Before she could tell Levi she didn't care who was watching, the lights in the room came up.

"It's time for the bouquet toss," a man's voice announced.

Grace scurried off the dance floor, followed by Levi.

"Aren't you going to try to catch it?" a woman she'd never met asked.

Grace shook her head.

No, she didn't think catching a bouquet would do anything to help bring her back to reality.

And reality was where she needed to be.

Chapter 35

A smile tickled Grace's lips as she woke. She'd been having a dream—a pleasant one, though she couldn't remember what it'd been about. Only the feeling it'd left her with.

It was the same feeling she'd had last night when Levi had kissed her.

She'd hoped for a chance to try that again, without an audience, but they hadn't had a moment alone together.

She slid out of bed and opened the door, the scent of coffee and waffles delighting her nose. Those smells meant Mama was up—and that Grace probably wouldn't get a second alone with Levi now either. But that was okay. They flew out this afternoon, and then they could have all the time they wanted together in Hope Springs. Assuming Levi felt this was as real as she did. And assuming she had the courage to ask him.

She paused in the doorway to the kitchen, watching Mama mixing up batter. There were times the woman drove her batty. But then there were other times, like this, when Grace realized how fortunate she was to have parents who cared about her so much.

Especially when she considered that they'd almost lost Mama to breast cancer only a few months after the whole Hunter incident. The thought that Mama could have died with that as her last memory of Grace was still enough to send Grace to her knees to thank the Lord for sparing Mama's life.

"There's my early bird." Mama looked up with a tired smile. "The day you were born at the crack of dawn, I knew you would be one."

"Morning, Mama." Grace padded across the kitchen to drop a kiss on her mother's cheek. "Why didn't you sleep in? I'm sure no one else will be up for a while yet." She glanced out the French doors, past the chaise lounge, to the spot where the river had just started to soak up the golden hues of the new day's sun.

"And when they do get up, everyone's going to need breakfast before church." Mama ladled batter onto the waffle iron.

"Please tell me you're at least going to take things easy after this. You'll burn yourself out."

Mama waved off her concern. "I'm planning the women's retreat for next month. So unless you're going to stay here and help me with that . . ." Mama gave her a pointed look, drawing a sigh out of Grace. Not this again.

She moved to pour herself a cup of coffee. "Mama, you know I can't. I have the bed-and-breakfast."

"And Levi?" Mama's gaze hit her full-on. "Don't think I didn't hear the two of you sneaking inside at an unholy hour the other night."

Grace nearly spit out the sip of coffee that burned her tongue. "We fell asleep talking."

But there was no point in explaining. Grace could read in Mama's eyes exactly what she was thinking. Because that was the same way Mama had looked at her the night she'd caught Grace and Hunter at the pond.

A flood of shame—fresh as the day it had happened—rolled over her, and she set her mug down with a shaking hand.

She and Levi had done nothing wrong.

"Grace, let's be real." The tiredness on Mama's face seemed to have doubled. "Levi Donovan is not the kind of man you're going to marry."

Grace swallowed, ignoring the papery feel of her burnt tongue. "Marry? Who said anything about marrying?"

Mama pried the waffle maker open. "That's the whole point of dating, isn't it? If you aren't thinking about marriage, then I don't know why you're with him."

"Well—" Grace stammered. "We haven't been dating that long. It's too early to think about that." And then there was the fact that they weren't *actually* dating.

"Honey." Somehow, Mama managed to hit her with a pitying look and ladle batter at the same time. "It doesn't matter how long you wait. A man like Levi Donovan isn't ever going to make a good husband. You probably don't realize this because you're so sweet and naive, but I looked him up, and he dates *a lot* of women. Plus, he said he doesn't believe in God."

Indignation filled Grace. Mama thought she was too naive to judge a man for herself? "As a matter of fact, I did know that."

Mama pressed a hand to her chest. "Then why in heaven's name are you with him? I know he's good-looking, but I had hoped you'd learned your lesson about letting your head be turned by lust like with Hunter."

A high-pitched buzz filled Grace's ears, and the smell of the grass that night at the pond, the dampness of the dew under her back swept over her. Mama's face was pinched again, same as it had been that night, her eyes a pool of disappointment and regret.

Was this what the rest of her life was going to be like? Living under the cloud of the mistake she'd made as a teenager? Constantly worried about disappointing Mama and Daddy again?

Or was she going to be brave enough to stand up to them? To tell them she could make her own decisions? That she'd learned from her mistakes?

"This is nothing like Hunter. And it has nothing to do with lust. Levi—"

"Please." Mama shook her head. "I saw the way his hands were all over you last night."

"We were dancing, Mama."

"Grace, this man is experienced. Do I have to spell it out? He's going to expect—"

"Mama, stop." Grace slapped the countertop with her palm. "Levi isn't like people think. He's kind and generous and loving." The words were out of her mouth before she realized they were true. She had told herself a thousand times that Levi wasn't the right kind of guy for her. And he may be a football player and a star and ride a motorcycle, but that didn't change who he was inside—a fundamentally decent and loving guy. She'd seen it in the way he treated his family, treated his brother especially. And the way he treated her.

"And his faith?" Mama shook her spatula at Grace. "You know it would break my heart and Daddy's to see you with an unbeliever."

Grace blew out a long breath. She couldn't argue with Mama on this one, as much as she wanted to.

"We talk about it," she said finally. "And I can see God working in his heart."

"That may be, but it's easy for a man to pretend to be what you want him to be. Until you're in too deep."

"Levi's not pretending." Grace bit her lip as soon as she'd said it. Technically, that wasn't true. Technically, this whole relationship was pretend.

Mama scrutinized her. "I know men like him, Grace. He'll say whatever it takes to get what he wants from you. And then he'll leave. He's done it to plenty of women before you, and I know you want to believe this time is different. But I can tell by the way he looks at you, honey. He's not in this for the long haul."

A jagged lump formed in Grace's throat. Mama was right. Levi had no reason to be in it for the long haul. He was in it for the weekend, like they'd agreed. She'd just let herself get swept away by the fantasy they'd created.

Mama set her spatula down and hugged Grace. "I'm only trying to watch out for my baby girl. I don't want you to get hurt." She brushed Grace's hair off her shoulder.

"I know, Mama." Grace swallowed down that lump. She had wanted to come back to reality, and here she was.

"It sure smells good in here."

Even without looking at him, she could hear the smile in Levi's voice.

As his footsteps approached, she scurried to hide in the fridge, pretending to rummage. "Mama made waffles."

"You'll spoil us, Mrs. Calvano. Need help finding something, Grace?"

"Nope. Here it is." She grabbed the first thing her hand landed on.

"Mustard?" Levi raised an eyebrow.

"Oops." Back into the fridge.

This time she came up with the orange juice, which had clearly been at the front of the shelf the whole time.

"You seem pretty exhausted." Levi was watching her, she could feel it. "We'd better get you to bed as soon as we get home."

Grace choked.

Levi's comment had been completely innocent, and yet heat flooded her cheeks at Mama's pointed look.

"We're all on our way to church, Levi," Mama said. "Feel free to watch some TV while we're gone."

"That's okay." Levi took the orange juice from Grace, then moved as if to put his arms around her.

She sidestepped him and opened the drawer to pull out forks and knives.

"I was planning to come along," Levi added. "If that's all right."

"Of course. Everyone's welcome at church." Mama's voice was sweet as the syrup she was setting on the table, but under it, Grace could hear her warning from earlier: *It's easy for a man to pretend to be what you want him to be.*

Chapter 36

He shouldn't have kissed her last night.

That had to be why she was acting so strange and distant today.

He should have waited until he'd had a chance to tell her the truth about his feelings, waited until she'd had a chance to tell him whether she felt the same way. Instead, he'd been selfish and impatient, his only thought that if he didn't kiss her right then and there, he would regret it forever.

Now, though, it seemed like the only thing worse than regretting something he hadn't done might be regretting something he had.

She'd sat next to him in church, rigid as the pews. And now that they were back at her parents', she was doing everything humanly possible to avoid being in the same room with him. He knew for a fact that she hadn't brought nearly enough luggage to warrant the half hour she'd been in her room, packing her bag.

If she didn't come out soon, they were going to miss their flight.

"Come on, Grace," Benjamin, who had volunteered to drive them to the airport, called down the hallway.

Finally, Grace emerged, pulling her carry-on behind her. She made a round of the living room, hugging each of her brothers and her father. Levi followed in her wake, shaking their hands.

"I hope we'll be seeing more of you." Grace's father clapped his other hand to Levi's shoulder.

Levi nodded. He did too.

When Grace reached her mother, the two women shared a long embrace.

"Promise me you'll think about what I said." Mrs. Calvano's voice was so quiet that Levi assumed whatever she was talking about was meant for Grace only. He tried not to hear.

Grace nodded, and then Levi was standing face-to-face with her mother.

He debated for a second: hug or handshake?

This was his last chance to make an impression on her. He stepped forward and wrapped his big arms around her small frame. "Thanks for everything."

A noise of surprise escaped her, but she lifted a hand to his back for half a second before pulling away.

They followed Benjamin out to the car, where Grace again insisted that Levi ride shotgun.

Benjamin kept up a steady conversation with Levi all the way to the airport, but the moment he drove away, silence fell.

"This was a nice weekend," Levi said as they stood in the security line.

She nodded.

"Your family is pretty cool," he tried as they sat in the terminal.

She nodded again.

"I think even your mom came around in the end." He gave it one more shot as they boarded. "It was probably the hug."

She pressed her lips together.

"Are we going to talk about it?" he asked as they settled into their seats.

"Talk about what?" She didn't look at him.

He angled his body to block out the other passengers filing into their seats. This wasn't the ideal place to do this.

"I kissed you last night, and I'm sorry."

She didn't say anything, so he pressed on. "I shouldn't have. I didn't mean to make things weird."

She slipped her hands under her legs. "It's fine."

"Obviously it's not. You can't even look at me."

"Can we not talk about it?" She tipped her head back against the seat, eyes closed. "I'm going to take a nap."

"Yeah." Levi gave up. "That's fine. We don't have to talk about it."

Where was she?

Strange sounds bombarded Grace's ears, and she struggled to open her eyes. The moment she did, she sat up straight. She must have fallen asleep—with her head on Levi's shoulder.

"Hey you." His smile was warm but tentative, and she prayed he wasn't going to bring up that kiss again. He'd already said it was a mistake. That was all she needed to know.

"I was just going to wake you." Levi pointed to the window on the other side of her. "We're about to land."

She slid closer to the window, watching a darkened Lake Michigan below them.

A jolt of turbulence sent the plane jostling, and Grace instinctively grabbed for Levi's arm but drew her hand back the moment she made contact.

When the plane landed with a bump, she forced herself to keep her hands in her lap.

Silently, Levi retrieved their luggage from the overhead compartment, then gestured her in front of him.

They were halfway through the airport when a woman in a shirt that plunged straight to her belly button snatched at Levi's arm. "Oh my goodness. You're Levi Donovan. I *have* to get your autograph."

An involuntary noise came from the back of Grace's throat, and she shuffled to the side.

Mom had been right. Levi was not the kind of man interested in a long-term relationship.

And Grace had been stupid to think otherwise.

But before she'd gotten two steps, a strong hand wrapped around hers and tugged her back.

"Sorry," Levi said to the woman. "My girlfriend and I are in a hurry."

The woman's face fell, and she sent Grace a wilting glare but moved on.

"We're home now, you know." Grace wriggled her hand out of his. "You don't have to pretend to be my boyfriend anymore."

Levi was watching her, but she refused to look at him.

"It got that woman to go away, right?"

Grace's smile was tight. He'd simply been using her to get what he wanted. Chalk another one up for Mama.

"I can drive if you want," Levi said when they reached her car in the parking garage.

Grace shrugged and passed him the keys. Maybe she could pretend to sleep on the drive too.

In the car, she closed her eyes and leaned her head against the passenger door.

Levi was silent so long that she started to doze for real.

"Actually, no, it's not fine," Levi burst out just as Grace felt herself sinking into sleep.

She bolted upright. "What's not fine?" She scanned the road, the car—everything appeared to be in order.

"Not talking about what happened last night. Our kiss. I'm not fine with that."

Grace turned to stare out the dark window. "It *is* fine. You already said it was a mistake. Apology accepted."

"What if I don't want you to accept my apology?"

"That would be kind of weird. You want me to stay mad?" She tried unsuccessfully to avoid looking at him, instead turning in time to see the way his face fell.

"Are you? Mad at me for it?"

She sighed. "No, not really."

"Good." He reached for her hand, threading his fingers through hers. "Because I wanted to ask if you'd be willing to go out with me sometime. For real."

He sounded so earnest, so sincere, so vulnerable. But Mama's words had been parading through her head all day, and no matter how she felt about Levi, there was one thing Mama had been right about. She could never be with a man whose first love wasn't Jesus.

She extracted her fingers from his. "I don't think that would be a good idea."

"You. Oh—" A muscle in his jaw worked, but he didn't say anything else.

"I think we both got a little swept up this weekend. With the wedding atmosphere and all. That's all it was."

"That's not all it was for me." Levi's voice was quiet.

"Levi—" She tried to be gentle. "You know you're not my type. And I'm definitely not yours."

"You know—" Levi cut a glance at her. "I'm getting a little tired of hearing that. Especially when we're obviously so good together. Everyone there saw it. Why can't you?"

"My mama didn't see it." The words slithered right past her lips before she could lock them in.

Levi's face darkened. "Is that what this is about? Your mama got to you?"

"No." She sounded too defensive. "I just think—"

Levi lifted a hand off the wheel. "Forget it. I understand. Don't worry, I won't bring it up again."

Chapter 37

"You're sure you'll stay home?" Mom's worried eyes peered up to Levi's face, as if searching for some sign that he was going to throw a party the moment she and Dad left. "Maybe we shouldn't go. That's a lot to ask of you."

"Mom, I promise." Levi leaned against the kitchen doorframe. "You two go. Get out of town for a few days. It's your anniversary."

"I know." Mom looked over her shoulder, toward the hallway. "But Luke's been feeling under the weather all week, and if you decide to go out—"

"Mom, I told you, I'm not going anywhere." Where would he go? Who would he go with? The one woman he wanted to spend time with would barely acknowledge him anymore. After spending all week tiptoeing around her at the bed-and-breakfast, barely speaking aside from an overly polite "good morning" or "excuse me," he was more than ready for a night at home. Just him and Luke—the bachelor brothers.

"Come on, Sandra. Luke will be fine. Levi will take care of him." Dad held Mom's purse out to her, giving Levi a look that said he'd better not let them down.

Mom sighed but took the purse. "I'll have my phone if you need me. And all the emergency numbers are on the fridge. I left a lasagna in there that you can heat up."

"Mom, you don't have to feed us. We're big boys. Now go." Levi leaned to give Mom a quick hug, then shoved her gently toward Dad, who steered her toward the door.

"We're counting on you." He didn't add, *So don't mess it up*, but Levi heard it all the same.

After Mom and Dad had finally left, Levi plopped onto the couch. He'd get some dinner going in a little bit, but first he needed to zone out in front of the TV.

Except he couldn't keep his head on the baseball game, not when thoughts of Grace kept invading it.

He had been so sure, after they'd fallen asleep talking under the stars, that they were right for each other. He'd never been able to talk to anyone else so easily and openly before. Had never felt so listened to—so *seen* and understood.

Grace had felt it too, he was sure of it. Otherwise, she wouldn't have snuggled close to him on the chair, wouldn't have fallen asleep tucked into his arm. Wouldn't have returned his kiss at the wedding.

But all it had taken was one word of disapproval from her mother—he was all but sure that was what had happened—and Grace was willing to forget about all of that.

She was willing to take the door of his heart that he'd started to open to her and slam it shut.

He'd been trying all week to convince himself that if that was how she was going to be—steered by her family's wishes instead of her own heart—then he didn't need her.

But that was a lie.

She had somehow coaxed out the best in him—parts of him he hadn't even known he had. And he wasn't sure how to hold onto them—how to keep being this new, true version of Levi Donovan—without her.

Levi reached for the remote control with a growl. What he needed was some food.

But he wasn't in the mood for lasagna. What he really needed was a big, cheesy, loaded-with-all-the-toppings pizza.

He pushed to his feet. Might as well ask if Luke wanted to get in on that.

But there was no answer when he knocked on Luke's bedroom door.

He checked the time. It was only seven. But maybe his brother had fallen asleep?

He knocked again, harder, then turned the doorknob and pushed the door slowly open.

"Hey, I was thinking pizza. You want—"

He froze as a low groan came from the bed, where Luke lay sprawled on his back, the low light streaming through the window illuminating the sweat beading his forehead. His lips were parted, and a low wheezing noise came from them every few seconds.

"Luke?" A current of panic went straight through his chest. This was not normal.

"Luke?" He shook his brother's shoulder gently enough to keep from hurting him but hard enough to wake him. "You okay, buddy?"

Luke's eyes opened, but it seemed to take him a moment to focus on Levi. "Yeah. I'm good." But he gasped around each word.

"You sure?" Levi crouched next to the bed.

"It's kind of hard—" Luke paused to gasp a few short breaths. "To breathe." He closed his eyes, wheezing as he fought for another breath.

Levi stared. His mind had gone entirely blank.

Luke opened his eyes again, making a pathetic sound, as if he were trying to cough but couldn't. Levi may not know much about Luke's condition. But he did know that the inability to cough and clear the lungs was one of the dangers. It was why Luke had the cough assist. But was it something he should use now? Or would that only do more harm at this point?

"Luke, buddy, do you want your cough assist?"

But Luke had closed his eyes again and seemed to be concentrating on just breathing. What did he do?

Mom and Dad never should have left him home alone with Luke. They never should have trusted him. They knew from experience that he'd only let them down. After all, he wasn't the kind of person who could make them proud.

They needed to be here. They needed to take care of what he couldn't.

Levi whipped out his phone, dialing Mom's number with a shaky hand.

His heart raced painfully as he waited, his own breaths coming in short gasps.

When Mom's voicemail snapped on, he dialed Dad. But there was no answer there either.

Levi snarled as he hung up and sent them both a text. *Call ASAP. Something's wrong with Luke.*

He stared at the screen.

Please answer. Please answer. He wasn't sure if it was a prayer or an attempt to send them a telepathic message, but either way, it didn't work.

After a minute, he jammed his phone into his pocket and stood, sliding an arm under his brother's shoulder.

"All right, buddy. Hang in there. We're going to get you to the doctor."

Chapter 38

Grace scrolled aimlessly through the list of bed-and-breakfast websites. She'd spent most of the week on the computer, ostensibly to get her own website done but mostly to avoid Levi. And to avoid noticing that he seemed genuinely hurt by her rejection.

She tried not to feel guilty. She'd only done what was best for them both. So why had a fissure opened in her middle? A fissure filled with longing and a wish that things were different. That *he* was different.

The thing was, it almost felt like everything about him was perfect for her—aside from the fact that he was the exact opposite of the kind of man she was meant to be with.

You have something against attractive, funny, caring guys?

That was the thing. He *was* all of those things that she'd ever wanted in a man. But he was also a player, a motorcycle rider, a bad boy.

Too much like Hunter, just like Mama had said.

Even if sometimes she thought maybe he really did want to date her—and not only for a week or two. Maybe he wanted to be with her long term.

But then she remembered what Mama had said—men like Levi Donovan weren't interested in long-term relationships.

Of course he'd been hurt when she'd said no. He wasn't used to being rejected. But he'd get over it soon enough.

She checked the time. Seven thirty on a Saturday night? He was probably out with another woman right now.

The thought churned her stomach, but she'd have to get over that. It wasn't fair to Levi to say she wouldn't date him but then expect him not to date anyone else either.

Her phone rang, and Grace dug through the pile of papers in front of her to find it. When she did, she set it right back down.

Levi.

They'd been together all week and barely said a word to each other. *Now* he wanted to talk to her?

Whatever it was, it could wait until Monday.

But something made her reach for the phone, pick it up, answer it, even as her head screamed at her to put it down.

Heaven help her, for reasons she was at a loss to understand, she felt like she had to answer it.

"Hello?" She tried for a friendly but slightly disinterested tone.

"Grace. I'm at the hospital with Luke, and I can't get ahold of my parents, and I didn't know who else to call. He's having a hard time breathing, and I don't know what to do." His words all ran together, but Grace's heart caught on the fear in his voice.

"I'm on my way. Keep trying your parents. I'll be there in fifteen minutes."

"No. You don't have to. Sorry, I was being stupid to call you. I don't know what I was thinking you could do."

"I can be there with you." She shoved paperwork off the desk until her hands landed on her car keys. "Fifteen minutes, okay? Maybe ten if I speed."

Levi's laugh was strained, and if she could have, she would have reached her arms right through the phone to hug him.

"And Levi?"

"Yeah?" His voice was hoarse.

"I'll be praying."

The moment she hung up, she scrolled through her contacts, dialing May as she sprinted to the car. When May answered, Grace broke the news as quickly and gently as she could. Despite the younger woman's muffled cry, Grace pushed ahead. "We need you there, May. You know more about Luke's condition than we do. Do you think you could meet us at the hospital?" She started the car and sped down the driveway.

"What if he doesn't want me there?" May's whisper carried a load of heartbreak.

"He needs you there," Grace said firmly. "We all do."

"Okay." May's voice rang with a strength Grace had never heard in her before. "I'll be there as soon as I can."

"Good." Grace threw the phone onto the passenger seat and floored the accelerator, careful not to push her speed too much above the limit but desperate to get to Luke and Levi as fast as humanly possible.

Twelve minutes later, she pulled into a parking space and sprinted for the emergency room doors. Inside, it only took half a second to spot Levi in one of the hard plastic waiting room chairs, his shoulders hunched over his knees.

As she rushed toward him, he looked up, and when he saw her, it was like his entire face crumpled. He stood, and in two strides he was in front of her, pulling her against him, burying his face in her hair.

Her arms rose to his back, and she squeezed as hard as she could, trying to get his trembling to stop.

Finally, he sucked in a shaky breath and pulled away, clearing his throat. "Sorry— I didn't mean to—"

She waved off his apology. "How's Luke?"

"They haven't told me anything yet." He raked both hands through his hair. "I'm going a little crazy here."

"Okay." Grace led him to a chair. "Have you gotten ahold of your parents yet?"

Levi shook his head, despair written across his face.

"We'll keep trying them. In the meantime, I called May."

"You what?" Levi's eyes went hard. "She left him. He doesn't need that right now."

"She's exactly what he needs. She knows his condition and his needs better than anyone other than your mama."

The swish of the emergency room's automatic doors drew their attention. May walked through, her stride purposeful in spite of the fear on her face.

Levi swallowed, then gave a grudging nod. "Fine. But she doesn't see Luke." He said it loudly enough for May to hear. Her footsteps stuttered for a second, but she closed the distance to them.

"What are they doing so far?" Her hands were shaking, but her voice was clear and efficient, and Grace marveled at her strength. She'd seen the way May still looked at Luke—that woman's feelings for him definitely had not diminished.

"I don't know." Levi glared toward the desk, where a woman in scrubs sat typing on a computer. "No one will tell me anything."

"Did you tell them about his BMD?"

"Of course." Levi's answer was scathing. "I'm not as useless as everyone thinks."

May ignored the comment. "Did you tell them not to give him oxygen unless absolutely necessary?"

"He couldn't breathe. Why wouldn't they give him oxygen?"

May spun and sprinted for the desk, leaning over it to catch the woman's attention. The woman immediately stopped typing and picked up the phone next to her.

Grace turned to Levi to see if he understood what was going on. But he looked as baffled as her. And a lot angrier.

The woman behind the desk hung up the phone, and after a short conversation with her, May started back toward them.

"Be nice," Grace said just loud enough for Levi to hear.

But his jaw was hard. "Mind telling me what that was about?" he shot at May.

"Luke's BMD affects his respiratory muscles, so he breathes more shallowly than most of us. His body is still able to keep the right balance of carbon dioxide and oxygen, but if you add oxygen, his body could think he has enough, and he'll stop breathing, which makes the carbon dioxide levels spike." Now she was the one giving Levi the hard look. "It could kill him."

Levi dropped onto the chair behind him with a thud. "I didn't know."

His face had gone chalky, and Grace sat next to him, placing a hand on his arm. "How could you have?"

"I'm his brother." His voice was tortured. "I'm supposed to know these kinds of things. Supposed to look out for him."

"It's okay." May spoke gently, her tone soothing. "I asked them to monitor his carbon dioxide levels. He'll be fine. You did the right thing bringing him here."

Her words didn't seem to have any effect on Levi. He dropped his head into his hands, and Grace rubbed his back, fighting off a wave of helplessness.

What can I do, Lord?

But the moment she asked, she knew the answer.

"Would you like to pray together?" she asked softly, still rubbing her hand up and down on Levi's back.

He turned red-lined eyes on her. "If you think it will help."

She nodded and closed her eyes, letting her hand still on his back but not lifting it off. She felt May settle into the seat on the other side of her.

"God, our loving Father," she started. "We know how much you love your children. Please be with Luke right now. We don't know what he needs, Lord, but you do. Give the doctors wisdom, give Luke healing, and give us trust. In Jesus' name we ask this. Amen."

Levi had played football for hours at a time, he'd taken hits so hard they made his head spin, he'd worked himself to the point of exhaustion, but his limbs had never felt as heavy as they did in this moment. He rubbed at his bleary eyes. He'd finally gotten ahold of Mom and Dad an hour or so ago. They'd had no cell signal for part of the drive. Which meant they now had to turn around and make the three-hour drive home.

In the seat next to him, Grace stirred, then stood. "I'm going to go get us some coffee."

He nodded, trying to work up a grateful smile, though his face was too tired to move.

In the next chair, May nodded too. As Grace walked off, May bent forward, bowing her head over her hands. She'd been doing that periodically all night. Praying, Levi assumed.

He hadn't quite been able to bring himself to do that, though Grace's prayer earlier had brought some small measure of comfort. Now what he wanted was an answer to that prayer. Sooner, rather than later.

As if she sensed his gaze on her, May raised her head and looked at him, her dark eyes filled with both strength and pain.

"Do you love him?" He didn't know why he asked, didn't know why it mattered to him, but it did.

May's eyes met his. "Yes." Her answer was simple and direct, but somehow it was more powerful than a profession of hundreds of words could have been.

"Then why did you leave him?" Let her try to explain that.

May watched her foot trace a line on the floor. "You're his brother. I couldn't stand coming between you two."

Levi gave a disbelieving laugh. So she was going to pin this on him. "It seems if you loved him so much, you wouldn't let an idiot like me stand in the way."

May stood and stepped in front of Levi. "Sometimes when you love someone, you do what's best for them. Even if it hurts you." She walked off in the direction Grace had gone.

Was that true? Could you love someone so much that you would leave them if you thought it was best for them?

A doctor in blue scrubs approached Levi, and he put the question out of his mind. He had more pressing concerns right now than theoretical questions about love.

"Luke Donovan's brother?"

Levi grimaced and stood, trying to brace for the worst, though he had no idea how to do that.

"Looks like it's pneumonia," the doctor said.

Levi allowed himself a quick, relieved breath. Pneumonia wasn't so bad.

"He's relatively stable right now, and we're pumping him full of antibiotics, but of course for someone with Luke's condition, pneumonia is quite dangerous."

Levi tripped against the seat behind him. It was?

"Could be touch and go for a few days," the doctor continued. "But it's good that you were able to alert us to monitor his carbon dioxide levels. Nice work. Your brother's lucky to have you watching out for him."

"Yeah." Levi grasped for the chair and sat.

If things had been left to him, his brother could have died.

Could still die.

And it would be all his fault.

Chapter 39

Grace rubbed her grainy eyes and checked the time.

Six a.m.

She must have dozed off, thanks to the slightly more comfortable chairs in the ICU waiting room. Luke had been transferred to the unit a few hours ago, and now she, Levi, May, and Mr. and Mrs. Donovan—who had arrived shortly before that, looking distraught and disheveled—were piled into the small waiting room. Levi had tried to insist that she go home, but she refused.

She may not have any intention of dating him. But she was still his friend, and she wasn't going to make him go through this alone.

"Good morning," he whispered from next to her.

"Morning," she whispered back, letting her eyes travel over the others. Next to her, May was curled up in her chair, feet up, eyes closed. On the other side of the room, Mrs. Donovan's head rested on her husband's shoulder, while Mr. Donovan stared blankly at a spot on the ceiling.

"Did you sleep at all?" she asked Levi.

He shook his head. His eyes were bleary and bloodshot, the skin beneath them a gray-blue.

"Close your eyes," she whispered. "I'll wake you if there's any news."

"I'm fine. You should go."

She tucked her hand into his. "How many times do I have to tell you I'm not going anywhere?"

Levi looked from their linked hands to her face. "Thank you."

"For what?"

He shrugged. "For being a friend."

"Always. Now close your eyes."

He shook his head, but when she glanced over a few seconds later, his eyes were closed, and his head lolled to the side.

She scanned the room for something soft to tuck under it for a pillow. But there was nothing.

Slowly, so she wouldn't wake him, she reached up and drew his head closer, until it rested on her shoulder.

Then she pulled out her phone and opened her Bible app.

For the next few hours, she alternated reading, praying, and dozing, her hand still resting in Levi's, his head still on her shoulder.

When he finally stirred, she craned her neck to smile at him. As if just realizing he'd fallen asleep, he bolted upright.

"Sorry. I didn't mean to fall asleep on you." He scrubbed his hands over his cheeks. "What time is it?"

Grace checked the phone in her hand. "Almost ten o'clock."

Levi blinked. "I can't believe I slept that long. You'd better get going."

"Levi, I told you—"

"You're going to be late for church."

Grace blinked at him. That was incredibly thoughtful, but also—

"Church started half an hour ago."

"Oh, I'm sorry. I didn't mean to make you miss it."

"Levi—" Grace took his hand back. "I wasn't planning on going."

"You weren't?" Levi's brow wrinkled. "I thought you liked church. You always go. You probably have perfect attendance."

"I do enjoy church, and I go every opportunity I can. But not to check off some attendance card. I go because I love to hear God's Word and sing his praises with my fellow believers. But right now, I think I can best serve God by being here for my friend in need."

As Levi watched her, something shifted in his eyes. "Will you sing for me?"

"Here?" Grace glanced around the room. May and the Donovans were awake but silent, and another woman who had come into the waiting room about an hour ago was crying quietly into her hands.

It wasn't a big audience, but it was an audience all the same. "I don't think . . ."

"Please. That song you sang in church?" Levi's eyes held hers, and there was no way she could say no.

She swallowed and closed her eyes, taking a deep breath. "Great is thy faithfulness . . ."

Levi's hand gripped hers, and she squeezed it, trying to pass the peace the song always brought her on to him.

When she got to the refrain, another voice joined hers. She opened her eyes to see May singing even as tears ran down her cheeks.

Grace kept singing, swaying to words that promised God's faithfulness no matter the circumstances.

When she sang the refrain a second time, Levi's parents joined in, as did the woman on the other side of the room. And on the final refrain, another, deeper voice joined theirs.

She turned to Levi, her mouth widening into a smile.

The man could *sing*.

And to hear the words coming out of his mouth—God was so, so faithful.

When the song was done, they all sat there, a sort of holy awe hanging over the room.

"Thank you," the woman across the room finally said. "I needed that reminder right now. My husband is in a coma. They don't know . . ." She brought a tissue to her eyes. "Sorry, I just— I really needed that."

Mrs. Donovan patted her husband's arm, then moved to sit next to the other woman. As they began to talk in low voices, Grace leaned toward Levi.

"You tricked me," she murmured.

His eyes shot to hers. "About what?"

"You can sing."

"When did I say I couldn't?"

"In the airport." She pointed a mock accusing finger at him. "You didn't say. You showed. In front of all those people."

He chuckled. "Got you to forgive me though, didn't it?"

She swatted at his arm, but he caught her hand and held tight to it. "Thank you for being here. It means a lot to me."

She nodded. "It means a lot to me too."

"Donovan family?" A doctor entered the waiting room, and everyone froze.

Grace clutched Levi's hand tight enough that she was surprised he didn't cry out.

"Luke's lung function has improved slightly," the doctor said. "We'll still have to be careful of infection, but I'm cautiously optimistic at this point. He's awake and can have visitors now, but I'd ask that you limit it to three at a time."

"Thank you, Jesus," Mrs. Donovan murmured. "Thank you, doctor."

Mr. and Mrs. Donovan rushed to the door, and Grace let go of Levi's hand and nudged him forward.

But he looked at the spot where May had collapsed onto her chair. "May should go."

May looked up at him, her mouth opening.

"Levi—" Mrs. Donovan started.

"It's what Luke would want," Levi said. "Trust me, he's been waiting a long time to see her again. Go, May. I'll visit with him later."

May gave him one more dumbfounded look, then jumped out of her chair and threw her arms around him.

Then she followed Mr. and Mrs. Donovan out of the waiting room.

"That was sweet of you." Grace bumped his shoulder as she took her seat.

Levi shrugged. "They love each other. I don't want to get in the way of that."

Chapter 40

Levi stood over Luke's bed, hand over his mouth to stifle the anguish that threatened to find its way out.

His brother had been doing so well yesterday—Levi had been in here talking with him—and overnight he'd taken a turn for the worse. The doctor said it was an infection in his lungs.

"Hey, bro." He barely managed to scrape up the whisper. "We're counting on you to fight this."

He pulled a chair up next to the bed. Luke's face was gray and slack, his eyes closed, his body still.

"I know you said you're ready to go home—" When Luke had said that to him two days ago, Levi had assumed he'd meant back to Mom and Dad's. He'd promised they were doing everything they could to get him healthy and back in his own room as quickly as possible.

But Luke had given his customary smile. "I mean *home* home. Whenever God calls me, I'm ready."

It had taken Levi a moment to realize he was talking about dying. About going to heaven.

It'd left Levi more than a little shaken.

"But I really need you to hang around here a while longer," he said now. "I need more time with my little brother." He looked down, rubbing at his forehead. "May needs you too. I see now that she loves you. She's going to stick around for the hard parts. Do you know she hasn't left this building once in four days?" Even Levi had gone home to shower and change yesterday, and he'd convinced Grace to do the same. He'd told her to stay home and sleep in her own bed too, but that part she hadn't listened to.

"Not to sound selfish," Levi said to Luke's still form. "But I really need you to pull through this because I need some advice. About a girl."

He waited for Luke's laugh—but the only sound was the whir of the medical equipment.

Levi wasn't sure how much more of this they could all take.

They'd been sitting vigil at the hospital for a week now. He hadn't seen Mom eat an actual meal since Wednesday. Dad seemed to age by the day. And even May and Grace were looking worn and disheartened.

Next to him, Grace read her Bible. Whenever he looked at her, she sent him an encouraging smile. But it didn't hide the worry in her eyes.

Restlessness driving him to his feet, Levi began to pace the room. His new hobby.

His eyes scanned them all. What good were they doing here?

"I think we should go to church," he announced, catching even himself by surprise.

"You do?" The question seemed to come from Grace, Mom, Dad, and May all at the same time.

"Grace says—" He looked at her for confirmation. "Church is a place of hope and encouragement, and I don't know about y'all—" He slipped the word in with a quiet smile at Grace. "But I could use some of that right now."

Grace stood. "I'll come with you."

"Me too." May stood as well.

He looked at Mom and Dad. "If you want to stay here with Luke . . ."

"We'll come." Dad held out a hand to help Mom up. "We have two sons, and we want to be there for both of them."

All Levi could manage was a short nod.

He didn't know why it meant so much to him that they all go together, but it did.

Dad drove everyone in the van, and Levi and Grace sat in the far back. Halfway to church, she reached for his hand. "This was a good idea."

He clung to those words—and to her hand—as they walked into church together a few minutes later. Dozens of people stopped to ask after Luke and say they were praying for him. So many of them had visited the hospital this week that Levi was beginning to think that though he was the famous brother, Luke was the popular one.

Instead of filling him with jealousy, as it may have once, the knowledge heartened him. Luke deserved their good opinion and their prayers. He was a part of their community, and he cared about each one of them.

By the time they'd spoken to all the well-wishers, the service had already begun. Levi glanced toward Dad—he must be having a heart attack at the prospect of walking in late. But instead, Dad looked more optimistic than Levi had seen him in days.

They filed into the sanctuary as the first song ended.

Last time he'd been in this church, he'd tried hard not to listen to the message. But today he wanted to soak up every word. If there truly was hope to be found here, he wanted to find it.

By the time Dan stood to deliver his sermon, Levi was starting to feel some of that hope. He leaned forward, ready to take in more of it, greedy suddenly for this message.

"Many of you know that I'm now a father of two," Dan began. He scrubbed his hands over his face. "Can I be honest with you? It's exhausting."

A laugh rippled through the congregation.

"With the newborn, there are the diaper changes and the feeding and the refusing to sleep at night. And with the preschooler, there's the temper tantrums and the constant questions and the refusing to sleep at night."

Sounded fun. Maybe Levi should advise Dan never to make a parenting commercial. But he'd seen Dan with his kids, and he knew that man loved his family fiercely. Which meant all of this was to make some sort of point.

"But you want to know what the hardest part of parenting is?" Dan looked directly at the spot where Jade sat with their children. "Saying no. When Hope comes to me and looks at me with those big eyes and asks me for something in that sweet voice, I want to say yes every time. But of course I can't. Because sometimes what she asks for might be something I know isn't what's best for her. Something that might even hurt her or be dangerous for her. Or what if she asks me for something good, but it's something I don't think she needs or should have yet? Or maybe she asks for one thing, but I have something even better planned for her? So I say no. And she may not like it, may not understand it, may throw a tantrum about it. But still my answer stands. No."

Dan looked down for a moment, as if searching for the words to express what he wanted to say next. Levi stilled as he waited. He had no idea where Dan was going with this, but he had the strangest feeling Dan's musings on fatherhood were somehow relevant to his own life, even if fatherhood didn't appear to be anywhere near the horizon for him.

"The hard part of being a human father," Dan said as he looked up, "is that I don't always *know* what's best for my kids. I do my best. I try hard. But sometimes I make mistakes. But God—" He smiled and shook his head, as if he could hardly contain what he was about to say. "God doesn't have that problem. He knows exactly what's best for his children. What's best for us."

Dan paced to the far side of the sanctuary, and Levi's eyes followed him.

"The hard part for us," Dan continued, "is that sometimes doing what's best for us means God says no to our prayers. Even when we think those prayers are exactly what we need. Maybe they're prayers for a job or prayers for a wounded relationship or prayers for a sick loved one. And we can't see any way God wouldn't answer those prayers with a yes. Because they're obviously for our good. But here's the thing—" He spread his arms wide. "We may think we know what's good for us—but God knows what's *best* for us."

Levi sat back hard against his seat. He needed God to answer his prayers for Luke. He had come here to hear that God was going to do that. And now Dan was telling him that wasn't going to happen?

Grace's hand, which was still in his, squeezed tight. Levi wanted to tune Dan out, but he forced himself to keep listening. Maybe he had misunderstood what Dan was saying. And Dan would clear it all up right now—tell him that as long as he prayed hard enough, God would do what he wanted.

"You know," Dan continued, "we tend to focus on those places in Scripture where God answered prayers—enabling David to slay Goliath, sending down fire on Elijah's offering to prove he was the only true God, healing the lame and giving sight to the blind. But there are plenty of examples in here"—he picked up his Bible—"of God saying no to his people's prayers too. And these weren't just any old Joe Schmoes God said no to—they were some of his most faithful servants. We might think if God was going to grant anyone's prayers, it would be theirs."

He paged through the Bible. "There was David, who prayed for God to spare his son's life. God said no. There was Paul, who prayed for God to take away the thorn in his flesh. God said no. And there was Jesus. Yes, Jesus, God's Son. On the night before his crucifixion, Jesus went into the garden and prayed, not once, not twice, but three times: 'My Father, if it is possible, may this cup be taken from me. Yet not as I will, but as you will.' And, well, we all know how God answered that prayer: that cup—the suffering he was about to experience—wasn't taken from Jesus. The very next day, he went to the cross for our sins."

The words rang in Levi's ears. Jesus? God had said no to Jesus' prayer? Then what hope did Levi have that God would answer his?

"So what good is prayer then?" Dan moved toward Levi's side of the sanctuary. "If God didn't give his own Son a yes, then what good does it do for us to pray?"

Dan's face broke into a smile again, and Levi had to resist the temptation to stand up right here in front of church and punch the guy. He didn't see what there was to smile about.

"So much good." Dan's smile widened. "It does so much good to pray. Because God hears every one of our prayers. It doesn't matter if you're Jesus or Joe Schmo. It doesn't matter how hard you pray or if you say the words just right or how much faith you have. Because prayer isn't about *you*. It's about God. About how he listens to you and how he, in his infinite wisdom and mercy, answers you, every time, whether that's with a yes, a no, or a not right now. His answer is always, *always* what is best for us. Even when it doesn't feel like it."

Levi wanted to believe that, he really did.

"How do we know that?" Dan seemed to pull the question out of Levi's head.

This time when he smiled, Levi felt a little less like punching him. "Because he tells us. Romans 8:28: 'And we know that in all things God works for the good of those who love him, who have been called according to his purpose.' Notice it doesn't say most of the time or sometimes or once in a while. No. *In all things*, God works for our good. That's why we can confidently pray, like Jesus did, 'not as I will, but as you will.' Praying for God's will to be done isn't a cop-out. It's not leaving some wiggle room for God, in case he can't do what we asked. It's saying, 'God I trust you. I trust that you know what's best for me. Please do *that* in my life.'"

Levi took a deep breath. That sounded like a big step. What if he prayed for God's will to be done, and God's will was to let Luke die? How would that be for his good?

He thought of Luke's words the other day: *God has a glorious home prepared for me, Levi. I'm ready to go there when he calls me.*

As the sermon ended and he stood with the others, Levi closed his eyes. *I want to want your will, Lord,* he prayed. *But I'm not sure I'm there yet. Please heal Luke.*

He opened his eyes.

That was the best he was going to be able to do for now.

Chapter 41

That had been intense.

Grace could almost feel Levi absorbing the sermon this morning, though as they walked to the car now, she wasn't exactly sure what his final verdict had been.

Mr. Donovan opened the door of the van, but Levi stood staring at it.

"I can't go back there right now," he choked. "I just— When I see him like that—" His hand fisted around the front of his shirt. "It's like I can't breathe. I need to go for a ride or something."

It was all Grace could do not to throw her arms around him. Instead, she slipped her hand quietly into his.

Mr. Donovan studied his son, and Grace held her breath. She'd gotten the feeling over the last few days that something was improving in Levi's relationship with his dad, but she felt like Mr. Donovan's response now might have the power to undo all of that.

After a moment, Mr. Donovan nodded. "I'll drop you off at home."

The tension in Levi's jaw eased. "Thanks." He ducked into the van, and Grace climbed in behind him.

All the way to his house, she debated. She didn't want Levi to be by himself right now. But he didn't necessarily seem to want company. And she had promised herself never to get on that bike.

By the time Mr. Donovan pulled into his home's driveway, she'd made up her mind. She'd go to the hospital and sit with the family.

Levi would be fine on his own.

"Be careful," she whispered as he unfolded himself from the van. But he didn't respond, and she wasn't entirely sure he'd heard her.

He shuffled toward the garage, shoulders hunched forward, head down.

Mr. Donovan backed the car out of the driveway.

"Wait." Grace unclicked her seatbelt as Mr. Donovan shifted into drive. "I'm going with him."

Mr. Donovan nosed the van back into the driveway.

"Thank you." Mrs. Donovan squeezed her arm as she clambered out of the van. Mr. Donovan nodded to her, and May added that she'd be praying for them.

As she stepped to the ground, Levi's Harley roared to life. Grace sprinted up the driveway as the Donovans drove away.

Levi was already sitting on the bike, helmet on, visor over his eyes, but she waved her arms wildly as she charged toward him, and he cut the engine.

Slowly, he pulled his helmet off. "What are you doing?"

Grace reached his side. "I'm coming with you. Where's that extra helmet?"

Levi's stormy eyes slid over her face in a long, searching look. She put on her most determined expression, and he finally gestured to the hard-sided case behind the seat. She popped it open, grabbing the helmet and pulling it over her head.

"So where to?" She pushed the visor up to watch him.

He shrugged. "I was just going to drive around. You're sure you want to ride? You don't have to, you know. I'll be fine."

"I know you will. I want to come. But I have a better idea than just wandering. You ever been to Rocky Point?"

Levi shook his head.

"Good." She lowered her visor and threw her leg over the bike. "Head out of town on highway twelve."

Levi nodded, put his helmet back on, and started the bike. Grace moved her hands easily to his waist, leaning with him as he gently steered out of the driveway and onto the street.

As they rode farther out of town and into the more sparsely populated countryside dotted with corn fields and orchards, she could feel the knots in his back loosen.

She liked to drive out this way whenever she had a problem. Seeing the wonders of God's creation always restored her soul—and Levi hadn't even seen the best part yet.

After over an hour on the bike, she pointed him down a nearly hidden road with thick forest on either side. Levi turned onto it, and they wound uphill through the trees until the road dead-ended at a parking lot. Levi pulled into a spot and shut the motorcycle down.

They sat in the abrupt silence for a few moments before Grace swung her leg off the bike and removed her helmet.

Levi followed, his eyes landing square on her. "That was *not* your first time on a bike."

"No." She tucked her helmet into the case on the bike. "Hunter had a bike."

"Oh." He didn't press the point. "So what is this place?"

"You'll see. You up for a hike?"

"Do I have a choice?" But he fell into step next to her with a soft smile.

She led him to a trail just wide enough for the two of them to walk side-by-side.

"Do you want to talk or just walk?" The thing she always appreciated about this place was the stillness—the chance to be alone with God—and she didn't want to take that from Levi. But if he wanted to talk, she was here to listen.

"Let's just walk for now." He offered her a grateful smile, and they lapsed into a silence so full and meaningful it almost felt as if they were talking without words.

Half an hour later, they emerged from the trees, right at the edge of a hill that sloped steeply down to Lake Michigan below, and Grace caught Levi's hand to stop him.

"There." She pointed to the right where, halfway down the hill, an arch of rock framed the view of the water below. The center of the arch was so impossibly narrow that there was no way the whole thing shouldn't crumble to the ground.

"How on earth?" Levi walked down the trail that led toward the arch. "That should not be possible."

Grace stepped to his side. "That's what I love about this place. It reminds me that things that are impossible with man are possible with God."

Levi's sigh was long and labored. "If God *wants* to do those things." He turned to her, looking completely broken. "Do you think God's answer to our prayers for Luke is going to be no?"

"I don't know." The whispered words were maybe the hardest she'd ever said. She so wanted to tell him that of course God would heal Luke. But she couldn't know God's will in this any more than the next person.

"I don't understand. Why would he say no?" Levi's voice cracked.

Grace moved closer to wrap her arms around him. "I don't know," she murmured. "There are so many things we'll probably never understand this side of heaven. But I do know God is the Great Physician. If it's his will, he can cure Luke of this infection. But more than that, he's already cured him of the infection of sin. He has a perfect home waiting for Luke in heaven."

Levi nodded into her hair. "That's what Luke said. But I'd rather if he stayed in his home here. Is that wrong? For me to want that?"

"Of course not." Grace rubbed her hand up and down his back. "Just remember that God might have something better planned. For Luke. And for you."

"I'm trying to trust that. But it's hard."

Grace held him like that for another minute, her heart giving way when a teardrop fell onto her shoulder. She sniffed and failed to hold back her own tears.

Finally, Levi cleared his throat and pulled away, passing the back of his hand over his cheek. "I'm sorry. I wasn't trying to take advantage of you."

She laughed, wiping at her own eyes. "If you recall, I'm the one who hugged you."

"Thank you." He turned to walk down the trail toward the arch. "For being honest about the fact that God might say no. I think I can accept that." He gave a dry, mirthless laugh. "Or at least I'm trying to."

Chapter 42

Over the past two hours, the weight of worry that had oppressed Levi since the moment he'd taken Luke to the hospital had lifted little by little.

He and Grace had hiked all the way to the rock ledge that passed within a few feet of the arch, followed the trail down to the beach, and splashed along the shore.

Every once in a while, the thought would creep back in: *What if God says no? What if Luke dies?*

And each time, he prayed silently: *Lord, please heal him.* And then added, painfully, *Not my will but yours be done.*

He couldn't remember a time ever before in his life that he'd prayed for God's will to be done—or at least not and really meant it—and it was slightly terrifying to put that much trust in a God he'd only recently started to see as relevant again. But it felt freeing too, to know that whatever happened was in God's hands. And if Grace and Dan were to be believed—if God's Word was to be believed—that was the best place for it.

"Here. This is for you." Grace held out a seashell in deep shades of orangey-red. "It reminds me of the sunset that night on the parasail. Remember how vibrant the colors were?"

Remember?

Of course he remembered. Just like he remembered how vibrant her smile was, how joyful her laugh was, how sweet everything about her was.

He cradled the shell in his hand.

Maybe after all of this was over, he'd start praying for his relationship with Grace. Because after all they'd gone through in the past week, his feelings for her had grown—not only stronger, but deeper, like there was a well in his soul that she was filling.

Her compassion, her faithfulness, her willingness to be there for others at her own cost—all of that had him more convinced than ever that she was the perfect woman.

What he wasn't quite so sure of was whether he was the perfect man for her. And he didn't want her to have anyone less than the one who was God's will for her.

So if—when—he prayed for their relationship, he'd pray for God's will to be done in that too.

"What's that?" She pointed toward something glinting in the sand down the beach.

But before they could check it out, Levi's phone rang.

They both froze.

After a moment, he pulled it out of his pocket, staring at it, every care, every worry, slamming back into his soul with a force that nearly bowled him over.

"It's my mom." Levi's vocal cords were too tight.

Grace took his free hand in hers, squeezing it around the seashell he still clutched.

Your will be done.

He lifted the phone to his ear.

"Levi?" Mom's voice was nearly hysterical, and Levi stepped closer to Grace, letting her hand around his anchor him.

He couldn't say anything. All he could do was wait.

"He's awake. He's awake." Mom's sobs drowned out the rest of her words, but it didn't matter. Levi's heart had taken off for the clouds.

He gathered Grace to him in a monumental one-armed hug, burying his face in her hair. "He's awake."

"Thank you, Lord," Grace murmured, wrapping her arms around him.

He turned his attention back to the phone. "So he's going to be all right?"

He barely heard as Mom explained that it was too soon to tell but that the infection seemed to be clearing, and Luke's lung function was improving. All he could think about was how he'd prayed for God's will to be done.

Was this God's answer? Was this his will? To bring Luke back to them?

When he hung up the phone, his arm was still around Grace, and hers were still around him.

Her eyes met his, and her smile was as big as his.

Slowly, she raised onto her toes, tipping her face toward him.

Levi almost bent down. Almost brought his lips to hers.

But she didn't know what she was thinking. She was just happy that Luke would be okay.

Gently, he took a step backwards. "We should probably get back."

"Yeah." Grace's eyes were still on his, their mocha color deeper and warmer than ever. "Let's go."

Chapter 43

There was something in the air tonight. Grace couldn't put her finger on what it was. But everything around her seemed to crackle with life: Her friends milling in Jared and Peyton's backyard. The birds calling from the trees. And Luke, seated in the wheelchair he'd use until he regained his strength, May at his side, both of them smiling so widely she wasn't sure they noticed the rest of the group surrounding them.

And then there was Levi, playing catch with Jackson, occasionally offering him pointers, but mostly just seeming to have fun. Every once in a while, he stopped to toss a Nerf football to little Hope.

And he never once stopped smiling.

Which had, in turn, put an impossible-to-erase smile on her lips too.

The change that had come over him in the two weeks since that day at Rocky Point—Grace had never seen anything so profound, and she wasn't sure what to make of it. Aside from the fact that it made her long even more for what she couldn't have.

She'd almost kissed him that day on the beach, but he'd pulled back.

He'd been right to do it—she knew he had. And yet, working with him for the past two weeks, it had been impossible not to wonder what it would be like to walk over to him, grab the hammer out of his hands, wrap her arms around his neck, and taste his lips on hers.

"He's good with kids." Jade settled into the chair next to Grace.

"Who?" Grace tried to sound surprised, innocent, confused, though her face felt as if it had been stuffed into an oven.

"Do you have feelings for him? Never mind. That was a dumb question. Let me rephrase: What are you going to do about your feelings for him?"

Grace leaned her head back on the chair and closed her eyes against the image of Levi in front of her. But that was no good because the image in her mind was of him kissing her.

She let her lids spring open in time to catch Levi fist bumping Jackson. "I'm not going to do anything."

"Why not?" Jade fixed her sharp gaze on Grace.

"Because—" Grace spluttered. "Because he's obviously not my type." Though it was taking more and more work to convince herself of that every day.

"The same way Dan wasn't my type? And I definitely wasn't his?"

Grace tucked her feet under her and shook her head. "That's different."

"How?"

"Because . . ." She harrumphed. "It just is. I have a plan for what my future husband will be like. And it's not Levi."

Jade gave her a probing look. "You know what I think? I think God takes one look at our plans, and he laughs and shows us how much better what he has planned for us is."

"You're saying you think God wants me to be with Levi?" The thing was, Grace had been feeling more and more lately like that might be true. But she'd chalked it up to her own desires.

"I'm saying you need to trust God. Even if he leads you somewhere you never would have thought of going on your own."

That may be true. But it didn't mean it wasn't terrifying. "How will I know?"

"Trust me, you'll know." Jade patted her hand. "Now, I'm off to get a cupcake. You want anything?"

"No thanks." Grace closed her eyes and leaned back against the chair again.

She would just know, would she? A sign or a roadmap or something would be much more helpful.

"Hey you." How was it that the sound of his voice was enough to make her limbs tingle? She let herself open her eyes a crack.

Levi stood a good five feet from her chair.

He'd been careful about that lately. Careful to leave enough distance between them. Careful not to enter her personal space. Careful not to so much as brush his hand against hers.

And after sitting by his side, holding his hand, every day for a week while Luke was in the hospital, she missed Levi's touch with a fierceness she couldn't explain.

"Mind if I sit?" Levi's voice was adorably hesitant.

"Of course not." Thankfully, the acceleration of her heart rate didn't come through in her words.

He lowered himself into the chair Jade had vacated but instead of relaxing back into it, leaned forward, bracing his elbows on his knees, clasping his hands in front of him. He looked at her, then looked toward the spot where Jackson and Hope were now tossing the Nerf ball.

Grace sat up a fraction. What was he thinking? She wanted to ask, and yet she didn't want to know.

"Hey, I didn't get a chance to thank you." She let herself touch his arm, but only for a moment.

"Oh yeah? And what do you have to thank me for this time?" His grin was joking, but there was something under the surface of his gaze that sent her heart skipping.

"I saw Tori's interview today. You called her, didn't you? There were things in there we didn't talk about that day. Things about the bed-and-breakfast. And about me."

Levi shrugged. "I told you, Tori's good at what she does. Good researcher."

"Is that so?" Grace pulled out her phone and scrolled through the article, which she had left open. She read: "Former Tennessee Titans quarterback Levi Donovan, whose family's company is involved with the renovation, offered high praise for Ms. Calvano: 'Grace is joyful and passionate, and she loves people. That comes through in everything she does, including preparing this place for guests. I know she will touch the lives of everyone who stays here.'"

She swallowed. She'd been just as moved all sixteen times she'd read it. "Where do you suppose Tori researched that?"

"I thought people should know about you, that's all."

That urge to kiss him came over her again, and Grace stood abruptly so she wouldn't act on it. "I think I'm going to . . ."

"I wanted to ask you—" Levi stood too. "There's this thing next weekend. A fundraiser for muscular dystrophy. I go every year. But I thought maybe this year you might want to . . ." His voice trailed into uncertainty.

"Levi, I—"

"Excuse me, everyone." Luke's voice sounded over the hubbub of conversations taking place across the patio, and everyone turned to him.

"Sorry to interrupt." He had pushed up out of his wheelchair and was leaning heavily on his cane, the effort of remaining upright clear on his face.

"What is he doing?" Levi muttered. "He's not strong enough yet." He left Grace staring after him as he strode across the patio toward his brother.

"I wanted to say thank you to all of you for coming to visit while I was in the hospital and for your prayers," Luke said. "I can't tell you how much that meant to me. And to my family." He nodded to Levi, who had reached him but hung back. From his alert expression, Grace could tell he was ready to step in and plunk his brother back in the wheelchair at the first sign of trouble.

"Growing up, I didn't always have a lot of friends, and I thought that was just the way my life was always going to be. And I was fine with it." Luke looked around at the group gathered there, smiling at each one of them. "But now I know how much richer life can be with people in it. People who love you and support you and pray for you." He wobbled a little, and Levi took a step forward, but Luke waved him off.

"And that's why I wanted to do this here. With all of you." He let out a quick breath. "May, could you come here a second?"

May looked surprised, but she stood and took the hand he held out, her smile quizzical but tender.

"My plan was to go through life alone," Luke said, and Grace felt a lump solidifying in her throat. Was he about to do what she thought he was about to do?

"And I was so certain that was God's plan for me too. He wouldn't want me to burden anyone with my illness."

May shook her head, looking like she had something to say about that, but Luke kept talking. "But you showed me that I wasn't a burden. You made me feel like a . . . like a gift. I mean, I knew my mom and dad felt that way. And probably my brother—" He threw a look over his shoulder at Levi, who gave him a tight smile that anyone who didn't know him might mistake for tension. But Grace knew it hid a well of emotion he was working to hold back.

Luke turned to May. "Aside from my salvation, you are the greatest gift God has ever brought into my life. And I don't ever want to lose you."

He adjusted his grip on her hand and moved one leg back, his cane shaking roughly. Grace raised her hands to her mouth. He was going to fall trying to get down on one knee.

But then Levi was at Luke's side, supporting his arm, slowly helping him lower into position.

Grace pressed a hand to her chest, her eyes following Levi as he patted his brother's shoulder, then took a step back.

That man might not be right for her, but he was something special.

"May."

Grace forced her attention back to Luke, so she wouldn't miss his big moment.

"I don't know what God has planned for the rest of my life. I don't know how long it will be. I don't know how long I'll be able to walk or how my disease will progress. But I do know that I want to spend the rest of my life with you. Will you marry me?"

May was crying too hard to answer, but at her emphatic nod, the entire group broke into cheers.

Grace wiped a tear from her own cheek as Levi rushed forward to help Luke back to his feet. The moment Luke was upright, Levi clapped him into a strong hug.

"Thanks, bro, but I'd like to hug my fiancée now if you don't mind." Luke's voice was loud enough for everyone to hear, and Levi let go of his brother, not a hint of embarrassment on his face as he moved out of the way.

May instantly stepped into his spot, her arms going around Luke in a long embrace with a sweet kiss that elicited more cheers, before she and Levi helped Luke back into his wheelchair.

Levi turned to May and held his arms out to her, wrapping her into a quick hug that brought another lump to Grace's throat.

She gave her eyes a determined swipe, then approached to congratulate the happy couple along with everyone else.

An hour later, as the group started to disperse, Grace found herself alone in the kitchen, where she'd offered to load the dishwasher. Mostly, she'd needed time to think.

The patio door slid open.

"Hey you." There was something about the way he said it that always made her smile.

"Hey yourself."

"Want some help?"

"Just finished." Thank goodness. She wasn't sure she could handle being alone with him right now. Not when her feelings were more mixed up than ever.

She couldn't be with him. And yet she wanted to be.

She knew he was Mr. Wrong. But he felt so much like Mr. Right.

"I think I'm going to head home, actually." She dug her keys out of her pocket. "You?"

He shook his head. "I'm Luke's ride, so I'll stay until he's ready to go."

"He's over the moon. I'm happy for him."

Levi gave her a thoughtful look. "Me too."

"I'm glad about that. I wasn't sure you would be."

"Guess I've learned a few things lately."

"Like?"

"Like I'm fortunate to have a brother like him. And like I didn't have a right to make assumptions about May based on what other women had done. And like—"

But she was stuck on that last one. Was that what she'd been doing to Levi? Making assumptions about him based on what Hunter had done? On the kind of person Hunter had been? Because, when she really thought about it, Levi wasn't anything like Hunter at all.

"I didn't answer your question from before." She didn't mean to interrupt what he'd been saying, but she had to do this right now. "About the fundraiser."

"Oh." Levi dropped his head. "Don't worry about it. I shouldn't have asked."

"No. I mean yes." She took a breath. "I mean, I want to go. With you."

Chapter 44

"I need your advice." Levi stood in the doorway of his brother's room.

Luke was in his wheelchair, reading a book, but he closed it and looked up with a smirk. "That's a first."

"Yeah well. There have probably been plenty of times that I should have asked you for advice, but I was too stupid to realize it."

"True." Luke gestured for Levi to come in, and Levi took the opportunity to snatch the pillow off Luke's bed and chuck it at his brother. Luke caught it easily. "So how can I help the great and mighty Levi Donovan?"

"Knock it off. If anything, you're the great and mighty one. Coming back from death's door like that." He pointed a finger at his brother. "Don't ever do that to me again, by the way."

"I'm only great and mighty because of the One who makes me great and mighty. Same for you. You know that, right?"

"Yeah. I do." Levi had continued to go to church ever since that day when Luke was sick and he hadn't known what else to do. And every time, he was sure he was going to hear something that would bring back all the old doubts. But instead, every time, his certainty that God was real—that God loved him—only seemed to grow.

"Anyway, this advice you desperately need . . . I assume it's about Grace?"

"I don't desperately need it." That wasn't true. "Okay, I do. And yes, it's about Grace." He was supposed to pick her up for the fundraiser in an hour, but he was petrified.

"I'm afraid I'm going to screw this up," he admitted to Luke. "She's already made it clear that she doesn't want to date me."

Luke eyed him as if he were a simpleton. "You're about to go on a date, so I think you can conclude that you've passed that hurdle."

Levi shook his head. "As a friend. I asked her to the fundraiser as a friend. But the truth is—" He swallowed. Even thinking the words felt monumental.

"The truth is you're in love with her," Luke filled in.

Levi watched his hands. It would be safer to deny it.

But he nodded. "Madly in love, actually."

"And have you told her that?"

Told her that? Was his brother crazy? "Of course not."

"What are you waiting for? A personal invitation?"

Yeah. Sort of. Shouldn't he be?

"Look." Luke maneuvered the wheelchair to the bed. "You said you wanted advice. So here's my advice: Love isn't always easy. Sometimes it's scary. But it's what we were created for. And you have the best example out there to follow."

"What? You and May?" His brother did seem to have things figured out in the love department.

"No, you doof. Jesus. He's your example of love."

Levi thought about that for a minute, then stood. "Thanks for the advice, man. And for, you know, being my brother." He moved toward the door.

"You're welcome. And Levi?"

Levi looked over his shoulder.

"Let's have these talks more often."

"You're sure everything's all right?" Grace must have asked the question half a dozen times on the drive down to Chicago. She threw in one more now as the limo Levi had rented traveled toward Navy Pier.

"Of course. Why do you keep asking?"

"You seem different tonight." Quieter than usual, with a sort of nervous energy cascading from him—which, in turn, was making her nervous.

"Sorry. I've just been thinking."

"About what?" She craned her neck to look at the skyscrapers towering over them. Ahead of them, a line of limos crept toward what she assumed was their final destination.

"You." He said it quietly, but it drew her eyes to him.

"What about me?" She bit her lip against the words, but they were already out.

"I was thinking," Levi said, sliding forward on the seat and taking her hands in his, "that you look beautiful."

"Oh." Grace glanced down at the floor-length silver evening dress she'd borrowed from Jade. "Thanks."

Why was she disappointed? The man had complimented her. She shouldn't have expected something more substantial—something deeper.

"You look nice too." Nice was putting it mildly. Levi looked like a celebrity in his tailored suit coat with a white t-shirt underneath. Then again, he *was* a celebrity.

Too often, she forgot that.

Levi cleared his throat. "And I was also thinking—"

"Sir, we are next in line." The driver's voice came over the intercom. "Please be ready to exit."

Grace's eyes tracked to the window, catching on a beautiful couple walking down a red carpet surrounded by a sea of people and flashing cameras.

"Wait. We're not going to have to do that, are we?" Her stomach seesawed. There was no way . . .

"It'll be fine." Levi scooted toward the door, pulling her with him. "I'll be right at your side the whole time. But maybe—" He lifted a hand toward her face and pushed the corners of her lips up. "Try to look like you're not mortified to be seen with me. Ready?"

Before she could say no, the door of the limo opened, and he stepped out, then reached back to help her out.

Grace had no idea how she was supposed to walk in these heels, let alone walk in front of all these people, but Levi wrapped a firm arm around her back and steered her toward the glass doors.

Every few seconds, another camera flash went off, and Grace heard a few people call Levi's name. He waved and smiled, and she turned to marvel at him. How did he do this all so naturally?

Finally, they reached the building and slipped inside.

Levi's arm remained tightly around her—and she was in no rush to step out of it.

"You did great." His smile made her want to cinch up closer to him. "You can relax now. That was the hardest part of the night."

But Grace knew she couldn't relax. Because the hardest part of the night was going to be denying her undeniably real feelings for Levi Donovan.

Chapter 45

Coward.

The word had been ringing in Levi's head since in the limo when he'd told Grace she was beautiful instead of saying what he'd meant to say. Luke had told him he needed to tell her. He *knew* he needed to tell her.

But he'd taken one look into those deliciously warm eyes and realized—if she didn't feel the same way, he would be devastated.

All through dinner, all through the speeches, all through the auction, and even now, holding her in his arms as they danced, he'd been trying to convince himself to go through with it.

Man up, he scolded himself. *If you can take a hit from a three-hundred-pound defensive tackle, you can tell this woman you love her.*

He gulped in a breath. "Hey, Grace?"

"Mmm hmm?" Her head was pressed to his chest, but she picked it up to look at him.

Oh man. He was a goner.

Again.

His mouth went dry. "You want to get some air?"

"Sure." She dropped her hands from his shoulders and slipped out of his arms.

Nice move. Wouldn't it have been easier to tell her while you held her?

But he led her toward the glass doors that led out onto a wide balcony overlooking the lake. The late August night had started to cool, and a sharp breeze blew in off the water. Levi let the fresh air fill his lungs. Much better than the stifling air inside. He peeled off his jacket and settled it over Grace's shoulders.

She wiggled her arms into the oversized sleeves, and he had to laugh.

"What?" Grace grinned at him. "Do I look silly?"

"Nope." Levi stepped closer, daring to press a hand to her cheek. "You look perfect."

Her eyes came to his, and he knew. He *had* to do this.

"Grace, there's something I've been wanting to tell you all night. But I haven't known how."

"Oh no. Do I have spinach in my teeth?" She lifted a hand toward her mouth, but he caught the hand.

"Your teeth are perfect. Your eyes are perfect. Your face is perfect. Your heart and your mind and your soul are perfect."

"Levi I'm not perfect. You know that I—"

"Fine. You're not perfect."

Grace looked satisfied.

"But you're perfect for me." He lifted her hand to his lips and brushed a gentle kiss over it. "What I'm trying to say, Grace, is I love you."

"Oh." Grace didn't move.

"It's okay." His heart was somewhere down below in the lake, drowning. But he could take it. "I realize you probably don't feel the same way. I just wanted you to know."

Still she stood, frozen.

"I'm sorry." He dropped her hands. "I shouldn't have said it. I didn't mean to make things awkward for you. I'll call the driver. We'll go home and pretend this never happened." He pulled out his phone, fumbling at the screen.

What had he been thinking, taking Luke's advice?

Tell her, his brother had said.

Well, now he'd told her—and had likely completely destroyed their friendship in the process.

Grace's fingers covered his phone screen, and she gently tugged the device away from him.

"Grace, what—"

But when he looked up, her face was raised to his.

Before he could figure out what was happening or how to react, her arms were around his neck, and her lips were on his.

He almost fought it.

He didn't want her to kiss him because she felt obligated.

But the feel of her lips on his was so right.

This was no kiss of obligation.

It was a kiss of sheer delight.

Grace pinched her lower lip between her fingers as she stood alone on her porch in the early morning mist. That kiss with Levi last night had been . . . sensational.

Which one? She giggled to herself. They may have kissed a few more times as they'd danced. And in the car. And when he'd walked her to her door.

Each one had felt more right than the last.

Until she couldn't deny it anymore.

Levi Donovan loved her.

And she loved him.

She giggled again.

All right, God. You may have known what you were doing when I prayed for you to send Mr. Right to my doorstep.

She'd been too blind to see it at first, since Levi had come in a different package—a motorcycle-riding, football-playing package—than she'd expected.

A familiar tickle went through her tummy as she spotted his truck at the end of the long driveway. The faintest glow of sunlight dusted the leaves that arched over the driveway, and it gave the whole scene a golden glow.

Or maybe that was the joy in her heart.

Levi sprang out of the truck, and before she could even say hello, he had taken the steps two at a time and caught her up in his arms.

"I missed you," he murmured into her hair.

"It's been less than eight hours." But she knew what he meant as she brought her hands to his broad back. That was about eight hours too long.

He lowered his face, catching her lips between his in a long, drawn-out kiss that left her breathless when he pulled away.

Breathless and tugging him closer for another.

"Sorry I called you so early," she said when they finally pulled apart.

"You can get me up early to do that anytime." Levi brushed a hand over her cheek, sliding his fingers into her hair.

"There's another reason I wanted you to come too."

"Yes, boss." Levi gave her a mock salute with the hand that wasn't in her hair. "We have cabinets to install today."

"True." She laughed but then wrapped her arms around his waist. "But also, I love you."

Levi's exhale was loud enough to be comical. "You do?"

She lifted her face to his and answered with another kiss.

Chapter 46

This was going to drive Grace crazy. She was supposed to open this place in less than three months, and she still didn't have a name for it. Which made it impossible to advertise.

Fortunately, Tori's blog had drummed up so much interest that she already had a handful of reservations, even without a name, but this was getting ridiculous. She didn't know why the decision was so paralyzing.

"Hey you." Levi came straight to the desk she'd set up to the side of the stairway so that she'd be able to greet guests the moment they arrived. He swiveled her chair and nuzzled his face into her neck. "Want to take a break for some lunch?"

"Yes, please. I'm not getting anywhere here."

"Still?" Levi pulled her to her feet. "How about The House Without a Name? Then you don't have to worry about it."

"That's helpful." She brought her lips to his. "What would I do without you?"

"I don't know." He drew her closer, kissing her again. "Good thing I'm not going anywhere."

Grace's eyes met his. Though the past week had been blissful, filled with kisses and long conversations, one thing had hung at the back of her mind—Levi had never made a secret of the fact that he had no intention of staying in Hope Springs.

"You're not?"

He brushed her hair off her shoulder. "You're here. Why would I want to be anywhere else?"

There was only one way to respond to that. She twined her arms around him and concentrated on putting the depth of her feelings into the kiss.

His kiss said he was doing the same.

When she pulled away from him, she studied him. "You're sure you'll be happy here?"

"Like I said, you're here."

"Yes, but Levi—"

"And my dad asked me to stay and partner with him—help him expand. Plus the football team needs a coach, so . . . I'll have plenty to keep me busy."

"In that case—" She gave him a playful smile. "It just so happens that I have an announcement too."

"Yeah? What's that?"

Another kiss distracted her from answering for a moment.

"I've decided to include TVs in at least some of the rooms. I realized that night we watched the movie was the start of things for me . . ."

"Really? That early?"

"Yes. Why? When did you start to realize you had feelings for me?" Not that it mattered that she'd liked him before he'd liked her.

"Oh, way before that. The first day I met you."

"You did not." She slugged him.

"Want to bet?" Levi brought his lips to hers again.

Grace considered taking him up on that bet but decided she liked the kissing better. Her fingers played with the ends of his hair.

The sound of a throat clearing from the doorway had them jumping apart.

"I'm so sorry. I didn't hear the—" Grace choked on her own words as her eyes fell on the open door.

"Mama?" Grace smoothed her shirt, though it wasn't rumpled, then rushed forward and pulled Mama into a quick hug. "What are you doing here?"

"I wanted to surprise you." Mama squinted toward Levi, who had stepped forward as well. "Looks like I succeeded."

Grace ignored the comment, as well as Levi's half-amused smirk.

"It's nice to see you again, Mrs. Calvano." Levi held out his hand, and Mama gave it a halfhearted shake.

"Would you like a tour, Mama?"

Mama's eyes traveled over the freshly finished fireplace, the newly laid floors, the recently hung window treatments, and Grace held her breath. Mama had grown up in this house—what would she think of the changes Grace had made?

"Actually, I could use a little rest."

Grace nudged her disappointment aside. She didn't need Mama to approve of this place in order to be proud of it herself. She led Mama upstairs to the Garden Room.

"Hmm." Mama stopped in the doorway. "This was my old room."

"I know." Grace moved to close the curtains so Mama could sleep, but she couldn't resist asking, "Do you like it?"

"I sure wouldn't have minded having my own bathroom as a kid." Mama laughed and sat on the bed.

Grace smiled. That might be the closest thing to a compliment she was going to get, but she'd take it.

"So what does bring you here, Mama?"

"Can't a mama want to spend some time with her only daughter? We didn't get a lot of time together at Simeon's wedding. Everything was so crazy."

"Of course you can, Mama. I'm glad you're here. But I'm not sure how much fun I'm going to be. We only have a couple months until the grand opening, and there's a lot to do yet."

"That's what you hired Levi for, isn't it? Or do you pay him simply so the two of you can stand around and kiss all day?"

There it was.

"Mama, we don't—"

Mama held up that finger that always quieted her. "You're a grown woman Grace. If you want to kiss a man, that's your business. I thought I made my feelings about that man being Levi Donovan clear. But if you want to ignore my advice, that's your choice."

"Mama, I'm not ignoring you. I just think—"

But Mama waved her off. "We'll talk about it later. Right now, I really do need to rest."

"Your mom all settled?" Levi looked up from the sandwiches he'd been preparing as Grace returned to the dining room. With the kitchen pulled apart, they'd moved the refrigerator in here.

She nodded but didn't say anything.

"You want mustard on your sandwich?"

"Sure."

He set down the cheese he'd been about to slice. She never had mustard. He'd only asked to see if she was paying attention.

Guess he had his answer.

He stepped around the table to stand directly in front of her. "Hello?"

"Huh? Oh." She shook herself. "Sorry. What'd you say?"

"I asked if you wanted mustard."

"Oh. No thanks."

"I know." He wrapped her in his arms, but she squiggled out of his grip after a quick hug. He frowned at her as she knelt and rummaged in a box full of dishes. "What's wrong?"

"Hmm? Nothing."

"Grace, do you really think I don't know when something is wrong?" He moved to her side and rested a hand on her shoulder. "Are you embarrassed that your mom saw us kissing?"

"What? No." But she kept her eyes on the cups in her hand.

"We weren't doing anything wrong, you know. Anyway, you've been meaning to talk to your mom about us, right? This will give you the perfect opportunity." Grace had confessed the other day that one of the things that had been holding her back from giving in to her feelings sooner was her mother's disapproval. So now they could get that all squared away.

"Yeah." But she still wasn't meeting his eyes.

"Grace? You *are* going to talk to her, right?"

She sighed, and his heart dipped.

"You don't understand," she said. "It's not that easy."

"No." He pulled her to her feet and turned her to face him. "I don't understand. I love you. You love me. What does any of that have to do with your mother?"

She wiggled out of his grip and retreated to the other side of the table. "Just give me some time. Please. I promise I'll tell her. But until then, maybe you should lie low."

He blinked at her. "That's what you want?"

She bit her lip, then nodded.

"Okay." He passed her the plate with her sandwich. "Then I'll lie low. Just don't take too long. I'll miss you."

He picked up his own plate and carried it to the front porch to eat.

Chapter 47

Why was this so difficult?

Grace had had three days to talk to Mama about Levi.

She and Mama had gone shopping and out to eat. They'd walked along the beach and gone to church. But never once had Grace worked up the courage to say Levi's name to Mama.

And aside from across church this morning, she hadn't seen him all weekend. He was keeping up his part of the bargain, lying low. Now it was time for her to do her part. And since Mama was leaving tomorrow, this was her last chance.

"Mama?" Grace settled onto the love seat in her sitting room, where Mama was resting with her feet up and eyes closed.

Mama had been napping a lot since she'd gotten here, which wasn't at all like the energetic woman Grace knew. Then again, she was getting older, and she'd just organized a huge women's retreat. She deserved some rest.

Mama opened her eyes. "This has been a nice visit, hasn't it?"

"It has, Mama." Grace licked her lips. "I was wondering if we could talk about something. About Levi, actually."

There. She'd brought him up.

Mama sat up, giving her a cautious look. "I noticed he hasn't been around the last couple days. I took that as a good sign."

"That's because I asked him to lie low. Until I could talk to you." When she said it out loud, it sounded horrible. She was fortunate Levi hadn't written her off then and there.

"I see." Mama's mouth went tight.

"Why don't you like him?"

Mama sighed. "If you must know, I do like him. I just don't think he's the right man for you."

"And you don't think I can decide that for myself? Did you choose Simeon's spouse for him? Or Zeb's?"

"Of course not. But this is different. You're my little girl. And—" She folded her hands in her lap, looking suddenly afraid and vulnerable.

It was enough to scare the indignant comment right off Grace's tongue and back down her throat. She waited.

Mama's exhale was long and drawn out and seemed to carry the weight of her years. "And I know what it's like to have your head turned by the wrong man. To be so in love with the idea of a man that you fail to see his shortcomings. Until it's too late."

A truck running her over couldn't have hit Grace harder. She clutched at the couch cushion. "What are you talking about? Daddy is—"

"I don't mean your daddy," Mama rushed in. "He's a wonderful, loving, God-fearing man."

"Then what are you talking about?"

Mama's hands twisted in her lap, and she refused to look at Grace. "There was a boy in high school. Ezra Talbot. I was so in love with him." Wistfulness and pain twined in Mama's voice. "But he never noticed me. Not until the end of senior year. And then, for whatever reason, he swooped in and swept me off my feet. I was blindsided. But I thought I was so, so in love." She blinked and let her eyes come to Grace's. "So in love that I conceived a child with him."

Grace's lips parted, but there were no words. She stared at Mama, and Mama stared back at her.

Finally, Grace found her voice. "What happened?"

Mama shrugged. "Soon as Ezra found out, he didn't want anything to do with me. I couldn't bear to tell my parents, so I arranged for my cousin Mary Beth in Tennessee to invite me for the summer. Her parents helped me arrange for the baby to be adopted." She drew in a shuddering breath, dropping her face into her hands.

Grace stared. She'd never seen Mama like this. She rested a tentative hand on Mama's shoulder. "You're saying I have another brother somewhere?"

"A sister." The word came out strangled.

Grace clutched Mama's arm. "I have a sister? Do you know where she is? What happened to her?"

Mama shook her head. "I didn't want to know."

"Does Daddy know? About the baby?"

"No one else knows." Mama brushed a piece of hair off Grace's forehead. "Now do you understand why I don't think Levi is right for you? I don't want you to go through the same thing I did. That night we found you and Hunter at the pond . . ."

The shame Grace had always experienced at the memory of what she'd nearly done with Hunter washed over her, but so did a new feeling. It was like being freed from a heavy weight that had chained her in place for years.

"Hunter was a mistake, Mama. One that I deeply regret. But one that I know I'm forgiven for. And you're forgiven for your sin too."

Mama pressed her lips together. "I know. But I also know how tempting it can be—"

"Mama," Grace said firmly. "I have no intention of ever making that mistake again."

Mama clutched at her hand. "I know *you* don't want to make that mistake again, Grace. And I trust you. But men like Levi—"

"Mama, Levi is—"

"There's something else, Gracey," Mama interrupted, her voice oddly quiet.

Grace froze. Mama only used that nickname when she had to deliver bad news.

Mama sat up straight and tall, the same way she'd taught Grace to, but she looked frail and older than her fifty-six years. She patted Grace's hand. "It's back."

"What's back?" But Grace knew the answer before Mama spoke, and already tears were gathering at the back of her throat.

"The cancer." Mama's voice was matter-of-fact, as if she were remarking on the return of the geese at the end of winter.

"But you had a mastectomy. You had radiation. You went through all that—" That year had been horrible and hard on all of them, but they'd come through it. Mama had survived. She was still here. She had so many years ahead of her yet. Work to do here on earth yet. That's why God had spared her. That's what she'd always said.

Mama reached over and pulled Grace into her arms. But Grace pulled away. She didn't want Mama to hold her. Mama only held her when something was wrong.

"It's everywhere this time." Mama took Grace's hand. "The doctor says there's nothing they can do. I probably have a couple months at the most. That's why I came. That's why I have to know you'll be okay. That you're not going to yoke yourself to the wrong man. Promise me, Gracey. You won't marry Levi."

This time when she reached for Grace, Grace fell into her arms, the first sob erupting into Mama's shoulder.

Forgive me, Levi.

"I promise." The words nearly tore her heart in two. But as much as she loved Levi, she couldn't deny Mama's last request. Couldn't let Mama die disappointed in her.

Chapter 48

After three days of lying low, Levi had to face it—Grace wasn't going to talk to her mom about him. She'd rather sacrifice her own happiness—and his—than risk disappointing her mother.

He rolled over and punched his pillow. He'd known, hadn't he, when he started to have feelings for Grace, that it was a mistake? Known that he couldn't live up to the ridiculous checklist she'd created for her future husband. Known that as soon as she realized that, she'd be done with him.

He just hadn't expected it to happen so quickly.

Nor had he expected it to hurt this much.

He tried to be thankful. He'd dodged another bullet. This one stung a whole lot more than Rayna, he could admit that. But he'd get over Grace—maybe not today or tomorrow, but someday.

And this time, he'd keep his pledge to remain a bachelor. Maybe date casually every once in a while. No strings. No obligations. No love.

That was what he'd wanted once, wasn't it?

He rolled to his other side, trying to shake the feeling that he'd changed. That he'd gotten a taste of what life could be like with genuine love. And he wanted more of it.

It would pass soon enough.

He closed his eyes. But the inside of his eyelids became a movie screen, playing images of Grace—Grace laughing with him, Grace mock scolding him, Grace kissing him.

Levi opened his eyes, growling into his pillow.

He wasn't going to get any sleep tonight. He slid out of bed, pulled on a t-shirt, and eased his bedroom door open.

He didn't know where he was going. Just that he couldn't stay here right now. Couldn't hold still.

A run.

That was what he needed.

He tiptoed through the house, careful not to wake Luke and his parents, and slipped out the front door. The night was darker than he'd expected, cloudless and filled with stars but no moon.

He tilted his head up, remembering the night he and Grace had spent lying on that chair under the stars, talking about everything under heaven. Talking about heaven itself, even. That was the night he'd first seen God's love in such a real and tangible way. And it was the night he'd known—she was the one.

Clearly that had been wishful thinking.

What would happen, he wondered, if he marched over there right now, told Mrs. Calvano that he didn't care what she thought, and asked Grace to marry him?

He laughed at himself. He already knew what would happen.

Grace would say no, and he'd end up more broken than he was right now.

The sound of a car drew his gaze to the street. It had to be after one in the morning. And Hope Springs was the kind of town that turned in by ten o'clock every night.

The car pulled to the curb in front of the house. For half a beat, Levi prepared to defend his family's home from an intruder.

And then his eyes picked out the silhouette behind the wheel. It was dark, but not dark enough to keep him from recognizing her.

In spite of himself, his heart sped up as if he'd gone on that run he'd been planning to take.

He waited for her to get out of the car, to explain what she was doing at his house in the middle of the night. But she just sat there, staring straight ahead, her hands still gripping the steering wheel, even though she'd shut off the engine.

After a minute, she dropped her head to the wheel, and then her shoulders started to shake.

Levi was across the yard in an instant, knocking on the passenger window.

Grace shot upright with a quiet scream, but when her eyes fell on him, she pressed the unlock button.

Levi didn't wait for a further invitation but slid into the car.

Angry. He wanted to be angry with her.

But one look at her face, and he was reaching across the seat and pulling her to him. He didn't know what was wrong, but he did know he couldn't bear to see her hurting like this.

She clutched at his shirt, her tears wetting it, as she drew in deep, shaky breaths. He stroked her hair, not saying anything, trying to just be there for her the way she'd been there for him through everything with Luke.

"I'm sorry," she said finally, letting go of his shirt and pushing herself out of his arms. "I had no right to do that."

"Of course you have the right." He skimmed a hand over the tears still tracking down her cheeks. "Do you want to talk about it?"

"Mama has cancer. She's probably not going to make it much longer."

"Ah, Grace." Levi tugged her back to him, tucking her against his chest and cradling the back of her head in his hand. "I'm so sorry."

She nodded into his chest. "I wanted to talk to her, Levi. About us." Her swallow was audible, and he rubbed her back.

"It's okay. I shouldn't have asked you to."

"No. You were right. And I did try. But she's dying, Levi." She shuddered against him. "I just can't have her last memory of me be disappointment that I didn't listen to her. Even if I know she's wrong. I'm sorry."

He ducked his head to kiss the top of hers. His heart was breaking for her. And he wasn't so unselfish that it wasn't breaking for himself too. "I understand."

She tilted her head to look up at him. "You do?" Her eyes were dark and surprised and grateful.

He thought of what May had said in the hospital. *Sometimes when you love someone, you do what's best for them. Even if it hurts you.*

"Yeah." Oh, he wanted to kiss those lips. But he resisted. "I love you, Grace. Enough to let you go."

She dropped her head to his chest again, silent tears soaking his shirt and shaking her shoulders. But after a moment she slid gently out of his arms. "I'm going to go back to Tennessee with Mama. To be with her until the end. I don't know if I'll be back. Daddy might need someone to stay and take care of him—afterward."

"What about the bed-and-breakfast?" Her life's dream. But he knew she loved her family enough to give it up for them. And he only loved her more for it.

"I guess we'll have to put a hold on things for now." Her voice broke. "I may have to look into selling at some point."

"You go. Do what you have to do. I'll take care of things here. Whenever you're ready, it'll be in shape for you to either open up or sell."

Grace studied him. "You'd do that for me?"

"I thought you already knew." Levi picked up her hand and kissed her palm, then closed her fingers around it. "I'll do anything for you. Even this." He opened the car door and stepped out. "Goodbye, Grace."

Chapter 49

"Can I get you anything else, Mama?" It took Grace's breath away, sometimes, how quickly Mama's health had deteriorated. When Grace had returned home with Mama a month ago, Mama had insisted on taking Grace out shopping or to make the rounds of the church's shut-ins she continued to minister to. But within two weeks, Mama had weakened so that they'd had to order a hospital bed for her. They'd pushed the large oak dining table aside to make room for it, and there was a constant stream of people in and out to visit Mama.

Grace's favorite times were in the evening, when she and her brothers gathered around, laughing and telling stories like it was a party. And in a way, she supposed it was. A party to celebrate Mama's life—and to rejoice in the eternal life waiting for her.

But then there were moments like this, moments when the house quieted and she had a second to just look at Mama, lying there in bed, still so spunky in spite of her weakness, that a wave of sadness nearly knocked Grace over. She knew it was selfish. Though Mama would never admit it, she was in more and more pain by the day, and she was ready to go home to her Father. But Grace wanted to keep her here. Wanted to have her Mama there on her wedding day—though without Levi, she wasn't sure she ever wanted that day to come.

He'd texted every few days, usually with questions about the finishing touches for the bed-and-breakfast. And he'd called a couple of times as well, just to see how she was doing. How Mama was doing. But as much as she appreciated the calls, appreciated the fact that he never crossed the boundaries of friendship, they always left her hurting, aching for more.

She'd thought Levi was selfish. But she was the selfish one. Because as much as she knew she could never be with him, not after she'd promised Mama, she also wanted him to still love her. The way she still loved him.

Mama held out a hand to Grace. "I'm fine, Gracey. Are you okay?"

Grace half-laughed. "Don't you go worrying about me now, Mama."

But Mama shook her head. "Until I draw my last breath, I'll still be your mama. And I know when something's bothering you."

"Of course something's bothering me, Mama." Grace took Mama's hand, then settled herself onto the edge of the bed. "I don't want to say goodbye to you."

"Oh hush." Mama frowned at her. "You know our goodbye is only temporary. I'll see you again soon enough. I think what's really bothering you is Levi Donovan."

"What? Mama, I—"

But Mama raised her index finger, and Grace closed her mouth. "I've been your mama for twenty-nine years, so don't you go thinking you can pull something over on me. I know that look in your eyes when you think of him. It's the same look your daddy gives me, same look I give him. You're in love with Levi Donovan." Though her features had grown gaunt, Mama's eyes were as sharp as ever.

Grace couldn't hold her gaze. She didn't want to lie to Mama, but she didn't want to disappoint her either. "I'm trying not to be," she whispered.

"Oh Gracey." Mama's weak arms pulled Grace closer. "I didn't know. I thought it was . . ." She shook her head. "Never mind that. Does he love you too?"

Tears stabbed at the back of Grace's eyes, but she blinked them away. Now was not the time to make Mama feel bad. "Enough to say goodbye. I told him I couldn't be with him, Mama, and he understands." Oh goodness, she was going to cry after all. She sniffled, and Mama fell silent so long that Grace thought she'd fallen asleep.

She moved to stand up, but Mama reached for her again. "Does he make you happy, Gracey?"

"Levi?" Grace gave a soft laugh. "Yes, Mama. Happier than I've ever been before. But it's more than that. Deeper. It's like . . ." She searched for a way to explain it.

"Like your souls are connected."

"Yeah." Grace's voice caught on the word. "But that doesn't change anything. I made a promise to you, and I intend to keep it."

"I thought you were smarter than that." Mama's voice was flat, and Grace looked up to find a wan smile on Mama's lips. "If you love him, you shouldn't let me stand in the way."

"But you said . . ."

"I was wrong."

Grace was pretty sure she'd never heard those words from her mama before.

"It's okay, Mama. We already agreed—"

"Grace, you listen to me." Mama raised her finger yet again. "I've made plenty of mistakes in my life. But I'm not going to let keeping my daughter from the man who loves her with a sacrificial love be one of them. I'm sorry I interfered."

"You didn't interfere, Mama."

But Mama gave her a look.

"Well you did. But I know it's only because you want what's best for me. And I'm thankful for that."

Mama closed her eyes, her hands settling over her middle. "All I ever wanted was to know you'd be okay, Grace. That you'd be taken care of when I'm gone. I thought I had to be the one to set that up. But it turns out God had a better plan than I did all along. You'd think I would have figured that out by now, after all these years, wouldn't you?" Mama sighed. "Better late than never I guess."

"Get some rest, Mama." Grace brushed a kiss over Mama's forehead. "We can talk about it more later."

"There's nothing more to talk about." Mama smoothed Grace's cheek. "We both know I'm right."

Chapter 50

Awe.

That was the only word that could describe how Levi felt right now, as he sat in church.

Awe that two months after doctors had been sure Luke was going to die, his brother was sitting next to him this morning, his wheelchair a thing of the past. Awe that though he'd had to let go of Grace, he felt more alive and complete for having loved her—for still loving her, even if he could never be with her.

But most of all, awe at the love of God that seemed to bounce off the walls and hang in the air this morning. Every song seemed to point to that love, to call it out, to surround him with it, and to his own surprise, he was soaking it up, basking in it, wanting to hold onto it.

He'd grown up in the church, had known about God since he was a young boy. If he was honest, it wasn't only that he'd questioned whether there *was* a God over the last few years. It was that he'd wondered how God was relevant to his life, whether God cared about him, loved him.

His dad had been right—as he'd become successful, he'd made himself into his own god. Thought he could earn his own way through life. And maybe he could—if life was only about football and money and chasing after fleeting pleasures. But the past few months had shown him that there was more at stake than life itself. There was eternity.

And he couldn't earn that himself. Not with all the skill or money or fame in the world.

He was about as unworthy of heaven as a person could be.

And yet, Jesus had saved him anyway.

Grace. That was what that was called, he remembered. Grace.

He'd been so sure that what he needed was Grace, the woman.

When what he really needed was grace, the undeserved love of God.

When I was lost, stumbling in the dark, Nate's worship band sang from the front of the church.

You came, you lit a fire in my heart.
A fire so bright that now I can see,
And darkness no longer has a hold on me.
I am free. Free in Jesus.

Levi closed his eyes. Those words. That was exactly how he felt.

Like he'd spent years stumbling in the dark, crashing into obstacles, bouncing off of walls, careening toward nothing. But now he could see. Now he knew the fire of Christ's love. Maybe for the first time in his life, he knew what it really meant. It meant he was free.

By the time church was done, Levi was buzzing with energy. He declined Jade's invitation to join the group for lunch. He was nearly done with things at Grace's bed-and-breakfast, and he wanted to wrap them up, both because he wanted it to be ready for whatever she decided to do with it and because Dad had a new job he wanted Levi to get started on.

When he reached the bed-and-breakfast, he headed straight for Grace's private sitting room. He knew she hadn't been planning to do any remodeling in here, but he couldn't resist making a few updates for her.

He told himself that it was because he wanted to do something nice for her, to thank her for helping him find his way back to what was important—his family, his friends, and his faith. But he knew it was also at least partly selfish. Being in this part of the house made him feel closer to her. And he maybe secretly hoped that every time she looked around at the walls he'd painted her favorite shade of lavender, she'd think of him. Unless she decided to sell—in which case having this area spruced up should help.

The thought of not coming here every day—of not seeing Grace every day—made his heart ache. But it wasn't the sharp ache of disappointment. More the sweet ache of knowing he was doing what was best for her.

It was what he prayed every day—that God's will be done in her life.

Not that his thoughts hadn't been filled with her every minute for the past month. Or that it didn't nearly kill him every time he texted or talked to her not to say those three words that flashed in his head the whole time. Not to beg her to please, please ignore the wishes of her dying mother and say she'd be with him.

But even he wasn't *that* selfish.

His phone buzzed in his pocket, and though he didn't recognize the number, he answered—just in case.

"Levi?" The voice was familiar, but he couldn't place it.

"Yes?"

"This is Heather Calvano."

"Mrs. Calvano." Levi snapped to attention, as if he'd just been caught snooping through Grace's private things. "Is Grace okay? Are you okay?"

"Yes. Yes. Everything's fine." Though Mrs. Calvano's voice was weaker than he remembered, she managed to convey her impatience.

"Oh. Good." Levi was at a loss. As far as he knew, there was no playbook for talking to the mother of the woman you loved but couldn't be with because of said mother. "Do you mind if I ask why you're calling then? If this is about me and Grace, I can assure you that there's nothing—"

"That's the problem," Mrs. Calvano cut in.

"I'm sorry. That's the . . ."

"Problem. Yes. Did you know that my Gracey loves you?"

Levi backed into the coffee table behind him, dropping onto it with a thud. "I did know that, yes."

"And she says you love her too?"

Levi blew out a long breath. "Yes, but—"

"No buts."

Levi drew himself up. Mrs. Calvano might be Grace's mother, and she might be dying. But that wasn't going to stop him from saying this. "*But*—" he emphasized. "I understand why you don't approve. And I understand why Grace doesn't want to go against your wishes. So you don't have to worry that I'm going to do anything about my feelings."

"That's a shame." Mrs. Calvano's voice had gone quiet. "Because I was wrong."

"You were . . ."

"Wrong." The word snapped through the phone. "You sure could work on your listening."

"Yes, ma'am." Levi scrubbed a hand over his unshaven cheek. "Sorry. You're catching me by surprise here."

"I'm catching myself by surprise too. I thought it was my job to protect Gracey from men like you. But that was just me letting my own past mistakes get in the way."

He heard her draw in a labored breath. "You don't want to hear about all of that. All you need to know is that Gracey is going to need you. She's a strong girl, and feisty."

Levi chuckled, picturing all the times she'd proven that. "That she is."

"But she's soft too. Sensitive. Always trying to make sure everyone else is taken care of before herself. I need to know you're going to put her first, before yourself. Can you promise me that?"

Levi closed his eyes, an image of Grace filling his whole being. "Mrs. Calvano, the only one above Grace in my life is Jesus." He'd never thought of it in those terms, but it was true, he realized now. His rekindled love for his Savior burned with a fierceness that had taken him completely by surprise. Not even his love for Grace could hold a candle to it. But he knew that was the way Grace wanted it too.

"That's all I wanted to hear." Mrs. Calvano's voice trailed off, and Levi was at a loss as to what to say next.

He was searching for a way to end the conversation when she spoke again. "And you plan to marry her?"

A bright, unbridled hope flared through him. Until a few minutes ago, he hadn't even allowed himself to hope for a moment alone with her. And now her mama was talking marriage.

"Yes, ma'am. If she'll have me."

"Good. Then I think my work here is done. You take good care of my baby girl, Levi Donovan."

"I will." Levi swallowed against a sudden swell of gratitude for Grace's mother, who even as she faced her own death was taking care of everyone else. "And Mrs. Calvano?"

"Yes?" She was sounding weaker.

"I think I know where Grace gets her habit of putting others before herself. You've raised a wonderful daughter."

"Thank you, Levi. Son."

Levi pressed his fingers to the insides of his eyes as he hung up. That might be the first and last time he'd ever hear that word from the woman he hoped would be his future mother-in-law.

Chapter 51

"You're sure you'll be all right, Daddy?" The airport buzzed around them, but Grace set down her luggage. In the two weeks since Mama's death, Grace had been busy helping with funeral arrangements and receiving guests who came to offer condolences and keeping Daddy and her brothers fed and cared for. But now the boys had returned to their lives—and Daddy insisted it was time for her to do the same. But she couldn't bear to think of him going through his days alone.

"You know I'd be happy to stay with you." She tried again. "Make your favorite hot chicken every day."

Daddy laughed. "I don't think that would be too good for my heart. Or for yours." He gave her a shrewd look, and Grace ducked her head.

"Your Mama told me about how she tried to keep you from seeing Levi." Daddy poked a finger under her chin to lift her head. "She also told me to make sure you didn't let that stop you from being with him. You can't stay here with me to hide from that."

"I'm not hiding," Grace mumbled, even though some small part of her knew that wasn't true. Because going back to Hope Springs meant facing Levi—and the possibility that he'd already moved on and found someone else.

"Gracey." Daddy pulled her into a hug. "You've spent so much of your life taking care of others. Now it's time for you to go and live your someday."

"I'm scared." The whisper slipped out before she could stop it. Daddy had enough worries of his own. She didn't need to burden him with hers too.

He squeezed her tighter, then let go and passed her the luggage. "I know. But you know what I always say."

"Do not be afraid; do not be discouraged, for the Lord your God will be with you wherever you go." Grace quoted Daddy's favorite verse from Joshua.

"That's my girl." Daddy patted her cheek. "Now go. With my blessing. And Mama's."

She nodded and steeled her shoulders, pointing herself toward the gate.

"Wait. Grace." Daddy passed her a piece of paper. "Mama wanted you to have this. She said she doesn't know who adopted your sister. But the adoption agency was in Nashville."

"She told you?"

Daddy nodded as Grace peeled the piece of paper open. It had the address of an adoption agency. And a name: Lydia.

"She didn't know if they kept the baby's name or not," Daddy said. "But she thought it might be a starting point."

"A starting point?"

"To look for her."

Grace watched him. He'd aged over the past month and a half, but he still stood straight and tall. She'd always thought of him as an unmovable force. "Do you want me to look?"

Daddy gazed out over the bustling crowd. "I still can't believe she kept that secret for almost forty years. But I'm glad she told me in the end. And this daughter is a part of her. So yes, I'd like to get to know her." Daddy cleared his throat and nudged her away. "Now get going before you miss your plane. I'll talk to you soon."

Grace obeyed, tucking the slip of paper into her pocket. She had no idea how easy or difficult it would be to find someone who had been adopted nearly forty years ago. But for Mama's sake, she was going to try.

She was so caught up in her thoughts that the flight passed in a blink. As she stepped off the plane, she took a deep breath. She was glad she'd been able to be there for her family.

But it was good to be home.

She made her way toward the coffee shop Jade had offered to pick her up from.

But she stopped short thirty feet from it.

That was not Jade.

Unless Jade had gotten a major makeover.

The moment he spotted her, Levi was on the move, dodging bodies, weaving against the current of people to get to her.

Never once did he take his eyes off her, and his face wore a mix of concern and joy and love—at least she thought it might be love.

Grace's pulse hummed as she waited for him to reach her, and her lips rose into an involuntary smile. But most of all, her heart sang.

And then his arms were around her in a bear hug of football player sized proportions.

She could barely breathe, but she didn't care. His arms around her offered her comfort and reassurance she hadn't even realized she needed.

"What are you doing here?" Her voice was muted by his shirt, but he must have heard her because she felt a chuckle rumble through his chest.

"I may have bribed Jade to let me come pick you up."

"Bribed her with what?"

"A night babysitting Hope and Matthias."

It was her turn to laugh. "You know, you probably could have gotten a lot more out of her for that."

"This was all I wanted."

He loosened his hold on her, leaning back so he could look into her eyes. "I'm so sorry about your mom. I've been praying for your family."

"Thank you." She swallowed hard. A lot of people had told her they were praying for her family over the past weeks, but none had meant quite as much as this. Levi took her bag as they headed for the exit.

She considered slipping her hand into his but decided against it.

Just because he'd come to pick her up, just because he'd hugged her, didn't mean he wanted to start over where they'd left off. She'd walked out on him over a month ago. And she wouldn't blame him if he couldn't get over that.

"I have a surprise for you." Levi nudged her shoulder as they stepped into the parking garage.

"Oh yeah? What's that?"

"You'll see." They walked in silence, Levi grinning the entire time. Finally, when her curiosity was about to get the best of her, he paused at a silver sedan. "Ta-da."

She stared. Why was he showing her some stranger's car?

Levi rolled his eyes and pulled out a key fob. He pressed a button, and the car's trunk popped open.

"This is your car?"

"Yep."

"You didn't get rid of the bike, did you?"

He stowed her bag in the trunk, then turned to her. "Why?"

She shrugged. "It's just so . . . you."

"And you like the bike."

"I mean, I—"

"You like it," Levi crowed. "I knew it. And to answer your question, no, I didn't get rid of the bike. Just thought it was time to get something a little more practical too."

"Okay . . ." She slid into the passenger seat as he opened the door for her.

She didn't remember ever telling him that "drives a sensible car" was item number five on her checklist for Mr. Right. He now officially checked every box, even if not in the way she'd expected.

Tell him, a voice urged. *Tell him you want to be with him.*

Grace opened her mouth. "Did I tell you I have a sister?" Those were not the words she'd been planning to say. But now that they were out, she knew she needed to talk about it.

Levi looked at her in surprise. "You do?"

She launched into the story of Mama's confession, of how she'd lived all those years with a secret of that magnitude eating at her heart.

"Wow," Levi finally said as they drove into Hope Springs. "That's a lot to take in."

"You're telling me." She chewed her lip. "I haven't said anything to the boys yet. I thought I'd wait and see how the search goes."

Levi turned to glance at her. "And you're sure you want to find her?"

"Yes. I mean, I think so. I don't know." She laughed. "Sorry, my emotions have been a little mixed up lately."

He took his hand off the wheel to give hers a quick squeeze, letting it linger a moment. "You're allowed. You've gone through a lot. But if you want to try to find your sister, I'll help."

A fresh rush of love for this man washed over her.

"Look—" Levi spoke up as he signaled to turn into the driveway of her house. "I have another surprise for you. But I'm not sure you're going to like it. And if you don't, you can tell me. I promise I won't be upset."

"Why wouldn't I like—" But as Levi stopped the car, tears filled her throat and kept her from saying anything else.

At the side of the driveway was a beautiful wooden sign carved with the words, "Heather House Inn."

Grace brought a hand to her mouth, pressing her lips tight in a vain attempt to hold back the sobs.

"I know I had no right to name your place. But it came to me the other day, and I just thought, with the heather on the hills behind the inn, and your mom's—"

"My mom's name." She managed to control her tears enough to say it. "It's perfect. I don't know why I didn't think of that. It's what this place was meant to be all along. Thank you."

Levi nodded and continued down the driveway to the house. "You ready for the tour?"

"I have one more surprise for you." Levi had loved every minute of taking Grace through the completed bed-and-breakfast. Watching the sparkle come back to her eyes, the flush to her cheeks, the joy to her voice—it made every ounce of sweat and effort worth it. "Close your eyes."

"I'm not sure if I can handle any more surprises today." But she dutifully closed her eyes and let him take her hand in his.

Perfect.

She'd used that word a hundred times as he'd shown her around the place. But *this* was what was perfect.

The two of them.

Together.

He only prayed she felt the same way. If not now, then maybe someday.

He steered her carefully through the kitchen to her living space at the back of the house. Opening the new French doors that led into her sitting room, he took her elbow and gently pulled her into the room.

Nerves tried to wriggle into his gut. What if she didn't like it? But he pushed them aside. It was too late to undo it now. And if she hated it, he'd put it all back the way it had been before.

"Open your eyes."

Without a second of hesitation, her eyes sprang open.

"Oh my goodness. Levi." Her hands went to her mouth, and she took a step back. She shook her head. "I don't . . ."

There was no holding the nerves back now. She didn't like it. "I'm sorry. This is your space. I shouldn't have—"

But she threw herself into his arms, nearly knocking him off his feet with her petite form.

"Are you kidding?" She was laughing and crying all at once. "I love it. It's just so . . . me."

She stepped out of his arms, and he forced himself not to grab her back up as she took a slow tour of the room, exclaiming over how he'd chosen the perfect colors and the perfect furniture. She paused especially long at a wooden sign he'd purchased from the little store Sophie and her family ran at Hidden Blossom Farms.

She ran a finger over the words: *Faith, Hope, Love.* "Daddy's message at Mama's funeral was based on 1 Corinthians 13:13. Same as their wedding day," she said. "It's perfect."

Then her eyes fell on the flamingo Levi had won at the Messtival, drawing out a laugh. "And so is this." She picked it up and hugged it, then tucked it back onto the shelf.

When she'd finished her tour of the room, she returned to his side. "I don't know why you did all of this for me, Levi. But thank you."

"You don't know why I did it?" Levi caught her hands in his, letting his eyes roam her face. "It's because I love you, Grace. I love you so much that it feels like you're a part of me sometimes." He lifted a hand to her cheek. "The best part."

"Levi, I . . ."

"Did you know your mama called me?"

Grace's head popped up. "She did?"

He nodded, leading her to the white love seat he'd picked out for this room. "A couple days before she died. She apologized. Said she'd been wrong to keep us apart. Was pretty adamant that we be together, actually."

Grace shook her head. "And here I thought I was going to miss Mama meddling in my love life. She told me the same thing, but I didn't know if . . ."

He caught her hands in his, pulled them to his heart. "Here's the thing, Grace. I love you. And I'd love for you to consider being in a relationship with me someday. But not because your mom told you to. Not to please me either. I want this to be completely your decision. Okay?"

Grace shook her head, and he forced himself not to fall to his knees right here and beg her to give him a chance. He'd told her it had to be her decision, and he'd meant it. "I understand."

"No." Grace brought his hands to her heart now. "I don't think you do. The part that isn't okay is that I'm done waiting until someday. I want to be with you now."

"But—"

Grace touched a finger to his lips. "Trust me, Levi. I'm not doing this to make Mama happy or to make you happy. I'm doing it because you make *me* happy. And I don't want to waste another moment waiting for someday. I love you *now*."

Chapter 52

"You look more nervous than I do." Luke slapped Levi on the back as Dad adjusted the bow tie threatening to cut off Levi's air supply. Why Luke had insisted that his groomsmen wear the torture devices was beyond him, but being that it was his brother's wedding day, Levi was trying to go along with it.

"I think I might be." Levi tugged at the bow tie. "At least your girl already said yes. You're sure you're okay with me asking Grace today? It's your big day. I can wait."

"I doubt that you can." Luke grinned at him. "Besides, I shouldn't be the only one who gets to be this happy today. How much longer? I can't wait to get out there." Luke's excitement was almost tangible as he moved a little closer to the door of the church conference room where they'd been getting ready.

Across the hall, May and her bridesmaids were doing the same. Levi couldn't count how many times he'd been tempted to pop over there and talk to Grace. But he'd held himself back.

It may not be his wedding day, but he still wanted to be surprised the first time his eyes fell on Grace today. He wanted to experience that heady rush of joy that washed over him every time he saw her. To imagine what it would be like when it *was* their wedding day. Because over the four months they'd been officially dating—since that day she'd said she didn't want to wait until someday to be with him—he'd grown more and more certain. Grace Calvano was the woman he wanted to spend the rest of his life with. The woman he wanted to wake up next to in the morning and lie down next to at night and spend every waking moment of every day with in between.

"There you are." Dad finally finished adjusting the bow tie and clapped a hand on Levi's shoulder. His eyes met Levi's. "I'm proud of you, son." Dad cleared his throat. "Of the man you are. I'm glad you found your way back."

Levi rolled his shoulder out from under Dad's clasp. Now was not the time to get all mushy. Even if Dad's eyes had grown misty and his own felt a bit prickly. "Thanks, Dad."

A knock drew everyone's attention to the door, and Dan poked his head in, giving Luke a thumbs-up. "It's time."

As the men filed out of the room, Levi grabbed Luke's arm. "Hey. Before we go out there, I want to say thank you."

"For what?" Luke moved his cane forward a step, and Levi could tell he was in a hurry to get to his bride.

"For, you know, being there for me. Even though I wasn't always there for you."

"You're here now." Luke threw a quick arm around Levi's back. "And that means a lot to me. Now if you don't mind, I've got a bride to meet."

"What are you waiting for then?" Levi opened the door and waited for Luke to pass through, then followed him down the hallway to a door at the front of the church. Levi patted his jacket pocket. He'd been careful to put Luke's rings in there. He didn't want to get them mixed up with the one in his pants pocket.

The one for later.

As he took his place next to Luke at the front of the church to wait for the bridesmaids to file in, Levi let his gaze drift over all the people gathered in the seats. The church was full, and Levi's heart was fuller. All these people were here to wish his brother and May well in their new life together. They were all here as witnesses to the vow that Luke and May would make before God to love and honor and cherish one another until the end of their days.

Neither of them knew when that would be. But both of them were willing to step out in faith, trusting that God would guide their lives.

A year ago, Levi had almost entirely written off that kind of faith.

And now?

Now God had restored that faith to him—strengthened it, actually. As a kid and into his teens, he'd mostly believed because it was what his parents had told him to do. But his faith had never been tested, never really become his own.

Now, after years without God, he could genuinely say that his faith was real, and that it mattered more than anything else in his life.

As the processional began, Levi watched two of May's friends start down the aisle, met halfway by Luke's two other groomsmen. And then Grace was gliding toward him, her face a picture of pure radiance, her smile seeming to glow from the inside out as her eyes met his.

He had no idea if the music was still playing, no idea if people were watching them, no idea even if he was still upright. The only thing he knew was that he was approaching the woman who had woven herself inextricably into the very fiber of his being.

"Hey you," he whispered as he tucked her hand into the crook of his elbow.

"Hey yourself." She let him lead her to the altar, where he reluctantly let her take her place with the bridesmaids as he took his with the groomsmen.

But all through the ceremony—as Dan offered his message, as Luke and May exchanged vows, as he handed the rings over to them—his eyes kept coming back to Grace. And every time, hers were on him too.

By the time the service was over, he was ready to drop to one knee right here in front of the entire congregation.

But he knew Grace wouldn't like that. She would want something more private. Quiet. Just the two of them.

Still, he couldn't wait much longer or the words would burst from him.

He managed to wait until they had walked back up the aisle and congratulated Luke and May with hugs all around.

But as guests began to filter out to greet the beaming bride and groom, he tugged Grace's hand. "Will you come with me for a moment?"

She looked from him to the guests. "Now? Don't we need to get to the reception to make sure everything is ready?"

"We will. I just want a minute alone with you first. Luke knows about it." Levi tugged her hand, pulling her to the new stairway that had been put in alongside the church after the old, worn one had been damaged in the tornado.

"Levi, we really should—" She tried to slide her hand out of his, but he kept pulling.

"I know. I promise, we'll go right back up. It's just I—" He stopped in the sand at the bottom of the steps. He'd been planning to lead her down the beach, to the water's edge, but he was done waiting. He was going to do this right here, right now.

He dropped to one knee, ignoring the sand spilling into his shoe.

"Levi." Grace's hands clutched at his shoulders.

He'd spent months trying to come up with the right thing to say when this moment came. But now that it was here, there was only one thing that mattered. "Grace Calvano. You told me once that you wanted to get married and have a family someday. With the right man. I know I'm not the man you expected, not the man you—"

She dropped into the sand in front of him, on her knees. "Levi Donovan. You are exactly the man I want."

His heart was already soaring, but he had to do this properly. He took the ring out of his pocket. "In that case, I want to make today our someday. Will you marry me?"

"I will." She launched herself into his arms, her lips meeting his as they tipped over. Their kiss was filled with laughter and sand and so much love Levi was pretty sure his heart had burst into ribbons of confetti.

When they finally pulled apart, Levi brushed a patch of sand off her arm. "We should probably get back up there."

"In a minute." Grace brought her lips to his again. "I've been waiting a long time for this someday, and I'm going to savor it."

Epilogue

Grace ran her hands down the smooth white satin of her dress.

How many times had she put on a bridesmaid dress, wondering when it would be her turn to wear white? And now here she was.

Was this how Mama had felt, looking at herself in this dress all those years ago when she'd married Daddy?

Like she was the most blessed woman in the world to be marrying a man who loved her so completely?

She picked up the picture of Mama that sat on her dresser. "I miss you, Mama," she whispered. "I wish you were here to share this day with me."

She swiped a quick finger under her eye before she could ruin the makeup Jade had so carefully applied only moments ago. The ceremony would start in a few minutes, and Grace was ready.

So ready.

There was a tap on the door, and Grace called, "Come in."

Daddy popped his head in the door but froze the moment his eyes fell on her. He blinked. Then blinked again and cleared his throat.

"Daddy." She went to him, and he wrapped her in the same hug he'd been giving her since she was a little girl.

"You look just like your Mama on our wedding day." Daddy's voice was choked up but also filled with joy. "She would be so proud of you."

"Thank you, Daddy. That means a lot." She hesitated, then made herself ask the question that had been weighing on her. "And you?"

"What about me?"

"It's been nine months since Mama . . ."

Daddy patted her hand. "I'm happy, Grace. Mama's in heaven with our Savior—and someday I'll get to be there too. But today I'm so happy I get to be here for this."

"You ready?" Jade ducked into the room. "Oh my goodness, look at you." She circled Grace. "You look like that dress was always made for you."

Daddy held out an arm, and Grace looped her hand around it as he led her into the kitchen, where her bridesmaids were lined up, waiting their turn to step through the French doors that led out to the backyard of the Heather House Inn, which had been transformed into the perfect outdoor wedding venue. The Heather House Inn had been open for six months now, and the rooms were almost always full. But Grace had blocked off this week for her family, and she was so grateful for the time she'd gotten to spend with her father and her brothers over the past few days. Her only regret was that she hadn't been able to locate her half-sister yet. But she wasn't giving up.

The processional music began outside, and a flutter of something went through Grace's middle. Not nerves. More like pure, unbounded joy.

She burst into laughter.

Daddy cut a glance at her, the same way he had from the pulpit when she was little and would start acting up in church.

But she couldn't help it. God had been so *good* to her. There was nothing else she could do.

Fortunately, she managed to get her giggles under control seconds before she stepped through the French doors and onto the patio.

Because the moment she saw Levi, tears shimmering in his eyes, she was in tears too.

It was too much. This love she felt surrounding her. She didn't know what to do with it all. What she'd ever done to deserve it.

Nothing.

That was the beautiful thing. She'd done nothing to deserve this love. But God had given it to her anyway.

As she reached the front of the aisle, she turned to kiss her daddy on the cheek, then took Levi's hand.

That first day when he'd knocked on the door of her house, she'd had no way of knowing that he'd come knocking on the door of her heart too.

No way of knowing that God had knocked it out of the park, answering her prayer to send Mr. Right to her doorstep.

But now she could see that God had a plan for her all along. What was it Jade had said? God saw her plans and laughed, then showed her that his plans were even better.

She really should listen to her friend more often.

Levi led her to the spot where Dan stood, waiting to marry them.

As he began the service, Grace committed to remembering every word, remembering every detail, of this day. The way Levi's calloused yet gentle hands felt in hers, the way the breeze played with the loose hairs around her face and blew her veil across her shoulders, the way the scent of the heather drifted up from the hill to remind her of Mama, the way the crash of the waves on the beach below formed the perfect backdrop to Dan's message about faith, hope, and love.

"But the greatest of these is love," she and Levi whispered along as Dan read.

All too soon, the ceremony was over, and they were greeting their friends and family, enjoying the meal Leah had catered, and dancing under the stars long into the evening.

Finally, when the grounds had grown quiet, with the last of the guests on their way home and Grace's family tucked into their rooms inside, Grace got the moment alone with her new husband that she'd been waiting for all day.

"Hey you." Levi drew her into his arms, teasing her lips with a slow, lingering kiss.

"Hey yourself." She wrapped her arms around his neck, letting his breath play across her lips.

"So how was your day?" Levi pulled her down onto a chair with him, settling her onto his lap, and snugging her in tight.

"I'd say it pretty much met the definition of perfect." She traced the outline of his lips with her finger. "This someday was well worth waiting for."

"My wife," he whispered. "Our someday is just beginning."

Not Until Now

A HOPE SPRINGS NOVEL

VALERIE M. BODDEN

Two are better than one, because they have a good return for their labor:
If either of them falls down, one can help the other up.

Ecclesiastes 4:9-10

Chapter 1

"Now what, Lord?" Kayla whispered the words into the silence of her car, an unfamiliar restlessness gathering in her soul as she eased the hand accelerator toward the steering wheel to pick up speed on the highway.

She'd always believed God opened and closed doors in a person's life for a reason—but she was struggling to understand the reason he'd literally closed the doors of the camp for disabled children that she'd worked at for the past decade. The place that had gotten her through the hardest time in her life. That had given her a purpose again. That had helped her find him again.

Even so, she trusted he would open another door eventually. "It'd be nice if you'd let me know what kind of door to look for," she muttered, although she knew that wasn't how God tended to work. More likely, she'd walk through the door without realizing it, not seeing it until she had the benefit of hindsight.

In the meantime, she'd focus on enjoying this visit with her brother and sister-in-law in Hope Springs. The small tourist town on the shores of Lake Michigan always eased her spirit. And with Vi's baby due in a little over a month, she could be there to help out. Her heart filled with joy once again that after years of worrying it would never happen, Vi and Nate's dream of starting a family was at last coming true. And that she was going to be an aunt. She had every intention of spoiling her niece or nephew rotten.

Her own biological clock gave a tiny twinge, but she ignored it. The doctors had reassured her after the accident that she'd still be able to have children. But in order to have children, she'd have to marry, and in order to marry, she'd have to date—and in order to date, she'd have to give up some of her independence. An independence she'd worked too hard to regain after her spinal cord injury to give it up for any man.

She settled back into her seat, letting herself pour out her hopes and fears and joys and disappointments to the Lord as the miles passed. By the time she neared Hope Springs, the sun was setting, but her soul felt like new life had been breathed into it. Whatever happened next was in God's hands.

She turned onto the road that would take her the last ten miles into the town, lowering the car's visor as the angle of the setting sun directed its beams directly into her eyes. The car in front of her was driving slower than the speed limit, but she didn't mind. She opened her window a crack, inhaling deeply even as she shivered in the frigid November wind that whistled into the car. The scent of pine and cold tickled her nose, and she smiled. She would enjoy Thanksgiving and Christmas with Nate and Vi, then figure out her next step from there.

"See, Lord, I can be pa—" She gasped as the car in front of her swerved once, then veered off the road and into the ditch, where it traveled a good fifty yards before coming to a stop.

Shoving the hand control forward to slow her own car, Kayla jerked the wheel toward the shoulder. Jamming the car into park, she grabbed her phone and punched in 911. As soon as it started to ring, she hit speaker and tossed the phone into the center console, then opened her door. Reaching toward the passenger seat, she gripped her wheelchair frame and flipped it over herself and out the open door. With her other hand, she shoved a wheel onto the frame. Then, balancing the chair against the door, she yanked the other wheel across the seat and rammed it on before she shoved her seat cushion into place.

"911. What's your emergency?" The voice came from the phone she'd stashed in the console.

"There's been an accident on Highway 10." Thank goodness she'd driven this way enough that the roads had become familiar to her. "A car went in the ditch."

Kayla barely heard the woman's reply that a squad car was on the way as she braced her hands on the seat to scoot her bottom as close to the edge of the car as possible. Bracing her left hand on her wheelchair and gripping the steering wheel with her right, she shifted her body into the chair. Quickly, she lifted one leg at a time onto the chair's footrest, then backed away from her car. She scanned the scene but could see no indication of what had caused the accident. The road was deserted, and though it was cold, there was no ice.

She eyed the shallow ditch, then with a quick decisiveness leaned back and gave a tug on her wheels to pull her chair into a wheelie. With her hands firm on the hand rims, she guided the chair in a controlled roll down the small hill and through the dried grass toward the car.

When she reached the car, she let her front wheels drop. Through the driver's window, she could see a woman's form slumped over the steering wheel, and her breath caught. "Please, Lord, no."

"Please help." The faint sound of a child's voice yanked Kayla's attention to the back seat. A little girl with tear-streaked cheeks gazed at her with wide eyes.

Kayla turned her wheelchair so she could open the girl's door. "Help is coming. Are you okay?"

"Mommy!" The girl bolted out of the car and tugged open the driver's door, clutching her mom's arm and shaking it.

Kayla reached gently for the girl. "Help is coming," she repeated. "They'll help your mommy." *Please, Lord, let that be true.* "Can you tell me what happened?"

The girl blinked at her, and Kayla wasn't sure she'd understood the question. But just as she was about to ask again, the girl said, "We were coming home from riding lessons, and I asked Mommy if we could get ice cream, and she said no, and I said, 'pretty please with a cherry on top,' and she said, 'Ruby Jane.' And then she took both hands off the steering wheel and grabbed her head and didn't say anything else. And then we went off the road. I didn't mean to make her mad." The girl's eyes filled with tears again.

Kayla reached for her hand and held it tight. "I'm sure she wasn't mad. Your name is Ruby Jane?"

"Just Ruby. Mommy only calls me Ruby Jane when I'm sassy."

"Okay, Ruby. My name is Kayla."

In the distance, the sound of sirens cut through the sharp air. "Here comes the ambulance. Let's get out of their way." She and Ruby moved away from the car as an ambulance pulled onto the shoulder and paramedics scrambled out.

"Kayla?" One of the paramedics did a double take. Nate and Vi's friend Jared. "Are you all right?"

She nodded. "I was following their car when it went off the road."

"Did you see what caused it?"

Kayla shook her head. "Nothing that I noticed. But Ruby said her mom grabbed her head before driving off the road."

Jared nodded, giving her a grim look. His eyes went past her to Ruby. "And you're Ruby? I think I've seen you at church."

The girl nodded.

"Are you hurt?"

The girl nodded again, and Kayla's stomach dropped. How could she not have thought to check the girl for injuries?

"Where does it hurt?" Jared moved closer and squatted in front of Ruby.

She held up her hand, revealing a band-aid on her finger. A relieved laugh escaped Kayla.

"Anywhere else?"

Ruby shook her head.

"Good." Jared straightened. "Can you tell me your mom's name?"

"Bethany Moore." Ruby's voice was timid but proud.

"All right, good job, sweetie. Why don't you go with Kayla and wait over there? We're going to help your mom." He jogged toward the car, where another paramedic had already begun working on Bethany.

"Come on." Kayla led Ruby toward her own car. It was too cold for the little girl to stand out here without a jacket.

"What are they doing to her?" The girl's eyes went straight back to the car in the ditch the moment Kayla had gotten her settled into the back seat.

Kayla glanced over her shoulder, to where the paramedics were lifting Bethany onto a stretcher. "That's my friend Jared, and he's really good at helping people who are hurt, so you don't have to be scared. He's going to help your mom." She sent up a quick prayer for God to guide Jared's hands.

"Where are they taking her?"

Kayla bit her lip. "They're going to bring her to the hospital to get her more help."

"What about me?" The girl sounded so lost that Kayla wanted to sweep her into her arms. But she didn't want to scare her more. The truth was, she had no idea what would happen to the girl now.

"Can you stay with her?" Jared called as they reached the shoulder with the stretcher. "Ethan's on his way in another rig. He's going to want to check the girl. And the police are going to need your statement." They slid the stretcher into the ambulance.

"Of course." The words were barely out of her mouth before Jared climbed into the ambulance, pulling the door closed behind him seconds before the ambulance roared off, its sirens shrieking and lights flashing in the gathering dusk.

"Mommy." Ruby's voice cracked, and this time Kayla leaned over to pull her into a hug.

"It will be okay. We'll go see her in a few minutes." She didn't know where the *we* had come from. But she *did* know she wasn't leaving this little girl until she knew Ruby wouldn't be alone.

A police car and a second ambulance rolled to a stop, and Nate and Violet's friend Ethan jumped out of the ambulance and jogged toward them, a police officer close behind.

"Hi, Kayla." He squatted next to her wheelchair and looked at the girl in Kayla's arms. "Who's your friend?"

"This is Ruby." Kayla shifted so Ethan could get a better view of the girl.

"Hi, Ruby. How old are you? Wait—" He held up a finger. "Don't tell me. Twenty."

"I'm seven." The girl giggled, and Kayla could have hugged Ethan. She supposed knowing how to comfort kids came with the territory, since he was a dad.

"Seven?" Ethan feigned shock. "You're way too brave to be seven. Does anything hurt?"

The girl shook her head, and Ethan pulled out a pen light and shined it into her eyes, then unwound the stethoscope from around his neck. After listening to her heart and checking her pulse, he felt her arms, legs, and head. "Well, it looks like you're as healthy as a horse."

The girl giggled again.

Instead of getting up, Ethan settled onto the gravel, as if he were going to stay for a chat. The police officer, who had been examining the crashed car, came up behind him. "Can you tell me what happened?"

"Mommy was driving me home from riding lessons, and I was asking for ice cream." Guilt flooded the girl's face again, and Kayla rubbed her back. "And she said my name, and then she grabbed her head like this—" Ruby lifted her hands to her temples and squeezed her head. "And then she drove off the road."

"Did she say anything else after that?" Ethan asked.

Ruby shook her head. "I kept calling for her, but she wouldn't answer me. I prayed that God would send someone to help us. And he did."

Kayla let out a shaky breath. *Is that why you brought me here right now, Lord?*

"He sure did." Ethan glanced at Kayla with a quick smile, but his eyes were somber. She wanted to ask what he was thinking but didn't want to scare the girl. Ethan hopped up from the ground and held out a hand to Ruby. "Want to take a ride in my ambulance?"

Ruby looked to Kayla. "Can you come with me?"

"Of course." She had no idea if that was allowed or not, but one way or another, she was sticking with this girl.

"Actually, I need you to stay and give your statement," the officer chimed in.

"I don't want to go without Kayla." Tears splattered onto the little girl's cheeks.

Kayla turned to Ethan. "Can you wait a few minutes?"

Ethan nodded. "For my friend Ruby? Of course."

"Let's go over here." The officer gestured toward his car, and Kayla followed, making sure to give Ruby a reassuring thumbs-up over her shoulder.

After she'd recounted how the car had gone off the road, the officer lowered his voice, asking, "And was the driving erratic before the incident? Crossing the center line, changing speed abruptly . . ."

Kayla bit her lip. "The car was going a little slowly, but nothing erratic that I noticed."

The officer gave a knowing nod. "Probably drunk," he muttered.

Kayla's heart sank. She had only too much experience of the cost of drunk driving. But she didn't want to believe that any mother would drive drunk with her child in the back seat.

An overwhelming desire to protect the girl overcame her. "What will happen to Ruby?"

The officer shrugged. "We'll notify family. I found the mother's phone, but she doesn't have any emergency contacts listed. Hopefully, the little girl knows her dad's name. Otherwise, it could take a bit to track someone down."

They made their way back to Ethan and Ruby, who had Ethan's stethoscope tucked into her ears and was holding it to her own heart. She pulled it off and looked up as Kayla and the officer reached them. "Can we go see Mommy now?"

"Yes. But I need to call your dad to have him meet you at the hospital," the officer said. "Do you know his name?"

Ruby shook her head. "I don't have a daddy."

The officer nodded, as if he'd suspected as much. "What about your grandma and grandpa?"

"My grandma and grandpa are in heaven."

Kayla's heart melted a little more for the poor girl. "How about an aunt or uncle or—"

The girl brightened. "I have an uncle!"

"Yeah?" Kayla reached to squeeze her hand. "That's good. What's his name?"

"Uncle Cam." Pride filled the girl's voice. Cam must be some uncle.

"Do you know where he lives? Close to here?"

"Far away, Mommy said. That's why he doesn't come to visit."

The radio on the officer's shoulder crackled to life, and a voice spewed out some codes Kayla didn't understand. The officer closed his eyes for a second, shaking his head. "I need to get to that. Take her to the hospital and have them contact child services to start processing her. We'll try to track down the uncle, but we don't have much to go on . . ."

"Wait." Kayla pointed to the phone in his hand. "Ruby, does your mom have your uncle's phone number?"

Ruby shrugged. "I think so."

"It's locked," the officer said, before speaking into his radio to say he was en route to the next emergency. He passed the phone to Ethan. "Have them give it to CPS. Maybe they can get someone to unlock it and track down the uncle." With that, he dashed for his car, taking off in a spray of gravel a second later.

"All right. Ready for that super cool ambulance ride?" Ethan turned to Ruby, who gave Kayla an uncertain look.

"Will you come with me?"

"I can't leave my car here, but I'll be right behind you, okay?"

As Ruby nodded, Kayla's eyes fell on the phone in Ethan's hand. "Ruby, do you know your birthday?"

Ruby gave a proud nod. "Yep. April 10."

Kayla held out her hand for the phone, then quickly tapped 0410 on the lock screen, letting out a sound of triumph as the phone unlocked. She held it up to show Ethan, then quickly scrolled through the contacts until she came to the name Cam.

She glanced at Ethan. "I'll make the call, then meet you at the hospital." She had a feeling this wasn't the kind of conversation a little girl should overhear.

"You're sure you want to make the call? We have people who can—"

Kayla shook her head. She didn't know why she felt it was important that she be the one to call, but she did. It was like the moment she'd opened Ruby's car door, she'd forged a connection with her. She felt responsible for whatever happened to her next.

Ethan studied her for a moment, then nodded and led Ruby to the ambulance.

Kayla waited until it pulled onto the road, then drew in a breath and tapped the number.

Hopefully in the next three seconds she'd receive some divine insight into how to tell a complete stranger that his sister had been in an accident.

Chapter 2

What was wrong with him? Tonight was a big night. Cameron should be content, if not ecstatic.

He took in the spacious living room of his boss's mansion—big enough to fit three of the houses he grew up in.

The place was packed with mingling and laughing people, all of them here to congratulate Cameron on the multi-million dollar merger he'd just brokered.

The truth was, he would have preferred a small celebration to this over-the-top soiree. But George Holt had a flair for the dramatic. And putting up with the party was a small price to appease George. If Cameron played his cards right and continued to oversee deals like this, the law firm of Holt, Barrow, and Wright would someday be Holt, Barrow, Wright, and Moore. Maybe sooner, if tonight went well.

"Are you ready?" His girlfriend Danielle leaned over him, her hand coming to his pocket, where she knew very well the little ring box was, given that she'd put it there herself.

He nudged her hand away. "I'm ready." He blew out a breath, trying to figure out why he felt sicker and sicker the closer they came to this moment.

It was the next logical step. The key to his future: perfect job, perfect promotion, perfect life.

He only felt sick because they were doing this so publicly. If he had his way, he'd ask Danielle at a small, intimate meal, with candles on the table and soft music playing in the background. But like her father, Danielle preferred drama and attention.

He swallowed down the agitation in his stomach and touched the box in his pocket.

"You're sure you don't want to use my mother's ring?" He knew better than to ask again, but he had to try one more time.

Danielle made a face. "We've had this conversation a thousand times, Cameron. The diamond in that ring is barely visible."

"It was all my dad could afford at the time," he muttered. "It has sentimental value."

Danielle laughed. "Not to me. I never met your parents, remember?"

Cameron bit his tongue before he could lash at her that that was because they were *dead*.

"Lucky for me—" She batted her fingertip against his nose. "*You* can afford more. Anyway, you already bought this one. Let me see it again."

With a sigh, he pulled it out of his pocket and discreetly opened it to reveal the three-carat round cut ring she had picked out.

She smiled, then whispered for him to put it away before he ruined the big moment.

As he tucked the ring back into his pocket, it hit him—he was about to tie himself to this woman forever. And suddenly he knew he couldn't do it.

It wasn't so much that he was afraid of commitment. But he *was* afraid of committing to the wrong person. And right now, he was afraid that might be Danielle.

He swallowed hard, then leaned closer to her. "Danielle, I think we need to—"

"Excuse me, everyone." George's voice boomed from the top of the high balcony that overlooked the living room, and Danielle gripped Cameron's arm.

"This is it," she whispered, her breath too hot in his ear.

"But I need to talk—"

She hushed him with a wave of her hand.

"Thank you all so much for coming tonight to celebrate my protege, Cameron Moore," George was saying from the balcony.

Hearty applause broke out across the room, and Cameron lifted a hand in thanks. He needed a way out. Right. Now.

"When my daughter first brought Cameron home, I thought he was going to be some young punk who didn't stand a chance—at the firm or with my daughter." Laughter echoed off the marble staircase. "But with this deal, Cameron has more than proved he deserves his place in the firm." He cut off as a ringtone blared into the room. It took Cameron a moment to realize it was coming from his own pocket.

"Sorry." He fumbled in the pocket of his suit coat for the phone, not managing to get his hands on it until it had blasted its brassy beat into the room two more times. He nabbed the button to dismiss the call and tucked the phone as discreetly as possible back into his pocket.

Danielle gave him a withering look, but her father laughed. "On the clock even now, eh, Cameron? This guy would do anything short of sell his soul to get a deal done." A smattering of laughter rippled across the room.

The blare sounded from Cameron's pocket again.

Oh, for Pete's sake.

This time he managed to snatch it out of his pocket on the first attempt.

"Silence it," Danielle hissed from next to him.

He nodded, scrolling to the volume settings and setting it to vibrate instead. As he did, he gave a cursory glance at the number of the missed calls.

Bethany.

His stomach turned. He hadn't realized he still had his sister's number in his phone. He hadn't spoken to her in ten years or more. And he'd gone through at least half a dozen phones in that time. Apparently, her number had followed him from one to the next.

"What do you say we get the man of the hour up here?" George called. "I believe he has an announcement of his own that might make us closer . . . But I'd better stop talking before I steal his thunder."

Danielle squeezed Cameron's arm tighter. "This is going to be amazing," she whispered, nudging him toward the stairway and putting on a bland look so she could pretend to be surprised when he pulled out the ring.

"I really think we should talk—"

But Danielle shoved him harder. "Don't embarrass me, Cameron." She managed to get the words out without moving a muscle of the smile plastered to her lips.

He swallowed dryly. He could do this. Danielle was the right woman for him. He just had a momentary case of cold feet. Perfectly normal.

As he stood, his phone jangled against his chest, a muffled vibrating sound coming from under his coat.

Danielle's eyes shot fire. "I told you to silence it." Again, her lips didn't move even a fraction.

"I did," he whispered back, pulling the phone out. His sister's number again.

Three calls in a row after a decade of no contact. A rock settled in his stomach. Something was wrong, that much he was certain of.

And as much as he didn't owe her a single thing—not even a simple phone call—he couldn't ignore it.

"So, without further ado, I give you Cameron Moore." George's voice was muted as Cameron's heart pounded in his ears.

"I'm sorry." Cameron whispered the words to Danielle. "I have to take this." He slipped past her and out the massive front door, vaguely aware that George was calling after him.

The LA night was cool, but a prickly sweat broke out on his forehead as he answered.

"Bethany." He made his voice hard, unyielding, even as a tiny part of him—the part that had worshiped his big sister as a child—let off the tiniest glimmer of hope. "This had better be important. I swear, if you need—"

"I'm sorry." A woman's voice, tentative but calm and sounding nothing like Bethany, came through the phone. "Is this Cam Moore?"

Cameron dropped onto the sprawling stairway, leaning his head against the wrought-iron railing. He'd always known this day was coming. Ever since the first time he'd caught Bethany sticking a needle in her arm. Thought sometimes that she deserved it, actually. But that didn't mean he was ready for it.

"This is Cameron, yes. Who is this? Where's Bethany?" The questions came out oddly croaky.

"This is Kayla Benson. I'm sorry to have to tell you this, but your sister was in an accident."

He couldn't pull in air. Couldn't exhale what was already in his lungs. So he just sat there, lungs burning.

"Um. Are you still there?" The voice on the other end of the phone was overly gentle.

"Is she dead?" They were the first words he could think of.

"The doctors are working on her now. They don't know if . . ."

"They don't know if she'll make it." He nodded, his heart suddenly turning to stone. He'd always figured that one day Bethany would take things too far, that she'd end up costing herself her own life. The same way she'd cost their father and mother their lives. "Was she high?"

The woman made a strange sound, and Cameron couldn't tell whether it was a denial or an affirmation. Not that it mattered.

"I can stay with your niece until you get here."

"My niece? What niece?" Cameron tried to process the word. If he had a niece, then that meant Bethany had . . . a daughter? Was that even possible?

"Yes. Ruby. I said I'd stay with her until you could get here."

"Get there?" Why did he feel suddenly like a parrot, unable to form his own sentences?

"Yes. How long do you think that will be?"

Cameron's head cleared suddenly. Bethany had brought this all on herself. It was too bad she'd decided to bring a little girl into it too, but that wasn't his problem. He had his own life. And it had nothing to do with Bethany. "Look, I'm kind of in the middle of something here. I need to go."

"What about Ruby?"

He rubbed his face, remembering suddenly that Ruby had been the name of the doll he'd bought at a garage sale and given to Bethany for her tenth birthday. He'd only been five at the time and hadn't realized until years later that Bethany had no longer played with dolls by then—but even so, she'd kept it in her bed long enough that her friends had teased her about it. To which she'd always answer that it was special.

But just because his sister had named her daughter after a doll didn't obligate him to care. "I don't know. What about the kid's dad?"

"She doesn't have one."

Cameron curled a lip. What did he expect? But that still didn't make the kid his problem.

"You'll have to find someone else, then. Thanks for the call." He pulled the phone away from his ear.

"Wait. No." The woman's shout was loud enough for him to hear even with the phone three feet away.

He lifted it again. "I can send some money. Would that help?"

"Money?" Disgust dripped off the woman's words. "The girl's mother is in the hospital, she has nowhere to go, and you think money is going to fix it?"

In his experience, money fixed most things. Which was why he worked so hard to earn it. "You can hire someone to watch her. Or you can watch her—use the money for whatever you need."

"Me?" The woman sounded incredulous. "She doesn't even know me. I just happened to witness the accident. She needs *family*. And as far as I can tell, that's you."

Family. He almost snorted. His sister had never understood the meaning of that word. Anyway, he was no more family to this girl than this Kayla person was.

"Look, Cam, I know I don't know you or your situation," the woman was saying now. "But I have to believe you know the right thing to do is to be here for your niece."

"You're right." He pushed to his feet. "You don't know my situation. And you have no right to expect me to— I didn't ask you to call me."

"She's a little girl, Cam." Kayla's voice was equally heated. "She didn't ask for this either. And she doesn't get a say in what happens next. Unlike you."

Something hit Cameron in the gut. He'd felt helpless like that once. Like all these things were happening around him that he had no control over. And even if that had been Bethany's fault, was he going to take it out on a little girl?

He did some mental calculations. He could move a few meetings, maybe get George to cover for him for a few days. "I can be there on Monday."

"Monday? That's three days away." He couldn't tell if that was disgust or amazement in her voice. "Where's she going to go until then?"

"I don't know. What do you want me to do, just drop everything?"

"That's exactly what I want you to do. Your niece needs you *now*."

He let out a sharp breath. Something about the idea of being needed did him in. He shook his head even as the words came out of his mouth. "Yeah. Okay." He dropped his chin to his chest. "Where is she?"

"At the hospital in Hope Springs."

"*Where?*" He'd never heard of the place.

"Hope Springs." She repeated the name louder, as if maybe he hadn't heard her the first time.

"What state is that in?"

"Wisconsin. You really don't know where your sister lives?"

The door behind Cameron opened, and he turned to find Danielle barreling down on him, fire flaring from her eyes. He made what he hoped was an apologetic face and held up a finger, turning his back on her as he spoke into the phone again. "I'll catch the next flight I can, but I probably won't get there until early morning. Can you stay with her until then?"

"I'll stay with her." Kayla's voice was gentle. "You're doing the right thing."

He shook his head. He highly doubted that anyone else would see it that way.

Least of all himself.

Or Danielle, judging by the anger pulsing across her face the moment he hung up.

She crossed her arms in front of her. "We'll skip over the part where I was totally humiliated for a moment. Where exactly are you going?"

"My sister was in an accident, and I have to go to Wisconsin to take care of my niece." Cameron reached for her, but she jerked away. He sighed. He wasn't necessarily a hugger, but right now he felt so mixed up that a little bit of comfort would go a long way.

"What are you talking about? You don't have any family."

No family that he cared to acknowledge anyway. "My sister and I haven't talked in years. I didn't know I had a niece until just now." That part still didn't seem real. None of this did.

"So why do you have to go then?" Danielle pursed her full lips. "They obviously don't mean very much to you if you've never even met your niece."

"No. I know. But they're still my family. I feel like I have to go." He couldn't explain even to himself why he felt that way. Bethany had never brought him anything but heartbreak, so why he felt any obligation whatsoever was beyond him. All he knew was that he couldn't shake what Kayla had said about his niece needing family.

He'd known that need more than once in his life.

"This is just something I have to do. I'll be back before you know it. I'll go, get things sorted out, find someone who can take care of the girl, and then I'll be back."

"And we'll have an even bigger party and do this." She raised an eyebrow and wiggled her ring finger.

The slither of doubt from earlier went through him again, but he pushed it aside. Maybe some time away was what he needed. A chance to put things in perspective. To realize he just had cold feet.

Absence made the heart grow fonder, wasn't that what they always said?

He leaned to kiss her cheek, but she turned away at the last second.

He shrugged. He didn't have time for her drama. "I'll be back before you know it. Tell your father I'll manage everything remotely. I'll call Mary to set it up." His secretary was a whiz at things like that.

He turned and marched down the steps, toward what, he didn't even know.

Family, he supposed.

Chapter 3

So this was where his sister had ended up.

Cameron scrubbed at his face, glancing at the clock on the dashboard of the budget line sedan he'd picked up at the airport. Not his usual wheels, but apparently it was the best they could do on short notice in this backwater.

Four a.m.

In the dark, the little town was completely still, except for the rhythmic in and out of the waves along the shore of what his phone's GPS told him was Lake Michigan. He wouldn't have figured the sleepy town as Bethany's kind of place. How had she even found it, let alone come to live here?

He followed his phone's directions to the hospital, where he pulled into a parking spot, then just sat. Exhaustion had set in on the plane, but he hadn't been able to sleep, his thoughts swirling between Danielle, Bethany, his parents, the woman on the phone—and even the niece he'd never met. He hadn't even thought to ask how old she was.

Well, sitting here wasn't going to get this over with any faster. He shoved his door open and stepped into the morning dark, a shiver immediately working its way up his spine as a sharp wind cut through the dress shirt he hadn't bothered to change out of before rushing to the airport. He ducked back into the car and grabbed his suit coat. At least it helped cut the wind a tad. If he was going to be here more than a day or two, he'd have to invest in a winter jacket.

But hopefully it wouldn't come to that.

He'd find his niece and make arrangements for her, then get back to his normal life.

With Danielle?

Of course with Danielle.

He'd realized on the plane that cold feet were only a feeling. And he well knew that feelings couldn't be trusted.

Logic could.

And his relationship with Danielle was nothing if not logical. She was as ambitious and as dedicated to the firm as he was. She understood the long hours and the constant interruptions. And, like him, she didn't want a family. Their relationship made sense.

See? Already the trip had given him some perspective. That was all he'd needed. Now he could get things figured out here and go home and continue to live his life as he'd planned.

He pushed through the hospital's revolving door, and a wave of memories assaulted him—powerful enough to stop him in his tracks for a moment. Dad. The ambulance. The sirens. The doctors shaking their heads. Mom's desperate cry. And Bethany nowhere to be found.

He shook the thoughts off and made his way to the front desk, where a much too bubbly receptionist directed him to the ICU. A minute later, he stepped off the elevator and strode past the empty counter toward the open waiting room door. A dark-haired woman sat on a worn-looking couch on the far side of the room. His eyes went to the young girl—maybe three or four years old, though he had no experience guessing children's ages—lying on the couch next to her. With blonde hair framing her face and a pert upturned nose, the kid was the spitting image of a young Bethany. At least he knew he was in the right place.

"You must be Kayla."

"Shh. She just fell asleep." The woman shot him a dirty look, her whisper scolding. "She's exhausted."

"All right." He lowered his voice. "I'll take her off your hands."

Kayla gave him a doubtful look. What did she want—identification?

"Bethany is out of surgery, but she's in a coma." Her voice was laced with sympathy. "I can stay with Ruby while you talk to the doctor."

"I don't see any doctors around, do you?"

"If you wait a minute, I'm sure they'll—"

He gave an impatient shake of his head. He wasn't ready to deal with whatever had happened. Or with what would happen next. "I'll call later and talk to someone."

He closed the distance to the couch but stopped abruptly as he reached them. How was he supposed to wake the girl up? Shake her? Shout at her? Turn on his phone alarm and let it blare in her ear?

"Can you wake her up, please?" He didn't know why he was still whispering if he wanted the girl to wake up.

Kayla looked at him as if he were crazy. "Don't wake her up. She's been through a lot."

"How am I supposed to get her to my car then?"

"Carry her." She said it like it was the most obvious answer in the world.

He sighed, studied Ruby's still form, then slid his hands under her and lifted. She was heavier than he'd expected, and he grunted.

The girl curled into him, her head coming to rest on his arm. For some reason, the movement made all of this way too real, and Cam nearly staggered with the fact that he was suddenly responsible for keeping another human being alive. He drew in a slow, quiet breath. If he could finesse deals with multi-million dollar companies, surely he could manage one little girl for a few days.

"Where am I going?" he asked Kayla.

"Oh, uh." Kayla pulled out her phone and tapped a few times. "I asked Ruby for her address before. It's 301 Southridge Court."

He gave her a blank look.

"I'm headed that direction anyway. Why don't you follow me, and I'll lead you to the house?"

He could only stare at her, baffled by why this complete stranger who had already given up her entire night was now offering to do more. But his niece wasn't getting any lighter in his arms. And all he really wanted right now was to find a bed and crash. "All right. Thanks."

She nodded, and he turned toward the door, angling his body so he wouldn't bash Ruby's legs—or her head—on the doorframe. He was all the way to the elevator when he realized Kayla wasn't behind him. He considered getting on it without her, but after all she'd done, that seemed too rude. Besides the fact that he hadn't written that address down.

Readjusting his grip on Ruby, he tromped back to the waiting room, stopping in the door as his eyes fell on Kayla using her arms to push her body up and off the couch and into a wheelchair that he'd only vaguely registered before. When she was seated, she lifted first one foot then the other and placed them on the chair's footrest. Her hands went to the rims of the wheels, and she spun the chair toward him.

"Ready?" Her voice was still hushed, her smile calm, as if she hadn't done anything out of the ordinary.

He nodded mutely and stepped back from the door to let her through.

But as he followed her onto the elevator, he couldn't help but wonder. Who *was* this Kayla woman?

The elevator lurched to a stop, and Kayla rolled out, glancing over her shoulder to make sure Cam was following. Ruby's head lolled against his arm—they'd make a cute picture if it weren't for the fact that Cam looked as if he'd rather be anywhere but here. Since the moment he'd walked into the waiting room upstairs, looking like a slightly rumpled version of a guy straight from the pages of *Forbes* or *GQ*, Kayla had been questioning her decision to call him. Everything from his suit to his stance to his surly expression exuded power. He was the kind of man who was used to getting his way. The kind of man who would run right over you if he had to.

Show a little grace, she scolded herself. She didn't even know the man.

As they exited the hospital into the dark of the early morning, weariness pulled on Kayla's eyelids, and she suddenly realized how tired she was. All she wanted was to get to Nate and Vi's and plop onto their guest bed—but not until she saw Ruby safely settled in.

"I'm parked over here." She gestured to the handicapped spots near the doors.

She waited for the usual, surprised, "You drive?" but Cam simply nodded.

"I'm over there." He bobbed his head toward the next row. "I'll pull up behind you."

"Okay." Kayla moved toward her car. "Make sure you put her in the back seat. And put a seat belt on her."

Cam stopped, looking as if he was about to say something, then shook his head and strode off, his back still rigid.

Ten minutes later, Kayla pulled up to the address Ruby had given her. The house was small but cute—at least from what she could tell in the dim streetlights. As Cam's car pulled in next to hers, she grabbed her wheelchair and assembled it, then transferred into it. By the time she was done, Cam had extracted the still-sleeping Ruby from his car.

"How do we get in?" His half-whisper cut through the dark.

Kayla held up the keys the police had pulled out of Bethany's car. Thankfully, there were only two on the key chain, so they wouldn't have to spend all morning figuring out which one it was.

Cam readjusted Ruby to hold out a hand for the keys, and Kayla started to pass them to him, then hesitated. What would the little girl think when she woke up with a strange man in her house? Would that add to the trauma she'd already experienced?

"Maybe I should come in with you. Just until Ruby wakes up. So she won't be scared when she sees you."

She thought she heard a low chuckle in the dark, but it could have been a bird. "Am I that scary?"

Maybe. But Kayla didn't let the word slip off her tongue. "She's been through a lot today. Waking up to a strange man in her house probably isn't going to help."

"Suit yourself. Can we just get inside? It's freezing out here. And she's not exactly a feather."

Kayla snorted. She highly doubted the broad man was having any trouble carrying his tiny niece. But she wheeled toward the front door. Fortunately, the doorway was at ground level, and she didn't have to worry about getting onto a porch in the dark. She slid the key into the lock and turned, grateful when it opened on the first try. She rolled back, gesturing for Cam to pass through with Ruby.

Kayla followed, popping up over the low doorframe with ease and nudging the door closed behind her.

"I can't see a thing," Cam muttered.

Kayla felt along the wall for a light switch. When her fingers fell on it, she flicked it tentatively. A weak light that didn't quite fill the space revealed that they had walked into a small, cozy living room.

"Do you want to put her on the couch for now?" Kayla whispered, pointing to the worn sofa along the far wall.

Cam didn't answer but moved toward the couch and lowered Ruby onto it.

Then he strode out of the room, into what Kayla assumed must be the kitchen. She stared after him for a moment, then let her eyes rove the living room. There wasn't much furniture: just a couch, a large, cushy armchair, a single side table with a small lamp on it—the only source of light in the room as far as Kayla could tell—and a small TV.

Kayla's gaze fell on a blanket crumpled next to a dollhouse made from a cardboard box, and she wheeled toward it, reaching down occasionally to scoot a toy out of her way.

She picked up the blanket and brought it to the couch, draping it over the girl and brushing her hair off her face. Something raw and maternal stirred in her middle, but Kayla pushed it away. It wasn't that she wanted her own child—it was just that she knew the challenges this girl was in for in the days ahead.

Please let her mother live, Lord. She'd been saying the prayer all night, but it had an extra urgency now that she'd met Ruby's uncle. Clearly he wasn't an ideal candidate to raise her.

A low clunking came from the kitchen, and Kayla lifted her head, listening. After a second, there was another clunk. And then another. It almost sounded as if someone was opening and closing cupboards. She supposed Cameron might be looking for some food. Her own stomach was rumbling as well.

She gave Ruby's hair one last stroke, then wheeled toward the kitchen.

Sure enough, Cam was opening cupboard doors, rummaging through the contents, then closing the doors again.

When he'd opened the third cupboard, Kayla spoke up. "You're going to wake Ruby. What are you searching for?"

Cam threw her a dark look and opened the next cupboard. "Bethany's stash."

"Stash of what?"

"Drugs." He lifted out a stack of plates and ran his hand along the back of the cupboard.

"Her tox screen was negative. It was a brain aneurysm." Which he'd know if he'd bothered to talk to the doctors.

Though she knew an aneurysm was life threatening, Kayla had been beyond relieved to learn that Ruby's mother hadn't been driving drunk.

Cam stilled with his hand on a cupboard door. Though his back was to her, she noticed the way his shoulders dipped.

But then his back stiffened again. "That doesn't mean she doesn't have a stash." He opened the last cupboard, shoved the glasses aside, then closed it.

"Didn't find anything?" Kayla didn't know why she felt vindicated. It wasn't like she knew Bethany. But the way her brother seemed so dead set on believing the worst of her made Kayla want to stick up for her.

"She must keep them somewhere else." Cam turned his back on her and stalked into the hallway, which she assumed led to the bedrooms and bathroom.

Kayla watched his retreating form for a moment, then shrugged and made her way back to the living room. He could go on his witch hunt all he wanted. All she cared about was that Ruby wasn't alone and scared when she woke up.

In the living room, Kayla gave the couch a longing look. She ached to lie down and go to sleep herself. But there really wasn't room for her on there with Ruby already sprawled across it.

She shifted in her wheelchair, making herself as comfortable as possible, then tucked her chin to her chest and let herself close her eyes.

Chapter 4

The house was a shoebox, and Cameron had prowled every last inch of it. Still, he hadn't found his sister's stash.

Which meant either Bethany had gotten better at hiding it or—

Or she was clean.

He didn't know why that thought left him unnerved. Maybe because it was too late. The damage was already done.

As he crept back to the living room, his eyes fell on the window. Outside, streaks of peach and lavender had just started their slow crawl across the sky. Cameron rubbed at his aching temples. He needed sleep. Badly.

But there was nowhere to lie down, unless he wanted to use his sister's bed. His eyes traveled to the ratty old couch, where Ruby was still asleep, a blanket now draped over her—courtesy of Kayla, he supposed. Which only went to prove that she'd be a much better caregiver for Ruby than he was.

His gaze flicked to Kayla in her wheelchair. Her head was tucked into her shoulder, and her eyes were closed, but he couldn't tell if she was sleeping or just resting. He wondered again what she was doing here. Why she was helping them. Why he was letting her.

Maybe because he had no earthly idea how to take care of a kid. He supposed he had to feed it and water it, but beyond that, what was he supposed to do?

Bethany had better recover quickly so he didn't have to worry about it.

What if she doesn't recover? The nagging voice had been tugging at his brain since Kayla had said the word aneurysm. He was no doctor, but an aneurysm was a pretty big deal, as far as he knew. *What if she died?*

He shoved the thought away. More than once over the years, he'd thought about how much better his family's life would have been if that had happened long ago—before she'd cost them everything. But he'd never really meant it.

And if she died now, he'd be saddled with a kid he didn't want.

With a ragged sigh, he rubbed at his cheek—Danielle would hate how scruffy it was—and fell into the oversized armchair, which nearly swallowed him. He was so tired it didn't matter.

It felt like two minutes later when a sound jolted his eyes open. Something warm weighted his legs down, and he glanced at his lap to find a white cat curled on his black pants. He gave it a hard shove, and it flew off his lap with a protesting meow.

"Mommy." The voice was small and plaintive, and it took Cameron a minute to remember where he was, to figure out that it must be his niece talking.

"It's okay, Ruby. You're at home now." Kayla's voice was low and soothing. "I came with you. And your Uncle Cam is here too."

"Uncle Cam?" Ruby turned her wide eyes on him, and he realized with a start that in place of Bethany's dark eyes she had his silvery-blue eye color.

"Cameron." The correction came out automatically. Danielle hated the nickname, so he'd stopped using it.

Kayla's eyes darted to his, filled with disapproval. Well, what? It was his name—he had a right to be called what he wanted.

"Where's Mommy?" The little girl's lip trembled, but she didn't cry.

"She's still at the hospital, sweetie." Kayla reached for the girl's hand. "The doctors are still helping her."

"When will they be done?" The girl's hair stood up in funny tufts, and for a moment, Cameron had a flash of Bethany at that age, all fun and innocence. He missed that girl sometimes.

Kayla tugged the girl closer to her, throwing a desperate look at Cameron.

He shrugged at her. It wasn't like he knew what to do.

"Do you want some breakfast?" Kayla asked the girl.

"Then can we go see Mommy?"

"Of course," Kayla started, but Cameron cut in with a flat, "No."

Ruby broke into tears, and Kayla sent her to the kitchen, promising to be there in a moment, then turned to regard him.

"What?" He crossed his arms. Why did he feel like he had to be on the defensive? She was the one intruding in his life, which until last night had been perfectly ordered.

"You're not going to take her to see her mom?" Her voice was quiet but seething.

"I've got a lot to do." Namely finding Ruby's father so he could take responsibility for his kid and Cameron could go home.

"Are you at least going to go over there yourself? I could stay with Ruby if you want—"

But he cut her off. "I'll call the doctor later."

"She's your sister." Kayla bit her lip as if she hadn't meant to say the words. "Sorry. It's none of my business."

He nodded. That was the truth.

"Do you want me to stay to help with breakfast?" Her voice was less forceful now, but he could see the effort it cost her.

Yes, actually. He wanted her to stay and do all of it. But he really had no desire to spend more time with her. He shook his head, skirting her wheelchair and making his way to the front door. He pulled it open. "Thanks again. I've got it."

She pressed her lips together as she watched him, as if trying to decide whether he could be trusted to care for the girl. But after a moment she called, "Ruby, I need to go. I'll see you soon."

He raised an eyebrow. He had no plans to make Kayla a regular visitor here.

"Bye, Kayla." Ruby came charging into the room and threw her arms around Kayla, who squeezed her back as if Ruby were her own niece.

Then Kayla rolled silently past him and did a quick wheelie over the doorframe.

He closed the door behind her, then blew out a long breath.

Now what?

"I mean, he acted like it was all one big inconvenience that he couldn't be bothered with." Kayla blew a piece of hair off her forehead as she helped unbox a set of Victorian silhouettes for Vi's antique shop. "And the way he treated Ruby—I don't think he said a word to her. Oh wait— I take that back. He corrected her when she called him Cam. Apparently he goes by Cameron." She rolled her eyes. Because clearly his name was the most important thing right now.

"Maybe he's not around kids much," Vi offered, rubbing a hand over her own adorably rounded belly.

"Yeah, maybe," Kayla mumbled. She should try to assume the best of him, she knew that. But something about him made that nearly impossible.

"And he acted like he didn't even care that his sister is in a coma. He doesn't plan to visit her. Or to take Ruby." So much for assuming the best of him. But she couldn't help it. Circumstances had prevented Nate from seeing her when she was in the hospital, but she knew he would have given anything to be at her side.

"Everyone deals with trauma in their own way," Vi said calmly.

Kayla blew out a breath. She knew Vi was right. Kayla had reacted to her own accident with anger in the early years, while Vi had dealt with the death of her first husband by refusing to move on for a long time.

"You're right," she murmured, turning her attention back to the silhouettes. She came across one of a mother pushing a baby carriage. "You should hang this in the baby's room."

Vi took it from her with a smile. "I can't believe this is finally happening." It was true, apparently, what they said about a pregnant woman's glow, as Vi's cheeks were practically radiant.

Kayla reached to squeeze her hand. "You two are going to be the best parents. And I'm going to spoil your kid rotten."

"He or she will be like you then." Nate strode into the store from the back room, and she stuck her tongue out at him. Laughing, he crossed the room and bent to give her a hug. "Sorry I missed you this morning. We had an early rehearsal. And as far as spoiling our kid, don't forget that turnabout is fair play."

"Good luck with that." He knew very well that she had no intention of having kids of her own. "Maybe I'll get a hamster someday and you can spoil that."

Nate and Vi exchanged a look, and she knew she was about to get the whole "never say never" lecture.

Fortunately, Vi's phone rang, cutting them off. As Vi answered it, Kayla took the opportunity to escape to the back room with the empty box. After she'd broken it down, she pulled out her phone. She'd put Cam's number in it last night, in case she needed to reach him while he was on the way. Maybe she should call him now and make sure he'd at least remembered to feed Ruby lunch.

Her finger was hovering over his name when Vi stepped into the room. "That was Jade."

Kayla tucked her phone discreetly back into her pocket.

"I told her about Bethany's accident. I guess Dan already knew. He went to visit Bethany this morning. And he said he'd check on Ruby tomorrow after church. So you can stop worrying."

"Oh, that's great." Knowing the pastor was going to check on Ruby took a weight off Kayla's mind.

But—

"What is it?" Vi eyed her, and Kayla had to laugh. Though she and her sister-in-law had only known each other for seven years, Vi knew her better than probably anyone else.

"I just hate the thought of Bethany being in the hospital alone, you know? Do you think it'd be weird if I went to visit her, considering she's a complete stranger?"

"Yes." Nate popped into the room. "But when have you ever let that stop you?"

"Hey." Kayla wheeled across the room to slug her brother's arm. But she knew without a doubt that if she ever needed anything, Nate—and all his friends—would be there for her. It was too bad Bethany didn't seem to have a family like that.

Well, then we'll have to be her family. She pictured Cam's sour look when he'd said he didn't need any more help. *Whether Cam likes it or not.*

Chapter 5

"I'm bored."

Cameron ground his teeth as he looked up from the ratty old box he'd brought up from the basement. It was the three hundredth time Ruby had uttered those two words today. Somehow, they'd survived their first day together yesterday, mostly because he'd plunked her in front of the TV and told her not to bother him while he worked.

"Can we play checkers?"

Apparently TV only worked as a babysitter for one day.

"I'm busy."

"But Mommy says it's your favorite game."

Cameron set down the stack of useless papers, mildly surprised that Bethany had ever mentioned him. What else had she told the kid about their past? Had she mentioned that checkers had been her favorite too, until getting high had become more important than spending time with her little brother?

"It was my favorite when I was a kid. Not anymore."

The cat jumped on the table, and Cameron shoved it off with a snarl.

"What's your favorite now?"

"Working."

The cat jumped up again, and he shoved it harder this time.

"That's silly." Ruby came farther into the room. "What are you working on?"

Cameron eyed the papers in the box. When he'd called the hospital yesterday, the doctor had made it clear that the bleeding in Bethany's brain had been severe enough that there was a chance she'd never wake up—and even if she did, she might never be the same—which was why he'd been searching through paperwork since dawn. He needed to find Ruby's birth certificate or Bethany's will or . . . or *something* that would lead him to a better guardian for his niece. And allow him to get back to his life.

So far, he'd found nothing useful.

"Did your mom ever tell you anything about your dad?"

Ruby shook her head, her blonde hair flying. "I don't have a daddy."

Cameron tried to hold back his exasperation. "Of course you have a dad. Everyone has a dad." Even him—even if his dad had died way too young, thanks to Bethany.

"Not me," Ruby said proudly. "The stork brought me."

Cameron rolled his eyes. *Way to teach the girl how the world works, Bethany.*

"What year were you born?" Maybe he could do some digging through public records.

The girl shrugged.

Was talking to little kids always this frustrating? "All right. How old are you?"

She gave a proud grin, revealing two missing bottom teeth. "I'm seven."

"Seven? Really?" Wow. He needed to work on his skill in judging ages. Then again, he didn't suppose he'd ever need it again.

"When can we visit Mommy?" Her grin fell away, replaced by pleading eyes.

Cameron nearly pulled his hair out. If she wasn't complaining she was bored, she was asking to visit Bethany. She couldn't seem to get it through her head that he had no plans to see his sister—at all.

"I don't know." He pushed the words out through gritted teeth. "Go watch TV."

"You're not as cool as Mommy said." Ruby flounced toward the living room.

Cameron snorted. Yeah, well, his sister wasn't as cool as he'd once thought either.

A light weight landed in his lap, and he looked down to find the stupid cat curling into a ball. The moment he shoved it off, it jumped back up.

"You really don't know when you're not wanted, do you?" But it wasn't worth the fight. He left it curled there as he pulled out his phone and scrolled through his calls from yesterday. Danielle had called three times, but he hadn't had the energy to call her back. He hit her number and waited, trying to figure out how to break it to her that he'd be here a few more days at least. But there was no answer. He hung up, wondering vaguely if she was still angry that he'd left. But what choice had he had?

He girded himself to dig into the paperwork again, but the doorbell rang. Rubbing a hand over his unshaven face, he pushed to his feet, sending the cat flying, and strode around Ruby's scattered toys to the front door. He'd have to have her clean those up later. He opened the door to find a man who was probably in his early thirties—about Cameron's own age.

"You must be Cam." The man held out his hand, but Cameron regarded him coolly. He had no interest in meeting his sister's latest supplier-boyfriend. That was the way it had always been with her. Though this guy didn't look the part, in his dress shirt and jeans, clean-cut hair, and clean-shaven face.

"I'm Cameron, yes."

The man withdrew his hand when Cameron didn't shake it. "I'm—"

"Pastor Dan!" Ruby shot straight past Cameron and out the door.

Pastor? Cameron felt his eyebrows raise. That would explain why the guy didn't look like a dealer. But what was Bethany doing hanging around with a pastor? Obviously, this pastor guy didn't know much about her life.

"Hey, Ruby." Pastor Dan smiled at the girl. "I was just visiting your mom, and I promised I'd come see you next."

"You saw my mommy? Did she say she misses me?"

Dan gave Cameron a look over the top of Ruby's head. "I did see her. She's pretty sleepy, so she couldn't talk to me, but I could talk to her. And I know she'd want me to tell you she loves you very much. How are you two doing?"

"I'm bored." Ruby pouted. "Uncle Cam won't play checkers with me."

"Maybe I could play a game with you? If it's okay with your uncle." Dan gave Cameron a questioning look.

Right, like Cameron didn't see right through the pastor's plan to get into the house so he could check up on them. But if it meant a few minutes of peace for him while the pastor played with Ruby, it would be worth it.

Besides, if anyone knew who Ruby's father was, it might be the pastor. He stepped aside and gestured for Dan to come into the house.

They moved into the kitchen, where Cameron poured two cups of coffee, passing one to Dan, who'd taken a seat next to the box of paperwork. Cameron leaned against the counter next to the sink, crossing his arms in front of him as he waited for an opening to talk to the pastor around Ruby's mile-a-minute commentary.

When Ruby was finally crowned champion—thanks to a couple of "mistakes" on Dan's part—Cameron sent her to her room to get dressed, though it was already two o'clock in the afternoon. Even with his limited interaction with kids, he was pretty sure the whole who-is-Ruby's-father conversation shouldn't happen in front of the girl.

"And try to wear something that matches this time," he called behind her. Unlike the wild purple flowery pants and orange striped shirt she'd worn yesterday.

When he heard her door click shut, Cameron sought for a way to bring up his question.

"Have you taken Ruby to visit Bethany?" Dan asked before Cameron could ease into a conversation.

He shook his head, his jaw tightening. He didn't need the preacher to tell him what he should or shouldn't be doing.

"I'm not going to lie, Bethany looks pretty rough with all those tubes and monitors," Dan said. "But it might do Ruby good to see her. As long as you're with her."

Cameron grunted, his shoulders tightening. That was not in the plans.

"Look. Do you know who Ruby's father is? Because he's the one who should be taking care of her. Especially if Bethany doesn't—" He closed his eyes. Saying the words was harder than he'd anticipated. He cleared his throat. "Doesn't wake up."

Dan watched him, as if trying to decide how to respond. "I realize this must have all come as quite a shock to you."

Cameron shrugged. Shock was one word for it. Burden, inconvenience, hardship—those were others. "Yeah, well, my sister and I aren't exactly close. I didn't even know I was an uncle."

"So maybe this is your chance to get to know your niece. I've only started meeting with her and Bethany recently, but she's a pretty fun kid."

"I'm sure she is." If there was such a thing. "But I've got a job to get back to." A life. And Bethany and Ruby weren't part of it.

Ruby sprang back into the room, dressed in a rainbow-striped sundress over a pair of thick jogging pants.

Cameron rolled his eyes. Hadn't Bethany taught the kid to dress herself like a normal person?

"Nice outfit," he muttered.

"This is Mommy's favorite dress." Ruby twirled. "She says it's because I'm her rainbow after the storm."

"I can see why." Dan pulled out the chair next to him and gestured for Ruby to sit. "I was going to say a prayer for your mom. Do you want to join me?"

Ruby nodded. "Can I say one too?"

"Of course." Dan gave Cameron a questioning look. "Join us?"

Cameron shook his head. He couldn't remember the last time he'd actually prayed, but even if he were a praying man, he wouldn't waste his prayers on Bethany.

Dan waited another moment, then folded his hands and ducked his head. Ruby did the same.

Cameron remained planted at the counter, shoulders knotting as Dan began the prayer. "Dear Lord, we come before you today on behalf of your daughter Bethany."

Cameron barely resisted the urge to laugh at that. Bethany was about as much a child of God as Judas had been.

But Dan continued his prayer. "You know her hurts, Lord, and you know how to heal them. We pray that you would do so quickly, so Bethany can get back to having fun with her Doodlebug."

Ruby giggled, and Cameron worked to steel his heart against the reminder that once upon a time Bethany had been a sweet little girl too.

"Your turn," Dan said to Ruby.

"Dear Jesus—" Ruby sounded sure, confident, as if she spoke to God all the time. "Please bless Mommy and help her get better. Thank you that Uncle Cam came here to take care of me. Please bless him and help him not to be so grumpy."

A laugh burst from Dan, but he covered it with a cough.

Cameron's arms pulled tighter across his chest, but he could feel a tiny muscle at the corner of his mouth trying to lift. He forced it down.

"And please help me be a good girl and listen to him. Even when I don't want to. Amen."

"Amen." The chuckle still sat in Dan's voice, and he looked to Cameron, making no effort to disguise his amusement. "No one prays quite like a kid."

Dan turned to Ruby. "I have to go, but I'm going to keep praying for your mom. And you pray too, okay?"

Ruby nodded and reset the checkerboard, though Cameron didn't know who she thought she was going to play with.

He followed Dan to the front door, where the pastor turned to him. "I don't know how much money Bethany has saved or anything, but obviously she's not going to be working for a while. The church has some funds for emergencies like this, if she needs help covering her bills . . ."

"I can take care of it." Cameron had no desire to be beholden to anyone, even a church, on his sister's behalf.

Dan gave him a shrewd look, as if he knew exactly what Cameron was thinking, but didn't say a word. "All right. Well, let me know if you need anything at all."

Cameron stepped outside with Dan. It was worth one more shot. "You're sure you don't know anything about Ruby's father? A name, a location, anything?"

Dan sighed. "Like I said, I've only been meeting with her for a couple months. She's never said anything about Ruby's dad. And I've never seen her with a man."

Cameron spiked his fingers into his hair. So basically, he was stuck with Ruby.

"Maybe instead of seeing this as an inconvenience, it might help to see it as a blessing. A chance to get to know your niece." Dan clasped his elbow for a second.

"I don't have time for that," Cameron insisted.

"Sometimes, what we think we need time for and what we really need time for are two different things. Fortunately, God seems to have a way of showing us which is which." And with that, the pastor was gone.

And Cameron was left staring after his vehicle, trying to figure out what his words had meant.

"Uncle Cam," Ruby called from the kitchen. "Want to play checkers now?"

"No." Cam closed the front door and stalked to Bethany's room, which he'd taken for his own.

He knew where he needed to spend his time—and it wasn't in Hope Springs.

But it looked like he was stuck here. For now.

Chapter 6

"I'm ready."

Cameron eyed Ruby. It'd been a relief to have her at school all day the last few days, even if packing her lunch and getting her out the door in the morning had taken all his problem-solving skills, especially when she couldn't find her left shoe this morning. He'd finally given up and sent her off wearing one pink shoe and one white one, figuring it at least complemented the rest of her mismatched outfit.

"Ready for what?" He took in the tan pants and cowboy boots she'd changed into. "The rodeo?"

Ruby giggled. "You're funny sometimes, Uncle Cam."

He smirked. He hadn't been trying to be funny.

"I'm ready for my riding lesson. Remember?"

He vaguely remembered her saying something about horses at dinner last night, but he'd been in the middle of reading work updates his secretary had sent. He glanced at the document open on his computer. It still needed plenty of attention. "I don't have time to take you tonight."

He finished typing the sentence he'd been in the middle of. Because of course she couldn't have waited for him to finish his thought before she interrupted him.

"I *have* to go. The parade is in less than two weeks, and Miss Emma said we all had to practice."

He neither knew nor cared who Miss Emma was or what she'd said. But Ruby looked at him, her eyes welling with tears she wouldn't let fall.

He growled to himself. If she started crying, he would have no idea what to do. He supposed he could work in the car while she did her horse thing.

"Fine. Get your coat."

Before he knew what was happening, Ruby flew across the room and threw her little arms around his shoulders as far as they'd go. "Thank you. You're the best."

Cameron just sat there. He'd never been hugged quite like this before. He cleared his throat. "All right, come on. Let's go."

Ruby removed her arms from around him, and he shoved his chair back, something odd still buzzing in his chest over her thank you hug.

His phone rang as he was grabbing his shoes, and he pulled it out of his pocket, stifling a groan as Danielle's name appeared on his screen. Not that he didn't want to talk to her, but their calls had become painfully familiar in the few days he'd been here: she'd ask when he was coming home, he'd say he didn't know, she'd go icy silent, he'd offer reassurances that he was doing everything he could to get back to her as soon as possible, and then they'd say goodbye. She wouldn't ask how his sister was doing. Wouldn't inquire about Ruby. Wouldn't even grill him about why he'd never mentioned his family to her.

He gave an irritated head shake. It wasn't like he wanted to share all of that with her—or with anyone, for that matter. And he surely didn't need or want her sympathy.

He considered letting the call go to voice mail, but that would only open its own can of worms with Danielle.

"Uncle Cam, I'm going to be late," Ruby called.

"Just a minute." He answered the call and lifted the phone to his ear, holding it in place with his shoulder as he tugged his shoe on. "Hey, baby." He worked to make his greeting sweet. "I only have a minute. I need to get the kid to riding lessons, apparently."

"Riding lessons?" Danielle's voice was spiked with icicles. "Oh, I wouldn't want to keep you from that. Obviously, that's much more important than anything I could have to say."

Cameron rolled his eyes but concentrated on injecting extra syrup into his response. "You know that's not what I meant, baby. I just mean I may have to call you back later."

"Don't bother." Danielle's voice switched from cold to businesslike. He wasn't sure which was worse. "Just write this down. While you've been playing house, I've been doing some actual investigating into Ruby's father. Barry Anderson, 176 Howley, Sharpesville, Wisconsin."

"Really?" Cameron jumped up from his chair and snatched a pencil and a sheet of paper covered with some sort of drawing off the counter. He flipped it over and scribbled down the information. "How did you find this?" He'd searched through every piece of paper in Bethany's house and had never come across the name. He'd even finally located Ruby's birth certificate, but no father was listed.

"Simple. I managed to get a report of her credit card activity for the last several years, which led me to an apartment complex in Sharpesville."

Cameron bit his tongue against pointing out how illegal that had been.

"And from there I called the apartment manager, who remembered a Bethany Moore. Said she hung out with this Barry guy a lot. I put two and two together . . ."

"So this guy may not be—" He lowered his voice in case Ruby was listening. Though he wasn't sure why he was trying to keep it from her that he was looking for her father. She'd find out sooner or later. Sooner if this lead proved to be good. "Ruby's father?"

"That's your job to figure out, Cameron. At least it's a lead. Which is more than you've gotten. Call me when you have more information."

The phone clicked dead before he could reply.

"Uncle Cam," Ruby marched back into the room. "We have to go *right now*." She grabbed for his hand, and he shoved the piece of paper he'd written on under a stack of mail before following her to the door.

Although Ruby kept up a constant chatter on the drive to the stables, Cameron had no idea what she said. His thoughts were too busy swirling around Danielle's information. If this Barry guy really was Ruby's father, Cameron could be on his way home in days. Which he was thrilled about, of course. He pushed away the nudge of conscience that said he was flouting his responsibility. He didn't have any responsibility to Ruby or to Bethany—and certainly not more responsibility than Ruby's father.

"Uncle Cam, you passed it." Ruby's words penetrated his brain.

"What? Oh." He glanced to the left side of the road, where a homemade wooden sign reading Hope Riders arched over a long driveway. There was no way he could make the turn now.

He continued down the road, eyes straining for a good place to turn around. But the driveways were few and far between on this country road. Finally, he turned into another long driveway, this one boasting a sign for Hidden Blossom Farms. Large groves of bare trees suggested it may be an orchard of some sort, though in the dark it was impossible to tell.

When he at last pulled into the right driveway, he caught a glimpse of Ruby bouncing in her seat in the rearview mirror. "So you like riding?"

"It's the best!" Her enthusiasm reminded him again of the way she'd thrown her arms around him and called him the best, and he grinned.

Then he flattened his lips and yanked his eyes back to the big white building in front of them. He did not need to go getting attached to this little girl. After all, he'd be on a plane back to his Ruby-free life soon enough.

Chapter 7

Kayla wiped her clammy hands on her jeans and pulled in a deep breath of the animal-hay-earth-leather scent of the arena. She'd only come because Nate and Vi's friend Emma, who owned the stables, had mentioned that Ruby rode here on Wednesday nights. And after spending the past five days worrying about the little girl, Kayla had needed just a peek to make sure Ruby was all right. That her uncle was actually taking care of her.

The problem was that Nate had mentioned Kayla's fear of horses—the result of a close encounter with a kicking horse when she was a kid—and now Emma was dead-set on getting her close to one of these creatures to help her overcome her fear.

Kayla glanced toward the arena door as Emma led a giant black horse toward her. Still no sign of Ruby. Which meant that Cam had probably put his own needs before the little girl's the same way he had when he'd refused to take her to see her mom. Kayla had gone back to visit Bethany every day this week, and each time the nurse had reported that the woman's only other visitor had been Pastor Dan. Kayla didn't know why she was surprised.

She may not have known Cam long, but it had only taken that first phone call for her to know the kind of man he was—the kind who didn't worry about anyone but himself.

That's not fair, she chided herself. She tried to turn her thoughts in a more charitable direction. She supposed it would be life altering to suddenly be called to take care of your niece halfway across the country. And as much as she knew she would do it for Vi and Nate in a split second, she also prayed she'd never have to know what it was like to lose her brother or sister-in-law.

Help me have more compassion toward Cam, Lord, she prayed. Though it would be a lot easier if he did a better job with Ruby.

She rolled her eyes at herself. That wasn't exactly more charitable. She reminded herself that Cam and Ruby were really none of her business.

Except, it felt like Ruby *was* her business. Kayla had been the one to see the accident. She'd been the one to get help. She'd been the one to watch the girl until Cam could get here. And in that short time, Ruby had managed to make a home in her heart.

"This is Big Blue," Emma said, stopping a few feet in front of Kayla.

The animal was even bigger than she'd imagined, and it studied her with its enormous eyes. Kayla had to sit on her hands so she wouldn't turn her chair right back around and race out of here.

"I know he looks intimidating," Emma said, "but he's a big softie. And he's trained to respond to voice commands. So you don't need to be able to use your legs to ride him."

Ride him? Kayla gaped at Emma. She was kidding, right?

Before she could ask, the arena door opened, and Ruby came bouncing into the building. The moment she spotted Kayla, she ran into the ring, patting Big Blue on the way past like he was no more frightening than her cat.

"Kayla." Ruby's smile was wide and gap-toothed and contagious. "I didn't know you rode horses too."

"I don't."

"But she will." Emma winked at Ruby, who giggled, then turned to Kayla. "Hold out your hand and let him smell it."

When Kayla hesitated, Ruby held her own hand out for the horse. Big Blue took a breath loud enough for Kayla to hear, then nickered softly.

"See." Ruby reached for Kayla's hand. "He's nice."

Kayla followed Ruby's lead in moving her hand to the horse's velvety nose.

The animal's hot breath slid across her skin, and Kayla let a nervous giggle escape. "It tickles."

"All right, Miss Ruby," Emma said after a minute. "Why don't you go join the other dressage riders so you can go over the routine for the parade." She turned to Kayla. "Have you had enough for one night, or did you want to try to mount him?"

Kayla contemplated the animal. She hated to back down from a challenge. But maybe this was the kind of challenge that needed to be conquered in baby steps. "Next time?"

"Absolutely." Emma clicked her tongue at Big Blue, who followed her toward the other end of the arena.

"Do you want to watch me?" Ruby asked Kayla.

"Of course." Kayla scanned the handful of parents waiting on the small set of bleachers near the door. She wanted to talk to Cam anyway, encourage him again to let the poor little girl see her mom.

But she didn't spot him among the other parents.

"Where's your uncle?"

Ruby's face fell. "He's waiting in the car. He said he had to make some phone calls."

"Ah." It figured. But it didn't matter. If Cam wouldn't show his niece that she mattered, Kayla would. She popped her chair into a wheelie to cross the soft arena sand. "I'll be by the bleachers. Show me what you've got."

According to the clock, Ruby's lesson should have ended fifteen minutes ago, but still she hadn't emerged from the arena. Nor had anyone else for that matter.

With a sigh, Cameron shoved his car door open and marched toward the building. He was ready to give this Miss Emma a piece of his mind. His time was valuable, and he didn't need her wasting it by not being punctual in dismissing her classes.

But the moment he opened the door to the arena, he froze. A couple dozen parents and kids sitting on a set of bleachers swiveled his direction. A blonde woman standing in front of them turned to him and smiled. "Can I help you?"

Cameron cleared his throat. There was no reason he should feel suddenly self-conscious. It wasn't like this was the boardroom of a Fortune 500 company. It was a rinky-dink stable in a rinky-dink town. "I'm looking for Ruby Moore."

A small hand waved from the bottom row of bleachers. "Over here, Uncle Cam."

Cameron's eyes went past Ruby to the woman seated on the far side of her. What was Kayla doing here? There was no way she rode, was there, given that she used a wheelchair?

"Sorry we're running late," the blonde woman he assumed must be Miss Emma said. "We were going over the details for the parade. It's the Sunday after Thanksgiving. Lineup time is four o'clock. We'll need adults to help pass out information and candy. I hope you can be there."

Cameron opened his mouth. That sounded like absolutely the last thing on earth he would do.

But he caught Kayla's grimace. Clearly, she expected him to refuse.

"Sure," he heard himself saying. "I'll be there."

"Great." Emma spoke for a few more minutes, then dismissed the group. Instead of running to him so they could leave, Ruby sat talking to Kayla.

At this rate, Cameron was going to have the art of the annoyed sigh perfected by the time he left Hope Springs. He marched over to his niece. "Ruby, time to go."

"One minute, Uncle Cam." Ruby turned to Kayla again.

"No minutes. Now." He cut off abruptly as he realized how much like his own dad he sounded. It was a voice he hadn't heard in way too long, and it sounded odd coming from his own mouth.

"Ruby, why don't you go ask Miss Emma about your idea to braid the horses' tails for the parade. I want to talk to your uncle for a minute."

Cameron shoved his hands in his pockets. What if he didn't want to talk to *her* for a minute? Had she thought of that? But he kept his feet planted as Ruby sprinted off, though he gave Kayla a look meant to convey that he didn't have time for this.

"It's been almost a week since the poor thing has seen her mother," Kayla launched into her lecture. "Are you ever going to take her?"

He shook his head. "Not that it's any of your business, but no, I'm not."

Kayla crossed her arms, her jaw tightening. "Whatever your issue is, she's just a little girl. She needs her mom. And it might help Bethany to hear her daughter's voice. I really think you should take her."

And he really thought she should mind her own business, but he bit back the words. "Her father can take her if he wants."

"Her father?" Kayla gave him a blank stare. "She doesn't have a father."

Cameron rolled his eyes. Not this again. "Of course she does. And I think I've tracked him down."

"So you're going to just dump her off on some stranger she's never met?"

"In case you've forgotten, *I'm* some stranger she'd never met too. And this guy isn't a stranger, he's her dad."

"Well—" Kayla's eyes sparked. "Has it ever occurred to you that there may be a reason Bethany never told Ruby about her father? Like maybe he's not a great guy."

Cameron glanced away. Of course it had occurred to him. Knowing the sort of men Bethany usually dated, he was almost sure that was the case. But that wasn't his problem. His sister should have thought of that before she let this guy knock her up.

He brought his eyes back to Kayla, squaring his shoulders with resolve. "I'm sure it will be fine." He started toward the other side of the arena, where Ruby was having an animated conversation with Miss Emma.

"Cam, wait."

He didn't know why he listened, but he did, turning around in time to see Kayla tip her chair back into a wheelie and roll through the arena sand with her small front wheels in the air.

She stopped in front of him. "I wish you'd reconsider this."

"And I wish you'd butt out." The retort flew off his tongue.

Kayla's eyes widened, and he was sure she was going to yell again.

Instead, she clamped her lips tight, then spun her chair toward the door. "If that's what you want. But at some point, you might want to stop thinking about yourself and start thinking about what's best for Ruby." Her words were quiet as she rolled past him. His gaze followed her as she continued to the door, then leaned forward to pull it open and maneuvered her wheelchair through it without a backward glance at him.

Cameron collected Ruby and led her to the parking lot. Fortunately, by the time they got outside, Kayla was nowhere to be found. If he never saw that woman again, that would be fine by him.

Chapter 8

Kayla bit her lip as she contemplated the application in front of her. She'd reread every one of her answers at least three times.

"Still working on that?" Vi waddled up behind her.

Kayla sighed. "No. It's done."

"So why are you still staring at it?" Vi pulled out a chair at the kitchen table and lowered herself onto it. "Man, I will be glad when I'm carrying this little person on the outside instead of the inside."

"I don't know why." Kayla shook her head at her computer screen. "I can't make myself hit 'submit.' I keep thinking about leaving you guys just when you're bringing this amazing new life into the world. I promised I'd help out at the store, and . . ."

"We'll be fine. You know that."

Kayla nodded. She did know. "And Mom and Dad aren't getting any younger."

Vi outright laughed at her. "Kayla, your parents are currently climbing Mount St. Helens. I think they'll be okay if you leave for six months."

"What about Ruby? I mean, Cam's obviously not concerned about what's best for her. What if he does contact her father? Who's going to make sure she's all right and that—"

Vi laid her hand on top of Kayla's to silence her. "I know you care about that little girl. But Cam is technically her guardian right now. You can't control what he does. Anyway, you don't know—he may come through after all. You have to give him a chance."

Kayla snorted. Vi only thought that because she'd never met Cam. Nor been told by him to butt out. That was gratitude for you, after all she'd tried to do to help him and Ruby.

Vi gave her a probing look. "Cam aside, you know that Ruby is in God's hands." She refused to take her gaze off Kayla, who had to look away.

"What's this really about?" Vi asked softly.

Kayla let her breath out, long and slow. "I don't know." But that wasn't quite right. "It's just, I've wanted to do a mission trip like this for so long, you know?"

Vi smiled. "I thought that was the point."

"Yeah, but what if I don't get accepted? There's a good chance they'll say the trip isn't wheelchair accessible or I'll slow them down or something."

Vi laughed as she patted Kayla's hand. "If that's the case, then they sure don't know you. Anyway, if you apply and don't get accepted this time, it doesn't mean you're not cut out for mission work. It just means this wasn't the right trip. God has a way of opening doors when and where they need to be opened, you know. But you're never going to find out if this is the door for you if you don't hit that submit button." She braced her hands on the table and groaned as she pushed to her feet. "Seriously, I don't know how women go through this whole process more than once."

As she shuffled out of the room, Kayla studied her application one more time. Her hand went to her mouse, and she hovered it over the submit button.

Then, drawing in a quick breath, she clicked.

"It's up to you, Lord," she whispered. "Is this the door for me or not?"

Chapter 9

The sick feeling that had lain heavy in his stomach since he'd driven out of Hope Springs after dropping Ruby off at school this morning intensified as Cameron stared at the apartment complex in front of him. He'd driven past it half a dozen times before he'd made himself turn into the parking lot.

This was where Ruby's alleged dad lived. All he had to do was go in there, tell the guy he was a father, ask him if he wanted to come to Hope Springs or have Ruby brought here, and then pack his bags and hop the next flight back to LA.

So what was stopping him from getting out of the car and doing just that?

Has it ever occurred to you that there may be a reason Bethany never told Ruby about her father? Like maybe he's not a great guy. Kayla's words from the other night had echoed relentlessly in his head for the past two days.

But if Bethany was friends with the pastor, then maybe that meant she had changed. And if she had changed, maybe that meant her taste in men had changed. Maybe she and her partner had split amicably—or better yet, maybe the guy was looking for an opportunity to be part of his daughter's life. Who was Cameron to deny him that?

And if things were too bad, Cameron could turn around and walk away. He hadn't committed himself to anything yet.

With a forced resolve that didn't feel like resolve at all, he pushed his car door open. At the locked entrance, he scanned the list of apartments, pressing the buzzer for the one labeled Barry Anderson. It took a moment before a guy's voice sounded over the speaker. "Yeah?"

"Is this Barry Anderson?" Cameron took a step closer to the microphone.

"Yeah. Who's this?"

"Did you know a Bethany Moore?" Cameron crossed his fingers, though he wasn't sure whether he was hoping the guy would answer in the affirmative or the negative.

"Bethany Moore? I don't think I . . . Oh wait, Bethy. Yeah. Haven't seen her in, what? Seven, eight years? Why do you ask?"

"I'm her brother. Could I come in?" He really didn't want to talk about this over the intercom. And besides, he wanted to get at least a glimpse of the guy before he told him about Ruby. He owed her at least that much as her uncle.

"Uh, yeah. I guess." The guy sounded surprised, but after a second the door buzzed open. The hallway was narrow and dark and smelled strongly of stale cigarettes and cat urine, but at least it didn't look seedy. When he reached apartment 105, Cameron gave a quick rap on the door.

Less than a second later, a guy dressed in faded jeans and a tan sweater opened the door. His hair was slightly greasy and his face weather-roughened, but Cameron let himself breathe a little easier. This guy didn't look so bad. Probably just the kind of hard-working guy who would make a good dad.

"So what's this about? Is Bethy in trouble or something, because—"

"She was in an accident." Cameron glanced past the guy into the apartment. It wasn't exactly glamorous—tired furniture, stained carpeting—but at least there weren't beer bottles laying all over the place or something. Which, given Bethany's history with men, was a pleasant surprise.

"Oh man. I'm sorry to hear that." Barry took a step back. Absently, he pushed his sleeves up. "I mean, that's terrible. Is she okay?"

But Cameron's eyes had locked on Barry's exposed forearms.

Fresh track marks.

They were unmistakable. He'd seen them enough times on Bethany to know.

Apparently catching the direction of Cameron's gaze, Barry tugged his sleeves down. "Is she okay?" he repeated.

Cameron looked him in the eye. "I'm afraid not. She died. I thought you should know." He turned and stalked down the hallway.

"Wait, man. When's the funeral?" Barry called after him. "I want to come."

But Cameron lifted a dismissive hand and picked up speed, shoving the door hard in front of him. In the parking lot, he sprinted to his car. Then he just sat there, hands gripping the steering wheel so they wouldn't shake.

He couldn't leave Ruby with a junkie. He'd give up his own future before it came to that.

As he turned the key in the ignition, an odd sense of relief washed over him. Until he realized he'd have to tell Danielle what he'd done.

Unless he didn't. He could just as easily say it had been a dead end.

Feeling unaccountably lighter than he had in days, Cameron tried to enjoy the drive back to Hope Springs. The sky was ridiculously blue today, and the few trees that still held leaves were putting on a brilliant display of color. Not to mention the lake, which he caught glimpses of every once in a while, glittering brighter than a thousand gemstones. It wasn't the Pacific, but there was something peaceful and soothing about it all the same.

Cameron relaxed into the drive, until he spotted the line of brake lights ahead of him. He slowed to a stop behind a long line of cars, grumbling to himself as he spotted the sign: "Construction ahead. Expect significant delays."

His eyes went to the clock. He'd planned his little trip so that he'd have just enough time to get to Sharpesville and back before Ruby got out of school. He'd already been cutting it close. But now there was no way he was going to make it back on time.

With a groan, he pulled his phone out of his pocket.

Too bad he only knew the number of one person in Hope Springs.

Chapter 10

The nerve. One day the guy is telling her to butt out, two days later, he's calling and asking her to do him a favor and pick up Ruby from school and hang out with her. Apparently, her interference was welcome as long as it suited him.

Not that she minded spending time with Ruby. Thankfully, the little girl had known where to find the spare key under a rock in the flower bed, since Nate's band was currently practicing at his house—not exactly conducive for the homework she'd just helped the little girl with.

"What should we do next?" Ruby bounced out of her chair.

Kayla checked the time. Cam hadn't known when he'd be home, but he'd thought it would be at least an hour. Which meant they might have time for a plan that had been lurking in the back of her mind since she'd gotten Ruby from school.

"Do you want to visit your mom?"

"Really?" Ruby brightened so much that it was almost heartbreaking. How could Cam keep this little girl from her mother? "Did Uncle Cam say it was okay?"

Kayla bit her lip. "I didn't have a chance to ask him." That was true, right? "We'll be there and back before he gets home."

Ruby wrinkled her brow. "Isn't that lying?"

"Don't worry, we'll tell him when he gets back." By then, it'd be too late for him to do anything about it. And she could show him how much good it had done Ruby. Surely he'd start taking her then. "Go get your shoes. I'm going to grab my purse."

Ruby still looked uncertain, but she nodded and moved toward the closet with a little skip in her step.

"Good girl." Kayla wheeled to the kitchen counter to collect her purse. She yanked it toward her, already backing her wheelchair away—every second counted if they wanted to get out of here before Cam got home—but the purse must have snagged on the mail or something, because Kayla was suddenly surrounded by an avalanche of scattered papers.

She bent to pick them up, gathering them into a messy pile. But she paused, a lump coming to her throat as she spotted a drawing of a chair with what looked like two big wheels on the sides. In the chair sat a blob-shaped person with an overly large head and a giant smile. Too sweet.

Kayla was about to add the paper to the pile in her hand when her eyes landed on words scribbled at the bottom in messy but definitely not childish handwriting: Barry Anderson, 176 Howley, Sharpesville, Wisconsin. But it was the two words under the address that made her mouth go dry: *Ruby's dad???*

An unaccountable anger went through her. Was that where he was right now? Looking for a way to shirk his responsibility and pass Ruby off to some guy in Sharpesville. Even after Kayla had expressed her concern that it may not be in Ruby's best interest, given that Bethany had kept any and all knowledge of her father from the little girl. People didn't just do that for no reason.

So much for Vi's theory that Cam would surprise them and come through for Ruby after all.

Honestly, she didn't know why she was so angry. It wasn't like she hadn't seen this coming. Well, if Cam thought he wasn't going to hear about this when he got home . . .

It's none of your business, she reminded herself. Except, hadn't Cam made it her business when he'd decided to ask her to watch Ruby while he ran out of town chasing down someone else to take on his responsibilities?

Kayla was still clutching the paper when Ruby marched into the kitchen. "Are you coming? My shoes are on."

Kayla hastily shoved the paper to the bottom of the stack and set it on the counter. No need to upset Ruby about this. With any luck, she'd be able to convince Cam that it was wrong to take the girl to a man her mother didn't want to have her. Or better yet, the man would have turned out not to be Ruby's father.

"Yeah, kiddo. Let's go."

Kayla gave the papers one last nasty look—as if they could control what was written on them—then followed Ruby to the front door. They bundled into coats against the late fall chill, then rushed outside. But they were only halfway to her car when Cam turned into the driveway.

Ruby waved wildly to him, but Kayla groaned. There was no way they could carry out their plan now.

Cam's face was drawn as he stepped out of the car, but he gave her what she was pretty sure was meant to be a grateful smile. She returned it with a stony look. As far as she was concerned, he could keep his gratitude if he was going to involve her in his plans to send Ruby off.

"Where are you two headed?"

"We're going to see Mommy." The words rocketed out of Ruby before Kayla could open her mouth.

"Oh you are?" Cam shot Kayla a hard look, which she met head-on. She had nothing to be ashamed of.

"Yep. Do you want to come?" Ruby asked cheerfully.

Cam shook his head. "Go inside, Ruby. I need to talk to Kayla for a minute."

"And then can we go?" Ruby sounded so hopeful, and Kayla willed Cam to be a decent guy just this once.

"No."

"But—" Ruby's face fell, and it was all Kayla could do not to plop the little girl onto her lap and wheel right past Cam to her car and take off for the hospital.

"Inside. Now." Cam stuck his keys in Ruby's hand, then pointed at the house. Ruby nodded and dropped her head, then dragged her feet to the door.

As soon as it had banged closed, Cam rounded on Kayla. "What do you think you're doing? I simply asked you to watch her for a little bit."

"I'm doing what's best for Ruby." The words shot off Kayla's tongue. "You might consider trying it sometime."

Cam's hands fisted at his sides, but she noticed with triumph that he couldn't hold her gaze. "Believe it or not, that's what I'm doing."

Kayla shook her head. She was not going to let him get away with thinking that. "Is that why you were in Sharpesville looking for her dad today?"

Cam's head jerked toward her. "How did—"

"You left it scribbled on a piece of paper on the counter. One of Ruby's drawings, just to add insult to injury."

"Yeah, fine. Whatever. That's where I was. I told you I had a lead on him."

Kayla waited, but when Cam didn't continue, she had to ask. "Did you find him?"

Cam gave her a long look, his expression unreadable. Finally, he blew out a breath. "It was a dead end."

Relief coursed through her. "Good."

Cam shook his head. "You're unbelievable. Do you know that?" He stepped around her wheelchair and walked toward the house. "Thanks for watching Ruby."

Kayla turned her chair toward him. "You're welcome." She thought about adding another plea for him to take Ruby to see Bethany. But maybe she'd already yelled at him enough for one day. She could always butt in again another day.

Chapter 11

Cameron flopped back on the lumpy mattress that passed for Bethany's bed—his bed these days—and held his phone above him. He'd avoided calling Danielle for the past two days, but he couldn't put it off any longer, if her increasingly irate texts were any indication. He dialed her number, then pulled the phone to his ear. He was not relishing the thought of this conversation.

But Danielle sounded cheerful when she answered. "Guess what? I made us reservations at Oshiki."

Cameron pulled his phone away from his ear and stared at it. Why was she talking about their favorite sushi place?

"For Thanksgiving," she was saying when he put the phone back to his ear.

Oh right. It was Thanksgiving this week.

"Yeah, baby, listen. I don't think I'm going to make it back for Thanksgiving."

"Why not?" Her voice went hard. "When I didn't hear from you, I assumed it was because you were making arrangements with the kid's father to get her off your hands."

He sighed. "No. I'm sorry. I should have called sooner. I went to Sharpesville, to find that Barry guy."

"And?" Danielle had never been one to sit and listen to a full story. She wanted only the pertinent facts.

"I found him, but—"

"Good. Then, what, you need a few more days to get things set up? I can probably move the reservation back if I—"

"No." Cameron's fingers tightened on the phone. "I found him, but—" He hesitated. If he told her that he'd decided not to tell the guy about Ruby, she'd go through the roof. Not to mention that she might try to contact the guy herself and convince him to come take Ruby. "He wasn't Ruby's father. He'd never even heard of Bethany."

"That's— Odd." Danielle sounded like she'd gone into lawyer mode. "The guy I talked to seemed so sure. Maybe this guy is lying. We could make him take a paternity test or—"

"No, Danielle. I believe him. And you know I can always tell when people are lying. It's a dead end. I'm sorry."

Silence pulsed from the other end of the phone.

"But—" He tried for a conciliatory tone. "You could come here for Thanksgiving. Meet the kid. She's not so bad, you know. Kind of fun sometimes even." He laughed. "The other day she—"

"Cameron, I don't care *what* she did." Danielle's words were sharp. "If you want this relationship to work, I think you need to spend more of your time focusing on a way to get home. Maybe don't call me for a few days, until you make some progress."

The phone clicked dead, and Cameron dropped it and pressed his hands into his forehead. He knew she didn't mean it. He'd give her a couple of days and then call—by then she'd cool down, and maybe he'd have something to report. But as he sat up, he couldn't help but wonder: Why was he working so hard to keep Danielle happy when he'd been having doubts about their relationship even before he came here?

Because she's part of your plan for the perfect life, remember?

He pushed to his feet, tugged on his shoes, and strode for the front door, grabbing the winter jacket he'd finally broken down and purchased. Right now, he needed to do something physical.

"Where are you going?" Ruby blinked up at him from the spot where she was playing with that ridiculous cardboard dollhouse, her green plaid shirt standing out in strong contrast to her mustard-yellow pants.

"Outside."

"Can I come?"

He shrugged. "Knock yourself out."

"Really?" Her eyes widened, as if he'd given her permission to go to the Bahamas.

"Yeah. Just stay out of the way." He marched out the door and around the house, to the small shed in the backyard, where he pushed past sandbox toys and miscellaneous planters to grab a rake.

Today was as good a day as any to attack the leaves strewn across the yard. The air was sharp, but the sun was out, and the breeze was almost warm. He focused on the rhythm of the rake, letting his mind go blank. The movement felt good—and the mindlessness even better.

It took him a moment to realize he wasn't the only one working. On the other side of the yard, Ruby was struggling with a rake nearly twice her height. He watched for a moment as she managed to scatter the leaves more.

Shaking his head, he scraped a few more rakefuls onto his own pile. But his eyes went right back to Ruby, who was still wrestling diligently with her own rake.

"Try holding it like this," he called, holding his rake in front of him to show her his hand placement.

She studied him, then slid her hands into the completely wrong position. With a sigh, Cameron dropped his own rake and moved to her side.

"Like this." He pushed her right hand up and her left hand down, then moved the rake back and forth a couple times to give her a feel for the motion.

"Oh, I get it now." Ruby grinned at him, then pulled the rake across the ground herself, missing half the leaves but managing to form the start of a small pile.

"Good." He returned to his own rake.

"Uncle Cam?"

"Yeah?" He kept raking.

"Who taught you how to rake?"

"My dad, I suppose." He paused mid-stroke. "Your grandpa."

"Really?" Ruby's eyes lit up. "You knew my grandpa?"

"Of course. I'm your mom's brother. So her dad was my dad too."

"Mommy said my grandpa was funny. Was he funny, Uncle Cam?"

Cameron's heart squeezed, thinking of his dad with his corny jokes and his booming laugh. "Yeah. He was funny."

"That's good. You're funny too."

Cameron returned to raking. He'd never thought of himself as a particularly funny guy. "How am I funny?"

"You act all mean and tough. But you're really nice." Ruby giggled.

Cameron shook his head. "Keep raking."

But as he watched her wrestle with the rake, he had to admit to himself that her words had been just what he'd needed to hear. He'd made the right decision, not telling Barry about Ruby. Besides, chances were, the guy wasn't Ruby's father anyway. And even if he was . . . no, Cameron had made the right decision.

He thought of Kayla, accusing him of not caring what was best for Ruby.

The truth was, as much as he didn't want to care about anything associated with Bethany, he did.

He actually cared about this little girl quite a lot, despite his best intentions.

Then why won't you take her to see her mom? He heard Kayla, as if she were right there in front of him, piercing him with that judgmental look she was so good at.

He sighed, stopping to lean on his rake. "Hey, Rubes?"

She giggled. "That's a funny nickname."

"Yeah. You want to go see your mom after this?"

Chapter 12

Kayla peeked at Bethany's still form over the top of the ragged copy of *Little Women* she'd been reading out loud to the comatose woman. Bethany looked to be slightly older than Kayla, which meant she was likely Cam's big sister. Whom he didn't seem to care an iota for.

She thought with satisfaction of the expression on his face when he'd said the lead on Ruby's father had turned out to be a dead end. She probably shouldn't gloat about that, but at least it meant she could still see Ruby around sometimes. Still keep Bethany informed of how her daughter was doing. Since Cam continued to refuse to bring Ruby to visit her mother.

Kayla wasn't sure how her visits to Bethany fit into Cam's request that she butt out, but quite frankly, she didn't care. The poor woman didn't deserve to be left here alone, whatever Cam seemed to think. Besides, Ruby needed her mother back, and Kayla was convinced that the main reason she'd come out of her own coma was the love and support of all the people who'd visited her. That and all their prayers. Thankfully, she knew Bethany was covered in prayer as well. Dan had said a prayer for her in church this morning, and all of Kayla's friends had promised to continue to pray as well. *Please help her to heal, Lord*, Kayla prayed again, then dropped her eyes to the book, reading out loud.

"'I don't believe I shall ever marry. I am happy as I am, and love my liberty too well to be in a hurry to give it up for any mortal man.'"

Kayla put her finger in the book to mark her page and looked up again. "Jo sure nailed that one, didn't she?" Sometimes Kayla felt like she was the only person in the world who didn't think she needed to get married, so it was good to have this confirmation from Jo March—even if she was a fictional character.

"'I love my liberty too well,'" she repeated, opening the book again and picking up with Laurie's response: "'You think so now, but there'll come a time when you will care for somebody, and you'll love him tremendously, and live and die for him.'"

Kayla paused again. "That's not the way it is for everyone, Laurie," she murmured. Then she looked at Bethany with a laugh. "Sorry, I'll stop injecting my own commentary."

She started reading again, but after a few minutes a tap on her shoulder made her jump.

"I'm sorry." The woman talked in the low, soothing voice that was common to nurses everywhere. "Bethany has more visitors, and we don't want to tire her out with too many. Would you mind stepping out for now?"

"Of course." Kayla dog-eared the page of her book. "We'll continue tomorrow." As she followed the nurse toward the exit, she let herself hope, for only a second, that the visitors were Cam and Ruby. But as fast as the hope had entered her thoughts, it dissipated. Cam had made his feelings on that perfectly clear yet again the other night. It was probably Dan and Jade who had come.

The nurse pushed the door open, and Kayla followed her down the hallway, her wheels quiet on the smooth, shiny floor. As they rounded a corner, Kayla dodged out of the way of a bustling nurse. When she looked up, her eyes caught on two forms waiting at the end—one tall and broad, the other small and bouncy.

Her heart gave a small leap. *Thank you, Lord.*

She lifted a hand off the rims to wave to Ruby, who sent her an enthusiastic return wave. Cam looked less pleased to be here. But at least he was here, finally doing the right thing.

As she wheeled to a stop in front of them, Ruby sprang toward her wheelchair and wrapped her small arms around Kayla's shoulders. Kayla hugged her back without reserve.

"What's that?" Ruby pointed to the book in Kayla's lap.

"Oh." Kayla glanced at the book, then at Cam. Well, she had nothing to be embarrassed about. "I was just reading this book to your mom."

"Is it good?"

Kayla nodded. "One of my favorites."

"It was Bethany's favorite too." Cam's voice was low and gravelly, and he cleared his throat. "Come on, Ruby."

He started down the hallway.

"Cam." Kayla didn't mean to call after him, but there was no way to take it back.

He turned, waiting silently for her to continue.

"I'm glad you came. Do you want me to wait here, in case . . ." She eyed Ruby. Even though she was convinced that it would do the girl good to see her mom, it might be a little intense. She might not want to stay in there as long as Cam. Or she might need someone to talk to afterward.

"Yes!" Ruby immediately cheered.

Cam shook his head. "We'll be fine, thanks."

But she was pretty sure she heard the slightest tremor in his voice.

Cameron resisted the urge to look over his shoulder as he strode down the hallway toward Bethany's room, Ruby skipping at his side. He didn't need to know if Kayla was still there, still watching him with that mix of compassion and loathing.

They stopped outside the room number the nurse had given him. Cameron grabbed the door handle but found he couldn't open it. A small hand slipped into his, and Cameron looked down to find Ruby gazing up at him. His first instinct was to pull away, but the fear in her gaze stopped him.

"It's okay," he whispered, then pushed the door open.

His eyes fell on the bed. Bethany's blonde hair spilled against the white pillowcase, and a ventilator tube was taped to her mouth. An IV traveled into her arm, and other wires ran in and out of her bed, feeding into monitors that cast a slightly eerie glow on her face.

Next to him, Ruby let out a whimper that sounded like, "Mommy."

Cameron supposed he should do something to comfort the girl. But he had no idea what that would be.

A nurse bustled into the room and squatted at Ruby's side. "You can step closer. I'm sure your mom would love it if you talked to her."

Ruby nodded and let go of his hand, saying a tentative hello to her mother. The nurse gave her an encouraging smile, and Ruby started telling Bethany about school.

The nurse gestured for Cameron to come closer as well.

He looked from the nurse to Ruby to Bethany.

"Excuse me," he murmured, turning and bolting out the door. He stopped halfway down the hallway, his breaths short and quick.

She hurt you, he reminded himself. *She tore your family apart. She's the reason you don't have a mother or a father.*

But as hard as he tried to clutch his anger to him, he couldn't stop picturing Bethany's still form in the bed.

He looked at the door to her room. He shouldn't leave Ruby alone in there. But at the thought of going back in, his whole body began to tremble and his stomach heaved.

He sprinted toward the far end of the hallway, making it to the restroom just in time to lose his lunch.

Chapter 13

Kayla wheeled out of the visitor's lounge into the hallway, glancing at the door to the men's restroom. She didn't know why she'd stayed at the hospital after Cam had so clearly dismissed her—but she hadn't been able to shake the thought that Ruby would need her after she saw her mom. It hadn't occurred to her that maybe Cam would too.

But the way he'd run down the hallway just now, looking like he was going to be sick—maybe he needed someone too.

It was never easy to see someone you cared about lying helpless like that. And despite his earlier refusals to visit his sister, his reaction proved that he did care about her on some level. Not that Kayla expected him to admit it.

The door to the bathroom opened, and Cam emerged, looking shaky and gray. She wanted to call out to him, let him know she was here if he wanted to talk, but something stopped her. She watched as he pivoted toward the desk and said something to the nurse there. She nodded and picked up her phone. Cam stood there for a moment, then lifted his hands behind his head and made his way to the window.

Kayla peered down the hall toward Bethany's room. Ruby must still be in there. By herself.

She attempted to work up anger toward Cam at that, but she couldn't. He was obviously struggling to cope with all of this himself.

With one more glance toward him, Kayla turned down the hallway and made her way toward Bethany's room.

The nurse she'd talked to earlier was checking Bethany's monitors and smiling at a chatting Ruby. Kayla's heart squeezed at the way the girl held her mom's hand. This was obviously exactly what she'd needed.

After a moment, the nurse ducked out of the room, and Kayla pulled her wheelchair up to the end of the bed.

Ruby looked her way. "Where's Uncle Cam? He didn't say hi to Mommy."

Kayla fiddled with the blanket covering Bethany's feet. "Sometimes grownups have a hard time dealing with seeing people in the hospital. Your uncle is waiting in the lobby for you. But I'll hang out with you and your mom until it's time to go."

Ruby nodded and turned back to her mom. "When is she going to wake up? It's more fun to talk to her when she answers."

"I know." Kayla fought down the lump that tried to climb up her throat. "The doctors hope she'll wake up soon. But they just don't know." She bit her lip. Maybe that was enough for now. Anyway, it was way too early to give up hope that Bethany would wake up. "Why don't you tell your mom all about the parade next weekend?"

Ruby launched into a renewed one-way conversation with her mom until the nurse came over and said it was time to let Bethany get some rest.

Kayla could have wept when Ruby raised onto her tiptoes to kiss her mom's cheek. *Please let Bethany wake up, Lord. This little girl needs her mother.*

She followed Ruby to the lobby, where Cam was in the same spot as when she'd left him.

"Uncle Cam." Ruby broke away from her. "What are you doing?"

Cam turned, and Kayla's heart twisted the tiniest bit as she noticed his red eyes. He rubbed his nose. "I had to talk to the doctor."

"Did he say Mommy's going to be better soon?"

Cam's eyes met Kayla's and he gave a subtle head shake that made her stomach drop. "He said they're going to do everything they can to help her."

Ruby nodded as if that was all the assurance she needed. Cam looked as if he were about to say something else but then apparently thought better of it and silently led the way to the elevator. He moved to the back corner to give Kayla room to maneuver her wheelchair in the confined space.

The moment the door closed, Ruby crumpled, a big sob tearing out of her little body. "I don't want to leave Mommy."

Cam stared at her, confusion and annoyance warring on his face. "We have to."

"No," Ruby pounded her fists on the elevator door. "Let me out. I want to go back to Mommy."

"Oh, sweetie, it's okay." Kayla bent over and reached for the little girl in the cramped elevator. "You can come see her again soon. How about we go get some ice cream?"

Ruby's sobs lightened, and she turned teary eyes on Kayla. "Really?"

"Really." Kayla didn't bother to confirm with Cam. She was taking this poor little girl for ice cream whether he liked it or not.

Chapter 14

Cameron fiddled with the spoon in his empty ice cream bowl. When they'd arrived at the oddly named shop—something about a chicken—he'd insisted he wasn't hungry, but Kayla had ordered him a sundae anyway, and somehow it turned out that ice cream had been exactly what he'd needed.

Kayla had kept up a steady stream of conversation with Ruby, which had allowed Cameron's mind to wander. He only wished his thoughts didn't keep bouncing back to Bethany's helpless body lying in that hospital bed.

Seeing his sister like that had been . . . honestly, he hadn't expected to react like that. He was supposed to be angry, to never lose sight of the fact that it was all her own fault. But seeing her lying there, all he could picture was the summer days they'd spent in their tree house and the way she'd let him tag along when she went to the neighborhood pool and the way she'd taught him to sneak cookies when Mom was in the basement doing laundry.

"Told you the ice cream was good." Kayla turned to him, and he worked to pull his thoughts back to the present. Because it wasn't the past, Bethany wasn't that innocent little girl anymore, and he wasn't her adoring little brother.

"I come here every time I'm in Hope Springs," Kayla added. "Usually more than once." She ran the spoon around her own empty dish.

"You don't live here?" Cameron looked at her in surprise. He'd assumed she was a lifelong resident of this small town, but he didn't know why. Probably because she gave off that small town vibe.

What vibe, nice? his head asked.

No. Nosy, he corrected his silly thoughts.

"At the Chocolate Chicken? No."

Ruby burst into giggles at Kayla's joke, and Cameron let a reluctant smile play with his lips too. "I meant Hope Springs. But that's good to know."

Kayla nudged Ruby, then turned to Cameron. "No, I don't live in Hope Springs. I'm from Wescott, on the other side of the state, but my brother and his wife live here. I try to visit them a couple times a year."

"So you just happened to be driving by when Bethany and Ruby . . ."

Kayla shook her head. "I didn't just *happen* to be driving by. God put me in the right place at the right time."

"You believe in God?" Ruby bounced in her seat. "Me too. Pastor Dan is teaching me about him."

Kayla smiled at her, but Cameron noticed the way her eyes went to him, as if waiting for him to chime in that he believed in God too.

He kept his mouth shut. Sure, he believed in God in an existential, impersonal way. Kind of how he believed in gravity. He knew it was there and supposed it affected him, but he never gave it much thought. And he certainly didn't talk about it. Not even with Danielle.

"You're not leaving soon, are you?" Ruby licked at the ice cream dripping down the side of her cone. She had to be the slowest ice cream eater ever. "I would miss you."

Kayla grabbed a napkin and ran it over Ruby's mouth. Cameron had to admit to himself that he was impressed that she didn't flinch at the gooey mess.

"I honestly don't know how long I'm staying," Kayla said. "But for a while. At least through Christmas. My sister-in-law is expecting a baby, and I want to be here when he or she is born. I can't wait to be an aunt."

"Hey." Ruby's eyes lit up. "If you're going to be an aunt and Uncle Cam is an uncle, maybe you can be an aunt and uncle together."

Kayla's laugh rang across the restaurant as she ruffled Ruby's hair. "That's not quite how it works. But I'm happy to be a pretend aunt to you." She gave Cameron a defiant look, as if daring him to contradict her.

Whatever. She wanted to be a pretend aunt, she had his blessing. It looked like they weren't getting rid of her anytime soon anyway. For some reason, the thought didn't completely aggravate him.

"So what do you do in Wescott?" He hadn't meant to ask, but his curiosity had taken over.

Kayla looked surprised at his interest. "Actually, that's part of the reason I'm visiting for so long. The camp I worked for just closed down. I'm trying to figure out where God is going to lead me next."

"A camp? That's so cool." Ruby's face was already covered with ice cream again. "What kind of camp was it?"

"It was for kids with disabilities."

"Like you," Ruby said cheerfully, and Cameron winced, wondering if there was room for him under the table. Apparently, political correctness was another thing Bethany had failed to teach her daughter.

But Kayla smiled at the girl. "Yep. Some of the kids use wheelchairs. Some have crutches or walkers. And others look just like you. But I helped them learn how to do things independently."

"Why do you use a wheelchair?"

"*Ruby*." Someone was seriously going to have to teach this girl some manners. "That's not—"

But Kayla cut him off. "That's a good question. I was in an accident when I was a teenager and I broke my back, so I can't walk. That's why I use a wheelchair." She said it cheerfully, as if remarking on riding a bike.

"Oh." Ruby popped the last of her cone into her mouth and spoke around it. "Do you ever wish you could still walk?"

Oh, for goodness' sake. Just when he thought her questions couldn't get more inappropriate. But he looked to Kayla. Was she going to handle this question with as much grace?

Kayla considered Ruby. "That's a pretty deep question for a seven-year-old. I guess I don't really think about it much anymore. This is just how I am now. And I like being me—"

"I like you being you too." Ruby grinned an ice cream–covered grin at her.

"That's good." Kayla returned the girl's grin. "Because I like you being you too."

All right. Before the two of them became blood sisters or something, instead of just pretend aunt and niece, it was time to get home.

He eyed Ruby. "Go wash your hands."

Kayla looked at him as if he were crazy. Well, what? He couldn't let her in the rental car like that.

"I'll go with you," Kayla said to Ruby.

Oh. He supposed sending a little kid to the bathroom alone wasn't necessarily the safest move, though in a town like Hope Springs it didn't seem like too big of a risk.

As Cameron waited for them to return, he made his way past the cozy round tables toward the shop's large window, stopping to glance at a shelf of eclectic metal sculptures—mostly of roosters, with a cow or two thrown in. He shook his head—he sure was a long way from LA. At the window, he looked out on the street lined with specialty shops. The sidewalks were mostly empty, and he wondered how any of these small places stayed in business, though he supposed this was their off season. Even so, he'd bet most of these places were inefficient at best, bleeding money at worst. Especially if, like his parents, they let their feelings get in the way of their business sense.

"All better," Ruby announced to the entire restaurant as she made her way back to him with her now mostly clean hands held high.

He hushed her, looking around at the few other customers in the shop. But they all smiled at Ruby as if she were the most precious creature they'd ever seen.

Yeah, Hope Springs was definitely a different kind of place. One he wasn't quite sure he'd ever get used to, though he had to admit that the slower pace made a nice change from his hectic LA life.

Not a nice change, he scolded himself. *Just a change.*

And that hectic LA life was exactly what he needed to get back to.

He followed Ruby and Kayla to the exit, waiting for Kayla to move aside so he could open the door for her. When she reached for it herself and tugged it open, he stepped in front of her to grab it out of her hands.

But she didn't let go. "I've got it. I'm not helpless." Her voice was hard, and Cameron let go of the door, raising his hands.

Helpless was the last thing he thought she was. "Just trying to be polite," he muttered. He stepped through the door she still held, with Ruby behind him. Then he watched as Kayla maneuvered her wheelchair through while keeping the door open with one hand. At one point, her wheel got caught, but he resisted the urge to help, and she managed to get over the threshold. If you asked him, she could have saved herself a lot of trouble by letting him help, but whatever.

They'd parked a couple blocks down, and Ruby nattered on about wanting Kayla to ride some horse named Big Blue as they made their way to the vehicles. When they reached Cameron's car, Kayla said goodbye to both of them, then continued to her own vehicle, parked a few cars back.

Cameron pulled open Ruby's car door and waited for her to climb in, watching the long, powerful movement of Kayla's arms on her wheelchair rims.

He shook his head again at her accusation that he thought she was helpless. Honestly, she was probably the most capable woman he knew. And that was saying something, given the women he worked with. In a lot of ways, her capable looked very different from theirs. Not because she used a wheelchair but because it was tempered with a compassion he'd seen in few people. And even less in people who made it a habit to yell at him.

"Kayla." He ducked into the car to tell Ruby to stay put, then jogged to catch up with Kayla.

She gave him a curious look.

He swallowed. "I wanted to apologize for the other night. For, you know, telling you to butt out. I know you only have Ruby's best interests at heart. There are just things you—" He cut off. "Anyway, I'm sorry. You were right about taking Ruby to see Bethany. It was obviously good for her."

Kayla offered a gentle smile, though it didn't erase the surprise in her eyes. "Apology accepted."

He stuck his hands in his coat pocket. "Good." He took a step backward, then stopped. "And you were right about Ruby's dad." He kept his voice low, in case little ears had big hearing. "I found him, but there's a reason Bethany didn't want Ruby to know him. He's a junkie."

Kayla gasped. "Oh no. I'm sorry." And she truly did look sorry, though it obviously wasn't her fault. But then she frowned. "Are you sure? How do you know?"

He shook his head and laughed darkly. She was unbelievable. First she told him not to find the guy because he might not be the sort of person Bethany would want to raise her kid. Now she was questioning his judgment when he said she'd been right.

"His arms had fresh track marks." He considered telling her how he knew what fresh track marks looked like, given that his sister was a junkie too. But that wasn't really something he wanted to discuss. There was a reason he kept his family life private.

"Anyway, I just thought you should know that I won't be searching for him anymore. So you can stop yelling at me."

Kayla's laugh sparkled into the cold air, brighter than the sunshine. "I can't make any promises."

Chapter 15

She couldn't do this. Kayla looked from Big Blue to Emma to Ruby to the bleachers, where Cam sat with his phone pressed to his ear. Why in the living world were his eyes on her every time she glanced that way? Was he waiting to see her fail?

It didn't matter. There was no way she could get up on this big beast of an animal. Not even for the satisfaction of seeing Cam disappointed.

She glanced his way again. He was leaning forward now, elbows on his knees, phone still pressed to his face, forehead wrinkled as his eyes went from Big Blue to her.

Then again . . .

"Let's do this."

"Yay! I knew you could do it." Ruby did a little dance in the arena sand and Emma smiled and led Big Blue to the wheelchair-accessible mounting ramp she'd pointed out to Kayla earlier.

Kayla tipped her chair back into a wheelie, then, with one last defiant glance at Cam, who, now that she looked closer, may not have been watching her after all, powered through the sand to the ramp. A few quick pushes on the hand rims got her to the platform at the top.

Emma had positioned the horse parallel to the platform so that its side was to Kayla. She drew in a deep breath. She knew there was a lift if she wanted to use it to put her on the horse. But she'd spent the past three days practicing the transfer onto a dummy horse. This was no different. Aside from the fact that she was getting onto the back of a thousand-pound living, breathing, moving animal.

"Just a sec," Emma said as Kayla positioned her chair alongside the horse. "Where did Miss Sarah go? I need her to hold— Cam!" Emma's shout made Kayla jump, her head jerking to where Cam now stood facing the arena, his phone still pressed to her ear.

Why was Emma calling for him?

"Can you come here a second?" Emma called.

A look of impatience flashed across Cam's face, but he said something into the phone, then hung up and vaulted the low arena wall in one smooth move.

Okay, not his first time in an arena.

He strode toward them, his loafers kicking up little clouds of dirt onto his khakis.

"What is it?" He crossed his arms in front of him.

"I need you to hold the horse steady while I help Kayla mount."

Kayla was about to protest that maybe they should do it another day, when Emma could have a qualified instructor hold the horse, but Cam nodded and grabbed the horse's harness, muttering to it in a low voice as he stroked its muzzle.

That she had not seen coming, although she supposed he *had* revealed a tiny bit of his soft side the other day at the hospital and the Chocolate Chicken. She'd assumed it was a one-time thing.

"All right," Emma climbed onto the ramp and took up a position next to Kayla. "Just like we practiced."

Kayla wanted to argue, but Cam's steely eyes were on her. She wouldn't let him see her fail. And anyway, Ruby believed in her.

She glanced at the little girl, who had clambered up the ramp after her and stood watching expectantly. "You can do it, Kayla."

She could still hear Cam whispering to the horse. He looked up with an almost-smile. "I've got him."

Kayla nodded, scooted to the front of her wheelchair and pulled in three quick breaths, then exhaled and lifted her right leg with her arms, hoisting it up and over the saddle. The horse barely moved.

"Easy," Cam's low, soothing voice intoned to the animal.

Readjusting herself in her wheelchair, Kayla gripped the saddle horn with her right hand and braced her left fist against her wheelchair seat. With one quick move, she straightened her left arm, at the same time pulling on the saddle horn with all her strength.

"You did it!" Emma's cheer reached her before she even realized that it was true—she was sitting in a saddle.

"I knew you could!" Ruby was dancing at the top of the ramp.

"Good job." Cameron patted the horse's nose, leading Kayla to believe his words were more for Big Blue than for her. But that didn't matter.

She had done it. She'd conquered her fear.

Emma handed Kayla what looked like the end of a seat belt. "Clip this around your waist."

Her hand shaking just the slightest bit—though she was no longer sure if it was from fear or adrenaline—Kayla snapped the seat belt into place as Emma tucked her toes into the stirrups.

"Are you ready?" Emma asked.

Kayla didn't hesitate this time. "Yes."

"All right." Emma turned to Cam. "You can let go."

He gave the horse's nose another rub, then let go and headed back toward the bleachers.

Emma jumped down from the ramp and took hold of Big Blue's lead rope. "You know what to do," she said to Kayla.

Gripping the reins in her hands, Kayla said in as commanding a voice as she could muster, "Big Blue, walk."

Kayla gasped as the large animal moved beneath her.

And then she started laughing.

Because for the first time in fifteen years, she felt like she was walking.

Cameron had meant to do some work after holding the horse for Kayla. Mary had sent him six reminders today about a brief he needed to get filed. But his laptop remained unopened on his lap. He told himself it was because he was impressed by the large animals or by the horsemanship Ruby showed at such a young age. But that didn't explain why his eyes kept straying to Kayla.

How could they not? That look on her face—like she was in complete awe—tugged at him. He was almost envious. When was the last time he'd felt like that about anything?

He shook his head and opened his laptop. He didn't need to feel awe. He didn't need to feel anything, really. What he needed to do was get this brief done. For the next half hour, he studiously avoided looking up, though that didn't keep him from hearing Kayla's delighted laughter—until he pulled out a pair of earbuds and popped them in.

There.

Now he could focus on the documents in front of him. Black and white, logical, emotionless documents.

The work wasn't necessarily interesting—mostly tedious—but it did the job in getting his focus back where it belonged.

Until the lesson was over and both Ruby and Kayla were in front of him.

"Ruby says you haven't bought a turkey." Kayla pointed an accusatory finger at him.

"Huh?" He tried to take his attention off her pink cheeks and bright eyes long enough to figure out what she was talking about.

"For Thanksgiving." Her stern voice made an odd contrast to her cheerful glow. "What are you doing for Thanksgiving tomorrow?"

He gave her a blank stare, and the determination on her face intensified.

What was it to her what they were doing for Thanksgiving? It wasn't like Ruby was going to starve if they didn't have turkey.

"We'll probably order a pizza or something." He made sure his tone wasn't defensive. He had nothing to feel defensive about.

But Kayla's look said she disagreed. "You are *not* feeding Ruby pizza for Thanksgiving. You're coming to Thanksgiving with us."

"Us?"

"My family and friends. We're helping serve the community Thanksgiving meal right after church."

Cam eyed her. Did she think he needed handouts? "Thanks, but I don't need charity."

Kayla shook her head. "You wear thousand-dollar suits. I didn't think you needed charity. I meant you guys could come help and then join us afterward at my brother and sister-in-law's house for our own dinner."

"Oh. I don't know," Cam hedged. "We couldn't—"

"You're coming. No arguments. Thanksgiving is a day to be with family and friends, right Ruby?"

Ruby nodded, flashing Cam her best smile. "Please, Uncle Cam. Kayla said they have apple pie, and that's my favorite."

Cam opened his mouth to say no again, but Kayla caught his eyes. "Please. I'd really like you to be there."

By "you," Cam knew she meant Ruby. But for whatever reason he found himself relenting slightly. "We'll see."

Both Ruby and Kayla cheered, and Cam fought to keep his lips in a straight line. He was *not* going to be influenced by that.

"Okay, so we have church at ten, if you're interested. Then the community dinner is around noon at Hope Church. And then dinner at Nate and Vi's at six or so." She pulled out her phone, her fingers zooming across the screen. "There. I texted you their address."

"I think you need to review the definition of 'we'll see,'" he said wryly, checking his phone as it dinged with Kayla's text.

"See you tomorrow." Kayla laughed and rolled back toward the arena.

Chapter 16

"I'm interested to meet this Cam guy."

Kayla stopped arranging the vegetable tray she'd been refilling and brought her attention to her sister-in-law. She'd been ruminating on Dan's Thanksgiving sermon from this morning, about being thankful for the unknowns and uncertainties. About trusting God to work things according to his timing, rather than demanding to know everything right now. Because God unfolded everyone's life one page at a time. And though Kayla wished sometimes that her story would turn to the next page already, it had been a reminder she needed to hear. Maybe there was a reason God had kept her on this page for now.

A Ruby-shaped reason, perhaps.

"Why do you want to meet him?" Kayla was on guard. Vi tended to get these crazy ideas about Kayla and men.

"Well—" Violet didn't miss a beat in her carrot chopping rhythm. "He sounds like a study in contrasts. He acts like Ruby is an inconvenience but then takes her to her riding lessons. He doesn't care about his sister but then can't handle seeing her in the hospital. He doesn't like you but then holds a horse so you can get on it."

"He doesn't— Those were all—" Kayla spluttered. She saw exactly what Vi was trying to do.

Anyway, it wasn't like it mattered much. She'd seen the look on his face when he'd said "we'll see" to her invitation last night. He had no intention of coming to Thanksgiving with her and her friends.

And poor Ruby was going to have to eat pizza for Thanksgiving. Maybe Kayla could at least make her a plate and bring it over there later. She supposed she could consider making one for Cam too.

"He's attractive, though, right?" Vi dumped her pile of carrots onto the tray.

"What—" Kayla stared extra-hard at the veggies. "I don't know. Why do you say that?"

"Because you get two little pink spots on your cheeks every time you talk about him." Vi's voice was teasing, but there was no way Kayla was going to let her think she was even a little bit right.

"I do not." She prayed her face wouldn't heat up. But if it did, it was only because Vi's charge was so ludicrous. "I have no interest in Cam. Zero. Zilch."

"Relax." Vi laughed at her. "It's not a crime to be interested in a man."

"Well, I'm not." Anyway, she had a feeling that it might be a crime to be interested in *that* particular man.

"But seriously." Vi rubbed her rounded belly, then picked up the vegetable tray and stepped toward the other room. "I know you worry about giving up your independence. But believe me, when you meet the right man, you won't feel like you're giving anything up. More like you're gaining a part of you that you didn't know was missing."

The kitchen door swung open as Vi was about to exit, and Nate rushed in. "Need more milk." He looked from his wife to Kayla. "What'd I miss?"

"I was just telling Kayla how wonderful marriage is."

Nate smiled and bent to kiss his wife. "I'll second that."

As Vi left the room, Kayla cleaned up their mess.

"So, why were you talking about relationships?" Nate's voice came from above her.

Kayla shrugged. "Your wife has some crazy notions."

Nate laughed. "That she does." He moved to the fridge and grabbed two gallons of milk. "So this guy you invited to dinner—"

Kayla rolled her eyes. "Not you too. He's Ruby's uncle. End of story. I have zero interest in him. I just didn't want Ruby to have pizza for Thanksgiving."

"Whoa." Nate held up his hands. "I was just going to say that this is all probably a pretty big adjustment for him."

"Oh." Kayla let her shoulders relax. "Yeah, I suppose it is." Though over the last couple days, he seemed to be doing better with it than he had at first. Remarkably well, actually.

Nate stepped closer. "But now that you bring it up, *are* you interested in him?"

Kayla's fist darted to slug her brother on the arm. *That* should answer his question.

"I can't wait. I can't wait. I can't wait." Ruby danced through the church parking lot, her purple dress flapping over the nearly matching pink and white striped tights.

"Come on." Ruby sped up. "We're late."

Yeah, over an hour late—mostly because Cameron had changed his mind about whether or not to come every five minutes this morning.

And he was about to change it again. Volunteering had never been his thing. And volunteering with a bunch of strangers sounded even less appealing.

But before he could call to Ruby to come back, she opened the church doors and disappeared inside.

Cameron sighed. He honestly didn't know what had possessed him to tell Ruby to get in the car—aside from the fact that Danielle had ignored his call this morning and that Ruby had asked six billion times if they were going and that she had the next four days off of school and he had no idea what he was going to do to keep her from driving him crazy.

The moment he opened the church door, the smell hit him: turkey, stuffing, potatoes. His mouth watered even as his stomach turned.

Thanksgiving had been his favorite holiday until the year he was twelve and Bethany was seventeen. He could still remember the smell of mom's turkey, the sound of the parade on TV and Dad's jovial laugh as he wrapped his arms around Mom and danced with her right in the middle of the kitchen. They'd sent him to go let Bethany know it was time to eat.

He'd knocked once, not bothering to wait for a response before pushing the door open. But the moment he stepped through, Bethany started screaming at him. He backed out quickly, but not fast enough to avoid seeing the needle shoved in her arm. He'd stood frozen in the hallway, no idea what to do, when Dad had come up to find out what all the commotion was about. Cameron told Dad what he'd seen, Dad called for Mom, and the two of them slipped into Bethany's room, locking him out. By the time they emerged, the turkey was blackened, the potatoes stuck to the pan, the stuffing inedible.

But it hadn't mattered because Mom and Dad had left that night to take Bethany for her very first stay at a rehab center.

Cameron distinctly remembered them telling him that everything was going to be fine—that Bethany had made a mistake, but we all made mistakes. That she would go away and come home all better.

The worst part was, they had believed it. Every single time. Until it cost them everything.

"Ruby." Cameron forced his mind to his sister's daughter as she disappeared down the stairs off to the side of the lobby. He couldn't do this. Not today.

But Ruby either didn't hear him or she chose to ignore him.

The door opened behind Cameron, and he stepped aside to get out of the way of an older gentleman.

The man stepped through the door and looked around. "Nice place."

Cameron grunted a response. He supposed it was. Somehow, in spite of its large size, it managed to give off a warm, cozy feel, with its tall windows letting in plenty of light and the comfortable looking furniture grouped around a large fireplace on the other side of the lobby.

The man stepped to Cameron's side. "You look lost, son."

"Not lost. Just thinking."

"I s'pose this is as good a place to do that as any." The man started toward the steps. "Ya comin' or not?"

Cameron wanted to say, "or not," but he couldn't leave Ruby here by herself. He followed the older man to the stairs.

"Been a long time since I celebrated Thanksgiving," the man said as if they were old friends. "Wife died six years ago. Haven't been able to bring myself to celebrate since then. But this morning, I woke up, looked out the window, and said, 'Sam, you get your grumpy ole butt out of bed and you get some turkey. Not eatin's not gonna change anything and ya can't hide from the past forever. So here I am."

Cameron made a sound at the back of his throat, no idea how else to respond. He didn't avoid Thanksgiving because he was trying to hide from the past. It was just that it was easier not to think about it. That wasn't the same as hiding. Was it?

At the bottom of the stairs, a festive signboard pointed the way to the fellowship hall—though the sign was made unnecessary by the growing aroma of food combined with the clatter of voices and dishes.

The moment they reached the large room, the other man made a beeline for the buffet. But Cameron stopped in the doorway, scanning the dozen long banquet tables crammed into the room, each nearly full. How was he ever going to find Ruby in this crowd?

"Cam. Glad you could make it." Pastor Dan strode toward him, hand outstretched. "Kayla mentioned you might come by to help out. My sister Leah is in charge of this shindig." He pointed to a blonde woman who was scooping turkey onto an elderly woman's plate. "She can let you know what we need help with."

"Have you seen Ruby?" Cam still hadn't spotted her, and an unfamiliar uneasiness went through him. He wasn't sure he liked it.

"She's in the kitchen."

Of course. Because that would be a safe place for a seven-year-old. He started in the direction Dan was pointing.

"Don't worry. Kayla's in there with her," Dan said to his back.

Ah. Cam did an about-face and headed toward the woman Dan had pointed out as his sister. He didn't know why he was suddenly reluctant to see Kayla, but he had a feeling it had to do with the way her glowing cheeks and breathless laugh had refused to leave him alone as he'd tried to fall asleep last night. Just because things with Danielle were rocky didn't mean he wanted to be thinking about some other woman. He wasn't that kind of guy.

He was sure Ruby was fine in the kitchen. He'd stay out here and help until this thing was over. Maybe he and Ruby could grab a bite to eat here and then beg off going to Kayla's brother's house.

But he was kept so busy clearing tables and emptying garbage cans for the next few hours that he didn't get a chance to sit down, let alone eat.

Though it certainly wasn't the type of work he was accustomed to, there was something oddly satisfying about it. Every once in a while as he passed the kitchen, he caught a glimpse of Ruby talking a mile a minute to Kayla, who was always smiling.

He tried to picture Danielle in Kayla's place but came up only with the pinched look she wore whenever someone failed to get right to the point. Still, that didn't make her a bad person. Just one who wouldn't do well with Ruby's constant chatter.

"Hey." Kayla had apparently sneaked up behind him. It was the first time she'd said anything to him today, and he wondered if she'd been avoiding him as studiously as he'd been avoiding her.

He looked up from the trash bag he was tying. "Hey."

"I'm glad you came."

He shrugged. "I'm glad you kept Ruby entertained."

She laughed, bringing her eyes to his. "More like she kept me entertained."

"You have to admit she's a little exhausting."

"Who's exhausting?" Ruby skipped over to Kayla's side.

"Your uncle Cam's just a wimp." Kayla raised an eyebrow at him, but before he could respond, a whistle pierced the air.

Cameron spun to find Dan standing at the front of the room, which had emptied of everyone aside from the handful of volunteers.

"Thank you all for making this event a success. We fed over three hundred people today. And that's thanks to all of you giving so generously of your time. Now, go home and enjoy your families."

A strange surge of satisfaction went through Cameron. It was similar to the satisfaction of completing a big deal—but sweeter somehow. Even though he wasn't going to get a bonus from it—unless sore feet counted as a bonus.

Kayla turned to them. "Ready to eat?"

This was the part where he should back out, say they couldn't make it. But as he looked from Kayla's bright eyes to Ruby's bright smile, he couldn't do it. "Let's go."

Chapter 17

He'd come. Kayla wasn't sure what to do with that fact.

And he'd not only come, but he'd worked hard all afternoon. She didn't think she'd seen him once without dishes or a trash bag in his hands. And he hadn't once acted like it was beneath him.

Which meant she might have to rethink some of her assumptions about him.

But she'd worry about that later. For now, there was the more pressing problem of all the delicious food being passed around the table.

Next to her, Cam filled both his own plate and Ruby's with the dishes Kayla passed his way, looking a little shell-shocked. And she didn't blame him. She'd just introduced him to nearly everyone she knew in Hope Springs.

There were Nate and Vi, of course. And then there was Vi's sister Jade, who was married to Pastor Dan, along with their daughter Hope, who was a little younger than Ruby, and their one-year-old son Matthias. Plus Dan's sister Leah, her husband Austin, and their teenage son Jackson.

And that was just family.

Most of Nate and Vi's other friends had also made it: Emma; Sophie and Spencer and their twins; Tyler and Isabel and their three kids; Ethan and Ariana and their daughter; and newlyweds Grace and Levi and Luke and May. The only ones missing were Jared and Peyton, who were currently in China to meet their adopted daughter.

"So Cam, where are you from?" Vi asked from the other side of the table.

Kayla eyed her sister-in-law, trying to decide if she was up to something, but as far as she could tell, Vi was just being polite.

"Originally, Texas. But I've lived in LA since law school."

"You're a lawyer?" Kayla didn't mean to sound surprised. Actually, it made sense, the way he was always on his phone or his computer. "What kind?"

"Corporate law. Mostly mergers and acquisitions."

"That sounds . . . interesting?" Oops. It wasn't supposed to come out as a question.

"Yeah, it's—" Cam shook his head with a slight laugh. "Really not. A few high-stress moments followed by a lot of paperwork, mostly."

"What would you rather do?" Kayla didn't mean to ask the question, but there it was.

Cam gave her a blank look, as if he didn't understand what she meant.

"You know, like what did you want to do when you were a kid?" She tried to clarify. "Like, I wanted to be Supergirl."

Cam laughed. "I never had any superhero aspirations."

But she wasn't going to let him off the hook that easily. "Okay, then. What *did* you want to do?"

Cam studied his plate so long she was sure the conversation was over, but then he met her eyes. "My dad had a landscaping company. I worked with him in the summers when I was a kid. Always loved it." He turned away abruptly and stabbed at a piece of turkey but didn't lift it to his mouth.

Kayla already knew his parents were dead, since Ruby had no grandparents, and her heart went out to him. "You should do that then. Start your own landscaping company, I mean."

Cam shook his head, looking at her like she'd lost touch with reality. "It doesn't work like that."

"Sure it does. You just have to—"

"It's not going to happen," Cam said sharply.

Kayla bit her tongue. She'd gotten carried away. It was none of her business if Cam wanted to keep doing a job he hated.

"What about you, Kayla?" Emma asked from her other side.

Kayla shot her a relieved look. Anything so she didn't have to keep talking to Cam.

"I heard the camp closed," Emma said. "Embezzlement or something?"

Cam's head lifted at that, and he gave her a hard look. Well, it wasn't like she'd been the one stealing money.

"Our director," she told Emma. "I never would have believed it if he hadn't confessed."

"I hope the organization reported it," Cam cut in, his voice blistering. "The guy deserves to be prosecuted."

Kayla shrugged. "They haven't figured out what to do yet. To be honest, I feel sorry for him. He was going through a rough divorce and gave in to temptation."

"That's no excuse." Cam's hand was clenched tight around his glass.

Why did he care so much? It wasn't like he had any involvement with the organization. Maybe because he was a lawyer?

"No, it's not," Kayla agreed. "But he has repented and asked for forgiveness."

Cam's smile looked more like a sneer. "Of course he has. That's easy enough to say. Especially when you're facing the possibility of prison."

Kayla shrugged. "It's enough for me. Personally, I hope he doesn't end up in prison, but that's up to the courts. Either way, I forgive him."

"Of course you do."

Before Kayla could decipher whether Cam's mutter was meant to be sincere or sarcastic, Emma cut in. "So what are you going to do now, Kayla? Any leads on a new job?"

"Actually, no. Or well, yes. There are a few places I've considered applying, but I don't know. I feel like God has something else for me right now. I just put in an application for a six-month mission trip to Malawi."

"That's awesome. Sounds like it's right up your alley."

Kayla dropped her gaze to her plate. "I hope the organizers see it that way. That they don't think this thing"—she tapped her wheelchair's frame—"will get in the way."

"If it hasn't stopped you from skydiving and winning marathons, I don't think it's going to stop you from this either." Jade joined the conversation.

Cam's eyes swiveled to Kayla. "Skydiving?" Was that admiration in his voice—or disapproval?

Not that it mattered.

"Twice," she said, enjoying the shock in his expression a little too much. "Anyway—" She turned back to Emma and Jade. "I'll find out if I was chosen in a few weeks. So I guess I'll figure out what's next from there."

"Doesn't it bother you not to have a plan?" Cam looked horrified at the possibility.

She shrugged. "A little bit, maybe. But I've encountered more than one unexpected event in my life." She gestured at her motionless legs. "I've found that God always has a way of working them out."

Cam opened his mouth, but Ruby beat him to speaking. "Want to play a game with me, Kayla?"

Kayla smiled past Cam. "I'd love to." Her eyes flicked to Cam. "How about it? Up for a game?"

"That's three games in a row," Cameron crowed, moving his gingerbread man onto the castle. Apparently, Candy Land was his game.

Ruby pouted at him. "Don't you know you're supposed to let the kids win sometimes?"

"What fun would that be? Then you'd feel cheated." Cameron gathered up the game cards. "I think it's time to get you home to bed."

Ruby yawned. "But I'm not sleepy."

Kayla laughed from her spot on the floor next to Ruby. When they'd first gotten out the game, the tables had still been covered with food, so Ruby had suggested they play on the floor. Cameron had been searching for a way to tactfully remind her that Kayla used a wheelchair so she couldn't just go crawling around on the floor, but Kayla had beaten him to the punch by lifting her feet to the floor, then lowering her body to the ground. Actually, she'd gotten down here more smoothly than Cameron, who couldn't remember the last time he'd sat on the floor.

As she reached for her wheelchair now, he considered offering to help. Surely he could scoop her up and set her in it in a matter of seconds.

But he'd learned his lesson when he'd tried to hold the door for her at the Chocolate Chicken.

As he watched her hoist herself back into the chair, he couldn't help but be impressed. He wasn't surprised she'd won marathons—she obviously had the arm strength for it. But skydiving?

That crossed the border into crazy-town. He was more of a two-feet-on-the-ground kind of guy.

Which was the reason he didn't go off and do something nonsensical like leave the high-paying job that afforded him the lifestyle he'd always admired to chase some dream of opening a landscaping company.

Maybe in Kayla's world not knowing what was coming was okay. But not in his. He had a plan, and he wasn't going to change it—despite this temporary hiccup in Hope Springs.

Still, he had to admit that he'd ended up enjoying the day with Kayla's family and friends.

He attended plenty of parties in LA, of course—most of them much bigger and fancier than this had been. And yet, sometimes those felt more like performances, like putting on a show so that the other guests would like you and want to do business with you. Here, everyone seemed to genuinely know and care about one another.

Why they'd extended that care to him and Ruby, he wasn't sure. But he couldn't deny that it felt nice.

Chapter 18

"So I was right." Vi passed Kayla the Santa hat she was supposed to wear to the parade.

Kayla was sure she was going to regret asking, but she couldn't help it. "About what?"

She stuck the Santa hat on her head and examined the full effect of the costume in the bedroom mirror. She still wasn't quite sure how Emma had talked her into being Mrs. Claus. All she knew was that when Emma had shown up at church this morning with the costume and a plea that the mom who was supposed to be Mrs. Claus had gotten sick, she hadn't been able to say no.

"Cam is good looking." Vi grinned at her in the mirror, and Kayla reached a hand behind her to swat at her sister-in-law, but for a pregnant lady, Vi was pretty agile.

"You're married to my brother, you know."

"And he agrees with me."

"Nate thinks Cam is attractive?"

Now it was Vi's turn to swat at her. She hit her target, knocking the hat off Kayla's head.

Vi started to squat to get it, her hand on her back, but Kayla turned her chair and reached for it.

"He agrees with me that you and Cam have good chemistry," Vi said as Kayla resettled the hat on her head.

Kayla snorted. "If by chemistry you mean we make each other want to explode, then I guess you're right."

"That's not what it looked like to the rest of us."

"The rest of—" She should have figured that Vi and her friends would jump to conclusions.

"I promise you that the only thing we have in common is Ruby."

Vi patted her shoulder. "Relationships have started on less."

Kayla shook her head. "You're impossible." She spun her chair and headed out of the room.

"I'm just saying, don't be surprised if he asks you out at some point," Vi called behind her. "And don't do what you always do."

Kayla stopped her chair and looked over her shoulder. "And what do I always do?"

"You know." Vi made a vague gesture. "Chase a guy away before he ever has a chance."

Kayla rolled her eyes. "I don't do that."

Or, well, she did, but for good reason. It was either chase them away or risk losing herself.

"I'm leaving now." She wheeled to the front door.

But Vi's words chased her all the way to the church parking lot, where they were to line up for the parade. Was her sister-in-law right? Did Cam like her? And if he did, how did she feel about it?

Not good, she decided. *Not good at all.*

Even if a little tingle went through her at the thought that he'd be here in a few minutes.

"Wear this too." Cameron passed Ruby a scarf.

She dutifully took it. "Uncle Cam, I can barely move."

"It's cold out, and I assume we're going to be out there a while." He used to walk alongside the trailer he and dad decorated with small Christmas trees every year, so he wasn't completely unfamiliar with the concept. Although that had been in Texas, where a sweatshirt had been enough to keep him warm—wouldn't Dad laugh to see him now in a winter jacket on top of a heavy flannel on top of a thermal shirt?

He shook his head as he bundled an equally well-layered Ruby out the door and into the car. He'd found himself thinking about Dad and his business a lot over the last few days. And he needed to stop—before his feelings of nostalgia convinced him Kayla had been right in suggesting that he leave law to open his own landscaping business. It wasn't logical to give up a prestigious, high-paying job in favor of the challenges and uncertainties of running a small business—no matter how much he might enjoy it.

But as he drove toward the church to line up for the parade, he found himself looking at the yards they passed with a critical eye. That one had several dead trees in need of removal. And the one over there could benefit from a new retaining wall. Not to mention that the low, squat shrubs in front of nearly every house did little to add to their curb appeal.

Cameron slowed as he pulled onto Church Street. People, horses, fire trucks, and floats lined the road, but instead of feeling crowded, it had a festive air. Cameron eased into the church lot, searching for a parking spot. His phone rang as he pulled into one, and it took him a moment of digging through his various layers before he found it tucked into the pocket of his flannel.

Danielle.

"Come on, Uncle Cam. We're going to be late."

"I know. Just a sec." His eyes fell on Emma with the horses. "Why don't you go join Miss Emma? I'll be there in a minute." As soon as Ruby had clambered out of the car, he pulled the phone to his ear, his eyes tracking his niece as she ran toward the group from the stables.

"Hey, Danielle. I'm glad you called." He didn't mention that he'd been waiting three days for her to return his last call.

"Have you made any progress?"

Cameron sighed. He knew she wanted him to come home. He wanted that too. But it might be nice if she'd ask how things were going for once. "Nothing new yet. Honestly, I'm not sure what else we can do. I think I just have to ride this out and hope that Bethany wakes up soon."

"Ride it out?" Danielle made a disbelieving click. "And what about me, Cameron? I'm supposed to sit around here waiting for you?"

Cameron rubbed at his jaw, his eyes following Ruby as she reached Miss Emma and pointed in his direction. He lifted a hand to wave, though he doubted they could see him in the dark. "You could come here. I know you have plenty of vacation time and . . ."

"Wisconsin is not my idea of a vacation, Cameron." Danielle did not sound amused.

"It's not that bad." As long as you wore layers. Cameron snickered to himself, patting at his puffy jacket. "And then you could get to know Ruby and see that kids aren't so bad. Maybe we'll even want one of our own someday."

"I hope you're not serious, Cameron." She said the words with deadly precision. "Because I've already made my feelings on that perfectly clear. As have you, I thought."

"I know." He'd been kidding—mostly. He knew Danielle would never change her mind about that. And neither would he. Right?

He spotted Ruby, now marching toward the car with a whole pack of people behind her, including Miss Emma, who appeared to be waving some kind of red fabric at him. He squinted, trying to figure out what it was.

"I'm sorry, Danielle, I have to go for now. Someone's waving a Santa suit at me."

"A what? Cameron—"

"Talk to you soon." He hung up before she could protest again.

As he opened the car door, he let out a breath. But he didn't have long to brood about the conversation as Emma, Ruby, and a group of giggling girls descended on him.

"You have to be Santa," Ruby said at the same time that Emma shoved the red suit at him.

"Please," Emma added. "You're my last hope. My Mrs. Claus canceled this morning. And now my Santa just called. Apparently there's a nasty stomach bug going around."

Cameron eyed the suit. "I don't—"

"You have to do it, Uncle Cam." Ruby and the other riders looked up at him so earnestly that he felt his resolve weakening.

"So, who's Santa?" A woman's voice called from behind him. He didn't have to turn to know it was Kayla, but he did anyway, laughing as he spotted her costume. Apparently, Emma had found her replacement Mrs. Claus.

He held up the suit. "I guess I am."

Great. Now Kayla felt self-conscious around Cam.

Thanks, Vi.

If her sister-in-law hadn't put it in her head that Cam liked her, then she could be sitting calmly next to him in this horse-drawn wagon that had been modified to look like a sleigh, waving to the crowd that had braved the frigid night. Instead of analyzing his every move and word to figure out if it held hidden signs of attraction.

The good news was that so far she'd seen nothing to indicate that Vi was right.

Even so, Kayla couldn't help weighing her own words and actions to make sure she wasn't giving him the wrong impression. The last thing she needed was for him to think she returned his feelings—if he had any in the first place. Which he didn't.

Kayla forced her thoughts off Cam and his feelings or lack thereof and scanned the group of horse riders in front of them for Ruby.

"She's a good rider." She nodded toward where Ruby was drawing her horse to a halt.

Cam directed his gaze in Ruby's direction. "I'm not surprised. We rode a lot as kids. One of my dad's biggest clients was this huge ranch."

Huh. One of the things Vi might have been right about was that Cam was a study in contrasts. He made it clear that he didn't want anything to do with his sister, and yet when he talked about his past like this, Kayla heard the nostalgia and something deeper—rawer—in his voice. She debated asking him if something had happened but decided against it. During a parade while dressed as Santa and Mrs. Claus probably wasn't the best place for a heart-to-heart.

"Are you warm enough?" Cam clapped his gloved hands together, then shifted the blanket that sat across their laps so that it covered her more.

"I'm good." She kept waving to the crowd on her side of the sleigh.

"How can you tell?" He slapped a hand to his mouth, looking mortified. "Sorry. That was a Ruby question."

"No. It's fine." She never minded answering questions about her injury—and it was always preferable to people simply staring. "I do have to be careful because I can't feel when my feet are cold. But usually as long as I don't start shivering, I know I'm okay.

Plus, I'm wearing wool socks and multiple layers, and I'm pretty much as covered up as a person can be." She eyed him. "Though maybe not quite as much as you."

He laughed and pulled his gray stocking cap tighter over his ears. "Hey, give me a break. I'm still adapting to this cold climate. I don't know how you handle it. I'll be glad to get back to the California sun."

Kayla nodded, relief going through her. She was being stupid to worry that Cam liked her. He lived in California. And he'd be going back just as soon as Bethany woke up.

"Hi, Santa. Hi, Mrs. Claus."

Kayla turned her head toward the voice and found a little boy waving at them, his parents standing behind him with their arms wrapped around each other. They would have made a perfect Christmas card.

A tiny wave of sadness went through her at the knowledge that she would never sit and watch a parade with a family of her own.

But she dismissed the thought immediately. Of course she would. She'd always have Nate and Vi and her little niece or nephew.

And that was all she wanted.

She shifted away from Cam the slightest bit, mainly to remind herself that she didn't need the warmth of another person next to her.

Chapter 19

"Don't you dare." Cameron eyed the cat crouching on the floor, shaking its haunches in preparation to jump onto the bed where Cameron sat with his computer on his lap. He'd already shoved the dumb creature off him a dozen times tonight.

But with a twitch of its tail, the cat jumped, coming to a light landing next to his leg. He nudged it off the bed, then checked the clock on his computer screen. It was nearing midnight.

He should go to sleep. He'd been staring at this screen for way too long without making any progress. He had three conference calls tomorrow, and for the first time in his career, he felt unprepared.

Possibly because somehow his computer browser kept clicking over to sites about starting a landscaping company. Which was completely the opposite of where his attention needed to be.

It needed to be on his actual job. On returning to California. On Danielle, who was apparently refusing his calls again—he'd attempted to reach her four times today and gone straight to voice mail each time. He'd tried not to be relieved that she hadn't answered.

With a weary groan, he stretched, then closed his laptop. Staring at his screen more wasn't going to get him any further tonight. His eyes fell on the Bible that had sat on Bethany's nightstand since the day he'd arrived. He hadn't been able to figure out what it was doing there, since his sister had never been the Bible-reading type. He reached for it, paging through it more out of curiosity than anything else. He raised his eyebrows at the highlights and penciled notes.

A section highlighted in purple caught his attention, and in spite of himself, his eyes tracked over the words. "Do nothing out of selfish ambition or vain conceit. Rather, in humility value others above yourselves, not looking to your own interests but each of you to the interests of the others."

Cameron almost choked on his sarcastic snort. The Bethany he knew was the very definition of selfishness and vanity. She'd never put another person before herself a day in her life.

He snapped the Bible shut and shoved it into the nightstand drawer. It was time to go to bed.

He was just pulling off his shirt when he heard the door across the hallway open and little footsteps running toward the bathroom. He shook his head. It wasn't Ruby's first late-night bathroom run. He kept telling her not to drink so much water before bed.

But instead of the sound of the bathroom door closing, he heard a strange sort of coughing noise. He pulled his shirt back on.

"Ruby?" He tugged his own door open. "You— Oh." He clapped a hand over his mouth and nose as Ruby stood over the emptied contents of her stomach.

"That's— Oh—" He fought off a gag as Ruby started crying. "It's okay." Though he didn't see how. "Do you have to throw up anymore?"

She shook her head.

"All right. Go change your pajamas and get back in bed. I'll bring you some water and then . . ."

Yes, and then what?

He had no idea how to take care of a sick kid.

He pulled his phone out of his pocket on the way to the kitchen, scrolling past Danielle's name with an ironic laugh. He could only imagine what she'd say if he asked for advice on taking care of a puking kid. Instead, he tapped on Kayla's name. He had no idea if she was a night owl or not, but it was worth a shot.

You still up?

Her reply came instantly. *What's wrong?*

He shook his head. How did she know? Then again, he'd never texted her at midnight before, so it probably wasn't too much of a leap. *Ruby threw up all over the place, and I have no idea what to do.*

Does she have a fever?

Check for a fever. Yeah. That was a good idea.

He grabbed a plastic cup out of the kitchen cupboard and filled it with water. He brought it to Ruby, whose hand shook as she drank it.

A small sliver of worry slid into his gut. That wasn't normal, was it?

He hurried to the bathroom, careful to give the puddle in the hallway as wide a berth as he could without looking at it. It only took a minute of rummaging in the closet to locate a thermometer.

"Bingo." He didn't know why it should give him such a sense of achievement, but he'd take it.

He brought the device to Ruby, who moaned slightly as he tried to figure out how to operate it. Finally, he realized that it was the kind that went under the arm.

It seemed to take forever to beep, but when it did, he pulled it out. Ruby moaned again.

99.4, he texted Kayla. *She keeps moaning.*

Poor thing. It's probably the stomach bug that's going around.

That made sense. And a stomach bug was nothing to worry about, right?

Okay, thanks. I need to try to clean this up and then email my secretary to reschedule my meetings tomorrow.

He shoved his phone in his pocket and went to search out some paper towels and carpet cleaner. And hopefully a pair of gloves too.

But his phone buzzed again almost immediately. *I can come watch her for the day if you need to do your meetings.*

Cameron stared at the phone. Not for the first time, he wondered who this woman *was* that she kept helping them without asking for anything in return.

He didn't want to take advantage of her. But he really *did* need to be on those calls.

You're sure? he finally texted. *It would only be for a couple hours, and I'll technically be here the whole time.*

I'm sure, Cam. I was going to go read to Bethany, but I'm sure she'd understand if I spend the day with her daughter instead. Now get that cleaned up and go to bed.

I will. Thank you, Kayla. He hesitated, then typed out the rest of his thought. *You may really be Supergirl after all.*

She sent a smiley face emoji, and he was about to put his phone away when he got one more message. *Oh, and give Ruby a pail. Just in case.*

Cameron groaned but then grinned. Supergirl, indeed.

Chapter 20

Kayla looked up from her book at the sound of Cam's bedroom door opening. The cat curled in her lap picked up its head momentarily, then settled back onto her legs.

"How's she doing?" he whispered, glancing toward Ruby's sleeping form on the couch.

"She seems to be doing a little better. Just fell back to sleep."

To be honest, Cam looked like he could use some sleep himself, his usually tidy hair slightly askew and faint traces of blue under his eyes.

"Did you get any sleep at all?"

He shook his head. "She puked three more times during the night, so no. I had no idea kids could be so gross."

"Or that you could worry about them so much?"

He waved off her comment, but he wasn't fooling her with that tough guy act.

"How was the call?" She'd heard the low murmur of his voice from out here, which she had to admit had made rather soothing background noise.

"Don't ask. Let's just say I'm lucky the deal didn't fall apart right then and there. Speaking of—" He pulled his phone out of his pocket and checked the screen. "I'd better get on my next call. It shouldn't be longer than an hour."

She nodded. "Take your time. I'm plenty content here." Wait. Did that make it sound like—? She quickly held up her book. "I mean, with my book."

"Thank you again for doing this, Kayla." He smiled, then disappeared into the bedroom.

Kayla settled back into her book, reading until Ruby opened her eyes half an hour later.

"How are you feeling?"

Ruby rubbed her stomach. "I'm hungry."

"I know you are, sweetie. But maybe we should wait, just to make sure you aren't going to get sick anymore." Poor Cam had already cleaned up after her so many times. And Kayla was quite sure that was outside his usual wheelhouse, though she was proud of him for stepping up.

"I'm bored." Ruby sat up partway, and Kayla wheeled closer to the couch so she could adjust the pillows behind the girl.

"We can fix that. I can read you a book or we can watch a movie or play a board game."

"Can we play Barbies?"

"Sure. How about we play right here, though, so you can rest. I'll bring them over." She crossed the room and grabbed the box that held Ruby's Barbie collection. She wheeled back to Ruby, positioning herself so that she faced the girl. "You have a lot of these. Who do you want to be?"

"I'm Barbie." Ruby dug in the bin. "And you can be Ken." She passed Kayla a Ken doll.

"All right. What should Ken and Barbie do?"

Ruby gave her a goofy smile. "Go on a date."

A laugh burst from Kayla. They were starting young these days. "A date, huh?"

Ruby nodded but giggled. "They're boyfriend and girlfriend."

"Ah, I see." Kayla pretended to walk Ken across the couch, then made her voice deep. "Hello, Barbie. Would you like to go on a date with me?"

"Yes, Ken." Ruby made her voice even higher pitched, then dissolved into giggles.

But after a moment, she stopped and laid back on the pillows. "My tummy hurts again."

Kayla brushed the hair off her forehead. "Maybe no Barbies for now. How about I read to you instead?"

Ruby nodded, and Kayla moved to the small bookshelf in the corner to choose a book.

"Do you have a boyfriend?" Ruby's question came out of nowhere, and Kayla turned to peer at the girl over her shoulder.

"Nope."

"Do you want a boyfriend?"

Kayla turned back to the bookshelf. "Nope."

"Why not?"

Kayla paused, her finger on the spine of a book. "I'm too independent, I think."

"What does independent mean?"

Kayla pulled a book off the shelf and flipped through it. "It means I like to do things for myself. Make my own decisions."

"And you can't do that when you have a boyfriend?"

Kayla put the book back, pulling another off the shelf. "I suppose you can, but—" How in the living world was she supposed to explain this to a seven-year-old? "It's just different."

"Well, I still want a boyfriend." Ruby sounded so earnest that Kayla had to laugh.

"No boyfriends for at least another twenty years." Cam's voice from the other side of the living room made Kayla jump.

Heat rushed to her cheeks. How long had he been standing there? And how much of their conversation had he heard?

Not that it mattered. Anyone who knew her knew she wasn't interested in a relationship. It was no secret.

She set the book on her lap and turned her chair to face him. "We were just about to read."

He nodded, but the way he was looking at her was odd. He shook his head as if clearing away a thought. "Actually, my last call got canceled, so if you want to go, I've got it from here."

"Oh." How did she say she'd like to stay without it coming across the wrong way?

She didn't, that was how. "Okay." She set the book on the arm of the couch. "Feel better, Ruby."

"I will. Thank you for taking care of me."

"Anytime." She brushed the girl's hair off her forehead, then collected her bag and wheeled to the front door, Cam following behind her.

"Wait!" Ruby's call was urgent, and both she and Cam spun toward her.

"What's wrong? Do you have to throw up again?" Cam made a face but stepped toward Ruby.

But she shook her head. "I have a great idea."

Cam stared at her. "All that commotion was for an idea?"

"Yep." Ruby was unapologetic. "It's a really good idea. Kayla should come to the zoo with us on Saturday."

"Oh. Uh—" Cam glanced over his shoulder at Kayla for a millisecond before turning away. "I thought you wanted to bring a friend."

"Kayla is my friend," Ruby insisted, and Kayla's heart went all syrupy.

"I'm sure Kayla has other—" Cam looked over his shoulder again, his expression a clear plea to help him out.

But there was no way Kayla could say no to such a sweet invitation. "I'd love to come if you don't mind."

Cam studied her for a long moment. Then he shrugged. "We'll pick you up at nine."

Chapter 21

"It's zoo day! It's zoo day!" Ruby danced around the kitchen. She'd made a remarkable recovery after Tuesday's illness, and she was definitely back to her old, noisy self. Cameron was surprised at the intensity of his relief about that. It was odd to him how unsettling it had been to see her sick.

He gave her a mock frown and pointed to her soggy bowl of cereal. "Eat. Or we're not going anywhere."

Which, honestly, might be the best course of action. What had he been thinking, letting Ruby invite Kayla along?

But he supposed he did owe her, after the way she'd come to his rescue watching Ruby so he could make his conference calls.

And he'd overheard her telling Ruby that she wasn't interested in dating, so he didn't have to worry that she'd get the wrong impression about their relationship. Not that it even was a relationship—more like an acquaintanceship.

"When can we see Mommy again?" Ruby followed her question with a big slurp of the milk left in her cereal bowl.

"We just went yesterday." This time, Cameron hadn't run out of the room, though he'd remained planted in a corner while Ruby talked up a storm to her mother.

"I know, but the doctors said it's good for her to hear my voice. It will help her wake up."

Cameron held in a sigh. The doctors also said that if Bethany was in the coma much longer, her chances of coming out of it fell dramatically. Though that part he hadn't shared with Ruby.

What if Bethany didn't wake up? The thought had been circling his head all night.

What would happen to Ruby? Since he was Bethany's only living relative, did that mean the state would automatically give Ruby to him? And did he want her?

The truth was, he didn't know. He never would have guessed it three weeks ago when he arrived, but there were parts of taking care of her that weren't all bad. Kind of enjoyable, even. Like the way she gave that goofy gap-toothed grin or made a surprisingly witty comment that forced a chuckle out of him. Or wrapped her little arms around him in an unexpectedly powerful hug.

But did he want to give up his whole life, everything he knew—including, quite possibly, his girlfriend—to become a father to her? That was a big step. One he wasn't sure he was prepared—or qualified—for.

"I'm ready." Ruby wiped the back of her hand over her milk mustache.

He sighed. Figuring out the future could wait.

For now, they had a trip to the zoo to get on with.

Cam seemed different today, but Kayla couldn't quite put her finger on what it was. She'd noticed it almost the moment he'd picked her up this morning, and it had lasted through the hour-long car ride and the past two hours at the zoo.

Maybe it was the fact that he was wearing jeans instead of his usual dress clothes. Or that he didn't have his phone attached to his ear. Or that he actually smiled every once in a while.

Whatever it was, it gave him a relaxed, less aloof air. And for some reason, that was making her uncomfortable, though she was more than happy to see Ruby enjoying herself.

"Can we get some popcorn? And then go see the giraffes? They're my favoritest favorites." Ruby skipped between them, and Kayla caught the look of envy a woman walking past with two screaming toddlers shot them.

Kayla was tempted to call out to the woman that they weren't the happy family they must look like. Even if it almost felt like they were.

That was it. That was what was making her so uncomfortable. The fact that they looked like all the other families here—and that she couldn't convince herself that she didn't like it.

"That popcorn does smell good." Cam veered toward the popcorn stand off to the side of the path. "Three bags."

"Make that two," Kayla cut in. "I'll get my own."

Cam gave her an odd look. "I've got it." He turned back to the teenager working the cart. "Make it three."

"Cam, I said I'll get it myself." She didn't know why it was such a big deal to her, but it was.

"Kayla, it's fifty cents. I think I can spring for it. I owe you for watching Ruby the other day."

The teenager looked uncertainly between Cam and Kayla. "So a dollar fifty, then?" He passed three bags of popcorn through the window.

Cam paid, then passed a bag to Ruby before grabbing up the other two and carrying them toward a table on a stone terrace that overlooked a small pond.

Kayla let out a huff as she followed. She was being stupid, but for some reason it really bothered her that Cam had bought the popcorns. She knew he was right that she'd more than paid him back by watching Ruby. But that was something a friend or even a babysitter did. Buying popcorn was something a date did. And this was *not* a date.

And she didn't want it to be one.

At the table, Cam passed her a bag of popcorn, but she set it down.

"I'm going to run to the restroom while we're stopped." She needed a minute to herself. Besides which, since she couldn't feel her bladder, she'd had to train her body to follow a schedule, and it was almost time.

"Do you need to go, Ruby?"

The little girl shook her head. "I went before we left home. Uncle Cam forgot to tell me, but Mommy always does, so I knew."

Kayla smiled at the girl, then wheeled away, feeling Cam's eyes on the back of her head. She didn't look over her shoulder.

Thankfully, by the time she'd finished in the restroom, she had managed to talk some sense into herself. She could even laugh at herself for getting so freaked out at the thought of family and dating. Neither Cam nor Ruby were thinking like that. She'd just let her imagination get away with her—or, more like Vi's imagination.

She'd go back out there and they'd continue on with their trip to the zoo—just an uncle and his niece and their friend.

She maneuvered out of the bathroom and toward the terrace where she'd left them.

Cam sat at the table, his phone pressed to his ear, and Kayla rolled her eyes at herself. All those worries about why Cam was acting so differently today—and here he was on his phone again.

She scanned the terrace for Ruby but didn't spot her among the few other families gathered there. She craned her head over her shoulder in both directions but didn't see her there either.

She sped toward Cam's table.

"Cam!" Her voice was sharp, but he didn't stop talking or even look up.

She shoved her chair closer and yanked the phone out of his hand.

That got his attention. "What are you—" He cut off as his eyes fell on her. "What's wrong?"

"Where's Ruby?" She barely managed to keep the panic out of her voice.

"She went to throw her popcorn bag away." His eyes darted across the terrace. "She was just here . . ."

His eyes met hers, horror-struck. "Where'd she go?"

"It's okay." Kayla needed him to stay calm, which meant she needed to stay calm herself. "We'll find her."

Cam sprang up from the table so quickly that Kayla had to roll her wheelchair backwards so he wouldn't plow into her.

He grabbed his phone from her and lifted it to his ear. "I'm going to have to call you back."

Without waiting for a response, he hung up, then spun in a slow circle, his eyes tracking across the landscape.

The moment he turned toward the pond, he froze, then sprinted toward it.

Kayla's heart leapt to her throat.

A thin sheen of ice skimmed the surface, not thick enough to hold a mouse, let alone a child.

Ruby wouldn't have . . .

Would she?

Kayla took off after Cam, who had scrambled down the side of the embankment that rimmed the shore.

He looked up, relief mingled with fear in his expression. "She didn't come down here." He rushed back up the bank.

"She couldn't have gone far. It's only been a few minutes." She focused on keeping her voice calm to steady both of them. "You go that way—" She pointed over her shoulder. "I'll go this way. Make sure you ask anyone you see. Find someone from the zoo if you can, and have them let the rest of the zoo's employees know."

He gave a terse nod, already striding away.

"Cam!" she called to his back.

He turned but didn't stop walking.

"We'll find her. Call me the second you have anything."

Chapter 22

Cameron raised his voice, fighting to call his niece's name over the pulse thumping hard and fast in his throat. His sister, the perennial screw-up, had managed to keep Ruby alive and intact for seven years. And now he'd been with the kid for less than a month and he'd already lost her.

"Ruby!" The name came out as a sharp gasp, and a woman holding a little girl's hand gave him a strange look. He jogged over to her, half expecting her to run away at his likely crazed expression.

But she stood her ground, tugging the girl closer to her.

"Sorry, ma'am. But have you seen a little girl walking around? She's wearing a—" What had she been wearing? Her coat, right? He saw it hanging on the hook by the door every day, watched her put it on before school. It was . . . "A blue coat. With snowflakes on it."

The woman shook her head. "Sorry. I haven't."

"Okay. Um." Why couldn't he think straight? He dealt with crises at work on a daily basis. And they'd never clouded his head like this. He took a breath. He had to take the emotion out of the situation. What he needed was some logic. Except, somehow that was a lot harder to pull up when it came to his missing niece than a stranger in a boardroom.

"Why don't you give me your number, and if I see her, I'll call you." The woman's voice was kind as she passed him her phone.

"Yeah. Okay. Yeah, that's a good idea." It took Cameron three tries to type his number in with his shaking hands, but he finally passed the phone back to the woman.

"What's your daughter's name?" the woman asked.

"Oh. She's not my— It's Ruby. Her name is Ruby."

"That's a pretty name." The little girl who had remained quiet throughout his exchange with her mother smiled shyly at him. "I'll say a prayer that you find her."

"Uh—" Cameron scratched at his cheek, backing away. He shouldn't be wasting time chatting. He needed to keep looking for Ruby. "Thanks."

He turned and set off at a jog again. "Ruby!"

A bear in the enclosure next to him lifted its head.

But there was no sign anywhere of his little niece.

Please, God. Let us find her. He didn't know where the prayer had come from, didn't remember the last time he'd prayed, but it was the only thing he could think to do.

Ten minutes later, Cameron's feet dragged to a stop. Prayer or not, they were never going to find her.

What if someone had kidnapped her or—

No. He couldn't let his thoughts go there.

He'd alerted zoo security, and they were checking every visitor who left the zoo.

His phone rang, and he snatched it out of his pocket, exhaling hard as he read Kayla's name on the screen.

"Please tell me you found her."

"By the giraffes." Her laugh was shaky and weak. "We should have known."

"I'll be right there."

The moment he hung up, his feet kicked into a sprint, and he followed the signs that pointed the way to the giraffe enclosure.

When he finally spotted Ruby and Kayla watching a giraffe amble past, relief and anger collided in his chest. How could the little girl put him through something like that?

He slowed to a walk, though his heart continued to pump like mad.

"Hi, Uncle Cam." Ruby's oblivious greeting sent him over the edge.

He opened his mouth to yell at her. But her eyes, a perfect reflection of his own, welled with tears, and next thing he knew, he was crouching and pulling her to him in a hug. "Are you okay?"

Ruby nodded against his jacket, her little arms squeezing his neck. "I'm sorry. Do you forgive me?"

Cameron hesitated, then nodded. "Don't ever do that again, okay?"

As Ruby nodded again, then skipped back to the giraffes, Cameron could only look at Kayla and shake his head. He wondered if she was thinking the same thing he was: parenting sure was heart-wrenching work.

It was one more reminder of why he didn't want to do it permanently. He'd never be able to handle all the messes. All the cleaning up. All the sleepless nights.

All the smiles. All the hugs. All the giggles.

He shook off the thought. Sure, that stuff was nice. But it didn't make up for the hassle of having your days completely consumed by caring for another human being.

Did it?

Chapter 23

Cameron strained for a glimpse of Ruby among the children flooding out of the school Monday afternoon. Ever since almost losing her at the zoo the other day, he'd found himself fighting off a sense of unease whenever he didn't know right where she was. He knew it was silly—she was obviously among these talking and giggling kids. But that close call had left him more than a little shaken.

If he'd lost her, he didn't know . . .

Cameron shook his head. He *hadn't* lost her, thanks to Kayla.

Finally, he spotted Ruby trailing behind the other kids, head down and feet dragging. Cameron frowned. That wasn't the Ruby he knew at all—the one who was always at the center of the group, laughing and talking away. He hoped she wasn't sick again.

He waved as she got closer to the car, but she didn't look up.

Now what did he do?

He'd gotten used to dealing with happy, bubbly Ruby—even when he got annoyed sometimes at *how* cheerful she could be. But he had no idea how to deal with sullen, sulky Ruby.

She kept her sullen expression as she slid into the back seat.

"Hey, Rubes." He injected an extra note of cheer into his greeting. "Feeling okay?"

"Yes." Her voice was flat.

"Oh." If that wasn't the problem, then what? "How was your day?"

"Terrible." Ruby clicked on her seat belt, then crossed her arms in front of her.

"I'm sure it couldn't have been that bad." He pulled out of the parking spot. "What was so terrible about it?"

"I'm a sheep."

Cameron angled his head so he could see her in the rearview mirror. "You look like a girl to me."

"Very funny." She didn't bother to stick her tongue out at him, instead sinking deeper into her seat. "In the play. I wanted to be the star. But Cassidy got it. Like always. I'm just a dumb old sheep."

"Oh." Cameron was at a loss. He didn't have the vaguest idea how to deal with a problem like this. "I'm sure the sheep is important too."

Ruby made an impatient noise. "I hardly even say anything. I crawl onstage, baa, and then crawl back off. It's the lamest part ever."

Cameron nodded. It did sound a little bit lame, but even he was smart enough to know he shouldn't say that. What would Kayla say if she were here? Something that would cheer Ruby up for sure.

But whatever it was, he couldn't come up with it.

They drove the rest of the way home in silence.

"Do you want a snack before homework?" They'd settled into an afternoon routine that was as normal to him now as reading the daily briefs had been only a few weeks ago.

"No." Ruby was still sulking as she unzipped her backpack. "Here. I forgot to give you this the other day."

Cameron took the note, frowning. A note from the teacher? Maybe there was more going on here than a bad part in a play.

"Our school bake sale is Tuesday, December 4," he read aloud. "You are signed up to bring—" His mouth opened, and he jerked his head up to Ruby. She looked at him blankly, and he lifted the paper again. "Six dozen cutout cookies."

She nodded.

"Ruby, December 4 is—" He pulled out his phone to confirm. "Tomorrow."

She nodded again.

"How long have you known about this?"

She shrugged. "I lost the paper in my desk."

"Where are we going to get six dozen cookies on short notice?" He pulled out his phone. "What's the name of the bakery?"

"We have to make them." Ruby gave him a look like that should have been obvious.

He shook his head, tapping the word "bakery" into the search bar. "I don't know how to make"—he glanced at the paper again—"cutout cookies." Actually, he didn't even know what cutout cookies were.

"I know how. Mommy makes them with me every year."

Cameron looked up from his phone. Bethany made cookies? He had such a hard time, sometimes, trying to reconcile the Bethany he knew with the one Ruby seemed to know.

He glanced back down at the phone, clicking on the website for the bakery. *Please let it still be open.*

He frowned at the listing. It had closed twenty minutes ago. "The grocery store probably has some. Maybe not six dozen, but . . ."

"I told you, Uncle Cam. We have to *make* them. Everyone else does. I can't be the only kid who walks in with grocery store cookies."

"I'm sure you won't be the only one—"

But she stopped him with her look. The one that said he was disappointing her again.

He sighed. "Fine. We'll figure it out. But if they end up tasting like feet, don't blame me."

She giggled, then clapped a hand over her mouth and refastened the frown on her face. But he let a grin lift his lips at the temporary reappearance of the Ruby he knew and loved.

Wait.

Loved?

He let the shock of the word go through him.

Yeah, he loved his niece. The wonder of the revelation nearly stole his voice.

But he pulled out his phone and managed to say, "I think we're going to need some backup."

Chapter 24

Kayla's arms quaked with fatigue, but she didn't ease up, instead pushing harder to spin the wheels of her racing wheelchair on the rollers that acted like a treadmill for the chair.

But as hard as she tried to focus on nothing but the rhythm of her gloved hands against the rims, her thoughts kept getting caught in a loop. A loop that involved Ruby, Bethany, and way too much Cam. Cam steadying her horse. Cam asking if she was warm enough at the parade. And most of all, Cam hugging Ruby to him at the zoo the other day. She was willing to bet that even he hadn't realized how much he cared about the little girl until that moment.

She had to admit that if ever her heart had been in danger of falling for Cam, it had been then. Fortunately, she'd withstood the test.

"Training again?" Vi waddled into the room.

Kayla didn't answer, knowing full well that her sister-in-law hadn't come in here to discuss her training regimen.

"You know it won't help, right?"

Giving up, Kayla straightened, letting the wheels spin on their own. Her lungs pumped with hot breaths, and she ran her forearm over her hairline. "What won't help?"

"Running away."

Kayla gestured at her wheels, which were still spinning, slowing as the friction of the rollers worked against their momentum. "Hard to run away when the wheels aren't going anywhere."

"You know that's not what I meant."

"I have no idea what you meant," Kayla said honestly.

Violet laughed. "All right. I'll spell it out for you. You like Cam and you're freaked out and you're trying to ignore it, but it's driving you crazy so you're throwing yourself into your training to try to convince yourself you're happy alone."

"I *am* happy alone."

Vi studied her. "Maybe. But there's a part of you that wonders if you could be even happier with him."

Kayla made a noise that was supposed to indicate just how far off Vi's theory was. She was just the right amount of happy the way she was.

"Why not see where it goes at least?" Vi asked. "Give him a chance."

Kayla rolled her eyes. "For one, he hasn't asked for a chance." Was that what was bothering her? Kayla pushed the thought away. That was preposterous.

"And for another, he lives in LA."

"I think Hope Springs is growing on him. Or you could always move. I hear it's sunny in California."

Kayla shook her head. "Honestly, Vi, I don't even know what I want with *my* life right now. Let alone getting involved with someone else's." That was the biggest issue. Until she figured out what she was going to do next, she didn't feel equipped to figure out who she wanted to do it with—if anyone.

"That's fair enough." Vi lowered herself slowly onto Kayla's bed, her belly bulging in front of her. Apparently their conversation wasn't over. "Just remember that there are very few things you can't do with another person at your side. In fact, most things are easier that way. 'Two are better than one, because they have a good return for their labor: If either of them falls down, one can help the other up.'"

Kayla knew it didn't pay to argue with Vi when she used Scripture—especially the verse from her wedding. Instead, she gestured to Vi's belly. "How's our little one today?"

The distraction worked. Vi rubbed a hand over her belly, with a rueful laugh. "I think he might be a musician like his daddy. He's decided my ribs are a xylophone."

Kayla laughed with her. "You think it's a boy then."

Vi bit her lip but nodded. "Yeah. I don't know why, but I just get a feeling."

"Well, I still think it's a girl."

The opening notes of Nate's song "He Holds Me" rang out from Kayla's phone, which was on the bed where she'd left it before she'd folded herself into her racing chair.

Vi reached for it, then looked at her with an impish grin. "It's Cam."

"Yeah, right."

"No, really." Vi held up the phone so Kayla could see the screen. "Told you he was interested."

"And I told you *I* wasn't interested. Let it go to voice mail."

"You're answering this." Vi held the phone out to her, but Kayla shook her head. "Or I am."

Kayla studied her sister-in-law. But she knew Vi didn't bluff.

"Fine. One second." She used her teeth to grab the Velcro that held her thumb against her glove, then tucked her hand under the opposite armpit to pull the glove off.

"It's going to go to voice mail," Vi warned.

Kayla shrugged but quickly unwrapped her other gloved hand and held it out.

Vi hit answer before dropping the phone into Kayla's hand, then waved and waddle-flounced out of the room.

Kayla stuck her tongue out at her sister-in-law's back before lifting the phone to her ear.

"Are you there?" Cam was asking.

She tried not to let the sound of his voice play with her heart. And failed.

"Yeah. I'm here."

"Good." Relief seeped from Cam's voice, and she was instantly on alert.

"Why? What's wrong?"

"I have to make six dozen cutout cookies by tomorrow." Panic laced his words. "Those are the ones in different shapes, right? Oh, and Ruby didn't get the part she wanted in the play, and I didn't know what to say to her."

A relieved laugh escaped Kayla's mouth, both because nothing was wrong with Ruby and because Vi had been wrong. Again.

Cam wasn't calling because he liked her. He was calling because he needed her baking skills. Or what there was of them.

"Do you need some help over there?"

"Yes, please." His voice was warm, and it wrapped around her like a hug.

She shook off the feeling—she didn't need a hug—and focused on the task at hand. Six dozen cookies and cheering up a disappointed little girl.

"Do you have everything you need?"

"I have no idea. What do I need?" His cluelessness was slightly exasperating—and slightly endearing.

"Just a second." She set the phone down so she could extricate herself from her racing chair and transfer to her regular wheelchair, then grabbed the phone again and brought it to the kitchen.

"Do you have a good cutout cookie recipe?" she asked Vi.

Her sister-in-law gave her a knowing look that Kayla pointedly ignored, then pulled out a recipe book that had to be about a hundred years old. She flipped to a page near the back. "This was my grandma's recipe."

Kayla thanked her, then read off the ingredient list to Cam. She could hear him searching Bethany's cupboards in the background.

"I have everything except powdered sugar."

Kayla pulled the phone away from her ear and turned to Vi. "Do you have powdered sugar?"

Vi gave her that same knowing look and nodded.

"All right. I can be there in twenty minutes," she said into the phone.

"Thank you, Kayla. You're my hero. I think we might have to promote you from Supergirl to Superwoman."

She snorted and hung up. She could barely look at Vi, who had not wiped that knowing expression off her face.

"Don't look at me like that. I'm helping out for Ruby's sake."

"I know." Vi winked and Kayla couldn't help but laugh, even as she snatched a towel and tossed it at her sister-in-law.

Chapter 25

"Kayla's here!" Cameron called from the spot he'd taken up at the window when every attempt to get Ruby to smile again had failed.

Ruby simply nodded from the spot where she'd plopped on the couch. Cameron had half a mind to march down to that school and give whoever had decided his niece wasn't good enough to play anything but a sheep a piece of his mind. But he had a feeling that wouldn't help. He could only hope Kayla would know what to do.

He watched as she reached across to the passenger seat and grabbed her wheelchair, attached the wheels and cushion, and transferred into it.

It wasn't the first time admiration for her—for the way she dealt with her disability, the way she never complained, the sheer strength she showed every day—had struck him.

She opened the back door of the car and reached inside, pulling out a plastic bag, which she set on her lap before wheeling toward the house.

Her eyes landed on him, standing in the picture window, and she waved.

He supposed he should be embarrassed that she'd caught him watching her. But he waved back, then moved to open the front door.

"I hear we have some cookies to bake." Kayla popped the front wheels of her chair over the doorframe, carrying the scent of the cold, but also something sweet and coconutty. He moved to close the door, but she had stopped dead right inside it.

"What do you have against Christmas?"

He blinked at her—why would she think he had anything against Christmas? "Nothing. Why?"

She waved a hand wildly to encompass the whole room. "Where are your Christmas decorations?"

He pulled out his phone and checked the date. "It's only December 3." Honestly, decorations hadn't even occurred to him.

"Exactly. Christmas is only three weeks away. What do you say, Ruby? Should we decorate after we make the cookies?"

Ruby gave a listless shrug, and Cameron gave Kayla a helpless look. There was no getting through to Ruby tonight.

But with a determined set of her mouth, Kayla opened the bag on her lap and rummaged in it. She pulled out a bag of powdered sugar and passed it to Cameron, then wheeled over to Ruby and reached back into the bag. This time she came out with a white headband with woolly ears attached. She held it out to Ruby, who shook her head and crossed her arms.

"I heard you get to be a sheep in the play," Kayla said brightly, "so I thought this might help you get into character."

"I don't want to be a sheep."

Kayla shrugged and stuck the headband on her own head. It should have looked ridiculous, but she actually looked kind of cute like that.

"Did I ever tell you about the time I auditioned for the role of Dorothy in The Wizard of Oz?" Kayla steered her wheelchair into the kitchen, and Ruby followed. Cameron brought up the rear.

"Look how organized this is." Kayla shot Cameron an approving smile. "There might be hope for you yet."

Yeah. He'd gotten ingredients out of the cupboards. He was practically a master chef. Still, he had to appreciate her attempt to be nice. Sure beat all the times she had yelled at him in the past few weeks.

"Anyway—" She turned back to Ruby, the sheep ears bobbing. "I wanted the role of Dorothy so badly. I practiced every day. My mom even got me a pair of red sparkly shoes that I wore everywhere. I thought I did a good job at my audition, so I was sure the part would be mine. I wore my red shoes to school the day they announced who got what parts. And when they called my name, I stood up, all ready to take the stage as Dorothy. Except I didn't get the part of Dorothy."

She paused dramatically, and Cameron had to hand it to her. She had certainly drawn Ruby into her story. Him too, if he was being honest.

"What part did you get?" Ruby whispered.

"A tree," Kayla said, keeping a straight face. "Not one of the cool talking trees. One of the trees that stood in the background and didn't do anything."

"That's lame. Almost as lame as a sheep." Ruby collapsed into a chair.

"Lamer," Kayla said. "But you know what I did?"

"Quit?"

"No." Kayla tapped Ruby's nose. "I decided that if I was going to be a tree, I would be the best tree there ever was. I would eat, sleep, and breathe being a tree. I only wore brown and green. And I made people call me 'Tree' instead of Kayla."

Ruby giggled, but Kayla kept a serious face. "And you know what? It worked. I was the best tree anyone had ever seen. And the very next year, I got to be the big bad wolf when we did a play of the three little pigs."

Cameron couldn't help bursting into laughter. Kayla was tough and feisty, sure, but the big bad wolf?

She gave him a look of mock hurt. "I'll have you know that people are still talking about my performance as the wolf."

Cameron raised an eyebrow. "What people?"

She shrugged. "My parents, mostly."

He laughed harder, and Kayla grinned as she tapped the headband on top of her head. "That's why I thought you might like this. To practice being the best sheep this town has ever seen. What do you say?"

Ruby eyed the headband, then nodded. Kayla pulled it off her head and slipped it onto Ruby's.

"Baa," Ruby said immediately.

Cameron and Kayla laughed together, and Cameron's heart lightened. That was one crisis averted.

Now for the next. "Should we make these cookies?" He moved to Kayla's side at the table. "Tell me what to do."

She pulled a ratty old book out of her bag. "I brought Vi's recipe. She said it's been in her family for like a hundred years. Why don't you mix the dry ingredients? Ruby and I will get the wet ingredients going. Then we'll put it all together."

Ruby baaed at her.

"Oh, sorry. Sheep and I will get the wet ingredients started."

Ruby gave a satisfied nod and let out another baa. Cameron suppressed a groan. That was going to get old fast.

But as he glanced at Ruby and Kayla with their heads bent close together, he had to admit, it was a small price to pay.

The oven timer dinged, and Kayla looked up from the artificial branch she'd been trying to wrangle into some semblance of an actual tree.

"I'll take care of the cookies. You two keep figuring this thing out." She backed her chair carefully through the scattered piles of artificial pine branches.

"I can get them." Cam started to get up from the floor.

"Absolutely not." Kayla gestured to the mess surrounding them. They were having a doozy of a time trying to figure out how this tree went together. "This is your job."

And anyway, she needed a second to remind herself that none of this was real. Because with the sugary sweet scent of baking cookies filling the house, soft Christmas music playing in the background, and the Christmas decorations scattered around them, it'd almost started to feel like she, Ruby, and Cam were a cozy little family.

"I'm not sure when you became boss," Cam muttered.

"Right about the time you called in a panic and said you needed help with the cookies."

"Touché." Cam shrugged, then attempted to fit his branch into the tree's thin trunk. It snapped into place with a satisfying click.

They all looked at each other in surprise, then let out a cheer.

"Smooth sailing from here," Cam said. "Could you pass me another one of the long ones, Rub—sheep?"

Ruby baaed, then passed one to him. Cam threw Kayla an exasperated look. "Thanks for that."

But she could tell that he was grateful to see Ruby back to her cheerful self.

In the kitchen, Kayla pulled the golden cookies from the oven. She took her time scooping the cookies onto the cooling rack and loading the pan with another batch of reindeer and candy canes and angels, working to talk some sense into herself as she did. This was all an illusion. Yes, she was friends with Ruby. And maybe with Cam. But there was nothing beyond that. And there never would be. But every time she almost had herself convinced, a Ruby giggle or a Cam rumble tickled her ears, and she had to start all over again.

When she finally returned to the living room, any sense she'd managed to talk into herself disappeared in the face of Cam's and Ruby's wide grins. They stood in front of the tree, holding their arms out toward it as if they were models showcasing a masterpiece rather than a scraggly, precariously leaning Christmas tree.

Kayla clapped her hands. "It's beautiful."

Cam looked nearly as pleased as Ruby.

Kayla reached into a box of decorations. They needed to focus on getting this done so she could go home and stop letting herself get carried away by this little fantasy family.

She pulled out a clump of tangled lights and passed it to Cam. "Here's your next job."

He groaned. "You really do like being the boss, don't you?"

Kayla nodded without looking at him. If he meant, did she like being independent and not losing herself to any man, then yes, yes she did.

She and Ruby wrapped the tree in garland, then sorted through the ornaments. There weren't a lot, and they were largely homemade, but Kayla could tell that each one meant something to Bethany. But every time she asked Ruby about one, the little girl just baaed at her.

"Serves you right." Cam laughed when she sighed after the fifth time it happened.

Kayla shot him a fake glare, then turned to Ruby. "What if you were a talking sheep, so you could use words *and* baas?"

Ruby tilted her head, then said. "Baa. I'm hungry, baa."

"Well, that's a slight improvement," Cam muttered, pulling out his phone. "No wonder. It's 7:00. How about a pizza?" He gave Kayla a defensive look. "We don't have it every night."

She gave him a gentle smile. "I didn't think you did."

"Baa. Sometimes we have cereal. Baa," Ruby said cheerfully.

Kayla laughed as Cam ducked his head. "Yeah, that's true."

"Cereal for supper sounds tasty." She wanted to tell Cam that he had nothing to be ashamed of. He was taking care of Ruby, making sure all her needs were met—but more than that, he was providing her with a happy home even in the worst circumstances any kid could be asked to go through. That was worth a lot.

They continued decorating as they waited for the pizza, then cleared a space at the kitchen table to eat.

"Baa. Can I pray? Baa?"

Cam looked to Kayla with a question in his eyes.

"I would love that." Kayla folded her hands, noting that though Cam didn't fold his, he did give his attention to Ruby.

"Dear Jesus. Baa," Ruby began. "Thank you for our supper. Baa. And thank you for Mommy. She's the best mommy in the world, and I really want her to be better for Christmas. Baa. Oh, and thank you that Uncle Cam was smart enough to call Kayla for help with the cookies. Amen. Baa."

Kayla's laugh joined Cam's as she looked up, accidentally meeting his eyes. He held her gaze for a moment, but fortunately Ruby knocked her milk over, giving Kayla an excuse to look away.

Dinner was easy and fun, the conversation flowing mostly from Ruby, with Cam and Kayla piping in here and there. They were just putting away the leftovers when there was a loud crash from the living room.

"What in the living world?"

All three of them froze for a second, then flew toward the living room.

"Mrs. Whiskers," Ruby cried. "Baa."

"Oh no." Kayla pressed a hand to her mouth to hold back the giggle. It wasn't funny. Only, it kind of was.

The cat had obviously attempted to climb the tree and gotten herself tangled in the garland, which was still draped around her. Her tail was puffed out to twice its normal size, and her ears lay flat against her head. The tree was toppled against the far wall.

Cam let out the first laugh, and Kayla couldn't hold it in any longer. In a moment, Ruby's infectious little girl laugh joined theirs.

The cat looked at them all as if they were crazy, then stalked off, the garland trailing behind her—which only made them all laugh harder.

It took a full five minutes to get their giggle fit under control, but at last Cam stood the tree back up. A few ornaments had fallen off—fortunately, none were breakable—and the tree leaned even farther now, but other than that, it was none the worse for the wear.

When they'd finished fixing the tree, Cam announced that it was time for Ruby to get ready for bed.

"Baa," the little girl pouted around a yawn. "What about frosting the cookies?"

"I'll stay and help Cam frost them." The words blurted from Kayla's mouth. She should really take them back. More alone time with Cam was *not* what she needed.

But between Cam's grateful look and Ruby's content yawn, she couldn't bring herself to change her mind.

"Baa. Baa. That means, will you tuck me in?" Ruby set her sleepy eyes on Kayla with a sweet smile.

Warmth filled Kayla's chest at the question, but she looked to Cam to see how he felt about it.

He nodded with a smile almost as sweet as Ruby's. "That's a great idea. I'll go get things ready to frost the cookies."

"But I want you to tuck me in too, baa. I want you and Kayla to do it together."

Kayla let herself peek at Cam out of the corner of her eye. She half hoped he'd say no.

"Yeah. Okay." Cam started toward Ruby's room, and Kayla fought to remind herself yet again that though Cam and Ruby were family, she was not. She was just a friend lending a hand.

But as they read Ruby a story together and listened to her say her prayers and turned on her night light, that family feeling only grew stronger. And when Ruby hugged first Cam and then her, Kayla was pretty sure she'd lost the fight right then and there.

Chapter 26

Keep your eyes on your cookie.

But even that didn't erase the thought Cameron had been fighting off all night: *This was what family felt like*. He remembered the feeling from his childhood—from before Bethany ruined everything—and it brought a sharp but almost pleasant ache to his chest to feel it again now.

Except they weren't a family. Sure, Ruby was his niece. But he was only taking care of her temporarily. And Kayla was . . . a friend, he realized with surprise. He certainly hadn't come to Hope Springs seeking to make friends. But Kayla had been a force to reckon with as she muscled her way into their lives. And right now, he was glad she had.

Because otherwise all the cookies would look like the one in front of him, with frosting blobs oozing over the sides and obscuring the cookie's shape so that it looked more like a frog than an angel.

He examined the spread of perfectly frosted cookies in front of her. "How do you do that?"

She looked up from the snowman she'd been giving a red scarf and smiled. "Natural talent, I guess."

"Yeah. I guess I got skipped in that department."

Kayla studied his cookies. "I mean, they have . . . They're really . . ." She bit her lip, as if searching for something nice to say.

He loaded his spoon with a big glob of blue frosting. "Think faster." He angled it toward her and used a finger of his other hand to pull it down, like a loaded catapult.

"You wouldn't." But Kayla dropped her own spoon and held up a hand to shield herself. "Your cookies are really interesting."

"Interesting?" Cameron pulled the spoon back farther. "That's a nice way of saying you can't think of anything nice to say."

Kayla's laugh bounced off the walls, and she clapped a hand over her mouth, glancing toward the hallway. But it'd been at least an hour since the last time Ruby had gotten out of bed to say she needed to go to the bathroom or get a drink or check her backpack, so he was optimistic she was finally asleep.

He couldn't resist. He let the spoon fling forward, sending the frosting straight for Kayla's face.

She shrieked and covered her head, catching most of the frosting on the back of her hand, although a small splatter landed on her cheek.

"You did not just do that." But she was laughing even as she licked the frosting off her knuckles.

"I think I did." He smirked at her, wondering what had come over him. This was so totally not like him. It was way too spontaneous and loose and . . . fun.

Huh.

When had he stopped being fun?

He loaded up another spoonful. If he was going to have fun again, he might as well go all in.

"Cam," Kayla shrieked. "We have so many cookies to do yet." But she grabbed her own spoon and loaded it full of red frosting.

Cameron glanced down at his blue t-shirt. "Wait. This is my favorite shirt."

Kayla blinked at him. "It's just a plain shirt. There's nothing on it."

"But it's comfortable."

She shook her head. "Should have thought of that before you started this."

Frosting flew through the air toward him, and he lifted an arm to block it while also flinging his spoonful at her. Apparently, this time he caught her by surprise because the frosting splattered right on her cheek. He ended up with an armful of frosting, but none hit his shirt.

"Missed me." He grinned and reached for another cookie to frost.

But he was just loading his spoon with frosting—for the cookie, not a weapon—when a wet blob plopped onto his forehead.

He looked up slowly, already feeling the frosting sliding toward his eyes. A blob dropped onto his shirt.

"Really?" But he couldn't help the giant laugh that burst out of him when he saw the expression on Kayla's face. Triumph mixed with amusement mixed with . . . he didn't know exactly what that was, but it made her look almost sparkling. Or maybe that was the tears falling on her cheeks as she laughed so hard.

She held up a hand as he reloaded his spoon. "Truce?" she gasped.

He studied her. She was wiping at her eyes and not paying attention to him at all, which meant he could easily get another shot in. But maybe there was such a thing as *too* much fun. Especially when they were supposed to be getting these cookies done. "All right. Truce."

They fell silent as they returned to frosting the cookies, but every once in a while, one or the other would let out a low chuckle.

"Can I ask you something?" Kayla's question came out of the blue, and he looked up at her as she set aside the angel she'd expertly decorated and started on a snowman.

He dropped a glob of frosting on his own reindeer. "Shoot."

"What happened between you and Bethany?"

Oh.

That question he wasn't prepared for. He'd managed to avoid talking about his sister with anyone in nearly twenty years. But the way Kayla was looking at him with those big, warm eyes full of compassion made the words tumble out against his will. "It started when she broke her arm in volleyball and had to have surgery. I guess that would have been her junior year of high school because I was twelve at the time. They gave her pain meds after the surgery, and I guess she liked how they made her feel." He swallowed.

Kayla's hands stilled on the cookie she was decorating.

He made himself go on. "A few months later, I caught her shooting up. Heroin. My parents were devastated. They checked her into rehab, even though they couldn't afford it."

He snatched for a cookie and started decorating it to give his hands something to do.

"It became a cycle. They'd check her in, she'd check out. They'd welcome her home, tell her everything was forgiven." He shook his head. "The last time, they gave her a job at Dad's landscaping company. She was out of rehab for so long that time that even I started to believe she was better." Bitterness coated his tongue. How could he have been so foolish? He'd *known*, in his head, that she couldn't have changed. But he'd *wanted* so badly, in his heart, to believe that she was still the big sister he'd adored. "They'd put her in charge of accounting because she'd always been good with numbers, and they thought it would give her confidence if they showed how much they trusted her." He set his mutilated cookie aside. "Turns out she was playing them. They had no idea that she knew how to forge my dad's signature. She'd write out checks to bogus accounts, her dealers, herself. . . . She was smart enough to cover it all up. By the time they realized, it was too late. Things had already been tight, but this was the last straw. They lost the company. And—" This was the worst part. "They let her get away with it. They didn't want to press charges. Said they just wanted her to get the help she needed."

He lifted his eyes to find Kayla watching him.

"It looks like she did." She gestured around the small kitchen.

But Cameron shook his head and dropped a fist onto the table. "No. She didn't. She ran away to who knows where. Left us with her mess." He stretched his neck, staring at the ceiling. "Dad had a heart attack the month after he filed for bankruptcy." Cameron didn't dare to look away from the ceiling. "Mom lost everything. I tried to help her out, but I was putting myself through college by then, and . . . Anyway, she had a stroke a couple years later." He blew out a hard breath. This part killed him every time he thought of it. "She was alone. A repairman found her body a few days later."

"Oh, Cam." Kayla's hand landed on his, sending warmth up his arm. "I'm so sorry."

"Yeah." He cleared his throat. "Sorry. I shouldn't have— I've never—"

"I'm glad you told me." Her hand left his.

"So that's the story of me and Bethany." He tried to make his voice light. "More than you bargained for when you asked, I'm sure."

Kayla backed her wheelchair away from the table. "Maybe, but all families have their share of problems."

Somehow, he doubted that hers did. She was voluntarily staying with her brother right now, wasn't she?

She grabbed a plastic food storage container off the counter and passed it to him. "I guess that explains why you weren't so keen on coming when I first called you to tell you about Bethany."

He laughed softly. "Yeah. Not so keen at all. But I'm glad you bullied me into it. It's been good to get to know Ruby."

"Hey." She pointed at him. "I didn't *bully* you. I just told you what you needed to hear."

"If that's what you need to tell yourself."

Her expression softened. "You know you're doing a good job with her, right?"

He shrugged. "Honestly, I'm just trying not to screw her life up too badly."

Kayla bit her lip.

"What? You think I'm screwing it up?"

She shook her head with a gentle laugh. "No. I'm just wondering if you've thought about what you're going to do if Bethany doesn't wake up."

He sighed roughly. "I've thought about it. But I honestly don't know. Finding Ruby's father was supposed to be the answer, but obviously that didn't pan out. I just don't know if I'm the best one to raise her permanently, you know? I'm still hoping Bethany will wake up and I can . . ."

"Get back to your life in California," she filled in.

He shrugged. He supposed so. That was where his life was, wasn't it? Even if Hope Springs was starting to feel more like home every day.

Kayla wheeled slowly toward the front door. She didn't know why she was so reluctant to leave.

But for some reason, that conversation with Cam had been so real and so raw and so . . . she didn't know what, but it made her want to keep talking to him. To learn more about how he ticked and why he was the way he was. To encourage him to see that even in all those terrible things his family had gone through—was still going through—God had a plan.

"You know—" She spun around so suddenly that she nearly ran Cam over. He took a step back, giving her a mildly curious but not annoyed look. "God has a plan even in this."

Cam looked skeptical. "How can you know that?"

"Because he promises that in his Word. And also because I've seen him working out his plan in my own life."

"By sticking you in that thing?" Cam gestured roughly at her wheelchair, horror overtaking his face a second later. "I'm sorry, Kayla. I don't know why I—"

"It's okay, really." She patted her seat cushion. "And actually, yes, by sticking me in this thing."

He studied her, disbelief written in his eyes. He leaned against the wall, arms crossed in front of him. "How so?"

"My parents brought me up in the church, taught me to be a good girl, all that. But I always felt like I had such big expectations to live up to. Nate was like this, I don't know, uber-Christian, always at youth group, in a Christian band, living for Jesus, you know? So I decided since I couldn't live up to all that, I'd be the exact opposite. I started going to parties, drinking . . ." She closed her eyes, remembering how close her path had cut to the one Bethany ended up on.

When she opened them, she found Cam's wide eyes on her. She didn't want to ruin his opinion of her, but she needed him to realize how God could work even their failures to his glory. "When I woke up after the accident, I was mad. Mad at God, mad at Nate, mad at my parents. Mad at the doctors and nurses, even. But now I can see how God used all of this to woo me back to him. To show me that he is the source of all good things in my life. Plus, because of my accident, I ended up at a job I really loved."

"Which you no longer have because of someone else's greed," Cam pointed out.

Kayla shrugged. "I admit I haven't figured out how God is using that yet. But I trust that he is. Anyway, it gave me a chance to meet you and Ruby—" She cut off and looked away, heat rushing to her face. She hadn't meant that how it sounded. "I mean— You know, so I could rescue you when you need to make cookies and such."

Worst save ever.

But she had a feeling that trying to fix it more would only make the situation worse, so she spun her chair back toward the door. At least she could still make a graceful exit.

Except she turned too sharply and knocked into the small table that held a vase with artificial flowers and a small lamp. Flinging her upper body forward, she was able to catch the lamp, but the sound of shattering glass told her the vase's fate.

She closed her eyes. So much for that graceful exit.

"Do you happen to have a broom?" She didn't dare turn around to look at Cam as she asked.

"Don't worry about it." His voice was kind. Overly kind? The kind of kind that meant he knew how flustered she was? "I'll get it."

But she shook her head. "I'm not helpless, Cam. I can clean up my own mess."

"Suit yourself."

As his footsteps retreated, Kayla forced herself to sit up straight and push her shoulders back. She had nothing to be embarrassed about. Accidents happened.

Especially when you have a crush on someone.

A crush? No way. Her feelings for Cam were more like—

Nothing. Her feelings were more like nothing because she had no feelings for Cam.

"Here you are."

A broom appeared at her side, and she grabbed it out of the air without looking at the person who held it there. It was a lot easier to convince herself she didn't have feelings for him when she didn't look at him.

She swept the glass fragments as quickly as she could, maneuvering her chair to make sure she got all of them. She kept her eyes on the job, though she was pretty sure she could feel Cam watching her.

Her suspicion was confirmed when he stepped in front of the pile she'd swept together the moment she brushed the last pieces onto it.

She held out a hand for the dust pan, but he squatted in front of her, holding it angled behind the pile of glass.

"I can get it, you know." She didn't mean to sound so testy. But really, she just needed to finish this up and go home and bury herself under the covers. And not come out again until she got her stupid heart to stop thinking it wanted something she knew for a fact it did not want.

"I know you can. And I know you're Superwoman. But that doesn't mean you have to do everything yourself. Sometimes other people want to be useful too, you know."

"Have it your way." But as she swept the glass onto the dust pan, she had to admit that it was much easier this way. The verse from Ecclesiastes that Vi had quoted earlier popped into her head. "Two are better than one, because they have a good return for their labor." She pushed it right back out.

"I think we got it all." Cam straightened. "And it didn't kill you to let me help." His smile landed on her, and the verse popped right back in.

She handed Cam the broom, then skirted around him to the front door. She had to get out of here before she started believing that maybe that verse applied to her after all.

Chapter 27

"Wow, Ruby, these look great." The white-haired teacher who had introduced herself as Mrs. Klein shuffled the containers Cameron had handed her, subtly shifting the one with the cookies he had decorated to the bottom of the pile. She turned to him. "So it's twenty-five cents a cookie."

"Oh, uh— Okay. I guess I'll take four then." He pulled out his wallet. It seemed a little odd that she'd expect him to buy the cookies he'd spent all night making, but whatever. He could spare a buck.

Mrs. Klein took his money and stuck it in a small metal box. "So this is the money box. It should have enough change."

He nodded again. This woman really was an over-sharer. He'd just made the cookies. He didn't need all the details of how they'd be sold.

"If you can, try to go for the upsell. I mean, don't be pushy about it, but you know, encourage them to buy a plate of brownies too or something."

"I can—" Wait. What? "You want me to sell the cookies?"

Mrs. Klein blinked at him. "You're signed up to do it this morning."

"I am?" He glanced at Ruby, who was grinning up at him. "I think someone may have forgotten to mention that."

"Oh dear." Mrs. Klein consulted a clipboard on the table. "I don't have anyone else coming in until lunchtime. Oh dear . . ." Her white eyebrows knit together. "I don't know. I guess we could . . ."

"I can do it." Well, now, what was he doing? He had at least three cases that needed his attention today. But the woman seemed so distressed, and it wasn't like it would be that hard to stand here and peddle cookies to kids. He could probably even manage to make some calls at the same time.

"Oh, can you really? That would be wonderful. Absolutely wonderful." The older woman patted his arm. "We'll be right in that classroom if you need anything."

"I'm sure I'll be fine."

Ruby skipped over to give him a hug, and he took the opportunity to whisper in her ear, "A little heads-up next time, please."

She giggled. "You're funny, Uncle Cam." And then she was skipping off to class behind Mrs. Klein. But she turned around after a few steps to add, "Baa."

Cameron gave her a thumbs-up. Thank goodness Kayla had known how to bring Ruby out of her funk yesterday. And how to make cookies. And how to listen to him talk about Bethany.

He didn't know what had possessed him to tell her so much. He'd always considered his past—and especially his sister—his biggest secret. And yet, it hadn't felt odd telling her. It had been a relief, actually. He'd woken up feeling lighter this morning than he had since he'd gotten here. Longer than that—since Dad had died, maybe.

He contemplated telling Danielle too.

But he quickly dismissed the idea. Danielle detested listening to other people's sob stories. And besides, maybe the reason it had been so easy to tell Kayla was that he knew he was leaving eventually and wouldn't see her anymore.

The thought drew him up short.

He'd grown so accustomed to seeing Kayla while he'd been here that he hadn't even considered what it would be like when he went back to California and she went wherever she ended up going. It made him a little sad to think about.

But he shook off the feeling. He had his life, and she had hers. They'd just happened to intersect at this small point in time.

He pulled out his phone to return a call from a CFO who was a real pain, but before he could dial, he had a line of students at the table.

"Whoa." He whistled to himself, fighting off the urge to run, until he remembered that they were just customers who wanted a product he was selling. Somehow, through all the jostling, shouting, and general chaos, he managed to get everyone what they wanted. When the bell rang for students to be in class, he let out a sigh of relief. The rest of the morning was much slower, and Cameron managed to make all the calls he needed to. When he'd finished, he found himself again perusing articles about starting a landscaping business. It looked like it would take a significant outlay of cash, which wouldn't necessarily be a problem since he'd always been a saver. The bigger issue was the risk. And the fact that Danielle would laugh him right out of the room if he suggested he'd like to make a career change.

At lunchtime, Cameron handed the cookie selling job off to a woman who introduced herself as the mother of one of Ruby's friends.

"You must be Ruby's uncle," she said. "I've heard so much about you."

She had?

"Good luck," he told her as kids swarmed the table. "These kids are little fiends when it comes to sugar." They'd already sold out of the cookies Kayla had decorated—and some desperate kids had even bought one or two of his monstrosities.

The woman laughed and touched his arm.

"Uncle Cam!"

He turned at the sound of Ruby's voice, using the opportunity to free his arm from the woman's hand.

"Hey there, little sheep."

The woman gave him an odd look, but he ignored her and squatted to be at eye level with his niece. "How was your morning?"

"Good. Want to come to lunch with me?"

Cameron debated. He still had those documents waiting on his computer. And yet . . . he was much more in the mood for lunch with his niece than for dealing with paperwork.

"That depends." He grinned at her. "What's for lunch?"

As he walked with her to the lunch room, Ruby grilled him. "Why were you talking to Mrs. McGregor? That's Cassidy's mom."

"The one who got the lead in the play?"

Ruby nodded.

"Well, it's not her fault her daughter got the part. And anyway, you can't be mad at Cassidy forever."

Ruby put a hand on her hip. "Yes, I can."

He started to argue, but then they were in the cafeteria, and she was leading him through the line. Turned out, it was spaghetti day.

When their trays were filled, he followed her to a table already holding six girls and one boy.

"You can sit there." Ruby sat in the chair next to the boy, pointing to the chair across from her.

Cameron squeezed past the close seats and took the spot she'd indicated, eyeing the boy. He didn't trust any boy who chose to sit at an all-girls table. He was definitely a ladies man.

"This is Jenna, Bree, Sierra, Maria, Libby, and Haley." Ruby pointed around the table at the girls. "And this is Braxton. My boyfriend."

Cameron choked on the drink he was taking from the tiny milk carton. "Your what?"

The girls at the table all giggled, but Braxton gave Cameron an impish smile. Cameron debated how much trouble he would get in for laying out a second-grader.

He kept an eye on Braxton for the rest of the meal, but fortunately the kid didn't attempt to make a move on Ruby. In fact, he seemed pretty oblivious to the fact that she was there at all. Mostly, he spent the meal staring longingly at a table full of boys who were having a contest to see who could down their milk the fastest.

By the end of the meal, Cameron nearly felt sorry for the kid. Ruby had clearly strong-armed him into this relationship.

"All right, Rub— Sheep. I have to get going." He slid his tiny chair away from the table and stood, grateful for the chance to stretch his cramped back. "Thanks for lunch."

"You're welcome." Ruby skipped next to him as they went to clear their trays. As he was setting his down, his phone buzzed in his pocket.

He pulled it out, giving the screen a quick look. A groan slipped unintentionally from his lips. He scolded himself silently. That should not be his reaction to a call from the woman he was supposed to marry. It was just that most of her calls these days involved either yelling or icy silence.

"Who is it?" Ruby asked.

"Huh?" He glanced at her. "Oh. My girlfriend."

Ruby stopped dead in the middle of the hallway. "You can't have a girlfriend."

He slowed to a stop as well. "Why not? You have a boyfriend."

She rolled her eyes. "That's different."

Yeah, because *he* was an adult. She was a second-grader.

"Okay, look, I have to take this. I'll see you after school." He reached to give her a quick hug, but she wriggled out of his arms.

"But you can't have a girlfriend because you have Kayla."

"I have . . ." He scrubbed his hands over his face. Oh boy. "Ruby, you know Kayla and I are just friends, right? Actually, mostly she's your friend. I just happen to be there too."

Ruby gave him a penetrating look. Fine, he and Kayla had become friends too. Pretty good friends if the way he had spilled his guts to her last night was any indication.

But that didn't change the fact that he had a girlfriend. An almost-fiancée.

He waved goodbye to Ruby, swallowed hard, and answered the call as he burst out the school doors into the gray day, determined to have a nice conversation with Danielle.

"I thought you were going to ignore me again," Danielle said by way of greeting.

"Sorry about that." He worked to sound placating. "You would not believe the morning I had. We were up all night frosting cookies, and then I get her to school this morning and find out that I'm supposed to be the one selling them." He laughed. All in all, it hadn't been such a bad day. And he felt a little more connected to Ruby now that he had spent some time in the place she hung out every day.

"I think I've been more than patient, Cameron." Danielle's words crashed like bricks through the phone.

So much for a nice conversation.

"I know. You've been the best." Well, maybe not the best. But she was doing the best she could.

"It's been a month. When are you going to be home?"

He rubbed his temple. "Danielle, you know I just can't answer that. I would if I could, but my sister's condition hasn't shown any improvement, and the doctor's don't know if . . ."

He trailed off as he reached his car and leaned against it instead of getting in. Just once, he wished she'd ask how he was doing. Ask if he needed anything. At least offer a semi-sympathetic comment about what he was dealing with. Listen to him like . . . like Kayla had last night.

He shook off the thought. Danielle wasn't that kind of person, and he knew that.

"Can you at least tell me if you'll be home by Christmas? I want to plan our engagement party, but I don't want to be humiliated a second time."

Cameron sighed. "I mean, if there's a miracle, maybe. But otherwise, I don't see how."

"I see." Danielle clipped the words. "I'm not sure how much longer I can do this, Cameron."

Do what? he wanted to ask. He was the one who was here, taking care of a little girl every day while managing his work schedule and her riding lessons and even cleaning up vomit.

And suddenly, he realized—he didn't know how much longer he could do it either. Not taking care of Ruby—he'd realized last night that he'd do that as long as needed.

"Then maybe we shouldn't do this anymore." The words popped out without warning, but once he'd said them, he knew they were exactly what needed to be said.

"So you'll come home?" Danielle's voice wore the triumph of scoring a major deal.

But Cameron shook his head, scrubbing a hand down his face. "No. I mean, maybe we shouldn't do *us* anymore." He bit his lip. He didn't want to hurt her.

"What?" Danielle sounded more dismissive than upset. "Cameron, don't be stupid. Just come home, and everything will be fine."

He watched the gray clouds above him. "No, Danielle, it won't. I saw it before, but I didn't want to admit it to myself." Absence hadn't made his heart grow fonder. It'd only made him more certain of what he'd already known that day Kayla's call had rescued him from going through with the proposal. "We're just not right for each other."

"Is this about the ring?" Danielle made the clicking sound she always made when she was annoyed. "Because I told you, I never met your mom. And anyway, there's an expectation that someone in our position would have a certain quality of—"

"It's not about the ring, Danielle." He drew himself up short. "Well, actually, it is. About what the ring means. About the fact that I've never told you about my family because I was afraid of what you'd think. About the fact that I've never even told you my dreams."

"Your dreams?" Danielle's tone was cavalier. "We have the same dream. Success. Money. Prestige. And in case you haven't noticed, we're well on our way."

Cameron shook his head. "I think I want more than that." Though he honestly didn't know what that would be. Only that somehow Hope Springs was offering him a taste of it. "I'm sorry." And he really was. "I never wanted to hurt you."

"You're not hurting me." Ice tipped Danielle's words. "Call me when you come to your senses."

After the line went dead, Cameron stood staring at the school building for a long time. Had he really just given up the life he'd had all laid out? His plan for a perfect job, perfect promotion, perfect wife? After this, there was a decent chance George would fire him.

He sighed as he climbed into his car. What was it Kayla had said when he'd asked if it bothered her not to have a plan? Something about God always having a way of working the unexpected out?

Well, good luck to you, God, he thought as he pulled out of the parking lot.

Chapter 28

Kayla chewed her lip, eyeing the phone in her hand as she sat up in bed Sunday morning. Ruby had mentioned wanting to go to church more than once. It would make total sense for Kayla to text Cam and invite them. So why was she having such a hard time making her fingers tap on his name?

It wasn't because she was afraid he'd reject her invitation. That was up to him, and he hadn't seemed too resistant when she was talking about God the other night.

It was more that she was afraid he'd get the wrong impression and think she was looking for an excuse to see him.

"Stop being so stupid," she muttered to herself. "Are you really going to let that keep you from inviting him and Ruby to hear the Gospel?"

She tapped out the invitation, then hit send before she could change her mind.

Rather than staring at the screen to wait for a reply, she clicked over to her email. She gave a cursory scroll through the various marketing messages before she noticed a message from the organization running the mission trip she'd applied for. Her mouth went dry as she tapped to open it.

The moment it appeared on the screen, her eyes darted over the words. Then she sat staring at her phone, dumbfounded.

She'd been accepted.

"Thank you for answering my prayers, Lord," she whispered. "Now I know what you want me to do next."

It was a relief, but also—

Something felt off. The excitement that should be sending her into a happy dance was tempered by the fact that she would have to leave Hope Springs behind—right when Nate and Vi had their baby, right when she was getting to know everyone here so much better, right when Ruby needed her.

She shook off the feeling. Her visit to Hope Springs had never been intended to be permanent. If she didn't go on the trip, she'd have to find a job somewhere. And that likely wouldn't be Hope Springs.

Well, she didn't have to make a decision right now. She had a few weeks before she needed to let them know.

Using her arms to scoot to the edge of the bed, she transferred to her wheelchair to get ready for church.

The decision still weighed on her as she wheeled into the kitchen, where Nate greeted her with a cup of coffee.

"Thanks." It was just what she needed. "Where's Vi?"

"Still getting ready. Moving a little slow this morning."

"You try hauling a watermelon in your belly." Kayla shot to her sister-in-law's defense. "You'd be moving slowly too."

Nate held up his hands. "Trust me, I know. I don't know how she does it. She's pretty amazing."

"*Very* amazing," Kayla corrected, though she knew her brother was head over heels for his wife. "Only a few weeks yet. Are you getting excited?"

Nate's eyes lit up at the same time that he shook his head. "Nervous."

"You'll be a great dad, you know that."

"I do?"

"Yes, you do." Kayla set her coffee on the table and rolled closer to him. "Or if you don't, I do."

Nate blew out a breath. "I hope you're right."

"I know I am. After all, you're a great brother."

He gave her a thoughtful look, and she knew he was thinking about the accident. Even though he'd finally forgiven himself for it, she knew he still struggled to let go sometimes.

But after a moment his eyes cleared. "I am, aren't I?"

She swatted at him but then grew serious. "Speaking of which, can I ask you for some advice?"

Nate regarded her. "Of course you can. About Cam?"

"What? No." Kayla smacked his arm again. "About the mission trip. I was accepted."

"What? Kayla, that's great." He set down his own coffee to hug her. "I know how much you wanted—" He hesitated as he pulled back and his eyes fell on her face. "What is it?"

She shook her head at her own maddening confusion. "I *do* want it, but— I don't know. I also want to stay here."

"Here?" Nate raised an eyebrow. "As in, in Hope Springs?"

"No. Yes." She sighed and laughed at herself. "I don't know. But I mean, if I got accepted for the trip, I should do it, right? It's pretty clear that's what God wants me to do."

Nate picked up his coffee and took a slow swig, watching her over the rim. Kayla knew he was using the time to process her question and formulate an answer, but she wanted to tell him to just say something already.

Finally, he set the mug down. "I guess I would say don't confuse God giving you an opportunity with God telling you what to do. He's given you a free will and a brain and a heart for a reason. Whether or not you go on the mission trip won't change anything."

Right. Except possibly her whole life.

"Pray about it," Nate advised.

"What are we praying about?" Vi shuffled into the room, a hand pressed to her back. The poor woman looked so uncomfortable that Kayla hoped for her sake the baby would come sooner rather than later.

"Kayla got accepted for the mission trip." The pride in Nate's voice filled Kayla's heart. "Now she has to decide whether or not to go."

"I knew you'd be accepted." Vi patted her arm. "I'll pray for you. Are we ready for church?"

Kayla nodded, pulling out her phone on the off chance that Cam had responded to her invitation.

She told herself she was glad there were no new messages.

She was confused enough the way it was.

Chapter 29

"They smell funny. Baa." Ruby wrinkled her nose at the waffle Cameron dropped onto her plate.

He didn't know what had possessed him to try making them this morning. He'd barely conquered the fine art of peanut butter and jelly for Ruby's school lunches, yet for some reason, he'd thought it'd be a good idea to graduate right to breakfast pastries.

Maybe it was the nervous energy that had gripped him ever since he'd broken up with Danielle the other day. It wasn't that he thought he'd done the wrong thing. But blowing up his carefully laid plans—leaving himself with no clue of what was going to come next—had him a little shaken. He'd spent most of Wednesday debating whether he should call and beg Danielle to take him back. But that wouldn't have been right—not when he knew they weren't right for each other. Fortunately, by Thursday, he'd poured his energy into a new project: decorating the yard. But he'd finished that on Friday and spent yesterday restlessly pacing the house. Which had brought him to baking this morning, apparently.

"Yeah." He scooped the waffle back off Ruby's plate. "You don't have to eat that." He crossed the room and dumped the three waffles on his plate into the trash, then dolloped the remaining batter in there too. "The usual?"

"Yes, please."

He grabbed two bowls and the cereal box. Ruby closed her eyes and whispered to herself. Praying. He'd gotten used to it and, out of politeness more than anything else, waited to dig into his own cereal until she'd finished.

He saw her nod, the signal for when she had finished, but this time she didn't open her eyes.

"Ruby?"

She held up a finger to signal for him to wait a minute. He rolled his eyes but sat silently.

When she finally looked up, she grinned at him. "Sorry, I was saying an extra prayer."

"Ah." He scooped a generous bite onto his spoon. "What for?"

"That you would say yes to what I want to ask you. Baa."

Cameron shook his head. This girl was something else. "And what is that?"

"Can we go to church? Baa?" Ruby's eyes were full of pleading, and Cameron laughed in relief. That was an easy question. And an easy answer.

"Yes."

"Really?" Ruby's eyes widened.

Wait. He had meant to say no—in spite of Ruby's pleading eyes and Kayla's friendly text this morning. But he couldn't deny that Kayla's conversation the other night—about how God had used her injury for her good—had him intrigued. How long had he wondered what good could possibly come out of what had happened to his family?

He sighed. "Really. But you have to hurry up and change. Church starts in—" He picked up his phone and checked Kayla's text. "Twenty minutes."

Ruby shoved another bite of cereal into her mouth. "I'm already changed," she said, mouth full of food.

"Chew." Cameron eyed her flowery pants and taco print shirt, then let it go.

Twenty minutes later, as he pulled into the church parking lot, he had a brief flash of panic. Though his family had gone to church until Dad died, he hadn't been to one in years.

Maybe it had been a mistake to come.

"How about if I drop you off and come pick you up when it's done?"

Ruby made a face at him. "You have to come in with me. I'm seven."

All right. She had a point there.

He parked the car and let her lead him toward the church doors.

"There's Kayla." Ruby waved wildly toward the sidewalk, where Kayla was approaching the church with Nate and Violet, but the three appeared to be caught up in conversation and didn't look their direction.

Good. Though Cameron didn't know why he felt that way. He actually quite enjoyed spending time with Kayla.

Which may have been the problem.

"Can we sit with her, baa?" Ruby grabbed his hand and tried to tug him forward, but he maintained a steady speed.

"No. And I don't think sheep are allowed at church." He could use a break from all the bleating.

"Pastor Dan said I'm Jesus' little lamb." Ruby gave him a mischievous look. "Baa."

He couldn't help the laugh that burst out at that.

Apparently, the sound caught Kayla's attention because she suddenly turned her head in their direction, then sent them a wide smile. She said something to Nate and Violet, who waved to Cameron and Ruby, then continued toward the doors.

But Kayla started toward them, which made Cameron's stomach do a weird sort of dip he couldn't explain.

"Good morning." Her greeting was as bright and cheerful as always, and Cameron relaxed. Just because he'd confessed his deepest, darkest secrets to her the other night didn't mean anything had to be different between them.

"Can we sit with you, baa?" Ruby bounced up and down as Kayla reached them, then spun her chair to wheel next to them toward the building.

"Of course. I'd be honored." Kayla glanced at Cameron. "If it's okay with you."

He nodded reluctantly. It wasn't like he had any good reason to say no.

When they reached the door, Cameron hesitated. After the argument over the broom the other night, he wasn't sure Kayla wouldn't bite his head off for opening it for her. But he glanced around at the other worshipers filing into the building. He didn't need everyone here to think he was the kind of guy who wouldn't open a door for a little girl and a woman who used a wheelchair.

He pulled it open. Instead of reaming him out, Kayla offered a quiet "thank you" as she slid through the door. Cameron nodded silently, almost wishing she'd yelled instead. At least that he knew how to deal with.

He followed Kayla and Ruby through the lobby and into the sanctuary, surprised by the number of people who stopped to greet them—both people he'd met at Thanksgiving and others he'd never seen before. He didn't remember his childhood church being this friendly.

"I want to sit next to Kayla," Ruby said as they reached a row filled with several of the people who had been at Nate and Violet's house for Thanksgiving.

That was fine by Cameron. He slid into the row, taking a seat next to Violet as Ruby pounced onto the seat on his other side. Kayla remained seated in her wheelchair at the end of the row.

"Glad you could make it," Vi whispered, before folding her hands and resting them on her belly.

While she prayed, Cameron took the opportunity to examine the space. A large cross hung on the front wall, and windows that reached nearly to the vaulted ceiling lined the wall that looked out over Lake Michigan. Cameron's eyes rested on the rolling waves, and a sort of peace he wasn't accustomed to washed over him.

The haunting melody of a piano solo drew Cameron's attention to the front of the church.

After a moment, the piano was joined by a guitar and a bass, then drums.

"Today he calls you." The lone male voice was strong and somehow familiar.

Cameron peered more closely, then leaned toward Violet. "Is that your husband?"

She nodded, clearly enthralled with his singing, and Cameron sat back, letting the music wash over him. The style wasn't his usual music preference, but he found he enjoyed it.

When the song was done, Pastor Dan welcomed the congregation, then began the day's readings.

Cameron tried to pay attention, though it wasn't easy with Ruby wiggling next to him and his gaze constantly attempting to stray to Kayla. Though a slight smile lifted her lips, he couldn't help thinking that she appeared to be deep in thought about something. And for some reason, he wanted more than anything to ask her what it was.

As the congregation finished singing another hymn—which Cameron had only listened to, though Ruby had joined in on the refrain in her surprisingly powerful seven-year-old singing voice—the little girl leaned over and whispered, "Thank you."

Cameron looked down at her in surprise. "For what?" he whispered.

"For bringing me here." She leaned her head on his arm.

Cameron froze for a second. "You're welcome." He resisted the urge to pull his arm away, instead letting the warm, steady weight of Ruby's head anchor him in this moment.

At the front of the church, Dan approached the podium. But instead of standing behind it, the pastor slid it to the side and stepped in front of it, moving closer to the first row of seats.

"Fool me once, shame on you. Fool me twice, shame on me," Dan began. "Ever heard that saying?"

Heard it? Cameron shook his head. He'd lived it. As had his parents. Thanks to Bethany.

"Here's the thing," Dan continued. "That saying may be clever, with its play on words, but it's not what Jesus calls us to. He says, "Fool me once, I forgive you. Fool me twice—"" The pastor paused, glancing around the church. "I forgive you. Fool me three times, I forgive you again. In fact, in our reading for today from Matthew 18, Peter asked Jesus if he should forgive someone who had sinned against him even *seven* times."

Dan pulled a Bible off the podium, flipping it open. "I mean, that sounds pretty generous to me. Someone hurts you seven times, and you forgive them every time? You deserve a medal. But as Jesus answers Peter, you can almost see him shaking his head. Because Jesus has a slightly bigger number in mind. He says, 'I tell you, not seven times, but seventy-seven times.'" Dan closed the Bible and looked up at them. "Can't you just see Peter's eyes going big? Seventy-seven times? That's a lot."

Cameron glanced at Ruby, whose eyes were on the pastor, her mouth open the tiniest bit, the same way Bethany's always had been when she was concentrating.

Seventy-seven times, huh?

Cameron had easily forgiven his sister that many times. Not that he wanted to pat himself on the back or anything. But if Jesus was counting . . .

"Seventy-seven is a lot," Dan continued. "But actually, the phrase used here can also be translated another way. It could be translated as seventy *times* seven. In other words, four hundred and ninety times. Is there anyone you'd be willing to forgive *four hundred and ninety times*?"

Honestly, Cameron had probably come close to forgiving Bethany that many times—before she'd crossed the line and cost his family everything. At some point, enough was enough. Why should he keep forgiving someone who obviously didn't have any intention of changing, who would only hurt him again and again and again?

Dan peered around the congregation, as if he couldn't believe what he'd just said. "Surely Jesus was exaggerating here. He doesn't really want us to forgive people who have hurt us almost five hundred times, does he? That would be ridiculous, foolish, unrealistic, unreasonable, right? Right." Dan nodded. "Jesus *doesn't* want you to forgive anyone almost five hundred times."

Cameron shifted in his seat. He'd known Jesus couldn't possibly expect that.

"Actually," Dan continued, "he wants you to forgive them *endlessly*. His use of the number seventy-seven or seventy times seven wasn't meant to give you a benchmark. He was basically saying, 'However many times they sin against you, forgive them that many times.'"

Cameron let out a quiet, disbelieving breath. This preacher was obviously crazy—or Jesus was. No one could forgive someone who kept hurting them over and over. And no one deserved to be forgiven for that.

"If you're like me, that probably rubs you the wrong way." Dan paced to the far side of the sanctuary. "After all, aren't there some people who should never be forgiven? People who have hurt you so much, who have hurt you so many times. . . . People you'd be fine with never seeing again. . . . People you've forgiven before but who have basically spit in your face and gone on to do the very same thing to you again and again and again. . . . People you'd be better off if you'd never known."

Dan moved toward their side of the church, looking right at Cameron. He shifted in his seat, unable to shake the eerie sensation that the pastor knew he was thinking of Bethany.

He tried to tune out the sermon. He didn't need any more exhortations to forgive someone who didn't deserve to be forgiven, whatever the pastor said. But Dan's next words hit him right in the gut. "The hardest part is when that person is someone who is supposed to love you. A friend. A parent. A sister or brother."

Ruby wiggled against his arm, and Cameron glanced down. She grinned up at him, her smile so much like Bethany's that he had to look away, clenching his jaw tight. Bethany may have managed to produce a pretty good kid. But that didn't change the fact that she'd destroyed his life, destroyed the lives of their parents, with her selfishness. The same selfishness she'd said she was sorry for again and again and again. Yeah, fool him once . . . But after a while if you let someone keep fooling you, that just made you a fool.

"'Love your enemies,' Jesus says." Dan was still going. "It sounds like a paradox, right? But sometimes loving our enemies is easier than loving those who are supposed to love us but have hurt us. I mean, how often do you see your enemies? But your friends and family—the people who sometimes hurt you the most—they're right there all the time. And they have more opportunities to hurt you every day."

Cameron swallowed. Not anymore. Bethany would never hurt him again. He wouldn't give her a chance. A tiny pang went through his middle as Ruby shifted her head on his arm. He'd tried so hard not to let his sister's daughter work her way into his heart. But somehow she had, and he was going to miss her when he eventually went back to California. But that didn't change the fact that he wanted nothing to do with his sister once all of this was over.

"Think of Joseph," Dan said. "His brothers threw him into a cistern, sold him into slavery, and told their dad he was dead. But he forgave them. Or the prodigal son's father. His son took his inheritance while his father was still alive, then told his dad he didn't want anything more to do with him—until the money ran out. And his dad forgave him. Welcomed him home with open arms."

Not the brightest dad ever. Cameron couldn't help picturing his own father welcoming Bethany home.

"Or Jesus himself. His own family said he was crazy and tried to get him to stop preaching. Or even better—or worse, I suppose—he was betrayed by one of his closest friends. And what did Jesus do?" Dan looked around the sanctuary. "He forgave them. Even though they didn't deserve it. None of these people deserved it."

Dan paused so long that Cameron wondered if the sermon was over. But then he said quietly, "The next time you're struggling to forgive someone, whatever they've done to you—something big or something small—I want you to remember that there is someone else who doesn't deserve forgiveness. You. Me." Dan picked up his Bible, flipping it open near the end. "It's easy enough to think that we're a good person, that we aren't anywhere near as bad as those who hurt us. But James 2:10 tells us, 'For whoever keeps the whole law and yet stumbles at just one point is guilty of breaking all of it.'" Dan looked up. "I don't know about you, but I have stumbled at far more than one point. And because of my sin, I deserve death. Romans 6:23 says, 'For the wages of sin is death.'"

His pause was only the length of a heartbeat. "Fortunately, that verse doesn't end there. It goes on, 'but the gift of God is eternal life in Christ Jesus our Lord.'" Dan's smile beamed around the church. "You don't deserve forgiveness. I don't deserve forgiveness. The person who hurt you doesn't deserve forgiveness. But God gives it anyway. Because his Son came into this world to keep the law perfectly—without stumbling at a single point—and then to die a sinless death in our place. He did that so we could have the forgiveness that none of us deserve." Dan shook his head slowly. "And if God, who has never done even one thing wrong, can forgive me for my many wrongs—so many more than seventy-seven or even seventy times seven—even though I don't deserve that forgiveness, surely I can forgive those who sin against me even though they don't deserve it. God calls us to that forgiveness when he says, 'Forgive as the Lord forgave you.' Amen."

Cameron lifted his head as the people around him began to stand. He pushed slowly to his feet too.

The sermon had been good. He could admit that. But that didn't mean he thought Pastor Dan was right.

Sure, maybe Jesus could forgive people even when they didn't deserve it. It was probably easy for him. But Cameron was only human. It wasn't reasonable to ask him to simply forget what Bethany had done to their family.

Not now.

Not ever.

As they settled back into their seats for the final hymn, Cameron slid farther away from Ruby. He knew Bethany's sins weren't her daughter's fault. But right now he needed a little distance from any reminders of his sister.

The moment the service ended, Ruby broke into conversation with Kayla, who looked past the little girl and caught Cameron's eyes with a smile. It was only for a moment, but it was enough to make his heart do a strange sort of leap. Cameron ignored it.

He nudged Ruby out of the row, and they followed Kayla toward the back of the church. But instead of exiting into the lobby, she stopped at the back row, where a couple was busy wrapping a baby in blankets.

Kayla squealed and returned the hugs the couple offered. "Let me see your little bundle."

"This is Ella Lynn." The man held up a squirming baby, probably not quite a year old, though Cameron knew better than to trust his own judgment when it came to children's ages.

Kayla rubbed a finger over the baby's tiny hand, and something about the movement was so tender that it tugged at Cameron.

"How old is she?" Ruby asked.

"She's nine months."

Well, who knew? He must be getting better at determining ages than he thought.

"Come on Ruby. We should get going." He tried to step around Kayla's wheelchair, but she glanced up, as if she'd forgotten he was there.

"Oh. Sorry. Jared, this is Ruby's uncle, Cam. Cam, this is Jared and Peyton and their brand-new daughter Ella Lynn. Jared is one of the paramedics who responded to Bethany's accident."

"Oh." Cameron wasn't quite sure how to react to that. He held out a hand. "Thank you."

Jared shook his hand. "How's your sister doing?"

Cameron's eyes flitted to Ruby. "She's doing . . . okay. Still about the same, but . . ."

Jared nodded solemnly. "We'll keep praying for her."

"Yeah." Cameron shifted awkwardly. "It was nice meeting you. Congrats on your little one."

He took a step toward the lobby, grabbing Ruby's hand to tug her with him.

"Wait. You're coming to lunch at the Hidden Cafe, right?" Kayla's eyes landed on his.

"Oh. Uh. Thanks, but—"

"Please, Uncle Cam," Ruby half-whined. He gave her a look, and she changed tactics. "I'm hungry. Your waffles were bad and I didn't have time to eat much cereal."

Kayla lifted an eyebrow. "You made waffles? I'm impressed."

"Don't be. They looked like shoe leather."

"And smelled like feet," Ruby added with a giggle.

Cameron couldn't hide his own laugh. "They kind of did."

"That settles it." Kayla clapped twice. "You two are coming to lunch with us."

Cameron considered arguing more. But the truth was, he was hungry. And enjoying his time with these people.

And, between Kayla and Ruby, he had a feeling he would have lost any argument anyway.

Chapter 30

"Oh, for crying out loud." Kayla gave an exasperated laugh at herself. That was the fourth time she'd dropped her napkin during this one meal. She started to roll her wheelchair back from the end of their long table at the Hidden Cafe, but Cam beat her to it.

"I've got it." He leaned over, giving her a full breath of his fresh, slightly spicy smell.

As he sat up, she tried not to notice how good he looked in his dark suit and the sapphire tie that brought out the flecks of warmth in his eyes. Or the way his suit hugged his shoulders, emphasizing their width. Or the way a lock of his hair fell onto his forehead, giving him a more playful appearance than usual.

A strange tingle went straight up the back of her neck—the same tingle that had been plaguing her every time he looked at her since they'd gotten here.

It had been a long time since she'd allowed herself to acknowledge attraction to any man, but Cam sure was making it rather difficult not to today.

Which was a problem.

Because she had no intention of giving up her independence for any man. Not even one as charming and attractive and funny and . . .

She stopped herself. Listing his good qualities was not going to help here.

"So, Kayla," Emma said from her other side.

Kayla turned to her friend with such a profound feeling of relief that she was afraid Emma would read it on her face.

But Emma seemed oblivious as she gave Kayla a huge smile. "I have a proposition for you."

"Yeah? What's that?"

Emma's grin grew. "I've been looking into starting a social interactions program at Hope Riders. But I don't have time to oversee it myself, and I was thinking . . ." She waggled her eyebrows at Kayla.

"Me?" Kayla stared at the other woman. Was Emma offering her a job?

"Of course, you."

"You'd be perfect for that." Cam cut in, and Kayla swiveled her head toward him in surprise. "I would?"

"Of course she would," Emma said to Cam, who gave a satisfied nod.

"And then you could stay in Hope Springs forever," Ruby added.

Kayla smiled at her but then turned back to Emma. "Is this something you want to start right away?"

"The sooner the better. Our grant funding just came through, so I need to get it going pretty quickly."

Kayla bit her lip. "I really appreciate the offer, and I'm definitely interested, but can I think about it a bit? I just found out this morning that I was accepted for the mission trip, so . . ."

"You were?" Emma popped up to hug her. "Oh, Kayla, that's wonderful. And no pressure at all. Whatever you decide, I know God is going to bless."

"Looks like you're in high demand." Cam gave her a warm look—or maybe it wasn't his look that was warm so much as her cheeks.

She ducked her head.

She had more important things to think about right now than her ridiculous feelings. Like how in the living world she was going to make this decision.

She spent the rest of the meal trying to weigh the pros and cons of each opportunity—but only ended up with a swirling head.

"All right, Ruby, time to go."

Kayla looked up in surprise at the sound of Cam's voice. She hadn't even registered that most of the others had left already.

"Bye, Kayla." Ruby jumped up from her seat and threw her arms around Kayla's neck.

"Bye, sweetie." Kayla was seized by the ridiculous urge to tell the two of them not to go. After spending so much time with them over the past couple of weeks, it felt odd not to be certain when she'd see them again. But it would be odd to invite them to the movie she'd been planning to see with Nate and Vi, so she simply lifted a hand and waved as they started for the door.

"You're just going to let them walk out?" Vi hissed from next to her.

"Yes, I am." She turned to her sister-in-law, whose hand was pressed to her belly. "And so are you."

Vi snorted. "You don't know me very well, do you?" She lifted her head to look past Kayla, raising her voice to call, "Cam! Ruby!"

The two of them stopped, their matching eyes falling on Vi.

"We're going to the movies. If you want to join us." Vi's voice seemed overly loud in the small restaurant.

Kayla dropped her eyes to her lap, then to the floor, then to the table—anywhere that wasn't Cam.

But after a moment, she couldn't bear not knowing his answer, so she looked up.

Ruby was already on her way back toward the table. Cam stood frozen to the spot, though his hand was extended toward Ruby, as if he'd tried to stop her.

His eyes met Kayla's, and she held her breath, one hundred percent unsure what he would do. One hundred percent unsure what she wanted him to do.

After a moment, he shrugged, dropped his arm, and followed Ruby.

"If you need to work, we can take Ruby without you." Kayla didn't know why she blurted the words. But at least this way Cam couldn't think the invitation had been directed at him.

"Nah, that's okay. I'll come."

The way Ruby's eyes lit up went straight through Kayla. And the fact that Cam looked nearly as pleased only made the feeling grow stronger. Somehow, over the last few weeks, Ruby's uncle had gone from complete indifference toward his niece to adoring her—even if he maybe wasn't quite ready to admit it to himself.

As they slipped out of the restaurant into the gray December afternoon, Vi gave Kayla a sly look. "Why don't you ride with Cam, Kayla?" Her sister-in-law's voice was all innocence. "Nate and I need to stop at the antique shop on the way to pick up a table I want for the house."

Kayla shot her sister-in-law a look that should have burned the sweet smile right off her face. But Vi seemed completely unperturbed. Right, as if Kayla hadn't heard the stories about how Vi had contrived to get her best friend Sophie alone with Spencer so the two could realize they were still in love.

Well, if that was Vi's plan here, she was going to be sorely disappointed.

"Sure." Kayla made her voice breezy and calm. No need to let Vi think it ruffled her in the least to spend more time with Cam and Ruby. Because it didn't. She turned to Cam. "If you two don't mind."

Ruby jumped up and down. "Come with us! Come with us!"

Cam's smile was sincere. "That's fine with me."

"All right then, that's settled." Vi took her husband's arm and waddled toward their car. "We'll see you there in a little bit."

Kayla followed Cam and Ruby to Cam's vehicle. When they got to it, Cam stepped in front of her to open the passenger door.

She gave him a look and prepared to tell him that she was perfectly capable of opening a car door on her own, thank you very much, but then he moved to open Ruby's door as well, poking her lightly in the side as she climbed past him, eliciting a giggle from her and a hearty chuckle from him.

Kayla laughed too—she couldn't help it. She moved into position to transfer into the car, trying not to feel self-conscious as Cam stood by, watching her first lift her legs into the vehicle, then boost her torso inside.

But he smiled as he reached for her wheelchair. She'd shown him how to take it apart when they went to the zoo last weekend, so they could stow it in the trunk.

As Cam got into the car, he gave Kayla another smile—he really needed to stop doing that—then looked over his shoulder at Ruby. "All buckled?"

"Baa. Let's go."

Kayla smirked at Cam when he huffed out a breath. Apparently Ruby was taking her acting advice seriously.

They had just pulled into the theater's parking lot when Kayla's phone dinged with a text from Vi.

Not feeling so great. I think we're going to head home. Have fun though!

Kayla rolled her eyes. She should have seen this coming. It was straight out of Vi's playbook.

But there was nothing she could do about it now.

Her fingers tapped out a quick reply. *I know what you're up to. And it's not going to work.*

Though as she glanced at Cam's smiling lips, she realized—she was going to have to take care to make sure that was true.

Cameron hadn't felt this relaxed in a long time.

Maybe it was the dark of the movie theater or the fact that he'd turned his phone off completely so that even its buzzing vibration couldn't interrupt his afternoon. Or maybe it was the sound of Ruby and Kayla giggling together all through the movie.

He'd tried to be annoyed—their laughter had made him miss more than one line of the movie. But instead he found himself smiling every time he heard them.

Ruby's full-bellied laugh was almost contagious—and Kayla's lighter, more lilting one wasn't far behind.

As the credits rolled and the lights came up, Ruby leaned over. "Uncle Cameron." Her whisper was urgent.

"Yeah?"

"I have to go to the bathroom." She squinted her eyes, as if she were in agony.

"Oh. Uh. Can you wait until we get home?"

She shook her head.

"I'll take her," Kayla offered.

"Thank you." Cameron honestly had no idea how a person was supposed to parent a child alone. He could definitely see that parenting was easier as a tag-team sport. Not that he and Kayla were parents. Or even a team.

As he cleaned up their garbage, his thoughts drifted back to Kayla's friends at lunch. So many families—all happy and whole and content.

But not all families were that way. And there was no guarantee that those that were would stay that way. He knew that better than anyone.

He threw away the trash, then waited in the hallway for Ruby and Kayla. Three other guys stood there too, apparently doing the same thing.

A young woman came out of the restroom, a toddler in her arms, and walked up to one of the men, smiling. He pushed off the wall and fell in step with her, wrapping an arm around her back and leaning over to tickle the toddler.

Something clenched in Cam's gut—a brief flicker of doubt. Was it possible that he did want that?

"Can we go look at the lake?" Ruby bounced toward him and slipped her little hand into his. Hers was still wet from washing it, but he didn't pull away.

Cam shrugged. He had plenty of work to catch up on, but honestly, he was in no rush to get to it. "It's up to Kayla."

"That sounds fun. I haven't been down to the marina since I got here."

They emerged from the theater to find that the cloudy afternoon was already dimming. As they made the short trek to the top of the hill that led down to the marina, Cam hesitated, glancing at Kayla in her wheelchair. That was a steep hill.

"You can manage this?" He didn't want to insult her, but he also didn't want to watch her lose control of her wheelchair and go plummeting into Lake Michigan.

"Yep." She popped her front wheels up, balancing on the large back wheels, then started down the hill at a controlled pace.

Cam shook his head as he followed her. He shouldn't have doubted her. The woman seemed to have no concept of just how extraordinary the things she did were.

At the bottom of the hill, they made their way onto the wide breakwater that extended into the lake, creating a safe harbor. A sharp wind blew off the water, and Cam reached over to pull Ruby's hood up.

By the time they'd made their way to the end of the breakwater and back, he could barely feel his fingers. He glanced at Kayla, who was now going to have to wheel all the way back up the hill.

But this time he knew better than to ask if she could do it. Instead, he walked alongside her as she attacked the hill as if it were nothing more than a speed bump.

"I can see how you've won marathons." He paused at the top of the hill to let Ruby, who had fallen behind after stopping to examine every crack in the sidewalk, catch up.

Kayla smiled, her breathing only a hint labored. "Honestly, I'm pretty out of shape right now. I've been starting to train again, although if I go to Malawi, I guess I won't be doing any races."

For some reason, the thought of her going that far away drew Cam up short. It made no sense—he'd be going back to California sooner or later, so what did it matter to him where she wound up?

"Does the Chocolate Chicken have hot cocoa?" He looked from Kayla to Ruby. "Or am I the only one who needs to warm up?" And who was having too much fun to go home quite yet.

Kayla grinned at Ruby. "I believe it does."

Chapter 31

Darkness was already falling as they exited the Chocolate Chicken, and though the evening was chilly, Kayla had to admit that she couldn't remember ever feeling so warm and cozy and . . . content. And the Christmas lights twinkling from all the storefronts only added to the peaceful atmosphere.

The sound of bells jingling carried in the clear air, and Ruby pointed down the street. "That's the carriage that went past our house three times last night."

Kayla read the chalkboard sign on the sidewalk. "Carriage tours nightly until Christmas Eve. Tour the best of Hope Springs' Christmas lights." She turned to Cam. "Why does it go past your house?"

Cam gave her a mysterious smirk. "Wouldn't you like to know."

"That's why I asked. Ruby?" She'd certainly have better luck with the little girl. "Did your neighbors decorate their houses?" When Kayla had left their house the other night, she hadn't noticed any decorations—or at least not any that would qualify as "the best of Hope Springs."

Ruby giggled and shook her head but didn't say anything.

"Seriously, what's the big secret?"

Both Cam and Ruby burst into laughter.

"I guess we'll just have to show you." Cam gestured to the carriage as it pulled to a stop in front of the Chocolate Chicken, the horses' breath steaming the air in front of them.

Yeah, she could probably be persuaded to extend this day a little longer. But after this, she *had* to go home, before Vi's plan really did work.

They waited for the current passengers—a young couple with pink cheeks and arms wrapped adorably around each other—to disembark. Then Cam boosted Ruby into the carriage. Once she was settled, he moved out of the way to let Kayla get into it. She eyed the narrow foot rest. There was no way she'd be able to get her feet stable on there and pull herself up. Maybe if she skipped it and hoisted herself directly onto the floor of the carriage? But it was high, and the opening was narrow. She doubted she could get the leverage she needed.

But she'd never been one to give up without a fight. She maneuvered her wheelchair into the best position she could manage, then reached for the side of the carriage and put her considerable arm muscle into pulling herself up. But the angle was off, and after a moment, she let herself drop back into her chair. She readjusted and tried again, but after another half-dozen attempts, she rolled her chair back from the carriage.

Given enough time, she knew she'd get in there eventually—she hadn't yet met the vehicle she couldn't transfer into. But it was cold, and she wasn't going to make Cam and Ruby wait here all night.

"You two go." She kept her eyes directed toward her lap. She knew she shouldn't be embarrassed, but she was. After Cam had been so impressed with the way she'd powered up the hill. Well, now he knew she wasn't Superwoman, after all. "I'll drive down your street later and see what's so mysterious that you can't tell me."

"Don't be stupid." The roughness of Cam's voice caught her by surprise, and she looked up to find him glowering down at her. "If I didn't know how stubborn you were, I would have offered to help long before now."

She gave a shaky laugh. "I'm not stubborn. I'm independent."

He shook his head. "Part of being independent is knowing that there's no shame in asking for help. You're stubborn."

"Please come, Kayla." Ruby's plea was much kinder than Cam's.

Kayla lifted her eyes to his. "All right, fine. Would you mind helping me?"

His glower transformed into a grin. "Thought you'd never ask. Just tell me what to do."

She let out a long breath. She didn't like the feeling of being carried—the lack of control—but it was the only option. "I can't get the right angle to transfer myself. I think you're going to have to lift me."

Cam nodded as if she'd asked him to do something totally normal, then stepped forward and slid one arm under her legs and the other behind her back. She inhaled sharply as he lifted, having no choice but to wrap her arm around his shoulder, telling herself that she didn't feel a tiny tingle all the way through her skin and down to her fingertips. That she didn't notice the ripple of muscle as he pivoted toward the carriage.

"I'm really sorry about this." She turned her head away from him so she wouldn't be staring at his firm jawline, wouldn't be awash in his spicy scent.

"Don't be silly." At least he hadn't called her stupid this time.

With a slight grunt, he angled her through the opening and raised her onto the carriage seat, setting her down as gently as if she were made of porcelain.

Then he stepped back and pushed her wheelchair underneath the awning of the Chocolate Chicken. "I assume that will be fine there for a little bit?"

Kayla nodded. "Yeah." She tried to get herself to think straight, but Cam's eyes were on her, and she wanted suddenly to know what he was thinking. Had he felt the same electricity she did when she was in his arms?

But then he looked away and climbed into the carriage, settling next to Ruby.

Kayla let out a sigh—of relief, of course.

Cameron fisted his hands in his coat pocket, working hard to look anywhere but at Kayla. Holding her in his arms for those few moments had been disconcerting. The way her warm, coconutty scent had cloaked him, the way her hand had rested lightly against his neck, the way her hair had brushed his cheek—it had all thrown his senses, not to mention his feelings, into confusion.

Be logical, he reminded himself.

Logic said that what a woman smelled like—or looked like sitting in the moonlight or sounded like laughing with Ruby or felt like in his arms—had nothing to do with anything. Feelings might get caught up in those things. But logic didn't. Logic said this was just a carriage ride. Logic said they were both doing this for Ruby. Logic said Kayla didn't have feelings for him any more than he did for her.

Logic said the only reason he was thinking like this at all was because of Ruby's ridiculous suggestion the other day that he couldn't have a girlfriend because he had Kayla.

You don't have a girlfriend anymore.

That was true . . . but it also didn't mean he was looking for one.

The driver made a clicking noise to his horses, and the carriage started forward with a slight jerk, leading Ruby to squeal and Kayla to lurch forward. Instantly, his hand was out of his pocket and on her arm, steadying her.

Only for a second, but it was long enough for him to feel the jolt.

"Thanks," she murmured.

"It's fine." He cleared his throat and pulled his hand back, even as his heart took up the rhythm of the horses' clattering feet.

As the carriage turned away from downtown toward the residential streets, he forced himself to focus on the decorations glinting from the houses. But the closer they got to the house, the more he felt the anticipation building. He didn't know why he was so excited for Kayla to see what he'd been working on, but he couldn't keep his grin from growing as the carriage approached their street.

Ruby apparently felt the same way, as she started bouncing on the seat next to him. "Close your eyes," she said to Kayla.

"Seriously?" Kayla's eyes flicked from Cameron to Ruby, and now he felt his smile reach for his ears.

"Really." He reached across the space between their seats and pulled her hat over her eyes.

"Hey." But she laughed and held her hands over her eyes as well. "This had better be good."

When the carriage finally arrived at the house, Cameron asked the driver to stop for a minute.

"All right, open your eyes," Ruby said.

"Are you sure?" Kayla kept her hands over her face.

"Yes!" Ruby stood and pulled Kayla's hands down, then shoved her hat onto her forehead.

Cam watched as Kayla's expression went from confused to surprised to delighted. "Wow! You did this?" She turned to him, and he couldn't deny the warmth that went through him at the admiration in her gaze.

He shrugged. "You're not the only one who knows how to put up Christmas decorations."

"Clearly not. Wow, Cam. This is amazing."

"Thanks." Cam let his eyes go to the yard, where he'd wrapped the trunks of every tree in blue lights, then draped white lights from the branches. He'd also created his own trees by stabbing shepherd's hooks into the ground, wrapping them in lights and then extending more lights from them in a pyramid shape. But his favorite part was the tunnel of lights he'd created along the walkway to the front door. Icicle lights on the eaves completed the effect.

It wasn't too bad, if he did say so himself.

"I take it you entered the decorating contest. Seriously, you might give Leah and Austin a run for their money this year. I have to get a picture of this." Kayla readjusted in her seat to dig into her coat pocket.

"There's a decorating contest?"

Kayla stopped rummaging for a second and stared at him. "You didn't know about the contest? You just did this for fun?"

He shrugged. Was it that hard for her to imagine him doing such a thing? "I always loved decorating the yard with my dad. This brought back good memories. And Ruby insisted on the icicles. We had to go back to the store to get them."

"Got it!" Kayla held up her phone triumphantly. She pulled off her glove and tapped the screen, then frowned. "Oh. I turned it off during the movie. One second. You guys move over so I can get you in it with the house in the background."

Cam and Ruby shifted. "Is this good?"

"You need to get closer. Maybe Ruby should sit on your lap."

All right. He'd never held a kid on his lap in his life, but sure, why not? Ruby got up, and he shifted to the far edge of the seat, then boosted her onto his lap and wrapped an arm around her so she wouldn't fall off. To his surprise, it didn't feel odd at all to be holding a kid. "How about this?"

But Kayla was staring at her phone, one hand pressed to her mouth, shaking her head.

"What's wrong?" He leaned forward, nearly dumping Ruby off his lap, but cinched his arm tighter so she wouldn't fall and gently took the phone from Kayla's hand.

He flipped it around to read the text that was open.

Took Vi to hospital. The doctors said placental abruption. They want her to deliver right away. Pls pray.

"That was from an hour ago. Why didn't he call me?" Kayla's voice was teary as she grabbed the phone back out of Cameron's hand and examined the screen. "Oh. He did. Six times." She glanced at Cam, fear pooling in her eyes.

A sick feeling settled in his stomach as Kayla tapped her screen, then pressed the phone to her ear. There had to be something he could do to help.

He set Ruby back on the seat next to him, then turned and tapped the carriage driver's shoulder. "We need to get back to where you picked us up."

"We haven't gone down Church Street yet." The driver spoke in a low-key monotone.

"Skip it. Take us back to the Chocolate Chicken."

The driver nodded and clicked to the horses.

Cam settled back into the seat, then leaned forward and took Kayla's free hand in his. "It's going to be okay." He had no idea what possessed him to whisper the words. He had no way of knowing that.

She gave him a weak smile as she left a message.

When she'd hung up, she turned to him. "Do you think you could drop me off at the hospital?"

He shook his head. He was absolutely *not* going to drop her off at the hospital.

"We're coming with you."

Chapter 32

Kayla numbly took the coffee cup Cam held out to her.

Shell-shocked. That was the only way to describe how she felt.

Like she had just watched everything in her world blow up in her face.

The doctors were still working on Vi, but they were pretty sure she'd make it.

The baby, though.

Tears came to Kayla's eyes again, and she swallowed them down with a scalding drink of coffee and a swipe at her cheeks.

The poor baby.

And poor Vi and Nate.

Grief for the hole that Vi would feel when she learned what had happened to her baby—it had been a boy, they'd learned—tore at Kayla's ribs.

"Do you want to stay or go home?" Cam's voice was low and soothing, and Kayla wondered yet again if this was the same man who had come barreling into this same hospital only a month ago, no interest in seeing his own sister, clearly impatient at the idea of caring for his niece. Now he leaned over and tucked Ruby's jacket under her head, which was pressed against the arm of a chair. The little girl had brightened them all for a while, until she'd grown too sleepy and curled up in the chair.

"I'm going to stay. But I can get a ride with Nate or someone else." The small waiting room was so crowded with friends that a nurse had come in a while ago and asked if some of them might like to come back another time—but not a one had budged. "You go. Get Ruby home to bed."

Cam's eyes held hers. "Ruby wouldn't want to leave you."

She swallowed. What about him? Did he want to stay too?

"Really, Cam. I'll be fine. Thank you for bringing me."

He nodded, then stood and slid his arms under Ruby's sleeping form. Kayla tried not to remember what it'd felt like to have those arms around her, lifting her into the carriage.

She should have been humiliated, disgusted at herself that she'd needed to ask for help. Instead, all she'd felt was warm—safe.

It was a feeling she couldn't let herself get used to.

She was plenty warm and safe all by herself. She didn't need a man to make her feel that way.

"Call me tomorrow," Cam said. "Let me know how they're doing."

On his way out of the room, he rested a hand briefly on Nate's shoulder, and Kayla's heart squeezed so tight she didn't know how it didn't pop.

Then Cam and Ruby were gone, and Kayla was left feeling . . . alone. Which made absolutely no sense, seeing that she was surrounded by friends.

She wheeled her chair in front of Nate's seat. Her brother looked up, his eyes bleary. "What am I going to do, Kay?"

She took his hand. The truth was, she didn't know. "We're all here for you, Nate. And for Vi."

The waiting room door opened, and a tired-looking doctor entered the room. "Mr. Benson?"

Nate gave Kayla a panicked look, and she squeezed his hand, closing her eyes and trying to issue a desperate prayer as Nate stood. But her soul drew a blank.

"Is she all right? Can I see her?"

The doctor ran a hand down his face, and Kayla's heart went cold. But the doctor nodded. "She's stable. You can see her now."

Nate let out a whoosh of air, as if he'd been punched, and fell back into his seat. "Thank you, Lord." But then he lifted his eyes, meeting Kayla's in horror. "How am I going to tell her?"

Kayla opened her mouth, grasping for the words of comfort she knew he needed to hear. But she was empty. Her quick prayer for something helpful to say went unanswered, and an unsettled feeling stirred inside her.

How could God have allowed this to happen to the people she loved most in the world? To people he'd already asked so much of? Who served him faithfully day after day?

None of it made any sense.

As she looked at Nate, she could only shake her head and swipe at her own eyes. "I'm so sorry."

She'd let her brother down.

And God had let them all down.

Chapter 33

Cameron growled at the document open on his laptop. For the life of him, he couldn't remember why he was supposed to care about it.

All he could picture right now was Kayla. Kayla smiling. Kayla laughing. Kayla crying over the loss of her little nephew.

That last one was the one he kept getting caught up on. The way she'd wiped the tears off her cheeks as fast as they fell. The way she'd tried to hide her face from him. The way every fiber of his being had ached to pull her into his arms and hold her tight and tell her it was okay to let them see her hurt.

She'd texted early Monday morning to say Vi had pulled through, and he'd been amazed by the power of the relief that had gone through him. How was it that these people he'd only known for a month had come to mean so much to him?

It wasn't logical.

But then, it seemed that nothing here was logical. It wasn't logical that his thirty-six-year-old sister had had a brain aneurysm, wasn't logical that Vi and Nate had lost their baby, wasn't logical that though it had only been five days since he'd seen Kayla, he missed her with a fierceness he'd never experienced before.

He closed his laptop. The house was too quiet, and Ruby wouldn't be home from school for two hours yet. His eyes fell on the picture Ruby had been drawing this morning—of her mother playing with her in the snow.

All week, Cameron's conscience had asserted itself louder and louder, Dan's sermon knocking around his thoughts like Ruby's super ball. Was the pastor right? Was it time he forgave Bethany? Time he was there for her the way Kayla and her friends had been there for Nate and Vi?

With a sudden decisiveness, he shoved the dining room chair back and jumped to his feet, sending the cat that had been curled up on his lap flying with a scolding yowl.

He grabbed his jacket and keys and twenty minutes later was standing in Bethany's hospital room, hands jammed in his pockets. Now what? He glanced around the room, then grabbed a chair from the far corner and pulled it up to the bed.

He stared at his sister for a long while, too many memories swimming through his thoughts. Memories of playing hide and seek with the whole family. Memories of movie nights gathered around the small TV in the family room. Memories of telling her everything would be okay when her first boyfriend broke up with her.

Memories of the first time she'd returned from rehab, promising she was all better. And of the second time. And the third. Of Mom and Dad welcoming her back every time.

Memories of the day he came home from school to find Dad in tears—his strong dad in actual tears—because Bethany had betrayed them.

Abruptly, Cameron shoved to his feet, sending his chair skidding across the floor behind him. "I'm sorry. I just can't." He spoke the words out loud, right over the top of his sister. "I can't forgive you for what you did. Mom and Dad gave you everything. They forgave you and welcomed you back and picked you up every time you fell. And because of you, they weren't there—" He tipped his head back to stare at the ceiling, his vision blurring. "They weren't there to do any of that for me. I had to figure it all out myself." His voice cracked, but he wasn't done. "You took them from me, Bethany, and nothing can change that."

He watched her still form for another minute, warring against the part of himself that felt sad and scared for her. She didn't deserve that.

"You managed to raise a pretty amazing little girl, I'll give you that." He pinched the bridge of his nose. "And I'll keep taking care of her as long as I need to. But it's not for you—" He shook his head, wiping away a single tear that had managed to creep onto his cheek. "It's for her. And for Mom and Dad."

Chapter 34

She shouldn't have let Nate and Vi talk her into coming to dinner at Dan and Jade's house tonight. They'd said being around friends would help, and though she doubted it, she'd come along, because if Nate and Vi could see everyone and talk and handle their grief, then what right did she have to stay home and be sad? But the cloud that had hung lower and lower over her all week felt like it was pressing on her now, stifling her, pushing her into the ground.

She forced a smile onto her face as she picked up Vi's empty plate to bring to the kitchen. She had to be strong for her sister-in-law.

"I can get that." Vi reached for it, but Kayla shook her head. It was the least she could do.

"You sit. I've got this."

Vi gave her a grateful pat and returned to her conversation with Sophie.

Kayla kept the smile plastered in place as she maneuvered past the others to the kitchen, not looking toward where Cam was handing Ruby a piece of cake. Tonight was the first she'd seen of him since he'd left the hospital last Sunday, and she didn't know why she felt like she had to avoid him now.

She suspected it was because as hard as she'd tried not to let him, he'd seen her cry. Seen her weak. Seen her in need.

Something she worked hard not to let anyone see—ever. She was supposed to be the strong one. Didn't people always tell her that—how much they admired her strength?

Straightening in her chair, she made her way to the kitchen, where Jade was loading the dishwasher. Jade directed a discerning look her way as she added the dishes to the machine. "How are you doing?"

"Me?" Kayla put on her toughest strong-girl smile. "I'm doing fine. Just trying to keep Vi off her feet."

"Good luck with that." Jade squeezed Kayla's shoulder. "They're going to be okay, you know that, right?"

Kayla swallowed painfully. "Of course. I'll go grab some more dishes."

But as she reached the living room, her eyes caught on Vi, absently rubbing a hand over her stomach, the same way she'd done when she was pregnant. With a silent shudder, Kayla left the room and wheeled down the hallway to Dan's office. She knew he wouldn't mind—she just needed a few seconds to pull herself together.

The moment she'd closed the door, she dropped her head to her hands and loosed the dam of tears she hadn't allowed herself to cry at the funeral they'd held for her little nephew—Isaac Matthew—three days ago. The same question that had plagued her since then swirled through her head: Why?

She could see the good that had come out of her accident, but how could babies dying possibly be for anyone's good, let alone Nate and Vi's? Why would God let something like that happen?

The part that hurt the most was that she had no answer. Just a profound sense of sadness that something had been taken from her that she was afraid she might never get back.

It made no sense. She kept trying to talk herself out of the feeling. She'd already gone through her crisis of faith once, a long time ago. She couldn't have a second one. Now she was supposed to be the one who was there for others through their own crises.

The creak of the door behind her made her wipe her eyes quickly. "I'll be out in one second." She worked to make her voice bright, but even she could hear the tears in it.

She heard the door click shut and offered a silent thank you. At least whoever it was had realized she wanted to be alone.

But footsteps crossing the wooden floor abolished that hope. She wiped her eyes harder. Dan must need something from his office. "Sorry, I didn't mean to—"

"Are you okay?" It wasn't Dan's voice. It was Cam's.

Kayla kept her head down, unwilling to let him see that she'd been crying. Again. "Of course. I just needed to . . ."

A wooden desk chair rolled up in front of her wheelchair, and through her eyelashes, she watched Cam sit in it, then slide it closer to her.

His hands moved toward her, and she couldn't find the wherewithal to move out of the way. She let out a long breath as his hands wrapped around hers.

"You're not okay. And that's okay." His voice was gentle. "Someone told me that after my dad died—I don't remember who. And I remember thinking at the time what a load of hogwash that was. But after a while, I realized it's kind of true. It's okay not to be okay. And it's okay to let others know you're not okay."

Kayla let herself look up at him. He was watching her with those clear blue eyes, warmer than she'd ever seen them but also filled with compassion.

"I feel silly," she admitted. "Nate and Vi are handling this better than I am. I should be the one supporting them, you know? The strong one."

Cam's thumb caressed the top of her hand. "You don't always have to be the strong one."

"Yes, I do. That's who I am. People tell me all the time—you're so strong, Kayla. I never could have gone through what you did, Kayla. You're an inspiration, Kayla."

Cam studied her. "Even inspirations are allowed to be sad sometimes, I think. Especially when something bad happens to someone they love. Right?"

Kayla's eyesight went bleary again, but she managed a small smile. "Maybe." She pulled her hands out of his to wipe her cheeks, then immediately wished she hadn't. The feel of his hands on hers had given her a warmth and hope she'd been needing all week. "I just— I gave you that whole speech about how God has a plan in everything. And I'm really struggling to believe that right now. Honestly, it feels like everything I believe has been turned upside down, and I don't know how to right it again."

She clapped a hand over her mouth. It was one thing to let him see her weak but another to let him know she was questioning her faith, especially when his own seemed so tender. The last thing she wanted to do was lead him away from the Lord. "I'm sorry, I didn't mean that. I just mean—" She closed her eyes. "I don't know what I mean." Defeat pulled on her shoulders.

"Maybe that's okay too," Cam said softly. His hands went around hers again, and she shivered a little. "Actually, it's a relief to see you struggling."

Kayla lifted her head to him. "That's . . . mean?"

He laughed. "Sorry. No, I mean, I'm not glad you're struggling. But I'm glad you told me. It makes me feel better to know I'm not the only one who ever has doubts. Because the other day at church . . . man, I was sure I was the only one. But it's nice to know you're human too."

Kayla gave him a slow, sad nod. "The humanest, unfortunately."

Cam leaned forward, lifting a hand to wipe a tear off her cheek. "I don't think that's such a bad thing." His voice was low, barely above a whisper, and as Kayla's eyes came to his, she found herself leaning forward. His hand was still on her cheek, and she closed her eyes.

What is happening here? What are you doing?

But she was tired of questions. She let her lips part.

Cam's hand slipped from her cheek and the sound of chair wheels on the wooden floor accompanied his throat clearing.

Kayla's eyes sprang open as her face spontaneously combusted.

What had she been thinking?

He hadn't wanted to kiss her. He'd only been trying to offer some simple comfort, and she'd read way more into it than she should have.

"Kayla, I'm—" He scooted his chair closer again, but she shook her head and held up a hand.

"We should get back out there. I have to check if Vi needs anything."

She spun her wheelchair toward the door without waiting for a response. She was in the hallway before she heard him push the desk chair into place.

But she didn't look back.

You are quite possibly the world's biggest idiot.

Why hadn't he kissed her?

His heart was hammering angrily at him, but his head told it to chill out. He hadn't kissed her because, for one, he'd just gotten out of a relationship and wasn't looking for another. And for two, he hadn't been at all sure that she really wanted to kiss him. She'd never given any indication of having feelings for him before. Likely, she had only leaned in because he'd offered her some measure of comfort in her grief. And he didn't want to take advantage of that.

Idiot. Apparently his heart didn't agree with his reasoning. *It* had definitely wanted to kiss her, even if his head said no.

Next time, he bargained. If she ever gave him a next time.

He followed her to the living room, trying to ignore the curious—maybe somewhat distrustful—look her brother sent his way. Cam tried to offer him an innocent looking smile as he took a seat next to Ruby at the table where she was coloring with the other kids.

He picked up a crayon and started coloring a picture of some princess or another. Though Ruby watched those movies all the time, he couldn't keep them straight.

But his eyes kept going to Kayla, who was either studiously ignoring him or completely unaffected by what had just happened. He found himself hoping it was the first.

"So Ruby—" Emma turned to his niece. "Did you write a letter to Santa?"

Cameron's head jerked up. Christmas. Santa. He hadn't even thought about that. Unless Bethany had some hidden store of gifts he hadn't run across, he needed to get Christmas presents for Ruby.

"Baa." Ruby grinned. "That means, 'nope.' Mommy always says Santa knows, so I don't need to ask for anything. And he always does. Last year, he got me the bike I wanted."

"If you did write a letter, what would you ask for?" Cam kept his question casual.

Ruby shrugged. "I don't know. Whatever Santa wants to bring me. Baa."

He groaned silently, thanking Bethany in his head for teaching her kid not to be greedy.

Surreptitiously, he pulled out his phone and tapped Kayla's name. *Help! I didn't think about Christmas presents. What do I do?* He added lots of panic face emojis, then sent the message.

He watched as Kayla pulled her phone out, read it, laughed to herself, then lifted her eyes to his, looking slightly bemused but not at all awkward. Thank goodness. They could move on and pretend his idiotic move of dodging her kiss hadn't happened.

Go shopping, I guess?

He rolled his eyes at her response. Thanks, Einstein. *Where do I shop? What do I get? You have to help me. Please!!!*

As he waited for her to read it, he fired off another message. *I don't want to ruin her Christmas.* There. Let her try to resist that.

He could tell the moment she got the second message, because she stopped tapping and looked up at him, biting her lip.

Then she dropped her head and tapped again.

Please, he urged silently.

All right. I'm free Tuesday. When her text came through, he let out a quiet exclamation of triumph, and Ruby gave him an odd look.

"What, Uncle Cam?"

"Oh. Nothing. Something for work." He ducked his head and picked up another crayon.

But when Ruby went back to coloring her own picture, he let himself glance toward Kayla. She looked a little brighter as she talked with Vi and Jade, and he let himself wonder: Would he get a chance to kiss her on Tuesday?

Chapter 35

Kayla was going to chew a hole through her lip. She'd been staring at the email from the mission organization for the past half hour, trying to convince herself to respond.

She knew what she had to do.

She couldn't go on the trip.

Because as much as she'd always wanted to do this, now wasn't the right time—not when she was questioning everything, wrestling with her own doubts. How was she supposed to spread the Gospel when she felt like her own faith was so fragile that all it would take was a feather to knock it down? When she couldn't even put two sentences together to pray right now? When the whole time she'd sat at church on Sunday, she'd been wondering if God really did care?

The doorbell rang, and Kayla set her laptop aside gratefully.

Until she realized that meant she had to see Cam. But he'd been at church on Sunday too, and things hadn't gotten awkward. Sure, that was mainly because they hadn't said a word to each other. But what was she going to say: *Sorry I almost kissed you the other night?*

It was better if they both acted as if it had never happened.

Kayla took a breath and pulled the door open. Today was going to be a totally ordinary day. Just two friends shopping together to make sure that a little girl had a good Christmas.

Ordinary, aside from the flippy thing her stomach did the moment she spotted him standing there in his jeans and sweater. She forced herself to ignore it.

"Good morning." Cam pulled a coffee cup from behind his back. "This is a bribe."

Kayla's fingers accidentally brushed his as she took the cup from him, and she pulled her hand back quickly, telling herself the warmth was from the coffee, not his touch. "I'm not sure you understand how a bribe works. You're supposed to give it to convince the other person to say yes. Not *after* they've already agreed to help."

"Ah, well. Then consider it a thank you." Cam's eye twitched, and she almost could have sworn it was a wink—but that was crazy.

She reached for her jacket and slipped her arms into it. Cam watched, waiting patiently, but didn't step in to help, she noted with satisfaction.

"So, where to?" he asked as she joined him outside.

Kayla bit her lip. She'd been debating that very question. Hope Springs had a plethora of shops—but they were mainly specialty places like Vi's antique store and Ariana's fudge shop and home decor places. If they wanted toys, they were going to have to go to the mall—which was over an hour away.

She wasn't sure she could handle being alone in the car with him for that long.

But then she thought of the look on Ruby's face Christmas morning. She supposed she could put up with a little awkwardness for Ruby's sake.

"Let's go to the mall." She followed him to the car and transferred into the passenger seat, then leaned down to take apart her wheelchair at the same time as he did. She caught his spicy scent as their heads almost collided, and she sat up quickly.

"Sorry," Cam mumbled. "You get it."

"That's okay. You know what to do." She picked up her purse and pretended to dig for something until he grabbed the wheelchair and brought it to the trunk.

This was not off to a non-awkward start.

And it didn't get any better when Cam got into the car and pulled out of the driveway. An odd, sort of electric, silence hung between them as Cam followed her directions out of town.

Kayla tried to focus on the scenery. But the silence only grew more charged.

They could not go through the whole day like this.

Which meant they were going to have to talk about it. It might make things more awkward for a minute or two—but then they could get back to normal.

She drew in a breath for courage, but before she could say anything, Cam turned to her. "What did you think of Dan's sermon on Sunday?"

Kayla's mouth snapped shut. Okay, they could talk about that instead.

"It was good." That was a safe answer—Dan's sermons were always good—though she honestly wasn't sure how much of it she'd caught. As hard as she'd tried to focus on what he was saying, the weight of her doubts had drowned out everything else, even the refreshment of the Word she knew she so desperately needed to hear. "What did you think of it?"

"He sure does harp on forgiveness a lot, doesn't he?"

Kayla laughed. Now she remembered—the sermon had been based on the parable of the unforgiving servant, who was forgiven his large debt but then refused to forgive the man who owed him a smaller debt. "Yeah, I suppose so. But that's because forgiveness is kind of the whole point. Without God's forgiveness, won for us by Jesus, we'd all be condemned to hell."

Wow, where had that come from? Kayla had been so sure that her doubts would keep her from sharing God's Word. But to her relief, she realized that whatever else she was wrestling with, she still believed this.

Cam nodded, but his face creased into a frown as he turned onto the road she pointed to. "I went to visit Bethany the other day. Without Ruby."

Kayla tried to keep up with the thread of the conversation. Was he done talking about forgiveness? She felt like there was so much more she should have said. But maybe what he needed right now was someone to listen. "How was it?"

He gave a dry laugh. "Pretty awful."

Her heart went straight to him. Despite his issues with Bethany, she knew he cared about his sister. "I'm sorry. I know it has to be difficult to see her like that." As much as it hurt that her brother and sister-in-law had lost their baby, at least she still had *them*. Cam didn't know if his sister was ever going to wake up—and what kind of state she'd be in if she did.

But Cam shook his head. "I yelled at her." His eyes flicked to Kayla, then back to the road, as if he wasn't sure he wanted to see her reaction. "I meant to go there to forgive her. But then there were all these memories. They weren't all bad, but somehow that made it worse, you know? I just don't see how—" He broke off, reaching to turn the heat down a notch. "I try to tell myself that she's different now. She's going to church and as far as I can tell from her house and the way she's raised Ruby, she's probably changed. But that's not the Bethany I know. The Bethany I know tore my family apart. Am I really supposed to forgive her for that?"

Kayla considered his question. It would be easy to offer a simple, "Yes, of course." But she knew better than anyone that it wasn't as easy as that. "If you mean, do I think it's what we're called to do as Christians, then yes, I do," she said finally. "But if you mean, do I think it's always possible—that takes a greater strength than we have. We can only do that through Christ in us."

"Well, then, I'm not sure I have enough Christ in me." Cam sounded impetuous, and Kayla let out a soft laugh.

"It's not about how much Christ you have in you, Cam. It's about letting him work in your heart. And it takes time."

For goodness' sake, she might as well be talking to herself. Wasn't that what she needed to do with her doubts? Let Christ work in her heart?

Cam nodded, and they fell into silence again. But this time it wasn't that electric, charged, awkward silence. It was the silence of two people contemplating hard truths.

"How about this?" Kayla held up a unicorn necklace, grateful that navigating the stores had dispelled any lingering awkwardness between them, putting them squarely back in the friendship zone.

Which was right where they belonged.

Cam glanced up, his arms loaded with the bags of gifts they'd already purchased. His smile may have made her insides do a little flippy thing again, but she was getting better at ignoring that. Soon enough, it would go away entirely.

And she wasn't even *thinking* about almost kissing him anymore.

"It's perfect." Cam grinned wide enough that she had to look away.

"What do you think? Are we set?" she asked after they paid, counting off in her head. They'd found books, a doll stroller, a plush pony, and now the necklace.

"There's one more thing I thought of. But I don't know. I mean, I think she would like it, but . . ."

"Maybe if you actually tell me what it is, I can help."

"I'll show you." Cam started down the crowded corridor of the mall, and Kayla fell in next to him with her wheelchair, trying not to notice how mindful he was to lead them on the path with the fewest obstacles.

"What is it with you and all the mystery? Why can't you just tell me?"

"I like surprises." His eyes sparkled as he turned into a large department store. "And so do you."

"You don't know that." But she couldn't deny that he was right, and in spite of herself a little flutter of pleasure went down her neck at the fact that he knew that about her without being told.

"I saw this online, and it made me think of Ruby and that box she has." He followed the signs to the toy department, glancing down each aisle until he'd apparently found what he was looking for.

"What do you think?" He held out his arms the same way he and Ruby had when they'd shown off the scraggly tree they'd put together. But this was no scraggly tree. It was a three story dollhouse, nearly as tall as he was.

"Wow, that's . . ."

"Don't you dare say interesting," Cam warned.

Kayla laughed. "No. I was going to say big."

He turned to look at it, frowning. "Is that a bad thing?"

"Not necessarily. But where would she put it? I'm not sure it would fit in her room. Or the living room."

Cam's shoulders fell. "You're right."

He looked so sweet, pouting about not being able to get his niece the gift he'd chosen, that Kayla wheeled closer. "It was a really nice thought, though. What about a smaller dollhouse?" She scanned the shelves and pointed to one that was more reasonably sized but still cute. "Like that one."

"That one's puny."

"Well, Ruby's pretty small herself. Unless you were planning to play with it?"

He hit her with a surprised laugh. "What do you think I do all day?" But he examined the smaller dollhouse more closely. "I guess this one is nice too." He picked up the box and started back down the aisle. "Come on. We have one more stop."

"Another?" Kayla never would have guessed Cam could outshop her—not that she was going to give him the satisfaction of telling him that. "Now where?"

"You'll see." He grinned at her.

She treated him to a dramatic eye roll but couldn't deny that her curiosity was growing as she followed him back through the mall. They'd already hit every store that could possibly have anything for Ruby.

Without warning, Cam slowed to a stop. "Hold on a second." He took a step backwards and peered in the window of a jewelry store. Kayla backed up her wheelchair to see what had captured his interest. It was a display of Christmas gifts for men—mostly watches, but also some rings and cuff links.

"My dad used to have a compass like that," Cam said quietly, pointing to a silver circle etched with the cardinal directions. "My mom gave it to him when they first started dating. It was engraved with his favorite verse: 'Be strong and courageous.' I always wondered what had happened to it. I didn't find it when we cleaned out the house after mom died. Bethany probably . . ." He shook his head, giving her a rueful glance. "Sorry. Let's keep going."

"Do you want to go in and look at it?"

Cam gave it one more look, then shook his head again. "No. Come on, let's keep going."

"And where are we going again?"

He laughed. "Nice try."

She frowned as he turned right. According to the sign, all that was in this direction was the food court. "I don't think there are any stores down this way."

"I know." Cam's grin grew. "But there's lunch. My treat."

Nope. No way. She'd never agreed to lunch. That was too much like a date. "We don't have to get lunch. I'm not hungry . . ." Okay, that was a total lie. She'd worked up quite the appetite with all their shopping.

Cam waved off her argument. "Well, I'm starving. And I don't want to eat alone. So what'll it be? Personally, I'm leaning toward one of those gigantic cinnamon rolls."

"For lunch?"

"Yep. Come on, you know you want one."

Kayla shook her head, but her mouth watered. Fine, he was right about this too.

Ten minutes later, as the fluffy dough, aromatic cinnamon, and sweet frosting melted on her tongue, she couldn't remember for the life of her what her objection to eating with him had been.

Until she caught a glimpse of him watching her with a warm smile.

She cleared her throat to keep that earlier awkwardness from creeping over her again. "I assume you know how to wrap the presents?"

Cam laughed. "A bold assumption. But, yes, I think I can handle the wrapping. I'm not completely helpless. Unless you want to—" He broke off as his phone cut through the noise of the food court.

"Sorry." He pulled it out of his pocket. "I would have turned it off, but I wanted Ruby's school to be able to reach me, just in case . . ."

Kayla waved off the apology. "That was a good idea." Man, when had this guy become such a good parent? And why did it make her heart do all those extra cartwheels just when she'd gotten it under control?

But Cam's smile faded as he looked at the screen. "It's not the school. It's the hospital." He lifted his head, his eyes meeting hers, panic lasering out of them.

"It will be okay," Kayla said out of habit, even though she was less certain of that than she'd ever been. Her heart thundered for poor Ruby. For Cam. For Bethany.

Please, Lord. It was only two words, but it was two words more than she'd managed to pray in over a week.

Cam lifted the phone to his ear, his other hand falling onto the table, and instinct drove Kayla to grab it before she realized what a bad idea that was. But Cam was her friend, and she needed to be here for him—and right now, taking his hand was the best way she knew to do that.

She watched his face as he listened. His forehead creased, but he nodded. "Okay," he finally said. "What does that mean?"

He listened some more, his fingers clutching at hers. Kayla swallowed, silently wishing for him to hurry up and finish the call so she'd know what was going on too.

"Thank you. We'll be there as soon as we can." As he lowered the phone from his ear, he slid his other hand out of Kayla's to hang up the call.

She let him sit staring at the phone for a full three seconds before she couldn't stand it any longer. "What is it?"

He looked up at her with an odd expression. "Bethany opened her eyes."

"Oh my goodness. Cam!" Before she could consider her reaction, Kayla was wheeling around the table and throwing her arms around his neck.

She heard him swallow as he leaned closer and squeezed her to himself. "They said it doesn't necessarily mean she's waking up. But they're hopeful."

Kayla nodded against his shoulder, trying to blink away the ridiculous tears that insisted on puddling in her eyes.

This was exactly the kind of news she'd needed today. It didn't make everything better, didn't erase all of her doubts—but it did ease the ache in her heart.

"Come on." She didn't even try to hide the tears as she pulled back. "Let's go get Ruby and take her to see her mom."

Chapter 36

The elevator dinged at Bethany's floor, and Ruby dove out of it, followed by Kayla. But Cameron was paralyzed. As much as he'd been waiting for this moment, he wasn't sure he was ready for it. Wasn't sure he was ready to face his sister awake. Wasn't sure he was ready to give up Ruby. Wasn't sure, even, that he was ready to return to his real life.

Kayla spun her wheelchair, apparently realizing he wasn't with them. "You coming?"

"Yeah." He forced his feet to step off the elevator, barely making it through as the doors closed.

"Ruby, hold up," Kayla called, and Ruby skipped back to them.

"Hurry up, Uncle Cam," the girl commanded. Apparently the excitement of getting pulled out of school to see her mom had made her forget that she usually communicated in baas these days.

"I will. Come here a second, though." He'd been trying to figure out all the way here how to explain to his niece what the nurse had told him on the phone.

He crouched down to be at eye level with her. "I don't want you to be upset if your mom doesn't open her eyes right now. The nurse said she's still really sleepy. And even if she does open them, she might not be able to do anything else, like smile or talk. She might be confused and not know who we are. Do you understand?"

Ruby nodded solemnly. "It's fine if she doesn't know who I am because I know who she is."

Cameron hesitated. Maybe this wasn't a good idea, after all. What if it traumatized Ruby to see her mom like this? But it might traumatize her more if he made her go home now. It wasn't the first time he'd wished for some sort of manual to tell him what to do.

"Okay," he finally said. "Let's go see her." He straightened slowly and let Ruby take his hand. They started down the hallway but after a second, he realized that Kayla wasn't with them.

He turned around to find her with her hands on the rims of her wheels—but she wasn't pushing them. "Aren't you coming?" He could understand if she didn't want to, especially given the memories it must bring back of her own accident. But he could really use her in there.

"Only if you want me to." She tucked her hair behind her ear, looking unusually vulnerable as she waited for his answer.

"Yeah." He gestured for her to catch up with them. "I really do."

Her smile was bright and gentle and supportive all at the same time, and together, the three of them made their way down the hall, Cam's heart picking up speed the closer they got to Bethany's room. Ruby might be able to handle this, but could he?

His gaze went straight to Bethany as they entered the room. But her eyes were closed, her form as still as always.

Well, the nurse had warned him that was likely.

Still, his heart broke a little for Ruby, who had made her way to the bed and picked up Bethany's hand. "Mommy?"

Bethany's eyes remained closed.

"I'm sorry, Ruby. They said—"

His words got caught in his throat as Bethany's eyes fluttered open.

"Mommy!" Ruby jumped up and down.

But Bethany's eyes skimmed right past her, past all of them, as if they were nothing more substantial than air.

"Mommy?" Ruby's voice shook. "It's me, Ruby."

But Bethany's eyes didn't go to her daughter, instead staring blankly at the far wall.

"Ruby—" Cameron took a step forward as Ruby turned away from the bed. He crouched just in time to catch her in his arms as she broke into tears. He ran a hand up and down her back, his tight throat barely managing to squeeze out the words, "It will be okay."

The much louder voice in his head was shouting that it would *not* be okay. In some ways, it had been easier to see Bethany when her eyes were always closed. At least that way, they could pretend she was only sleeping. But seeing her like this—eyes open but completely unaware—was surreal. Or maybe too real. It was like the time he'd walked in on her and her boyfriend in their parents' basement, both so strung out on who knew what that neither of them realized he was talking to them when he was standing right in front of them, yelling for them to turn down the music, which had been blasting at levels that should have burst their eardrums. Finally, he'd turned the music off himself and stalked away—and still neither had acknowledged his presence. It was like they were somewhere else entirely, completely oblivious to the real world around them.

A sudden, fresh surge of anger went through Cameron. It was one thing for Bethany to put him through that. But how could she put her little girl through it too?

He pushed abruptly to his feet, grabbing Ruby's hand. "I think we should go."

"But Uncle Cam, I don't want—"

"We're going." He pulled her toward the door.

Kayla backed her wheelchair out of the way. "Cam, don't you think—"

"No." He stepped into the hallway. "No, I don't think we should stay. It's obviously upsetting Ruby. And there's nothing we can do right now. We need to go home so Ruby can do her homework and we can have dinner and she needs to shower yet and brush her teeth and—" He couldn't stop talking. If he just kept this list going, then they could get back to all the things that had become a normal part of his day.

"Cam—" Kayla's fingers brushed his hand. "It's okay. You're right." She turned to Ruby. "Your mom would want you to get your homework done and be all rested for school tomorrow."

He nodded, hoping Kayla could read the gratitude in his eyes. "Yep. Come on, little sheep. You've got a date with some addition problems."

He waited for the giggle Ruby usually gave when he talked about her having a date with homework, but she stared at the floor silently. He cursed himself for bringing her in to see Bethany. He should have known it would be too much.

"I don't want to be a sheep anymore." Ruby scuffed the toe of her tennis shoe against the tile floor.

"Of course you do. The play is in three days. You need to be in character." He could hardly believe he was saying it, after all the times it had driven him crazy that she wouldn't break character to so much as eat breakfast.

"I don't want to be in the play," she said, putting out a lip.

"Why not?" Kayla wheeled closer to the girl, giving Cam a questioning look.

He raised a shoulder. Sometimes he forgot how in over his head he was here—and then something like this came along to remind him.

"Because Mommy's not going to be there." Her eyes filled, and Kayla reached out a hand to take one of Ruby's. Cam squatted on the little girl's other side.

"I know, sweetheart, and I am so sorry that she can't be. But your uncle Cam is going to be there. And I'm going to be there." Kayla's eyes went to his, and he wanted to tell her suddenly how much it meant to him that she was always there for them. But she kept talking. "And I told Vi and Nate about it, and they can't wait to see you. And I think Jade and Dan are bringing Hope and Matthias. And you know Jonah and Jeremiah and Gabby are in the play, so Isabel and Tyler will be there too. And you know what?"

Ruby lifted her eyes to Kayla, who grinned at her.

"You are going to get the loudest cheer any sheep has ever gotten." Kayla winked at her. "It'll be so loud that everybody will think you're a movie star."

Ruby's giggle was tiny, but it brought Cameron such relief that he could have gathered them both up in a hug.

Instead, he gave Kayla's arm the briefest squeeze, then stood and took Ruby's hand. "Now, about that date with your homework."

This time Ruby's giggle was stronger. "You can't have a date with homework, Uncle Cam."

He feigned shock. "Why not?"

"Because dates are for people."

He glanced at Kayla as they made their way toward the elevator.

Yes, dates were for people.

Chapter 37

Kayla tucked the pearl barrette into her hair, giving a satisfied smile at the effect of the white gems against her dark locks.

"Don't you look nice."

Kayla jumped at the sound of Vi's voice behind her. "I will never know how you get around so silently."

Vi gave a gentle laugh. "I see you went all out tonight." She gestured to Kayla's hair, the makeup she rarely bothered with, the black leggings and soft blue sweater she'd chosen after spending way too much time in front of the closet, the black boots that took a wrestling match to pull onto her feet.

Kayla shrugged. "It's a special night. I want Ruby to feel like it's a big deal."

"Mmm." Vi nodded, but Kayla could read the amusement in her eyes. "It's for Ruby. Not her uncle."

"What?" Drat. That sounded too rehearsed. She tried again. "Of course it's not for Cam."

So what if just saying his name made her smile? That didn't mean she'd gotten all dressed up for *him*. So what if the way he'd held Ruby close the other night at Bethany's bedside had melted her from the inside out. That didn't mean she'd given him one thought as she swiped on the thin coat of mascara. And so what if the way he'd looked at her when he'd dropped her off had nearly made her feelingless toes tingle and caused her to almost lean in again. That had nothing to do with the fact that she'd swept her hair off her neck and chosen her favorite teardrop earrings.

"All right, then." Violet nodded, obviously patronizing Kayla. "We're ready to go when you are."

"You guys go ahead. I'll drive over separately. I promised I'd take Ruby out for ice cream afterward."

She avoided Vi's too-knowing look as Nate came up next to his wife, slipping an arm around her waist. "Is she beautiful enough yet?" His teasing eyes went to Kayla. "I guess she'll do. Come on, slow poke."

Vi grinned at her husband over her shoulder. "She wants to drive separately. Which means you get me all to yourself."

"I like that idea." Nate nuzzled his wife's neck from behind, and Kayla made a loud groaning noise.

Except, it did her heart good to see the two of them smiling and laughing together. Even if she didn't understand how they did it—how they went on each day, knowing what they had lost.

Was it because they had each other that they were able to endure it? Because if one fell, the other could pick them up, like their wedding verse said?

She pictured Cam comforting her when she'd cried. Pictured the way her hand had gone to his when the hospital had called about Bethany. Pictured the way they'd shared their deepest secrets and toughest challenges with each other.

And then she shoved those pictures away and grabbed her keys. Before she left the room, she pulled the barrette out of her hair and the earrings out of her ears. There was no time to wash off her makeup, but at least she didn't look like she was trying to impress anyone.

She headed for the door without another glance in the mirror.

By the time she got to the elementary school, the auditorium was packed. Kayla let her eyes roam the space, trying to figure out where there was room for a wheelchair.

"Kayla! Over here." Cam hurried to her side, and she couldn't command herself to ignore the flare of pleasure that went through her at the knowledge that he'd been watching for her.

She followed him to a side row, where an open space had been left for wheelchairs. "Don't you want to sit closer to the stage?"

He shook his head. "Ruby picked out these spots just for us."

As they settled in, Kayla felt a small shiver work through her.

Cam glanced at her. "Cold?"

Sure, they could go with that as the reason, not his nearness. "I forgot my blanket in the car." Which was true. She generally put it over her legs whenever she had to get from a parking lot into a building, but she'd been so focused on getting inside before the play began that she'd forgotten all about it.

"Here." He shrugged out of his jacket.

"Oh, I don't need—"

But he'd already laid it across her lap, and the house lights dimmed as the stage lights came up.

"Thank you," she whispered, tucking her hands under it and letting them soak up the warmth of his body heat that the jacket retained.

Cam nudged her as students in costume filed onto the stage, and she took a moment to pick out Ruby, adorable in her sheep costume. Then she let herself peek at Cam, who was beaming as he snapped pictures with his phone.

They both leaned forward as Ruby crawled to the front of the stage. She stood staring out at the crowd, and Kayla had a piercing moment of fear. What if Ruby had forgotten what she was supposed to do? But then she said, clear and loud and very sheep-like, "Baa. Christmas is a time of cheer. Baa."

The audience laughed, and even from her seat near the back, Kayla could see the smile on Ruby's face. Cam turned to her with a proud grin.

And that was it.

Her heart was done for.

For the rest of the play, she had to work hard not to notice every time he shifted in his seat, sending his spicy scent drifting her way. Had to concentrate on not noticing just how close they were sitting. Had to pretend she didn't want to slide closer.

She shifted her wheelchair subtly away from him. The best thing she could do was ignore these feelings and trust they'd go away.

When the play was done and the cast was taking their bows, she and Cam and the rest of their friends scattered through the auditorium let out a deafening cheer for Ruby.

"She did good." Cam's smile was lopsided and proud and oh-so-perfect as he stood.

"She really did." After that performance, Ruby would get the lead in next year's play for sure. Kayla couldn't wait to see it—if she was still in Hope Springs, that was.

But she was having a harder and harder time imagining being anywhere else.

"Excuse me," a woman's voice said behind them, and Cam turned to look over Kayla's shoulder.

"You're Ruby's uncle, right? Cameron?"

For some reason, that made Kayla laugh, but she covered it up with a cough as Cam said, "Yes."

"I thought so." She stepped around Kayla as if she wasn't there. "My daughter is in Ruby's class, and I volunteer in there a few times a week. From the way she talks, I was pretty sure you'd be a superhero."

Kayla's fake cough grew louder, and Cam eyed her, but she could tell he was fighting off a laugh too.

"Nope. Just a regular uncle."

"I was thinking maybe you'd like to get together for coffee sometime. I know how tough it is to be a single parent. Maybe we could—"

"That's very kind. But I have a partner in crime already." Cam smiled at Kayla, and her heart sped right toward her throat. He only meant partner as in someone who helped with Ruby, right? Not *romantic* partner?

"Did you see me? Did you see me?" Ruby rocketed right into the middle of the group, nearly knocking the other woman off her feet.

"Oh, I'm sorry." Cam gave a deep bow. "I was expecting Ruby. Not a *movie star*."

Ruby's giggle turned into a squeal as Cam scooped her up and twirled her in a circle.

Kayla's heart beat faster as she watched them. Did she want to be Cam's partner? For more than helping with Ruby?

She knew the right answer was no.

And yet, with each passing minute, she became less and less certain that it should be.

As Cam set Ruby down, the little girl dove into Kayla's arms.

"You are officially the best actor I've ever seen." Kayla squeezed her tight, noticing with a tiny bit of satisfaction that she wasn't necessarily proud of, that the other woman had begun to back away.

Kayla's friends gathered around them, all offering congratulations to Ruby. Kayla rejoiced to see the girl bask in the attention. She knew Ruby still wished her mom was here—they all wished that—but at least the night hadn't been completely ruined for her.

"So—" Cam turned to Kayla. "I believe there was a promise of ice cream."

Chapter 38

Walking on air. Wasn't that the saying? Cam was certain it applied to him tonight as he escorted Kayla and Ruby toward the school doors. The play had been perfect. Ruby had been a hit. And Kayla had been . . . stunning.

If it weren't for the fact that he hadn't wanted to miss a minute of Ruby's performance, he wouldn't have been able to keep his eyes off her. And now that the play was over, he didn't bother trying to resist.

But the moment they stepped outside, his attention was stolen by the scene in front of him. It had been starting to flurry when they'd arrived, but now the air was thick with swirling flakes, and a good inch of snow already blanketed the sidewalk.

He stopped and held out a hand, observing as a few large flakes landed on it and immediately melted. Fascinating.

"What are you doing, Uncle Cam?" Ruby's voice made him realize that both she and Kayla had continued down the sidewalk.

"Sorry." He gave them a sheepish grin. "I haven't seen a lot of snow in my life."

"And what do you think of it?" Kayla was watching him with a curious expression on her face.

"It's sort of magical, isn't it?" The way it danced in the air, the way it sparkled under the lights, the way it covered everything over, making the whole scene look clean and new and pristine.

"The first snowfall always reminds me of that verse," Kayla said. "'Wash me, and I will be whiter than snow.' Though I admit I'm not a big fan of driving in it." She bit her lip as she peered toward the road.

"Tell you what." Cam turned to Ruby. "How do you feel about hot cocoa instead of ice cream? Seems a little more fitting. And we can have it at our house so Kayla doesn't have to drive as far."

Ruby eyed him. "Can I have marshmallows in my cocoa?"

He nodded.

"And whipped cream?"

He laughed and nodded again. The girl may have gotten her negotiating skills from him.

"Then we have a deal." Ruby shook his hand as Kayla's laugh sparkled in the night air, only making the scene more magical.

Then they continued to their vehicles, Cam rushing to get Ruby buckled in so they could pull up behind Kayla and wait for her. He was slightly worried about her trying to maneuver her wheelchair in the snow—though he should know better by now. By the time they reached her, she was already in the car and disassembling her wheelchair. When she was done, he waved for her to pull out ahead of them, then followed her to Bethany's house.

He'd no sooner pulled into the driveway than Ruby shot out of the car and straight into the snowy yard, dropping onto her back and doing some form of lying-down jumping jacks.

Cam moved to Kayla's car and waited for her to assemble her wheelchair, then locked his hands on the backrest.

Kayla studied him. "What are you doing?"

He shrugged. "It's slippery out here."

She looked for half a second like she was going to argue but instead offered a quiet, "Thank you."

"You're welcome." He waited until she'd transferred into the chair and lifted her feet onto the footrests before he let go.

"Come on guys, make snow angels with me," Ruby called. She was standing over the one she'd just made, clumps of snow clinging to her hair. She took two giant steps away from it and plopped down again, starting a new one.

"I'm good, thanks." The snow was pretty and all, but that didn't mean he wanted to play in it. Besides, there was no way Kayla could . . .

"What, are you afraid of a little snow?" Kayla rolled her chair to the edge of the yard, then leaned forward and stuck one mittened hand into the snow.

"What are you—" But before he could finish the question, she'd lowered her body to the ground.

"What does it look like I'm doing?" Kayla shot him a grin as she scooted a few feet farther into the yard, then lay back. An irresistible giggle escaped as she slid her arms through the powder above her head and then down to her sides. After a moment, she sat up and wrapped her hands around both of her legs, then pushed them back and forth through the snow. Cam shook his head—this woman never failed to surprise and amaze him. Not that he should be surprised by anything she could do anymore. Or by his growing feelings for her.

"Come on, Uncle Cam," Ruby called. "You have to try it."

Cam eyed the snow, eyed Ruby flailing her arms wildly to make yet another angel, eyed Kayla, smiling up at him, snow sparkling in her hair.

With a shrug, he took two steps into the snow and dropped to the ground next to Kayla. "Oh, that's cold." He shivered as the powder worked its way down his collar.

But as he slid his arms and legs through the snow, jumping jack-style, the way Ruby had, he couldn't help laughing. It was as fun as it had looked. After a moment, he sat up to examine his handiwork. Not too bad.

"Now what?" he asked.

"Now you get up and jump away from it so you don't wreck it." Ruby demonstrated on her own angel, and Cam followed her lead.

"Hey, Cam," Kayla called from the spot where she was still sitting in her own angel. Her voice was strange, almost shy.

"Yeah?"

She blinked up at him, looking uncertain. "Do you think you could lift me out of my angel so I don't wreck it by scooting?"

His heart filled. He knew how much she hated asking anyone to do anything for her, so it was no small thing that she'd been willing to ask him for help.

"Of course." He moved to her side, careful not to step in her angel. She scooted to the very edge of it, and he bent over to slide one arm under her legs and the other behind her back. Then he lifted, pulling her in close to him as he stood. Her arm went around his neck, and he could feel her hand brushing the snow off, sending sparks down his spine.

"Thanks." He let himself bring his eyes to hers.

"You're welcome." Her voice was barely a whisper, and his eyes went to her lips. He'd been waiting all week for another chance to kiss her. Was this it?

"Can we have cocoa now?" Ruby popped up at his side.

Apparently not the time for a kiss.

"Yeah." But Cam didn't take his eyes off Kayla's as he brought her to her wheelchair and set her down.

Maybe after they had their cocoa and put Ruby to bed, they'd have some time alone. The prospect warmed him all the way down to his frozen toes.

"That cocoa may have been better than the Chocolate Chicken's." Kayla emptied her mug and gave a satisfied sigh. She couldn't remember a time she'd ever felt cozier than this. When they'd come inside from making snow angels, Cam had insisted that she change out of her cold, wet leggings and had dug out a pair of Bethany's sweatpants for her. They were a little big for her atrophied legs, but they were warm and dry—and they reminded her yet again of how thoughtful Cam could be. She wasn't sure how it had taken her so long to see it. Or maybe he'd only come by that thoughtful streak recently—she'd certainly noticed the way his whole personality had softened over the past six weeks as he'd taken care of Ruby. It seemed that taking on parental duties had brought out the best in him.

She grabbed the three empty mugs and balanced them on her legs to bring them to the counter, then spent way more time than necessary loading them into the dishwasher. She needed a moment to separate herself from Cam and Ruby—to remind herself, yet again, that though they felt like a family sometimes, they weren't. To stop wondering what it would be like to actually raise a family with Cam.

She didn't want that. Didn't need it.

It would be too easy to lose her independence if she gave herself over to a relationship. Look at the way she'd asked Cam to help her out of her snow angel before. That wasn't like her at all. Even if she'd enjoyed being in his arms, it wasn't worth the price.

"Okay, movie star, time for bed," Cam announced.

"Will you help tuck me in again?" Ruby blinked at Kayla with those sweet, big eyes, so much like her uncle's—who was also gazing at her, looking hopeful.

She glanced out the window, where the flakes swirled faster. "I'm sorry, sweetie. I think I'd better go. I'm not sure how the roads will be." That, and if she kept looking into those eyes—either of them—she'd be unable to resist the pull they had on her heart.

Simultaneously, both Ruby's and Cam's faces fell. Cam recovered first. "At least say you'll come over Christmas morning. I know Santa would want you to watch Ruby open her presents."

"Please, please, please come," Ruby threw in.

There was no way to say no to that. "All right. I'll come. But only if you two will come to Christmas dinner at Nate and Vi's."

"It's a deal." Ruby held out her hand, and Kayla shook it, allowing herself one quick look at Cam, who was grinning as widely as Ruby.

As she wheeled out the door and into the night, Kayla realized—her parents would be at Nate and Vi's for Christmas. And her mom would jump to conclusions if she found out Kayla had invited a man.

She'd just have to hope Mom assumed that Nate or Vi had invited him.

Chapter 39

"Hey, Kayla."

Kayla jumped at the sound of her brother's voice in the dim living room, lit only by the colored lights of the Christmas tree.

"Nate. You scared the daylights out of me. What are you doing, sitting here in the dark?"

"Praying. How was the ice cream?"

She wheeled toward him, skirting the path around the furniture she knew by heart by now. "We ended up having hot cocoa and making snow angels."

"Sounds fun." Nate's voice was warm, but the shadows on his face traced out faint lines she'd never noticed before. "I never asked. Did you make a decision about the mission trip?"

Kayla bit her lip. The decision had been weighing on her, but she couldn't bring herself to respond one way or the other. The conversation she'd had with Cam the other day had led her to believe that maybe God could still work through her, in spite of her own doubts. But on the other hand . . .

"Have you ever felt like you've lost yourself?" she asked her brother.

Nate let out a soft breath. "You know I have, Kayla. For years. Why? Do you feel like that?"

She shrugged. "I don't know. Sometimes. I can't figure out what God is doing right now, you know? I was telling Cam a couple weeks ago about how God works everything for our good. But I just can't find the good in Bethany being in a coma or in Ruby being without her mother. Or in you and Vi losing the baby . . ." She trailed off. She hadn't meant to bring her brother's sorrow into this. A sigh dragged from her lungs. "I don't know, I guess it all makes me wonder if God . . ." The thought was so awful, she wasn't sure she could say it out loud.

"Cares?" Nate filled in.

Kayla nodded miserably. "I'm sorry. I'm not the one going through loss. I shouldn't have brought it up. You and Vi are handling it so well and—"

Nate's sharp laugh stopped her. "Kayla, there's not a day that goes by that I don't feel like I'm falling apart on the inside. And I know Vi feels that way too. To think that our baby is . . ." He looked away, swallowing.

Kayla gaped at him. "You do? She does? But you both seem so . . . steadfast."

Nate brought his gaze back to her. "That's God's doing, not ours. I've been where you are, Kayla, remember? Wondering how God could let something so terrible happen to someone I love. I know how much it hurts. I know the questions that are going through your head."

Kayla sniffed, a tear sneaking from her eye. "This is so stupid. I already went through my doubting phase. I should be past this by now."

Nate laughed. "Wouldn't that be nice? One time in your life that you question God and then you're good forever. But you're human Kayla. And sinful—sorry to break it to you."

She swatted at him, even as she hung on his words.

"I'm just saying, things come along in this world, things we can't understand and don't think are fair, and we start to wonder again if God really is in control. If he really does care about us. Sadly, doubt isn't one of those one-time things."

"So what do I do about it?" Kayla could hear the desperation in her own voice, but she didn't care. She needed to know how to get back to that place of faith she'd grown so comfortable in. "I keep trying so hard to hold on tighter, but I just can't."

"No, you can't." Nate leaned toward her. "But God can. He's holding onto you. Not the other way around. Even when it doesn't feel like it, he's there."

Kayla let out a long breath, nodding slowly. She still didn't feel one hundred percent better. But it was a relief, at least, to know she wasn't the only one who struggled with this stuff. And she knew Nate was right—God was holding onto her, even if she couldn't feel it right now.

"Thanks, Nate. You're a good brother, did I ever tell you that?"

Nate chuckled. "Not often enough." He cleared his throat. "And speaking of being a good brother, is there anything I should know about you and Cam?"

"No. Like what?"

"Like are the two of you seeing each other, or . . ."

"No." Kayla tried not to sound defensive.

"Oh." Nate shrugged. "I thought you liked him."

"I do." Well, she hadn't meant to blurt that out. Especially not to her brother.

"So what's the issue?"

"That *is* the issue," she said impatiently.

"I may be kind of dense about these things," Nate said. "But that doesn't sound like an issue."

Kayla huffed at him. "You know I don't have any intention of ever getting married or anything. I can't give up my independence for anyone. Not even him."

"And you think he'd ask you to give up your independence?"

Kayla shook her head. "He wouldn't have to. It just happens. Look at you."

"Me?" Nate gave her a truly baffled look. "What about me?"

"Well, you're not as independent as you were before you got married, are you?"

Nate snorted. "I think you're forgetting that before I got married I was in prison."

"Okay. Bad example. But don't you ever feel like you've given up part of yourself to be with Vi?"

Nate looked at her as if she was off her rocker. "I don't feel like I gave up part of myself. I feel like I found part of myself that I didn't know was missing."

Kayla gave him a dubious look, pushing away thoughts of all the times she'd been with Cam and Ruby and felt like everything in her was complete.

Nate pushed to his feet. "I'm going to go find Vi." He squeezed her shoulder. "Don't let fear hold you back if you think this guy might be worth it. But if he's not the right one, don't settle for anything less."

He disappeared from the room, leaving Kayla to sit in the dark.

She closed her eyes, sat still, and let a little whisper of a prayer work its way from her soul.

Chapter 40

Cam couldn't remember the last time he had enjoyed Christmas so much.

And it was only nine thirty in the morning.

But as Ruby opened her last present, a feeling of such complete contentment washed over him that he wasn't quite sure what to do with it. Except smile as wide as his mouth allowed.

As Ruby pulled the wrapping paper off, Cam glanced at Kayla, whose smile was also larger than life.

Ruby's deafening squeal pulled his attention back to the gift unwrapping.

"A *real* dollhouse. I love it." She bounced to her feet, then sprang into his arms for a hug. "Thank you, Uncle Cam." The moment she'd pulled out of his arms, she was wrapping her arms around Kayla. "Thank you, Kayla."

Cam's heart pushed against his chest as he watched the two of them.

"Don't you mean, 'Thank you, Santa'?" Cam wasn't going to be the one to blow the charade.

Ruby giggled. "I know Santa's not real. Mommy told me last year. I just played along for you."

"Oh, in that case, maybe you can help me with something." Cam pointed to a wrapped box that remained under the tree. "Can you be a little elf and deliver that to Kayla?"

"What? Cam—" Kayla's eyes met his in surprise, as Ruby skipped to the tree.

"Be careful with it." He winced as Ruby bobbled the box.

Thankfully, she managed to get it to Kayla without dropping it.

She gazed at him for a few more moments, then dropped her eyes to the box and tore the paper off—almost with more enthusiasm than Ruby had. She pulled the cover off the box.

"Oh." She stared at it for a moment, then reached into the box and pulled out a snow globe with a horse and carriage passing in front of a church. Cam tried to work out if that had been a good *oh* or a bad *oh*.

"It's like the carriage we rode." Ruby bounced on her toes. "Remember?"

Cam held his breath. He'd debated getting the snow globe. For him, that carriage ride had been the start of something. Something he dearly hoped could become more. But for her, it might only bring back memories of her brother and sister-in-law's loss.

But when she lifted her eyes to his, they were warm and open. "This is beautiful. Thank you."

He nodded. "Should we get to church?"

"Not so fast." Kayla gestured for Ruby to come closer, then whispered something in the girl's ear. Ruby giggled, then skipped toward the front door and rummaged through a plastic bag Kayla had dropped off there when she'd come in.

"What's going on?" he demanded.

But Kayla blinked at him demurely. "What, you're the only one who can have surprises?"

"This?" Ruby held up a wrapped box.

"Yep. Go ahead and give it to him."

"What? Me?"

"You're the only him here," Kayla pointed out with a laugh.

"Yeah, but you didn't have to—"

"Neither did you. Just open it."

He took the box Ruby passed him and shook it. It was light and didn't rattle. "Not breakable."

Kayla let out one of her adorable snorts. "Good thing."

He knocked on it. "Not alive."

He lifted it to his nose and smelled it. "Not food."

Ruby giggled, and Kayla shot him a look. "We're going to be late for church."

"All right. I'll open it already. If you want to ruin the surprise." He tore off the wrapping paper in world-record time, then lifted the lid off the box.

A laugh burst from him as he spotted the t-shirt—it was exactly the same as his old one.

"It's to replace the one I got frosting on," Kayla said. "I didn't want you to be without your favorite shirt."

Cam lifted it out of the box and held it up to himself. Oh yeah, this was going to be his new favorite shirt, simply by virtue of who had given it to him.

"Thank you." He set the t-shirt aside, looking forward to lounging in it later. But for now they had to get going to church.

By the time Ruby had gone to the bathroom one last time and found her shoes and gotten bundled, they had only ten minutes before the service began. Thankfully, the house was only five minutes from Hope Church.

As he followed Kayla and Ruby from the house, Cam's eyes fell on the yard, where their snow angels had been partially obscured by a fresh snowfall.

That feeling of contentment filled him again as he thought of Kayla's comment the other night, about sins being washed as white as snow. Standing out here on Christmas morning, he couldn't deny that truth—a truth that bathed him in peace.

It was the kind of peace he hoped would never go away.

He opened Kayla's car door—it was Christmas and she was just going to have to deal with the fact that he was a gentleman—then skirted around her vehicle toward his own car.

His hand was on his door handle when the sound of tires crunching on the driveway grabbed his attention. Kayla couldn't possibly have disassembled her wheelchair and pulled out already.

But it wasn't a car pulling out of the driveway—a vehicle he didn't recognize was pulling in. An Audi. Funny, that was the same car he'd rented more than once when traveling with . . .

Danielle.

His breath left him in a rush as he spotted her behind the wheel.

What was she doing here? In Hope Springs? On Christmas?

He glanced at Kayla, who had paused in the process of transferring into her car, then strode toward Danielle's vehicle.

She opened the car door, gingerly placing a ridiculous open-toed shoe onto the unshoveled driveway. As she stood, her eyes went past him to first Kayla, then Ruby, then the house. She made a face. "I can see the appeal of this place." Sarcasm clung to her, thicker than the snow on the driveway.

"What are you doing here, Danielle?"

"Can we go inside? It's freezing out here."

He considered asking whether she had considered that it was winter here when she'd chosen her strappy shoes and gauzy blouse but kept his mouth shut.

"We were actually on our way to church."

Her nose wrinkled harder. "You don't go to church."

"I used to. And I've started going again."

Danielle lifted an eyebrow at him. "I flew all the way from LA to see you. On Christmas. And you're just going to ignore me?"

Cam sighed. He wanted to say yes. To say that she shouldn't have come. Because they were over. But maybe he owed her more than that. Maybe he owed her an in-person conversation, at least.

"All right." He scrubbed a hand over his head, that peaceful feeling he'd been basking in sliding away as he turned toward his car. He hated the idea of letting his niece down.

"Ruby, I think we're going to have to skip church today."

Ruby bounced toward them, giving Danielle a curious look. "Why? It's Christmas. Everybody goes to church on Christmas."

Danielle peered down her nose at Ruby. "Not everybody."

"I can take Ruby, Cam."

Cam closed his eyes for a millisecond. What must Kayla be thinking was going on right now?

He glanced toward her car to find that she'd wheeled halfway down the driveway.

"It's no problem," she added quietly. "You can catch up with us at Nate and Vi's." Her eyes flicked to Danielle, and she offered a genuine smile. "And you're welcome to come too."

Danielle gave her a fake smile in return but didn't say anything.

"But I want you to go to church too, Uncle Cam." Ruby crossed her arms and stuck her lip out in a pout.

"I know. I'm sorry, Ruby. I have some things to talk about with Danielle, and—"

"Who is Danielle?" Ruby demanded.

"She's my—" Cam stammered. What was he supposed to call her now? Ex-girlfriend, he supposed.

"I'm Cameron's fiancée," Danielle cut in.

Cam froze at the look on Kayla's face. "What? No. Danielle, we're not—"

"You're right," Danielle simpered. "You haven't put the ring on my finger yet. But as soon as I get you home, you can ask me properly."

Cam spluttered. There were no words. Why couldn't he come up with any words? And why was she acting like nothing had changed? Like they hadn't broken up three weeks ago?

They hadn't talked once in that time. And now she was saying they were still getting married?

"Danielle," he finally forced out. "You know we talked and—"

She wrapped a hand around his elbow. "Seriously, Cameron, I'm freezing. We need to go inside." She turned to Kayla. "It was nice meeting you. Thanks for taking Ruby off our hands for a bit."

Her hand on Cam's elbow tightened as she took a step toward the house. "It's slippery. Don't let me fall." She didn't glance back once at Kayla and Ruby.

But Cam did. "You're sure you're okay taking Ruby?" He tried to meet Kayla's eyes, but she refused to look at him.

"Of course." Her voice rang with false cheer. "We'll see you later."

"Kayla." There had to be a way to make this better, right here and now.

She waved him off. "We're going to be late for church. I'll bring Ruby to Nate and Vi's afterward." She opened the back door of her car for Ruby, then started to transfer into the driver's seat.

As he opened the door to the house for Danielle, Cam told himself to make this conversation quick so he could meet up with Kayla as soon as possible and explain everything.

Assuming she'd give him a chance.

Kayla stared at the words of the hymn on the screen at the front of church. But she couldn't make her mouth form them. Not if she wanted to hold back the tears that had threatened from the moment that gorgeous woman had introduced herself as Cam's fiancée.

She'd been over it a thousand times in her head. And no matter how many times she looked at it, she couldn't be upset with Cam. He'd never once led her on. Sure, they'd spent a lot of time together—but that had been to take care of Ruby, nothing more, she could see that now. Anything else she'd read into it was her own fault.

Even that almost-kiss at Dan and Jade's had been her doing, not his. No wonder he'd pulled away.

Where he'd meant friendship, she'd imagined more.

She was a complete idiot—and she felt it acutely.

The worst part was, she'd never wanted a relationship in the first place. So there was no reason to feel so crushed now that she knew there was no possibility of one. If anything, she should be relieved.

She let her eyes slip to Ruby, singing next to her, and to Vi on Ruby's other side, swaying to the music Nate led. Looked farther down the row to Sophie and Spencer with their kids and Isabel and Tyler with theirs. In front of them to Ethan and Ariana with Joy, and Jared and Peyton with Ella, and Jade wrangling Matthias while passing Hope a coloring book as Dan smiled at them from his seat at the front of the church.

She directed her attention back to the song. Just because having a family made all of them happy didn't mean she needed a family to feel complete. She had always been independent—always would be, if she had anything to say about it. Then she'd never have to worry about losing herself.

Except that, with Cam, it hadn't felt so much like she was losing herself as like she was becoming *more* herself.

She swallowed hard and ignored the thought as Dan stood to deliver the sermon. That was where her focus needed to be. On God's Word, on the reason he sent Jesus into the world that first Christmas. So she could share that message with the people of Malawi.

She'd done some more soul searching and praying after her conversation with Nate the other night and finally sent in her acceptance yesterday, though she'd decided to wait until after Christmas to tell everyone.

Peace settled over her as she considered the opportunity she'd been given to watch God at work. To witness how he could use even her fragile faith to do the work of his kingdom. The peace was tempered only by the ache that rose every time she thought of leaving Hope Springs for six months. Of leaving Nate and Vi. And Ruby. And Cam.

Cam is already out of your reach.

She allowed herself one more moment of grief, then pushed it aside. No reason to let herself wallow in her heartbreak.

No, it wasn't a heartbreak.

More like a heart scratch.

And she'd be over it in no time at all.

Chapter 41

Cam paced the living room. He'd stopped noticing how small it was weeks ago, but he was painfully aware of it now, as he concentrated on the path between the still-leaning Christmas tree and the couch where Danielle sat gingerly, as if afraid she'd catch a contagious disease if she settled in.

"So, this is the place I couldn't tear you away from." She scanned the room, disdain clear on her face.

"What are you doing here, Danielle?" he asked again.

"I can't come to visit my fiancé for Christmas?"

He stopped and stared at her. "You know we broke up, Danielle."

She met his stare head-on. "And you know you only broke up with me as a negotiating tool. So I'm here to negotiate."

A disbelieving laugh escaped before he could think better of it. "It wasn't a negotiating tactic, Danielle."

She frowned at him, clearly doubting he was in his right mind. "Then what was it, Cameron? You haven't been yourself since you came here." She stood and crossed to his side, grabbing his arms and wrapping them around her waist. "Frankly, I'm worried. But I know that once we get you home, everything will be back to normal."

He sighed, disentangling his arms from around her and stepping away to look out the window. The word *home* sounded strange on her lips. Like it didn't belong to California anymore. "It won't, Danielle. Believe it or not, I'm more myself now than I've ever been."

She frowned at him. "That doesn't even make sense."

He shrugged. It wasn't like he could explain it either. But that didn't change the fact that he knew it was true. "I know. And I'm sorry. But I just don't see things working between us."

"You're being ridiculous. The Cameron I know wouldn't be so . . . I don't know, whatever you are right now. He would realize that we both want the same things. That's what makes us right for each other."

"Then maybe I'm not the Cameron you know," he said softly. "I'm sorry, Danielle. I really am. But those things I thought I wanted . . . they're not enough anymore."

"All right." Danielle crossed her arms in front of her as if getting ready to square off against an executive. "What do you want then?"

Cam hesitated. "I want a family. I want to spend time with them, the way my parents did with me, before they . . ."

Danielle's expression grew tighter. "A family is not on the table, Cameron. You know that."

"Yeah, I do. That's part of why I know we're not right for each other. Because I already have a family."

Danielle's eyes widened. "What, the girl? That's temporary. Mary said your sister woke up, so you can't use her as an excuse anymore."

Cam blinked at her. He'd never known Danielle to speak to his secretary. "Bethany has started to track people's movements with her eyes. But she's a long way from being able to care for Ruby. The doctors don't know if she'll ever get there."

Danielle stared at him, and he tried not to think about how, if it were Kayla he'd just said that to, she'd already have her arms around him.

"So, what, you're going to stay here and play daddy forever?"

Cam lifted his shoulders. "I don't know. Maybe." Honestly, the possibility didn't sound so bad.

"In case you've forgotten, you have a responsibility to my family. To my father. I haven't told him about our . . . issues . . . yet. I wanted to give you time to come to your senses. But if you're not going to . . ."

"I'm prepared for the consequences," Cam said calmly. "Your father can keep me on for the good work I do for him. Or he can let me go. Either way, I can't stay with you just to keep my job. It wouldn't be fair to you."

Danielle huffed out a breath. "What's not fair is that you're walking away from all of our plans. Our future. I already booked the Starlight, you know. Do you have any idea how humiliating it would be to call and cancel?"

Cam almost retorted that she should have thought of that when she booked a wedding venue before they were even engaged. But that wasn't fair. He'd given her every reason to believe he was going to marry her. He'd given himself every reason too . . . until it had been time to go through with asking her.

She whirled on him suddenly. "Does this have to do with that woman out there?" She gestured to the window, and Cam's eyes followed her hand, until he realized that she meant the woman who had been out there earlier.

"Kayla?" He swallowed. "She's been helping me with Ruby. Honestly, I don't know how I would have done any of this"—he gestured around the room—"without her. But I promise you that I was never unfaithful to you. Kayla and I were only friends."

"Were?" Danielle looked at him shrewdly. Ah, the pitfalls of having a lawyer for an ex-girlfriend.

He made himself meet her gaze. "I don't know what we are now. Or what I want us to be. But I do know that whatever does or doesn't happen with Kayla in the future, you and I don't belong together. You deserve someone who wants what you want and loves you exactly as you are. And so do I."

Danielle watched him for a moment, then looked away. "I thought I had found that person." She spun and strode down the hallway. He was going to ask where she was going, until he heard the click of the bathroom door closing.

He rested his head against the front window, staring at nothing. How was it that he'd managed to make two women look utterly betrayed in one day?

"Ruby seems like a sweet little girl." Kayla's mother pulled the garlic bread out of the oven. It was just the two of them in the kitchen as Vi tried to wrangle the rest of the guests to wash their hands and have a seat.

"She is." Kayla finished slicing the lasagna. "I admit she's stolen my heart."

"According to Vi, she's not the only one." Mom kept her focus on the bread she was slicing, but Kayla saw her gaze slide her direction for a moment.

"Vi doesn't know what she's talking about," she muttered, shooing Nate and Vi's dog away as he begged for a piece of lasagna.

"No?" Mom found a basket and started arranging the bread in it. "So you don't have any interest in Ruby's uncle?"

"He's engaged," Kayla said flatly, maneuvering her wheelchair to the refrigerator to pull out the Parmesan cheese.

Though she avoided looking at Mom, she could feel Mom watching her. "Since when?"

Kayla shrugged. "Always, I guess. I met his fiancée this morning." She didn't even have to struggle to get the words out. Which only proved that she was over it already.

"Oh sweetie, I'm so sorry he did that to you."

But Kayla shook her head. "He didn't do anything wrong, Mom. I may have misinterpreted some things, but honestly, he's never said he wanted anything more than friendship. Sometimes not even that." She laughed a little, thinking back on their earliest encounters. She was pretty sure he would have been content if she'd gone and dived into the lake. But somehow, over time, they'd started to . . .

Become friends. That was all.

"Kayla—" Mom's voice was soft.

"Really, Mom. It's fine. I'm not upset about it. Anyway, I'm not going to be here much longer."

"You're not?"

"Nope." She grabbed a spatula and slid it into the lasagna pan. "I accepted the mission trip. I'm going to Africa." She grinned as the realization sank in—she was really doing this.

Mom studied her. "You're not going as a way to run away, are you? Because that's not—"

"That's not why. I decided the other day. Before any of this. I just realized . . . It's not about me. I mean, I've really been struggling to deal with Nate and Vi losing the baby. . . . And then I was talking to Cam—" She ignored Mom's look. She couldn't help it if so much of her life recently had involved him. "And I found that God helped me speak to Cam's doubts even in the midst of my own. And I was overwhelmed that I serve a God who is that powerful. And I just . . . I want to let him work through me. I want to do the work he has prepared for me. You know?"

She let herself glance at Mom, taken aback by the tears shimmering in her eyes. She'd rarely seen her mom cry, even after the accident. "I do know." Mom leaned down and kissed Kayla on top of the head. "I'm so proud of you."

Kayla ducked her head before she could get teary too. "I'm a little scared," she let herself admit.

"I'd be worried if you weren't," Mom said with a laugh. "It's a big thing you're doing. But you'll have all of us here praying for you."

Vi poked her head into the kitchen. "How's the food coming?"

"All set." Mom smiled as Vi gave them a thumbs-up, then disappeared again.

"Come on." Mom squeezed Kayla's shoulder. "Let's get this food to the starving masses."

"Right behind you." Kayla placed a large cutting board across her lap, then reached for the pan of lasagna and rested it on the board, making sure it was secure before rolling toward the dining room.

She'd only made it a couple of pushes when the doorbell rang.

"Who else are we expecting?" she heard Nate call to Vi.

"Grace and Levi, but not until later." Vi looked up as Kayla entered the room with the lasagna and set it on the table.

Vi raised her voice, calling, "Come in."

They all watched the door, but it didn't swing open. Vi frowned, pausing in pouring juice into the kids' cups. "You want to get that, Kayla?"

Kayla wheeled to the front door, pulling it open. "You guys know you don't have to ring the—"

She broke off as her words were swallowed by her confusion. "Cam?" She peered behind him, but he appeared to be alone. "Where's your fiancée?"

"She's not my— Can we talk?"

"Cam!" Nate's shout carried from the dining room. "Come on in. We're about to eat."

Cam nodded but gave her a questioning look. "After lunch?"

Kayla rolled back from the door to let him in. "There's nothing to talk about. Come on, everyone's waiting to pray."

"Kayla, I want to explain." Cam's voice was low as he stopped in the doorway.

"Honestly, Cam." She made herself meet his eyes. "You don't owe me any explanations. Everything's fine." She didn't give him a chance to argue more as she wheeled toward the table.

She heard his sigh as he followed her.

Nate had grabbed another chair and was in the process of sliding it into place next to Ruby. Cam thanked him and sat, then leaned over to wrap an arm around his niece, pressing his face against her hair. As he straightened, he tickled her side, making Ruby let out a high-pitched giggle. Everyone around the table laughed, but Kayla found she had to look away to blink a few times.

When everyone had settled in, Dan began his prayer. "Savior of the world," his soothing voice rang out. "Though you are God from all eternity, you humbled yourself to come into this world as a man that first Christmas. You put yourself—the very maker of the law—under the law to keep it perfectly for our sake. You experienced all the hurts and the hardships and the griefs of your people out of your great love for us. Help us as we celebrate Christmas to remember that your story doesn't end in the stable—it ends at the cross, where you took upon yourself the sins of us all, so that we now have the promise of eternal life with you in heaven. In the name of our newborn King, Amen."

Kayla had to swallow before she could join in the chorus of "Amens." Something in the prayer had loosened the knot in her soul just a little further. Sometimes she forgot that Jesus knew what it was like to be a human. That he had gone through the same hurts and sorrows as she did. That he had done it out of love for her.

When she lifted her head, she found Cam's eyes on her, concern clear in them. She tried to ignore him, to focus on dishing food onto her plate and scooping it into her mouth and keeping up a conversation with Jade.

By the time the meal was done, she needed an escape. She picked up a stack of dirty dishes, placing them on the cutting board she'd set on her lap again. Maybe while she was in the kitchen, Cam would go home. Or at least follow Dan to the living room to continue the conversation they'd been having about football.

She stalled as long as she could unloading the dishes but eventually had to return to the dining room. Where she found Cam collecting his own stack of plates.

Silently, she grabbed the empty lasagna pan and wheeled back toward the kitchen. A moment later, Cam was there too, but fortunately Vi was right behind him with her own stack of dishes. Kayla silently begged her sister-in-law to stay right where she was.

"I asked Ruby what she thought of her presents," Vi said brightly, "and she said they were perfect. You two make a good team."

Kayla forced herself not to look at Cam, instead shooting Vi a warning look. She hadn't yet had a chance to talk to her sister-in-law alone and tell her about Cam's fiancée, and she could only imagine what Vi might say next.

But Cam beat her to it. "Yeah, we do. Kayla, could we talk now?"

Vi's eyes swiveled from Cam to her. Kayla could read the questions in them, but she shook her head.

"It's not necessary. Truly."

"Why don't you guys use the nursery?" Vi said. "It's probably the only place you're going to get some privacy. I'll keep an eye on Ruby."

"Thank you." Cam gave Vi a warm smile.

But Kayla shook her head again. "I'm going to help clean up. I—"

"Kayla." Vi gave her a stern look. "I've got plenty of help." As if to prove her point, Jade, Leah, and Sophie entered the room carrying more dishes.

"Please, Kayla." Cam's voice was soft, but not so soft that the other women didn't look from him to her curiously.

Fine. It was better than standing here and trying to explain to everyone what was going on.

"I'll be right back," she muttered to Vi. Then she made herself follow Cam out of the kitchen.

Chapter 42

For the second time today, Cam found himself pacing a tiny room, this one a heartbreaking reminder of what Kayla's brother and sister-in-law had lost—and of Kayla's grief over that loss.

And he had only made things worse by hurting her more.

He gripped the back of his neck, trying to figure out where to start. "I owe you an apology."

Kayla rolled away from the crib she'd been running her hands over. "You don't, Cameron."

Cameron? Since when did she call him by his full name? "Call me Cam. And yes I do. I should have told you sooner. I don't know why I didn't, actually." It hadn't been intentional . . . at least, he didn't think it had. It was just that his life in California had seemed so separated from his life here that Danielle had never really come up. And his relationship with Kayla had developed so slowly, from those initial days when they couldn't stand each other to a partnership in doing what was best for Ruby to a genuine friendship. It hadn't been until after he'd broken up with Danielle that he'd considered there might be more.

Still, that didn't excuse him.

"That you have a fiancée?" Kayla shrugged as if it was no big deal. The kind of thing people forgot to mention all the time. "You don't owe me any explanations. I never thought— It's not like we're— I promise you that my only feelings are for Ruby."

"She's not my fiancée." On that account, at least, he could set the record straight. "We were never engaged. I mean—" If he was going to do this, he needed to be completely honest. "We were supposed to get engaged, but I was having doubts. I tried to ignore them. It was the next logical step. We had the same goals, the same aspirations, not to mention her dad is my boss and he was starting to talk partnership."

Kayla looked away from him. "I get it, Cam. She was perfect for you."

"No." Cam said it more forcefully than he meant to, but he needed her to understand this. "I tried to make myself think so. But I knew she wasn't. I was supposed to propose at this big party—she had it all planned out, but she wanted to play it off like it was a big surprise. That was the night you called to tell me about Bethany, and . . . well, it never happened."

Kayla ogled him. "*That's* what I interrupted? Your proposal?"

Cam laughed. "Yeah." He moved closer so he could look into her eyes. "And it may be the best interruption that's ever happened to me. I was trying to convince myself to go through with something I knew wasn't right, because it had been part of my plan for so long. One more step on my road to a perfect life. And then you called and threw all my plans out the window when you convinced me I needed to be here for Ruby, and—"

"You could have finished your proposal first," Kayla exclaimed.

But Cam shook his head. "That's what I'm saying. I'm glad I didn't. Because I came here, and I met Ruby. And I met you. And somehow the two of you changed my life."

He saw Kayla's neck bob as she swallowed. "But Danielle—"

"I broke up with her weeks ago. When I realized that I couldn't go through with marrying someone I didn't love just because it was supposed to be part of my plan. The funny thing is—" He bent to gather her hands in his. "I didn't even realize I was starting to have feelings for you until after that."

"Cam . . ."

But he wasn't done. "I want to go out with you, Kayla. Or stay in with you. It doesn't matter. I just want to be with you. I know we haven't known each other for long, and for a lot of that time, you couldn't stand me . . ."

He paused as she laughed, then squeezed her hands tighter. "But I want to get to know you better. I want to spend more time with you—and not just to take care of Ruby. Unless your feelings really are only for her . . ." In which case, he would feel like a supreme idiot. But at least a supreme idiot who had taken a chance and gone for what he really cared about. Maybe for the first time in his life.

"Cam . . ." Kayla pulled her hands out of his, and his heart fell. It was what he deserved, but he'd still hoped . . .

"I've decided to go to Malawi."

Malawi? It took him a moment to catch up. Where had Malawi come into the conversation? And then he remembered . . . she'd been accepted to the mission trip. When Emma had offered her a job, he'd been sure she'd take the job over the trip—it's what he would have done. And she hadn't mentioned it in so long that he'd kind of forgotten about it.

"I hope this isn't because of Danielle. Because I promise . . ."

But Kayla was shaking her head. "It's not." She bit her lip, as if trying to decide whether to say anything else. "It's because of you."

His shoulders dropped. He couldn't blame her. But . . .

Maybe that meant it wasn't too late to convince her to change her mind.

"Truly, Kayla, I'm so sorry. If I could go back and do things differently . . ."

She was laughing gently, and he stopped. He hadn't thought there was anything particularly funny about his apology.

"It's not because of this, Cam. I started thinking about going after we went shopping last week."

"You're going so you don't have to shop with me anymore?"

She laughed harder this time. "No, you goofball. I'm going because of our conversation that day."

Cam stared at her. She had lost him. "I don't remember saying anything particularly wise that day."

She snorted. "It wasn't you, Cam. It was God. I mean, not like he said something. But he showed me that he could use even weak little me, with all my failings and doubts, to share his Word. *That* was how I knew I wanted to go on this trip. To see him at work in me and through me."

"Oh." He still couldn't say that he understood completely. But he *could* see how much it meant to her. "When do you leave?"

"January 2."

"Okay." He swallowed back the urge to ask her not to go. "That gives us a week. And then we can write, call, text. It's only six months, right?" Although right now, that seemed like an eternity.

Kayla shook her head. "I don't know if that's a good idea, Cam. I don't think I'll be anywhere that I can communicate regularly. And by the time I get back, you could be in California."

"But—" He was not letting this go without a fight. If he'd recently figured out what he didn't want, he'd also figured out what he did. And it was all right here—in her.

"I'm sorry, Cam. I just— I don't know what I want right now. I thought I did, before I met you. But now . . . Can we just leave things as they are? Be friends?"

He swallowed painfully. "Of course we can."

"Thank you." She squeezed his hand quickly, then pulled away. He kept himself from catching hold of her arm and begging her to reconsider. If this was what she wanted, then this was what he would do.

"Come on. We should get back out there." She bobbed her head toward the door. "Ruby is probably wearing Vi out." Sadness hung on her smile. "Man, I'm going to miss her." She hesitated, her eyes on his, and he held his breath.

But then she turned and wheeled out of the room. And he had no choice but to follow.

Chapter 43

She couldn't do this. Kayla sat in her car in the driveway of Cam and Ruby's house.

She was supposed to leave tomorrow, and she'd spent the past week rushing like mad to get everything ready. But she'd promised Ruby at church on Sunday that she'd come for one last meal with them.

But for the life of her, she couldn't figure out how she was supposed to say goodbye.

She drew in a slow breath. She could do this. She assembled her wheelchair and transferred into it, then grabbed a small bag off the back seat and made her way to the front door.

Ruby had it open before she could even ring the bell.

"What's in there?" Ruby instantly pointed at the bag on Kayla's lap.

"It's a surprise." Kayla popped her front wheels up and through the doorway. "It sure smells good in here."

"Uncle Cam is cooking."

Kayla eyed Ruby, trying to tell if this was one of her silly jokes. But the girl wasn't giggling.

"Seriously?"

"Yep. It's fabitas."

"Fajitas," Cam called from the kitchen.

No matter how hard she tried, Kayla couldn't keep her heart from speeding up whenever she heard his voice.

"Dinner is served." He appeared suddenly in the living room, and Kayla's heart decided it needed to accelerate to marathon speeds. He was wearing jeans and the t-shirt she'd given him. And a semi-sad smile.

"But I want to know what surprise Kayla has in her bag."

"Surprises are always better if you have to wait." Kayla tucked the bag next to the front table, which held a new vase—this one with real flowers—she noticed. "I'll show you after dinner."

Ruby took two seconds to pout, then grinned and flounced toward the kitchen.

Kayla gasped as she wheeled into the room after Ruby. The table had been set with a tablecloth and candles and place cards written in Ruby's sprawling handwriting.

"Oh wow. This is beautiful." She gave Ruby a hug. "Did you do this?"

Ruby nodded. "Welllll. I made the name tags. But Uncle Cam lit the candles. But he said I can blow them out later. Unless you want to."

Kayla laughed. Oh, how was she going to say goodbye to this little joy-bringer? "That's okay. I think you should do it."

Cam carried a steaming dish of chicken and peppers to the table, and Kayla inhaled. "Hey, it doesn't even smell like feet."

Cam's laugh was rich and full and it wrapped right around her. She had to stop soaking up all this wonderfulness—it was going to make it too hard to leave.

Kayla slid her wheelchair into the spot marked for her, noting with relief that Ruby had placed herself next to Kayla. But the relief dissipated as Cam took the seat across from her—now she'd have a perfect view of his eyes. Of the way the candlelight reflected in them, making them look warmer and brighter than she'd seen them before.

Cam offered her another smile, then folded his hands in front of him. "Would you like to pray? Or should I?"

The question sent joy right through Kayla. But there was no way she was going to be able to get through a prayer without breaking down in tears.

"Can I do it?" Ruby bounced in her seat.

"That sounds nice." Kayla bowed her head.

"Dear Jesus," Ruby began. "Thank you that Mommy can talk to me with her eyes now." Kayla nodded in silent agreement. She'd rushed to the hospital the other day when Cam had texted that Bethany had begun to blink for yes and no. It had brought tears to Kayla's eyes—and Cam's too, she was pretty sure—when Bethany had blinked "yes" when the nurse asked if she recognized Ruby.

"And thank you that Kayla came over tonight," Ruby continued. "And that Uncle Cam cooked fabitas that smell good. Please keep Kayla safe on her trip. I'm going to miss her because she is my best friend. But I know we can still be best friends even if she's far away. And I hope she gets to tell lots of people about you. Amen."

"Amen." Kayla managed to choke out. She sat blinking at her lap but it was no use. She had to quickly wipe at her eyes before she could take the fajitas Cam passed her way.

As they ate, Ruby filled Kayla in on all the things she'd missed as she'd been busy packing and making arrangements over the past week. Apparently, Ruby had started to work on jumping her horse. And Cam had signed her up for swimming lessons. And at school she'd auditioned for the spring play and gotten the part she wanted.

As Ruby continued her cheerful chatter, Kayla tried not to dwell on the fact that she'd miss all of these things. Ruby and Cam had become such a part of her life over the past two months that she was having a hard time imagining her life without them. But they'd all be fine. She knew they would.

Her eyes went to Cam. He was watching her with that same tender expression he'd worn when he'd told her that he wanted to be with her.

She'd relived that conversation a hundred times a day over the past week. But she couldn't see any other way it could have turned out. She was leaving for six months. And even when she got home, she didn't know what was next for her. She couldn't go to Africa with the need to keep up a long-distance relationship hanging over her head. Maybe when she got back . . .

But by then he'd likely be in California—he could even be in a new relationship.

The thought made the fajitas turn in her stomach. She made herself finish what was left on her plate anyway. Cam had gone to a lot of effort to make this meal. And truth be told, it was delicious.

The moment they'd cleared the table, Ruby was at Kayla's side. "Can we have our surprises now?"

"Ruby," Cam warned, but Kayla laughed.

"I think we've waited long enough to make them special." She wheeled to the living room and picked up the bag, reaching inside it. "Let's see, I think there's one in here for Ruby, isn't there?" She pretended to feel around. "Yep. There it is."

She pulled out the box she'd wrapped this morning.

"Unicorn wrapping paper," Ruby squealed right before she tore it to pieces. She barely paused to throw it aside as she opened the box. "Oh wow! I love it! I love it! I love it!" She pulled out the plush giraffe and squeezed it to her. "I'm going to name it Kayla."

"I'm honored." Kayla reached back into the bag and passed Ruby another wrapped box. "This one is for your mom. But if you want to open it for her, I bet she wouldn't mind. You can give it to her next time you visit."

Ruby tugged the wrapping paper off the box and opened it. "It's a book."

"*Little Women*. It's the book I've been reading her. I thought maybe someday she could read it to you."

"Thank you, Kayla. What else?" Ruby looked toward the bag.

Kayla laughed. "I'm afraid that's it."

"And a good thing too." Cam stepped forward. "It's time for you to get ready for bed, Rubes." He held up a finger, as if anticipating Ruby's objection. "No arguing. You go back to school tomorrow."

"I wasn't going to argue," Ruby said. "I was going to negotiate."

"Negotiate?" Kayla laughed. "Where did you learn that?"

"From Uncle Cam," Ruby said proudly, then turned to Cam. "How about I get to stay up five extra minutes tonight and then I'll go to bed five minutes early tomorrow."

Cam shook his head. "Nice try."

"Can Kayla at least help put me to bed?"

"Of course. If she wants to." Cam looked to her.

"You know I do."

"All right. Your negotiations worked," Cam said to Ruby. "You got what you wanted all along. Now go get ready."

Ruby made a face but scampered off toward the bathroom.

Silence fell between them, and Kayla searched for a way to fill it. But all the things she wanted to say were things she shouldn't say. Like how much she'd miss him. And how much the last two months had meant to her. And how much she wished he'd still be here when she got back . . .

"You're all packed?" Cam rescued her from her dangerous thoughts.

Kayla nodded. "About three times over. I'm so afraid I'm going to forget something that I keep unpacking to recheck. I even made Vi go through it with me."

"What time does your flight leave?"

She groaned. "Four a.m." Which meant she should get home and get some sleep since she'd have to be awake by two.

Silence fell between them again, and Kayla studied her fingernails. She had one more gift—but that one she wasn't going to give him until she was on her way out of the house.

"You're going to do great there, you know."

She shook her head. "I'm trying to trust that. But to be honest, I'm pretty nervous. Hope Springs is the farthest I've ever been from home on my own . . ." What in the living world was she doing traveling halfway around the world?

"Kayla, I know you. And I know how strong you are. You're going to go over there and you're going to share the Gospel, and it's going to be amazing. Somehow you always know exactly what to say."

Kayla swiped at her eyes. "Thank you, Cam." She hoped he knew she meant for everything. "You're not so bad at knowing what to say yourself."

"I'm ready," Ruby called from down the hallway.

Cam gestured for Kayla to lead the way to Ruby's room, and she tried to give him a brave smile. But the whole time they read a story and Ruby said her prayers and Cam tucked the blankets tight around her, saying he was making her into a fajita, Kayla had to fight back the burning in her throat.

When she wheeled to Ruby's bed and Ruby threw her arms around her, she gave up holding it back.

"Don't be sad, Kayla." Ruby patted her cheeks. "I'm going to pray for you every day."

Kayla nodded and gave the girl one more squeeze. "And I'll pray for you every day too."

"And Mommy and Uncle Cam?"

Kayla let go of the girl and retucked the blankets around her. "You better believe it."

"See you when you get home." Ruby yawned and snuggled deeper into her blankets. "I love you."

Kayla managed a shaky breath. "I love you too, Ruby. Sweet dreams."

She wheeled out of the room before her few tears turned into a torrent.

In the living room, she ran her hands over her cheeks. She must look like an absolute mess right now. "Sorry." She gave Cam a rueful smile. "I know it's not forever, but I'm going to miss her so much."

"I know."

"I should—" She fumbled. What had she been about to say? Cam's eyes had captured hers, making her forget everything but how warm and inviting they were.

With supreme effort, she looked toward the door. Yes, that was what she'd been about to say. "I should go."

"Do you have to? We could watch a movie or something." Cam's voice held just the slightest note of pleading, nearly weakening her resolve.

But staying would only make saying goodbye harder. "I have to get up to go to the airport in a few hours."

Cam nodded and gave her another sad smile, as if he'd known all along that would be her answer.

"Here." She picked up her coat and dug in the pocket, pulling out a small, wrapped box. "This is for you. But don't open it until after I leave."

"What is it?"

She laughed. "For someone who likes surprises, you sure don't seem to understand how they work."

He stepped forward and reached toward her. But instead of taking the box, his hands wrapped around hers. She stared at them for a moment, letting the tingles from his touch travel up her arm, then met his eyes.

"Kayla," he whispered. And then he was leaning down toward her and she was stretching up toward him, and their lips were meeting. The kiss only lasted a moment, but it was enough for Kayla's heart to break and mend a thousand times. Everything about it was right and wonderful and . . . fleeting.

Cam straightened and unwrapped his hands from hers, bringing the gift with him. "Thank you."

Kayla nodded wordlessly, then rolled her chair to the front door and pulled it open. It took every ounce of effort she possessed to say the words she'd been dreading.

"Goodbye, Cam."

She made herself roll out the door and down the sidewalk, made herself get in the car, made herself turn it on and back out of the driveway. Made herself acknowledge, as she drove away, that it might be the last time she ever saw him.

Chapter 44

Cam stood outside the hospital, staring up at the gray sky. It seemed like the past three weeks had been a string of one gray day after another, as if Kayla had taken the sunshine with her out of the country.

He reached into his coat pocket, wrapping his fingers around the compass she'd given him before she left—engraved with the words, "Be strong and courageous," just as Dad's had been.

He was going to need courage to do this.

He tried to conjure up what Kayla would say, if she were here with him. Probably something wise, like how he couldn't do this on his own—how he could only do it through Christ in him.

All right then, Lord, he prayed in his head. *I know you've forgiven me.* The beautiful, shocking truth of that message had worked its way into his heart over the past weeks, reawakening parts of his soul that he'd closed off for far too long. *Now please help me forgive Bethany, as you have called me to do.*

With a nod and a quick breath, he made his way into the hospital and up to Bethany's room, his steps resolute.

But when he entered her room, he faltered. He hadn't anticipated that she might be sleeping. It gave him a startling flash of all those weeks she'd lain in bed, completely motionless, and they hadn't known if she'd ever wake up. But this wasn't the motionless sleep of a coma, and after a moment, as if she sensed him there, her eyes fluttered open.

"Cam?" Her speech was halting—she'd only started to talk a week or so ago, and she struggled with finding the words she wanted—but she pushed herself up against the pillows, so that she was almost sitting. "Where's Ruby?"

"Still at school. Listen, Bethany. I have something I need to say, and I don't want you to interrupt me because, frankly, I'm not sure I'm going to be able to get through it." His words came out too fast, but he couldn't slow them down.

Bethany blinked at him, and he wasn't entirely sure she was understanding what he said. The doctors said she would likely continue to be easily confused for quite a while yet.

He gulped in a breath. "I have been so mad at you for so long. I've held onto that anger so long because I thought it was a righteous anger. I thought you didn't deserve to be forgiven for what happened to our family. I thought I'd go through my whole life holding it against you." He had to stop and just breathe for a second.

But he wasn't going to quit, now that he'd started. "I was wrong," he said simply. He studied her, watching him, studied his own heart, beating steady and sure. "I forgive you." He blew out a breath. There. He'd said it. And, more than that, he'd meant it.

"Okay," Bethany said, as if he'd told her the nurses were bringing her a bowl of Jell-O.

Cam blinked at her. And then realized it didn't matter. He hadn't forgiven her for her sake. Hadn't done it to hear how thankful she was or to get an apology from her. He'd forgiven her because as someone who knew forgiveness, he could no longer withhold it.

"Okay," he agreed. "Do you want to go back to sleep?"

She shook her head. "Stay. . . . Please."

Cam nodded and plunked into the chair next to her bed. "Do you need anything?"

She shook her head. "I miss . . . that woman."

Cam tipped his head, trying to figure out who she could mean. "One of the nurses?"

Bethany shook her head, frowning as if concentrating. "With the . . . book."

"With the— Oh." His heart squeezed. "Kayla. Yeah. Me too."

"She has a nice voice."

"Yeah, she does." Oh, how he missed hearing her voice.

"You're . . ." Bethany searched his face. "In love?"

Cam started to shake his head but then stopped himself. "Maybe I am," he said slowly, wondering how Bethany had figured it out before he had. "But it doesn't matter. She's in Africa. For six months."

"Write to her," Bethany said simply, not even pausing to search for the words this time.

"I don't know if I should. I told her I was fine with just being friends."

Bethany's lips tipped into a smile. "Friends . . . write."

"Yeah." Cam grinned. He supposed they did.

Chapter 45

"Mail for you," Jasmine, one of the other missionaries, singsonged, dropping an envelope into Kayla's lap as she sat reading her Bible on a blanket under the shade of an acacia tree.

"Thank you." Kayla put a finger in her Bible to hold her page and smiled up at Jasmine. Though the woman was a good seven or eight years younger than Kayla, she'd become a close friend over the past twelve weeks.

"It's from Cam again," Jasmine pointed out—unnecessarily, since Kayla's eyes had picked out his handwriting the moment the envelope had landed in her lap.

"Yep."

"Well, are you going to read it?" Jasmine prompted.

"Yep. As soon as you give me some privacy," Kayla quipped.

Jasmine laughed and waved as she made her way back toward the small thatch-roofed building that housed the mission. "Don't get so caught up in it that you miss dinner again," she called over her shoulder.

Kayla laughed as she tore into the envelope. When she'd received Cam's first letter a month after she'd arrived here, she hadn't known what to do with it. She'd been missing him, thinking about him every day. And yet, she'd been afraid that opening his letter would only make things harder. She'd left it tucked into her Bible for a whole week before she'd worked up the nerve to open it.

And when she had . . . it had felt like Cam was sitting right there next to her, talking to her, making her laugh. Just like he had in Hope Springs.

In the weeks since then, she'd begun to look forward to his letters more than she cared to admit. He sent news and pictures of Ruby, who apparently was quite a swimmer and had stolen the show in her play. And he shared updates on Bethany's recovery—and even an occasional message from her, which was so good to hear.

She'd debated writing back—what if it only encouraged him to think there was more between them than there could be—but in the end, her desire to say hi to Ruby had won out. Or at least she had told herself that was the reason she'd picked up her pen.

As she let her eyes fall on his letter now, her heart took up the familiar song at the sight of his words on the page.

Dear Kayla,

Your last letter made me laugh because it was the very thing I had been thinking about and was planning to tell you. But you phrased it better than I ever could have: "Faith doesn't mean understanding everything God does. Faith means believing everything God says." That's . . . deep. And also so simple, when you think about it.

Kayla nodded and lifted her head to scan the horizon. The sun was just lowering over the distant hills. She'd seen more heartbreak and suffering here than she ever had at home. And yet, she'd also seen more joy and hope and trust as well. It was at the funeral of a young mother, as the pastor had read the familiar words of Psalm 23, that it had occurred to Kayla: She didn't have to know *why* God had allowed this woman to die to believe that he had saved her and that she would dwell in the house of the Lord forever. Just like she didn't need to know why God had allowed her accident or Bethany's coma or the death of Nate and Vi's baby to believe that in all of those things he was with them.

She dropped her eyes back to the paper.

Ruby was excited to hear about the play you're planning to do with the schoolchildren. She says if you need a sheep, she could come and be one. And she volunteered me to bring her.

Kayla laughed. Oh, how she longed to see them.

Over the past week, Bethany has made huge strides. All she can talk about these days is going home. The doctors say that should be possible in a week or two if she keeps progressing like this.

Kayla drew in a breath. She was so happy for Bethany. And yet, she couldn't help the tiny swoop of disappointment. If Bethany was recovered enough to go home, then Cam wouldn't need to care for Ruby anymore. Which meant he wouldn't need to stay in Hope Springs.

She pushed the thought aside. Now was not the time for her to focus on her own selfish desires—now was the time to rejoice with Bethany.

Anyway, I hope you're doing well there. Ruby says she misses you, and so does Bethany. And . . . I miss you too.

With prayers for you always,

Cam

Kayla let herself read the letter again, then tucked it into her Bible and pulled herself back into her wheelchair. She'd better get dinner before the others ate it all.

As she filled a dish with nsima, the thick maize porridge they had with most meals, she tried to stop dwelling on the fact that by the time she returned to Hope Springs, Cam would likely be gone. It was no surprise—she'd known that even before she left. And it wasn't like she had any plans to remain in Hope Springs once she found a job... wherever she found one. She let herself toy briefly with the idea of looking for one in LA. But she dismissed the thought quickly. For one, she'd never enjoyed big cities. And for two, that might be rather presumptuous, given that she'd told Cam she wanted to remain just friends and he hadn't pressed the issue once since then.

"I know that look." Jasmine elbowed her as she pulled up to the table. "It was a good letter, huh?"

Kayla shrugged. "It was fine."

"Mmm hmm." Skylar nodded on the other side of the table. "Fine. That's why you have stars in your eyes."

"Why I— I do not."

"Come on, Kayla. You have to admit that Cam is more than a friend. He writes every week—and every time you get a letter, you get all . . . in-love looking." Jasmine wiggled her eyebrows at Kayla.

"In-love looking?" Kayla scoffed at her friends. "That's not a thing. And even if it were, I do not get anything of the kind. Because I'm not in love with him." In *like* with him, yes. In wanting-to-spend-time-with-him, yes. In a talk-all-night-and-share-your-deepest-secrets kind of friendship, yes. But not in love.

Thank goodness.

"Don't worry, she'll figure it out sooner or later," Skylar stage-whispered to Jasmine, who nodded with a giggle.

Kayla ignored both of her friends and shoveled another bite of nsima into her mouth, trying hard not to let the word *love* linger in her heart.

Chapter 46

"We're going to need at least two more strings of lights," Cam called to Bethany as he looped the strand of lights in his hands over a tree branch at the edge of the patio he'd just finished installing in Nate and Vi's backyard. The July humidity clung to him, making sweat trickle down his neck.

He was also going to need a shower when he was done with this job.

He glanced at the time. It'd be cutting it close to finish the job and get home and back before the party tonight, but he was not going to miss this for anything.

"I'll make a quick run to the store," Bethany said, standing from the spot where she'd been planting a rosebush next to a statue Nate and Vi had placed as a memorial for their baby. "I'd better write it down." Though she'd made a remarkable recovery and often seemed almost her old self—the Bethany he'd known before she'd gotten involved with drugs—she still struggled with short-term memory issues. "You want to stay here, Rubes, or come with me?"

Ruby looked up from where she'd been playing in the dirt. "I'll come with you."

Cam watched mother and daughter walk hand-in-hand toward the front of the house, marveling again at how similar they were—both with long blonde hair swinging behind them and that cheerful, almost bouncy walk.

Over the past few months, as he'd gotten to know his sister again, he'd grown in love and respect for her—for the way she'd cleaned up after learning she was pregnant with Ruby, the way she'd left a situation where she knew she'd face constant temptation to make a home here, the way she'd worked so hard at rehab so she could get home to Ruby.

Her recovery had gone so well, in fact, that she'd been ready to take on full-time responsibility for Ruby a month and a half ago. Cam had gone so far as to pack his bags and load them in his trunk. But when it came down to it, he couldn't leave. Not when it felt like every beat of his heart belonged to Hope Springs.

To being with Ruby. And even with Bethany. And maybe, someday, with Kayla.

LA may have been where his house was. But Hope Springs was *home*.

He'd flown back to California only long enough to sell his house, wrap up a few loose ends at the office so he wouldn't leave George in the lurch, and apologize once more to Danielle—who was now seeing an artist and seemed genuinely happy.

And then he'd come back home, crashing with Ruby and Bethany until he'd closed on his own house two weeks ago. That didn't mean his relationship with Bethany was perfect—there were times he still had to fight off the old anger about what she'd done to their family—but he prayed day by day to let it go and cling instead to forgiveness. And each day it got a little easier.

The sound of the patio door sliding open drew his attention.

"Wow, this looks great." Vi stepped onto the patio and surveyed his work. "You're definitely good at this, Cam. If you give me some business cards, I'll put them out at the antique shop."

"Thanks." He brushed his hands on his pants, taking a moment to examine the warm brown and red tones of the pavers that formed the patio and complemented the outdoor fireplace he'd constructed. "I need to get a couple more strings of lights up, and then everything should be done."

"Great. We're going to be leaving for the airport in a few minutes."

"Remember, don't tell her."

"I haven't spilled the beans yet," Vi said. "And you haven't spilled mine, right?" She rubbed at her slightly protruding belly.

"Not a word." He'd been sorely tempted a few times to include Nate and Vi's good news in his letters, because he knew how happy it would make Kayla, but he'd held up his end of the bargain.

Vi smiled. "It's going to be so good to see her, isn't it?"

"It really will." Speaking of which—Cam turned to get back to work. Unless he wanted to see her in this smelly, dirt-covered state, he had to get this job done.

Why was she so nervous?

Kayla watched out the plane's window as the ground below quickly drew closer.

But it wasn't the landing that was sending butterflies through her nerves. It was being home. Which made no sense at all. As wonderful and transformative as the mission trip had been—and as much as she was going to miss the people she'd met—she couldn't wait to see her brother and sister-in-law. And Ruby and Bethany and all her friends.

And Cam.

Except, Cam wouldn't be here. He'd written six weeks ago to say he was all packed and ready to go back to California. Although he didn't say much about his life there—and she could never work up the courage to ask—she assumed it was going well. In his last few letters, he had seemed different somehow . . . happier maybe. Apparently California life was agreeing with him. And now that she was home, he'd have no reason to keep writing to her.

Kayla pushed the gloomy thoughts away as she transferred into the narrow wheelchair the flight attendant had rolled to her seat. By the time she'd maneuvered off the plane and transferred into her own chair on the Jetway, Kayla's nerves had transformed into anticipation. She was *home*.

Months of pushing her wheelchair across rutted dirt paths and patches of thick grass had left her arms stronger than ever, and she quickly powered up the Jetway, through the airport, to the baggage claim area. Fortunately, it wasn't a busy airport, and Nate and Vi had said they'd be . . .

Right there.

The moment she spotted them walking toward her, she covered her mouth to keep the squeal back.

But as Vi bent to give her a hug, she couldn't keep from letting out a small squeak. "You didn't tell me." She touched a hand to Vi's rounded belly.

"It was kind of a surprise to us. And we wanted it to be a surprise to you too." Vi was laughing as she squeezed Kayla tight. "It's so good to see you."

Kayla squeezed back, then hugged her brother. "Seriously, you guys, how could you keep news this big from me?" She felt like Ruby, wanting to bounce in her chair.

"Oh, trust me, there's bigger news." Nate failed to hide a mischievous smile.

"What is it?" Kayla was still smiling from the first news.

But Vi hit her husband's arm, then matched his mischievous expression. "You'll have to wait and see."

"Oh, come on, you can't do that to me."

"Watch us." Nate grabbed her bag from the baggage claim, then led the way out of the building.

The entire way to the parking lot, Kayla continued to beg them to tell her whatever this other news might be—and she would have kept going all the way to Hope Springs, but a pleasant drowsiness fell over her almost the moment they pulled away from the airport. "I'm just going to close my eyes for a minute," she mumbled.

She woke up to Vi's gentle shaking.

Her eyes sprang open. "What? Oh." She looked out the window. They were parked in Nate and Vi's driveway. "Sorry. I think I fell asleep."

"Yeah." Vi laughed. "We thought you might want to wake up for your surprise."

"Surprise?" Kayla was instantly alert. "Now?"

Vi hit her with that mysterious smile again and got out of the car. Nate opened Kayla's door and slid her wheelchair into place for her to transfer.

As she did, she noticed all the cars parked on the street in front of the house. Way more than she'd ever seen there before aside from when . . .

Ah, so that was the surprise. A party.

Kayla lifted a hand to her hair. She didn't even want to know what it looked like after spending the past two days traveling. Oh well, she knew her friends would welcome her, messy hair and all.

She followed Nate and Vi to the front door, ignoring the prickle of disappointment that came from knowing that one person would be missing. Getting to see everyone else would more than make up for that.

"Welcome home." The cry was so loud and so warm and so welcoming, that Kayla let out a genuinely surprised laugh. And now her disappointment really was gone, as she gazed on the faces of all the people she'd grown to love during her time in Hope Springs. There were hugs all around and laughter and question on top of question about the trip.

When she'd finally greeted everyone and had been forced by Vi to go to the kitchen and fill a plate with food, Kayla looked around the crowded house. This was so wonderful, but her heart was aching to see Ruby—and to speak to Bethany in person. Maybe Vi hadn't thought to invite them. Which was fine. Her sister-in-law had done more than enough already. She could always go visit Ruby and Bethany tomorrow.

"Kayla, do you have a second?" Emma popped up at her side. "I was hoping we could talk."

"Of course." Kayla set her plate down and gave Emma her attention as the other woman leaned against the counter next to her.

"You know I started that new social interactions group before you left, right?"

Kayla nodded. As much as she'd loved the trip, she'd had her moments of wondering if she should have accepted the job after all. Especially since now she was going to have to start her job search from scratch.

"It hasn't exactly been going great," Emma said, with a wry laugh. "Actually, I'm not going to lie. It's been going pretty terribly. I've had two coordinators quit already. I think they didn't quite realize what they were getting into, and the group is . . . challenging. What I really need is someone who has some experience." She gave Kayla a pointed look, and this time Kayla didn't miss the cue.

She shook her head, laughing.

Emma raised an eyebrow. "Is that a no or a yes?"

"Sorry." Kayla touched Emma's hand. "It's a how-does-God-do-that. I spent most of the flight home making a list of all the possible places I could look for a job. I wanted to hit the ground running. And instead God ran a job right at me."

Emma smiled. "So a yes?"

Kayla bit her lip. It all felt so right. Hope Springs had seemed so much like home before she'd gone to Malawi that she couldn't imagine living anywhere else. But— "Can I pray about it, just to be sure?"

"Of course." Emma straightened and squeezed her shoulder. "Take all the time you need."

Kayla picked up her plate again, marveling at the way God worked things out sometimes.

"Where's Kayla? Where's Kayla?" The little voice Kayla would know anywhere came from the living room, and in an instant, Kayla had set her plate down and was wheeling past the others to sweep Ruby into a hug.

"I missed you." Ruby's arms threatened to cut off Kayla's airflow, but she didn't care. She'd hug the little girl all day if she could.

"I missed you too. I think you grew two feet while I was gone."

Ruby giggled. "Silly, I always had two feet."

"I think she means two feet *taller*, Ruby." A blonde woman came up behind Ruby, and Kayla recognized her instantly.

"Oh my goodness. Bethany. It's so good to see you on your feet. You look wonderful."

The woman gave her a shy smile. "It's nice to finally meet you. And be able to thank you."

Kayla waved off the gratitude, but the woman leaned down to hug her, sandwiching a giggling Ruby between them.

"I don't know what would have happened without you . . ." Bethany sniffed and wiped at her eyes as she stood, and Kayla had to swallow back her own emotions. Who would have thought that seeing Bethany's car go off the road that day would have changed her life so dramatically?

"Did you get to tell lots of people about Jesus?" Ruby asked as she unwrapped herself from around Kayla's neck.

"I sure did. It was . . ." But there were no words to describe what it felt like to see someone come to know their Savior. It was like watching a plant leave the shackles of its seed behind and soak up the sun.

"That's good. But now you're going to stay here forever, right? Just like—"

"Ruby!" Bethany's voice held a warning Kayla didn't understand, and the little girl clapped a hand over her mouth.

"Sorry, Mommy."

Bethany smiled at her daughter and wrapped an arm around her. "Come on, let's go get you some food."

Kayla stared after them, completely baffled as to what that had been about but also completely overjoyed to see Ruby reunited with her mother. After a moment, she realized she'd never eaten her food either and made her way to the kitchen after them.

She picked up her plate just in time to see Bethany pull her phone out of her pocket. Bethany grinned as she looked at the screen, then showed it to Ruby, who jumped up and down.

"Where are you?" Bethany said as she held the phone to her ear. "Ruby almost just gave you up."

She listened for a moment, her smile growing wider. Then she said, "Will do," and hung up.

She bent down and whispered something in Ruby's ear that made the girl giggle, then run to Kayla.

"Come with me." Ruby grabbed the plate of still untouched food out of Kayla's hands and set it on the table.

Kayla gave Bethany a curious look, but Bethany wore that same mischievous smile Nate and Vi had worn earlier.

"Where are we going?" she asked Ruby.

"Outside."

"Why?"

But Ruby shook her head. "I can't tell you."

"Why not?"

"It's a surprise." Ruby was bouncing her way toward the front door.

"Another surprise?" What could possibly be left to surprise her with?

But she followed Ruby to the door.

Ruby burst outside and gestured impatiently for Kayla to follow.

With a shrug, Kayla popped her wheels over the threshold and made her way toward the small ramp that lay over part of the steps leading off the porch.

Out of the corner of her eye, she thought she caught a glimpse of something moving near the driveway, and she turned her head.

Her hands lifted off her wheelchair to cover her mouth as a disbelieving, joyous laugh-cry made its way up from her core.

This couldn't be real. He couldn't really be standing there.

Cam.

Holding a bouquet of flowers and smiling that oh-so-perfect smile and bouncing on his toes the same way Ruby did.

Her eyes met his and she had two seconds to enjoy the warmth and the hope in them before he was striding toward her, his long legs carrying him so fast that she still hadn't quite registered what was going on when he leaned down and wrapped her in a tight hug.

"I missed you," he murmured into her hair.

All she could do was nod around the tightness in her throat as her hands rested on the firm muscles of his shoulders. He was solid and real and . . . *here*.

As he pulled back, he handed her the flowers.

She cradled them in her arms, but she was too busy trying to figure out what was going on to look at them. "What are you doing here?"

"Nate and Vi invited me," he said with a sly smile.

She hit him lightly with the flowers. "You know that's not what I mean. What are you doing *here*, in Hope Springs?"

Cam glanced past Kayla, to where Ruby stood in the doorway. "You want to tell her, Rubes?"

"Uncle Cam lives here," Ruby burst out, bouncing and clapping her hands in front of her.

"You— What? Since when?"

Cam looked to Ruby again, raising an eyebrow. "What's it been? Six weeks?"

"Six weeks?" Kayla squinted, trying to remember the exact date of the letter in which he'd said he was moving. "But in May you said you were going back to California."

Cam shrugged. "I couldn't do it. I realized my life is here now. With Ruby and Bethany and—" He looked up. "Ruby, why don't you go inside. If anyone is looking for us, we'll be inside in a little bit, okay?"

"Okey dokey." Ruby saluted him, then pulled the door closed behind her.

Kayla tried to sort out which question swirling around her brain to ask first. It wasn't easy, the way her heart was skipping around her chest and distracting her from all rational thought. Cam was here. Not in California. *Here.* "What about your job?"

"Come here." He jogged down the porch steps, gesturing for her to follow.

She hesitated. She honestly didn't know if she could handle any more surprises today. But the excitement in his eyes led her to roll down the ramp and follow him to the driveway.

He paused in front of some sort of work truck parked there. "Ta da."

Kayla blinked at the vehicle, uncomprehending. And then her eyes focused on the logo. "Moore Landscaping."

She gasped. "Cam! You did it? You started a landscaping company?"

He ducked his head but then lifted it with a smile. "I'm in the process. Your brother and Violet were technically my first clients. But it's a start. Bethany has been helping . . ."

"Cam, this is amazing. I'm so happy for you. Wait. You did some work here? Can I see it?"

He nodded, looking pleased. "It's the back patio." She followed him through the grass to the backyard, where the old, cracked concrete patio had been replaced by beautiful pavers in rich, warm tones. Strings of lights led from the house and across the patio, drawing her eyes to a stunning outdoor fireplace.

She rolled onto the patio, letting herself admire his handiwork.

"Wow, Cam. This is beautiful." Finally, she turned to him and asked the question that had been begging to be asked since Ruby had said he lived here now. "Why didn't you tell me about any of this?"

"I know how you like surprises." He grabbed a patio chair and pulled it up in front of her wheelchair, sitting close enough that their knees nearly brushed. "And also, I didn't want to freak you out."

She laughed. "Why would I be freaked out?"

"Because—" He reached for her hands and wrapped his around them. "I told you before you left that I was fine with remaining just friends. But the truth is, Kayla, I moved here because I want to be closer to Ruby and Bethany, yes. But I also wanted to be close to you. Because . . ." He cleared his throat. "Because I love you. And I'm sorry if that freaks you out, but there it is."

Kayla drew in a breath filled with the warm, delicious smell of him. "It doesn't freak me out," she said quietly.

"It doesn't?"

She shook her head, not sure herself why it didn't. But it came to her then, and she almost laughed with the wonder of it. "It doesn't. Because I love you too." It was a love that had been deepening for so long that she couldn't believe she hadn't realized it until now.

He lifted his eyes to hers, and she could read the joy and the hope in them. She didn't want him to look away—ever.

She leaned forward, wrapping her arms around his neck and drawing him closer. Her eyes fell closed as his soft breath brushed her lips. And then his lips were there, warm and caressing and . . . perfect. Her hands slid to his face as his slipped into her hair. It felt like she had been waiting for this kiss her whole life, she thought, as she pulled him closer. And also like it was always meant to be right now.

Chapter 47

Cam's fingers slid happily through Kayla's hair as she snuggled closer to him on the couch in his living room as they watched *It's a Wonderful Life*. Even though Christmas was over a month away yet, Kayla had insisted that they had to watch it now, to get them in the Christmas spirit. Cam had readily assented. Any excuse to curl up with her was fine by him.

The four months since she'd returned from Malawi had been nearly perfect, and he'd soaked up every moment with her, finding it impossible sometimes to remember that he hadn't known her his entire life.

"I love you," he whispered, nuzzling his chin into her hair.

She tilted her head up to brush a kiss onto his lips. "I love you too."

They both jumped as her phone dinged with a text. Nate had called an hour ago to say that Vi had gone into labor but that they shouldn't come to the hospital yet since it would likely be a while. He was supposed to text them when it got closer.

Cam peered at the phone over Kayla's shoulder.

"Wait. Is that . . ."

Kayla squealed and nodded.

It was a picture of Vi holding a baby, all pink and swaddled in a blanket, a wild tuft of hair sticking up at the top of its head.

Another text came through seconds later. *Liliana Kay Benson. 7 lbs. 3 oz. 20 inches.*

Nate sent a picture of himself grinning as if he were about to burst.

"I'm so happy for them." Kayla nuzzled into Cam's arms for a second, then sat up. "Want to go meet my niece?"

"You know I do." Cam turned off the movie. "I hope we have a family like that someday."

Kayla's head whipped toward him. "You do?"

Cam froze. He'd been thinking that for months now—pretty much since the moment he'd first told her he loved her—but he hadn't meant to bring it up yet. He knew how much her independence meant to her, and he didn't want to rush her into anything. He'd been thinking maybe at Christmas, he'd ask her . . .

But he nodded. "Yeah, I do." He hesitated, then took her hands in his. "But I know you're not ready yet. So don't worry, I'm not going to pressure you or anything."

Kayla tilted her head at him. "You know I'm not ready?"

"I mean—" Cam fumbled. "Are you?"

"You'll have to ask me to find out." Kayla's voice took on a teasing tone, and her eyes sparkled.

"What? Now?"

She shrugged. "Or whenever you're ready. It doesn't have to be now."

Oh, it was going to be now. If she was ready, there was no way he was going to wait another day.

He jumped up from the couch and sprinted to his bedroom, to the box he had tucked into the nightstand.

"Cam?" Kayla's voice carried to him as he popped back into the hallway.

She gave him a relieved smile as he hurried toward her. "You really shouldn't disappear on a girl after saying something like that."

"Sorry. I had to get something." He clenched the box in his hands. It wasn't even a proper ring box. Just an old check box he'd found lying around Mom's house when he'd cleaned it out.

When he made it back to the couch, he hesitated, joy, nerves, and a wild, unbridled hope colliding so hard in his heart it made him dizzy.

Slowly, he reached for her hand, then lowered himself to one knee.

Kayla covered her mouth with her other hand. "You're really doing this now?"

He nodded, his smile feeling huge and yet wobbly at the same time. He blinked once. Looked away. Blinked again.

Kayla's hand came to his cheek, rubbing against the stubble there, and he realized he hadn't shaved today and was wearing jeans and a t-shirt. Not exactly the romantic proposal he had been imagining.

And yet . . .

He knew he wanted to do this right here, right now.

"Kayla." His voice came out raspy, and he brought his eyes to hers to find that she was blinking back tears.

Ah man. He was never going to get through this without falling apart.

But he drew in a slow breath. Cleared his throat. Squeezed her hand tighter, then let go and opened the check box, revealing a simple princess cut diamond ring. The stone was much smaller than what he could afford. And it hadn't cost him a thing. But he knew none of that would matter to Kayla.

She would understand the value of this ring.

"This was my mother's wedding ring." His voice cracked. For Pete's sake. He had to pull it together. But how could he, when the woman in front of him had come to mean everything to him? "And I would be honored if you would wear it. If you would spend the rest of this life at my side." He pulled the ring out of the box and held it out to her. And now, instead of tears, he could barely hold back the laugh. He was really doing this. And nothing had felt more right in his life. "Kayla Benson, will you marry me?"

Kayla's laugh mingled perfectly with the tears on her cheeks. Instead of answering, she leaned forward, slid her hands around his neck, and pressed her lips to his.

But when she pulled back, she gave him a serious look. "Are you sure about this? You know our marriage might not look like other people's. We might have to make adaptations or—"

Cam grabbed her hands tight in his. "Kayla, whatever we have to do, we'll do it. If we can't have children, we'll adopt or we'll spoil Ruby and Liliana or, I don't know, we'll figure it out. All I know is, whatever it takes to make you happy, I'll do it."

"I can have children, Cam."

He let out a breath. "Well, there you go, then. Now, are you going to answer my question?"

But that serious look still lingered in her eyes. "That doesn't mean there won't be other challenges."

"Of course it doesn't." He laced his fingers through hers. "Just like any marriage. And we'll work through them. Together. End of story."

She nodded, a grin slowly pulling up her lips, and he let himself breathe a little easier. "So are you going to answer the question now?" He didn't mean to be impatient, but . . .

Kayla laughed, her playful tone returning. "You want an answer right now?"

"I can wait if you're not ready to answer. Five minutes or so enough?"

Kayla shook her head, her laugh still bouncing in her eyes and filling his heart to bursting. "I'll answer you right now. Yes, Cameron Moore, I will marry you."

"Call me Cam," he murmured, slipping the ring onto her finger before bringing his lips to hers.

Epilogue

"You look like a princess." A wide-eyed Ruby entered the room at the back of Hope Church where Bethany was just finishing up weaving a white ribbon through Kayla's dark hair as she twisted it into a braided updo.

"Thank you." The truth was, in this dress, with its halter neckline and tulle skirt, she felt like a princess. And in a few minutes she'd be rolling down the aisle to her prince.

She slid her hands down the white fabric that billowed around her legs. She'd had the seamstress remove just enough of the tulle so that it wouldn't get in the way of her wheelchair wheels.

She took in Ruby's matching dress and the flowers braided into her hair. "And you look like the world's most beautiful flower girl."

Ruby smiled and twirled, letting her dress flare around her legs. "Uncle Cam says you're going to be my auntie after this. But I want you to be my friend."

Kayla laughed. "I'll be both, silly."

The sound of a baby crying from the other side of the room pulled their attention to the stroller in the corner. "The best-laid plans," Vi sighed, reaching into the stroller to pick up five-month-old Liliana. She'd laid the infant down twenty minutes ago with the hope that she'd sleep through the ceremony. "I'm so sorry, Kayla."

"Don't be ridiculous. You know I want Liliana to be part of this too. If you don't mind holding her during the ceremony, I think that'd be precious. Or you can give her to Mom if you'd rather."

The baby let out a lusty cry and turned her face toward Vi's dusty rose bridesmaid dress.

Vi groaned. "Do you really need to eat now, little one?" She checked the time, then gave Kayla a desperate glance. "There's no way I can be done feeding her in the next five minutes, but if I don't, she's going to scream through the whole ceremony."

"Vi, relax. You know that little girl means the world to us. We can wait a few minutes to start the ceremony." She turned to Ruby. "Can you go tell your uncle Cam that we need about fifteen minutes?"

Ruby gave a solemn nod, then skipped toward the door.

Kayla bit her lip. She was anxious to see her groom. Maybe she should go over there and explain things to him herself.

She was halfway to the door when it shot open and Cam burst through, looking like her very own prince in his white tux and blue tie that intensified his eyes. "What's this I hear about my bride keeping me waiting?"

"Cam," Bethany scolded. "You can't be in here. You're not supposed to see each other yet."

"Oh, trust me," Cam said, never taking his eyes off Kayla. "We're supposed to see each other. Right now. Come with me?" He nodded toward the door, and Kayla followed.

The moment they were in the hallway, he stopped and reached for her hands. "You are the most beautiful—" He swallowed. "I can't believe how fortunate I am." His eyes welled, and Kayla couldn't help it. A tear dripped onto her cheek.

"You're going to ruin my makeup," she scolded. "And you should know that I'm the fortunate one here. I was so sure that if I ever gave my heart to someone, I'd lose myself. But somehow, with you, I feel like I've found the part of me that makes me even more whole."

"I know exactly what you mean." He bent to give her a long, slow kiss.

They pulled apart as the door to the dressing room behind them opened and Nate strode out. He looked from Cam to Kayla. "What's going on out here?"

"Nothing, sir," Cam said in a mock serious voice. "I promise your sister and I were behaving ourselves."

"Glad to hear it." Nate clapped a hand to Cam's back. "Do you think I could talk to Kayla for a minute?"

"Yes, but only a minute." Cam stepped back into the dressing room. "She has an anxious groom waiting for her."

Kayla forced her eyes off her future husband as the door to the dressing room clicked shut. "What's up, big brother?"

Nate opened his mouth, shook his head, tried again. "I just wanted to say that I'm proud of you."

Kayla smiled and took his hand. "I'm proud of you too."

Nate gave her a surprised look. "I didn't do anything."

"No." She shoved him. "Just made that amazing, tiny little human in there." She pointed toward the women's dressing room.

Nate's eyes went all dreamy. "She's pretty incredible, isn't she?" He shook himself. "But we're not here to talk about me. This is your day. And I'm so happy for you. I've never seen anyone live life as fully as you do, Kayla. The things you've overcome. The way you let your faith shine." He cleared his throat. "Anyway, I hope Cam realizes what an amazing woman he's getting."

"Oh, don't worry, he does." Kayla laughed. "He tells me that way too often."

"Good. Because you deserve only the best."

Kayla shook her head. "I don't deserve anything. But I'm grateful God has given it to me anyway."

"I know how you feel." Nate looked up as the dressing room door opened. His expression morphed into a goofy grin, and Kayla didn't have to look to know it must be Vi and baby Liliana.

"We're ready," Vi said. "Finally."

A surge of adrenaline went through Kayla as Nate opened the guy's dressing room door, calling that it was time to get this show on the road.

Cam came out of the dressing room, lighting her up with a smile that said how sure he was about this. And just like that, she wasn't nervous anymore. Just so ready for this moment. To get married. Right now.

As the guys disappeared down the hallway to wait for them at the front of the church, Kayla's dad fell in step next to her wheelchair.

As the first strains of "Jesu, Joy of Man's Desiring" filtered into the lobby, Ruby stepped into the church, sprinkling flower petals every few feet as she made her way down the aisle. Kayla clasped her hands at her heart as Ruby walked, remembering all the times Ruby and Cam had felt like family. And now they really were.

God was so good.

"You ready for this?" Dad whispered as Bethany and then Vi, holding a wide-eyed baby Liliana, started down the aisle.

"So ready."

Dad nodded, not saying anything, but leaned down and gave her a quick hug that said everything.

She hugged him back and then they were on their way down the aisle and the only thing she noticed anymore was Cam, standing and waiting for her, his smile so big it almost made her heart burst.

When they reached his side, Cam shook her dad's hand, then escorted Kayla to the low, backless bench Spencer and Tyler had fashioned for them after Cam had said he wanted to be able to look into his bride's eyes as they said their vows. Kayla maneuvered her wheelchair in front of it, then with Cam's hand on her shoulder and Bethany at her side to help sweep the dress under her, transferred to the bench. Bethany moved the wheelchair out of the way and then it was just her and Cam, sitting on the bench in front of Dan.

The ceremony was a blur of "yeses" and "I wills" and Dan's sermon on Genesis 2:24 worked its way right into Kayla's heart. She squeezed Cam's hand as Dan read the words: "That is why a man leaves his father and mother and is united to his wife, and they become one flesh."

Comfort settled in Kayla's soul as Cam met her eyes. She'd thought melding two people into one flesh meant that each of them had to lose part of themselves. But it turned out that becoming one with Cam made her more herself than she'd ever been before.

Before she knew it, Dan was introducing them as Mr. and Mrs. Moore, and Bethany was bringing her wheelchair to her. She reached to transfer back into it, then turned and looked at her husband, glowing at her side. She'd always insisted on doing everything herself. But he was now part of her.

"Will you lift me into the chair?" She bit her lip. They hadn't rehearsed this part.

Cam gave her a lopsided smile. "I would be honored." He stood and tucked an arm under her legs and one around her back, then lifted her into the air.

But instead of setting her into the wheelchair, he bent his head just enough to bring his lips to hers in a gentle kiss.

The congregation burst into applause as he lowered her into the wheelchair. As he started to straighten, she grabbed the front of his tux and pulled him back down to her for another kiss. The applause intensified, and Kayla couldn't stop smiling as she finally let go of Cam, and they made their way down the aisle, his hand on her shoulder.

The moment they reached the lobby, they were inundated with guests offering hugs and congratulations. Kayla soaked it all in, grateful for her family, her friends, this community that had welcomed them so readily.

When the last guest had left the building, Cam turned to her. "That was easier than I thought it would be."

Kayla couldn't help the giggle. "You thought marrying me would be hard?"

"Marrying you? No. Sitting up there in front of everyone and trying to express how I feel about you? Yeah."

"Well, you did a beautiful job."

"You made it easy." He leaned down for another kiss, then pulled away to look into her eyes. "What now?"

"Now, we go take pictures."

"And then?"

"And then have dinner and our reception."

"And after that?" Cam's eyes danced.

"After that we have our honeymoon."

"Mmm." He kissed her again. "And then?"

"And then—" Kayla nuzzled her face into his neck. "We go through the rest of our lives together."

"Well then." Cam stood and took her hand. "Let's get started. Right now."

Not Until Then

A Hope Springs Novel

Valerie M. Bodden

For now we see only a reflection as in a mirror; then we shall see face to face. Now I know in part; then I shall know fully, even as I am fully known.

1 Corinthians 13:12

Chapter 1

This wasn't happening.

Bethany scanned the checkout counter around her, as if her purse would magically appear on it.

All she wanted was one day of the year where she had it together. It didn't feel like too much to ask that it be today.

But apparently she was bound to make a mess even of her daughter's birthday.

"That will be $21.99." The cashier—an older woman with kind eyes—repeated.

"I . . . Uh . . ." She felt at her shoulder again—the spot where her purse should have been. In the rush to get everything ready for Ruby's party, she must have forgotten it.

She rubbed at her temple. She couldn't show up to her own daughter's tenth birthday party without a gift. Not when everyone else would have one—probably one they'd purchased weeks ago. It was bad enough she was buying it at the grocery store, but she didn't have much choice; it was on the way to Ruby's school and it was almost time to pick her up.

She blinked at the necklace—a figure of a horse and a girl face-to-face within a heart. She had two choices: grab it off the counter and run out the door—or put it back on the shelf. There was a time in her life when the first would have seemed viable. But not anymore. Not even for Ruby.

"I'm sorry. I forgot my wallet. I guess I'll have to put it back." The words weighed her whole body down.

"Do you want me to set it aside for you?" The cashier slid the necklace into her hand and set it next to the register, sympathy in her voice.

"That would be nice, thank you." Bethany knew the woman's name, she was sure of it, but she didn't have the energy to search her mind for it right now. "I probably won't be able to get it until tomorrow. I have to get to my daughter's birthday party. Maybe I can give her an 'I owe you.'" She tried for a weak smile. At least she didn't have to worry about crying. The aneurysm had stolen that ability from her right along with a good chunk of her short-term memory.

"Here." A man's voice spoke from behind her, and someone reached past her to hand the cashier a credit card. "I'll get it."

"I...Um..."

Before Bethany could stop her, the cashier had already taken the card and run it through the register.

"That's very kind of you," the older woman said, beaming into the space behind Bethany. "Oh, doesn't this feel like the beginning of a romance movie? You make sure to get his name, dear." The woman winked at Bethany.

Bethany opened her mouth as she turned to look at the man. His left arm was in a sling, and he wore a gray flannel shirt, but the thing that struck Bethany the most was his face—all hard lines and angles, not a trace of a smile.

Say something, Bethany's brain screamed. But the words wouldn't arrange themselves in a straight line in her head.

"Here you are, dear." The cashier passed Bethany a small bag and handed the card back to the man.

Bethany was halfway to the door before she finally managed to turn and blurt, "Thank you," the words sticking together like paste as they came off her lips.

She didn't wait to see whether the man would acknowledge her gratitude.

Outside, the wind grabbed at her hair, and she pulled the zipper on her sweatshirt up higher against the early April chill as she scanned the parking lot. Usually she took a picture of where she'd parked, but she'd been in too much of a hurry today.

There. She let herself breathe out as she spotted the boxy maroon four-door only two rows away. Finally, something was going her way. Maybe that meant Ruby's birthday wouldn't be a disaster after all. She should have just enough time to stop home and wrap the gift before she had to pick her daughter up from school and bring her over to the stables for the party.

As she strode toward the car, she reached into her pocket for her keys.

When her fingers didn't brush against metal in her jeans pocket, she checked her sweatshirt.

Then she checked all the pockets again.

Empty.

Which meant she'd left the keys in the car.

"Please tell me I forgot to lock it," she muttered to herself as she reached the vehicle. With a quick prayer, she tried the handle.

It lifted—but the door didn't budge.

She peered through the window, letting her head rest against the cold glass as she spotted the keys dangling from the ignition.

"Really? Today of all days?" She hadn't slept well last night; she was sure that was the explanation for her increased forgetfulness today. But knowing why it was happening didn't change the fact that she was going to ruin her daughter's birthday. Poor Ruby hadn't done anything to deserve a mother who could barely remember to make a meal, let alone plan a perfect birthday party.

Be grateful, she reminded herself. She was still here to celebrate Ruby's birthday. Two years ago, that hadn't been at all certain. The aneurysm may have made things more difficult, but it hadn't taken her life.

She closed her eyes and offered a quick prayer of thanks—as well as a plea for help out of yet another situation. Then she let out a long breath and opened her eyes. This wasn't the first time she'd locked her keys in her car. Which was why she'd given a spare set to her brother Cam and his wife Kayla. She hated the idea of calling them to come to her rescue—again. But for Ruby's sake, she'd do it.

She reached for her back pocket, just as she spotted her phone—in the car's cupholder.

She groaned and pounded her fist against the car window.

Something like this would never happen to any of the perfect moms of Ruby's classmates—whose names she would probably never manage to remember.

She shook her head. Feeling sorry for herself wasn't going to help.

Okay, what else could she do? She could go in the store and ask to use someone else's phone—except it wasn't like she could remember any phone numbers to call. She had to look up her own any time she needed it, for goodness' sake.

She had no choice but to call a locksmith. But first she'd better call the school to let them know she was going to be late getting Ruby—again.

She tried the car door handle one more time, jiggling it up and down. "Aargh." She smacked the window again.

"Everything okay?" A man with his left arm in a sling, his right draped in shopping bags, frowned at her from the middle of the aisle.

"Yeah. Fine."

He stared her down. "You're sure? Because it kind of looks like you locked your keys in your car."

"I did." She sighed so hard it hurt. "It's my daughter's birthday."

The man gave her a strange look.

Right. There was no reason for him to care.

"Anyway—" She gestured toward the store. "I have to go call a . . ." Ugh. The word had escaped as she'd been talking. "Someone to unlock it."

"That could take hours." The guy moved closer. "I can get it open for you." Tension radiated from the set of the guy's jaw, and Bethany was torn between an instinct to run away and the need to get into her car.

"You're not going to break the window, are you?" Although if that was the quickest way to get her to Ruby, maybe it would be worth it.

The man made a sound she thought might have been a laugh, though there was no trace of humor in it and his mouth remained flat. "Hang tight a second. I'll be right back." He unloaded his bags on the trunk of her car, then jogged back toward the store, his slinged arm jouncing awkwardly at his side.

Bethany squinted after him until he reached the door, the beginning of a headache twinging behind her eyes. She took a few deep, controlled breaths in an attempt to stave it off. Her head could pound as much as it wanted *after* Ruby's party. But she refused to spoil her daughter's birthday any more than she already had.

Minutes passed. Bethany squinted toward the store. Maybe she should call someone after all.

She was just eyeing the guy's bags, trying to figure out what to do with them so she could go inside and ask to use a phone, when he emerged from the store. He jogged across the parking lot, his stride powerful despite the long metal rod in his good hand.

"Sorry. Took some convincing to get the manager to let me borrow these." He held up the rod and a screwdriver.

"What are you going to do?" A vague uneasiness crept over her. She'd never seen this man before, as far as she remembered—which admittedly wasn't saying much. But what if he was a con artist or something?

"Trust me. I've done this a thousand times."

"You've broken into cars a thousand times?" She pressed a hand to her stomach. Now what kind of mess had she gotten herself into? They seemed to follow her around these days. Her doctor said it was because the aneurysm had affected the impulse control center in her brain. "Maybe I should—"

"It's okay. I'm a cop." The way he said it seemed sincere, but Bethany eyed him. She didn't see a badge or a gun.

"Off duty," he said as if detecting her suspicion. He wedged the screwdriver between the roof and the top of the car door. "From Milwaukee."

"Oh." But that would be easy enough to lie about, wouldn't it? It wasn't like there was a way for her to check. She peered around the parking lot. It wasn't exactly crowded, but there were a few people getting into and out of cars. She supposed if he tried anything, she could yell for help.

Besides, by now she had to be at least fifteen minutes late getting Ruby. She didn't have any choice but to trust this guy.

He grunted as he pulled down on the screwdriver, opening a small gap at the top of the door. Bethany winced. If he damaged her car . . .

"Pass me the rod." He pointed his chin toward the metal rod he'd leaned against the car. Bethany picked it up and held it out to him.

He glanced at it, then at the arm that hung in a sling. "That's not going to work. Here." He took half a step back, still pushing down on the screwdriver with his other arm. "Come over here and slide the rod through this opening."

"Me?" How was she supposed to know how to do this?

The man made an impatient sound, and she stepped closer, catching a whiff of something slightly warm and woodsy and spicy that made her think of curling up in front of the fire on a winter day. Angling her body in front of his, she slid the metal rod in through the opening he'd created.

"Good. Now, see the unlock button on the side of the door?"

Bethany shifted to get a better view, accidentally bumping against his chest. An odd sensation went through her at the contact, and she scooted out of the way. "I see it."

"Good. You want to press that with the end of the rod."

"I don't think I—"

"You can do it." The quiet assurance in his words tugged at her, even though he'd obviously only said it so she'd try. He didn't even know her.

She pressed her lips together and concentrated on guiding the end of the rod toward the button.

She missed twice, but on the third attempt, she landed right in the middle of it. She'd never heard a sound as beautiful as the click of the doors unlocking.

"Yes!" She let go of the metal rod and grabbed the door handle, pulling it open—barely acknowledging the clang of the rod against the ground as it tumbled out.

"Thank you so much!" She threw her arms around the man, who grunted and didn't return the gesture. It took her a moment to realize it was probably because the hug was completely inappropriate. Stupid impulse control.

"Sorry." She let go and stepped back, then bent to pick up the rod.

The man nodded tightly as he took it. "You're welcome." He gathered up his bags, then started toward the store.

"Do you want me to take that stuff back inside?" It was the least she could do, and he surely had places to go too.

"That's okay. You have your daughter's party."

Bethany gasped. How did he know about that? Had she told him?

Probably.

She suddenly realized she'd never called the school to say she'd be late. She jumped into the car and started the engine. At the last second, she remembered to open her window and call out one more thank you.

The guy lifted a hand in acknowledgment and kept walking toward the store.

As she pulled out of the parking lot, Bethany gave him one last look in her rearview mirror.

"That's not the way I expected you to answer that prayer, Lord. But thank you."

Chapter 2

James plopped his purchases onto the table of his sister's farmhouse. That had been the most bizarre trip to the store of his life. The forgetful woman with the blonde hair and dark eyes had refused to leave his thoughts all the way home.

Only because it had felt good to be able to help someone again.

You always have to be the hero, don't you? His ex-wife Melissa's voice cut straight through the good feeling. At least this time helping hadn't cost him anything—if only because he didn't have anything left to lose.

"I see you bought out the entire supply of junk food in Hope Springs." His sister Emma eyed the bags as she bustled into the room.

"If you didn't insist on stocking your refrigerator with all rabbit food, I wouldn't have to." He pulled a bag of potato chips out and carried it to the pantry, wedging it into place on a shelf between a jar of homemade spaghetti sauce and a package that said chia seeds, whatever those were.

"You know it's not fair that you can eat like that and stay in shape, right?"

"Could have something to do with the ten miles I run a day." He'd started running after Sadie . . . and never stopped.

"Just you wait. By the time you leave, you're going to appreciate that health food can be just as delicious as junk food."

He snorted. By the time he left. If it was up to him, he wouldn't be here at all. Not that he didn't want to spend time with his sister—it must have been at least three years since he'd visited—but he'd only been here two days, and already he was going crazy. His job had been the only thing keeping him sane for the past five years. But when his captain had told him it was either take some of the years' worth of vacation he had accumulated or ride the desk for the next six weeks while his shoulder recovered, it hadn't really been a choice at all.

"How's the shoulder?" Emma plucked a package of beef jerky out of his bag and carried it across the room.

He rescued it just as she opened the lid of the trash can. "It's fine. I should be working. Give me something to do around here, at least."

"You know you're supposed to be recovering from a gunshot wound, right?"

"It was a graze. I'm fine."

Emma hit him with a hard stare worthy of their mother. He only supposed he should be grateful Mom didn't know anything about what had happened. Unless—

"You didn't tell Mom, did you?" There was no need to worry her, after everything she'd already been through.

Emma watched him the same way he watched a suspect during an interrogation. They'd both gotten that ability from Dad.

Finally, she relented and looked away. "No. But James, things can't go on like this."

"Like what?" He crossed his arms. He was just doing his job. Same as Dad had taught him.

"Captain said you didn't wait for backup."

"He called you?" Captain Burke may have been as close as a father to him, but that didn't give him the right to go interfering in James's life.

"He was Dad's best friend, James. He's worried about you."

"Whatever. He shouldn't have called you."

"It was either me or Mom," Emma said. "And anyway, he just wants to make sure you get the help you need. So do I."

"I knew I should have gone to Mexico," he muttered. Not that there was anything he wanted to do in Mexico. Or anywhere else. All he wanted to do was work. And the captain had made even that impossible.

Emma raised her hands. "Sorry. I'll back off. But it's been five years, James. You can't keep punishing yourself forever. Sadie wouldn't want—"

"Don't." They were not going there.

Emma pulled a package of chocolate candies out of his bags and slid some cans over in the cupboard to fit it. "I'm just saying, I'm here to talk, if you want. Or we have a great pastor at our church. I'm sure he—"

"Is that what you call backing off?" He wasn't going to talk about it. Ever.

Emma gave him a look but kept her lips shut.

"Just give me something to do before I go crazy."

"With one good arm?" But then Emma's face lit up. "I know. We're hosting a birthday party in—" She glanced at the clock on the oven. "About fifteen minutes. I could use some help with the pony rides."

James's stomach hardened. A birthday party meant kids. And kids meant remembering. "I'll pass, thanks."

"James, you can't avoid—"

"I'll muck out the horses tomorrow. And anything else you need done. Leave me a list. I'm going to go read." He grabbed the bag of chips out of the cupboard, then sprinted up the stairs to the guest room Emma had prepared for him. He was going to have to call and talk the captain into shortening his leave. Because there was no way he was going to survive here for six weeks.

James tossed his book onto the bed and stood. He'd been reading for an hour, and he wasn't sure he'd retained a word of the story.

His conversation with Emma had stirred up too many of the memories he worked so hard to forget every day. He'd tried thinking about other things: work, the new condo in Florida he'd helped Mom move into last year, even the woman from the store.

That thought was the only one that had provided a measure of distraction. He couldn't deny that she'd been beautiful, if a bit scatterbrained.

And affectionate.

That hug had been . . . warm and spontaneous and sweet.

And completely inappropriate.

But still, it had threatened to poke a pinhole into the Kevlar that he kept wrapped securely around his heart. Fortunately, she'd come to her senses and let go before that could happen.

He glanced out the window, wondering again if perhaps the party Emma was hosting was for the woman's daughter. After all, the woman had said she was on the way to her daughter's birthday party. And she'd purchased a horse necklace.

Or, well, he supposed he had purchased it.

He didn't know what had come over him. Only that the woman had looked so broken at the thought of disappointing her daughter. And the necklace she'd held—Sadie would have gone wild for it. Aunt Emma's house had always been her favorite place, and she'd thrown her arms around him and planted a big, wet kiss on his cheek when he'd said the next time they came here she could have her first horse ride.

James ripped his eyes away from the practice ring, where Emma was helping a young girl onto a pony.

His throat burned.

What he needed was some water.

He trundled downstairs to the kitchen, opening the fridge and pushing Emma's stash of vegetables aside to reach for a bottle of water. A movement caught his eye as he closed the fridge, and he was instantly on alert, spinning to face the intruder.

"Oh!" The woman from the store jumped backwards, bobbling the cake in her hands.

James lunged toward her just in time to steady the wobbling platter. He ignored the sear of pain that shot through his shoulder. "Sorry. I didn't mean to scare you."

The woman nodded. Well, that answered the question of whether this was her daughter's birthday party.

Slowly, he took his hands off hers, making sure she wasn't going to drop the cake before withdrawing all the way.

"Did your daughter like the necklace?"

"I . . . Yes." The woman looked startled. "Sorry. Who are you?"

Nice one, James. "I'm James. Emma's brother."

"I didn't know Emma had a brother."

"Oh." There wasn't much else to say to that. He didn't suppose Emma went around talking about her brother to random clients. "Anyway." He held up the bottle of water. "I was just getting this."

"Okay." The woman stared at him for a moment, then glided out of the house with the cake in front of her.

James watched her blonde hair ripple behind her, then let out a breath. There was something about her that raised a whole lot of questions in his head. Like why had she seemed surprised when he'd asked about the necklace? And why hadn't she acknowledged that he'd come to her rescue—twice—at the store? Not that he wanted to be thanked or anything. But she'd hugged him there and now acted like she'd never seen him before.

He ignored the tiny spikes of warmth that went through him at the memory of the hug. It didn't matter how much she intrigued him; she had a kid. And even if he had been willing to risk his heart on a woman again, he'd never risk it on another child.

Chapter 3

"Hurry up, Rubes." Bethany slathered peanut butter onto a piece of bread, then swiped at the alarm on her phone. She hated its incessant beeping. But it was the best way she'd found to make sure she didn't forget any part of her daily schedule.

Not that it meant she ever managed to get Ruby to school on time.

"I can't find any socks," Ruby shouted from her room.

"Check the dryer," Bethany called.

Ruby skidded into the room, their cat Mrs. Whiskers following close behind.

"Hurry," Bethany urged again, grabbing another piece of bread for the jelly.

But Ruby stopped in front of the counter and made a face at the sandwich Bethany was preparing.

"What?" Bethany glanced down to make sure she hadn't messed it up. But she was pretty confident she could handle making a PBJ.

"Do you think I could have a turkey sandwich tomorrow?" Ruby asked.

"Of course. Just—"

"Remind you," Ruby chimed in, continuing toward the basement laundry room.

"Right." Except something about the way Ruby said it bothered Bethany. "Wait. Ruby. Did you already ask me for a turkey sandwich before?"

"It's no big deal, Mom," Ruby called up the steps. "PBJ is great."

Bethany let out a long sigh and tucked the PBJ in the fridge. She could always have it for her own lunch. She shoved leftovers out of the way to find the turkey and cheese and rushed to make a new sandwich. If she hurried, Ruby would only be a few minutes late. And at least she'd have the lunch she wanted.

Ruby's feet pounded up the basement stairs. "There's nothing in the dryer."

Bethany closed her eyes. "I thought I did laundry yesterday."

She flipped her notebook open—the one she used to keep track of tasks she didn't do on a daily basis. "Laundry" was written on yesterday's page. But it wasn't checked off. She tried to remember what had stopped her from doing it, but like most recent events, all she could picture was a blank canvas.

"Can you wear a pair of mine? Or dig some out of your hamper?" She cringed. What kind of mom told her kid to wear dirty socks? Or forgot what she wanted for lunch? Or couldn't get her to school on time even once a week?

"Sure." Ruby offered her typical good-natured smile, and Bethany was reminded of her own mother's easygoing nature. Her gut clenched. It was her fault that Ruby would never know her grandparents.

She tried to stamp out the thought. Why was it that painful memories from her past were always too eager to push their way forward, when the moments in the present she wanted to hold onto refused to solidify into memories?

"Okay. I'm ready." Ruby reappeared from the hallway, wearing a pair of striped knee socks.

"You used to wear those all the time."

Ruby's eyes widened. "You remember that? Are you getting your memory back?"

"I—" Bethany's heart quickened. Could it be? She hadn't given her comment much thought—it had just come out. But the image in her mind was of a much younger Ruby wearing those socks. "I don't think so. Dr. Kellar would say it was a long-term memory. But I'm glad I have it." She offered Ruby what she hoped came across as a bright smile.

But Ruby's shoulders fell. "Oh."

Bethany held her smile firmly in place. "But I know how we can make a new memory." She pulled her phone out of her pocket. "Say memories."

"Can we just go, Mom? I'm going to be late." Ruby slung her backpack over her shoulder.

"First say memories," Bethany insisted. She wasn't going to let every moment of the rest of her life pass her by just because she couldn't remember them.

"Memories," Ruby obliged.

Bethany couldn't tell if her daughter's grimace was supposed to be an attempt at a smile. But she kept the picture and tucked her phone in her pocket. "All right. Let's get you to school." She swept her notebook off the counter and flipped the page. Today she had—

She gasped.

The PTO meeting. She'd completely forgotten about it. And it started in—she glanced at the clock again—ten minutes ago.

She opened the door, waving Ruby through. But before Ruby got a toe out the door, Mrs. Whiskers charged past her, diving into the flower bed.

"Mrs. Whiskers!" They didn't have time for this.

"I'll get her, Mom." Ruby stepped outside, but Bethany grabbed her arm to stop her.

"It's muddy. I'll do it. You get in the car."

Ruby shrugged but obeyed, and Bethany tiptoed into the mucky flower bed, careful to avoid the puddles between the bushes.

"Come here, kitty." But as she reached for Mrs. Whiskers, the cat sprang toward the rose bush. Bethany lunged for her, sending a spray of mud into her shoe and up her leg. A thorn from the rose bush caught at her hand, but she pulled free and snagged the cat.

Holding Mrs. Whiskers unceremoniously out in front of her to avoid getting dirtier, she marched to the house and tossed the cat in the door. She glanced down at her jeans. Spatters of mud traveled up one leg, and her sock was drenched. But Ruby was already so late. Bethany was just going to have to go through her day like this.

Shoving her hair out of her face, she dropped into the driver's seat.

"Is Mrs. Whiskers okay?" Ruby asked from the back seat.

"She's fine." Bethany gritted her teeth and forced herself to take a long, slow breath before backing out of the driveway.

Every time she got in the car, she worried all over again that she was going to have another aneurysm while driving. She didn't remember last time, but poor Ruby did. Bethany could only thank the Lord that he'd kept Ruby safe when their car had gone off the road. And pray that it didn't happen again.

Thankfully, Ruby's school wasn't far. And the route was one of the things her messed up memory allowed her to retain. But by the time she'd parked the car and taken Ruby to the office to get yet another tardy pass—the school secretary didn't even ask for an explanation anymore—she was a good 30 minutes late for the PTO meeting.

She bit her lip, debating whether to skip it. It wasn't like she contributed anything anyway. But she used to be super involved in it—before the aneurysm. And she was determined to remain just as involved in Ruby's life and school. Straightening her shoulders, she requested a visitor badge, then marched down the hallway to the library, where the meetings were held.

She tried to slip into the back unnoticed, but there weren't many people here today, and it felt like every head in the room swiveled in her direction. Bethany ducked her chin and slid into a seat, tucking her mud-splattered pant leg under the chair.

"Glad you could join us," the woman at the front of the room called. Though her voice was kind enough, Bethany still heard the judgment behind it. She tried to come up with the woman's name. She should know it, since their daughters were in the same dressage class, but it refused to come to her.

To the room at large, the woman said, "So Sabrina and Amy are going to take care of the bake sale, and Justine said she'd work on teacher appreciation gifts. Marybeth, you're in charge of the concession stand for baseball season. And I'll speak to local businesses about donating items for the silent auction."

Bethany's head spun just listening to all the responsibilities these women were taking on. She'd had a hard enough time just getting to the meeting—late.

"Tiffany?" One of the women asked, and Bethany nearly shouted out loud. Yes! Tiffany was the woman's name. Fortunately, her impulse control seemed to be functioning properly at the moment, and she remained silent.

"Yes?" Tiffany smiled at the other woman.

"Are we going to talk about the field day? I understand Tess isn't going to be able to run it this year."

"That was next on my agenda," Tiffany said. "And you're right. Tess has decided to step back this year to focus more on some of her other volunteer work. So if anyone else wants to step up and organize the field day . . ."

She scanned the room, skimming right over Bethany.

Something jerked Bethany's arm into the air. "I'll do it."

Tiffany's gaze swung back to her, and she made a small surprised sound. Her mouth was round, eyes wide. "Are you sure? I mean, you have time?"

Bethany resisted snorting. Some days it felt like all she had was time. Sure, she helped with Cam's landscaping business, but that was more busywork than anything. More to give her something to do than to help him. Other than that, the biggest thing on her schedule was helping to muck out the stalls at Emma's stables once a week to help pay for Ruby's dressage lessons. Not that her brother hadn't offered to pay for them, but she already felt bad enough taking a salary from him for the little help she provided.

"I have plenty of time," she assured Tiffany.

"Um. Okay." Tiffany sounded uncertain as her eyes traveled to the other women in the room. "Do you want someone else to help? It's a big job."

"No thanks. I've got it." If all these women could handle their responsibilities on their own, so could she.

"Okay. Great." Tiffany's smile looked like it had been smeared onto her face. "Then I guess if we don't have further business, we can adjourn."

Bethany pulled out her phone and started to tap a reminder note. A bubble of doubt worked its way through her. How on earth was she going to do this?

Before she'd finished typing, Tiffany swooped down on her. "This might be helpful," She held out a thick manila folder. "It's Tess's notes—about where to get the food and equipment, what to set up where, how to collect tickets, all that stuff."

"Thanks." Bethany swallowed and took the folder, the bubble of doubt growing to a full-out balloon. She took a breath. She just had to be organized, break it down into little tasks, that was all.

"If you have any questions or need anything—"

"I've got it. Thanks." Bethany didn't mean to sound curt, but Tiffany wasn't asking any of the others if they needed help.

"All right." Tiffany's smile skirted the edges of genuine. "Thanks again for inviting Kimberly to Ruby's birthday party."

"Of course." Bethany tried to recall what Kimberly had given Ruby as a gift, so she could thank Tiffany, but she drew a blank.

"I'm having a birthday party for Kimberly in a couple weeks. I hope Ruby can make it."

"I'm sure she'd love that." Bethany relaxed a little. She didn't know Tiffany well, but she seemed nice enough. It wasn't her fault that her perfect hair and perfect makeup and perfect parenting made Bethany feel like a failure.

"Great. I'm taking the girls to the indoor water park in Green Bay. I thought we'd stay two nights so they can really enjoy it."

Bethany blinked at Tiffany. Green Bay? Two nights? Ruby had never even been away from home for one night, aside from at Cam and Kayla's. "I'll have to—"

"Sorry. I have to catch Amy before she leaves. I'll text you the details." Tiffany was already scurrying away as she finished the sentence.

Bethany sighed, glancing at the thick folder in her hands.

Her impulse control had chosen a great time to disappear.

What did she know about organizing a field day? She'd be lucky if she remembered to buy a ticket for herself, let alone got everything set up for everyone else.

She chewed her lip, flipping through the folder. Maybe she should give it back to Tiffany, tell her she didn't have time after all.

She closed the folder and took a step toward Tiffany. But just then the alarm on her phone blared from her pocket. She snatched at it, heart thudding as the eyes of everyone in the room flew to her. She'd meant to silence her phone before the meeting, but in the rush she must have forgotten. Big surprise.

It took two attempts to silence the annoying beeps. Bethany peeked at the screen, then at Tiffany, who was watching her with a sympathetic smile.

She looked back at the screen.

Next up on her schedule was mucking out stalls at the stables.

So she could either go shovel manure or go tell Tiffany she couldn't do the field day.

With one more glance at the folder in her hand, she marched toward the door.

She'd take care of the manure now.

And figure out a way to handle the field day later.

Chapter 4

"James Henry Wood, put that pitchfork down right now. And get your arm back in the sling."

James rolled his eyes at his sister's command and stuffed the pitchfork into the next section of hay, bouncing it a few times to sift out the soiled portions. He ignored the sharp pull through his shoulder as he lifted the dirty bedding into the wheelbarrow that he'd positioned in the aisle outside the stall.

"I told you, I need to work."

"And I told you, my friend Bethany is coming to muck the stalls today."

James snorted. "If that's how you treat your friends, I'd hate to be your enemy."

Now Emma was the one rolling her eyes. "She does it to pay for her daughter's dressage lessons."

"Just credit my work to her then." What did it matter to him who got credit for the work?

"I would, but she won't accept that. She wants to earn it herself."

James could respect that. But what else was he going to do with his day?

Emma had encouraged him more than once to take the horses out. But every time he considered saddling one up, all he could think of was how badly Sadie had wanted to ride.

"When is she coming?" he asked Emma.

"Should be here any minute now."

"I'll save some stalls for her."

Emma sighed. "Will you at least put the sling back on?"

"Fine." He maneuvered the uncomfortable contraption into place. "Happy?"

"I'd be happier if you were happy. But this will have to do for now. I have to run up to the Ploughman's farm to pick up some hay. Just don't scare Bethany, okay?"

James made an impatient sound. He had no intention of talking to this Bethany, let alone scaring her.

Emma watched him for another minute, then strode out of the barn.

James pulled in a breath of the sweet-sharp scent of hay and animals and waited until the echo of her footsteps had faded before he pulled his arm out of the sling. Dull pain pulsed through his shoulder. But pain was good. It kept his mind on the here and now.

Outside, a horse nickered softly from the pasture. The sound had frightened Sadie the first time she'd heard it, and she'd climbed into James's arms, trusting him to keep her safe.

He bent and scraped his pitchfork harder against the ground. He needed to work, not remember. He threw himself into the rhythm of finishing the stall, then stepped into the alley to fetch a fresh bale of straw.

But he jerked to a stop as his eyes fell on the woman standing there. It was the woman from the store. And the birthday party.

"What are you doing here?" The question may have come out more like an interrogation, but the strange woman had popped into his head at the oddest times over the past few days, and he had been working hard to banish thoughts of her.

"That's my job." She gestured to the pitchfork, propped against the wall next to him.

"I guess that means you're Bethany." He didn't know why he liked having a name to go with her face. "Emma said you were coming. Don't worry. I left plenty of stalls for you. I just thought I'd help out. It's either that or go crazy with nothing to do. I hope you don't mind."

James closed his mouth at the look the woman was giving him. Was he babbling? The last time he'd strung that many words together had probably been when he'd argued with the captain not to make him take this time off.

"Who are you?" Bethany asked.

James blinked at her. He was sure he'd introduced himself the other night. "James. Emma's brother." When she showed no sign of recognition, he added, "From the store. With the necklace." He lifted a hand to the strap of his sling, as if it were a necklace. "And your daughter's birthday party. I almost made you drop the cake." *All right, stop.* It was starting to sound like he'd kept detailed records of all their interactions.

"Right." But the tone of her voice rang false.

She didn't remember him at all.

Ouch. But it wasn't like it mattered.

Bethany watched him a moment longer, then disappeared into the next stall, emerging with the water bucket and feed tub, which she placed to the side. Then, without sparing him a glance, she marched to the far end of the barn, returning with a pitchfork and shovel.

James ducked into his stall, spreading the straw as he heard the scraping of the shovel next door. When an even layer of bedding covered the floor, he stepped into the aisle, noting that Bethany had scooted the wheelbarrow to a spot between their stalls.

"I'm moving the wheelbarrow," he called, sliding it to the far side of the stall she was working in, so he could reach it from the other side. Bethany didn't reply but emerged into the alley to deposit a fresh load of soiled straw into the wheelbarrow. He supposed he'd take that as confirmation that she'd heard him.

He fell into the rhythm of the work: Bend. Scoop. Toss. Bend. Scoop. Toss.

From the stall next door, he heard Bethany's movements, matching his own. After twenty minutes or so, he finished the stall and emerged into the alley. Bethany came out of her stall at the same time.

They both eyed the over-heaping wheelbarrow. Bethany made the first move toward it, but James shook his head.

He had no doubt she was perfectly capable of moving it, but what kind of man made a woman push a pile of manure? "I'll get it."

"Aren't you supposed to be wearing that?" She pointed to his sling.

He frowned. He didn't need another sister. "No."

Bethany shrugged and ambled down the alley to the next stall that needed to be cleaned.

James grabbed the wheelbarrow handles, wincing at the pull on his wound. On his way past the stall Bethany had entered, he couldn't help peeking inside. Her hair fell over her face as she worked, but her movements were fluid and graceful.

The wheelbarrow hit something and lurched to the side. With a sharp tug, he attempted to right it, sending a bullet of pain through his shoulder—and a crash of metal to the floor. The soiled contents spilled across the concrete.

"Are you— Oh." Bethany emerged from the stall and looked from James to the pile of manure and dirty straw, her eyes widening and a hand shooting up to cover her mouth. But she wasn't quick enough to stifle the giggle. "Sorry." She giggled again and clapped a second hand to her mouth. After a moment, she pulled her hands away, revealing a stunningly big smile. "I didn't mean to laugh. It's just—" She shook her head. "I'm always afraid that will happen to me."

"And has it ever?" He righted the wheelbarrow, then walked over to the post where he'd propped his shovel.

She watched him as if she were deep in thought. "Not that I remember," she finally answered, before picking up her own shovel and helping him scoop the mess into the wheelbarrow.

"Trust me, I don't think it's the kind of thing you'd forget." He grunted as a fresh shot of pain stabbed at his shoulder. Bethany gave a pointed look at his sling but didn't say anything.

James kept scooping.

It only took a minute to fill the wheelbarrow again.

"Maybe I should take it this time." Bethany's smile hadn't diminished at all as they'd worked.

James snorted. His pride wasn't exactly wounded, but he wasn't going to admit defeat. "I've got it."

By the time he returned with the empty wheelbarrow, Bethany had pulled the food and water buckets out of all the remaining stalls and was standing at the ready with her pitchfork.

As the morning went on, they made their way down the stalls, working next to each other, pausing to empty the wheelbarrow when it got full. Neither of them spoke, and yet the silence wasn't oppressive. It was more like . . . Well, he didn't know what it was like. Only that it left him feeling less weighed down than he had in years.

"Thanks for the help," Bethany said after they'd cleaned up their shovels and pitchforks. "This usually takes me all morning."

He shrugged. "I needed something to do. If Emma had her way, I'd just sit around here all day 'recovering.'" He made air quotes around the last word. "I'm not so great at sitting still." That's what Melissa hadn't understood when he'd returned to work almost right away after Sadie. . . . She'd wanted him to stay home and just sit with her. But what purpose was there in that? The only thing sitting did was give him time to remember, to hurt. And that didn't benefit anyone.

Bethany gestured at his sling. "What happened to your arm?"

He hesitated. Emma had said not to scare her. "Got hurt at work."

"What do you do?"

"I'm a detective." And a good one. Who should be on the job. Not standing here talking to some strange woman.

I could think of worse ways to spend your time, his heart prompted. James ignored it, but for some reason he couldn't make himself turn away.

An alarm sounded on Bethany's phone, and she pulled it out of her pocket. "Sorry." She read the screen, then looked up, seeming embarrassed. "I have to go."

"Okay." He almost said, "See you later," but then realized it would probably be best if he didn't see her again. So he turned and walked away.

Chapter 5

Bethany groaned as her alarm woke her from a dream. She didn't remember it, exactly, only that it had left her with a pleasant, warm feeling. One that made her want to stay in bed and dream a little longer.

But the alarm was insistent—and annoying. She rolled over to turn it off, scrolling through the other notifications that had come up on her phone. There were a few emails, a reminder to take her medication, and a calendar alert that it was Easter Sunday. She blinked at the screen a few times. Was it really Easter?

A vague sense of unease settled over her, like there was something she was forgetting. The feeling had become her normal state, but she still hated it.

She reached for her notebook to double-check she hadn't missed anything.

There it was, at the bottom of yesterday's schedule: *Hide Easter eggs.*

Had she done that?

She tried to remember. Tried to picture stuffing the colorful plastic eggs and finding the perfect hiding spots for them.

But she knew she hadn't.

Ruby had had a dressage competition all day yesterday, and by the time Bethany had gotten home, made dinner, and gotten Ruby to bed, she'd had a terrible headache. So she'd showered and gone to bed herself.

Without checking her notebook one last time.

Nausea rolled over her.

What kind of mother forgot to hide Easter eggs?

Maybe Ruby was still asleep, and she could hide them right now. But it took only a moment of listening to pick up the sound of the TV.

There was no way she could sneak past her daughter to get the plastic eggs from the basement—not to mention that she had nothing to fill them with.

Ugh. She covered her face. Did she have to go out there and explain to her ten-year-old daughter why there would be no Easter this year?

Unless . . . Maybe there was an Easter egg hunt somewhere in town today. She picked up her phone and did a quick search. But it seemed everyone had done their egg hunts last weekend. She was about to turn off her phone when another calendar alert popped onto the screen: *Brunch. Emma's. 11:00.*

"Thank you," she whispered, then tapped out a quick text to her friend. *Any chance you're planning to do an Easter egg hunt? I completely forgot.*

The reply came quickly: *Happy Easter! I didn't have one planned, but I know I have some plastic eggs around here. I'll hide them before church.*

Bethany let out a long breath. *You're a lifesaver.*

She took her time getting dressed, not quite ready to face her daughter yet. She might have come up with a backup plan, but Ruby was a bright girl. She'd likely see right through it.

Finally, she couldn't put it off any longer. She had to get Ruby some breakfast and make sure she was ready for church.

"Happy Easter," she said brightly as she entered the living room and turned off the TV. "Time to get ready for church."

"Happy Easter." Ruby stood and stretched. "Are you making cinnamon rolls like you always do?"

Cinnamon rolls. That was the other thing she'd forgotten.

She focused on keeping her smile in place. "I didn't want to ruin our appetite for lunch at Miss Emma's. We're going to do our Easter egg hunt there too. I thought it'd be more fun on the farm. Don't you think?"

Ruby shrugged, looking away. "I'm ten, Mom. I don't need to hunt for Easter eggs."

"Of course you do." Bethany dropped a kiss on top of her daughter's head as she moved toward the kitchen. "How about some cereal before church?"

She could feel Ruby watching her, but she didn't turn around. "Sure, Mom. Cereal sounds good." She heard Ruby shuffle down the hallway and forced herself to take another deep breath as she pulled bowls and spoons from the cupboards.

Easter wasn't about the food or the eggs. She knew that. And Ruby knew it too.

Still, she tried to imagine any of her friends, any of the moms of Ruby's classmates, anyone, forgetting to make the day special for their child. But she couldn't come up with a single person who would—except herself.

"What are you doing?" James paused in the doorway after his morning run, watching his sister bustle around the kitchen. Though the day had dawned with frost on the grass, sweat sucked his t-shirt to his skin under his sweatshirt, and his shoulder throbbed. He subtly tucked his arm back into his sling before Emma looked up.

"Happy Easter!" Emma's smile reflected joy. "He is risen!"

James grunted. He knew the traditional response. But any reason he'd had to worship God had been stolen from him five years ago. "Those Easter eggs?"

Emma rolled her eyes. "No. They're Arbor Day eggs." She pointed at a pile of bright wrappers on the table. "Make yourself useful."

"Huh?"

"Stuff those in the eggs, would you? I think another twenty or so should be good."

"Hey." He stepped to the table. "Is that my candy?"

"Relax. It's for a good cause."

"What cause?" James tucked a chocolate into a yellow egg and snapped it shut.

"I'm having some friends over for brunch after church, and we're going to have an Easter egg hunt for the kids."

"And you decided to wait until the last minute so you'd have to steal my candy?" That didn't sound like his sister, the consummate over-planner.

"Would you let the candy go? I'll buy you some more next time I go to the store. Anyway, the egg hunt was a last minute addition." She hesitated. "You know my friend Bethany?"

Something in James pinged, but he ignored it. "The one who helps with the mucking?" Working in the barn on his own the last couple of days had felt oddly lonely—but he wasn't about to ask Emma when Bethany would be back. He stuffed a piece of candy into an egg and snapped it shut.

"Yeah." Emma slid a few more eggs his way. "She forgot to hide eggs for her daughter. So I said I could hide some here."

"Ah." *Look, Daddy, I found a blue one. That's your favorite color.* James shook off the memory and snapped the egg shut harder than he'd meant to. He stared at the crack that now splintered one side.

"Here." Emma took the egg from him and swept the candy out, tucking it into a new egg. "So what did you think of Bethany?" she asked with a sly grin.

He shrugged, keeping his face blank. It was obvious where this was going. But he wasn't interested in playing along. "She seems like a hard worker. Quiet. Maybe a little scatterbrained."

Emma chucked an egg at him. It bounced off his shoulder and fell to the floor.

"Hey. What was that for?"

"She's not scatterbrained," Emma said. "She had an aneurysm a couple years ago. She almost died."

James looked up sharply. That was not what he'd expected his sister to say. "Is she all right?" He pictured her mucking stalls and carrying around water pails. She'd seemed so capable. And yet a wave of protectiveness went through him. His ex-wife would have called it his hero complex.

"Physically, yes," Emma answered. "But she has some short-term memory issues. And some language difficulties. I think she gets frustrated sometimes. But she's come a long way." Emma closed the last egg, then swept them all into a big basket.

"Wow. I had no idea." He tried to digest the information. "What did she used to be like?"

Emma shrugged. "I didn't meet her until she was in a coma after the aneurysm."

James blinked at his sister. She'd always been friendly, but . . . "You befriended someone in a coma?"

"Of course not." Emma laughed. "My friend Kayla did. She was the first on the scene when Bethany's car went off the road. Anyway, one thing led to another and now she's married to Bethany's brother."

"Wow. That's crazy."

"Crazier things have happened." Emma studied him. "You know . . . Bethany's an amazing woman. You should really get to know her."

James shook his head. That was one crazy thing that was not going to happen. "So where are you going to hide those?" He nodded to the basket of eggs on her arm.

"Outside. I think." Her eyes went to the clock. "But I'll have to do it fast. Church starts in half an hour."

"Here." He held out a hand for the basket. "You go. I'll hide them."

Emma's face fell. "You're not coming to church?"

He didn't mean for his laugh to sound bitter. "No."

"James—" Emma reached for him, but he pulled away, grabbing the basket from her.

"I'm not going to change my mind, Emma." God had closed the doors of the church to him the day he'd buried his daughter. And as far as he was concerned they could remain closed forever.

"Maybe not today." Emma pecked him on the cheek. "But I pray that someday God will change your mind for you. And your heart."

James didn't bother answering. There was little to no chance of that happening. Ever.

He followed Emma out the door and watched her get into her truck. "Thanks, James," she called. "I know Bethany will appreciate it. And don't hide them anywhere too hard." With a wave, she closed her door and started down the long driveway.

James pulled the first egg out of the basket, surveying the expansive property for a good hiding spot—and trying not to think about Emma's parting statement that Bethany would appreciate this. He wasn't doing this for her. He was only doing it for . . . Well, he didn't have a good reason for doing it. But it wasn't for her.

As she sang along with the closing strains of "I Know that My Redeemer Lives," Bethany closed her eyes and let the words wash over her.

This. This was what mattered.

Not whether she'd hidden the Easter eggs. Not whether she'd made cinnamon rolls. Not even whether she ever regained her full abilities. What mattered was Jesus.

That was something she needed to do a better job of remembering. In fact . . . as the service ended, Bethany pulled out her phone and tapped out a quick reminder: *Jesus matters most.* She set it for every day at 6:00 a.m. There. Now she couldn't forget.

Tucking her phone into her pocket, she gave her daughter a hug, then wished her friends a Happy Easter as they all filed into the lobby.

"We're all set," Emma whispered as she sidled up to Bethany, careful not to let Ruby overhear.

Bethany offered her friend a smile she hoped conveyed the depth of her gratitude. She wondered again how God had managed to bless her with such an amazing group of friends. Her first years in Hope Springs, she'd been so careful to keep to herself so she wouldn't end up with the wrong sort of people again—people who would lead her right back into temptation. But then she'd had an aneurysm and been in a coma—and when she'd woken up, she'd been surrounded by not only the brother she'd thought she'd lost forever but a whole army of friends he—or rather, his now-wife—had managed to amass for her. She didn't know what she would have done over the past two years if it hadn't been for all of them. She wished sometimes that she didn't have to rely quite so heavily on others—but today wasn't one of those days. Today, she was simply grateful.

"I hope you're ready to hunt for eggs," Emma said to Ruby. "I had my brother hide them, and he's an expert."

Ruby offered Emma a polite smile. "I'm too old to hunt for Easter eggs."

"Ruby! Miss Emma went through a lot of work—"

"It's okay, Bethany," Emma said gently, then turned to Ruby. "I know *you're* too old to hunt for eggs, but what about Ella Lynn and Liliana and Matthias? They're going to need help from you and the rest of the big kids."

Ruby's smile turned genuine. "I can help them. Hey, Liliana," she cooed, moving toward the toddler in their friend Violet's arms. "You want me to help you find some Easter eggs?"

"You're a genius," Bethany whispered to Emma. "Thank you." She pushed down the feeling that she should have been the one who knew how to make the Easter egg hunt appealing to her daughter.

Emma squeezed her arm. "Come on. Let's go get this hunt started. I told my brother not to hide them anywhere too difficult, but if he's anything like my dad, it could take all day to find the eggs."

Bethany laughed. Her dad had always enjoyed searching out the hardest spots to hide eggs too. Like the year he'd hidden Cam's basket in the trunk of the car. Dad had chuckled for days over that one. Bethany's laugh dried as a wave of regret swept over her. That must have been the last year they'd celebrated Easter before her first trip to rehab. An ache opened in her chest as she wished she could get that time back—wished Mom and Dad could be here to celebrate Easter with the granddaughter they'd never gotten to meet.

"Happy Easter." An elbow nudged her, and she grinned at her brother, his greeting chasing away the sad thoughts. She'd see her parents again someday in heaven. And right now, she could be grateful that her relationship with Cam had been restored.

"Happy Easter. Where's Kayla?" But she spied her sister-in-law directing her wheelchair toward them. Cam stepped aside for her, and Bethany bent to hug Kayla, then set a hand on her sister-in-law's belly. "How much longer?"

She probably asked every time she saw them, but Kayla practically glowed as she answered, "Only two more weeks."

"You're going to be such a good mom." It didn't matter that Kayla used a wheelchair. She was good at absolutely everything she did.

Behind Kayla, Cam cleared his throat.

"And you're going to be a good dad." Bethany stood and slugged his arm.

"That's all I wanted to hear." Cam gave a satisfied nod and rested a hand on his wife's shoulder.

Bethany's eyes lingered on them for a moment. The kind of happiness they'd found together was . . . something she didn't need.

Besides, she was happy already. With her friends, her family, and her daughter. She didn't need anything else.

"Come on, Rubes." She moved toward her daughter. "Let's go find some eggs."

Chapter 6

James stepped out of the shower and scrubbed the towel over his face until his freshly shaved cheeks were raw. Hiding the Easter eggs had been easy enough, except that with every egg, a barrage of memories had slapped at him. The time they'd taken Sadie to the zoo to see the Easter bunny—who had scared her when he'd taken off his head. The first time she'd tried to eat a hard-boiled egg—with the shell on. The time she'd thrown a tantrum right in the middle of church on Easter Sunday—and the way the pastor had joked with them after the service and even given Sadie a jellybean.

He tossed the towel on the floor and pulled on his clothes. Should he have gone to church with Emma? After all, it *was* Easter.

But he shook his head against the thought.

He'd shown up for God every single Easter—nearly every single Sunday—his entire life. And the one time he'd asked God to show up for him, he'd been answered with a big fat *no*. And with that one no, God had destroyed James's life.

James pulled on a pair of jeans and a flannel shirt, picked up his dirty running clothes and his towel, and stepped into the hallway. A strange rattling came from the kitchen, and James tossed his dirty clothes into the guest room, then charged down the stairs to let his sister know he'd successfully completed his mission. "You can call me the master egg—" He spluttered to a stop. It wasn't Emma in the kitchen.

It was Bethany. His heart did a weird sort of patter against his ribs.

Because of what Emma had told him about Bethany's struggles. No other reason.

Bethany glanced over her shoulder at him, then turned back to the cupboard. "Sorry. I was looking for the . . ." Her hands stilled, and she dropped her head to stare at the counter.

James watched her. Was she going to finish that sentence?

"Band-aids," she burst out triumphantly, as if the word had just come to her. "My daughter has a bad habit of scratching at her scabs."

He should turn around and go back upstairs to hide in his room for the duration. But instead his feet led him toward her. He opened the cupboard next to her and pulled out the box of band-aids.

"Thanks." She blinked at him. "I'm Bethany."

"Yeah." He should have asked Emma what to do when face-to-face with Bethany's memory issues. "I'm James."

She studied him. "You've told me that before, haven't you?"

He shrugged. "It's no big deal." At least maybe this meant she also didn't remember him tipping over the wheelbarrow full of manure the other day.

The door behind Bethany burst open, and Emma flew through. Her eyes skipped quickly from James to Bethany, and she grinned. James took a step backwards.

"Good. You found them," Emma said to Bethany. Then to James, "Come on. The kids are about to start hunting for the eggs. We need you to make sure they don't miss any."

James shook his head. That hadn't been part of the deal. Emma knew the rule. No kids.

"You hid the eggs?" Bethany's smile was gentle and grateful, and it seemed to hold a strange power to make James speechless.

"Come on," Emma repeated. Bethany smiled at him again and turned toward the door. He felt his feet pulling him after her.

But the moment he stepped outside, he knew it had been a mistake. There were kids *everywhere*.

He tried to retreat, but Emma was there, blocking his escape. She took his elbow and led him forward.

"Everyone." Her voice carried across the yard. "This is my brother James."

The group of adults and kids that had been scattered near the porch all peered toward him. James raised an awkward hand, said "hi," then tried to wriggle away. But Emma didn't let go of him.

"You already know Bethany. And that's her daughter Ruby, one of my best dressage riders." Emma pointed to a young girl who embodied the phrase "spitting image of her mother."

James's throat tightened as he nodded in the girl's general direction. Everyone had said Sadie had his eyes, but the rest of her features she'd gotten from her mother.

"And this is Bethany's brother Cam and his wife Kayla," Emma continued, pointing to a tall man whose hands rested on the shoulders of a pregnant woman in a wheelchair. They both smiled at him.

He nodded back. He didn't need to know who all these people were. It wasn't like he was going to be spending any time with them.

"And then that's Kayla's brother Nate." Emma insisted on continuing the introductions. "And his wife Violet and their little Liliana."

The toddler waved a pudgy fist at James. He looked away, the slice of his swallow sharp against the memories of Sadie's pudgy arms around his neck.

He didn't know how much longer he could handle being out here.

But Emma pointed to another happy family. "And this is Sophie and Spencer and their twins Rylan and Aubrey. And Spencer's brother Tyler, his wife Isabel, and . . . Where are the kids?"

Tyler laughed, pointing toward the side of the house. "Playing with the kittens. Where else?"

James shifted on his feet. From the time she'd turned four, Sadie had asked almost every day if she could get a cat. He'd always answered that she could have one when she was older. Except, she'd never . . .

He forced his attention to Emma. He still didn't care who these people were. But it gave him something to focus on other than the jackhammer pulverizing his heart.

"That's Austin and Leah. And their son Jackson." Emma pointed to a tall young man. "He's in his second year of college." The adults all beamed at the kid, who ducked his head.

"Let's see. Who did I miss?" Emma glanced around the yard.

"It's fine, Emma. I'm sure everyone wants to get on with the party. Not stand around and wait to be introduced to me." He took a step toward the house, reaching subtly behind him for the doorknob.

"That's where you're wrong." A guy with a toddler propped in his arm stepped forward and held out his hand. "I'm Dan. This little guy is Matthias, and that's my wife Jade and our daughter Hope." He nodded toward a woman who offered James a warm smile. The girl's smile was equally as warm. James ducked his head but shook the guy's hand.

"What about Grace and Levi?" The woman Emma had introduced as Violet asked. "I thought Grace would have sung at church this morning, but I didn't see them."

"They went to Tennessee to celebrate Easter with her family. And Ethan and Ariana took Joy to Disney."

A car turned in at the end of the driveway. "There's Jared and Peyton and Ella Lynn," Emma said, letting go of James's arm as she stepped forward.

James let out a breath. Finally, he could escape.

He made a quick, stealthy turn and disappeared inside, easing the door closed behind him as he heard someone—it sounded like Bethany's voice, he thought—asking everyone to gather for a picture.

He thundered up the stairs, pretending he didn't hear his sister calling behind him.

He spent the next three hours reading and trying to ignore the joyous sounds—and delicious smells—drifting up the stairs. Part of him said he was being stupid not to go down there and fill a plate. But the smarter part of him said it wasn't worth the risk. He could eat later—whatever the loud rumblings from his stomach might say in protest.

It took forever, but the chatter downstairs at last grew quieter, and he heard the sounds of car doors closing and engines starting. He waited a good fifteen minutes after he heard the last car pull away to emerge from his room. Pausing to listen at the top of the stairs, he heard the sound of water running from the faucet but no voices.

If having to help Emma with the dishes was the price he had to pay for leftovers, he'd gladly do it. And he'd even put up with a lecture about how he shouldn't have disappeared earlier. As long as she'd saved him some mashed potatoes.

"It's about—" For the second time that day, he clamped his mouth shut as he reached the kitchen and found not Emma, but Bethany, her hands immersed in a sink full of dishwater.

He stopped and looked around. Who else was still here? "Sorry. I thought everyone had left."

"They did." Bethany looked up with a smile, not taking her hands out of the water. "It's just me."

"My sister left you to do the cleanup?"

"I volunteered. She took Ruby out to the barn to work on a new dressage movement."

"I was just going to grab some food. But I can help you with the dishes first." What else was he going to do? Sit here and eat while she worked?

"That's okay. I like the quiet." She turned back to the sink.

Was that a hint that she wanted him to leave? He supposed he could get some food later. It would be less awkward for both of them. He turned to head back up the stairs.

"Wait, um . . ." Her voice reached for him. "Emma's brother."

He paused on the bottom step, unable to keep the edges of his lips from tipping up. "James," he supplied.

"I knew that."

"Oh really?" He turned toward her with an eyebrow raised—a gentler version of the look he'd hit a suspect with if he knew they were lying.

"No." Bethany laughed self-consciously. "Sorry. I have—"

"Short-term memory loss," James filled in. "Emma mentioned it."

Bethany nodded and rinsed off the plate in her hand. "How many times have you told me your name?"

He shrugged. It was four. But it didn't matter. "It must be hard." Though some days he wanted nothing more than to lose his memory. It had to be better than recalling everything with near-photographic detail.

Bethany stilled, as if formulating an answer, but then turned to the sink without saying anything.

He was about to tromp up the stairs—foodless—when she said, "It's hard, yes. But it's taught me that God puts people into our lives for a reason."

James grunted. Yeah. To steal them away again.

"Were you going to get some food?" She glanced at him over her shoulder, her smile catching him in the chest. "Or did you forget?" She laughed lightly at her own joke.

"I . . ." He gestured toward the stairs, but her eyes didn't leave his. "Yeah. I was."

He dug the leftovers out of the fridge and loaded them onto a plate. He popped it into the microwave, unable to keep his gaze from sliding to Bethany as he waited for it to heat up.

A small smile played on her lips as she washed another plate, and he had the strangest desire to know what she was thinking.

He turned to the microwave, staring at his food as it rotated in a slow circle. When it was done, he debated carrying it upstairs to eat in his room. But that seemed rude. Not to mention he'd been trapped up there all day. And it was oddly peaceful here in the kitchen.

He set his plate on the table and pulled out a chair. Bethany peeked at him over her shoulder—that smile still hovering quietly—then went back to the dishes.

James wondered vaguely if he should attempt to make conversation. But Bethany looked completely content in the silence, and he relaxed into his seat. It was nice being with someone who didn't constantly urge him to "talk about it."

By the time he'd wolfed down his meal, Bethany was on the last few dishes.

He carried his plate to the sink. "I can finish up the rest."

"That's okay. I'm having fun."

He gave a short laugh. "You have a strange concept of fun." Not that he could talk—he wasn't sure he remembered what *fun* was anymore. "At least let me dry. Can't let you have all the fun yourself."

She gestured to the towel on the counter. He slipped his arm out of his sling, picked up the towel, and took the bowl she passed him. They fell into an easy rhythm, silent except for the splashing water and clanking dishes. Every once in a while, when he stepped closer to her, he caught a scent of peaches that made him think of summer and sunshine. He let his mind go pleasantly blank, the memories that had been hunting him down all day finally relenting. He'd never realized doing the dishes could be so therapeutic.

"Last one." Bethany passed him a china serving platter. James reached for it, but Bethany let go a second before his fingers could grasp it.

He lunged for it as it careened toward the ground, exhaling as his fingers closed around it. But something about the dish felt strange—too soft. He glanced down to find Bethany's fingers wrapped under his.

"That was close," she breathed.

"Yeah." He should let go of the dish.

"Guess what, Mom!"

James wrenched his hand away as the door flew open and Bethany's daughter burst through it, followed by Emma. Fortunately, Bethany managed to keep her hold on the platter. Unfortunately, the look on Emma's face said she thought there was something very different going on from what was really happening—which was nothing.

Bethany reached past him to set the wet platter on the counter, then turned to her daughter. "What?"

"Miss Emma says I'm ready for loops at the next competition." The enthusiasm in Ruby's voice punched straight at James's gut. Sadie had been so enthusiastic about everything too—from getting ice cream to spotting an ant on the ground.

"That's great." Bethany wrapped her daughter in a hug.

James dropped the towel on the counter, the heaviness of his own empty limbs weighing at his sides. He slid his left arm back into the sling.

"Don't think I didn't see that," Emma mock scolded. "But since you came out of your room, I won't yell at you about the sling."

"How good of you," he muttered.

"Do you have my eggs?" Ruby asked her mom.

"Um . . ." Bethany glanced around the room.

"Right here." Emma swept a small bag of plastic eggs off the counter. "I thought you had more than this."

Ruby shrugged. "Hope didn't find that many, so I gave her some of mine."

"That was nice of you." Bethany tucked her daughter's hair behind her ear, and James suddenly saw Sadie's wild curls that would never stay put.

"I thought I said not to hide the eggs in spots that were too hard." Emma directed a laughing frown at him.

"It wouldn't have been any fun if they were too easy to find. And anyway, they weren't *that* hard."

"In the downspout?" Emma lifted an eyebrow.

He chuckled. "All right. But that was the only really hard one."

"Not for me!" Ruby reached into her bag and pulled out a blue egg. "I found it!"

"Bummer." James didn't mean to talk to her, but the words came out before he could stop them. "I was hoping no one would find it, so I could have the candy myself."

Ruby stepped forward, holding out the egg. "Here. You can have it."

"No. That's—"

But she was already pressing it into his hand. Her fingers were warm and not nearly as sticky as Sadie's five-year-old fingers had been—but still the shock of the contact paralyzed him.

"Um. Thanks." He tucked the egg into his sweatshirt pocket, then retreated to the stairs. He was halfway up before he heard Emma apologizing for him. Vaguely, he wondered what she was telling them. But it didn't matter. From now on, he'd be staying as far away from Bethany and her daughter as possible.

Chapter 7

Bethany squinted at the man glowering on her doorstep. She should know his name, but . . .

"James," he said, as if he recognized her struggle. "Emma's brother."

"I know."

He made a face but didn't say anything.

"What are you doing here?" She supposed she could have asked that more politely, but it was too late to rephrase it.

"I was supposed to give you this the other day when you were at the stables. But I forgot, and I was coming into town anyway, so . . ." He passed her a book.

"Oh. Um. Thanks."

"Emma said it was for your women's Bible study tonight," he supplied.

"Right." She had completely forgotten she needed to buy a book for that.

"Okay. Well." He gestured toward his truck in the driveway.

"Hi, James." Ruby bounded to the door, sliding between James and Bethany. "Did you eat your candy?"

James took a step backwards, not looking at Ruby. "Not yet. I should—" He turned and jogged down the walkway, then jumped into his truck.

"I don't think he likes me," Ruby said matter-of-factly.

Instantly, Bethany's defensiveness sprang to life. "Of course he likes you. Who wouldn't?" Although she had to admit that the way he'd rushed away the moment Ruby appeared had been weird. "He's probably in a hurry."

"He seems sad." Ruby watched the truck as James pulled into the street. "We should do something to cheer him up."

Bethany laughed. That was what she loved about her daughter—she was always worried about other people's feelings. "For now, you have homework to do. And I have a chapter to read before I get you some dinner and then head to Bible study."

"Yay. Uncle Cam said he's bringing a movie tonight. And we're going to make popcorn."

Bethany ruffled her daughter's hair. "I'd say you got pretty lucky in the uncle department." And Bethany had gotten pretty lucky in the brother department. After the way she'd torn their family apart, he'd had no reason to come to her rescue by watching Ruby while she was in the hospital. More than once, she'd shuddered to think what might have happened to her daughter without Cam and Kayla.

More than once, she'd wondered if Ruby would be better off if they were still raising her. She pushed aside the thought. She had to trust that God had kept her in Ruby's life for a reason.

Two hours later, with her Bible study chapter read—and annotated to help her remember—Bethany greeted her brother, made him promise not to let Ruby stay up past her bedtime, then joined Kayla in the car.

"You look happy," Kayla said as she used her hand controls to back the car down the driveway.

"I do?" Bethany shrugged. She didn't have any reason not to be happy.

"Yes." Kayla grinned at her. "Any reason in particular?" The way she said it made it sound like she already knew the answer.

But Bethany had no idea what it could be. "Not that I can think of."

Kayla shook her head, still grinning. "So it has nothing to do with James?"

"James?" Bethany gave her a blank look. What *was* she talking about?

"Emma says you've been spending a lot of time with her brother. So . . ." Her voice went up with expectation.

Oh. James, Emma's brother. His face popped into her head. "We haven't been spending time together."

But she did need to come up with a way to remember his name. Her doctor had suggested linking people's names with their most prominent feature. The trick had helped her remember the names of the new friends she'd met after her aneurysm. Like, Kayla was the "Wheelchair Queen," complete with a crown in Bethany's head. And Emma was "Cowgirl Emma" in Bethany's mind for the riding boots she always wore.

So what was James's prominent feature? The sling on his arm? Or the lips that rarely smiled? Maybe the muscles that flexed under his flannel shirt as he scooped out the horse stalls? Muscle-man James?

A giggle made its way out before she could stop it.

"I knew it," Kayla crowed as she slowed for a stop sign. "You like him."

"No." Bethany refused to acknowledge the tiny jump of her stomach. "I was just trying to come up with a name association for him. Like how you're the Wheelchair Queen."

"And?" Kayla asked. "What'd you come up with?"

"Um . . ." Bethany had to stall. She certainly couldn't tell her sister-in-law about Muscle-Man James. "James the Gray."

"Gray?" Kayla glanced her way. "I didn't notice any gray hair."

Bethany laughed "No. Me either." Though, if she had to guess, he was probably around her own age of forty. "Gray because he never smiles."

"Ah." Kayla turned into the church parking lot, her eyes sliding slyly to Bethany. "Maybe you can change that."

Ruby's words from earlier about cheering James up suddenly came back to her.

But she had plenty of her own problems to worry about. She didn't have time to figure out why James was sad—or what she could do about it.

She opened her car door and waited for Kayla to assemble her wheelchair and transfer into it—she'd learned long ago that her sister-in-law didn't need help with this, or most tasks—then walked next to her toward Hope Church, her thoughts lingering on James.

But once inside, she pushed him out of her mind and turned her focus to Jade, who was leading the study.

"Last week, we wrapped up our study of the book of Esther," Jade said. "So, keeping with our theme of 'Being a Woman God Uses,' I thought we'd look at Ruth next."

Bethany nodded as she opened the book about Ruth that James had brought her earlier and reviewed the notes she'd made. She so wanted to be a woman God could use. But she didn't know how that was possible. Not anymore. Maybe when she'd first come to Hope Springs. When she'd gotten past her addiction and turned her life around. But now, with the limitations her aneurysm had left her with, she had a hard enough time getting through the day without making too many mistakes—without forgetting too many words or leaving her daughter at school because the alarm on her phone hadn't gone off. How was God supposed to use that?

Shaking off the thoughts—this Bible study wasn't about her, it was about Ruth—she returned her attention to Jade. How long had she been talking? What had Bethany missed?

"When Ruth left her homeland and everything she knew," Jade was saying, "she did it out of love for her mother-in-law. She had no idea that God had a larger purpose in mind for her. She had no idea that out of her family—a family she didn't even know she would have yet—would come the Savior."

Bethany let the words slip down to her soul. It had only been a few months before her aneurysm that she'd started coming to church. And every time she heard the Word now, it felt like the first time. Not because she didn't remember it. But because it had taken on such rich meaning in light of everything she'd been through. If God had a larger purpose for Ruth, maybe it meant he had a larger purpose for her too.

James the Gray popped into her head again. But she popped him right back out. She may not be certain of her purpose, but one thing she was certain of—he was not part of it.

Chapter 8

"Guess what day it is?" Emma sing-songed, bursting into the kitchen with her Bible in her hand, at least a dozen sticky notes poking out of it in various places.

James looked up from the protein bar he was eating. He'd never admit it to his sister, but some of her health food was okay. Not great, but edible. He used the sleeve of his flannel shirt to wipe at a wet spot on the table. It felt good to move his arm freely again, now that he'd decided to completely forgo the sling.

"Uh. Wednesday?"

"Uh huh." Emma's grin rivaled the Cheshire Cat's. "And you know what Wednesday means."

"Not really." All the days seemed pretty much the same here.

Emma gave him a look like she was disappointed. He finished his protein bar and threw away the wrapper. He needed to get out to the barn to take care of the stalls. Wait. Wednesday.

Bethany.

"You just remembered, didn't you?" Emma pointed at him, her grin growing into a laugh.

"Remembered what?"

"Don't try that on me." Emma filled a bottle with water. "I have a doctor appointment this morning. I was thinking maybe you and Bethany could take Ace and Fancy Lady out for a ride after you clean the stalls." He noticed how she very purposefully didn't look at him as she said it.

"You're about as subtle as a basket of snakes, you know that?"

"What?" She turned to him with an innocent look he would recognize as fake even if he weren't a detective. "Fancy Lady gets loopy if she doesn't get ridden. And Ace needs the exercise. He's starting to look more like a cow than a horse."

"Right." James headed for the door.

"So you'll do it?" Emma called after him.

"You know I never could say no to my sister," he said over his shoulder. He heard Emma's snort, followed by her thank you, before the door closed.

He strode toward the barn, telling himself that was *not* extra energy in his step. He wanted to get the work done, that was all.

But the sound of tires crunching on the gravel driveway drew him to a stop, and he couldn't seem to control the way his lips responded to spotting Bethany's car. He'd seen her in passing the other day when she'd brought Ruby to her dressage lesson. They hadn't even talked. But the way she'd smiled had stuck with him ever since.

She has a kid, he reminded himself.

But Ruby had stuck in his head too—the way she'd waved at him from atop her horse when she'd spotted him from across the arena, the way her grin was warm and open in spite of the fact that he'd been rude to her the other day. He owed her an apology. Maybe he could pass it on through Bethany.

The car door opened, and Bethany stepped out. She didn't seem to notice him, so he let himself watch her.

Her hair fluttered in the breeze as she tucked her keys into her pocket, then closed the car door and tilted her head back with her eyes closed. A smile played across her lips, and he found himself wanting to know what it was about. After a few seconds, she lowered her head and opened her eyes—which seemed to land right on him. Her smile grew as she waved and started toward him.

He considered fleeing into the barn ahead of her, but his feet didn't want to move.

"Hey, James," she called when she was almost to him.

"Hey—" He broke off, staring at her. "Did you just remember my name?"

Bethany's laugh knocked against his ribs. "I guess I did. I had to come up with a name association. That's all."

"A name association?" He held open the barn door for her.

"Yeah. Like linking your name to something familiar."

"Do I want to know what you associated me with?" He fell into step next to her as they walked toward the back of the barn.

Again her laugh swept over him. "Probably not." She threw a smile at him, then slipped into the equipment room.

James remained outside the door for a second—just long enough to remind his heart that it was not allowed to develop feelings for this woman, even if her smile and her laugh and the way she said his name were all trying to storm the hard spots in his heart.

Then he followed her into the room. They silently collected their equipment and silently walked to the stalls and silently started working. But it was the most comfortable silence James had ever experienced. No demands. No expectations. No one telling him he should talk.

But the more they worked and the more comfortable he grew, the more he realized he couldn't go riding with her. He'd just ride each of the horses in turn. Because if he spent more time with her, he was going to want to spend *yet more* time with her. And that was a problem.

He heard Bethany grunt, and he stepped out of the stall he was working on to find her lugging a straw bale nearly as big as she was.

"I would have gotten that." He rushed forward and took the bale from her, its sharply sweet scent mingling with her fresh summery one.

"Thanks." She was breathing heavily from the exertion. "Sometimes I forget how heavy those are."

"No problem." He carried the bale to a spot between their stalls and cut the twine. Bethany grabbed her pitchfork and started scooping new bedding into her stall. After a moment, she glanced at him, and he realized he was still watching her. With a jerk, he hustled back into his own stall.

Yes, he was definitely going to exercise the horses alone.

"I'll clean up," he said as they completed the stalls. "You can head out."

"That's okay." Bethany collected her shovels. "It'll go faster together."

"Really," he insisted. "I don't have anything else to do today, aside from exercising Ace and Fancy Lady."

"You're going to ride?" Her eyes lit up, and James realized his mistake. He couldn't *not* ask her, not now that he could see how much she would love it.

"Yeah. Do you ride?" *Say no. Say no. Say—*

"My dad used to take us out when we were kids. Those are some of my best memories. I haven't been in years though. Not since . . ." Her wistful expression faded to one of regret. "Anyway, have fun."

She turned, and he almost let her walk away.

"Wait." The word came out kind of strangled, but Bethany stopped and turned around, giving him a perplexed smile.

"You wouldn't want to help, would you?" he asked. "Ride Ace while I ride Fancy Lady?"

"For real?" Bethany looked like he'd offered her a million dollars.

He shrugged, but it was impossible not to smile at her unchecked enthusiasm. "I mean, if you want to."

"Yes." She shot forward, her arms wrapping around his shoulders. He winced as she pressed against his wound.

"Sorry." She let go and jumped backwards. Her cheeks were flushed, and she ducked her head. "I didn't mean to— Sometimes I struggle with . . ." She toed the ground and let out a frustrated sounding breath. He waited, having no idea what she was going to say. Finally, she looked up. "I can't remember what it's called. When you do something without thinking about it first?"

"Spontaneous?"

She shook her head, frowning in concentration.

"Impromptu?"

Another head shake. A deeper frown.

He sought for another word. "Impulsive?"

"Yes!" Her shout was exuberant. "Impulse control. I have impulse control issues. Since the aneurysm. I didn't mean to hug you."

"Oh." What was he supposed to say to that? "It's okay." Fortunately, he was able to keep a lid on his heart, which was saying it was more than okay.

Chapter 9

There were a lot of things Bethany had done in her life that she regretted.

This was not one of them.

As Ace carried her along the trail that led from the barn toward the wooded part at the back of Emma's property, Fancy Lady and James right in front of them, Bethany drew in a long breath. The late morning air smelled earthy and damp and sweet with the scent of lilacs that had just begun to bloom. Around them, grasses waved in the gentle breeze, and up ahead, leaves in new green unfurled on the trees. The sun warmed the top of her head, and peace warmed her insides.

Thank you for this day, Lord. Her contentment burst out of her in a silent prayer. There was a time when it had looked like she wasn't going to have any more days—and now here she was, riding a horse and marveling at the beauty of God's creation. There may be a lot of things her aneurysm had taken from her—but she wouldn't let it steal her joy in rediscovering God.

Ahead of her, James reined in his horse and pulled it to the side of the trail so that Bethany and Ace could stop next to him.

"How are you doing?" The way he watched her, as if he wanted to make sure she was all right—really all right—did something strange to Bethany's stomach.

She pressed a hand to it. "I'm good. Though Ace keeps trying to graze."

James laughed, and she wondered if it was the first time she'd ever heard it—because she was pretty sure she would have remembered how gloriously rich it sounded. "Emma said he was getting chunky. Should we keep going, or do you want to turn around?"

"Definitely keep going. But first—" She leaned to the side in her saddle so she could finagle her phone out of her pocket. She opened the camera app, then lined James and Fancy Lady up on the screen. "Say horses."

James gave her a perplexed look but said "horses," and Bethany snapped a picture.

"Helps me remember," she explained, taking one of Ace's head and neck in front of her.

"Here." James leaned toward her and held out a hand. "Let me get one of you."

The strange feeling in Bethany's middle grew. James wasn't making fun of her for taking pictures of everyday things—he was helping her.

He snapped a couple of pictures, then passed the phone back to her. She tucked it into her pocket, and they started on the trail again. It was wide enough here that they could ride side-by-side, and the horses fell into step next to each other, Bethany tugging on Ace's reins every few minutes to keep him from grazing.

"Where did you learn to ride?" The question slid from her mouth easily even though she hadn't taken the time to formulate it in her head first as she usually did.

"Emma was horse crazy even as a kid. She convinced my parents to let her take lessons. Which meant I, of course, insisted on taking lessons too. Had to do everything my big sister did."

Bethany smiled. "Cam was like that with me too." At least until she'd gotten involved with drugs. She could only thank God that he hadn't followed her down that path.

"I hope it didn't drive you as crazy as it drove Emma. She hated when I copied what she did. My parents always told her she should be flattered that I wanted to be like her."

Bethany laughed. "Sometimes I think it's sad that Ruby won't know what that's like since she's an only child."

James nodded, but his jaw tightened, and he fell silent.

They continued to ride side-by-side until they came to a spot where the trail narrowed and disappeared into the woods.

"After you." James reined in Fancy Lady to let Bethany and Ace take the lead on the single-file trail.

As the trees closed overhead, Bethany felt like she was being transported into another world.

A dappled kaleidoscope of sunlight circled across the ground. The shadows and light moved with the breeze, playing tricks on her eyes and making the whole world shift.

She grasped for Ace's mane and closed her eyes for a second. When she opened them, everything spun. The motion of the horse beneath her made her head swim. Which way was up and which was down?

She moaned, closing her eyes again in an attempt to get her bearings. She felt like her body was moving in the opposite direction of the horse.

"Bethany!" The voice from behind her sounded garbled and far away.

"I'm okay." She forced the words out past the waves of nausea rolling over her. "Just . . . dizzy."

"Rein him in," called the voice behind her. "And hold on."

Somehow, she managed to obey, giving the reins a gentle pull. She couldn't tell if the movement below her had come to a stop since the world was still spinning and bright pops of color filled her vision. She needed to get to the ground. Right now.

She gasped as she slid to the side, but a pair of firm arms wrapped around her and slid her off the saddle. Oh. That was so much better. Her feet touched the ground, but the arms didn't leave her. She opened her eyes, and her vision cleared enough to make out James standing in front of her. His hands were on her elbows, steadying her.

"Can you stand on your own?"

She nodded but pressed a hand to her head as the motion reignited the spinning. She closed her eyes, concentrating on taking deep breaths. James's hands were firm on her arms, and when she opened her eyes, concern cloaked his face.

"Sorry about that. Sometimes motion gives me . . ."

"Vertigo?" James supplied.

She nodded, causing a few bright pops of color to explode in her vision. "I'm better now."

But the look on James's face said he didn't buy it. "Let's sit for a minute."

"No, really. I'm fine." Embarrassment suddenly washed over her. What must he think of her, unable to keep her seat on the gentlest horse Emma owned? And now she couldn't even stand on her own? She wriggled out of his grasp, and he let her go, though he kept his hands poised in front of her, as if he expected her to tip over at any moment.

"Where are the horses?" She turned her head, but the motion blurred her vision and the world slipped sideways again.

Next thing she knew, James's arms were around her, and he was lowering her to the ground. "Put your head between your knees."

Too dizzy to protest, she obeyed. She heard him rustling around behind her.

"Here. Lie back." With a hand on her shoulder, he guided her to lie on something soft.

She moaned quietly and lifted her forearm to cover her eyes. When would the spinning stop?

She had no idea how much time had passed—or whether she'd fallen asleep or remained awake—before she lowered her arm and tentatively opened her eyes.

Thankfully, the world seemed to have righted itself, and the gentle swaying of the leaves above her didn't make her nauseous.

She turned her head to the side to find James sitting next to her, staring into the distance.

"Sorry about that," she murmured.

He startled, as if his thoughts had been far off, but smiled as he turned to her. "Nothing to be sorry about. Feeling better?"

"I think so." She positioned her arms to push herself into a sitting position. But before she'd started to exert herself, James had scooted to her side and placed a hand behind her back, easing her up.

"Thanks." She gave him a brief smile but looked away at his intense expression.

"Any more dizziness?"

She waited a moment before answering to be sure this time. "Nope. I don't think so."

"Let's wait a little longer, just to be safe." James took his hand off her back, and she shivered.

"Cold?"

"No. Just damp from lying on the ground."

"I'd give you my flannel, but . . ." He reached behind her and then held it up. Deep streaks of mud covered the blue and white fabric.

"Oh no. I'm sorry."

He balled the shirt up. "Don't be. It served its purpose."

"Uh oh." Bethany spotted Ace, contentedly grazing at the side of the trail. "I think Ace may have *gained* weight from this walk."

James chuckled, the sound warming through her.

"You should laugh more." The words plopped off her lips. Oops. That would have been a good time to practice some impulse control. "I mean—"

But James gave her a thoughtful look. "It's been a while since I've had much to laugh about."

Bethany watched, waiting for him to elaborate. When he looked away, she considered asking, but she knew better than most that some things were too hard to give words to.

They sat in silence for a few more minutes, the sounds of the calling birds and scurrying squirrels supplying a soothing backdrop.

Bethany's phone rang, and she reached for it, surprised to find it still tucked into her pocket. She was reluctant to break the peace. But it could be Ruby's school.

Her eyes fell on the screen. Not Ruby's school. Cam.

He probably needed her to run an errand. She considered not answering—she could always take care of it later—but dismissed the thought. It was her job.

She lifted the phone to her ear. "Hey, Cam."

"Hey." He seemed breathless, and she heard what sounded like drawers opening and closing in the background. "Where are they?"

"Where are what? What are you doing?"

"Sorry. I wasn't talking to you." Cam's usually calm voice was frenetic, and Bethany sat up straighter. "Cam. What's wrong?"

Out of the corner of her eye, she saw James turn toward her, looking alert.

"Nothing. Sorry." Cam's laugh bordered on wild. "Kayla's water broke."

"Wow. Cam." Bethany covered her mouth. She was about to become an aunt.

"What is it?" James whispered, moving closer. "Is everything okay?"

Bethany nodded. "My sister-in-law's water broke."

"Ah." James's gaze shifted to the trees, but not before Bethany detected the trace of brokenness in his eyes.

"I think that's everything, right?" she heard Cam say on the other end of the phone.

"Yes." Kayla's laughing answer sounded much calmer than Cam.

"You take care of Kayla, Cam. I'll meet you guys at the hospital." She wasn't going to miss this for anything.

"Actually, that's why I called." A door closed as Cam muttered, "Oh man, I dropped that."

Bethany rolled her eyes. Anyone who met Cam right now would have a hard time believing he was an extremely capable businessman—who used to be a high-powered attorney. She supposed that was what happened when your wife was about to have a baby. Not that she would know—Ruby's father had been long out of the picture by the time Ruby was born. Bethany's drive to the hospital had been alone. As had every step of her parenting journey. Though she sometimes wondered what it would have been like to raise Ruby with a partner at her side, Ruby's father never could have been that man.

Her eyes strayed to James, who was again gazing into the distance.

"Anyway." Cam finally spoke into the phone again, and Bethany heard a door close and then an engine turn over. "Bill Jespersen called. There's some sort of problem with the stone we ordered. I was about to tell him I'd come check it out when Kayla's water broke. I think I might have hung up on him."

Bethany laughed.

"Glad it's so amusing to you," Cam said dryly. "But you know what a big client he is. We can't afford to lose him."

"Okay, Cam." She didn't remember who Bill Jespersen was, although for some reason she had a picture of a trout in her head. "I'll go deal with Bill Jespersen. You and Kayla go have that baby. And call me the minute you have news."

"You're sure? If it's too much, I can always call him and say I'll take care of it tomorrow."

Bethany tried to ignore the sting left by his question about whether she could handle it. "You're not going to take care of it tomorrow. You're going to be too busy being a dad."

Next to her, James seemed to twitch, and his shoulders visibly tightened. But her attention was pulled back to the phone as she heard Kayla tell Cam he'd missed the turn.

"Go," she said to her brother. "Take care of your family. I've got this." She hung up the phone, then started to push to her feet.

James scrambled up next to her, locking his hand around her elbow as she straightened. Even after she was upright, he held on, watching her.

An unexpected tingle went up her arm. "Thanks. I think I'm good now."

James let go slowly. "We should probably lead the horses, rather than riding."

As much as she wanted to protest so she could take care of things for Cam faster, Bethany nodded. A faint unsteadiness still clung to her, and if she had problems again, it would only delay her more.

James collected the horses, taking the reins of each in his hands, and Bethany fell into step on the far side of Ace. Though they couldn't talk with the horses between them, Bethany caught the way James checked on her every few minutes, and a new kind of warmth went through her.

By the time they got to the barn, her legs seemed to weigh an extra three hundred pounds, and she was bracing a hand against Ace's side to keep from stumbling.

James brought the horses to a stop, then came around to her side. Silently, he took her arm and led her to the decorative metal bench next to the barn door. "Sit."

"I have to—" But her legs ignored her protest and honored James's order.

"I know. Just sit for a minute. I'll be right back."

All Bethany could do was close her eyes and lean her head back against the barn wall. Just once, she wanted to be there when someone needed her. She was tired of letting everyone down. But she wasn't sure how she was going to walk to her car, let alone take care of things for Cam.

"Here." James emerged from the barn with a water bottle that he must have gotten out of the mini fridge in the back. He unscrewed the cap, then refastened it lightly and passed the bottle to Bethany.

"Thanks." How had he known she always struggled with those stupid caps? She downed a long swallow.

James's eyes didn't leave her the whole time.

As she lowered the bottle, the heaviness and nausea seemed to lift. "Thank you. I feel much better now." She pulled her keys out of her pocket.

"That's what you said before." James stood in front of her, blocking her way to her car.

"I know." She stood, which put her closer to him than she'd expected. He still smelled good. "I really am better. I have to go—"

"I can't let you drive in this condition." He held out a hand, as if he expected her to drop her keys into it.

"Cam needs me to—"

"I know." James plucked the keys from her fingers. "I'll drive."

"I— Really?" She felt like she was gaping at him, but she couldn't help it. He would do that for her?

"Come on." He waited for her to take a step, then fell in alongside her. "Where to?"

"To—" Wait. The name had been on the tip of her tongue. She'd repeated it to herself a thousand times on the walk back so she wouldn't forget. She could picture the trout in her head. But the name had escaped. "To, uh—" She shot him a look. "I forgot who it was." She couldn't call Cam back—not when he and Kayla were having a baby.

"You said Bill Jespersen on the phone." James's tone was calm and matter-of-fact, as if he hadn't just saved her life. Bethany turned to stare at him, but he simply shrugged. "I have a near-photographic memory."

"Wow." What she wouldn't do to simply have a regular memory, much less a photographic one. "That must be nice."

James's lips formed a grimace for a second before flattening. "Not always."

Chapter 10

Silently, James made the turn his phone told him to make. Bethany had found Bill Jespersen's address in the customer file on her phone. He glanced over at her, relieved to see that the life had returned to her cheeks. He hadn't seen anyone that pale since—

His knuckles tightened as he fought off the memory.

"This is my favorite view," Bethany murmured as they turned onto Hope Street, which ran parallel to the Lake Michigan shoreline. To their left, a steep hill dotted with flowers and a gazebo led down to the marina, where colorful yachts and sailboats rocked on the gentle waves. Beyond them, sunlight glinted off the water, making James squint. As they continued down the street, they passed quaint stores—a fudge shop, bakery, antique store—with a few people lingering outside.

"That fudge shop was how I knew I was going to love Hope Springs," Bethany said.

James glanced at her. "How long ago did you move here?"

"Eleven years ago," Bethany answered instantly.

"You remember that?" He didn't mean to sound surprised, but he'd expected her to at least have to think about it.

She shrugged, still looking out the window. "I can remember almost everything from my past." She turned to him with a rueful smile. "It's just new memories my brain doesn't like to make."

"Will it get better?" Maybe he shouldn't ask, but she fascinated him. Or, her condition did. Not her.

Keep telling yourself that.

"They don't know," she answered. "I see a— Um. A— Brain doctor." She rolled her eyes.

"Neurologist," he supplied, offering her a smile to let her know there was nothing to be embarrassed about.

"Thank you. She says it's improved since right after I woke up from the coma, but I can't remember that so . . ." She fell silent, then said, "I'm just grateful I remembered Ruby when I woke up. Can you imagine if I had forgotten her?"

James's hands dug into the steering wheel. There had been times over the past five years when he'd wished he couldn't remember Sadie—because if the memories of her disappeared, so would the pain—but he'd always taken the wish back instantly. It wouldn't be worth forgetting the pain if it meant forgetting the joy she'd brought him.

"Is something wrong?" Bethany peered at him.

He shook his head without looking her way. "Just checking the map. Looks like we need to turn . . ." He slowed. "Here."

He eased into the driveway, which was flanked by two stone lions, and pulled to a stop in front of a grand house right on the lakeshore. He whistled. "Cam sure knows how to pick his clients."

Bethany's eyes were huge as she looked up at the house. "Hopefully I won't screw this up."

"Why would you think that?" In spite of her memory issues, she seemed to be an incredibly capable woman.

But Bethany opened her car door and stepped out. James debated getting out too, just to get a better view of the house and the lake, but decided to stay put. This was Bethany's thing. He was only the chauffeur.

Bethany was halfway to the front door when a big guy in a golf shirt emerged. Bill Jespersen, presumably. Bethany held out a hand to the guy, but he ignored it, the boom of his angry voice reaching the car.

Instinct kicked in, and James shoved the car door open, quickly covering the ground between himself and Bethany. "Everything all right?"

Bethany looked over her shoulder, surprise—and possibly annoyance—scribbled across her features. Well, so what? He had a job to do, and it wasn't always making people happy—it was keeping them safe.

"No, it's not." Bill turned to him. "You work for Moore Landscaping too?"

"No." James shuffled closer to Bethany.

"Why would you?" The man threw up his hands in exasperation.

"What seems to be the problem?" James asked patiently. He'd learned in his years on the force that the key to diffusing a temper was remaining calm.

"What's the problem?" Bill shoved past Bethany and strode toward the backyard. James nearly grabbed the guy to remind him to use his manners but instead turned to Bethany to make sure she was all right. But she brushed past him, following Bill around the house. James waited a beat, then stepped in behind her. There was no way he was going to leave her on her own with this dude.

The backyard offered a stunning view of the lake, but Bill was gesturing to a large pallet of stone slabs. "Does this look like what I ordered?"

Bethany's nose crinkled as she examined the stone, and James realized she probably had no recollection of what the guy had ordered.

But James had already admitted that he didn't work for Moore Landscaping. So it wouldn't do any harm for him to ask. "Sorry, what did you order?"

"Slate," Bill spat at him.

"And this is . . ."

"Travertine," Bethany filled in, shooting James a look he decided was gratitude. She pulled out her phone and tapped it a few times, then scrolled for a moment. Finally, she looked up. "Are you sure you decided on the slate? Because our order form shows travertine."

"Your form is wrong." Bill crossed his arms. "And now my project is going to be weeks behind. My daughter is supposed to get married out here in two months, and my wife—"

"Miranda?" Bethany interrupted.

"Yes, my wife Miranda is freaking out about all the details."

"There's a note here that Miranda called to change the order to travertine." Bethany angled her phone so Bill could see it. He yanked it out of her hands, and James took a step closer to Bethany. She gave him a quelling look.

"Just a minute." Bill turned abruptly toward the house, Bethany's phone still clutched in his hand. "Miranda!" he bellowed, making both James and Bethany wince. He yelled the name three more times before he stormed toward the house and yanked open the French doors that looked out over the existing wood patio.

James eyed Bethany. "This guy's a piece of work."

"Why don't you go wait in the car? I've got this." Her tone was pleasant enough, but the stiff way she held her head spoke much more loudly than the words.

"Bethany, this guy is trying to intimidate you." James had seen the way the guy had sized him up when he'd gotten out of the car. He wouldn't do anything as long as James was standing here. But if he wasn't . . .

"I'm perfectly capable of handling this myself." Again the stiffness.

James opened his mouth to argue again, then changed his mind. "I'll be in the car if you need me." He turned back toward the driveway as Bill marched toward Bethany with a woman at his side. The woman, at least, was smiling, which set James a little more at ease.

He rounded the house and got into the car, staring out over the lake and trying not to think about why he felt so protective of Bethany.

It was his job to be a protector. That was all.

You always have to be the hero. His ex-wife's words slapped through his head to the rhythm of the waves hitting the shore.

Still, he remained on alert, listening for any signs of discord from the backyard. It was a good forty-five minutes before Bethany emerged around the side of the house and hurried toward the car. Some of the color that had returned to her face earlier had faded, and she rubbed at her temples.

She gave him a weak smile as she got into the car and fell back against the seat.

"Everything settled?"

"I think so." Bethany sounded exhausted. "Although I think those two may have some issues to work through."

James started the car. "Speaking of issues, I'm sorry if I overstepped. I just didn't like the way that guy was talking to you."

"That's okay." Bethany rubbed her head again. "I've dealt with much worse. I had it under control."

"I'm sure you did. My ex-wife always accused me of having an excessive need to protect people. Called it my hero complex."

Bethany looked at him in surprise. "I didn't know you were married."

Because he never talked about it. So how had she made him let his guard down enough to bring it up? "Yeah." Hopefully his short answer would clue her in that he wasn't interested in talking about it. Because talking about it would lead to talking about why they weren't together anymore. And that would lead to talking about Sadie.

And that he couldn't do.

Thankfully, before they could continue the conversation, Bethany's phone beeped. She pulled it out and read the screen, then squealed. "Cam and Kayla had the baby. It's a girl! Evelyn Rose."

Every muscle in James's neck clenched. *It's a girl.* She'd been so perfect. Ten fingers. Ten toes. Barely a strand of hair. But the sweetest smile, which the nurses said technically wasn't really a smile, but he'd seen it, right from that first moment.

Bethany's fingers flew across her phone, and she practically bounced in her seat. "Ruby is going to be so excited to meet her new cousin." She stopped typing and looked up. "Is that what time it is? Three twenty?"

James's eyes flicked to the dashboard. "I guess so."

"Oh no." Bethany's groan was pained.

"What's wrong?" Immediately his eyes went to her, but she was covering her face with her hands. "Bethany?"

She dropped her hands and scrolled through screens on her phone. "Ruby gets done with school at three. My alarm should have . . ." She made a sound of disgust. "I must have turned it off when I was talking to—uh—what's his name."

"Bill?"

Bethany nodded. "I don't remember turning it off, but that doesn't mean much." She tapped her screen again, then lifted the phone to her ear.

James listened silently as she explained to the person on the other end that she'd be late picking Ruby up, his shoulders tensing unexpectedly as the cutting tone of the woman on the other end came through the phone: "Again?"

Bethany closed her eyes but politely said "yes" and "thank you."

When she hung up, she let out a loud sigh.

"I'm sure she'll be fine," he tried to reassure her.

She frowned. "I know she will be. It's just, none of the other moms need an alarm to remind them to get their kid from school."

"None of the other moms have had to deal with the things you've dealt with."

Bethany's tight smile said she appreciated the words—but didn't believe them. "Do you mind if we swing past the school to get her before we go back to the stables to drop you off?"

James's muscles locked tighter. There was a reason he always declined the captain's requests for volunteers to visit schools. Seeing all those smiling, laughing kids—kids Sadie should be among—gouged him from the inside out.

He shook his head. He couldn't go there right now.

"Otherwise I can just . . ." Bethany said, and James realized he hadn't answered her.

"Yeah," he rasped, against his better judgment. "We can go pick her up."

Bethany directed him to the school, and too soon he was turning into the parking lot. His chest squeezed as if someone had cinched his bullet-proof vest way too tight. There was no room for his lungs to expand.

I had a great day, Daddy. But I missed you.

He pressed his foot to the brake and pulled in a shaky breath. *Compartmentalize.*

At least they were late enough that there were only a couple of kids lingering outside as their moms chatted. He pulled up along the curb and put the car in park.

"I'll be back in a minute." Bethany opened her door and jumped out.

Leaving him to fight the memories on his own.

Chapter 11

Bethany strode toward the school, working hard not to look over her shoulder at James. Was he that annoyed that she'd asked him to pick Ruby up, or was she mistaken about the tension that had rippled through him the moment she'd asked? She sped up. She didn't have time to worry about him right now.

There was only one small cluster of parents out here, their kids running around on the front lawn. Bethany should probably recognize the group of moms—but she wasn't about to stare at them long enough to figure it out. Which didn't keep her from feeling the judgmental looks stabbing into her back. She pressed the buzzer on the school door and announced that she was there to pick up Ruby.

"I'll send her out," the voice on the other end replied.

As Bethany waited, she sneaked a glance over her shoulder to make sure James hadn't left. The car was still at the curb, but James faced the other direction. Even though she couldn't see his face, the tension was clear in the rigid way he sat, his shoulders straining forward as if he could move the car by sheer force of will.

Hurry up, Ruby, she silently urged her daughter. She'd already been enough of a burden to James for one day.

"Bethany," a cheerful, airy voice called out.

Bethany cringed. She'd been so busy watching James that she hadn't noticed one of the women break away from the group and approach her. The woman's daughter stood next to her in a skirt and matching top that could have come straight out of the pages of one of those designer catalogs. Even her socks and shoes were perfectly coordinated.

"Hey, Kimberly." Fortunately, the daughter's name came easily to Bethany, since she associated her with the riding lessons she and Ruby took together. And that meant the mom was . . .

She searched through the files in her memory as inconspicuously as possible. "Tiffany." She gave herself an internal high-five.

"I'm sorry you weren't able to make it to 'bring your mom to school day' today," Tiffany said. "I hope you don't mind that I let Ruby do the activities with me and Kimberly."

"Bring your mom to school day?" So much for that high-five. She pulled out her phone and scrolled, but it wasn't on her calendar. She'd have to check her notebook when she got home—but she didn't remember ever hearing about it. But then, she supposed chances were high that she wouldn't remember. "I— Um. Thank you." A hole the size of Lake Michigan opened in her stomach. As much as she couldn't remember all the instances she'd let Ruby down, she knew this wasn't the first.

The school door opened, and Ruby burst through, looking cheerful enough as she bounded over to them.

"Hey, Rubes. I'm so sorry I didn't make it to bring your mom to school day. I must not have put it on my calendar. I feel terrible."

"It's fine, Mom."

Bethany studied her daughter. There was something about her expression that made Bethany believe it wasn't as fine as Ruby said. But maybe she didn't want to talk about it in front of her friend. Bethany would be sure to apologize later—as long as she remembered.

"Let's go. James is waiting in the car."

"Really?" Ruby's eyes lit up. "How come?"

But it was too long of a story to get into right now.

"I was just going to check—" Tiffany fell into step next to Bethany, and Kimberly walked next to Ruby, the two girls bending their heads together and giggling. Bethany had a sudden flash of what it had been like to have such uncomplicated relationships as a kid.

Her eyes went to Tiffany, who was still talking. "How are things coming for the field day? Do you need any help?"

Bethany's foot hit the ground wrong, and she stumbled but caught herself before she ended up on her face. The field day. She had started to go through the folder of notes but had gotten overwhelmed and set it aside with the plan to return to it later. Only she'd forgotten all about it—until now.

"It's coming great." If her years as an addict had taught her anything, it was how to tell a convincing lie. Not that she was proud of it. But what other choice did she have? She didn't need to give everyone one more reason to doubt her competence. Besides, she'd start on it when she got home and work on it all week and all weekend, and by Monday it really would be coming along great.

"Oh. Good." Tiffany looked surprised—and skeptical. "Because if you need any help, I can—"

"Thanks. I've got it." They reached the car, and Bethany opened the back door, gesturing Ruby in.

"See you Friday for the trip to the water park," Tiffany said to Ruby. Then she turned to Bethany. "You got all the details I texted you, right?"

"Um. Yes?" At least if Tiffany had sent them, there was no reason Bethany shouldn't have gotten them.

"Great. We'll leave right from school, so remember to bring your bag," she said to Ruby, as if the ten-year-old was the responsible one here. "We'll probably be back early Sunday afternoon."

"Oh, but—" Two days was a long time. What if Ruby got homesick or something? But watching her daughter wave excitedly from the back seat as Tiffany and Kimberly walked away, Bethany knew it wasn't her daughter who would be homesick. It was her.

***

"And they have three pools and ten water slides. They sound scary, but Kimberly says they're so, so, so fun."

James could barely keep up with Ruby's chatter—which hadn't stopped since they'd left the school. But Bethany seemed lost in thought, which had left James to respond to the girl.

"Oh," he grunted now.

"Have you ever been to a water park?" In the rearview mirror, he could see Ruby wriggling in her seat, and he glanced to make sure her seatbelt was still in position.

"Once." The tension in his shoulders cranked tighter. Sadie had been too young to do much more than wade in the kiddie pool, but she'd loved it. James had told her she'd be a dolphin when she grew up, which had made her giggle. His jaw locked, and his throat convulsed. *When* she grew up—it had never seemed like it should be a question of *if*.

"Did you like it?" Ruby pressed.

"Yes." James barely got the word past his gritted teeth.

He looked to Bethany. Perhaps she wanted to take over the conversation? Since it was her daughter, not his?

Apparently sensing his eyes on her, Bethany sat up. "Hey, Rubes? I'm really sorry again that I didn't come to bring your mom to school day. I don't know how I missed it."

"I told you, it's fine, Mom."

"No it's not. It should have been in my calendar, but . . . I don't know what happened. When did you give me the sheet about it?"

"Uhhh . . . a couple weeks ago?"

James had been a detective long enough to spot a lie when he heard one. A quick glance in the mirror showed Ruby was toying with a thread on her shirt, not looking at her mom.

"It's so weird," Bethany muttered again. "But I promise I'll make it up to you. Maybe some ice cream for dessert tonight?"

"It's okay, Mom. You don't have to make it up to me. It was a lame day."

Another lie. And that was definitely guilt in her eyes. But why?

James glanced at Bethany, who still looked troubled.

"So what did you two do today?" Ruby asked, as if she didn't find it the least bit unusual that he was driving her mom's car and had come along to pick her up from school.

"We went riding," Bethany said. "And then we had to go to see a client for Uncle Cam because—" She gasped. "I can't believe I forgot to tell you. You have a baby cousin!"

"What?"

James hadn't realized little girls' voices could go that high.

"Is it a girl like I thought? What's her name?"

"Um . . . I think it's a girl." Bethany picked up her phone.

"Evelyn Rose." The answer came out before James could think it through.

What should we name her?

It doesn't matter. As long as we get to keep her.

"James?" Bethany's voice cut through the memory.

"Sorry. What?"

"I was just asking if you were going to turn, because you passed the driveway."

"Oops. Sorry. I'll turn around." He pulled into the driveway of Hidden Blossom Farms, the cherry orchard down the road, owned by some of Emma's friends. Already, tiny buds of green and white dotted the branches. James glanced away from the signs of life and accelerated faster than was probably necessary back toward the driveway to the stables. He had to get out of this car—away from this reminder of what it had felt like to have a family.

The instant he pulled up in front of the house, he slammed the car into park and opened his door. Bethany got out too, crossing in front of the car, toward the driver's side.

She stopped directly in front of him. "Thank you for driving."

"Don't mention it. You're good now?" He let himself study her face, relieved that she looked fine.

"Much better, thank you. I don't know what I would have done if—"

"No problem." He gave a curt nod, waiting for her to move out of the way.

"Is everything okay?" She peered at him closely, as if searching for something. "You seem . . ."

"Nope. Everything's good." He pushed past her and sprinted up the porch steps and into the house.

Inside, he grabbed a glass and filled it to the top with water, then downed it in one gulp.

"Thirsty?" Emma popped into the room, chuckling.

He set the glass down. But the water had done nothing to wash away the mixed up jumble of Melissa and Sadie and Bethany and Ruby in his head.

"So . . ." Emma raised her eyebrows at him. "It looks like you and Bethany made a day of it. Aren't you glad I suggested you go riding?"

"Ah, let's see. She got vertigo and almost passed out."

"What?" Emma gasped. "Is she okay?"

"She is now, but it took a while. I had to drive her to take care of a client because Cam and Kayla were having their baby."

"I saw that! I'm so excited for them." Emma's eyes were bright, and James could tell she meant what she said, even though she had often wished for children of her own. That just made her a better person than him—but that was no surprise. "Anyway, the client was a total jerk." He wished he'd clocked the guy for the way he'd spoken to Bethany. "And that took forever, so then we had to go pick Ruby up from school. And Ruby talked all the way home."

Emma laughed. "That sounds like Ruby. She's always reminded me of—"

"Don't," James cut in sharply. He knew exactly who Ruby reminded her of because she reminded him of the same person. But Ruby would never be Sadie.

"You can't just never talk about her, James. It's not healthy."

He grunted.

"You like Bethany," Emma pressed. "I can tell."

James shook his head. He was not getting into this with his sister. It didn't matter *what* he felt about Bethany. She had a kid. And that was a deal breaker.

"Seriously, James. What are you going to do? Spend the rest of your life alone?"

"You're alone," he pointed out.

"Thanks for the reminder," Emma said dryly, and he sighed. That had been unfair. He knew how much Emma had always wanted a big family of her own.

"I'm sorry." He crossed his arms and leaned against the counter. "I'm just saying, I'm perfectly happy on my own."

Emma's gaze held his. "You're not happy, James. And sometimes I think you want to stay that way."

He shrugged. It didn't make much of a difference whether he was happy or miserable.

"It's okay to move on, you know," Emma said gently. "Melissa called me the other day. She's remarried and—"

He held up a hand. He already knew his ex-wife had moved on. Ironic, since she'd been the one who'd complained that he'd gone back to work too soon after Sadie.

He didn't begrudge her for wanting a new family. But that didn't mean he wanted the same thing. Losing everything once was more than enough.

Emma's hands went to her hips. "Is this how you think Sadie would want to see her dad? Afraid to smile or laugh or be happy for a single minute because she's not here? Your misery can't bring her back, you know. So don't you think it's time to start living this life

God has given you? Before it's too late?" She tried to stare him down, but James turned away.

Because he knew she was wrong. If God wanted him to live this life, then he shouldn't have asked him to live it without Sadie.

Chapter 12

"So are you going to see James today?"

Ruby's question caught Bethany off guard, and she accidentally pressed the accelerator harder than she meant to, making the car lurch forward.

"I don't know. Why?" But she couldn't pretend she hadn't felt the lurch in her stomach as well as the car.

"He's nice. You should ask him on a date."

"What? Ruby!" Now she braked faster than she meant to. Good grief. She was going to crash yet if Ruby kept talking such nonsense. "We're just friends." If that. Sometimes she couldn't tell. "Do you have your toothbrush?" It was high time to change the subject.

"Yep. And my swimming suit. And a towel. And pajamas. And clothes. And socks and underwear."

Bethany tried to recall what else had been on the list she'd made for Ruby. She still wasn't one hundred percent comfortable with being away from her daughter all weekend, but she couldn't very well withdraw her permission now. She knew Ruby would be in good hands—Tiffany was surely a more competent mom than Bethany would ever be—but she couldn't help feeling like it was a big step toward Ruby's independence. One Ruby might be ready for but Bethany definitely was not.

"And Kimberly's present," Ruby added.

Right. A present. At least Ruby was on top of things.

Bethany pulled into the school parking lot, glancing at the clock. They had five minutes to spare today, which might be a new record.

Tiffany waved to them from behind a car parked near the school, and Bethany pulled into the spot next to her.

"Oh good, you made it." Tiffany pounced on them the moment they got out of the car. "Kimberly already went inside. Ruby, why don't you go ahead too so you're not late. I'll get your stuff from your mom."

Bethany bristled. They were early today, thank you very much.

Ruby popped her arm through the strap of her backpack and turned toward the school.

"Ruby." Bethany didn't mean for her voice to come out harsh like that, but was her daughter really going to leave without saying goodbye?

Ruby turned around and Bethany held out her arms for a hug. With a not-so-subtle check of the parking lot, Ruby gave Bethany the briefest hug in the history of hugs. Then, with a cheerful "bye," she bounded toward the school.

"Have fun," Bethany called after her. "And be careful. Listen to Ms. . . ."

"Stemple," Tiffany filled in.

"I know. Listen to Ms. Stemple."

"I will. Bye, Mom. Have fun with James."

"I— Ruby—"

But with one last giggle, Ruby disappeared into the crowd of students surging for the door. Bethany could only sigh and watch her.

"They grow up too fast, don't they?" Tiffany came up next to her. "You're lucky. Kimberly stopped letting me hug her in public a year ago. No one ever tells you how hard it's going to be."

Bethany shook her head and opened the trunk of her car. Tiffany was clearly only saying that for Bethany's benefit. There was no way Miss Mom-of-the-Year had any concept of how hard it really was.

She pulled Ruby's bag and pillow out of the trunk and passed them to Tiffany, who loaded them into her SUV's already stuffed cargo area.

"That too?" Tiffany pointed into the trunk.

Duh. The present. Bethany reached for it. Ruby never would have forgiven her if she'd forgotten that.

Tiffany tucked the gift into the last remaining pocket of space in the SUV, then closed the hatch.

"So who's James?" Tiffany's voice pitched up, and she nudged Bethany. "The guy you were here with the other day? I've seen him around the stables."

"Oh. Um. Yeah. He's Emma Wood's brother."

"So you two are . . ."

Bethany stared at her. They were what?

"Together?" Tiffany concluded with a laugh.

"Oh." Bethany ignored the jump in her heartbeat. "Of course not. He was just— It's a long story."

Tiffany smiled, but Bethany wasn't sure she liked the way the other woman's eyes had lit up when she'd learned James and Bethany weren't together. "Well, I'd better get going. Enjoy your weekend to yourself."

"I will." But as she backed out of the parking spot, the word *yourself* hung heavily over Bethany. She knew she should probably be looking forward to some time alone, but the house was going to be so empty without Ruby. Maybe she'd invite her friends over for dinner tomorrow night. Cam and Kayla could bring baby Evelyn to meet everyone. A wave of nostalgia went through her as she directed her car toward home. She hadn't had anyone to introduce Ruby to when she was born. It was just the two of them against the world. She shook off the regret. They were surrounded by wonderful friends and family now. She cranked up the volume on the Christian radio station. Songs were one of the few things she could remember easily, and listening to them in the car usually meant that they'd stay with her for the rest of the day—a tangible reminder of God's love to carry inside her. It didn't take long before the music soothed her. Ruby would be fine. She would be fine. And in two days, they'd be together again. She blew out a breath. That wasn't so long.

The ringing of her phone cut through the music as Bethany pulled into her driveway. She glanced at the screen, smiling as baby Evelyn's picture came up. It hadn't taken Cam long to change his profile.

"Hey. I was just about to call and invite you all over for dinner tomorrow. Let baby Evelyn meet everyone."

"Sure. That would be great." Cam sounded exhausted but happy. "But listen, I was thinking, maybe you should show the mayor some options in limestone too. I know he doesn't . . ."

But Bethany missed the rest of Cam's sentence as she yanked the phone away from her ear to check her calendar.

Show samples to mayor, 9 a.m.

And now she remembered. When she'd gone to visit Cam and Kayla and baby Evelyn at the hospital the other day, Cam had asked if she could cover this meeting to show the mayor samples for the big marina job. And she'd said yes, of course she could.

Her gaze flicked to the time. 8:48. The pole shed Cam had recently built on the outskirts of town was only a ten-minute drive from here. She could make it.

She hit the speaker button on her phone and restarted the car.

" . . . think he'll wish he'd gone with something that matches the shoreline," Cam was saying.

"Absolutely." Bethany checked over her shoulder as she backed out of the driveway. "Match the shoreline. Got it."

"Thanks, Bethany. You're a lifesaver." A lusty baby cry cut through the phone. "Shh. It's okay," Cam cooed, and Bethany couldn't help grinning as she pushed her foot to the accelerator. That little baby already had her daddy's complete adoration.

But as soon as they hung up, her grin faded and the worry worked its way in. She'd forgotten the meeting. What made her think she wouldn't mess this whole thing up?

She shook her head. She wouldn't mess up. This was too important to Cam. She could do this.

But more questions wiggled into the cracks in her pep talk. What if she forgot to show the mayor the options Cam wanted? What if she forgot to take notes? Or took bad notes? Or— She forced herself to stop that line of thinking.

She was looking in the wrong place. She didn't need a pep talk. She needed a prayer.

Please give me the strength to do this, Lord. Please help me remember—

The prayer died on her lips as she spotted the brand-new wooden sign in front of Cam's building. Slashes of ugly red spray paint cut through the bright green letters that spelled out Moore Landscaping. She eased into the driveway, her hand going to her mouth. The same red spelled out a profane word against the bright white of the building's aluminum siding, and the window of her brother's office hung with jagged glass. In front of the building, Cam's work truck was also covered with spray paint and tilted at an odd angle, one tire completely flat.

Bethany's mind went blank, though she continued through the gravel parking lot toward the door. What was going on? What should she do?

Before she could decide, a black car tore around the far side of the building, spraying gravel as it gunned through the parking lot. Bethany slammed on the brake, freezing as the car ripped past her. She caught a glimpse of two young men before the car squealed out of the driveway.

Hands shaking, breath rasping, Bethany slid the car into park and pulled out her phone. Who should she call first: Cam or the police?

Dread hammered her ribs as she dialed Cam's number.

"Hey. So I guess—"

"Cam." Her voice froze up. She couldn't tell him.

"He didn't like the stone," Cam continued, and she wondered if maybe she hadn't said his name out loud after all. "Did you tell him—"

"Cam!" She said it loudly enough to make herself jump.

"What's wrong?" His voice became all seriousness, and she was suddenly reminded yet again of how much he had become like their dad.

"I don't know. There was this car. These people . . . They—" She halted, unable to get her thoughts straight. What was the word she needed?

"Wait. Bethany. Slow down. What people? Where?" Cam spoke slowly, and she knew he was trying to help her, but it only made her more frantic. Didn't he see how urgent this was?

"Here. Your building. The sign. The truck. They trashed it."

"Are you all right?" Urgency pulsed in Cam's voice.

"I'm fine. But, Cam—"

"I'll be right there. Just stay put. I'll call the police on my way."

Chapter 13

James patted Fancy Lady's side as he led her to the pasture. Maybe he'd take her out for a ride when he was done mucking. The thought made him lonely, and an image of Bethany slipped into his head. But she wasn't likely to be riding again anytime soon—not after almost falling off Ace the other day. His stomach turned every time he thought of it—followed immediately by the desire to find out how she was doing, make sure she'd seen her doctor about it. But he reminded himself that he wasn't supposed to care—that he *didn't* care. Caring was too dangerous.

He rubbed his hands over Fancy Lady's mane, then turned back to the barn. He'd just gotten started on the first stall when Emma rushed in.

"Morning, sleepyhead." Though she was usually the most chipper of morning birds, she'd still been sleeping when he'd gotten up. "I thought maybe you decided to take—" He caught a glimpse of Emma's face. "What's wrong?"

"Cam and Kayla's business was vandalized."

James let out a sharp breath. He'd been afraid it was something terrible, the way Emma looked. Though he supposed in Hope Springs vandalism was probably a relatively bigger deal than in Milwaukee—if only because it was rarer.

"The police are over there now," Emma said. "But I know they're really understaffed, and I thought maybe you could . . ."

But James was already shaking his head. Much as he hated to know someone was in trouble and not assist, this was way out of his jurisdiction.

"Bethany was there." Emma leveled her gaze at him. "The vandals almost crashed into her."

"What?" The shovel clanged as he shoved it against the wall. "Is she all right? Did you talk to her?"

"Kayla texted me, but I haven't been able to reach Bethany. She's probably talking to the police. But you—"

"What's the address?"

"701 Willowbrook. It's on the outskirts of town, over by the—"

"Got it." He'd already brought up a map on his phone. He jogged toward the door.

"James, wait."

He made an impatient sound but turned to see what his sister wanted.

"Tell them I'm praying for them."

He grunted, then jogged to his truck. His tires squealed as he pulled onto the road, and he pushed the truck faster than he should considering he wasn't in his squad car with the siren on. But if the department was understaffed, they probably didn't have anyone out patrolling.

The law's the law, son. No one is above it. His dad's voice jabbed against the inside of his skull. He eased his foot off the accelerator. But the need to see for himself that Bethany was okay pushed his foot back toward the floor.

"Sorry, Dad," he muttered.

The map had said it would take twenty minutes to get to the location, but James made it in thirteen. He slowed as he pulled into the driveway, anger hardening in his gut at the red paint covering the sign and building and truck.

A small cluster of people stood in front of the pole shed, and James searched them for—

A sharp stab of relief went through him as Bethany turned toward his truck. Her eyes widened, and she lifted a hand as he stopped the truck and jumped out.

He only barely resisted pulling her into a rough hug when he reached the group. Instead, he contented himself with a quick scan to verify she didn't have any injuries.

"James." Cam held out a hand, and James shook it. "Thanks for coming."

He couldn't take his eyes off Bethany. "You okay?"

She nodded, and he let himself breathe again.

"What are you doing here?" Her voice shook slightly—enough to make him resolve to catch whoever had done this.

"Emma told me what happened. I thought I'd see if there was anything I could do to help." He turned to the uniformed officer standing at Bethany's side and held out a hand. "Detective Wood, Milwaukee PD. I'm here on . . . vacation. But if you can put me to use, I'm happy to help out."

The officer eyed him before shaking his hand. "Captain Perry. We don't have much to go on. The vandals were here when Bethany got here this morning. She says she saw them, but she can't remember what kind of car they drove or what they looked like or how many there were." The captain's eyes slid to Bethany, and James recognized the look. Suspicion.

He stepped closer to Bethany.

Her body was rigid, hands clenched. "I'm sorry. I can't . . . remember. I'm trying." Her dark eyes swept to him, and he nearly took her hands in his. He moved toward the building instead, surveying the scene.

"At least it's not gang related." He peered at the artless bubble letters that formed the word.

"What makes you say that?" An older gentleman in khaki pants and a golf shirt stepped up beside him.

"Sorry." Cam stepped forward. "Mr. Mayor, this is James Wood, Emma Wood's brother. James, this is Mayor Harding."

James shook the mayor's hand, then pointed to the graffiti. "Gang graffiti is ugly. Plain paint, thin lines, gang tags and symbols. This isn't exactly the height of artistic ability, but you can tell they were trying. Probably some local kids. A prank or a dare. Have you crossed paths with any kids who might have had something against you?" he asked Cam.

Cam looked at him helplessly. "Not that I can think of. You think it was targeted?"

"Who would do that?" Bethany asked.

The captain peered at her again. "You're sure you don't remember anything?"

Bethany stared at the parking lot, as if trying to see a replay of the events, but after a moment, she shook her head. "It happened so fast," she whispered.

James moved toward the broken window. "Is anything missing?"

"A couple of leaf blowers from my truck, a hedge trimmer, and some solar lights." Cam scrubbed a hand over his face. "Thankfully, I had my laptop with me, and we don't keep any cash on site."

"Good. That's good." James glanced at Bethany, who was running her hands up and down her arms as if she was cold, despite the sunshine.

The captain's radio crackled and he stepped away from the group. James prowled the perimeter of the building. But aside from some scuffed up gravel with no clear shoe prints, the vandals had left no evidence.

The captain returned to them. "I've got an accident across town. I'll send you a copy of my report for insurance. We'll devote as many resources to this as we can, but we're down to two officers. Unless some evidence turns up . . ."

"I understand. Thanks." Cam shook the captain's hand. "We appreciate anything you can do."

"I'd better go get on the phone with the insurance company," Cam said as the captain drove away. "Mr. Mayor, I'm afraid we'll have to reschedule."

"Of course." The mayor clapped Cam on the shoulder. "I don't know what the world is coming to when things like this happen in Hope Springs." He turned to Bethany, who was still rubbing her arms. "I'm glad you're okay." And then to James, "Anything you can do to help is appreciated."

James nodded in surprise. He'd fully expected the same jurisdictional grandstanding he usually ran into.

The mayor got into his car and Cam went inside the building. And then it was only James and Bethany.

"Are you cold?" James moved closer, pulling off his flannel shirt and holding it out to her. A cool breeze cut through his t-shirt.

She looked at the flannel but didn't take it. "I can't . . . I know I saw them, but I can't remember. I keep trying, but . . ."

"It's okay." He settled the shirt over her shoulders, then planted himself directly in front of her. "Where were you when you saw them?"

Bethany's lips pressed into a line, and concentration creased her forehead. After a moment, she threw a hand in the air and pointed to the far side of the parking area. "Over there. I had just pulled in and I saw the graffiti and I didn't know what to do."

"Good. That's good." He took her hand and tugged her toward the spot she'd indicated. Reenacting a scene often helped to jog a witness's memory. Cold radiated from her fingers, and he was tempted to wrap his other hand around them too, to warm them. Instead, he let go as soon as they got to the spot. "You were here?"

"They came around that corner so fast. I was afraid they were going to crash into me." Her voice shook, and he pressed his hands into his pockets so he wouldn't take hers again.

"What kind of vehicle were they driving? What color was it?"

Bethany sighed. "I don't remember."

"That's okay." He kept his voice even. "Close your eyes." He waited for her to comply. "Here they come. They're tearing around that building. They're in a—"

Bethany's eyes popped open. "A car."

She grinned at him in triumph. "They were in a car. A small one. Sporty, I think."

"Good." A small car. That wasn't much to go on. But he needed to keep the momentum going. "What color is it?"

Bethany closed her eyes again, this time looking less tense. But it wasn't long before she opened them, frowning. "I can't remember. Dark, I think. Maybe blue? Or black?"

He didn't know how accurate he could expect her information to be—but it was better than nothing. Probably. "Does anything else stand out about it? A bumper sticker? License plate? Maybe a dent or something?"

Bethany shook her head but then closed her eyes, her brow furrowing. After a moment, she drew in a sharp breath and opened her eyes. "It made a funny sound. Like a whining noise."

"That's great. Good job." An identifying marker, something easy to spot, would have been better, but he wasn't about to tell her that. "Do you remember anything about the driver? How many people were in the car?"

Bethany shook her head but then stopped. "Wait. Yes. There were two of them, I think. Young."

"Boys?"

Bethany nodded. "Do you think you'll be able to find them?" Hope warmed her voice, and he wanted nothing so badly as to tell her yes.

But false hope could be worse than no hope at all. That much he knew for certain. So he gave her the only answer he could: "I'm going to try."

Chapter 14

She didn't want James to leave.

Bethany stood next to him, the warmth of his flannel shirt soft and comforting against her shoulders.

He made her feel safe. He helped her remember.

She tried to come up with another detail so he'd have a reason to stay, even after he'd finished searching the whole place, inside and out, and helping Cam board up the broken window.

"You're sure you're okay?" he asked.

Bethany smiled. Even *she* remembered that it wasn't the first time he'd asked since he'd gotten here. "I'm fine."

"And your vertigo from the other day?" he pressed. "Did you talk to your doctor about it?"

"I called. She said it was to be expected. She'll check me at my next appointment."

Worry still edged James's eyes, and Bethany laid a hand on his arm. "Thank you. For helping Cam and Kayla. It means a lot."

"Of course." James stared at the spot where her fingers rested on his skin, and she lowered her hand. Touching him had been unnecessary. But nice.

"I'm going to drive around town," he said. "See if I can spot anything. If it was a couple of kids, they're probably trying to figure out what to do with all the stuff they just scored."

"I'll come with you." The words popped impulsively out of her mouth. But she couldn't just sit here.

James frowned. "Absolutely not. No."

"I wasn't asking." She folded her arms in front of her and gave him her sternest look, which admittedly probably wasn't very intimidating to him, though it worked wonders when Ruby was misbehaving.

James shook his head. "It could be dangerous."

"You said it was a couple of kids. And anyway, maybe I'll recognize them if I see them."

James opened his mouth, then hesitated. But Bethany knew what he'd been about to say—how was she going to recognize them when she couldn't remember what they looked like?

"Plus," she added, "how are you going to know the sound I heard? I remember sounds better than anything else." She wasn't completely useless.

James sighed but nodded. "You have a point. But you do exactly what I say. No impulse control issues, okay?"

"I promise. Just let me go check on Cam quick." She was halfway to the door when she spun and pointed at him. "And don't even think of leaving without me."

"Wouldn't dream of it." The faintest hint of a smile found its way to his lips.

Bethany continued into the building, pausing to listen for Cam's voice. He'd been on the phone with the insurance company several times already this morning. But he must have finally gotten everything squared away because silence hung over the lawn mowers and gardening equipment that filled the garage space. She made her way to his small office.

But when she reached it, she stopped short. Her brother sat at his desk, head in his hands.

A memory slammed her—the same image, only instead of Cam it had been her father. *Why, Bethany? You know we would have given you anything you needed.*

Cam looked up, offering her a smile worn thin at the edges.

"Cam. I'm so sorry. I wish . . ."

"It's not your fault," he said firmly. He pushed back his chair and strode around the desk to pull her into a hug.

The movement was so unexpected that it took a second for Bethany to return the gesture. Though she knew he had forgiven her for the way she'd destroyed their family, he was rarely demonstrative like this. And she didn't blame him. This may not have been her fault, but she couldn't say the same for what had happened to their father's business.

"I'm just glad you're okay." He squeezed harder, then let go, looking her up and down. "You're sure you *are* okay, right?"

She nodded with an attempt at a laugh. "Scared the daylights out of me, but other than that I'm good. You?" She took a turn scrutinizing him. "You look exhausted."

"Someone could have warned me that babies don't believe in sleep."

Bethany laughed. "How are Kayla and Evelyn doing?"

"Good. I just called, and Kayla said Evelyn finally went down for a nap." He glanced toward the boarded up window. "I wish she wouldn't have to worry about this. She has enough . . ."

"Cam, your wife is the strongest woman I know. She can handle it."

"I know." He shook his head with a short laugh. "I called planning to tell her that everything would be all right, and instead, she was the one who ended up reassuring me."

"That's what partners are for." Or so she assumed. She'd certainly imagined more than once how nice that would be. She looked over her shoulder toward the door. Hopefully James had kept his promise not to leave without her. "There's nothing else you can do here. Why don't you go home and take care of your family. I'm going to go ride around town with James and see if I can recognize the guys who did this."

"Did you remember something?" Cam's eyes sparked with hope.

"Not much. But maybe if I see them again. Or hear their car . . ."

"I don't know, Bethany. That could be dangerous." Cam's voice took on that big-brother protective tone he'd adopted since her accident, even though she was the older sibling.

"I'll be with James. He's a cop. Nothing's going to happen to me."

Cam squeezed her arm. "All right. Be careful."

Bethany headed for the door. But as she stepped outside and spotted James, she had to slightly amend her promise to her brother. Nothing would happen to her physically, that she was sure of. But she couldn't be quite as certain about her heart.

Chapter 15

James massaged a kink in the back of his neck and glanced toward Bethany, who peered intently out her open window. They'd circled the entire town five times and driven out into the countryside on either end, but so far they'd come up empty.

How did he break it to her that this was pointless?

"What about that car?" Bethany gestured excitedly toward a black sedan down the block.

"It's pretty big." James failed to mask his frustration. She'd said it was a small car, and yet this was the seventh larger car she'd pointed out. Was she having doubts about the accuracy of her memories? Because he was.

"Let's just check." She leaned forward as James eased the truck closer to the car. "Are there two people in there?"

The car turned at the intersection in front of them, and James spotted an older lady—driving alone.

"I don't think it was her." He rubbed at his neck again.

"No." Bethany sank back into her seat. "Sorry. Again."

"It's okay." He almost reached to pat her arm but gripped the wheel tighter instead. "Driving around was always a long shot." He pulled into the driveway of the hardware store.

Bethany turned to him. "What are we doing?"

We.

James swallowed. He couldn't let himself enjoy the ring of that word. "If they bought the spray paint here, maybe someone will remember them."

"Smart." Bethany perked back up.

He shrugged. "We don't have a warrant, so . . ." Wait. Had he said *we* too? He opened his door. "But it's a small town. People like to talk. Maybe we'll get lucky."

He waited for Bethany to hop down from the truck, then kept an arm's length away from her as they strode toward the building. But he had to get closer to open the door for her, and her peach scent drifted past him, making him want to lean in. He waited until she was half a dozen steps into the store to follow.

"Where should we start?" She'd stopped to wait for him, and he couldn't avoid stepping close to her to keep from getting run over by a guy with a shopping cart.

He edged away as soon as shopping-cart-guy was gone. The smell of tire and grease drove out Bethany's sweet scent and made it possible to think again. "Over there." He pointed toward a man standing at the end of a row of checkout counters. Probably a manager of some sort.

"Excuse me," James called to the guy as they approached. "I'm Detective Wood. I was wondering if you remember anyone buying some red spray paint recently. Maybe two younger men?"

The manager eyed him, perhaps looking for a badge. There was a reason James hadn't specified his police department.

"Not that I remember," the guy said at last. "But I've been off for the past week. You can talk to Cheryl. She's always here." He pointed to a white-haired woman who was chatting with a young couple as she slowly rang up their purchases.

James and Bethany got in line behind them.

"Are you remodeling?" the cashier asked the couple.

"Sort of." The woman's smile was radiant as she looked to her husband and pressed a hand to her middle. "We're converting a room into a nursery."

"Congratulations!" The cashier stopped scanning their items to beam at them. "Is it your first?"

"Yep. Is it that obvious?" The man wrapped an arm around his wife's shoulders and dropped a kiss on top of her head.

James angled his face away, studying the packs of gum lining the end caps. Melissa had had terrible morning sickness throughout her entire pregnancy, so James had prepared the nursery himself—a sunny yellow that he later told Sadie was the reason she was such a cheerful baby.

"Really, Daddy?" she'd asked.

He'd laughed, tapped her nose, and told her no, it was actually because God had made her his little bundle of sunshine.

He still didn't understand why God had . . .

"James?" A hand on his shoulder made him jump. "Sorry." Bethany let go and gestured toward the cashier, who was waiting for them.

James blinked, relaxing his cramped fingers. With supreme effort, he summoned what he hoped would pass for a smile. "Cheryl?"

At the woman's nod, he moved forward. "Sorry to bother you." He glanced over his shoulder to make sure there was no one in line behind them. "I'm Detective Wood. I'm wondering if you might have seen a couple of young men buying red spray paint recently?"

Cheryl looked toward her manager, then down at her hands, which she had twisted together. "I'm sorry. I know I shouldn't have sold to them. They didn't have IDs, but they promised they were over 18. You're not going to arrest me, are you?"

"Of course not," Bethany cut in.

James glanced at her, then at Cheryl. "Do you happen to remember anything about them? What they looked like?"

"I . . ." Cheryl stared at her hands. "I don't think so."

"Please." Bethany slid closer to James and leaned toward the woman. "I know how hard it can be to remember, but this is really important. Maybe if you close your eyes." She glanced at James. "It helped me."

Cheryl looked from Bethany to James, who nodded. Slowly, she closed her eyes. Both James and Bethany leaned in, and Bethany's hair brushed James's arm. He didn't move.

"Wait!" Cheryl's shout made both of them jump. At least Bethany's hair was no longer silky against his skin.

"One had a scar right here." She drew a line above her eyebrow. "He seemed to be the leader. The other one was small and mousy. I felt sorry for him, to tell you the truth."

"Great. That's really great." Bethany reached across the counter and clasped the woman's hand. "Right?" She turned to James with a brilliant smile.

"It's good." James tried to temper her hope. They still had no idea where to look for these guys—if they even were the culprits. Buying spray paint didn't make them guilty of vandalism.

"Anything else?" James asked Cheryl. "Have you seen them before?"

This time, Cheryl closed her eyes without prompting. Bethany gave James a hopeful look, and he tried to put on an encouraging expression.

But after a minute, Cheryl opened her eyes. "I'm sorry. I don't think I've ever seen them around here before."

"And what day did they come in?"

Cheryl thought. "Sunday, I think. Or maybe Monday."

A guy with a cart full of plumbing parts approached the lane.

"Thank you. If you think of anything else, you can give me a call." James pulled out a card and passed it to her.

"Milwaukee?"

"Just helping out. You can reach me on my cell." The last thing he needed was for his captain to find out he was working a case way outside his jurisdiction—while on a forced vacation.

"And next time, make sure to get an ID," he warned.

Cheryl nodded. "I will."

On the way out of the store, he stopped to ask the manager about security footage, but the manager insisted they didn't have any. Which meant either the guy was holding out for a warrant—or he didn't feel it was necessary to have security cameras in a town as safe as Hope Springs.

"That was so great," Bethany bubbled as they exited the store. "Now we know what the guys look like."

"But not where to find them."

"True." Bethany frowned. "So what next?"

"There's not much else we can do." There he went with that *we* again. "I'll take you back to the shop so you can get your car."

"Wait. That's it? We're giving up?" Bethany crossed her arms as she waited for him to unlock the truck.

He pulled her door open. This was the part of police work he hated—hitting a dead end and knowing there was nothing he could do about it. "I'm sorry. I wish there was something else—"

"Let's at least drive around some more. Hope Springs isn't that big. They have to be here somewhere."

But that was just it. They could be anywhere. Including out of town. "The chances that we'll find them—"

"Please, James." Bethany reached for his arm. "Cam has done so much for me. I have to help him."

He had to say no. It was a fool's errand.

"All right." He puffed out his cheeks and expelled a breath. Apparently, he was willing to be a fool for her.

"Thank you." Bethany flung her arms around his neck and squeezed, then climbed into the truck before he could unfreeze.

"Sorry." But her smile didn't slip.

"That's okay," he croaked. Why could he still feel the imprint of her arms around him?

He closed the door and rounded the truck to the driver's side, getting himself composed on the short walk. Her hug had been nothing but a lack of impulse control, he reminded himself.

And his reaction had been . . . also a lack of impulse control.

He pulled his door open and climbed in, her grateful smile melting him the moment he looked in her direction.

"One condition." He started the truck and pulled out of the parking spot.

"What's that?"

"We get some food. I could eat a horse."

"Don't let your sister hear you say that."

He chuckled at her unexpectedly quick comeback.

"How about the Chocolate Chicken?" She opened her window as he pulled into the street, again peering intently at every passing car.

"Ice cream for lunch? Don't let Emma hear *you* say *that*."

Bethany's laugh filled the truck and seemed to seep in through his skin, filtering toward his heart.

"Wait! Did you hear that?" Bethany's face wore sharp concentration, and she swiveled her head back and forth.

"Hear what?"

"That whine. That's it!" She clutched his arm. "I'm sure of it."

James slowed the truck, listening. "I don't hear—"

"Shh." She pulled her hand off his arm to put a finger in front of her lips. "I heard it."

"Where?"

Her head swiveled more. "I don't know. Back there. Can you turn around?"

James bit back his doubts that she'd actually heard anything and turned the truck around, easing it slowly in the direction they'd come from.

"There." She pointed down a side street toward a small black car pulling into a driveway. "Hear that?"

But the car stopped, and James had to shake his head. Still, it might be worth getting a look at whoever had been in the car. He turned onto the street and sped toward the driveway. If whoever was in the car entered the house before James and Bethany got there, there'd be nothing he could do.

He pulled up along the curb as two guys got out of the car.

"There are two of them," Bethany breathed.

James put the truck in park. "Stay here." He strode casually toward the driveway. The guy who'd gotten out on the passenger side glanced toward him, then away.

"Excuse me," James called.

The kid looked his way again. James supposed he could be described as small and mousy. "Yeah?"

"I'm looking for Moore Landscaping. Can you tell me how to get there?"

Fear flickered in the kid's eyes, and his mouth tightened. "Moore Landscaping?" His voice squeaked an octave higher.

"Never heard of it." The bigger kid came down the driveway. "Sorry we can't help you." The scar above his eyebrow lifted as he directed a look at his friend. "We gotta get going." He raised a hand to scratch his nose, and James spotted the red rimming his fingernails.

Gotcha.

He allowed himself a slow, triumphant smile. "So you weren't over there earlier this morning?" he asked casually.

The small boy gulped loudly enough that Bethany probably heard it from the truck, but the bigger boy grabbed his friend's arm and pulled. "I said we gotta go."

The smaller boy tripped, catching himself at the last second.

"What's the rush?" James asked. He stepped closer to the car and peered into the back seat. "You two planning on doing some landscaping?" He pointed to the solar lights that covered the seat.

"That's my dad's stuff." The older boy smirked.

James smirked right back. "And I suppose the leaf blowers and trimmers are your dad's too?" He kept his eyes on the boys but raised his voice. "Bethany, could you call Captain Perry? These are our guys."

Both boys' eyes widened. The bigger one stepped toward the car, but James blocked him.

The smaller boy cowered. "Chris, maybe we should—"

"Shut up, Pete."

James smiled. Now he had names to put to the faces.

"You're not going to get far if you run. I'm pretty fast." He directed his comments to Pete. "Your best bet is to tell me what's going on."

"We were—"

"Shut up." Chris shoved his friend hard enough to knock him to the ground.

"Hey. That's enough." James sidled closer, getting a better read on the bigger boy. He was scared but afraid to show it—which made him act with a bravado James knew he didn't really possess. And which could make him do something stupid—especially if he was armed.

"Look. I get it." He kept an eye on Chris but spoke to Pete. "You were goofing around, right? You didn't think it was a big deal?"

"It was just a dare," Pete spluttered from the ground. "We wanted—"

"I said shut up!" Chris aimed a kick at Pete, but James was too quick for him, moving in to deflect the blow and pull the kid's arm behind his back in one smooth move.

"Hold still," he warned, loosening his grip but not letting go.

"You can't—"

A sharp siren split the air, and red and blue lights sped toward them.

Chris stiffened and tried to twist away, but James had his arm locked in place.

"Good timing," James called as an officer he hadn't met before sprang from the car.

"Let go of him," the officer shouted as he worked his way toward them, hand on his hip.

"Whoa man. I called this in. I'm Detective Wood, Milwaukee PD. Captain Perry asked for my help this morning. These are the vandals from the Moore Landscaping case. This one was about to beat his friend to a pulp."

The officer didn't relax his posture, and James didn't blame him—he wouldn't have either.

"We did it," Pete whimpered. "Please don't arrest us. My mom will kill me if I go to jail."

Chris aimed another kick at the ground, but James yanked him back.

"You'll find the stolen items in the car." James tipped his head toward the vehicle. The officer looked in the car, then pulled out his cuffs. James adjusted his grip so the officer could fasten them on Chris.

"He didn't tell me we were going to steal anything." Pete's voice wavered as the officer cuffed him too. "I'm really sorry."

"Do they have all of Cam's stuff?" Bethany appeared at James's side.

"Looks like it." James grinned at her. "Nice detective work."

"Thanks." Her cheeks pinked.

"Let me finish up here. Then we can go get that lunch. I could eat *two* horses now."

Chapter 16

Bethany studied her checklist. She was relatively sure she had everything ready for tonight's dinner with her friends. She'd made a big slow cooker full of pulled pork, along with a pan of Snickerdoodles, and her friends would all bring food too. They always ended up with more than enough to eat at these gatherings.

But she still felt like something was missing.

She scanned the room, spotting Ruby's dress shoes in the corner. She picked them up and carried them to Ruby's room.

That was what was missing. Ruby. Or, more like she was missing Ruby.

Only a little longer, she reminded herself. Yesterday had flown by, with their search for the vandals. And today had been filled with cleaning up the house. Tomorrow, she'd go to church, and before she knew it, Ruby would be home.

"Hello," a voice called from the front door. "We're here."

Bethany hurried to the living room, her heart filling at the sound of her sister-in-law's voice. Kayla wheeled through the front door, followed by Cam, carrying a car seat with a sleeping baby Evelyn snuggled inside.

"Give me that little beauty." Bethany rushed for her niece.

"Okay, but if you wake her up, she's yours," Cam joked.

"Deal. You guys go relax. I've got her." Bethany crouched in front of the car seat and carefully extracted Evelyn from the straps. The sleeping baby curled against her shoulder. Bethany closed her eyes, soaking in the sweet, milky scent. Every once in a while, she let herself dream about what it would be like to have another baby. But with her issues—not to mention the fact that she was single—that wasn't likely to happen. So she'd just have to spoil her niece.

Somehow, Evelyn remained sleeping through the bustle of everyone else arriving and cooing over her. Bethany reluctantly relinquished her hold on the baby to give the others a turn. She helped Leah set out the appetizers she'd brought, then found a spot for Peyton's bread and Ariana's fudge and Sophie's spinach dip.

"Got room for this?" Emma waltzed into the kitchen, carrying a tray of deviled eggs. "I barely managed to pry them away from James."

"They can go right here." Bethany slid the pulled pork to the edge of the counter to make room. She peered past her friend toward the living room. But she didn't spot James among the crowd gathered there.

"I thought— I meant to invite him."

She didn't realize she'd spoken out loud until Emma said, "Don't worry, you did. I thought he was going to come, but then—" She shook her head. "He has a hard time with things like this."

Bethany glanced around the space. It was just a group of friends sharing a meal.

But before she could ask what Emma meant, Kayla rolled into the room, baby Evelyn looking cozy and sweet in her lap. "That's too bad. I wanted to thank him in person for getting Cam's stuff back."

Talk turned to the vandalism, but Bethany's thoughts drifted to James. Their lunch together yesterday had been fun and comfortable. She appreciated the way he didn't seem to expect her to fill every moment with small talk. And when she did talk, she felt like he really listened, waiting patiently when she had to pause to search for a word.

Easy. That was how being with him felt. Easier than anything in her life had felt since the aneurysm.

But maybe it didn't feel that way for him.

Maybe that was why he hadn't come tonight. When Emma said he had a hard time with "things like this," did that mean things like her?

"I'm so hungry, Mommy," a little voice cried plaintively. Matthias tugged at Jade, and she shushed him but looked to Bethany.

"I think everyone's here." Bethany smiled at Matthias. "Do you want to ask your daddy to lead the prayer?"

Matthias nodded and rushed toward Dan, who scooped him into his arms and nuzzled his hair. The pang of missing Ruby strengthened in Bethany's middle.

"All right, everyone," Dan called. "This little guy says it's time to eat."

"I'm a big guy," Matthias interrupted.

"Right. Sorry." Dan tickled his son's side. "This big guy is hungry. Let's join together in prayer." He waited a beat as quiet fell over the room. "Dear Lord, we come before you today with hearts overflowing with gratitude. Thank you for bringing baby Evelyn Moore safely into this world. Lord, we ask that you would help us all to support Cam and Kayla as they raise her in you. Lead us to encourage them and share your love with Evelyn. Thank you for bringing us together as a family of believers."

Bethany nodded. These people really were her family, and she was so grateful for them.

"Thank you for the delicious meal we are about to eat," Dan continued. "And for Bethany's hospitality in inviting us here this evening. May our little family here continue to grow. In Jesus' name we pray. Amen."

"Finally!" Matthias shouted, and everyone laughed, making the boy giggle.

"Why don't you go first," Bethany offered to Matthias. "And you're next." She turned to Kayla. "I'll hold Evelyn so you can eat." She stepped forward to take the baby before her sister-in-law could protest. Bethany urged the others to fall in line as well.

"I can take her," Cam offered, holding out his hands for his daughter.

But Bethany shook her head. "Get some food with your wife. It's my turn to take care of you guys for a change."

Cam's laugh was incredulous. "I'd say you already did. I still can't believe you identified the vandals."

"James was the one who caught them."

"That's not what he told me."

She looked up. "You talked to him?" Bethany had called Cam and Kayla on the way to lunch with James, then went right to their house afterward, but James had declined to go with her.

"I called him." Cam studied her. "He said you refused to give up the search even when he told you it was hopeless."

"You know me. I've always been stubborn."

"Seriously, Bethany." Cam refused to laugh off her deflection. "It means a lot to us."

"Yeah, well." She rubbed her fingers over Evelyn's wisps of hair. "You guys mean a lot to me. Now eat."

But the glow of Cam's appreciation stayed with her as she scooted past everyone to take a seat with Evelyn in the living room. She'd just settled in with the baby nestled against her shoulder when the doorbell rang. That was odd. Pretty much everyone she knew in the world was right here.

Except Ruby.

A bolt of fear went through her as she jumped to her feet, the movement disturbing the baby, who immediately broke into loud wails.

"Shh." Bethany rubbed the baby's back as she hurried to the door, fear making her knees spongy. If anything had happened to Ruby . . . "Please don't let it be a police officer, Lord," she whispered as she wrenched the door open.

"Oh." Her relief came out as a long exhale. At least she knew this police officer wasn't here to deliver bad news. "James. You came."

He nodded, Adam's apple bobbing as his eyes rested on the crying baby she held.

Bethany repositioned the baby, who calmed a little. "Meet Evelyn Moore. My niece."

James's jaw tightened, but he nodded again.

So he had come, but apparently he wasn't interested in talking.

"Come on in. Grab a plate. We just started eating." She stood back and gestured toward the kitchen.

"Thanks." His voice was quiet but warm, and a strange thrill went through Bethany at the sound, as if she'd gone too long without hearing it.

His warm spicy scent competed with Evelyn's baby smell as he stepped past her.

"James." Cam strode across the room, a full plate in one hand, the other outstretched.

Everyone else greeted James as well and thanked him for helping to catch the vandals. In spite of baby Evelyn's renewed cries, Bethany couldn't wipe the smile off her face. It felt like Dan's prayer that they bring more people into the family had already been answered.

He should leave.

It was the tenth time he'd told himself that.

Most of Bethany's friends had already headed home. Only he, Emma, and Cam and Kayla and their baby remained.

Seeing Bethany with the baby on her shoulder when she'd answered the door earlier had nearly sent him reeling back to his truck. It had been too reminiscent of seeing Melissa holding a newborn Sadie. But the way Bethany's eyes had rested on his, warm and welcoming, had drawn him into the house.

And now he'd been here nearly four hours and couldn't quite convince himself to leave. Not that he was wrapped up in the conversation between Cam and Kayla and Emma about some new ministry at their church. At the other end of the couch, Bethany appeared to be listening politely, but he could tell her attention had drifted, and she seemed to be struggling to stay awake. Another reason he should leave. So why didn't he want to?

Probably for the same reason he'd decided to come in the first place.

Because for the first time in five years, his insides didn't ache every minute of every day. And he had a strange feeling that the only way to keep them from aching so profoundly was to spend time with these people.

All of them, or one in particular?

Bethany rubbed at her temples, as if massaging a headache. All right. It was time to stop being so selfish and leave so she could go to bed. Maybe the others would follow suit.

He stood and stretched. "Thanks, Bethany. This was . . ." He honestly wasn't sure what word fit at the end of that sentence.

"Are you leaving?" Her eyes drooped with exhaustion, and he reminded himself that was likely tiredness in her voice—not disappointment.

"We should go too." Kayla wheeled toward the spot where Evelyn slept in her car seat. James averted his eyes from the peaceful expression on the baby's face.

"Me too." Emma got up as well.

James moved to the door and held it open for the others, then stepped into the cool spring night that carried a hint of flowers.

"I'm glad you came." Bethany followed him outside, covering a yawn as she spoke.

His swallow felt oddly strained. "So am—"

Her pocket burst into song, and he chuckled as she grabbed for her phone.

"What's that one for? Bedtime?" He was getting used to the numerous alarms she set each day.

But she shook her head, her eyes wide. "It's not an alarm. It's Tiffany. Ruby's at the ... uh ..." He could tell she was groping for the word. "With her." Her hands shook so that she couldn't hit the icon to answer.

James caught her hand to still it. "Hey. I'm sure Ruby's fine." He tapped the answer button for her, his stomach knotting and unknotting and reknotting in quick succession. This was why he couldn't get involved with someone who had a kid. He couldn't go through this again. In fact, he should be heading for his truck, pulling away from the house like the others were.

But he couldn't leave her alone, not with that fear etched on her face.

"Ruby?" Bethany gasped into the phone.

James watched her face impatiently, unable to hear the other end of the phone call. When the tightness in her mouth relaxed slightly, he let himself take a breath.

"I'll be there as soon as I can." Her voice was urgent but not panicked.

James studied her again as she listened to the person on the other end. A few times, she tried to interrupt, but the other person clearly wasn't giving her room to speak.

Finally, she shook her head, her mouth set. "I'm coming to get her. I'll call you when I get there." She hung up, then rubbed at her temples.

"Everything okay?"

"Ruby threw up and wants to come home. Tiffany said I should wait until she brings Ruby home tomorrow, but I'm not going to leave her there when she's sick."

James eyed her. "How far away is it?"

She was already tapping something into her phone. She turned the screen to show him the map. Ninety minutes.

She was in no shape to drive that far. "Maybe you should wait until tomorrow. She'll probably feel better if she sleeps."

Bethany stared at him. "She's my daughter. I'm not going to leave her there when she needs me. Trust me, if you had a kid, you'd be doing the same thing."

James stumbled back a step as she disappeared into the house, leaving the door open behind her.

His heart thudded against his ears. *If he had a kid . . .*

But he knew she was right. If that call had been about Sadie, he'd be jumping in his car right now, no matter the time or how tired he was.

He crossed his arms over his chest and waited for her to emerge, that *if* knocking against his nerves. *If* it hadn't been raining that day. *If* they'd have left five minutes earlier. *If* he hadn't stopped.

A white streak in the doorway caught his eye. Some kind of animal, making a dash for the side of the house. A ferret? He crept toward the spot where it had disappeared behind a bush. Not a ferret. A cat.

And one who didn't seem to know what to do now that it was out here.

"Hey, kitty." He held out a hand to the creature. "Are you supposed to be out here?"

The cat slunk forward and sniffed his fingers, then slid its fur against them. With his other hand, James swooped under the cat's belly and picked it up. Instead of fighting him as James had expected, the cat purred and curled into him.

"Don't get too comfy," he muttered, carrying it toward the front door. He stepped into the light spilling from the house as Bethany emerged.

She stopped short, staring at him. "You're still here."

"You had a runaway." He held up the cat, as if that was the reason he'd stayed.

"Mrs. Whiskers," Bethany scolded, holding out her arms. "Thank you. Ruby would be devastated if we lost her."

James passed her the cat, their hands getting momentarily tangled in the handoff.

Bethany tossed Mrs. Whiskers inside and closed the door, locking it behind her.

"Your car or my truck?" he asked.

"What?" Her brow wrinkled as if he'd spoken a foreign language.

"I'm driving either way. But which vehicle would you rather take?" He stepped into her path, ready for whatever argument she was going to put up.

But the long breath she released sounded more relieved than annoyed. "We can take mine." She passed him the keys and moved to the passenger door before he could even register that he'd won the fight.

Chapter 17

Bethany fought to keep her head upright, eyes open. It took a second to register that her head had bobbed forward again, and she snapped it back, suppressing yet another yawn.

"I don't know why you're fighting it." James's voice was soft, like a lullaby. "Just close your eyes. I'll wake you up when we get there."

With effort, Bethany pushed her lips open to form words. "I'm keeping you company so you don't get—" A giant yawn shook her. "Tired."

James snorted. "I've sat up all night on stakeouts. I'm good. Seriously, just sleep." She thought he turned to look at her, but she was too tired to move even her eyes.

"Maybe for a minute," she murmured, letting the drowsiness overtake her. A soft sigh escaped her lips, and she thought vaguely that she shouldn't feel this relaxed when Ruby was sick. But James was taking her to Ruby. James would take care of them . . .

She jolted awake as something changed. The car had slowed. She swiveled her head to James. "Why are we stopping?"

"We're here."

"Already?"

He chuckled. "Time flies when you're sleeping."

"I'm sorry. I didn't mean to—"

His hand fell on her arm. "It's okay. I told you to. Feel better now?"

Bethany paused. Her headache had completely disappeared, and she no longer felt like someone was trying to glue her eyelids shut. "Much. Thank you."

She opened her car door, moderately surprised when he did the same. She'd figured he'd wait out here. Not that she minded him coming with her. It was kind of nice, actually.

Inside the hotel, a desk clerk asked how he could help. "I need to pick up my daughter. She's in a room with . . . Uh . . ." She had known the woman's name an hour and a half ago. But her brain was still foggy with sleep. "Sorry." She pulled out her phone to find the name.

"Tiffany." Authority rang from James's voice. "Tiffany Stemple."

"Oh yes." The clerk shuffled through some papers. "She called down to let us know you were coming. Room 206."

She thanked the man, then headed for the elevator across the lobby, but James caught her arm and gestured toward the staircase in the middle of the room. "Stairs will be faster."

With a shrug, she followed him. Whatever got her to Ruby fastest was good with her. She practically ran up the stairs to keep up with James's long legs. At the top, he led them to the left. They stopped outside room 206, and James raised a fist to knock, but Bethany wrapped her hand around his knuckles. "I'll text Tiffany," she whispered. "In case they're sleeping." It was nearly midnight already.

"Good idea." James lowered his hand, bringing hers with it. She let go and pulled out her phone, tapping a quick message to Tiffany.

A moment later, the click of a lock echoed through the door, and it swung open.

"James!" Tiffany brought a hand to her hair, smoothing it, though it was already perfect, before her eyes went to Bethany. "I told you that you didn't have to come," she whispered, her eyes darting back and forth between them. "There was no need to interrupt whatever you were . . ."

"Where's Ruby?" James cut in.

"She's sleeping." Tiffany stood back to reveal a roomful of sleeping girls, most of them on the floor, though Ruby was by herself on one of the room's two beds. Her hair was matted to her face, and her cheeks shone as if feverish, but even so relief coursed through Bethany.

She hurried toward the bed, careful to tiptoe around the sprawled girls.

"Don't wake her." James's whisper was closer behind her than she'd expected. "I can carry her."

Bethany eyed him. He was certainly strong enough, but Ruby was also sick. Did he really want to get that close to her? Before she could ask, James had slid his arms under Ruby and hoisted her against his chest. His lips pressed shut, and he looked as if he was holding his breath. Hopefully Ruby didn't smell too much like vomit.

Tiffany passed Ruby's bag to Bethany.

"Thanks for having her," Bethany said dutifully.

"Of course." Tiffany stepped into the hallway with them. "I'll give you a call later in the week to touch base on how things are going for the field day."

Bethany swallowed roughly. "That sounds good."

She followed James, who strode right past the elevator.

"Wouldn't the elevator be easier?" She watched Ruby's head, which lolled on James's arm.

"Nope." He reached the stairs and started down.

"Don't drop her." She raced to stay at his side.

He glanced her way, his lips lifting a fraction. "Don't worry. I won't."

When they got to the car, Bethany helped him maneuver Ruby into her seat and fasten her seatbelt. The girl stirred, and Bethany pushed her hair off her cheeks. "Mom's here. Go back to sleep."

Ruby obeyed, and Bethany got into her own seat. James started the car and pulled onto the road.

"Thank you." The words felt inadequate, but she had no others.

"Anytime."

It didn't feel like the flippant *anytime* a regular person would give. It felt more like a promise.

Bethany scoffed at herself. Of course it wasn't a promise. He was just being nice. Doing his job.

"So what's this field day thing Tiffany mentioned?" James's low voice provided a welcome interruption to the crazy line of Bethany's thoughts.

"It's a big activity day and fundraiser on the last day of school. I accidentally volunteered to organize it."

"Accidentally?" Amusement warmed James's voice.

"Maybe not accidentally. More like—" Drat. Why could this word never come to her?

"Impulsively?" James asked

"Yes." And how did he always know exactly the word she was searching for? "But don't tell Tiffany that," she rushed to add. "I think she already doubts that I can do it."

"Why would she doubt you?" The genuine question in his voice filled Bethany, until he asked, "How's it going so far?"

"Uh. Well." Bethany concentrated on the view out the window, though she couldn't see much beyond the side of the road in the dark. "I haven't started yet. But—" She didn't want him to think she was a total flake. "I know what I'm going to do." That was maybe a stretch, but close enough. She had some ideas. She only hoped she'd written them down, because none of them were coming to her right now.

"If you need any . . ." But he trailed off without finishing the sentence.

"Mom," Ruby's sleepy voice called from behind them.

"Hey, Rubes." Bethany twisted in her seat to check on her daughter. "How are you feeling?"

"Better, I think. Hi, James."

Bethany angled her head toward James.

"Hi." His knuckles stood out against the steering wheel, and he stared straight ahead. It wasn't the first time she'd wondered if he really did dislike her daughter.

If he did, then he was the one missing out. She turned to Ruby. "We're almost home. Why don't you get some more rest?"

"I had a dream about you."

"That's nice, sweetie. I'm here now."

"And you too, James," Ruby added. "You were walking down these big fancy stairs together. I think you were getting married."

A strangled cough came from the driver's seat, and Bethany wished this were a Flintstone car so she could slip right out the bottom.

She rubbed her eyes. "That was at the hotel, Ruby. James was carrying you down the steps, and I was walking next to him. We weren't getting married."

"Oh." Ruby fell silent, and Bethany turned slowly toward the front of the car, careful to avoid looking at James. She could only imagine what he was thinking.

"Do you mind if I turn on the radio?" She needed the distraction.

"It's your car." The words were clipped.

She turned on the radio and leaned back against her seat, letting herself lip sync to the lyrics.

"Mom?" Ruby trilled after a few minutes.

"What is it, Rubes?" She didn't turn around this time because she wasn't ready to look at James.

"Why don't you date?"

Oh, for heaven's sake! "I just— I don't—" She couldn't put together a sentence—not when she could feel James watching her. "I just don't." There. At least she'd put three words together.

She peered out the window, squinting desperately for landmarks. They had to be almost home by now.

There! The sign announcing that Hope Springs was five miles away. She only had to survive a few more minutes.

"I know!" The excitement in Ruby's voice sent a wave of nerves through Bethany. Heaven only knew what was going to come out of her daughter's mouth next.

"Oh look." Bethany pointed toward the marina, where the moon illuminated a sailboat painted in vibrant colors.

"You and James should date," Ruby said gleefully. "And then you really can get married and I can have a dad."

"Ruby!" Bethany's eyes went involuntarily to James.

He clutched the steering wheel so hard, she feared he might pull it right off. A muscle in his jaw worked, as if he were trying to crank it shut tighter.

"No one is dating or marrying anyone." She blew out a breath, making herself speak to James next. "Sorry. She clearly needs some sleep."

"No problem." His lips didn't move around the words, and he didn't say another thing the rest of the way. When they reached Bethany's house, he bolted silently out of the car and into his truck.

"Thank you again," Bethany called before he shut himself inside.

He nodded and pulled away.

At least she'd been right about one thing: no one was going to be dating or marrying anyone.

Chapter 18

James scanned the progress he'd made in cleaning the stalls, then checked the time. 7:30 a.m. Despite his early start today, there was no way he was going to finish before Bethany got here. Which meant he was going to have to see her. For the first time in a week. When she'd had to cancel helping at the stables on Wednesday because she'd come down with Ruby's stomach bug, he'd been relieved. Not that she was sick—but that he wouldn't have to face her after what Ruby had said.

He'd spent all week struggling not to think about the girl's blithe statement that he and Bethany should date and get married. *Then I could have a dad.*

As if he could so easily step back into that role. As if he'd want to, after the first time had shattered him.

He knew it wasn't fair to hold the words against Ruby; she had no idea that he'd ever been a dad.

But her words had been a wake-up call. He had to stop spending so much time with Bethany. Thankfully, his enforced vacation was almost over. Two more weeks and he'd be back to work. Or maybe he'd call the captain and convince him to take him back earlier. He jabbed his pitchfork into the soiled straw, ignoring the stab of protest from his shoulder. If he could muck a stall, he could take down a criminal. Hadn't he proved that when he'd caught those vandals last week?

With Bethany's help.

He shoved the pitchfork harder. Why did it seem everything he'd done since arriving in Hope Springs involved her? And why did the thought of going back to Milwaukee, where he would never see her, raise a grumpy protest in his chest?

His phone rang, and James wiped at the sweat on his brow before answering.

"Detective Wood?"

"Yes?" James set the pitchfork down, on alert. It hadn't been a number he recognized.

"This is Captain Perry. Of the Hope Springs police department. We met on the Moore vandalism case?"

"Of course, Captain. Did you get the report I sent over?" Not that it was required, since this wasn't his department and he'd given a statement to the officer on the scene, but he always felt better if he made a written record of everything.

"I did, thanks."

"Great." James tucked the phone between his ear and his good shoulder as he moved to the wheelbarrow. "If there's anything else I can do . . ."

"Actually, I hope there is."

"Yeah? What's that?" James hoisted the wheelbarrow and steered it toward the next stall.

"I was hoping I might be able to convince you to take a position here."

"What?" James picked up his head in shock, his phone sliding down his arm—straight toward the wheelbarrow full of dirty horse bedding. James swiped at it—but that meant letting go of the wheelbarrow with one hand. The whole thing tipped toward the right, and it was only his lightning reflexes that kept it from spilling all over the floor. A loud crack announced that the phone hadn't been so lucky. James lunged for it, inspecting it for signs it had gotten soiled before lifting it toward his ear. He held it a few inches away, just in case.

"Hello? Are you there?" The captain's voice sounded distant.

"Sorry about that. Dropped my phone."

"I'll take it as a good sign that you didn't hang up on me." The captain chuckled.

"Look, Captain, I appreciate—"

"I know I probably can't match your current salary," the captain interrupted.

"I don't care about the money." Being a cop had never been about earning a paycheck for him. It was about justice, about helping those who needed help, about honoring his father.

"Even better," Captain Perry joked. "Just give it some thought, would you? I spoke to your captain, and he thought the change of scenery might not be such a bad thing."

"What?" James's grip on his phone tightened to the point where he expected it to snap in half. Betrayal snapped harder. After everything he'd given the department, Captain Burke was ready to get rid of him?

"He told me what happened with your daughter." Captain Perry's voice took on that overly soft tone everyone used when they learned about Sadie. "I have a little girl, and I can't imagine—"

"Yeah." James couldn't have this conversation. "Thanks for the offer, but I have to run."

"Just think about—"

James hit the button to end the call and shoved his phone into his pocket.

Outside, a horse nickered, and in the barn, the scent of horse manure and hay closed in on him. He pressed a hand against the smooth wood of the nearest stall. He wasn't going to pretend there weren't things about Hope Springs he'd miss. But that didn't mean he was going to stay here and take a job with the tiny department. He was needed in Milwaukee.

At least he had thought he was. Apparently, Captain Burke felt differently.

He considered pulling his phone out and calling the betrayer right now—but there was too big a risk he'd say something that would get him fired on the spot. He needed to wait until he calmed down. Which might take a while.

With a growl low in his throat, he seized the wheelbarrow handles and charged toward the door. By the time he'd emptied it and started back toward the barn, he'd constructed a rough outline of what he'd say to his captain if he could talk to him right now. Based on that, it was best he wait longer to make the call.

He stepped into the barn, his eyes taking a moment to adjust from the bright sunlight outside to the dimmer artificial light in here.

"Hi, James."

His gaze jumped toward her voice. She stood next to the stall he'd been in the middle of cleaning before Captain Perry's call. Her smile seemed nervous, her posture uncertain. He slowed as he approached her.

This was another reason he couldn't take a job in Hope Springs—he couldn't afford to get closer to her and Ruby.

"Hi." His greeting sounded stilted, and Bethany must have noticed too because her smile faltered. He felt bad. She probably didn't even remember what Ruby had said. "Are you feeling better?"

She nodded and picked up a shovel. James let out a breath as she turned toward a stall. If she did remember, at least she wasn't going to bring it up.

"Listen." She didn't face him. "I wanted to apologize for what Ruby said the other night. I hope you know she didn't get that idea from me. She's just . . ." She tilted her head toward the ceiling, as if she'd find the word she was looking for scrawled across the wooden beams.

James followed her gaze. His eyes landed on a bird's nest clinging to the corner of the rafters. "Precocious?" The word slipped from his lips before he remembered that the last time he'd used it was to describe Sadie.

"I was going to say ridiculous." Bethany's laugh still held a tinge of nervousness. "But that works too. What are you looking at?"

He smelled her soft, peachy scent first, before he felt her move closer to him.

"A bird's nest." He pointed toward the rafters.

"Where?" Bethany shifted, and her scent wrapped all the way around him.

"Right there." He shook his finger toward the nest, as if that would help.

"I don't see it." Her scent drifted away from him, and he dropped his arm.

"Here." He grasped her shoulders lightly—though not lightly enough to avoid the jolt the contact produced—and moved her into the spot where he'd been standing. He reached over her shoulder to point so that she could follow the line of his arm, right up to the rafters.

"Oh." A childlike awe filled her exclamation as a baby bird stuck its head up from the nest.

James dropped his gaze and took a step backwards. "I'd better get back to work."

"You got a lot done already."

"Yeah." He grabbed his pitchfork and returned to the half-cleaned stall.

After a few seconds, he heard the scrape of Bethany's pitchfork in the next stall. They worked in silence, James's brain whirring as he mentally revised what he planned to say to Captain Burke. He'd managed to come up with something almost civil by the time they were done.

When they'd put everything away, Bethany looked at her phone. "It's a good thing we got done quickly. They're supposed to clean up the graffiti today, and now I can go over there and supervise so Cam doesn't have to worry about it."

James tried to follow what she was saying, but he must have missed something. There was no reason anyone should have to supervise the cleaners. Unless— "Who's they?"

"The boys," Bethany answered, as if it were obvious. "The ones who did the damage. Cam talked to their parents and said he'd ask the prosecutor to drop the charges as long as they cleaned everything up and paid for the broken window and the truck repairs."

"That's—" The word *stupid* was on his tongue, but he held it back at the look on Bethany's face.

"Generous," she filled in for him, grinning as if she'd found a word he couldn't. "Cam's a big believer in second chances," she continued. "Fortunately for me."

He tipped his head. "How so?"

Bethany looked at him with the panicked expression he recognized as belonging to someone who had said something incriminating—but then she schooled her face into a smile. "Oh you know . . ."

James studied her—he *didn't* know, but he decided to let it pass. It was none of his business.

"Anyway, I'd better get going. Ruby's spending the day at Kimberly's to make up for missing part of the party." Bethany pulled out her phone and tapped the screen a few times, then lifted it to her ear as she strode toward the barn doors.

"Hey, Cam," he heard her say. "I'm on my way over to the shop. You stay with Kayla and Evelyn." She pulled her keys out of her pocket, then disappeared out the barn doors.

Uneasiness stirred in James's belly. *Leave it,* he commanded himself. Those boys had been pulling a stupid prank. They were unlikely to be a serious threat to Bethany. Not to mention that she wasn't his responsibility.

Serve and protect. That's the job, son.

Yeah, it was. But he wasn't on the job. Just like he hadn't been on the job the day he'd pulled over to help at that accident.

If he hadn't had such a hero complex, maybe Sadie . . .

Stop.

He couldn't let himself go down the *if only* road again.

Because no matter how much he wanted to change the past, he couldn't. All he could do was attempt to forget it. And the only way to forget it was to stay busy.

"Bethany. Wait." James shot through the stable, squinting in the sunlight as he burst out the door. But Bethany was already in her car. He called her name again as the engine turned over. But she must not have heard him. Her car rolled down the driveway.

He should go back into the barn. The last thing he needed was to spend more time with Bethany.

Her car pulled onto the road.

James stared after it a few seconds. Then instinct took over and he jumped into his truck and followed her.

Chapter 19

Bethany lifted her eyes to the rearview mirror again as she turned onto Willowbrook Street. The black pickup behind her turned too, and her heart accelerated faster than the vehicle. She wasn't sure how long the truck had been behind her—she hadn't noticed it at first because there had been a couple of vehicles between them—but the truck had steadily gained on her, and she was pretty sure it had been following her for the past few turns at least.

Lots of people drive this way, she reminded herself. She'd been watching too many cop shows lately. People didn't get followed in Hope Springs.

She slowed for the turn into Moore Landscaping, waiting for the pickup to tear around her. But it slowed too.

She was about to slam her foot onto the gas pedal and take off when the pickup got close enough for her to make out the driver.

James?

It sure looked like him.

Heart calming a little, she made the turn, the black truck following close behind.

She pulled up to the building and turned off her car, taking a moment to get her breathing under control before opening her door.

By the time she got out, James was already standing in front of her car.

A rush of unexpected anger hit Bethany as he stood there looking all calm and collected after nearly giving her a heart attack. She slammed her door and marched toward him. "You scared me half to death, following me like that."

James looked surprised—but not apologetic. "Sorry. I thought you'd recognize my truck."

She shook her head. Never mind that he should have realized she wouldn't. "What are you doing here?"

James shoved his hands in his pockets and looked away. "Didn't like the idea of you here alone with those punks."

"I— Oh." Well, that was sort of sweet. But unnecessary. "Trust me. I've dealt with worse. A lot worse." She wasn't proud of that time in her life, but she'd learned to take care of herself in some pretty awful situations.

James looked doubtful. "I don't have anything else going on. I might as well make myself useful."

Bethany peered at him. "You're not very good at relaxing, are you?"

"Ha. I don't really believe in just sitting around." His eyes jerked to the road as a car squealed into the driveway, sending gravel shooting behind it. The vehicle roared toward them, and James stepped in front of Bethany. She grabbed his arm with a gasp as the car skidded to a stop a foot in front of them.

"Second chances," James muttered, shaking his head.

Bethany stepped out from behind him, her pulse knocking against the side of her neck. The kid had only been showing off. She was sure he wouldn't really have hurt them—but suddenly she was grateful to have James at her side. It'd been a long time since she'd had to deal with anyone threatening.

The kid wore a sneer as he got out of the car. He looked Bethany up and down, his gaze lingering long enough that she crossed her arms in front of her.

James stepped toward the kid, whose eyes finally went to him.

"You don't have jurisdiction here." He smirked.

"Get to work, Chris." James's voice carried authority without threat.

"Who's going to make me?" Chris's smirk morphed into a sickening laugh. "You, old man?"

James pointed at the kid. "You want to throw away your second chance? Go ahead. If it were up to me, you'd be in jail."

"James." Bethany grabbed his arm, sending him a warning look. "Do you have cleaner?" she asked the boy.

Chris stared at James another minute, then looked away. "Yeah. I got it." He moved to the trunk. "I'm not starting until Pete gets here though."

"Of course. Make him do the dirty work, like always." James curled a lip. "How long did it take you to convince him to do this in the first place?" James gestured toward the spray painted building. "I suppose it makes you feel tough to know you can make a kid half your size do whatever you say."

"You don't know me, man." Chris glared at James, and Bethany put herself between them.

With an impatient grunt, James stepped around her. "Trust me. I know you. I see guys like you every day. And I know where they end up."

"James." Bethany's voice was sharper than even she expected. "Maybe you should go."

James threw his hands in the air and shook his head, striding to the far side of his truck but not getting in. Instead, he crossed his arms and leaned against the door, his back to them as he faced the road.

Bethany let out a long breath. What would she have done if he'd followed her impulsive order to leave?

"Your boyfriend needs to chill." Chris twisted his face with that sneer again.

"He's not my boyfriend."

"Oh, really?" The boy's eyes traveled her body again, and she barely resisted the urge to run away.

She pulled her arms tighter. "And he's right that you don't want to throw away your second chance. Trust me." How many chances had her parents given her? Five? Six? And she'd thrown away every single one. Until it was too late.

The crunch of tires on the driveway drew their attention to another vehicle approaching—this one moving much more slowly and driven by a woman who looked to be around Bethany's age.

Chris snorted. "He brought his mom." His face wore contempt, but Bethany heard the ache under the words. He scuffed his feet toward the building, the cleaner and a rag hanging limply from his hand.

Bethany moved around his car to the spot where the woman was parking the other vehicle. After a moment, the woman got out, as did the boy sitting in the passenger seat.

"Come over here before you get started, Pete," the woman called before turning to Bethany. "Carrie Smith. Pete's mom." She offered a tight smile. "I can't tell you how sorry I am about all of this. And Pete has something he wants to say too."

Pete reached his mother's side just as James appeared next to Bethany. To her surprise, the boy looked relieved to see James.

"Go ahead, Pete," his mother prompted.

"Thank you for the second chance," Pete murmured. Though Bethany had to strain to catch the words, she could tell they were sincere.

"That's my brother's doing," she replied. "Trust me, you're not the only one he's given a second chance. I hope you won't take it for granted."

The boy nodded.

"Go get to work, Pete. The cleaning supplies are in the back," Carrie said firmly.

Pete moved to the trunk and pulled out a large bucket filled with spray bottles, sponges, rags, and gloves. He eyed James again before making his way toward Chris, who stood leaning against the building, arms crossed, smirking toward them.

"I'm so sorry," the woman said again as Chris reached over to slug Pete's shoulder—hard, from the looks of it. Next to her, Bethany felt James tense. But Pete simply set down the bucket and started working. After a minute, Chris did too.

"I don't know what to do." The woman—her name had slipped out of Bethany's mind already—sniffed and rubbed under her eyes. "He was always such a good kid. But then my husband left and Pete started high school and met Chris." She gulped loudly. "Never mind. It's no excuse. I'll do better."

"I'm sure you're doing the best you can." Bethany moved closer and squeezed the woman's shoulder. "It's not your fault."

"My dad died when I was about Pete's age." It took Bethany a moment to realize the words had come from James, they were so soft-spoken. "I don't know how my mom made it through those years. I sure didn't make it easy. Got into all kinds of trouble."

Bethany blinked at James, trying to picture him making trouble of any sort. Impossible.

"What changed?" the woman asked.

"Spent a night in jail."

"Oh." The woman squeaked at the same time Bethany's jaw came unhinged. There was no way.

"Not like that," James clarified. "My dad was a cop and his partner arranged it. Said that was where I was going to end up if I kept going the way I was. And then the next day he took me fishing. Caught a bass this big." He held his hands out, and all Bethany could do was gape. Had he always been this talkative?

"So you think he needs a night in jail?" Pete's mom wilted against her car.

"Nah." James peered toward the building, where Pete was scrubbing against a slash of red. "I think this will be enough to set him straight. That other kid though . . ."

"Chris?" The woman sighed. "He has a sad story. His dad died during a robbery. I don't know much about his mom except that she seems to have checked out. Rarely leaves the house, except to go to the liquor store."

"Oh dear." Bethany pressed a hand to her heart. It was no wonder the boy acted out. She'd had the most wonderful family in the world, and still she'd gone down the wrong path. How was this boy—who had no one there for him—supposed to find his way? "Is there anything . . ."

She forgot what she was going to say as she realized James was striding away from them, toward the boys. Purpose clung to his steps. Pete kept working as James approached, but Chris stopped and crossed his arms, a quick flash of fear instantly replaced with a grating smirk. Bethany held her breath, praying James wasn't about to do something drastic.

But when he reached the boys, he simply bent and picked up a scrub brush and some cleaner and started working between them. Pete acknowledged him with a quick nod, and after a second, Chris started scrubbing again, harder this time.

"I should get back to work." Pete's mom clicked her phone on nervously. "Do you think it'd be okay if I come pick him up around three?"

"Oh don't worry about that. I can give him a ride home."

"You would do that?" The woman stared at her as if she'd grown a halo.

"Like I said, I know what it's like to need a second chance."

"Thank you." The woman squeezed her hand. "God bless you."

"Believe me, he has." As the woman drove away, Bethany went to help James and the boys with the cleanup. They worked mostly silently, aside from an occasional instruction from James. It took a good two hours of steady work before the building gleamed almost like new. Fortunately, the sign only took another hour.

By the time they'd finished, Bethany's shoulders ached and her stomach rumbled.

"Do you need a ride home, Pete?" James asked as they finished gathering up the cleaning supplies.

"I have a better idea," Bethany cut in. "Why don't you take Pete and Chris fishing?" She wasn't sure where the idea had come from so suddenly, but sometimes her lack of impulse control was brilliant.

"Fishing?" James stared at her—and she very much doubted he was seeing a halo. Maybe horns.

"You know, like your dad's partner—"

James shook his head. "*That* you remember?"

She shrugged. "It's not like I control it. And I also remember that you don't have anything else going on today and you don't like to just sit around, so . . . Do you guys like to fish?"

Pete was already nodding enthusiastically, looking at James as if he were a hero. Chris shrugged. "It's kinda lame, but whatever. It's not like I have anything else to do."

Bethany met James's eyes. Surely he could see how badly these boys needed this.

James rubbed a hand back and forth over the top of his head. "I don't have any fishing poles."

"Emma does." She wasn't sure how she knew that, but she did. "You run to the farm and pick them up. I'll pick Ruby up from her friend's house. We'll meet you at the marina. And I'll bring food."

Chapter 20

How in the world had he managed to get talked into this? James tried to loosen the tension in his neck as he turned onto the road that led down to the marina. His job was to put criminals in jail—not take them fishing.

He understood what Bethany was trying to do—admired it, even—but she had to realize that most people who were given a second chance blew it.

He glanced toward Chris, in the passenger seat. He couldn't ignore the fact that the kid's father had been killed in a robbery—same as James's dad. But whereas James's mother had taken on the role of both mother and father for him, this kid apparently had no one.

James pulled the truck into a parking spot. It wasn't likely that one fishing trip was going to change these kids' lives.

But he was here now, so . . .

"Hi, James." Ruby hopped out of the car that had pulled in next to them, sticking her hand in his open window.

He nodded to her, then quickly looked away. She had her hair in pigtails today, and suddenly all he could see was the lopsided pigtails he'd put in Sadie's hair. She'd never seemed to care that they were uneven.

James got out of the truck and scooted past Ruby to pull out the fishing rods and tackle box he'd picked up from Emma's house. His sister had quite the impressive collection of fishing gear.

He passed a rod to each of the teen boys, then one to Ruby and one to Bethany, who didn't look in the least concerned that she'd roped him into spending the afternoon in the last way he wanted to spend it.

"Can we go over there?" Ruby pointed to the end of the breakwater, where waves splashed against the large boulders that lined the sides of the wide concrete walkway.

"Sure." James shrugged. It wasn't like it mattered if they caught anything. All he had to do was survive for an hour or two and then he could be free.

"Thanks!" Ruby's smile poked its way right through James's heart.

"Come on." She turned to Pete and Chris with that same smile, already assuming a friendship with them. Both boys followed her, Pete looking enthusiastic, Chris giving her a begrudging nod.

James reached into the truck bed to grab the bucket he'd brought just in case they caught something. When he turned around, he was surprised to find Bethany waiting for him. He took the bag of snacks she held, hooking it over his arm.

They fell silently into step next to each other, following Ruby and the boys. Even from a few yards behind, James could make out her mile-a-minute chatter.

"Next time you could maybe consult with me first before volunteering me for something like this," he said in a low voice.

"Sorry." Her voice held no hint of remorse. "She's good at that, isn't she?"

James followed her gaze to Ruby, whose fishing pole swung wildly toward Pete as she kept up her enthusiastic chatter. Pete dodged but laughed.

"At what? Gouging people's eyes out?" James asked as her pole got dangerously close to Chris.

Bethany snorted. "No. That." She waved a hand toward the trio. "Talking to people."

James shrugged. They used to call Sadie Little Miss Talks-a-Lot, but Ruby might give her a run for her money.

"She thinks you don't like her."

"I— What? Who?" James swiveled his head in every direction as if he'd find some mysterious "she" Bethany was referring to.

"Ruby." Bethany said her daughter's name quietly, but a mama-bear protectiveness roared under the word.

"I— It's not—" How could he explain to Bethany that looking at her daughter was like looking through a mirror that showed everything he'd lost?

But she didn't give him a chance to try. "You're the one missing out. She's the best, sweetest little girl. And if you can't see that, it's your loss."

Before James could answer, Bethany had sped up, quickly closing in on Ruby and the boys. She said something to Ruby, who slipped her hand into her mother's. The girl smiled over her shoulder at James, making his heart contract so painfully that he wondered if he was having a heart attack. But then Ruby turned around again and his heart released. The pain in his chest lingered though, even as he caught up with the group and prepared their lines and showed them how to cast and how to set the hook if they felt a bite. It wasn't until he tossed his own line into the water that it eased a little. He'd chosen a spot several yards from Ruby and Bethany, which put him next to Chris. But right now he'd gladly take a juvenile delinquent over the chatterbox who reminded him so painfully of what he used to have. He was sorry if that made Ruby think he didn't like her—but it was the only way he was going to survive the afternoon.

He cast his line again and gazed across the waves to the horizon, letting his mind wander to Captain Perry's offer. Today was one more proof that Hope Springs wasn't for him. In Milwaukee, he never would have gotten roped into fishing with a couple of vandals, a crazy woman, and her daughter. In Milwaukee, he could do the job and then go home, day after day. In Milwaukee, nothing changed. Nothing brought him great joy, maybe. But nothing brought him sorrow either. He rubbed at his chest.

"Ah! Help!"

The cry startled James from his thoughts, and before he had consciously registered that it had come from Ruby, he was sprinting toward her.

"What's wrong?" he called, though he couldn't spot any immediate danger.

"Something is trying to steal my fishing pole." Ruby strained to pull it toward her.

James let out a breath as he reached her, chuckling. "That's a fish."

"It is?" Ruby's eyes went wide.

"Reel it in."

"I can't." Ruby appeared to be using all her strength to hold onto the pole.

"Here." James stepped behind the girl and reached around her to hold the pole. "I'll hold onto it. You reel. Slowly." The fish tugged on the other end of the line. "Feels like a big one."

"Really?" Delight sang from Ruby's tone. "This is fun."

"Keep cranking." He readjusted his grip so she could turn the reel more freely. "There it is." He pointed into the water a few feet from the boulders that jutted out from the breakwater. "Chris, climb down there and grab the line. You need to lift it over the rocks so we don't lose it."

Chris didn't reply, and the fish was getting closer. James gave an impatient sigh. "Pete, can you—"

"I got it." Chris climbed nimbly over the rocks and reached for the line.

"Easy," James cautioned.

"I said I got it." Chris shot him a look but pulled the line out of the water carefully. The fish dangled precariously on the end of the line.

"Grab it so it doesn't fall off," James called.

"You want me to touch it?"

"Yes. And hurry up before it ends up back in the water."

Chris made a face but wrapped a hand around the fish's middle.

"Watch the fins," James warned. "They're sharp." He let go of the fishing pole and moved to take the fish from Chris as he reached the top of the breakwater. "Nice job."

Chris shrugged, but James saw the way his expression softened. Maybe Bethany had been right that this was what the boys needed.

He held the fish out to Ruby. "It's a walleye."

She giggled. "That's a funny name. Can I touch it?"

"You can hold it if you want." Ruby nodded, and he placed it into her hands. "Hold it tight."

"Say 'fish.'" Bethany pointed her phone at Ruby.

"Fish." Ruby called, just as the fish wiggled. James lunged forward and helped her catch it.

"Get in there, boys," Bethany called. "This was a team effort." Both boys looked embarrassed but also pleased. James inched backwards, but Ruby smiled at him. "You too, James."

"No, that's okay. I don't—"

"You heard the girl. Get in there." Bethany lowered her phone, waiting for him. "If it weren't for you, that fish might have pulled Ruby right out to the middle of the lake."

James shook his head but stepped up next to Pete. It was easier than arguing.

After they'd taken the pictures, James helped Ruby put her fish in the bucket and reset her line. The rest of the afternoon, he was kept hopping from one person to the next, helping pull in fish and untangle lines. By the time they decided to call it a day, Pete and Bethany had caught one fish each, Chris two, and Ruby four. James hadn't had a spare moment to catch anything of his own, but he didn't mind.

"This was the best day ever, wasn't it?" Ruby bubbled as they hauled their catch and gear back to the parking lot.

Pete smiled at her. "It was fun."

Even Chris nodded. "You're a good fisherman."

"Fisher*girl*," Ruby corrected, making Chris laugh.

James set the bucket of fish down when they reached the vehicles. "I only have one bucket, so who's going to take the fish home?"

"I don't know how to clean fish," Bethany said. "So you boys can take them."

Pete shook his head. "My mom would kill me. She hates fish."

"All right. Chris, you take them." James passed the bucket to the teen. "Do you know what to do with them?"

The boy shrugged. "I'll figure it out."

"I can teach you." The words were out of his mouth before he could think. Maybe Bethany's impulse control issues were contagious.

He tried to figure out a way to take it back.

"That's a great idea." Of course Bethany had jumped right on that one. "You guys come on over to my house, and James can show you how to clean and cook the fish. I'll make some potatoes to go with it too."

"Bethany, I don't think—"

"Of course you do. Come on. Follow us." She jumped in her car before James could say anything else.

He eyed Pete and Chris, who were both laughing.

"Shut up," he growled.

But he gestured for them to get in the vehicle, then did the same and followed Bethany to her house.

"I'm sorry we didn't have any potatoes." Bethany carried the leftover fish to the counter and divided it into bags for Pete and Chris to take home. There wasn't much left—the boys had scarfed it down after helping James clean and cook it, and even Ruby had eaten seconds and then thirds.

"It's really fine." James's smile was overly patient.

"I've already said that, haven't I?" she asked sheepishly. Sometimes it was hard to keep track of what she'd said out loud and what she'd only spoken in her head.

James shrugged. "Don't beat yourself up over it. There was more than enough food."

A burst of laughter came from the living room, where Ruby had coerced Pete and Chris into a game of Pictionary.

"Do you think this will make a difference? For those boys?" She leaned against the counter.

James tucked the milk jug into the refrigerator. "Maybe." He turned to face her. "Maybe not."

"That's not very optimistic."

"After some of the things I've seen, that's as optimistic as I get."

"But you came," she pointed out.

"As I recall, I didn't have much of a choice."

Bethany laughed and loaded dishes into the dishwasher. "You're a funny guy. Did you know that?"

"Can't say I've ever been accused of that before." But his smile made him look almost cheerful. "What makes you say that?"

She studied him. "I don't know." Or maybe she did know, but she wasn't quite sure how to put it into words. "You seem so . . . all the time. But under it all, I think you're really . . ."

James's brow wrinkled. "I'm not sure if I should take that as a compliment or an insult."

She puffed in frustration. What was she trying to say? "You're . . . softer than you seem."

The sound James made in response said she had offended him.

"No, I mean that in a good way." Bethany scrambled for the right words. "I mean—you're nicer than you seem."

James's full laugh sounded genuine. "Maybe you should stop trying to fix it. I think you're only digging a deeper hole."

"Maybe." Bethany rubbed ruefully at her forehead. "It's been a long day." She loaded the last few dishes into the dishwasher and added soap, then started the machine. When she turned around, James was wiping the kitchen table.

The sight sent a sudden, sharp pain through her middle. It was so *normal*. So like the family she'd grown up in. So like the family she used to assume she'd have one day.

So far from how things had turned out.

She'd done the right thing, leaving Ruby's father—or the man who was most likely to be Ruby's father—the moment she'd found out she was pregnant. She never would have been able to leave that lifestyle and get clean if she hadn't. But sometimes she wished she didn't have to do it all alone.

"Bethany?" James's voice swam through her thoughts.

"Sorry. What?"

"Are you okay? You were staring."

"Was I?" She pulled her eyes away from him, pretending not to feel the heat climbing up her neck. "Sorry. Just tired."

"Yeah. I should get those guys home." He passed her on his way to set the rag by the sink, and his homey scent made her think of a protector. Made her want to move closer.

She moved toward the living room instead.

"Hey, Bethany?"

She paused.

"Thanks for making me do this."

She grinned at him. "Anytime."

In the living room, Chris was frantically tapping his drawing board with the marker while Pete and Ruby called out guesses.

Bethany studied the picture. "It's one of those— Uh— The things that— They grow underground and you eat them."

"Potato," Pete called.

But Bethany shook her head, frustration building. It was just a stupid game. But she was so tired of never being able to come up with the right word. "It's— Uh— It's red."

"Radish." James came up behind her, and she almost leaned back against him in relief. Yes. That was the word.

"Yep." Chris held up his board triumphantly, waving around the picture.

"Nice job," James murmured to her.

She pressed her lips together before she could say something about making a good team. It was nice to be able to exert some impulse control for a change.

"All right, guys." James gestured toward the door. "Time to go."

"No." Ruby pouted, but Bethany sent her a warning look.

"Can we do this again sometime?" Ruby asked as the boys made their way toward the door. "Do you guys want to play charades next time? I'm really good at that."

"Sure, Ruby. Thanks for having us," Pete said politely as he stepped outside.

Chris grunted his agreement.

"You're welcome anytime," Bethany replied.

"Wait," Ruby cried. She ran out the door to give first Pete and then Chris a hug. Then she eyed James, as if weighing how to say goodbye to him. Bethany saw the way his shoulders tensed and his mouth flattened.

"Come on, Ruby. Time to get ready for bed."

"Coming."

Bethany let out a breath. At least Ruby hadn't gone for a hug and been rejected.

"Thanks for helping me catch so many fish." Before Bethany could stop her, Ruby threw her arms around James's waist.

"Oof." James didn't return the hug, instead standing stock still, his eyes closed, jaw set as if he were in pain.

For heaven's sake. What could be so terrible about a hug from a little girl? Maybe Bethany had been wrong in thinking he was softer than he seemed.

"Come on, Ruby."

Ruby let go, and James's eyes opened. They landed on Bethany's, then shifted away. But not before she saw the same torment in them as she'd seen in the mirror for years. But for her, hugs from Ruby had helped to heal the pain.

So how had the girl's hug brought it to the surface for James?

Chapter 21

"You're serious?" James pulled the phone away from his ear to stare at Captain Burke's name on the screen.

"All I'm saying is, a change of pace might be good for you. Get away from the memories."

James massaged his neck. He'd called to beg the captain to let him come back early, and now the guy didn't want him back at all. Didn't he understand that the memories followed him wherever he went? The only thing that saved him from them was working.

And spending time with Bethany and Ruby certainly didn't help. That hug from Ruby the other day—she might as well have punched a hole right into his lungs. And the way Bethany had looked at him afterward—as if she'd seen right into his pain. No, he couldn't stay here.

"Look, the captain there says you've been a great asset and they could really use you."

James snorted. "It was a vandalism case, not a serial killer."

"And thank the Lord for that."

James shook his head. He'd stopped thanking the Lord for anything long ago.

"The point is," Captain continued. "It sounds like you're making a real difference there. Emma told me you seem happy."

Emma.

He should have known better than to tell his sister about the job offer. Of course she'd felt the need to butt in.

"Look, are you firing me?"

"Of course not." Captain's voice held the fatherly note that had always warmed James. But right now it made him want to punch someone. "I'm just suggesting that you consider what's best for you."

"I already have. I'll be back in a week." He hung up and tossed the phone onto the table.

"What's eating you?" Emma swept into the room, carrying a large box.

"You talked to Captain?"

Emma set the box on the table. "He wants what's best for you, James. I do too."

"I think I can be the judge of that."

"Can you?" Emma raised an eyebrow. "Because it seems like you're doing a good job of ignoring the great opportunities that are right here in front of you. Including this job offer. What'd you tell Captain Burke?"

"That I'd see him in a week." James pushed past her toward the door.

"Wait. Where are you going?"

"To the store. You need anything?"

"No. Well, actually, some protein bars, since you keep eating them all." Emma smirked at him. "But also, since you're going that way, would you mind dropping this off at Bethany's for me?" She gestured to the box, which appeared to hold random junk.

"You want me to bring her trash?"

Emma laughed. "Ruby needs it for a school project."

"Ah." James stepped forward, digging through the box to find a broken coffee maker, a stack of horse magazines, and a bag of fake snow, among other things. He squinted at his sister. "Why can't you do it?" He wasn't much in the mood to do her any favors right now. Not to mention that the thought of seeing Bethany and Ruby again unsettled him.

"I have a doctor appointment. I was going to do it after, but I have to get back in time for a private lesson."

James frowned. "Didn't you just have a doctor appointment?" If she was trying to set him up with Bethany, she could at least come up with a new excuse.

Emma shrugged, looking away. "It's a follow-up. So you'll do it?"

He studied her. There was something she wasn't telling him. About her "secret" matchmaking efforts? Or about her health? "Is everything okay?"

"Of course." She smiled brightly. "Tell Ruby I'm sure I can find more stuff if she needs it."

James nodded slowly. He wanted to press the issue, make her tell him if something was really wrong—but he didn't have the courage. Besides, his sister was the healthiest person he knew—and the most straightforward. If something were wrong, she would tell him.

He picked up the box of junk. As he carried it out to the truck, his eyes fell on a bottle of glitter.

Look, Daddy. I glittered your belt.

He dropped the box into the back and jumped into the vehicle. If this was another one of Emma's matchmaking tricks, she was going to be sorely disappointed. Because he was immune.

Where was it?

Bethany strained on her tiptoes on top of the kitchen chair, searching through the cupboards.

"Ruby?" she called.

"Yeah, Mom?" Ruby appeared in the kitchen a moment later.

"Do you know where the thing is?"

"What thing?"

"You know. The thing. For the . . ." She pulled her head out of the cupboard and waved her hands vaguely. She had known the word a minute ago.

"Kimberly's going to be here soon." Ruby glanced over her shoulder.

"I know," Bethany snapped. "That's why I'm looking for it."

"Looking for what?" Ruby raised her voice.

"Don't take that tone with me," Bethany warned. "Or you can forget about your sleepover."

"But I don't know what you're looking for," Ruby wailed.

"The thing!" Now Bethany was raising her voice too, and she hated it. But she hadn't slept well all week, and her frustration with her language issue had finally reached a boil. She never should have told Ruby she could have a sleepover. Why had she thought she could be a normal mom and handle keeping two girls entertained all night? Most days she could barely handle one.

The doorbell rang, and Bethany threw her hands in the air. Of course they were early. "Whatever. I guess you guys won't have cookies. Go get the door."

Ruby spun on her heel and marched toward the door, but Bethany was pretty sure she heard her mutter something about forgetting the sugar anyway under her breath.

She closed her eyes and counted slowly to five before climbing down from the chair. She supposed she could always go buy some cookies. Or take the girls to the Chocolate Chicken. Maybe that would go a little ways toward making up for yelling at Ruby.

She moved toward the front door, zipping on a smile. No need to make Tiffany question whether she was competent to watch her daughter for the night.

"Hi there. I'm so glad you—" She went mute as she spotted James in the door, passing a box to Ruby.

He lifted his head. "Everything okay? I thought I heard yelling . . ."

Ruby burst into tears and dropped the box, taking off for her room.

James shot Bethany an alarmed look. "I'm sorry. I didn't mean to—"

"It wasn't you. It was me. I was looking for something and I couldn't think of the word and I yelled at her." Her own eyes stung, but she knew no tears would fall. Though she wished sometimes they would. A good cry might be a relief. "Rolling pin." The word came to her suddenly. "I was looking for a rolling pin." She covered her face. "What kind of mother am I?"

James stepped into the house and touched a hand to her forearm. "Remember what you told Carrie the other day?"

"No." Bethany sniffed with a dry laugh. "I don't even remember who Carrie is."

"Sorry. Pete's mom. The boy who did the graffiti and—"

"I remember Pete," she interrupted.

"Okay, well, you told his mom that you were sure she's doing the best she can. And I'm sure you are too."

Bethany shook her head. "There's a big gap between my best and a normal person's best. I just— I don't know if I can do this anymore. And Ruby's friend is going to be here any minute and what's it going to look like if Ruby won't come out of her room and . . ." She ran out of words and took a shaky breath.

"Hey. It's okay. You just need a break." James's voice was calm and soothing. "Why don't you go take a walk?"

"I don't want to leave Ruby home alone."

"I'll stay here with her. She'll be fine."

"But what if Tiffany and Kimberly get here while I'm gone?"

"Then I'll tell them you'll be right back. It's going to be fine," he repeated. "Walk around the block or something." He nudged her toward the door. "Trust me, it will help."

"If you're sure you don't mind . . ."

"I'm sure." James gently pushed her the rest of the way out the door and closed it firmly behind her.

Bethany pulled in a deep breath of the lilac-scented air and started walking.

She hadn't been wrong in thinking that having someone to share parenting duties with would make life easier.

It's fifteen minutes, she reminded herself. *Not forever.*

Chapter 22

F or crying out loud.

If Bethany's impulse control issues rubbed off on him one more time, James was seriously going to have to get his head examined.

What on earth had possessed him to offer to stay here with Ruby while Bethany took a walk?

But as much as he wanted to keep the question rhetorical, he already knew the answer.

It was the distress, the exhaustion, the *need* in Bethany's eyes. He couldn't bear to see it there and not do something—anything—to take it away. His hero complex at work again. Or maybe something else.

You're getting dangerously close to caring too much about this woman.

He plopped onto the couch with a sigh. Didn't he know it.

Fortunately, he only had another week to go, and then he'd never have to see her or Ruby again. He tipped his head back against the top of the couch and stared at the ceiling.

"Mom?" Ruby called from the hallway.

James closed his eyes for a second, then sat up. "She went for a walk," he called softly, not wanting to startle her.

"Oh." Ruby appeared in the living room as if she'd expected him to be there all along. "Why?"

Oh brother. What should he say to that? "She needed some fresh air."

"I didn't mean to make her upset," Ruby said quietly.

This might have been the first time James had seen the girl looking anything but cheerful, and he didn't like it. He considered telling a joke but instead said, "I know you didn't. And she knows too. She said it wasn't your fault."

Ruby frowned and slid onto the couch next to him. Every muscle in James's body tensed, ready to run away, but he was pinned between Ruby and the arm of the couch.

"Sometimes I wish she was like she used to be." Ruby played with a string on her sleeve.

"What did she used to be like?"

"I don't know. Different. Happy. Funny. We would do fun things together."

"Is that why you didn't tell her about bring your mom to school day?" James made sure not to allow any accusation to seep into his tone.

"I did tell—" Her face crumpled. "I didn't want all the other kids to say mean things and make her feel bad."

Oh man. The things this kid had to deal with. "That's fair. But don't you think she would have wanted to be there with you, even if it meant dealing with a few stupid kids?"

Ruby giggled. "Mom doesn't like the word stupid."

James laughed. "Sorry. But don't you think she'd put up with anything—even *silly* kids—to be with you?"

Ruby chewed her lip. "Probably."

"Trust me. I know she would."

"Are you going to tell her?" Ruby didn't sound scared. More like resigned.

"I'll leave that up to you. But believe me when I say you'll feel better if you do."

"You're just saying that because you're a grown-up. You're supposed to say it."

James laughed. "No, I'm saying that because I used to be a kid. One time I lied and told my dad I wasn't the one who threw a baseball through the window of his squad car. I felt sick for weeks until I finally told him."

Ruby seemed to consider that. "Was your dad mad when you told him?"

James thought about it. "He was disappointed that I'd lied. But he said he was proud of me for coming clean. He told me life would be full of hard choices between doing what's right and doing what's easy."

"Your dad sounds like a smart guy."

James chuckled. "He was. He's the reason I became a police officer. To be like him."

"Is he still a police officer? Or is he tired?"

"Tired?" James tried to make sense of the question. "Oh, retired? No. He's—" Was this an appropriate conversation to have with a ten-year-old? "He died in the line of duty."

"I'm sorry." Ruby patted his knee, as if she knew just what to do in such a situation.

"It's okay. It was a long time ago." He'd only been sixteen at the time. How had twenty-four years gone by since then?

"Is that why you're sad all the time?" The question was earnest and straightforward, and James looked at her in surprise.

"I'm not—"

The door opened, carrying Bethany in on a gust of fresh air. A healthy pink dotted her cheeks, and her hair had been tousled by the wind—but it was her smile that caught James off guard with the way it set his heart thumping.

Yep. It was time to go.

He tried to push to his feet, but Ruby used his leg as a springboard to vault toward her mom, shoving him back down into the cushions.

"Mom, I'm sorry." Ruby threw herself into Bethany's arms as they met in the middle of the room.

"Me too, Rubes. You didn't do anything wrong."

Ruby glanced toward James, who got to his feet. They didn't need him here for this. "I should go. Glad you're feeling better." He almost reached for Bethany's shoulder as he passed but diverted his hand at the last second and rubbed his neck.

"Thank you, James." Bethany's voice was soft and warm, and it sped his footsteps toward the door.

"Yeah. Thanks, James." Ruby's voice followed. "You know, you'd make a good dad."

"Ruby!" Bethany sounded mortified, but the word seared through James hotter and sharper than the bullet that had pierced his shoulder. He tore open the door but jerked to a stop just in time to avoid plowing over the woman and girl on the other side.

He gripped the door, trapped, trying to get his flight reaction under control.

The woman's eyes widened, and her lips curled into a smile. "James. I wasn't expecting to see you here." She glanced past him to Bethany. "Is now a bad time?"

"I was just leaving," James scraped out.

But before he could squeeze past her to get out the door, a furry streak bolted past him and into the bushes.

"Mrs. Whiskers," Ruby cried, running past them to follow the critter. "Come here, you silly cat."

But Mrs. Whiskers took one look at Ruby and darted for the nearest tree, scrambling up it in record time.

"Oh no. Mrs. Whiskers, come down," Ruby cried, running to the tree. The cat meowed but didn't move.

Ruby looked toward them. "We have to help her."

"She's too high," Bethany called back. "I don't have a ladder. She'll come down later."

Even from across the yard, James could see Ruby's lip tremble.

"I'll get her." He slipped past Tiffany and her daughter, working out the best route up the tree as he crossed the yard.

It took him a couple of attempts to get a grip—it'd been a long time since he'd climbed a tree—but once he did, the movements came back naturally enough.

"Be careful, James," Ruby called from below him.

He grunted. What on earth was he doing crawling around in a tree to rescue a cat that had nothing to do with him?

It shouldn't have mattered that Ruby had looked desolate at the thought of leaving her cat in the tree.

It shouldn't have.

But it did.

"Here kitty, kitty." James held out a hand. The cat eyed it but didn't move. He inched out farther on the branch. It seemed sturdy enough, but he listened for any cracks or pops. So far so good.

"Come on, Mrs. Whiskers," Ruby called. "Go to James. He's nice." She stood right under the branch James and the cat were on.

"Ruby, do me a favor and move back, okay? Just in case."

"Just in case what?" Ruby blinked up at him.

"Just back up." He reached for Mrs. Whiskers, managing to snag her leg. The cat didn't resist as he pulled her closer to him. When he tucked her against his shoulder, she started purring. James rolled his eyes. "Stupid cat." But then he remembered what Ruby had said about her mom's feelings about the word stupid. "Silly animal," he amended.

With the cat tucked securely against him, he contemplated how to get back to the ground. He snorted at himself. Maybe the cat wasn't the stupid animal here.

"Why aren't you coming down?" Ruby asked, still standing too close to the tree.

"I'm working on it," James shot back. "Move away from the tree."

It took longer than he would have liked, but he managed to lower himself enough that he could make the final jump. The instant he was on his feet, Ruby's arms were around him. It didn't feel as odd as it had the other day, and he found himself lifting one hand briefly to her back before he extracted the cat from his arms and passed her off to Ruby.

Now he could leave.

"That was heroic," Tiffany said as James tried to inconspicuously pass the little group gathered outside.

He shrugged, but Bethany's grateful smile slowed his footsteps. She opened her mouth as if to say something, but Tiffany beat her to it. "I have this huge bookshelf I've been wanting to move for months, but it's too heavy for me. If you're not busy, do you think I could borrow your muscles for a minute?"

"Uh . . ." How was he supposed to answer that?

"I'll sweeten the deal with cookies. I made them this morning."

"I guess. Sure." He didn't have much choice. It wasn't like he had anywhere else he needed to be. Although he suddenly had the oddest urge to stay right here.

"Great." Tiffany beamed at him, then turned to Bethany. "You're all good here then? You need anything?"

Bethany shook her head with a stiff smile. "I've got everything under control. I'll bring Kimberly home tomorrow morning."

"See you then." Tiffany sidled up to James, and Bethany's meager smile faded.

James waved to her. "See you later."

She nodded, then stepped inside and closed the door.

Tiffany hooked her hand around James's elbow, chatting animatedly about how she was redecorating her house. James tried to pay attention. But he found himself looking over his shoulder at Bethany's closed door, thinking of how cozy he'd felt inside.

Could she borrow his muscles? Bethany rolled her eyes as she stood to the side of the window, watching James's truck pull away and follow Tiffany's SUV. She wished she could forget that line. It was ridiculous. And also something she knew she could never come up with.

She had a hard enough time managing a normal conversation, let alone flirting.

Not that she wanted to flirt with James.

Besides, he and Tiffany had made quite the striking couple, strolling down her driveway, his jeans and flannel shirt a perfect contrast to her pencil skirt and dusty rose blouse.

Undoubtedly, it wouldn't be long before she heard the rumors around town.

She sighed. Ah well. It didn't matter.

She pulled out her phone and swiped to the list she'd made for tonight. *Make pizza.* Right.

But she had just turned on the oven when the sound of raised voices came from down the hall. She paused, listening.

The girls were probably just having fun—but why did it sound like they were shouting?

She slipped silently down the hallway. She wouldn't intrude unless there was a problem, but she had to get close enough to make sure everything was okay.

"That's not fair." It was Ruby's voice, and it was elevated. Bethany took a step closer to her daughter's bedroom door. There was enough stuff in that box of junk James had brought over that they shouldn't have to fight over it to complete their assignment.

"I met him first." Ruby was still shouting.

Bethany paused. This was about a boy? She rubbed at her temple. She definitely was not ready for that. But maybe it wasn't something she should get in the middle of. She could always talk to Ruby about it after Kimberly left tomorrow.

She turned toward the kitchen.

But Ruby's voice came again. "You already have a dad."

"Yeah, but he lives in Iowa."

"Well, I don't have any dad. Plus, he likes my mom better."

Bethany froze, bracing a hand on the wall. Were they fighting about . . . *James?*

She spun around and marched to Ruby's room. She had no idea what she was going to say—only that she had to put an end to this conversation. Immediately.

"Yeah right." For a ten-year-old, Kimberly carried sarcasm well. "*You* don't even like your mom better. Otherwise you would have told her about take your mom to school day."

Bethany pulled her hand back from the slightly ajar door, pressing it instead to her middle. Had Ruby intentionally not told her about the event? Because she didn't want Bethany there?

"You know what," Kimberly kept going, "I bet my mom and James will be dating by the time I get home tomorrow."

"Maybe you should go home right now!" Ruby shot back.

Bethany pushed the door open. "Hey, girls." She forced enough pep into her voice that she probably sounded like an over-the-top cheerleader. "Who wants some ice cream?"

Ruby toed the floor, not meeting Bethany's eyes. "We didn't have dinner yet."

Did she think Bethany had forgotten?

"I know that, silly." Bethany waved off her daughter's objection. "But if we eat dinner first, you'll be too full for ice cream. So I thought we'd go to the Chocolate Chicken now and then we can always have some pizza later if you guys are hungry. What do you think?"

"I think that's a great idea." Kimberly bounced off the bed, sending Bethany a syrupy smile. "You're the best, Ms. Moore." She flounced out of the room.

As Ruby slipped past, Bethany caught her arm. "We need to talk about this later."

Ruby nodded, not looking up. "I know."

"But for now," Bethany continued, "try to have fun with your friend. No more arguments, all right?"

Ruby lifted her head. "Yeah, Mom. All right."

"Good." Bethany gave herself a moment after Ruby had left the room to just breathe. She may not be an expert at sleepovers—but she seemed to have salvaged this one.

Chapter 23

Two more days and James could return to Milwaukee. He'd have the weekend to get things in order at his house, and then he'd get back to work on Monday.

It was what he'd been waiting for all summer.

So why was he sort of dreading it? Not the work part—but the leaving Hope Springs part. Much as he hated to admit it, this little town had gotten under his skin. So much so that for a second the other day, when he'd been rescuing Ruby's cat, he'd wondered what it would be like if he took the job offer here. A few more cat rescue calls, a lot less homicides.

And a lot more Bethany . . .

He shook his head, shoving out the kitchen door and instinctively checking the driveway for her car. She wasn't here yet.

Probably for the best.

He made his way toward the barn, trying not to picture her frown when Tiffany had asked him to come over and help move her bookshelf. Bethany had looked . . . jealous wasn't the word. More like wistful, as if she wished . . . what?

He ran a hand over his head. It didn't matter what she wished. He was leaving.

Which was exactly what he'd told Tiffany after he'd moved her bookshelf and she'd insisted on plying him with cookies, then suggested that they get coffee or dinner sometime. In retrospect, the comment probably shouldn't have taken him by surprise, given the way she'd been acting, but it did.

At first, when he'd stammered out that he couldn't, she'd asked if it was because of Bethany. Even after he'd forcibly—perhaps too forcibly—denied it, she hadn't seemed to believe him.

Which was ridiculous. Since it was true.

Sure, it was also true that even if he weren't leaving town, he would have turned Tiffany down. But that had nothing to do with Bethany.

He slid in through the barn door and moved down the stalls, inhaling the sweet hay and horse scent. That was definitely one thing he was going to miss about Hope Springs.

But would he miss Bethany?

The door behind him opened, and his heart accelerated at the same time his mouth became a map of involuntary muscles, all pulling upward.

She was here.

He turned, trying to tone down his smile. "Hey, how— Oh, it's just you." He made a face at his sister.

Emma didn't offer the quick comeback he expected. She must be tired this morning—it wasn't like her to pass up an opportunity to joke with him. As she got closer, his heart kicked into fight or flight mode. Her expression—it was the same one Mom had worn when she'd told them Dad had been shot. The same expression the doctor had worn when Sadie . . .

He took a step backward, the pounding in his throat too strong to get any words past. It felt like there was a veil of water between them, keeping her from reaching him, making her form wobble. But when she finally stood in front of him, he grabbed her shoulder.

"Mom?" The word scraped its way out of his hoarse throat.

"Mom's fine."

A sharp breath pushed out of him, as if his lungs had been punctured. As long as Mom and Emma were okay. Two more names popped into his head, sending his heart rate back up. "Bethany? Ruby?"

Emma smiled faintly. "They're both okay. But now I know how you feel about them."

He shook his head. He wasn't going to play that game right now. "What then?"

"Let's go sit down." Her voice was way too gentle, and James dropped his hand to his side. "No. Tell me."

Emma sighed but met his eyes. And then he knew. "It's you." The whisper sliced across his vocal cords like a knife blade. She moved closer, but he held up his hands, as if they could shield him from the words.

"The reason I've been going to the doctor is that they're concerned about a mass on my ovaries."

"No." He shook his head. "You said it was a follow-up appointment."

"They think it might be cancer," Emma continued. "But—"

"No." He shook his head again, as if he could somehow dislodge the words. It couldn't be true. He wouldn't let it be true.

"James, listen." Emma used the same voice he'd heard her use to soothe spooked horses. "It's not as bad as it sounds." She took a tentative step toward him, holding out a hand. "They want me to have surgery. A—" She swallowed hard but then gave him a wavery smile. "A hysterectomy. They're hopeful that they caught it early enough that that's the only treatment I'll need."

"When?" He crossed his arms in front of him, as if he were interrogating a suspect.

"Monday." Emma took another step toward him. "It's going to be fine, James, okay?"

He nodded once. "I'll call Captain Burke. Let him know I'm going to need more time off. I imagine it'll be at least a few weeks before you're on your feet again."

"No. I called Mom, and she's going to come for the surgery and then stay for a while afterward."

"Good. Mom can take care of you. And I'll take care of all of this." He waved a hand around the barn.

"I do have a staff, you know. And my friends will help out." She patted his arm. "Everything is under control. You need to get back to your life. Unless . . ."

"Unless what?" He folded his arms in front of him. She had better not start talking about what would happen if she didn't make it. Because that was not an option.

"Unless you've decided your life is here with a certain someone . . ." She waggled her eyebrows at him, and he wanted to punch her and hug her all at once. How could she goof around at a time like this? But he knew she was doing it for his sake.

He shook his head. "I'm staying. Until you're on your feet. Don't get any other dumb ideas."

"You're a good brother. Have I ever told you that?" Emma's lip trembled, and she pulled him into a hug.

He squeezed her tight, closing his eyes, his arms shaking. *You can't have her too, God. I won't let you.*

Chapter 24

All the things she forgot on a daily basis, and yet Bethany couldn't get the image of James and Tiffany walking away from her house the other day out of her head.

"It doesn't matter," she told herself firmly before getting out of the car at Emma's stables. So what if this would be the first time she'd seen James since then—it wouldn't change anything between them, especially since there *was nothing* between them. Which was exactly what she'd told Ruby after she'd taken Kimberly home the other day. Fortunately, her daughter hadn't brought it up again, and the argument didn't seem to have affected the girls' friendship.

She sighed as she made her way toward the barn. The day was warm and sunny, and she tipped her head toward the blue sky and pulled in a deep breath. She had more than enough to be thankful for.

She opened the barn door and stepped inside. The sound of a shovel scraping against the floor carried down the length of the building, making her smile. James was already hard at work. As always.

She made her way to the stall, where he seemed to be attacking the bedding with unusual vigor.

"Wow. In a hurry today?" she joked.

But when he looked up, the sharp blade of his gaze stabbed right through her. He was broken—more broken than usual. But why?

"I— Is everything all right?"

James shook his head but resumed scooping. "You talk to Emma at all?"

"Not today, no. Why?"

James stopped shoveling and straightened but kept his back to her. "You should talk to her."

"Okay. But her car isn't here. What's going on?" Did he want his sister to break it to her that he and Tiffany were now seeing each other?

He turned toward her so slowly that she was surprised he didn't tip over, like Ruby the first time she'd ridden a two-wheeler. A deep frown creased his features. Today he really was James the Gray.

"She has to have surgery."

"Oh." Bethany let out a breath. That wasn't so bad. Lots of people had surgery every day. "I'm sure—"

"They think it's cancer, Bethany." Hardness coated his voice, but his face dissolved into soft lines of fear.

It took Bethany a moment to process the words. But as soon as she had, she couldn't keep her feet from carrying her across the stall or her arms from wrapping around him.

James stiffened and disentangled himself from her grasp. "Just. Don't." He looked away.

Bethany swallowed. She hadn't meant to upset him more. "I'm sorry. I just—"

"Impulse control. I get it. Can we get to work?" He resumed scooping before she could answer.

She watched him for a minute, then moved to her own stall across the way, sending up prayers for Emma and for James as she worked.

When they had finished, they cleaned up silently. Then James left the barn without a word. Bethany stood there, listening to the sounds of the nickering horses.

It seemed wrong how peaceful it was in here when turmoil swirled all around. But then, sometimes it seemed like that was the way life was. Peace and chaos. Beauty and pain. Joy and sorrow. A collision of opposites. *But God is here through it all,* she reminded herself.

Chapter 25

James blinked up at the ceiling, faint gray light finally illuminating the contours of the room. He didn't know how long he'd been lying here awake—only that he couldn't stand it for another minute. He hadn't slept well a single night since Emma had broken her news to him, and exhaustion was a constant companion.

He rolled himself out of bed and pulled on a pair of running shorts and a t-shirt. Exhausted or not, a run was the only thing that would clear his head—though he'd found that even those hadn't helped lately to banish the thoughts, the guilt, the anger, as everything he'd lost—everything he could still lose—collided in his head. He crammed his earbuds into his ears, cranking up the volume on his music in the hopes of drowning the thoughts out.

He made his way downstairs, tiptoeing past Emma's door to keep from waking her. He had no idea how she was holding up the way she was. He'd walked into the arena on Friday and found her teaching her dressage riders, her voice cheerful, same as always. Not even a hint that her body had turned on her.

On the one hand, he'd been proud of her. And on the other hand, he'd had to walk out of there, his eyes catching Bethany's for a moment before he'd let the door slam behind him. He'd thought that she might follow him, but he was grateful she hadn't. The compassion in her gaze, the understanding—it was too hard to take. He probably owed her an apology for the way he'd snapped at her for hugging him the other day. But it had been either snap or break down completely. And he couldn't afford to do that.

As he slipped out the front door now, James sucked in a couple of deep breaths of the damp morning air before taking off down the long lane that led into the trees where he and Bethany had ridden together. He pushed himself hard, letting the music drive him forward, relishing the pounding in his heart that came from running, as it pushed out everything else.

He followed the trail until it branched into two paths, one slightly overgrown. James frowned at it before taking it. He didn't recall ever going this way, but if he got lost, at least his outside circumstances would finally match his insides.

Only half a mile down the trail, it became so overgrown that he had to slow to a walk so he wouldn't trip. Still he kept pushing forward, ripping his feet through the tangle of underbrush and holding his hands up to shield himself from the wispy branches of low-growing trees that overhung the path.

"Ouch!" He lifted a hand to his face as a spiny branch snagged his cheek. His hand came away with a small streak of blood, and he growled at it.

He should turn around and go back. But a strange compulsion pulled him forward. Now that he'd started down this path, he needed to see where it led.

In another three minutes, the path disappeared completely. But by now James could see an opening ahead. He shoved his way through a dense layer of bramble, stumbling before he regained his footing.

Swiping sweat out of his eyes, he took in the small pond in front of him, shimmering as the newly risen sun sent a ripple of gold across the surface. At the far end, a mother duck eyed him as she led her babies toward the shore. A light breeze cooled the sweat gathered on the back of his neck and sent a hushing sound through the grasses and leaves.

James let out his breath slowly and clasped his hands together behind his head.

It was beautiful. It was powerful and gentle all at once. It was—

James tilted his head toward the heavens. "What is this?" He shouted the words, leading mama duck to send him a reproving look and veer off with her ducklings. "You can do this? You can make all of this? You can take care of these stupid birds? But you can't keep my sister healthy? You can't keep my daughter—"

James broke off, shaking his head. What was he doing? Yelling at someone who would never listen. Someone who had shown time and again that he didn't care. James had wondered more than once if it was just that God was powerless, if he *couldn't* help. But looking at all of this, this morning, he knew. God wasn't powerless. He was heartless.

He spun away from the pond and plunged back into the brush, ignoring the twigs and branches that slapped at his face and arms, the weeds and bushes that grasped at his feet. He had to get out of here. The moment he reached the path, he drove his feet into a sprint, keeping up the punishing pace all the way back. He only slowed down when his eyes fell on Emma, sitting on the front porch, a blanket around her shoulders and a book—likely her Bible—in her hands.

He ducked into the barn to catch his breath and get his emotions under control. Emma had enough to worry about without adding him to the mix. He needed to be the strong one here.

When he finally felt his heart rate slow, he made his way toward the house. Emma looked up from her book—he'd been right that it was her Bible—as he clomped up the porch steps.

"Have a good run?" She offered him a gentle smile.

"Yeah." Hopefully he'd been far enough away when he'd yelled that she hadn't heard him. "Found a pond."

"That's one of my favorite spots to just sit and pray. It's so peaceful."

James grunted.

"I'm going to go get ready for church." She closed her Bible and stood.

James stepped out of her way, but she didn't move past him.

"I have a favor to ask." She looked tentative, and James's stomach clenched. Whatever she was about to say, he wasn't going to like it.

"Worship with me?" Her voice was upbeat, but her eyes were pleading.

He swallowed. He would do almost anything for his sister, but . . . "I don't exactly feel like worshiping right now."

Emma smiled gently. "You know what Dad always said: 'There are only two times to worship. When you feel like it and . . .'" She looked at him expectantly.

He shook his head but mumbled, "And when you don't."

"Please, James. I know it's a lot to ask. I just need—"

But he had already made up his mind. "I'll go."

He'd go to church. Because Emma needed him.

But it wouldn't change the way he felt about God.

Chapter 26

"Yikes." Bethany looked down as she nearly tripped over Mrs. Whiskers. The cat meowed up at her plaintively. "What's the matter with you?" She glanced toward the cat's dishes in the corner of the kitchen. Empty.

"Poor kitty." Bethany thought she'd taken care of her last night before bed, but she must have forgotten. She quickly filled the food dish, then carefully picked up the water dish and carried it to the sink. "Ruby," she called as she stuck the dish under the faucet. "Are you almost ready? We're going to be late." Not that that was anything new.

Her daughter's bedroom door opened just as Bethany shut off the faucet. She turned to give the dish to the cat. But she stopped so fast at the sight of her daughter's face that a nice big splash of water slopped down the front of her blouse.

"What is that?" She pointed at the pink blush that streaked Ruby's cheeks and the glittery green eye shadow that shimmered from her eyelids.

"Kimberly gave me some of her makeup."

"Some of her . . ." Bethany pointed toward the hallway. "You know you're not old enough for makeup. Go wash it off."

"But, Kimberly's mom lets her—"

"Now." Bethany gestured again, waiting for her daughter to march down the hall with a huff before releasing her own huff and refilling the water dish, wiping at the wet spot on her shirt with her free hand.

Oh well. She didn't have time to change. Hopefully it would dry before they got to church. And anyway, a wet shirt was a minor problem in the scheme of things. Especially when she compared it to what Emma was facing. And James.

She couldn't get his brokenness out of her head. Or the way he'd rejected her hug.

She sighed. The hug hadn't been an impulse control thing. Not really. More like it was the only way she could express what she was feeling.

Ruby reappeared in the kitchen, face sullen but makeup-free.

"Much better." Bethany grabbed her purse. "Let's go."

Ruby made a face but followed her to the car.

Bethany made sure Ruby had her seatbelt on before backing slowly down the driveway.

"Mom?" Ruby's voice was so quiet that at first Bethany thought she was hearing faint sounds from the radio.

"What is it?" she asked when she realized it was her daughter. She checked the time on the dashboard. It was just possible that they'd get to church on time.

"Is Miss Emma going to die?"

Bethany smashed her foot to the brake at the bottom of the driveway. Telling Ruby about Emma's possible diagnosis had been one of the hardest things Bethany had ever done. But she'd been careful to focus on the positive and hadn't once brought up death.

She turned to look at her daughter over her shoulder. "What makes you ask that?"

"Kimberly said people who get cancer die."

Bethany swallowed. "Some do." She didn't want to lie to her daughter. "But many don't. Just like some people who have an aneurysm die. But not everyone, right?"

Ruby nodded slowly but still wore lines of worry too old for her ten-year-old face. "What if she dies though?"

Bethany swallowed. She didn't want to consider that possibility. But she couldn't pretend it didn't exist. "Then she'll go to heaven. That would be pretty awesome for her, right?"

Ruby frowned. "But I want her to stay here."

"I know, Rubes. Me too. You know the best thing we can do for her, right?"

Ruby nodded and folded her hands. "Can we pray right now?"

Bethany glanced at the clock again. The minutes were ticking away. But how could she say no to praying for their friend? "Of course. Do you want to or should I?"

"You drive. I'll pray."

Bethany laughed. Leave it to her practical daughter to come up with a solution. "Sounds like a plan." She pulled the car into the street and headed toward church, Ruby's sweet prayer—for Emma, for James, for all of their friends, even for the horses—filling the vehicle and lifting Bethany's heart.

She might not always be the mother she wanted to be—but in moments like this, she was so very glad God had given her Ruby.

"Amen." Ruby's prayer concluded as Bethany pulled into the church parking lot—only three minutes late.

"Amen," Bethany repeated, parking in the first spot she found. "That was a wonderful prayer, Ruby."

"Thank you." Ruby hopped out of the back seat. Bethany grasped her hand and they speed-walked toward church.

They had just reached the sidewalk, the sounds of the first hymn floating out the open doors, when Ruby stopped abruptly, pulling Bethany to a stop too. "I forgot one."

"One what?" Bethany glanced toward the greeter holding the door open for them.

"Prayer."

"That's okay. You can keep praying in church." Bethany tugged her forward through the doors, mumbling a thank you to the greeter, who nodded with a warm smile. Ruby led them straight for the row where they always sat, with the friends who had become family.

At the front of the church, Dan was beginning his first Scripture reading, and Bethany directed her attention to him.

"Mom." Ruby's whisper was urgent, and she tugged on Bethany's sleeve.

"I told you to go to the bathroom before we left," Bethany murmured.

"No you didn't. But that's not it."

"What?" Bethany directed an impatient glance at her daughter. It was hard enough to concentrate without Ruby's constant whispers. But her gaze caught suddenly on the person sitting next to Ruby. James?

His eyes met hers, and she offered him a smile that he didn't return as he ducked his head.

Eyes wide, Ruby leaned toward Bethany and whispered, "God already answered one of my prayers."

Bethany nodded. One of hers too.

Maybe James had found the same thing she had. That when you were at your lowest, that was when you found out how much you needed the Lord.

Chapter 27

If his neck muscles were any tighter, James's head might pop right off his body. But he couldn't relax.

Not here. Not with his sick sister on one side of him. Not with Ruby, who reminded him way too much of what he'd lost, on the other side. Not with Pastor Dan up front, talking about how good God was.

You're doing this for Emma, he reminded himself, forcing his head toward one shoulder and then the other as the hymn ended and Pastor Dan stood gazing out at the congregation, a small smile on his lips, as if they were all one big, happy family. James crossed his arms over his chest. He wasn't buying it.

"I like to think I'm a relatively calm guy," Pastor Dan began. "Pretty unflappable. But the one thing that can ruffle my feathers more than anything is that little guy over there." He pointed toward a tow-haired boy sitting on a blonde woman's lap, a girl who was probably a little younger than Ruby sitting next to them. His family, James remembered from the Easter dinner. "Hey, buddy." Dan waved at the kid, who giggled and stuffed a piece of cereal in his mouth. "See—" Dan turned back to the congregation. "Matthias is going through his 'why' phase. You know the one—where every question I answer is followed by another: Daddy, why are fire trucks red? So people can see them coming. Why? So they can get out of the way. Why? So the firefighters can get to the fire faster. Why? So they can help people and put the fire out. Why? Because that's their job. Why? Argh." Dan clutched his head with a chuckle, and the congregation laughed along with him. "And he could happily do it all day long. Don't get me wrong. I know it's good for kids to ask why. I know it helps them learn about the world around them. But sometimes you have to admit that those why questions are a little pointless, right?"

He paused, growing sober. "Let that sink in for a moment. Those why questions are pointless. And yet—" He paced a few steps to the left. "How often do we demand answers to our own why questions? You know the ones: Why did we lose our job? Why were we in a car accident? Why is someone close to us sick? Why did someone die?"

James's neck muscles tightened to the snapping point as he dug his fists into his sides. Next to him, Emma patted his leg once and offered a soft smile. James could only grimace in reply. On his other side, Ruby wiggled, her elbow digging into his ribs. He glanced over at her, and she smiled up at him, whispering, "Sorry."

He was pretty sure his grimace deepened as he lifted his eyes from her to Bethany, who was watching him with lines of worry wrinkled into her brow.

He shook his head and faced the front, using every ounce of self-control to keep himself anchored in his seat. *You're doing this for Emma. You're doing this for Emma.* He tried to focus on the mantra, but Dan's words stabbed through.

"If it makes you feel any better, you aren't the first person to ask those why questions. In fact, we can look all the way back to Moses. God had promised him—*promised* him—that he would lead the people out of slavery in Egypt. And yet, the first time Moses went to pharaoh and asked for permission to leave—and pharaoh not only said no but made the Israelites work harder to produce bricks each day—Moses turned to God and said, 'Is this your plan? Is this why you sent me? Why are you bringing trouble on us? Why is this happening?'"

Dan walked to the small podium and picked up the Bible that rested on it. "Fast forward a little bit, and God brings all these plagues on the Egyptians so that finally pharaoh tells the Israelites, 'Get out of here already. We don't want you here anymore.' So the Israelites go, led by Moses, just as God promised. They get out of Egypt, they evade the soldiers pharaoh sends when he changes his mind again. Not just evade them, but God clears the way for them to walk through the Red Sea on *dry ground,* for heaven's sake. And then there they are, at the door of the Promised Land. And the leaders of the tribes go out to explore and they come back and, even though they know full well that God has promised this land to them, they say, 'There's no way we can take this land. The people in it are much too strong for us.' And the whole community takes up the tantrum."

He looked at the Bible in his hand and read, "'If only we had died in Egypt! Or in this wilderness! Why is the Lord bringing us to this land only to let us fall by the sword?' And then they start making plans to ignore God's promise and go back to Egypt. They're finally talked out of that foolishness, but then they're facing attack by the Amorites, and Gideon says to God, 'Pardon me, my lord—'" Dan looked up with an ironic smile. "At least he showed some humility." He turned back to the Bible. "'But if the Lord is with us, why has all this happened to us? Where are all his wonders that our ancestors told us about?'"

Dan paused. "Of course, those were all big, national things. Things that affected a lot of people. So maybe we can't always understand the politics behind them or the intricacies involved in them. Maybe it would be unreasonable to expect that we would. But what about the more personal suffering we face? Ever ask God why he allows those things to happen?"

James clamped his jaw together tight enough to send a shockwave through his teeth. Of course he'd asked God why. And he'd never once gotten an answer. And from what he was hearing here, neither had anyone else.

"The most famous person to ask why in the Bible is probably Job, right?" Dan set the Bible down and took a few steps closer to the congregation, his voice softening. "And who can blame him? The guy lost everything. His home, his animals, his servants, his children. All gone." Dan shook his head. "Frankly, I don't know what I would do."

James swallowed. Dan was lucky he didn't know what he would do. That he had never had to find out. He felt Bethany's eyes on him again but refused to allow himself to look anywhere but straight ahead. He didn't need to see her worry or compassion or kindness.

"Listen to Job's why questions: 'Why have you made me your target? . . . Why do you hide your face and consider me your enemy?'" Dan winced. "Cuts right to the heart of it, doesn't he? Isn't that what we so often think? That when bad things happen to us, it's because God has turned against us. Because he is evil. Because he's punishing us. Because he doesn't love us enough to keep us from hurting."

"Well." Dan flipped further in his Bible. "I have news for you. It's not because God doesn't love you. It's not because he's punishing you. It's not because he's turned against you. And it's certainly not because he's evil. How do I know that?" He paused. "Because of another why question. This one asked by Jesus—" Dan looked down at his open Bible. "My God, my God, why have you forsaken me?"

Slowly, Dan set the Bible on the podium and looked around the church. "God loves you and me so much that he took the punishment that we deserved for our sins and placed it on his own Son. He loves us so much that he sent Jesus to the cross so that he wouldn't have to turn against us. He loves you so much that he promises that even when bad things happen—things we can't explain, things we don't understand—he will use them for your good and his glory."

There it was. James had been waiting for that line of garbage the whole sermon. That saccharine promise that whatever happened to you, no matter how terrible, it was supposed to be good for you. And yet, somehow, no one ever seemed to be able to explain *how* it was good for you.

"I know what you're thinking." Dan's gaze swept the church, and James looked away. He very much doubted that the pious pastor up there knew what he was thinking.

"You're thinking *how*? How can losing my job be for my good? How can getting into an accident be for my good? How can getting cancer be for my good? How can losing someone I love be for my good?"

James wanted to stand up and scream, "It can't." But he held his seat, digging his fists into his legs, vowing not to listen to another word.

Except Dan's voice wasn't the type of voice that could easily be tuned out.

"You want the hard answer, or the easy one?" Dan asked.

James stared at the floor, watching Ruby's black shoes swing back and forth. *Do you like my new shoes, Daddy? Mama says they can be my church shoes.*

James shifted in his seat, clearing his throat.

"The hard answer is, 'I don't know.' I don't know how any of those things can be for our good." Dan's voice grew louder. "But the easy answer is that God does. He tells us in Isaiah 55:8-9, 'For my thoughts are not your thoughts, neither are your ways my ways,' declares the Lord. 'As the heavens are higher than the earth, so are my ways higher than your ways and my thoughts than your thoughts.'"

Dan closed the Bible and just stood there, as if to let the words sink in. James shifted in his seat again. All that proved was that God was smarter than he was. But it didn't mean God was good—it didn't mean he had James's good, Emma's good, Sadie's good, in his heart.

"You see, even if God told us the why, even if he explained every detail, we wouldn't get it," Dan continued. "We couldn't. We're just too small. Our concept of God's plan is just too puny. We're stuck in the here and now. God sees the big picture, the whole picture, all of time and eternity. And he promises that someday he will bring us to glory with him, and *then* we will see. 1 Corinthians 13:12 says, 'For now we see only a reflection as in a mirror; then we shall see face to face. Now I know in part; then I shall know fully, even as I am fully known.' *Then*," Dan said with a smile. "*Then* we will know how God used all of these things—all of our whys—for his glory. Until then—" Dan held his hands out to his sides. "We walk by faith and not by sight. We trust. We believe. We take him at his Word. I'm not saying it will be easy. I'm not saying we won't ever wonder why again. But I *am* saying that his promises are true. That he has our eternal good in his heart. And nothing can shake that. Amen."

As the sermon came to a close, James's head reeled. There was a part of him—an ever-so-small, ever-so-timid part of him—that wanted to believe what Dan said was true. That wanted to believe that everything he had lost had not been for nothing. But the thing was, he would gladly give up any future joy—any *then*—to have Sadie here with him now. Maybe that was blasphemy or sacrilege or who knew what, but it was how he felt.

Chapter 28

Peace washed over Bethany as Dan finished his sermon. How many times had she asked why over the past couple of years? Why had her aneurysm happened? Why did she have to face this struggle with words and memories? Sometimes her thoughts went back further: Why had God let her get hurt in volleyball, which had led to surgery, which had led to her addiction to painkillers, which had led to her spiral into other drugs? Why hadn't he stopped her from leaving rehab time and again? Why? Why? Why?

And even though she still didn't have the answer to those whys, she felt like she could finally let them go. That she could trust them to God, trust that he had been working through the hard things, even if she didn't know exactly how. The relief was enough to make her grin like a fool as she stood and joined in singing the next hymn.

Until she happened to glance over at James.

His arms were nailed to his sides, his mouth stretched into a stark line, his jaw clenched tight. He looked so much like a statue that she held her breath until she saw a muscle in his neck twitch.

As if he felt her watching him, his eyes came to hers—only for a moment. But it was long enough for Bethany to catch the depth of pain in them.

It wasn't the first time she'd noticed it, but today it pressed closer to the surface than ever.

Before she realized she'd moved, she felt the back of her hand touch the back of his. His eyes darted to hers, and she pulled her hand away with a jerk, resting her palm on Ruby's back instead. Blasted impulse control.

But she couldn't help it. She needed him to know that he wasn't alone. That she was here.

Not that it probably mattered to him.

As the song came to an end and they took their seats again, she was careful to squeeze as far toward the end of the row as she could, even though Ruby made a good barrier between them.

"Please join me in prayer," Dan was saying from the front of the church. "Today we ask God to watch over our sister Emma Wood, who will be having surgery tomorrow for a possible cancerous mass. We also pray for . . ." Bethany lost track of Dan's words as James stumbled to his feet and climbed over Ruby's legs and then her own with a mumbled, "Sorry."

Her eyes followed him as he strode down the aisle and out the sanctuary doors at the back of the church. She lost sight of him as he crossed the lobby and slipped out the exit. She turned around, her eyes meeting Emma's, who gave her a weak, worried smile. Bethany reached a hand out to Emma behind Ruby's back, and her friend took it with a gentle squeeze. Bethany closed her eyes as Dan began to pray. She may not be able to help James, but she could be here for Emma.

As Dan said the prayers and then they ended the service with another hymn, Bethany checked over her shoulder every few seconds to see if James would come back. Something in her said she should go after him, but that was crazy. She didn't know him well enough to go chasing him out of church. Not to mention that even if she did find him, what would she say? No doubt words would fail her, as they always did.

"He'll be okay," Emma murmured as they filed out of church, apparently catching her scanning the crowds for James. "It's just a lot for him."

"It's a lot for you too."

Emma looked at her thoughtfully. "I'm not going to deny that. But I have the peace of God. It makes a big difference."

Give him peace, Lord, Bethany prayed as their group of friends gathered in the lobby. It didn't feel like enough, but she knew from her own experience that prayer was more powerful than anything else she could offer.

"I say we do lunch at the Hidden Cafe," Spencer said to the group. "It's been too long." He turned to Emma. "If you're up to it?"

Emma nodded vigorously. "I'm always up for the Hidden Cafe. You know that. I just need to find my brother."

"I think that's him now." Cam inclined his head toward the exit. James was in the parking lot, striding toward the church doors. "It's hard for a brother to see his sister going through something like this." He shot Bethany a look. "But he'll get through it. We all will."

Emma sighed. "I know that. I just wish he did."

As the group filed toward the door, James looked up, surprise and more than a trace of dismay crossing his face as his eyes roved the crowd of people surrounding Emma.

Cam pulled the door open and gestured Bethany and Ruby through. Bethany hesitated, unsure how to greet James, but Ruby pushed out ahead of her.

"Hey, James. We're going to the Hidden Cafe for lunch. I'm going to get pancakes. Wanna sit by me?"

Bethany followed her daughter, mostly to keep from creating a traffic jam in the doorway.

James shook his head, hands in his pockets, watching the ground. "We can't. Emma should—"

"Eat," Emma interrupted, coming up alongside Bethany. "Emma should eat. She's starving."

James pressed his lips together but walked silently alongside the group as they made their way through the parking lot, breaking off with promises to meet at the cafe as each family reached their own vehicle.

Finally, Bethany and Ruby were the only ones still walking with James and Emma, and Bethany spotted James's truck right next to her car. She'd been in such a hurry when they'd arrived that she hadn't noticed it.

James led Emma to the passenger side of his truck, and Bethany waited, smiling as he opened the door for his sister. That was sweet. As he closed the door on Emma, Bethany moved aside to let him pass, but instead of rounding his truck, he opened her car door.

"Oh. Um, thanks." The gesture shouldn't have meant anything. It was just one person opening a door for another. But for some reason, it touched Bethany. This time when she brushed his hand, it was intentional. "It's going to be okay."

He gave a terse nod, looking away, and she dropped into her seat.

James closed the door behind her, and Bethany started her car, waiting for him to back out of his spot before following.

"I don't think he liked church very much," Ruby said.

Bethany puffed out a breath. Sometimes her daughter was a little too observant. "I think he's worried about Miss Emma."

"Then why wouldn't he pray for her?"

Bethany glanced at her daughter in the rearview mirror. She missed the days when Ruby's questions were simple, like "Why is the sky blue?"

"I'm not sure, Rubes. He probably needed some space or some air or—"

"He needs Jesus," Ruby said definitively. "And us."

"Ruby," Bethany warned. "Don't—"

"I'm going to tell him all the jokes I know until I make him laugh. Even if it takes all day."

Bethany shook her head with a chuckle. She wasn't sure who she should wish luck—her daughter or James.

She followed his truck into the nearly full parking lot at the Hidden Cafe.

Everyone was already gathered in front of the doors, and they all went in as a group. The hostess took one look at the size of their party and led them to the separate dining room at the back of the restaurant, overlooking Lake Michigan. The tips of the waves sparkled like jewels today, and Bethany stood for a moment, captivated. It wasn't that she didn't remember the view of the lake—it was that the view changed every time she looked at it.

"Come on, Mom." Ruby tugged her toward the table James and Emma already stood next to. Bethany's eyes flicked from James's sour grimace to Emma's playful grin—matched by Ruby's. The two maneuvered so that Bethany and James had no choice but to sit next to each other—or make it very obvious they were moving to avoid each other.

They'd just settled into their seats when Cam and Kayla joined them, baby Evelyn sleepily waving a fist in her car seat. Cam set the carrier down and unbuckled the baby, then passed her to Kayla, who nestled the little girl on her lap. Evelyn immediately cooed and sent the biggest smile in James's direction.

"She likes you," Ruby cheered.

James's lips moved into—well, Bethany couldn't place the expression, but it definitely wasn't a smile—and he directed his eyes toward the window.

"Can I hold her?" Ruby asked Kayla.

"Of course." Kayla readjusted her wheelchair so she could help Ruby position the baby on her lap. Cam leaned toward them. "You know what, Evelyn was telling me yesterday that she can't wait for you to teach her how to ride a bike."

Ruby rolled her eyes. "Evelyn can't talk yet, Uncle Cam."

"That's what you think." Cam winked at her, and Kayla laughed—and Bethany was struck again by how good they were, not only with their new baby, but with Ruby too. It seemed to come so much more naturally to them than to her.

Their food arrived, and Kayla took the baby back, holding her with one arm and eating with the other.

"Hey, James."

James looked startled as Ruby called his name. "Yeah?"

"Why did the turtle cross the road?"

James stared at Ruby blankly. Bethany rolled her eyes. He could at least pretend to play along.

"Because he was too slow to catch the bus." Ruby giggled and giggled.

James didn't crack a smile, but Emma laughed and shoved him. "That was a good one, Ruby. Don't mind James. He's never been very good at jokes."

"Well, I bet my mom that I could get him to laugh," Ruby announced.

Bethany winced as James's eyes came to her. "It wasn't a bet," she murmured.

But Emma laughed. "Count me in, Ruby."

For the rest of the meal, Cam, Kayla, Emma, and Ruby took turns telling jokes. Bethany listened and laughed along. She even pulled out her phone to snap some pictures of everyone smiling. But James kept his focus on his food, grimacing occasionally—or maybe that was supposed to be a polite smile.

When they'd all finished eating, Ruby popped up from her seat. "I've got it." She waited until they were all looking at her. Even James lifted his head, Bethany noted with satisfaction.

"What do cows like to do on Friday nights?" Ruby snickered, and Bethany couldn't help but smile. Ruby had told this joke enough times that even *she* remembered the punchline. But her daughter seemed to find it hilarious every time.

"Go to the moooo-vies." Ruby dissolved into giggles, which made everyone else, including baby Evelyn, laugh too.

Bethany accidentally glanced toward James. He wasn't laughing, but his face had relaxed into the smallest smile. Bethany grinned at Ruby. She'd say her daughter could count that as a win.

"Look at this happy group," the waitress said as she brought the check over. "You guys must be celebrating something fun."

James's face went pale, and Bethany felt her own smile wilt as she remembered what had brought them all here. But Emma's smile didn't falter. "We are. We're celebrating life."

"That's a great thing to celebrate." The waitress smiled. "I can take this whenever you're ready."

Cam reached for the bill. "This is on me."

Bethany knew she should argue with her brother. He already did so much for her and Ruby. But she also knew Kayla would take Cam's side and she'd end up losing. It was what happened every time.

But James seemed less inclined to accept Cam's offer. "I'll get it." He plucked the bill from Cam's hand.

Cam looked at him in surprise, then chuckled. "All right. How about we split it?"

James leaned forward, pulling a billfold out of his back pocket. He flipped it open and pulled out a credit card, handing it to Cam, who got up to take the bill and cards to the register.

"I think this little one needs her diaper changed." Kayla patted the still gurgling Evelyn.

"I'll come with you." Emma pushed her chair out.

And then it was just Bethany and Ruby and James at the table.

"Who's that?" Ruby's abrupt question made Bethany swivel her head.

But there was no one in the room that they didn't know. And then she realized that her daughter was pointing at James's billfold, which he still held open in front of him.

James's eyes flicked to Ruby in surprise, then back to the picture. He stared at it so long that Bethany wondered if he'd forgotten the question.

"My daughter." His knuckles stood out white against the billfold, but his voice was soft.

Bethany blinked at him. He'd never said anything about having a daughter, had he? And Emma had never mentioned a niece. At least as far as Bethany could remember...

The girl in the picture looked to be four or five. So where was she now? With her mother? Bethany thought James had mentioned he was divorced.

"She's cute." Ruby leaned over Bethany to get a better look. "What's her name?"

James cleared his throat. "Sadie." He touched a finger to the picture, then snapped his billfold closed.

"How old is she?" Ruby was still half draped over Bethany.

"Uh." James rubbed a hand over his chin and looked around, as if seeking an escape hatch. "She would be ten."

Bethany sucked in a breath, and his eyes came to hers. He gave the slightest nod, and her heart cracked clean through the middle. No wonder he looked so broken all the time.

Ruby's forehead wrinkled. "Ten? That's the same as me. You should get a new picture. She probably doesn't—"

"Ruby." Bethany let her hand fall on her daughter's shoulder, though she couldn't look away from James.

His throat rippled as he swallowed.

"What?" Ruby tucked her hair behind her ear. "You should bring her to Hope Springs sometime. We could—"

James shook his head and pushed back from the table. "Tell Emma I'll be in the truck."

"James—" Bethany wrapped her arms around her daughter, watching as James bolted from the building.

"Did I make him mad?" Ruby whispered.

Bethany kissed her daughter's hair. How would she ever live without her? "He's not mad, Rubes. He's sad. I think his little girl died."

Chapter 29

"It's going to be all right, James." Emma gave him a bright smile as she followed the nurse out of the waiting room Monday morning.

"I know." He tried to sound as brave as she did, but the moment she was out of the room, he dropped back into the uncomfortable chair.

A hand fell on top of his and squeezed. He turned, and his mom offered an encouraging smile.

"Aren't you worried?" he asked.

Mom's smile didn't slip. "She's my daughter, James. Of course I'm worried. But I also trust that she's in God's hands. Which are much more capable than mine."

"What if it's cancer?" he asked hoarsely. "What if they don't get it all? What if—"

Mom shook her head, silencing him. "What ifs are only going to drive you crazy. You know that."

Yeah. Better than anyone. But that didn't mean he didn't ask them. All the time. What if he hadn't stopped to help that day? What if Sadie hadn't—

"Excuse me, everyone." Mom stood abruptly and raised her voice over the murmurs of the others who had gathered in the waiting room: Sophie and Spencer, Leah and Austin, Dan, Grace and Levi, and Bethany. And he knew the rest of Emma's friends had promised to stop by throughout the day.

The murmurs stopped, and the gathered friends all gave their attention to Mom.

"I wanted to thank you all for being here for my Emma. For being family to her. She's told me so much about all of you that I feel like I know you already." She paused, and James marveled at her poise. This woman who had already had to say goodbye to her husband and now faced losing her daughter was chatting as if they were at a church potluck rather than in a hospital waiting room. "I asked Pastor Dan if he'd lead us all in a prayer this morning." She looked to Dan, who stood and gave her a warm smile.

James tensed as Mom took her seat next to him and wrapped her hand around his. He wasn't going to be able to run out on this prayer. Not that he could explain why he'd run out of church yesterday. It wasn't like he didn't want people praying for Emma. He might not think God was going to listen, but if there was the slightest chance . . .

But hearing Dan say it like that, in front of the whole church, had made it suddenly move from the realm of surreal to real, and he hadn't been ready for that. And now that they were at the hospital, now that Emma would be going under the knife in minutes—it didn't get any more real than this.

"Heavenly Father," Dan's voice was strong and yet soothing at the same time, and James wondered briefly if that was natural or if he'd had to train to speak like that. "We come before your throne asking for your guiding hand over the surgeons who are operating on Emma today. We ask that you would help them to remove the mass safely, we ask that you would grant her complete healing, we ask that you would bless her with a speedy recovery. Most of all, Lord, help her—and all of us—to know that she is in your hands. Let your will be done. And let us trust that your will is perfect. We ask all these things boldly and confidently, in Jesus' name. Amen."

James remained silent as a collective "Amen" went up around the room. For a moment, no one moved, and then the gentle murmuring started again. James managed to keep his seat next to Mom for another two minutes. But he couldn't take it any longer than that.

"I'm going to get some air. I'll grab you some coffee on my way back up."

Mom looked like she was going to protest but then nodded. "Coffee would be great. Thanks."

James kept a low profile as he slipped out of the room and headed for the end of the hallway. The last thing he needed was to be followed by one of Emma's well-meaning friends. When he reached the bank of elevators, he bypassed them, following the sign down the next hallway toward the stairs. He hated small spaces. And right now he needed to move, to push his body hard enough that his heart had to focus on pumping.

Because otherwise it might stop.

Bethany had never thought of herself as a ninja before.

But she felt like one now, as she slipped out the waiting room door ten seconds after James.

She'd tried to tell herself not to follow him. Tried to convince herself that he might be going to the restroom or something. Tried to tell herself that if he'd left because he wanted some alone time, it meant he wanted to be *alone*. Not with her. But then she'd seen the look on his mother's face and known: even if he wouldn't admit it, James needed someone.

She didn't know why she thought that someone should be her.

She only knew that he'd passed the bank of elevators and slipped around the corner. She scrunched her nose, trying to remember what else was down the hallway. Maybe he really was only making a trip to the restroom.

But she continued to the end of the corridor, glancing down the next hallway, which was dominated by a nurse's station—but no restrooms.

A door at the end of the hallway swung closed with a heavy thud, and Bethany noticed the exit sign above it.

Ah. He was taking the stairs.

Picking up her pace so she wouldn't lose him, she hurried down the hall and through the door, the hammering of footsteps echoing up to her. Fortunately, they were only on the third floor, so if she lost him here, he shouldn't be too hard to find at the bottom. Gripping the railing tightly, she scurried down the staircase and pulled open the door at the ground floor, coming out on a wide corridor. To the left, she could see the bustle of the hospital lobby. To the right, a side exit.

She made a decisive turn toward the exit.

She pushed the door open slowly, in case he was standing near it, but as she stepped outside, she had to second-guess her conclusion. There was no one out here.

She turned to go back inside, but a flicker of movement on the other side of a bush caught her eye. It may have been a bird, but . . .

She stepped outside, easing the door closed behind her, and made her way toward it.

She rounded the bush slowly, ready to discover that she was on a literal goose chase. But instead of a goose, she found James, sitting in the grass, knees bent up in front of him, head tucked down.

She inched forward until she was standing alongside him. When he didn't look up, she lowered herself to the ground next to him, letting her eyes rove across the hospital parking lot toward Lake Michigan across the street. There was a slight chop on the water today, sending frothy foam rolling off the top of the waves.

After a few minutes, James sat up. "What are you doing out here?"

"Enjoying the beautiful day."

James snorted. "Did my mother send you?"

"Nope. I came on my own. I wanted to make sure you were—"

"Okay?" James's laugh was ironic. "I'm not the one under the knife."

"Sometimes it's harder to be the one waiting."

James nodded but didn't say anything.

"It's going to be—"

James turned to her. "Don't say 'all right.' You can't know that."

Bethany glanced at him in surprise. "I was going to say warm out." Already the sun was giving the skin on her arms a toasted feel.

"Oh." James tipped his head skyward. "I guess so."

The silence lasted longer this time, the warmth of the sun and rhythm of the waves lulling Bethany into a sort of awake-sleep.

"I'm sorry about yesterday," James said abruptly, pulling her out of her doze.

"For what?" As far as she remembered, he hadn't done anything to apologize for.

"I didn't mean to upset Ruby. I just didn't expect . . ."

Bethany looked toward him, and he dragged a hand through his hair. "Tell her I'm sorry."

"I will." Bethany had lain awake half the night, thinking about James and his daughter, torn between a desire to forget what she'd learned and a desire to wrap her arms around him and tell him she was here for him. She sat on her hands, just in case. "You know, if you ever want to talk . . ."

But James was already shaking his head. "I don't talk about it."

Bethany nodded. "Okay. We'll just sit then."

Chapter 30

Ask her to leave. Tell her you want to be alone.

Except—did he really want her to leave? Did he really want to be alone?

As much as he shouldn't admit it, sitting here with her—not saying anything, just watching the waves, listening to the gulls, smelling the peachy wafts that floated from her—was more comforting than he would have guessed.

Just a little longer, he promised himself. *Then you have to go back inside. You have to be there for Mom and Emma.*

But another ten minutes had gone by when Bethany turned to him. "Do you think we should go back upstairs?"

Reluctantly, James nodded. He pushed to his feet, then held out a hand to help her up.

Her hand slid into his without hesitation, its warmth sweeping through him. He pulled her up quickly, then let go, but she closed her eyes and swayed, grasping for his arm. He reached for her before she could tip over.

"Sorry." She opened her eyes after a moment. "Happens sometimes when I stand up too fast." She still gripped his arm, and he didn't let go.

"I think I'm good now." She released his arm, but he held on for a moment longer, until he was relatively certain she wasn't going to keel over.

"Want to take the stairs or the elevator?" Bethany asked as he held the exterior door open for her.

As much as he hated elevators, he couldn't see trying to make her climb stairs right now. "Elevator."

Bethany didn't argue, and he led the way. He pressed the up button and it was only a few seconds before it chimed and the elevator door opened. He forced himself to get on but pressed his back to the wall as the door slid closed.

"Your mom seems sweet," Bethany said as the elevator bumped to a start. Her eyes came to him with a smile that fell away. "What's wrong?"

"Nothing. Just not the biggest fan of elevators."

"Really?" Bethany's brow wrinkled. "Why?"

"Claustrophobia. When we were kids, Emma used to trick me into going into her closet and then lock me in there. I haven't been able to handle small spaces since then. Especially ones I can't get out of easily."

Bethany burst out laughing, and the sound made James's muscles relax a little. He didn't mean to let his lips ease upward, but they did.

"Sorry." Bethany coughed, pretending to get her giggles under control, though James could see the mirth in her eyes. "I can't picture Emma doing that."

"You'd be surprised by the things she did to me. She's always been my—" His voice cracked unexpectedly, and he cleared his throat, staring at the numbers on the elevator.

"I know." Bethany moved closer and the elevator seemed to grow smaller—but not in a bad way. "She's become like a sister—"

The car went dark, and Bethany crashed against him. His arms went instinctively around her.

"What was that?" Bethany's voice came from right below his chin, and her peach scent drifted to his nose, temporarily stunning him.

Gently, he unwrapped his arms from around her as the emergency lights came on. "I believe that was the elevator breaking down." He gestured toward the doors, which hadn't opened.

Bethany's eyes widened. "That really happens?"

"Once in a while." He'd responded to a couple of calls to broken elevators over the years. It was never serious—they always got them running again eventually—but he'd shuddered at the thought of being trapped inside one for any amount of time.

He tugged at the collar of his shirt. He was fine. The small space couldn't hurt him. He needed to remain calm for Bethany's sake.

"So now what do we do?" She sounded completely at ease.

"Now we call for help." But he was suddenly reluctant to move away from her. What if the car began to plummet—he needed to be close enough to protect her.

He shook his head at himself. He knew enough about how elevators worked to know that wouldn't happen. So why didn't he want to leave her side?

The truth was—

No, it was too dangerous to examine the truth.

He stepped forward and pressed the emergency call button. It was only a moment before a voice replied, saying they were aware of the problem and had someone on the way to help. "Sit tight," the voice added.

It wasn't as if they had any other choice. There was nowhere they could go. Not up, not down, not forward, not . . . His chest tightened. He didn't like not having an escape.

He could feel Bethany's eyes on him, and he fought to get himself under control. This was not the time to lose it.

"So." Bethany had apparently taken the disembodied voice literally, as she slid to the floor and crossed her legs crisscross applesauce style—he'd learned that term from Sadie. "Might as well get comfy."

James nodded. "I guess."

"So this probably doesn't help your . . ." Bethany blinked up at him.

"Claustrophobia?" He crossed his arms in front of him. "I'm fine."

"You know what they say. The best way to deal with your fears is to face them."

"Maybe *they* should get stuck in an elevator then."

Bethany's laugh was warm and understanding. "Come on. Let's do something to take our minds off it."

"Like what?" he asked cautiously, eyeing her. If she was going to ask him to talk about Sadie again . . .

"How about tic tac toe? I have paper and a pen." She reached into her purse and pulled out a small notebook. She patted the floor next to her. "Come on."

He sighed but crossed the elevator and lowered himself next to her, pressing his back into the wall. Bethany drew a tic tac toe board and put an O in the center square. He took the notebook and added his X in the top left square.

By the time they were three games in, James felt himself start to relax. Sitting here, next to her, he could almost imagine they were still outside rather than trapped in a five-foot by five-foot box.

"This is getting silly," Bethany said after the sixth tied game. "Let's play something else."

"Like what?"

Bethany pressed a finger to her lip, and James found himself watching the way her mouth moved as she answered. "Would you rather?"

James tipped his head to the side. "Would I rather what?"

Bethany's laugh filled the elevator, making him smile a real smile for what felt like the first time in days. "No, silly, that's the name of the game. Would you rather? Ruby and I play it all the time. One person asks a 'Would you rather?' question, and the other person has to answer it. Like, 'Would you rather have to eat only chocolate for the rest of your life or eat only ice cream for the rest of your life?'"

"That's easy. Chocolate ice cream." James gave her a smug look, and Bethany shoved his shoulder lightly.

"No cheating. Okay, your turn."

James tapped his chin, thinking. This was just the kind of game Sadie would have loved. What would she have asked? "Would you rather wear only purple or only red?"

Bethany treated him to a laugh and a surprised look. "I did not see that question coming."

"Why not?" It wasn't a particularly deep one.

"It's just so . . ."

He waited, knowing it sometimes took her a while to find a word.

"Fun," she said finally.

"And I'm not fun?" He raised an eyebrow, though he already knew the answer to that. He used to be fun . . .

Bethany shook her head, but he saw the truth in her eyes. "No, it's not that. It's just . . . What was the question again?"

He snorted. "Nice change of subject. Wear all red or all purple?"

"Right." She rolled her eyes—at herself, he was pretty sure, and he wished she wouldn't do that. It wasn't like she forgot things on purpose or because she didn't care. She couldn't help it.

"Definitely purple," she answered.

"I knew it." He didn't know why that pleased him so much.

"You did? How?" She leaned toward him, and he suddenly noticed how pretty she looked, even in the elevator's emergency lighting.

"I guess I just associate you with the color purple."

"You associate me with a color?" Her eyes widened, and he realized that was probably the most ridiculous thing he'd ever said.

"I mean, it's a cop thing." Nope, *that* was the most ridiculous.

But Bethany grinned as if he'd made her queen. "I associate you with a color too. It's how I remember your name."

"Oh." So that was how she'd remembered at last. "What color?"

"Gray." She cringed as she said it. "Only because you always seemed sort of sad. But now I know why . . ." She drifted into silence.

"Yeah." Sadie had always refused to color with the gray crayon. *Gray is too sad, Daddy,* she'd told him when he'd asked why she'd made her elephant pink.

What would she think if she knew her daddy had become sad and gray?

"My turn to ask a question." Bethany's voice rang with forced cheer. "Would you rather go to the moon or scuba dive in the deepest part of the ocean?"

"Moon. So I could see if it was really made of cheese." It was the kind of answer he would have said to Sadie—the kind that would have lit up her face and brought out that deep belly laugh and made her call him silly.

Bethany's surprised laugh was nearly as rewarding.

"Nice. Your turn."

They each asked a few more goofy questions, and James let himself forget that there was a world outside this elevator. In here, he could tell himself everything was fine. And he could let Bethany's smile convince him whenever he started to doubt again.

"Okay, I've got another one," he said.

"Let's hear it."

Somehow, they'd slid closer together as the minutes had passed, and he kept catching whiffs of her tantalizing scent.

He inhaled. "Would you rather forget everything that ever happened to you or remember everything?"

Bethany's eyes widened, and he realized the question was probably too personal. "I'm sorry. You don't have to answer that. I'll come up with something else."

"No." Bethany shook her head slowly. "It's a good question. I just need to think about it for a minute."

"You do?" James turned toward her. "I would think the answer would be easy for you."

Bethany frowned. "Would it be easy for you?"

James sucked in a breath, considering. If he could forget everything, then this pain that was a constant reminder of all he had lost would finally disappear. But so would his memories of Sadie. On the other hand, remembering everything was no picnic either. "I guess it's an impossible question."

Bethany's smile was gentle. "There are things from my past that I wish I could forget. And things from my present I wish I could remember." Her laugh held a trace of sorrow. "But in the end, I guess it all makes up who we are, right? Even the things we've forgotten. Or the things we'd rather forget."

James swallowed, nodding as her eyes came to his. "I guess you're right."

She slid closer, and he shifted a little as her knee bumped his.

"What was she like?" Bethany's voice was gentle, like a ripple of wind on a spring day. Like Sadie's smile.

"She was . . ." He dropped his head back against the wall, staring up at the ceiling. A hand slipped into his and squeezed, and he could feel Bethany's compassion all the way to his heart. But that didn't mean he could do this. "I'm sorry, I can't." He worked too hard to push those memories away every single day. And talking about her would only make that more impossible.

"Okay," she whispered. They sat in silence for a few seconds, then she broke in. "I've got one. Would you rather clean horse stalls by yourself for a week or get stuck in this elevator with me for an hour, forced to play Would You Rather?"

James chuckled but considered the question. A month ago, it would have been a no-brainer. He'd preferred to clean the stalls by himself. And he certainly hadn't thought he could enjoy being stuck on an elevator. But now, if he was being honest . . . "I'm going to go with get stuck in the elevator."

"Really?" She wrinkled her nose, but her face lit up. "The horse stalls are bigger. And easier to get out of."

"But you smell better."

Bethany's laugh ricocheted off the elevator walls, taking a bounce and landing smack in the middle of James's heart.

"You'd better be careful," she teased. "Or I might have to change your name from James the Gray to a happier color."

He lifted an eyebrow, feeling much lighter-hearted than he should. "Like what?"

Bethany studied him, and suddenly he couldn't look away—didn't want to. In fact, he wanted to get closer and—

"Orange," Bethany proclaimed.

James blinked. "That was Sadie's favorite color." The words came out of him before he could remind himself that he didn't talk about her.

Bethany's smile was gentle. "Then it's the perfect color for you. James the Orange."

"I guess at least it's not James and the Giant Peach."

She gave him a confused look.

"Like the book. Never mind."

She shrugged and brushed her hair back from her face, exposing a small scar on her forehead he'd never noticed before. He reached for it and ran a finger lightly over it.

Bethany froze a moment before he did. What was he doing?

Would you rather, a voice in his head asked, *kiss her or—*

He pulled his hand back and grasped the railing that ran around the elevator. It was time to get some distance.

He had risen to a crouch when the elevator lurched suddenly, throwing him off balance—and right on top of Bethany.

"Oof." Her arms came to his shoulders as he scrambled to get his legs under him so he could un-crush her.

"Sorry," he grunted as his fingers accidentally got tangled in her hair.

"It's okay." She was laughing, and in the restored lighting, her eyes sparkled. "I guess they got the elevator fixed."

The elevator dinged and the door slid open just as James managed to get his fingers unwrapped from her hair and push himself to his feet.

"Well." Mom stood in front of the open doors, looking amused but not surprised. "I was just coming to see if I could get an update from the maintenance crew, but it looks like you're all right."

"Yep." James tugged his shirt into place, then reached down to help Bethany up. When she was on her feet, he held a hand to the small of her back to make sure she wasn't about to tip over as she almost had outside. He shook his head at Mom's knowing smile and moved his arm away as soon as he was sure Bethany was steady on her feet.

The instant he stepped out of the elevator, the reality he'd managed to pretend didn't exist while he was trapped in there with Bethany came crashing back over him. Forget the elevator—it was this antiseptic, sterile space that made him feel claustrophobic.

"How's Emma?" He managed to squeeze the question out of too-tight lungs.

Mom's expression sobered. "They did a biopsy. And—"

James tensed.

"It is cancer," Mom said gently.

Bethany's hand slid into his, and he held onto it for dear life.

"But they think they can get it all," Mom continued. "They're going ahead with the full hysterectomy. She may have to do some chemo or radiation down the road, just to be safe, but she should be out of surgery in a while."

"James," Bethany whispered.

But he shook his head and pulled his hand out of hers, striding past her and Mom to the waiting room. He wasn't about to give God one more thing to take away from him.

Chapter 31

"So." Mom set a big bowl of her famous potato soup in front of James and took a seat across the table in Emma's kitchen. Emma would be in the hospital another few days to recover, but she had insisted that James and Mom come back here. And since he had to take care of the horses, James couldn't really argue, though he couldn't push away the fear that if he left her there, he'd never see her again.

"So." James played with his spoon and inhaled the savory steam billowing off the bowl but didn't take a bite. The day had left him battered and exhausted.

"Should we give thanks?" Mom folded her hands in front of her.

James let himself nod. For one thing, he knew Mom wouldn't eat until they did. And for another, he didn't have the energy left to argue.

"Would you like to or—" Mom waved a hand over her soup.

"You go ahead." He might be willing to listen to a prayer, but he sure wasn't about to offer one.

Mom closed her eyes, and James followed suit.

"Dear Lord," Mom began. "Thank you for protecting Emma through her surgery and for guiding the doctors' hands. We ask you to be with her in her recovery. And be with James too. Show him that you have hope and a future planned for him—"

"Mom." The word shot out of James as he clenched his fists. This wasn't about him.

Mom didn't miss a beat. "Remind him that he is your child too and that you love him. In Jesus' name we pray. Amen."

"That wasn't necessary," James said as soon as she opened her eyes. "Just stick to praying for Emma."

"I pray for both of you every day, James." Mom stirred her soup. "And to be honest, you're the one I worry about more."

James shook his head, spooning up a bite of soup and shoving it into his mouth, wincing as the hot liquid scalded his tongue. He should have known Emma would tell Mom about the gunshot sooner or later. "It was only a graze. I'm fine."

"What graze?" Mom raised an eyebrow, and James realized too late that his wound wasn't what she'd been talking about.

"Nothing." He downed a gulp of milk to cool his burning mouth. "I'm good," he repeated.

Mom watched him but didn't push the conversation further, and James concentrated on devouring his soup as quickly as possible so she couldn't ask questions about his injury. His bowl was almost empty when Mom set down her spoon.

Uh oh. He knew what that meant: a lecture was coming.

"Seriously, Mom, it was nothing to worry about. Captain overreacted and sent me here. But as soon as Emma's on her feet . . ."

"Don't you think you've run away long enough?" Mom let her penetrating gaze rest on him.

James huffed. "Run away? I've been here for almost two months."

"I know." Mom reached across the table and set her hand on top of his. "And we both appreciate it. But I don't mean that you haven't helped us. I mean you haven't let us—anyone—help *you*."

"Because I don't need help. I already told you. I'm fine." He pulled his hand back and stood to carry his bowl to the sink.

"Emma says you won't talk to her about Sadie. You won't talk to me. What about Bethany?"

James looked at her over his shoulder. "What *about* Bethany?"

"Have you talked to her about Sadie?"

He rinsed his bowl. "She knows." Or well, she knew he'd had a daughter. That was enough.

"So the two of you are close?" Hope blanketed Mom's words. "Are you dating?"

James studied the water flowing into his already-clean bowl. "We're friends, I guess."

"Come on, James. I've been here less than twenty-four hours, and I can tell you see each other as more than friends." He heard Mom's chair slide back and her footsteps come toward the sink.

He turned the water off and set his bowl down, not looking at Mom as he cleared away the rest of the dishes. "I don't know what you think you saw, but—"

"Don't push her away, James. She cares about you, I can tell. And you may not want to admit it, but you care about her too."

James shook his head. That might be true. But it didn't mean he was going to let it go anywhere. "She has a kid, Mom. A little girl. Same age Sadie would be." He didn't mean to sound like a bitter old man, but the truth was, sometimes he felt like one.

"Did you ever think maybe there's a reason for that?"

"A reason?" he spun and stared at his mother. "What, like God hasn't had enough fun with me yet? He had to stick the knife in a little deeper?"

Mom winced. "You don't really believe that."

"Yes. I believe that. Same as I believe I will never date or have a family again, so it doesn't pay to push me."

"I'm not trying to push you. I'm trying to encourage you. Closing yourself off to others isn't the answer."

"And you know this how?" It'd been a long time since James had raised his voice to his mother, and he wasn't proud of it now. "Dad has been gone for over twenty years, and I don't see you moving on."

"Actually—" Mom glanced away. "About that . . ."

James froze.

"I met someone." Color rushed to her cheeks, and she suddenly looked ten years younger. "His name is William. He lives in the same retirement community as me. And he . . . he's really great. I think you'd like him." She fluffed her short curls with a nervous laugh. "Sorry. I wasn't sure how to bring that up, but . . ."

James couldn't quite process what he was hearing. "So you're dating this guy?"

"William." Mom nodded, looking more confident and less nervous. "Yes. We're dating."

"Oh." He swallowed. "Okay."

"That's all? Okay?"

James shrugged. What else was he supposed to say? Mom was a grown woman. She could do what she wanted.

"Why now?" He finally asked. "After all these years?"

Mom gave him a thoughtful look. "For a long time, after your dad died, I wasn't interested in opening myself up to hurt again. And then after a while, I realized that closing myself off from others wasn't the answer. But I never met anyone who could measure up to your dad."

"And William does?" A hard defensiveness rose in him.

"No," Mom said gently. "I learned that I couldn't measure other men against your dad. I had to see them as themselves, completely apart from him. William is a retired accountant who likes to golf."

James laughed in spite of himself—Dad had hated golf with a passion.

"But he's a lot like your father in all the ways that matter," Mom continued. "He loves the Lord, he's funny, he's compassionate. He puts my needs before his own." Mom's face softened. "He loves me, James. And I love him."

James swallowed. It felt strange knowing she was talking about a man other than his father. But at the same time— "I'm happy for you, Mom."

Her face relaxed, and she stepped forward to give him a hug. "Thank you." She pulled back. "And can I give you one piece of advice?"

"Just one?" James raised an eyebrow.

Mom laughed. "For now." Her expression grew serious. "It's worth the risk. Putting your heart back out there. God created us to love and support one another. So don't keep people from doing that for you."

James pressed his lips together and turned toward the stairs. He was glad taking the risk had paid off for Mom. But he was going to stick with his original plan. No risk. No reward. No heartache.

Chapter 32

Bethany shifted the giant bouquet of yellow roses to her left hand as she reached Emma's front door and knocked. She opened the door without waiting for an answer—Emma had just gotten home from the hospital yesterday, and she didn't want her getting up to answer the door.

"Hello, anyone home?" she called as she peeked her head inside, her stomach tightening at the thought that James could be here. She'd hardly seen him since Monday—since they'd been trapped on that elevator and she'd thought he might—

But it didn't matter what she'd thought. Whatever it had been—if it had been anything at all—had clearly passed. On the few occasions she'd seen him this week, he'd done little more than grunt hello and tell her that he'd already cleaned all the stalls so she could go home.

Footsteps—too light to be James's—hurried toward the door, and Bethany prepared to scold her friend for getting out of bed. But instead of Emma, it was her mother who came popping into the room, offering Bethany a bright smile. "Those smell heavenly."

Bethany smiled back—she liked Emma's mom. And it was clear where Emma had gotten her sunny disposition from. James must take after his father. Or a bear.

"Emma is napping. Do you want me to wake her?"

"No. Let her sleep. I'll go help in the barn first. If James didn't finish it all himself already. Again."

Emma's mom regarded her, as if thinking, and Bethany felt suddenly self-conscious. She hadn't meant to grumble against the woman's son. "I mean, it's great that he's—"

"He said he told you about Sadie?"

Bethany blinked at her. Sadie? That name didn't ring any . . .

"His daughter?" Emma's mom prompted.

"Oh." Bethany's heart squeezed. Every time she thought of James and his daughter—whose name she hadn't been able to recall no matter how hard she tried—fresh sorrow rolled over her. "I'm sorry. I'm not very good with names. My memory . . ."

"Emma told me about your aneurysm." Emma's mom pulled out a seat at the table and gestured for Bethany to do the same. "She said you have some short-term memory loss?"

Bethany glanced at the door over her shoulder but took a seat. "Yeah. So I should probably admit that I can't remember your name either." There wasn't much point in pretending otherwise.

Emma's mom smiled. "I'm Anne." She leaned forward. "So he did tell you about Sadie, then?"

Bethany shook her head. "My daughter happened to see her picture and asked about her. I know she died, but . . . he won't talk about it. I think it would probably help if he did."

Anne frowned, worry deepening her eyes. "I think so too." She rubbed a hand over the table. "It's been five years, but to him, I think it was yesterday. He says he's moved on, but what he's doing isn't living."

"Do you mind if I ask what happened?" Bethany asked tentatively. She didn't want to make the woman relive losing her granddaughter.

Anne's forehead wrinkled, but she nodded. "James and Sadie had gone on a daddy-daughter date to the zoo. On the way home, it started to rain, and there was an accident in front of them. James pulled over to help. He told Sadie to stay in the car, but . . ." She pressed her lips together, shaking her head.

"Oh my . . ." Bethany reached forward and clutched the woman's hand.

Anne looked up, offering a gentle smile, though her eyes glistened. "The driver didn't see her through the rain. She made it to the hospital, and James got to say goodbye to her. She told him not to worry, that God would take care of her, but . . ." Anne wiped a finger under her eyes. "I don't think he's been able to forgive God—or himself—since that day." She sniffed and rubbed at her nose.

Bethany could only watch helplessly. Her heart felt like it was being cranked in a vice and the only way to release the pressure was to cry—and yet her eyes remained dry.

"I'm sorry." Anne sniffed again. "That was more than you asked for."

"I'm glad you told me." As much as it hurt, it also helped her understand James better. "I only wish there was something I could do."

Anne patted her hand. "I think you already have, dear. Emma says that you and James are . . ."

"Oh." Bethany's face sucked up all the heat in the room. "Um, no, we're . . ." She searched for the right word. But she wasn't sure if there was one.

Anne patted her hand again, then stood. "I'm going to go check on Emma. I'll let you know when she wakes up."

Bethany didn't know how long she sat staring at the spot where Anne had been sitting before she finally got up and made her way out to the barn.

Her heart hurt and hammered at the same time as she opened the door. What if James was in here? What was she going to say to him? Now that she knew everything he'd gone through, it felt like she should have something profound to say, some sort of comfort to offer him. *Please give me the words I need, Lord.*

But her prayer proved to be unnecessary as she stepped inside and found the stalls all clean, the horses moving quietly, and James nowhere in sight.

Her eyes fell on a stall door that stood open, then tracked to the far end of the barn. James had to be out there with Fancy Lady.

Her heart drummed louder than horses' hooves as she made her way down the aisle, not stopping to greet Ace as he nickered for a sugar cube. It would be easier to leave. Easier to pretend she'd forgotten everything Anne had told her. Easier not to search for words she knew she'd never be able to find.

But she couldn't do that.

Not when James needed her.

Her heart jumped as she spotted him working Fancy Lady at the far end of the training ring. She let herself watch as he turned the horse, trotted her, circled back, and then cantered away. He did it all with grace and precision, holding complete control—the same way he seemed to hold complete control over his life.

A control he didn't need disturbed by someone like her—someone who was nowhere near in control of all the things in her life.

She should leave.

James turned the horse again, setting her on a course directly for the gate next to Bethany. He didn't seem to notice her. But she could tell the moment he realized she was there because his whole face dropped into a frown, and he glanced over his shoulder as if contemplating making a break for the woods. But he continued toward her.

She swallowed and held her ground. He may not want to see her. But she needed to know that he was okay.

"Whoa." He pulled Fancy Lady to a halt in front of the gate. "Hi." His greeting was neither warm nor cold—more indifferent than anything.

Bethany brushed off the hurt and opened the gate for them. "You didn't leave anything for me to do." She gestured toward the barn. "Again."

"I can do it myself."

"I know you *can* do it yourself. But that doesn't mean you have to. Or even that you should." Bethany reached a hand up to stroke Fancy Lady's nose.

James shrugged. "I'd better get her brushed down."

Bethany watched him closely. Now that she knew his stiff, controlled exterior guarded a heart that was aching for his little girl, she longed to wrap her arms around him and tell him it was okay to let go of that control. Okay to hurt.

But she moved out of the way, and he led Fancy Lady toward the barn.

Bethany hesitated. She could walk around the outside of the barn and give him the space he so clearly wanted.

Or—

She followed behind Fancy Lady, waiting until James had dismounted from the horse to step forward.

He startled as he spotted her. "I thought you'd left."

She smiled. "No such luck."

James took off the horse's saddle and bridle, then led her to her stall. Bethany grabbed the curry comb and brush off the pegboard hanging on the wall and followed. She passed the comb to him and watched as he rubbed it in circles over the horse's neck. He studied the movements of his hands as if one slip in concentration would mean disaster.

I still need words, Lord. Bethany waited, too many thoughts swirling in her head to form them into a sentence. Finally, a few worked their way free. "Emma was sleeping when I stopped by the house."

James grunted a reply.

"I talked to your mom."

James glanced up for a second, then back at the comb.

"She told me, James."

"Told you what?" The words were gruff, but at least they represented progress from the grunts.

"She told me about Sadie," Bethany said softly. "About what happened to her."

James's hand jerked to a stop, and he jumped back from the horse as if it'd kicked him. Fancy Lady pranced and sent him a reproving look that would have been comical if it weren't for the anger in James's eyes. "She shouldn't have—"

"Yes." Bethany said firmly, taking a step closer to him. "She should have. You won't talk about it, and—"

"That's right." James crossed around to the other side of the horse, and she heard the brush start working again. "I don't talk about it. Ever."

"You're so . . . so . . ." What was the word she needed? She balled her hands and closed her eyes, thinking. "Frustrating." She opened her eyes again and moved around Fancy Lady to stand next to James, who kept combing. "Your mom said it's been five years. You can't lock yourself off from the world forever. Sometimes you have to let yourself need other people."

In one fluid movement, he pulled the curry comb off his hand and thrust it at her. It took Bethany's brain a moment to catch up with the fact that he'd disappeared out the stall door.

"Wait! James!" She'd messed it up. Apparently those hadn't been the words she'd prayed for. She sped after him, but he was halfway down the alley, his long strides not slowing. "When are you going to stop being such a coward and running away every time someone asks you to be a little vulnerable?" The words spilled out before she could think them through, and she couldn't help the glimmer of elation at coming up with a word like *vulnerable* on the spot.

James stopped, his back going stiff.

Uh oh.

Maybe those weren't the words she'd prayed for either.

He spun in a slow half-circle. "A coward?" He laughed coldly and held up his arm. "I have the bullet holes to prove I'm not. It's my job to run *toward* danger."

"I know." Bethany took advantage of the fact that he'd stopped moving and hurried toward him. "That's not what I meant. Physically, you're probably the bravest person I know. But emotionally, you're . . ."

James crossed his arms—but she got the feeling he was trying to protect himself more than intimidate her. "I'm what? You have no idea what it's like to lose a child." His voice was hard, controlled, but it stopped Bethany from moving closer.

"You're right," she said softly. "I can't even imagine . . ." She swallowed at the look of anguish that twisted James's features.

"No you can't," he spat. Then he turned and fled for the door again.

Bethany hesitated. Maybe she should let him go. But something sent her feet flying after him. She caught up to him and snatched for his arm, pulling him to a stop. "I may not know what it's like to lose a child, but I know what it's like to need other people. I have to ask for help every day. I have to let other people do things that I used to be able to do myself. I have to make myself vulnerable even when it's hard."

"You want me to be vulnerable?" James's voice rose, and Ace pranced nervously in the stall next to them. "All right. How's this for vulnerable? My daughter is dead. She's dead, and it's my fault. She's dead, and I can't bring her back." He was shouting now. "She's dead, and there are days when I don't know how I can go on." He glared at her, his shoulders rising and falling with his breaths. "There. Are you still glad you asked?"

Bethany could only blink at him. That had been so raw and so open and so vulnerable. She pressed a hand to her heart, praying for words.

When none came, she did the only thing she could think of.

She stepped forward, slid her arms around his shoulders, and rose onto her tiptoes, bringing her lips gently to his.

He stiffened, his hands coming to her shoulders, and she thought he was going to push her away, but then he was pulling her in closer, and his arms were around her.

She concentrated on pouring every ounce of her compassion and her sorrow and her gratitude that he'd finally opened up into the kiss.

Wait.

The *kiss*.

She was *kissing* James.

With a gasp, she pulled back, glancing over her shoulder toward the far door. Would it make *her* the coward if she ran now?

James was watching her, not saying anything, which made the whole situation more confusing.

She touched a hand to her spinning head.

"I'm sorry. I shouldn't have— I just . . ."

James's lips lifted a fraction, and it set something loose in her chest. "Impulse control?"

She seized on that, nodding with a shaky laugh. "I should . . ." She gestured toward the door behind him, and he stepped aside.

Keeping her head down, she scooted past him, then dashed down the alleyway, out of the barn, and into her car. She didn't realize until she was home that she'd never gone back inside to visit with Emma.

Chapter 33

Ah, he was a mess.

Had been for three days.

Ever since that kiss with Bethany. It had been the last thing he'd expected her to do after he'd yelled at her like that. His first instinct had been to push her away, to ask her what in the name of all that was holy she thought she was doing.

But the feel of her lips on his, of her arms around his neck, had undone something inside him that had been coiled tight for years.

He hadn't let himself feel—really feel—anything for so long, and the full impact of his suppressed emotions had been too near the surface ever since.

Sorrow over the memories of Sadie knocked louder than usual, but it was coupled with something undefinable—something close to relief. Relief that Bethany knew about Sadie? Relief that he'd finally admitted that missing his daughter was killing him? Relief that Bethany had kissed him?

He wasn't sure. And he wasn't sure he needed to know.

Because it wasn't like they were ever going to kiss again. She may not be able to control her impulses, but he could.

Not that he'd had to worry about it the last few days, since she'd stayed away from the stables, texting that she had too much to do for Cam and Kayla. He'd wondered more than once if she was avoiding him.

Or if she'd forgotten the whole thing.

Either way, he was thankful. He had no idea what he was supposed to say to her the next time he saw her—which would be any minute now.

"Do you have the snaffle bits?" Emma called from the bench near the barn door that he'd made her promise not to stir from. She should be in bed, but this was the closest he could get to making her rest as he got things ready for today's dressage competition.

"Yep. Single-jointed, double-jointed, and unjointed. And the bridoon bits." He hefted a saddle and loaded it onto the trailer. The sound of tires on the driveway stole his attention, and he glanced over his shoulder—again. It wasn't Bethany—again. But she and Ruby had to be here soon. It was almost time to leave for the competition.

Following Emma's instructions, James helped the other kids load their horses onto the trailers. But still Bethany and Ruby hadn't shown up. Had Bethany forgotten? Had something happened to one of them? His heart roared that he needed to go make sure they were all right.

He took a deep breath.

There was no reason to overreact. And the fact that he *was* overreacting was only proof that he'd let himself get too close to them.

He pulled his truck keys out of his pocket and strode toward his sister. "Aren't Bethany and Ruby supposed to be here?"

Emma gave him a shrewd smile. "Didn't I tell you? You need to pick them up on the way." Her smile grew. "They always ride with me since Bethany doesn't like to drive long distances. And since you won't let me come . . . Unless you want to change your mind." Her eyes sparkled with mischief.

James shook his head. "You're staying here and resting. I'll give them a ride."

"If that's what you want," she lilted.

James growled but got into his truck, following the caravan of horse trailers down the driveway.

The things he did for his sister.

He navigated through the streets to Bethany's house, his thoughts refusing to budge from that kiss. Was it going to be awkward to see her?

Of course it's going to be awkward.

But it might also be . . . really nice.

He shook his head and opened the window. Maybe some fresh air would chase these thoughts away.

But if anything, the fresh air only fueled his need to see her. By the time he reached her house and rang the doorbell, nerves fired through his middle.

"Hi, James." Ruby was chattering the second she opened the door, and for some reason it set him at ease.

"Do you like my new boots? Uncle Cam and Aunt Kayla gave them to me for my birthday."

James dutifully examined the black leather boots. "They're very nice. Are you . . ."

He lost track of his words as Bethany entered the living room behind her daughter. Had she always been so beautiful?

"Hi." Her smile seemed shy, tentative.

"Hi." He cleared his throat and looked away. "Are you ready to go?" He directed the question to Ruby.

"Yep. Oh wait. I forgot my helmet." She charged out of the room.

James's eyes accidentally landed on Bethany's. Was it his imagination, or were her cheeks pinker than usual?

"Um. So." She straightened a precariously stacked pile of books on the coffee table. "How's Emma doing?"

"She's good. Mad that Mom and I insisted she stay home, but she'll get over it. I think she's worried I'll screw everything up. But all I have to do is get there and check everyone in. The kids have to do the hard part."

The kids.

The word felt unnatural coming from his mouth. He'd worked so hard to avoid anything having to do with kids for years. And now look at him. What was he doing here?

Ruby bounced back into the room, helmet dangling from her hand. "I'm ready. Let's go."

Something about the way she said it—as if the three of them went places together all the time—caught him off guard. Not in a bad way. More in an I-could-get-used-to-this way. He held the door open for them, then led the way to the truck. He tried to avoid glancing at Bethany as he fastened his seatbelt, but failed. She had tucked her hair behind her ear and he could see the scar he'd touched in the elevator. As if she sensed his eyes on her, she turned toward him. He swiveled his head quickly and started the vehicle. But when he reached to shift into gear, his hand accidentally bumped hers on the console between them.

"Sorry." Her hand slid away, and he had to resist the urge to grab it and pull it back toward him. Man. He had to forget about that kiss. She probably had. And anyway, it had been a momentary lapse of impulse control on her part. Nothing more.

"I'm so nervous," Ruby said suddenly from the back seat, drawing James's eyes to the rearview mirror. "I've been working on my loops, but I don't know if I'm ready."

James glanced to Bethany, but she seemed to be lost in thought. He supposed he could ignore Ruby's comment and hope the girl would decide to be silent—but that seemed unlikely. Besides, another peek in the mirror told him that she really was nervous.

"If my sister thinks you're ready, then you're ready," he said. "Plus, I've seen you ride. You're very good."

"You really think so?" Ruby sounded earnest and hopeful.

James met her eyes in the mirror. "I really think so."

"Thanks, James." Ruby settled back in her seat, and James nodded, an odd sense of satisfaction rolling over him. Only because Ruby had fallen silent and he could ride in peace.

It lasted all of thirty seconds.

"Can I ask you something?" Ruby sprang forward in her seat again.

"Who? Me? Or your mom?" *Please let it be Bethany.*

"You, silly."

"Um. I guess?" He could always decline to answer. It wasn't like this ten-year-old was the boss of him.

"Do you like Kimberly's mom?"

"Ruby," Bethany gasped.

So she *had* been listening.

"I'm sorry." Bethany's cheeks were definitely pink now.

"I, uh—" James scratched his eyebrow. "She's nice, I guess." Where was this line of questioning going?

"But do you, you know, *like* her like her?"

"Ruby Jane, stop." Bethany turned in her seat, and James caught a glimpse of the warning look she sent her daughter.

"What about my mom?" Ruby asked.

"Ruby Jane Moore!"

James couldn't help it. The horror in Bethany's voice made him laugh out loud. He tried to cover it with a cough.

Unsuccessfully, judging by the death ray Bethany shot him.

"I'm so sorry," Bethany repeated.

"Turn right at Sunset Drive. Your destination will be on the left," an electronic voice cut in.

"Thank goodness," Bethany murmured.

James chuckled. Saved by the GPS. Now he didn't have to answer Ruby's question.

At least not out loud. But that didn't stop his brain from thinking about it the whole time he got the riders checked in and the horses unloaded and everyone to where they needed to be. He got separated from Ruby and Bethany in the shuffle. But as much as he tried to tell himself that was a good thing, he couldn't resist searching them out the moment everything was settled.

He reached them just as Ruby's level was announced as the next event.

"I can't do this." Ruby turned to Bethany, looking panicked.

"Of course you can." Bethany sent James an equally panicked look.

"No, Mom. I'm too scared. I'm going to mess up."

"You know what I used to tell Sadie when she was scared?"

"What?" Ruby looked to him as if he had the answer to the secret of life.

"I'd tell her, the more scared you are to do something, the braver you are when you do it."

Ruby nodded slowly.

"And if that didn't work," he continued. "I'd bribe her with ice cream. That's how I taught her to ride a bike."

"Does that mean we can get ice cream if I do this?"

"That's up to your mom."

They both looked to Bethany. She rolled her eyes. "Like I can say no now."

"Goody." Ruby clapped her hands, and next thing James knew, her arms were around his waist. He lifted his arm to her back. The girl seemed to have her mother's propensity for spontaneous hugs.

"Ruby." Bethany's voice was full of laughter, and it made him accidentally smile too. "Let go of James and get on your horse if you want a chance for some ice cream."

Ruby squeezed him once more, then let go and moved toward her horse.

James helped her into the saddle. "You and your noble steed get out there and show us your stuff."

"Noble steed." Ruby giggled as she rode off.

James and Bethany made their way to the rail so they could watch.

Bethany grasped his hand as Ruby's name was announced over the loudspeaker.

"She's got this," he reassured her.

Ruby put her horse through the required moves, keeping her lines beautifully and guiding her horse through the half-circle loops flawlessly.

"Emma would be proud." James grinned at Bethany as they made their way toward the spot where Ruby was exiting the arena.

"Thank you." Bethany paused and touched his arm.

"Of course." He tilted his head. "For what?"

"For that pep talk before. You didn't have to tell her—us—about Sadie."

James blinked down at her, his gaze getting stuck on her lips. "Someone told me I need to be more vulnerable."

Her face remained neutral, and at first he thought maybe she hadn't heard him. But then she said, "Who?"

He nudged her shoulder. She was kidding, right? "You."

"I did?" She squinted as if trying to peer back in time.

James studied her. "The other day. At the barn. You yelled at me to be more vulnerable and then— You really don't remember?"

Bethany played with a strand of her hair. "I'm sorry. My memory—"

"Did you guys see me?" Ruby barreled into them, nearly knocking Bethany off her feet. James reached out a hand to steady her.

"You were great." Bethany hugged her daughter. "Let me take a picture of you."

Ruby smiled for her mom, then turned to him. "I did it! That means we get ice cream, right?"

"Yep." James looked at Bethany, who was nodding.

So ice cream she remembered. But the kiss that had shaken up his whole life?

Apparently that had been forgettable.

Chapter 34

Bethany's lip felt raw from chewing it all the way to the Chocolate Chicken. Ruby and James had spent the drive analyzing Ruby's performance—which had earned her a third-place finish.

But all Bethany could think about was the fact that for the first time since her aneurysm, she'd lied about not remembering something.

Of course she remembered the conversation she and James had had in the barn—and what had come after it.

She'd been trying for days to forget about the way she'd made a fool of herself, kissing him like that. But it'd been hopeless. The harder she tried to forget, the more she remembered—remembered the caress of his hands and the smell of his cologne and the taste of his lips.

But just because she remembered didn't mean they should talk about it. If she pretended to forget, then they could move on as if it hadn't happened at all.

"Mom!" Ruby's voice blasted through her thoughts, making her jump.

"Sorry. What?"

"We're here. You have to get out of the truck."

"Oh." Bethany startled to find James opening her door. She didn't mean to look into his eyes—they were bluer than usual today, a shade she couldn't think of a word for, and less troubled too.

"Are you okay?" he asked as he helped her down. "You seem quiet today. Quieter than usual, I mean."

She laughed. "And you seem less quiet than usual."

He looked taken aback but then laughed too. "My ex-wife used to say Sadie got her chatterbox tendencies from me. Don't look at me like that. It's true."

Bethany closed her mouth. She hadn't meant to look surprised, but chatterbox? James?

"I guess I haven't felt like talking much in a long time," he said quietly. But even the way he said that didn't feel as heavy as usual.

"I'm going to get bubblegum ice cream," Ruby announced as she hopped out of the truck.

"Ugh." Bethany wrinkled her nose.

But James laughed. "Sadie tried that once. She wasn't a fan."

The three of them strolled toward the ice cream shop together, and Bethany got the oddest sensation suddenly—this was what it would be like if they were a family.

But they weren't.

"What was she like?" Ruby asked. She was walking between them, and it took Bethany a moment to realize she was talking to James—and that she was asking about his daughter.

"Ruby, that's not—"

But James gave Bethany a soft smile. "It's okay." He glanced down at Ruby. "She was funny, silly, always giggling. She had the best laugh—" He cut off, clearing his throat and looking out over the lake.

Bethany's heart ached for him, and she had to clasp Ruby's hand to keep from reaching for his. But then Ruby clasped James's hand with her other hand, making the three of them a chain.

"She sounds special," Ruby said.

Bethany held her breath. This was past the point where James usually shut down or ran away.

But he smiled at Ruby. "She was. She would have loved to ride horses the way you do."

They had reached the door of the Chocolate Chicken, and Bethany was almost disappointed. Something was happening here. She didn't know what, exactly. But it felt like something she wanted to last.

"There you guys are." Tiffany and Kimberly raced toward the Chocolate Chicken from the other direction. "We thought maybe you got lost." Tiffany's smile faltered as her eyes went to the line of their linked hands, but she recovered within half a second. "I'll get a table for all of us over by the window if you'll place our order. I'll have a single scoop of peppermint, and Kimberly likes cookies and cream."

"I— Um. Okay."

Tiffany and Kimberly were already disappearing through the door James held open, and Bethany gave him a panicked look. She'd already forgotten what they wanted.

"Don't worry." James tapped his head. "Sometimes my nearly photographic memory is useful." His hand landed on the small of her back for a second as he ushered her through the door, and a jolt of nerves shot up her spine.

When they got to the counter, he ordered for everyone and insisted on paying, telling the server he'd cover anyone else who came in from Hope Stables too.

It only took a few minutes for their order to be ready. Bethany picked up Ruby's bright pink concoction and held it out to her. But just as Ruby reached for it, James stepped away from the counter with the rest of the order. His elbow hit Bethany's hand, and she lost her grip. The ice cream seemed to fall in slow motion, straight toward Bethany. She gasped as the blob hit her in the stomach, then slid to the floor, leaving a nice pink streak in its wake.

"I'm so sorry." James set his dishes down and pulled a wad of napkins out of the dispenser on the counter.

"It's okay." Bethany blotted at her shirt. What had she been thinking when she'd decided to wear white this morning? Her gaze flicked toward Tiffany, who was also wearing white—her outfit was still pristine.

Bethany gave up on her shirt and shifted to wiping the ice cream off the floor.

"Here. I'll do that. You go take care of your shirt." James squatted next to her, his eyes right in front of hers, his lips . . .

She looked at the floor. There was no reason for her to notice his lips. "I've got it. If you want to bring the others their ice cream, I'll be there as soon as I'm done."

James's hand fell on top of hers, stopping it. Gently, he took away her napkins. "Go. I'll clean this up and then order Ruby a new one."

Bethany stood slowly. She didn't need a dizzy spell on top of everything else. But she wobbled as she straightened and had to reach out a hand to steady herself. It contacted James's shoulder instead of the chair she'd been aiming for. He stilled, his other hand reaching up to grasp her elbow, and she had no choice but to hold on for another second before being certain that she was steady enough to cross the room.

"I'll be right back," she murmured, not quite sure if the fresh wave of dizziness was from standing up or if it was from the care she'd seen in his eyes as she walked away.

James's eyes flicked to the back of the Chocolate Chicken as he tried to make small talk with Tiffany. Fortunately, she seemed content to carry the conversation, and all he had to do was nod every few seconds.

Bethany had been in the restroom a while. What if she had fallen and hit her head in there? She'd seemed dizzy when she'd stood from wiping up the ice cream. He should have sent Ruby with her. Should he send her to check on her mom now? Or maybe he should send Tiffany.

But she was still talking. "The field day is the last big thing of the year, and then I can finally relax. Has your mom said how it's coming?" She directed the question to Ruby.

"How what's coming?" Ruby took a bite of the rocky road James had talked her into ordering in place of the spilled bubblegum flavor. He'd been surprised when Ruby had agreed to the suggestion.

"The field day, of course." Every once in a while, James caught a hint of condescension in Tiffany's tone—and he didn't like hearing it directed toward Ruby.

"It's good," James jumped in at Ruby's confused expression.

"Oh." Tiffany raised an eyebrow. "Bethany told you that?"

"Mmm hmm." James concentrated on stuffing a big bite of ice cream into his mouth so he wouldn't be forced to stretch the truth any further. Bethany had said she was planning to start on it weeks ago. Surely she had by now. Just because she hadn't mentioned it again didn't mean she hadn't done anything.

"That's a relief. To be honest with you, I was worried that she might not remem—"

"Nope. It's all under control." James wasn't about to let Tiffany insult Bethany right in front of Ruby. Or right in front of *him*, for that matter. Bethany couldn't help it if she sometimes couldn't remember things—even whole entire kisses.

His pulse kicked up a notch as he spotted her emerging into the seating area. Her forehead wrinkled as she scanned the tables, and he realized she didn't remember where Tiffany had seated them. He waved a hand over his head. Her eyes landed on him and her forehead unwrinkled as her lips lifted. James finished the last large bite of his ice cream so he wouldn't stare.

"Oh no. It didn't come out all the way." Tiffany pouted toward Bethany. "Here. I think I have some . . ." She opened her purse and pulled out a pouch, producing a small wipe that she passed to Bethany. "Stain remover."

"Thanks." Bethany looked embarrassed as she rubbed it over the spot that was now a faded pink. "I keep meaning to put some of these in my purse, but . . ." She shook her head with a rueful smile. "Guess I'd better write it down."

"Here." Tiffany reached into her organizer and passed a handful of the little packets to Bethany. "I have plenty more at home."

James smiled at Tiffany. That was kind. Maybe he'd misjudged her.

"Thanks," Bethany murmured again. The spot was almost completely gone from her shirt now, and she stepped away to throw the wipe out, then returned to the table.

"Hold on." She eyed Ruby's ice cream as she took the seat between James and her daughter. "I know I forget things, but that ice cream does not match the color on my shirt."

"James said rocky road was Sadie's favorite. So I decided to try it. It's good."

"I can't believe you got her to try something new." Bethany smiled at James as she scooped a bite of her own melty Sundae.

"Who's Sadie?" Kimberly asked from the other side of the table.

James froze. Just because he'd been able to talk about his daughter with Bethany and Ruby didn't mean he was ready to talk about her with the whole world. But both Kimberly and Tiffany were watching him with unabashed curiosity.

"Oh look." Bethany pointed toward the window. "There's a new store going in where the barber shop used to be."

"Thank goodness." Tiffany wrinkled her nose. "Every guy in town came out of that place with the same exact haircut."

James laughed at her comment but sent Bethany a grateful smile. He couldn't be sure whether she'd changed the subject to spare him from talking about Sadie or because the flurry of activity across the street had caught her eye, but either way, he was thankful.

"Can we go to the park, Mom?" Kimberly asked after they'd all speculated about what kind of store could be going in.

"Sure. I'll take you girls while Bethany finishes her ice cream. Care to join us, James?"

He glanced at Bethany. She still had most of her ice cream left. "I'll wait here with Bethany. We'll meet you over there."

Tiffany's smile dipped for half a second but then returned. "Of course." As they filed out of the shop, the two young girls seemed to be arguing, both of them looking at him over their shoulders.

"I wonder what that's about."

"No idea," Bethany murmured, sticking her spoon in her mouth. Her cheeks took on a rosy glow.

James felt his own face warming. Now what? Should he make small talk? Maybe about the weather? Or Ruby's ride today? Or the small matter of the kiss she'd forgotten?

"James?" Bethany's voice drew his eyes right to her. She was watching him, looking perplexed.

"Sorry. Did you say something?" He'd been a little lost in thought.

"No. But thanks for telling us about Sadie. It means a lot."

He swallowed and nodded. He wondered if she remembered that she'd already thanked him for that. Right before he'd discovered that she'd forgotten all about their kiss. "Thanks for listening."

"Always."

He looked out the window at all the families bustling by. He used to believe in always. But now he knew it could be ripped away at any moment.

He pushed back from the table to clean up the mess the others had left—and to catch a breath. What was he doing here, acting like Bethany and Ruby were his family—like he *wanted* them to be his family? He'd already had that once and, yes, he missed it with a sting sharper than a hundred bullet wounds. But that was his past. His future was as a single man. What he needed now was for Emma to hurry up and get better so he could get back to Milwaukee—where he'd never once questioned his family-less future.

He took a fortifying breath and made his way back to the table. Maybe he could rush Bethany through the rest of her ice cream. He lowered himself into his seat, sliding a few inches farther from her so he wouldn't be tempted to enjoy her peach scent.

"Oh. Ow." Bethany dropped her spoon into the dish and pushed her palms to her forehead.

"What? What is it?" James sprang toward her. Was it possible for her to have another aneurysm?

"It's okay." Bethany lowered her hands, and one of them fell on top of his. "Brain freeze."

He exhaled. "Don't do that to me. I thought . . ."

"Sorry." She smiled apologetically, and James had to look away so she wouldn't see how much she'd scared him.

But why? He was a cop; he was trained to deal with emergencies. He'd seen some awful things over the years, and he'd never flinched.

Except when it was Sadie.

And now Bethany.

People you love.

No. He didn't love Bethany.

He cared about her—as a friend—yes.

And this was only proof that even that was too risky.

He felt Bethany's eyes on him but resisted the pull as long as he could. When he finally gave in, there was such a depth of understanding in her gaze that he couldn't look away.

But then the bell over the door clanged and snapped him out of it. "I almost forgot to tell you, Tiffany was asking Ruby about the field day. I told her it was going great and you had everything under control."

If he'd wanted her to stop looking at him so sweetly, this had done the trick. Her eyes widened, and she scrambled to pull her phone out of her purse. "The field day! I completely—" Her mouth snapped shut, and then she whispered, "It's in two weeks. I'll never get it done." She dropped her head into her hands and massaged at her temples. "Why did I ever think I could do this? I'm going to have to tell Tiffany. Maybe she can still pull it together. Better than I can."

James's heart tugged. She was a smart, talented woman. She shouldn't feel this way about herself. "Or . . ." He glanced toward the window. Did he really want to make this offer when what he should be doing was putting more distance between them, not less?

But when he looked back to her, her eyes were so full of hope that he had no choice. "I could help you. I bet the two of us—and maybe a few of your friends can get it done on time."

"Really?"

James shrugged. "Sure."

Instead of impulsively hugging him as he fear-hoped, Bethany narrowed her eyes. "On one condition."

"You're going to put conditions on me helping you? I'm not sure that's the way this is supposed to work."

"Yes it is. My condition is that you have to let me help you too."

"Help me? I don't—"

"With the horses. No more finishing everything before I get there. Deal?"

Oh boy. That would mean even more time together. But he found himself grinning. "Deal."

Chapter 35

"How about this one?" Bethany passed her phone to James to show him the list of field day activities she'd found.

"A water balloon relay race? Sure. I think the kids would like that. But who's going to fill all those water balloons?" He rested his elbows on Emma's desk in her office at the stables, which they'd transformed into a headquarters for field day planning over the last few days. His arm bumped Bethany's, and she jiggled her eyebrows at him. He laughed—it was a sound she heard more and more often lately, and one she never forgot.

"You think *I'm* going to fill them?" He shook his head. "I have no idea how you roped me into this."

"You volunteered," she reminded him.

"Oh, you remember that?"

She nodded, not letting herself mention what else she remembered, though she was suddenly staring at his lips. She tore her eyes away and concentrated on writing water balloons on her list of supplies they needed to pick up. Fortunately, the list wasn't terribly long. They'd already arranged for all the food with the help of Leah and Peyton and Ariana and Sophie and Grace. And James had made a sign-up sheet for volunteers, which Ruby had brought to school and asked her teacher to hand out to parents.

She rummaged through the folder from Tiffany. "Food. Check. Games. Check. Prizes—" She looked up at James. "We need prizes."

"All right. Where do we get those?"

She paged through some sheets in the folder, frowning. "It looks like they usually order them months ahead of time." She sighed. She'd made such a mess of this whole thing. And every time she thought she might pull it off, another obstacle came up.

"Hey." James covered the paper she was reading with his hand. "We've got this. Come on." He stood, turning his hand palm up and holding it out to her.

Okay. As far as she could remember, she'd been the only one to ever initiate contact between them—and that only impulsively. This was . . . unexpected.

But he bounced his hand a little, and she let her palm come to rest in his. His fingers closed around it, warm and secure, making her wish that they always walked around like this.

But then he tugged her to her feet and she came to her senses and pulled her hand back. His hand hovered near her elbow. "No dizziness?"

She shook her head. "Nope. I'm good." Unless you counted the unexplained longing that had taken up permanent residence in her chest as they'd spent more time together. She let him lead her outside. "Where are we going?"

"Downtown. I'm sure there are plenty of places that would love to donate prizes."

"You think so?"

He opened her door. "It's worth a shot."

She climbed into her seat, using the few seconds it took him to reach his own door to calm the nerves that suddenly tingled through her. This wasn't a date. It was a volunteer project. *Her* volunteer project. And yet here he was, pouring his time and energy into it too. Why? For her?

She didn't usually consider herself a quick thinker, but she pushed that thought away as fast as it had entered.

James was just bored. Or he felt sorry for her. Or . . .

He got in the car and smiled at her.

Maybe he was doing it for her. The thought made its way back in. "Um." She tried to refocus her attention. "Maybe we could try the hardware store too? They might have something we could give away."

"Like nails?" James joked.

"No." She shoved his arm lightly, his firm muscles barely moving under her touch. She retracted her hand and folded it in her lap. "Like squirt guns or something."

"That's a great idea."

A glow started in Bethany's middle and worked its way toward her face. "Thanks."

They fell into an easy conversation about Ruby's volcanic science experiment that had made a mess all over the kitchen. Somehow talking with him was never intimidating or hard or tiring. She never worried about forgetting her words or taking her time to find the right one. With him, the words were just there—or he waited patiently until they were. From Ruby, their conversation turned to Emma and her frustration at not being able to work in the barn yet.

"It's a good thing she doesn't know about her surprise party on Saturday, or she'd probably get mad about not being able to help plan that too," James said.

"The party!" Bethany bolted upright so fast her seatbelt tightened. "I think I forgot to get a gift."

"You can always get one at the hardware store," James teased.

But Bethany groaned. "You must think I'm a terrible friend."

James didn't answer for a moment but slowed the truck for a stop sign. Then he looked over at her. "You have to stop thinking that I think you're a terrible anything. Or that anyone does. In case you haven't noticed, people around here really like you. They admire you. I—" He turned back to the road and stepped on the accelerator. Bethany's imagination tried to guess the ending to the sentence he'd left unfinished.

"Anyway," James continued, pulling on the collar of his shirt. "Everything worked out fine when you forgot Ruby's present, remember?"

"I forgot Ruby's present?" She gripped the console between them. She was sure she'd given her daughter something . . . though she couldn't remember exactly what it was. Maybe she was a worse mother than she thought.

"No," James said gently. "You gave her that horse necklace, remember? But you had forgotten your purse that day. And then locked yourself out of your car. You don't remember?"

She shook her head. "No. Sorry."

"It was the first day we met," he said softly.

She closed her eyes. It seemed impossible that she wouldn't remember that. And if she'd forgotten that, what else didn't she remember? Had she kissed him more than once?

Her internal debate over whether to ask him lasted all of three seconds. It was better to go on pretending the kiss—or kisses, as the case may be—had never happened.

And to make sure it didn't happen again.

"The lake is pretty today." James had to come up with something to think about other than how much he was enjoying this day with Bethany. They'd made a huge haul—jacks and tops from the toy store, bookmarks and stickers from the book store, squirt guns and Frisbees from the hardware store, and even a few trinkets from Violet's antique shop, where Bethany had also found a Victorian silhouette of a woman and a horse for Emma.

"I think that's one of the things that surprised me most when I moved here." Bethany squinted toward the waves, which slipped gently toward shore today. "I used to think a lake is a lake is a lake. But not this lake. It's like it has its own mood swings."

James laughed—it felt like he'd been laughing all day.

"So what is the lake's mood today? Happy?" James grinned at her. His sure was.

Bethany studied the waves. "I would say more like content."

"Content it is." He fell silent again but only for a moment. He couldn't explain this new desire to talk whenever he was with her—or his desire to draw her out, to learn everything about her. "I don't think I ever asked where you're from."

She frowned as if it was a hard question. "Texas, originally. A bunch of other places in between. But I think this is the first place that has felt like home since I was a kid."

James could see why she would think that. Hope Springs had something about it that said *home*.

But it's not, he reminded himself.

It could be, his thoughts argued.

"So what brought you here?" he asked, mostly to keep his thoughts off his own growing desire to stay.

Bethany looked startled. She didn't say anything for a few minutes, until they reached his truck and he opened her door. "I got pregnant with Ruby." She paused with one foot on the running board. "And I knew I had to get out of the situation I was in."

James's jaw hardened. He'd seen more than one woman who'd had to flee from an abusive "situation," but the thought that it had happened to Bethany made him want to throw up—or punch someone.

"He hurt you?" he managed to growl.

"No." Bethany climbed the rest of the way into the truck and tucked her hands between her knees. "He was . . . into things that I knew I couldn't have around my baby."

"Drugs." He couldn't keep the contempt out of his voice. He'd made too many arrests, been too personally affected by what addicts could do, to remain neutral.

Bethany nodded silently, staring straight ahead out the windshield, and James closed her door. He shoved his hands in his pockets and rounded the truck. He hadn't meant to make her feel bad about it. It wasn't her fault she'd gotten mixed up with the wrong guy.

"You did the right thing," he said the moment he opened his door. "Leaving Ruby's father, I mean. People like that don't change. I've seen it over and over again. The guy who shot my dad had been arrested for possession three times. He was out two weeks before he got high and killed my dad."

"Oh, James. I'm so sorry." Bethany's lip trembled.

Way to go. He'd been trying to reassure her—not leave her in tears.

"Hey. It's okay." He reached for her hand. "It was a long time ago. I just wanted you to know I'm glad you left that situation. I've seen too many beautiful, intelligent women get involved with guys like that and not know when to walk away."

Uh oh. Had he just called her beautiful and intelligent?

Well, she is.

If Bethany had picked up on what he'd said, she didn't show any signs of delight. If anything, she looked closer to tears as she extricated her hand from his and clasped it in her other fist.

He tried to recapture the lighthearted mood he'd managed to single-handedly ruin, but though Bethany offered strained smiles, her replies were short and halting, as if she struggled with every word. When they reached the stables, she silently accepted his offer to unload the donations they'd collected and headed straight for her car.

He watched her leave, trying to figure out what had gone wrong.

And reminding himself that actually it had gone *right*. If she wouldn't speak to him, he wouldn't be so tempted to stay in Hope Springs.

Chapter 36

Bethany tried to focus on Jade's words as she discussed a point Kayla had raised in their Bible study. All these women, living such lives of faith, having everything together all the time. She loved them all dearly—and yet sometimes she had to ask herself if she really belonged here.

"Could someone read the next two verses out loud?" Jade asked.

Bethany's hand sprang into the air.

Jade gave her a surprised smile. And no wonder—Bethany had never volunteered to read out loud before, as far as she could remember. But right now, she felt like she needed to prove she wasn't a waste of space. Like she had a purpose, even if it was just reading a couple of verses.

She directed her eyes to the Bible open in her lap and realized she'd forgotten which verses they were on. She skimmed her finger over the words, hoping something familiar would jump out at her. "Um." She licked her lips. Emma leaned over and pointed at the verse.

"Thanks," Bethany whispered, then read out loud. "For he has rescued us from the dominion of darkness and brought us into the kingdom of the Son he loves, in whom we have redemption, the forgiveness of sins." Her words slowed as she reached the end of the verses, their truth spreading like a warm blanket over her heart. After her conversation with James in the truck yesterday, she'd almost let herself forget this. She'd been dwelling on the sins of her past—the years she'd spent living in the "dominion of darkness"—instead of focusing on Christ's forgiveness. James might think former drug addicts could never change—but she knew the truth: in Christ, she had been set free from those sins.

Of course, that didn't mean James would want anything to do with her if he knew about her past. But that was fine. She didn't need him to have anything to do with her. She had Ruby. And her friends. And her Savior. That was what mattered.

She spent the rest of the Bible study concentrating on the discussion between the other women—and even contributing one or two tentative comments.

When they had closed with prayer, Emma leaned over to Bethany. "Is everything all right? Between you and James?"

Bethany fought unsuccessfully against the flush rising to her face. "There is no me and James, Emma. And I know this isn't the first time I've told you that, so don't give me that innocent look."

Emma laughed. "But seriously. He seemed upset after you left yesterday. I thought maybe he finally got up the nerve to ask you out and you—"

"He didn't ask me out."

"But if he had . . ." Emma prodded.

Bethany's heart jumped, but she shrugged as casually as she could. "I would have said no."

"What? Why?" Emma frowned. "You're as stubborn and hard-headed as he is."

"Thanks," Bethany said dryly. "I think it's best not to complicate things." She patted her friend's leg. "I'll see you tomorrow."

Emma's forehead wrinkled. "Tomorrow?"

"For the—" She caught herself just in time. But how was she going to cover up the slip? "Never mind. I was thinking tomorrow was Wednesday, not Saturday." She tapped the side of her head. "Good thing I have a calendar."

Kayla stopped her on the way out the door. "Nice save."

"Thanks," Bethany murmured dryly. "How's Evelyn?"

"You mean the nocturnal screaming machine who has forgotten how to sleep more than twenty minutes at a time?" Kayla's eyes widened. "Why didn't anyone tell me how hard this would be?"

Bethany could only stare at Kayla. She'd always seen her sister-in-law as a superwoman—and now supermom. Did she really struggle too?

"Oh my goodness. It's just me, isn't it?" Kayla pressed her hands to her cheeks. "I'm not cut out for it." A large tear dropped onto her cheek. She swiped it away. "I'm sorry. I don't know why I'm crying. I love her so much, but I'm so tired."

Bethany squeezed Kayla's shoulder. "Don't apologize. I think I cried every day for Ruby's first month. I had no idea what I was doing."

"I find that tough to believe." Kayla squinted at her. "You seem to find the whole mom thing so easy. And you raised Ruby all by yourself. I can't even imagine how difficult that was."

Bethany swallowed. "It *was* hard. It still is hard. But I have you all. And you have all of us too, you know."

"I know," Kayla sniffled. "But I feel like I should be able to do it all myself."

Bethany laughed. "I know you do—because that's who you are. But I've been learning that it's not so bad to ask for help. How about you drop Evelyn off at my house tomorrow afternoon, and you and Cam can—" When Kayla started to protest, Bethany cut her off. "Just for a little while. Anyway, we have—" She directed a subtle look toward Emma. "The you-know-what tomorrow night, so you won't be able to stay out very long."

Kayla sighed. "You win. Thank you."

As Bethany got into her car, she laughed to herself. Who would have thought she would be the one giving parenting advice? But it felt good to know that for once she'd helped someone else rather than being the one in need of help. Now all she had to do was survive caring for a baby on her own again.

Chapter 37

"Good morning."

James startled as an older man entered the kitchen. Instinctively, he shoved his cereal bowl out of the way and jumped to his feet, his hand going uselessly to his hip.

The man held up his hands. "Whoa! Relax, son. I'm William."

James didn't relax. Was that name supposed to mean something to him?

"Your mom's . . . friend."

"What are you doing here?"

"He came to surprise me." Mom bustled into the room, looking chipper and more youthful than she had in years, and slipped an arm around William's back. "Isn't that sweet? He got in around two o'clock this morning."

James eyed William and then his mom.

"He's staying in the office," Mom clarified.

James nodded. That was a relief, at least.

"Is Bethany coming by today?" Mom asked with a not-at-all subtle grin. "I noticed you two have been spending a lot of time together."

"I'm helping her with the school's field day. I told you that. And no, she's not coming today. We have everything done until we have to set up next week."

"Hmm." Mom nodded thoughtfully. "Then may I make a suggestion?"

"Can I stop you?" James crossed his arms in front of him.

"No." Mom mirrored his crossed arms. "Ask her on a date. Just the two of you. William and I would be happy to watch Ruby."

"Mom, it's not like Bethany and I are dating. We're just friends."

If they were even that anymore. He hadn't heard from her since she'd left Thursday afternoon, and he still hadn't figured out what had upset her.

"Come on." Mom pulled William toward the table. "William has grandkids, so he'll be good at keeping Ruby entertained."

"Yep. Six grandkids." Pride oozed from William's smile. "Oldest is twelve. Littlest one is four. Spunky as all can be. Takes after her mother."

James laughed, letting the dull ache surface but not overpower him. "Sadie was like that too."

Mom's smile was surprised and misty. "She took after you." She moved closer and squeezed his arm. "See, I told you Bethany was good for you. Go on. Call and ask her out."

James studied his mom and then William. He reached for his phone but hesitated with it in his hands. Was he really ready to take this step?

"What's the worst that could happen?" Mom asked. "She says no?"

James swallowed. That wasn't the worst that could happen. The worst that could happen was she'd say yes and they'd have a wonderful time and they'd grow closer and become a family and then God would decide to snatch yet one more thing from him.

"It's worth the risk, James," Mom said quietly. "You can't live your life waiting for the other shoe to drop. God doesn't operate that way. He's not out to get you."

James shook his head. He wished he could believe that. But so far, his life hadn't borne that out. Not with Dad, not with Sadie, not even with Emma—she might still be here, but the doctors wanted her to do a round of chemo, and James knew that God wasn't above taking her too.

He stowed his phone back in his pocket.

Mom's face fell. James ignored it as he took a step backwards. But his phone rang before he could make his escape. He pulled it out of his pocket and gave an ironic laugh as he caught sight of the number.

Bethany.

He pretended not to notice the way Mom's eyes lit up—or the way his own heart did.

"Hey." He didn't mean for his voice to have that little skip in it.

"Hey." Bethany sounded breathless. "I'm sorry to bother you, but Mr. Faber called, and he has the giant Jenga blocks ready, but he needs us to pick them up today because he's going out of town. I'd go get them, but I don't think they'd fit in my car and I'm—"

"No problem. I'll get them." A perfect excuse not to ask her out. Mom couldn't fault him for that.

"Oh thank you. Would you mind bringing them over here after you pick them up? I want to paint them the school colors."

That meant he'd have to see her. He frowned at the kick of adrenaline suddenly surging through him. "Sure, I'll be there in a little while."

He hung up and turned to Mom, who still had an arm around William and was grinning as if she'd orchestrated this whole thing herself.

Honestly, he wouldn't put it past her.

"Have fun," she said. "And stay as long as you want. We'll make sure Emma gets to—" She lowered her voice, though Emma was still in bed. "Her party."

"Would you stop grinning like that?" But James couldn't help smiling himself as he loped out the door. He was only going to see Bethany for a few minutes—but that was enough.

He tried to fight the anticipation, but by the time he picked up the blocks and got to her house, he couldn't wait a moment longer to see her. He knocked, then rocked from foot to foot as he waited for her to answer the door. A loud cry that sounded like a newborn pierced the air, and James glanced around. He *was* at the right house, wasn't he?

When there was no answer, he knocked again. Again he was met with that cry.

Finally, the door opened, and Bethany stood there, her hair askew, dripping spatula in one hand and crying baby in the other.

"Oh hi." She practically had to shout over the baby's cries. "I forgot you were coming."

"I'll try not to take that personally. You look busy."

"I told Cam and Kayla I'd watch Evelyn today, but I forgot how much work a baby is." She bounced a little, but the baby didn't quiet. "Here, will you hold her for a sec? I'm almost done mixing the brownies for tonight and then I can feed her."

"Oh. Uh. No, I don't think—" But Bethany had already shifted so that baby Evelyn was leaning toward him, and he had no choice but to either take her or let her fall to the ground. The baby was lighter than he remembered Sadie being—more delicate feeling—and he instinctively tucked her closer against his chest. She stopped crying for a second but then started in louder than before.

"Don't take that personally either." Bethany gestured him into the house and nudged the door shut with her hip. "According to Kayla, she does this all day and all night. I thought maybe she was exaggerating, but . . ." Her voice trailed off as she crossed the living room and disappeared into the kitchen.

James dropped his gaze to the little bundle in his arms. She looked so much like Sadie had as a baby—same full cheeks, same bright blue eyes. The only difference was the hair—Sadie had been a baldy for almost a year after she was born, but Evelyn had a fuzzy layer of light hair already. The baby opened her mouth wide in another wail, and James's heart cracked—for this little girl and for the one he missed so much.

"It's okay," he whispered, as much to himself as to the baby. He shifted her to his shoulder and patted her back in a slow rhythm. "Shh." He walked slowly across the room, putting a small extra bounce in each step. When he reached the far wall, he pivoted and paced back the way he'd come. By his third lap, her cries had slowed to occasional snuffles, and he took a deep breath, accidentally inhaling her milky newborn scent.

He closed his eyes against the memories that assailed him. But instead of the familiar stab—or maybe on top of it—the image of Sadie as a baby brought an odd sort of joy.

"Wow."

He opened his eyes to find Bethany staring at him, the unbaked pan of brownies in her hand. "I'm impressed."

James shrugged. "It always worked with Sadie."

"You're going to have to teach me. I sure could have used you around when Ruby was a baby. I mean—" She took a step backwards, her elbow knocking into the door frame and making her bobble the pan of brownies. "I'd better get these in the oven before I drop them."

James couldn't resist following her. "Where's Ruby?"

Bethany closed the oven door. "Riding her bike around the block."

"By herself?" James glanced toward the front window. How long had she been gone? Should she be back by now?

"With a couple of kids from the neighborhood." She frowned. "I miss the days when she screamed all night but stayed right where I put her. It seems so much harder now, especially since—" She broke off, looking stricken. "I'm sorry. You probably don't— You never got to—" She blew a piece of hair out of her face. "I'm making things worse, aren't I?"

But somehow, she wasn't. "No. It's okay. I know what you meant." His eyes met hers, but her gaze skirted immediately away.

She gathered a few dishes and carried them to the sink but then dropped them and turned to him. "Sorry. You probably want to go. I can take her. I'll clean this up later."

Handing the baby over would be the sensible thing to do. Leaving would be the smart choice.

The baby snuggled her head into his shoulder. "I can hold her a little longer if you want."

Evelyn let out a tiny cry, and he patted her back again.

"I think she's hungry." Bethany rummaged through a diaper bag on the counter, pulling out a bottle. She held it out to him. "Do you want to?"

He took the bottle and moved to the kitchen table, settling into a chair and adjusting the baby, whose cries had worked their way up to a full wail again. The moment the bottle touched her lips, she quieted. After a few sucks, a contented sigh slipped from her, and she closed her eyes, still drinking. It was unreal how natural this felt, how familiar, how comforting.

"You look good like that," Bethany said softly.

He let his lips turn up a little bit, but his throat was too full to say anything. The sounds of Bethany cleaning up and the baby sucking lulled him into a weird sort of half-awake state that made him start thinking strange things, like that maybe it was worth the risk to have a family again.

"Mom!" A tearful yell from the front door tore James out of his foolish thoughts. "I fell off my bike."

James jumped to his feet, accidentally pulling the bottle out of Evelyn's mouth. Instantly, her face puckered into a loud cry.

"It's okay. I've got Ruby." Bethany rushed past him into the living room, but James followed, tucking the bottle back into the baby's mouth as he walked.

"Looks like you got a little scraped up." Bethany squatted in front of her daughter, examining her shredded palms and bleeding knees. "But you'll be all right. Let's go get you washed up." She led Ruby down the hall—toward the bathroom, James assumed.

He sat heavily on the nearest seat, making sure not to jostle the baby's bottle. What had he been thinking, imagining that having a family again would be worth the risk?

It's only a few scrapes. She's fine.

This time. But next time it could be worse. It could be—

He had to get out of here.

But it wasn't like he could toss the baby on the floor and disappear.

Fortunately, after a couple more gulps, the baby stopped sucking, her lips going slack as her breaths deepened into little puffs. James lifted her to his shoulder and patted her back until she burped, then carefully laid her in the playpen in the middle of the room.

He was about to make his escape when Ruby bounded in, tears dried, knees bandaged.

"Hi, James."

If he hadn't seen her crying three minutes ago, he wouldn't have believed anything was wrong. "Like my bandages?"

He gave them a cursory glance. "Rapunzel. Nice." And also Sadie's favorite princess. "I have to get going. Tell your mom I'll put the Jenga blocks next to the garage."

"You got them? Cool. Can I see?" Ruby followed him out the door.

James sighed but silently began unloading the truck, taking as many blocks at a time as he could balance. Ruby picked up a block too, adding it to his stack after he set it down.

It only took a few minutes to empty the truck, but by the time they finished, Bethany stood outside, watching.

"Is it lunchtime yet?" Ruby asked. "I'm hungry."

Bethany laughed. "Sure, Rubes. We can have lunch."

"Can James eat with us?"

Bethany looked startled but then smiled toward him. "You're welcome to stay if you'd like. I can't promise a gourmet meal, but . . ."

James backed toward his truck. "Thanks, but I really have to go." He yanked on the handle and dove inside.

"See you tonight," Ruby called before he shut the door.

James glanced at the clock. It was noon. That gave him six hours to forget any notions of family that had been floating around in his head. Plenty of time.

Chapter 38

"Quick. Grab the brownies." Bethany pushed her car door open with a harried check of the time. They were running late, and she didn't want to be the one to spoil Emma's surprise party. Ruby popped out of the back seat, brownies in hand. "This is so exciting. Can I have a surprise party next year?"

Bethany laughed, hurrying her daughter to Sophie and Spencer's door. "It wouldn't be much of a surprise since you asked for it."

"I'll forget I asked. I promise."

"I highly doubt that." Bethany pulled the door to Sophie and Spencer's house open. It was dark inside, although she could hear rustling here and there.

"They're on their way," someone hissed. "Hide."

Ruby giggled, handed Bethany the brownies, and dived into the small space behind the couch.

Bethany glanced around helplessly at the shadowy forms already occupying all the spaces. Did they really have to hide? Surely it would be enough of a surprise that they were all here. But she knew when her friends did something, they went all out.

Her eyes fell on the coat closet as a series of car doors closed outside. She grabbed the closet door, yanked it open, and flew inside, pulling the door closed behind her.

"Ouch." The whisper came from right next to her, and she just barely kept from screaming as she recognized the voice and the warm scent. Of course she had crammed herself into a closet with James.

"Sorry," she whispered. "I can find somewhere else."

"No. There's no time. We can fit." There was a shuffling sound, then his hand fell on her arm and turned her so she had more room.

"How do we know when to jump out?" Hopefully it would be soon. She wasn't sure if it was the small space or his enticing scent or his tangible nearness, but her head was suddenly spinning.

"I guess Sophie has some sort of signal."

She shifted the brownies to her other hand but bumped his side. "Sorry. It's a little cramped in here. Hey. Aren't you claustrophobic?" Or was that someone else?

"Huh. You know, I didn't think about it."

"And?"

"And it's not bothering me right now."

A loud horn blasted from the other side of the door, and suddenly James's hand was on her arm, pulling her out of the closet with him.

"Surprise!" Bethany chimed in a few seconds late as she caught up with what was happening.

Emma stood in the doorway, clutching her heart but laughing.

"You guys." She shook her head. "I can't believe you got me."

"All those years of saying you couldn't be surprised," Spencer called from next to his wife. "We just had to bide our time and wait until you weren't expecting it."

"I should have known something was up when Mom finally decided to let me leave the house." Emma turned to her mom, who stood behind her with an older gentleman. "I really bought your story about William wanting to see the cherry orchard." She made her way around the room, thanking and hugging everyone.

"I'm going to put these in the kitchen," Bethany murmured after Emma had hugged her and James, giving them both a smile that said she thought there was something going on that wasn't.

"I can take them." James reached for the pan before Bethany could protest. He headed toward the kitchen, and she sighed.

She couldn't figure him out. One moment, he was looking at home feeding her niece in her kitchen—and the next he was running out the door as if his life depended on getting away from her.

"Look who's a happy girl tonight after spending the day with her aunt Bethany." Kayla wheeled over with a cooing baby Evelyn in her lap.

Bethany reached down to scoop the baby into her arms. "It's nice to see you happy, little one." She made a face at the baby, who giggled. "You like that?" She made the face again. "See, James isn't the only one who can get you to stop crying."

"James?"

"Yeah. Didn't Cam tell you?" Cam had dropped Kayla off at home to catch a quick nap while he picked Evelyn up from Bethany's house earlier. "James stopped by to drop off a game for the field day. I was in the middle of making brownies and Evelyn was hungry, so he fed her."

"Wow." Kayla raised her eyebrows. "Not every guy would feed a girl's niece to impress her."

Bethany snorted. "He didn't do it to impress me. He did it to help out."

"Even better." Kayla gave her a significant look. "Definitely a keeper."

"Who's a keeper?" Cam sidled up between them. "Evelyn?"

"Of course." Kayla reached for Cam's hand, and Bethany fought not to remember the warmth of James's hand in hers. "But also James."

"James?" Cam directed a perplexed look between his wife and Bethany. "A keeper for what?"

"Nothing," Bethany blurted.

Kayla laughed and rolled her eyes at her husband. "You're adorable when you're clueless."

"Thanks." Cam grinned, then turned to Bethany. "But seriously, do I need to have a talk with this guy?"

"A talk?" Bethany gaped at him. "Oh my goodness, no. There's nothing to talk about. Your wife is . . ."

"Incredible?" Cam filled in. "Amazing? Perfect?"

Bethany and Kayla both slapped his arm at the same time. Before Bethany could come up with the word she'd been looking for, a wolf whistle pierced the room. Everyone's eyes swung to Levi—the only one of the group who could whistle quite like that.

He stepped aside. "Take it away, Emma."

Bethany pulled out her camera and snapped a few pictures of her friend.

"Thanks, Levi." Emma's smile was misty as she looked around at everyone gathered there. "I asked Dan if he'd mind if I led the prayer tonight." There was quiet shuffling as people clasped hands and bowed their heads.

"Lord of glory," Emma began. "What an outpouring of love you have shown me tonight through all these people you have brought into my life. I am thankful for each one of them, Lord, and the ways they have touched my life. I don't know what your plans are for me in this world—whether they are days or weeks or months or years—" Across the room, a throat cleared. It was a sound Bethany instantly recognized, and she looked up to see James grasping the chair in front of him. His eyes met hers for a second, and she sent him a reassuring smile, but he shook his head and looked away.

"But the length of my life isn't what matters, Lord," Emma continued. "What matters is that it belongs to you. Teach me to serve you each day and to trust that whenever it is your will, you will bring me to your side in heaven. And in the meantime, let me never forget that I have the most amazing group of friends and family in the world. Amen."

"Amen." The word resounded from around the room as several people wiped at their eyes.

After a few seconds, the low murmur of voices picked up again, and everyone surged toward the kitchen to fill their plates. Bethany marveled at the selection. Having several friends who cooked or baked for a living meant no one ever went hungry at one of their gatherings. Sometimes she felt bad that her own contributions weren't more elaborate, but—

Wait.

Where were her brownies?

She scanned the dishes more closely. There were cookies and fudge and a big birthday cake. But no brownies.

Her eyes skimmed the room until they fell on James, sitting silently next to his mom and the gentleman she'd come with. She stepped out of line and made her way toward them. "Do you know where my brownies went? I thought you were going to put them out."

James shifted, looking uncomfortable. "Don't be mad. I tasted one earlier. When I took them into the kitchen."

"And what? You ate the whole pan?" Bethany stuck a hand on her hip.

But James shook his head, grimacing. "Not exactly."

And then she realized. "Oh my goodness. They're terrible, aren't they?"

"Not terrible," James hedged. "Just— I think it's possible you missed an ingredient. Maybe the sugar?"

Oh. Oh. Oh. How could she have done that? She rubbed at her forehead. "So where are they?"

"In a cupboard," James admitted sheepishly. "I was going to throw them away later when no one was looking, and then you'd think they'd been a big hit."

Bethany stared at him. "You were going to . . ."

"I know. I'm sorry." James half-stood. "I can get them out now if you want."

"No. That's . . ." Possibly the sweetest thing anyone had ever done for her. "I can't believe I did that."

"You were a little busy," James said. "And I interrupted you right in the middle of making them."

"Don't worry, dear," James's mother piped in. "I've had more baking fails than you could count. I forgot to add the eggs to James's birthday cake one year." She turned to him. "Remember that?"

"Yeah. I spit it out."

"Hey." His mother hit his arm, then smiled at Bethany. "At least now you know he likes you better than he likes me."

Bethany had no idea how to respond to that—and she didn't need James's mom to see the way her face was warming. She waved toward the kitchen. "I guess I should go get some food."

"Of course." James's mom smiled warmly. "And then come sit by us. We'd love to get to know you better."

"I— Um—" Bethany looked helplessly around the room. Maybe she could use Ruby as an excuse. But her daughter had already filled a plate and was sitting with a group of the other kids.

"Sure." Bethany finally murmured. "I'll be right back."

Chapter 39

James sucked in a deep gulp of the damp night air. As much as he was coming to understand why Emma loved this group of people, he couldn't handle another moment inside with everyone. Especially with the way Mom had spent the past hour chatting with Bethany—and he'd spent it not letting his heart get caught up in how much he was going to miss hearing her voice when he left. Unless he didn't . . .

"Mind if I join you?"

James winced at the sound of a male voice behind him. All he wanted was a few minutes of peace. A few minutes to get his head back on straight and remind himself of all the reasons he couldn't stay in Hope Springs.

He glanced over his shoulder, but Cam hadn't waited for an invitation and was already carrying a chair over to the edge of the deck, next to James.

"Nice night." Cam sat with a long sigh—the happy kind, James was pretty sure.

James didn't bother to reply. He had a feeling Cam hadn't sought him out to discuss the weather.

They sat silently for a few minutes, and James began to think that maybe Cam had simply needed to escape the chaos in the house too.

"So . . ." Cam sat forward. "Bethany said you were a big help with Evelyn today. Thanks for that. Kayla and I appreciated the break."

James shrugged. "No problem."

"Bethany told me about your daughter," Cam said quietly. "I'm so sorry."

James stiffened instinctively, but then found he didn't mind so much that Cam knew. Not that it meant he wanted to talk about it. "Thanks."

"So, you're great with babies, an old hand in the stables, and you even solve crimes. You ever considered that Hope Springs might be the place for you?"

James eyed him. "Emma put you up to this?"

Cam laughed. "She mentioned that the Hope Springs police department offered you a job, but I promise I'm out here of my own free will. I just thought you should know that we all appreciate having you around. My sister and Ruby seem rather attached to you."

There it was. James leaned forward and ran a hand over the smooth wood of the deck railing. "I don't know what you think but—"

"Bethany's sort of . . ." Cam interrupted. "I think she's vulnerable. I mean, she's smart. But she's been through a lot. With the drugs. And then she got cleaned up and had Ruby and was getting back on track. But the aneurysm . . . I wouldn't want her to go through more heartbreak, if she thinks there's, you know, more between you two than there is." Cam shifted, looking uncomfortable, but James had gotten stuck on one word.

"Drugs?"

Cam let out a breath. "She didn't tell you?"

"She said Ruby's father was an addict, but . . ." But she hadn't trusted him enough to tell him she had been one too. Of course, with the way he'd been spouting off about how addicts never changed, it was no wonder.

"It was a long time ago," Cam said. "The moment she got pregnant with Ruby, she left that all behind."

James nodded silently. So she'd not only left a bad situation, but she'd gotten herself cleaned up as well. She was so much stronger than he'd imagined.

"I'm sorry." Cam ran a hand over his head. "I shouldn't have—"

"I'm glad you did."

"Well, I'm going to go inside before I wreak any more destruction." Cam stood. "Do me a favor and don't hurt them. They've been through enough already."

James nodded. So had he.

He sat outside for a while longer, watching the stars appear one by one until he could make out the Little Dipper, which Sadie had called the Little Digger.

By the time he went inside, the house had cleared out considerably.

He didn't mean to seek her out, but his eyes went instantly to Bethany, and when she looked up and smiled, something funny twanged right in the middle of his heart, puncturing straight through his Kevlar. Was Cam right—did she think there was more between them than there was? Or—better question—did he?

"Hey, James." Sophie looked up from her conversation with Emma. "The guys were talking about going out fishing on Tyler's boat tomorrow if you're interested. Bethany said you helped Ruby catch a bunch. Maybe you can bring these guys some luck. They sure could use it."

"Hey." Spencer nudged her but then looked to James. "She's not wrong. You're more than welcome to come."

"Oh. Uh." He wasn't sure he was up to more socializing. "I was planning to run up to the Ploughman farm tomorrow to pick up some hay."

"I almost forgot!" Emma pulled out her phone. "Irene Ploughman texted me the other day. Their new calf was just born. She sent pictures of bottle feeding it."

"Really?" Though Ruby had been sitting on the floor looking sleepy, she bounced upright. "Can I see?"

"Sure." Emma passed the phone to Ruby.

"It's so cute. I wish I could do that."

"I'm sure Mrs. Ploughman would let you. You and your mom should go along with James tomorrow." Emma's triumphant smile shot to James.

Wait. How had his plan for some alone time backfired?

His sister, that was how.

"Can we?" Ruby pleaded—though James couldn't tell whether she was asking him or Bethany.

Neither of them answered at first, but then Bethany came to the rescue. "We have church tomorrow."

James relaxed. That made things easier.

Ruby frowned, but then her eyes brightened. "James can come to church with us first and then we can go to the farm after."

James's mom chuckled. "I like the way you think, Ruby. That's a great idea. Isn't it, James?"

"Uh." James looked helplessly from his mom, who nodded with certainty, to his sister, who grinned gleefully, to Ruby, who folded her hands in a pleading gesture, to Bethany, who wore a smile that bore a hint of . . . hope?

"All right. I'll take you to the farm."

"And you'll come to church with us?" Ruby persisted.

"We'll see," was the only answer he could give to that.

But Ruby seemed satisfied. "Good." She yawned.

"Time to get you home to bed." Bethany stood and laid a hand on her daughter's head. "Looks like we're going to have a big day tomorrow. Goodnight, everyone. Happy birthday." She leaned down to hug Emma, her eyes coming to James as she stood. "See you tomorrow."

Maybe he shouldn't, but he really liked the sound of that.

Chapter 40

"Hey, Mom?" Ruby asked from the back seat.

"Yeah, Rubes?" Bethany glanced at the clock with satisfaction. They were going to be on time for church today. If the person in front of her ever decided to drive faster than ten miles per hour. She tried to peer around the car to see what the holdup might be.

"If you and James get married, will Emma be my aunt too, since she's James's sister? Like how Kayla is my aunt because you're Uncle Cam's sister?"

"Um, yeah— What are you doing here, buddy?" she muttered to the driver ahead of her. Her thoughts caught up with her daughter's words as the car turned into a driveway, giving her room to accelerate. "Wait. What did you say?"

"I said if you and James get—"

"Ruby!" Bethany didn't need to hear the rest of the sentence again. "We've talked about this. James and I are not getting married. We aren't even dating. We don't even like each other."

Ruby started to protest, and Bethany amended her statement. "Not like that, I mean. We're just friends."

"Isn't that how relationships start?" Ruby sounded smug.

"I— What?" How old was her daughter anyway? When had she started thinking about things like relationships? "No. I mean, yes. I mean, not every friendship is the start of a relationship."

Ruby didn't say anything else, and Bethany let out a slow breath. With any luck, that would be the end of that. But then she heard Ruby's low song drifting from the back seat: "Mom and James sitting in a tree, k-i-s-s-i-n-g."

Oh goodness. It was a good thing Ruby couldn't see her face—it had to be glowing like a furnace. But there was no way her daughter knew about their k-i-s-s. She was just being silly.

But that didn't stop Bethany's thoughts from wandering back to the feel of James's lips on hers.

She tried to banish the memory, but it lingered as she pulled into the church parking lot and her eyes fell on the man himself, getting out of his truck. Her heart danced. "I didn't think he was going to come," she mumbled to herself, pulling into a spot a few spaces away.

Before she had turned off the engine, Ruby bounced out of the car. "Ruby, wait!" Bethany scrambled to grab her purse and follow her daughter.

"James," Ruby called.

Though he was already halfway to the church building, he stopped and waved. Bethany fully expected him to turn around and keep walking toward the church, but he waited for them. She fell into step next to Ruby, trying to ignore the flighty swirls in her stomach. Though James wasn't wearing a tie, he tugged at the collar of his white button down, then tucked his hands into the pockets of his jeans.

Bethany pulled her eyes off him.

"Mom didn't think you would come," Ruby announced the moment they reached him.

"Ruby—" Bethany was going to have to talk to her daughter about knowing when things weren't meant to be repeated. "Sorry, I—"

"That's okay." James's smile seemed to hold an edge of nerves. "I didn't think I would either."

"I'm glad you did." Ruby stuck her hand into his and marched him toward the church doors.

Bethany followed them. "Where's Emma?"

"She came with my mom and William. They're already inside." James glanced over his shoulder at her. "You look nice."

"Oh." She suddenly couldn't remember any words at all.

Ruby turned around with an I-told-you-so smile, and Bethany found her voice. "No, Ruby."

James looked at her, forehead wrinkled in confusion. "Did you say something?"

"Uh. Nothing. I mean, thanks."

You look nice? What had he been thinking?

Cam had already warned him that Bethany might think things between them were more than they actually were. Telling her she looked nice sure wasn't going to help with that.

But that didn't change the truth. She *did* look nice. More than nice. She looked tear-your-breath-out-of-you gorgeous.

"Hey, James, nice to have you join us." Dan held out a hand, and James shook it, surprised to find that he didn't resent being here today.

He let Ruby lead them to the row where Mom and William and Emma had joined Emma's whole posse of friends. James laughed to himself at his own description, but he had to admit that she was lucky to have this group around her. Every one of them had been there for her through this hard time.

People were there for you too, but you pushed them away. You're still pushing them away.

Ruby slid into the row, and James stood aside so Bethany could go next. But the moment he sat down, he realized he should have gone first and let Ruby sit between them. Because now he'd be smelling Bethany's tantalizing peach scent the entire service. He tried to put some space between them, but he was squeezed against the very end of the row.

A giggle came from next to him, and James looked over, assuming it was from Ruby. But Bethany had a hand over her mouth, her eyes sparkling. She leaned closer and pointed to something in the worship folder. "Sermon theme: Amnesia About God's Goodness," James read.

He chuckled along with her, just barely resisting the urge to wrap an arm around her shoulder and tuck her in close to him. As much as he appreciated the irony, he also felt an overwhelming need to protect her from all the struggles she'd faced.

As the service began, James found himself listening to the hymns and prayers and Bible readings as if he were hearing them for the first time. The sharp edge of anger that usually pulsed behind his heart when he thought about God was a little duller today.

As the final strains of the hymn "It Is Well with My Soul" faded, Dan walked toward the small podium at the front of the church, still humming the melody. Instead of standing behind the podium, he slid it aside and stepped in front of it, moving closer to the rows of gathered people. "I love that hymn, don't you?"

All around James, heads nodded, Bethany's more vigorously than any. Not that he was surprised. He'd seen her wear a shirt with those very words on it.

"So," Dan continued. "How is it with your soul today?"

A heaviness settled on James's shoulders at the question. It hadn't been well with his soul for a long time. And he couldn't see how it ever could be again.

"Before you answer that." Dan lifted a finger. "Let's talk about what it means for it to be well with our soul. It's maybe not something we think about all that often. It's not like we go around asking people how their soul is doing today. Like, 'Hey Joe, It is well with my soul today. How about yours?'" Around the church, a few people laughed.

James shifted, accidentally bumping Bethany's arm. "Sorry."

"It is well with my soul," she whispered back.

James smiled at her quick response, though at the same time a strange pang took hold of his middle. What would it be like if it were well with his soul?

"This hymn is so uplifting," Dan was saying now, "that you'd be forgiven for thinking it was written at the high point in the writer's life. But its author, Horatio Spafford, penned these words at the lowest point in his life. Lower than probably most of us could imagine. Not only had he lost all his property in the Great Chicago Fire of 1871, but two years later, his wife and four daughters were sailing for Europe when their ship sank, taking the lives of all four of his girls. Changing his life in a single moment."

Dan paused, and James clenched his jaw against the sharp jab to his solar plexus.

"On his way to Europe to get his wife, who had survived, Horatio passed right over the spot where his daughters had drowned."

James closed his eyes, but he couldn't block out the image of the side of the road, where Sadie . . .

A hand slipped into his, and he clutched at it, even as he considered getting up and walking out of church. But something made him feel like he wanted to hear the rest of the story. Like he *had* to hear it.

"And *that's* when he wrote these words, 'It is well with my soul,'" Dan said.

James let out a breath. *How?* How was it possible for anyone to say it was well with their soul after something like that? He sure couldn't.

"Is that how we respond to trouble and hardships and sorrow?" Dan asked. "Is our first reaction, 'You know what, even though this terrible thing has happened, it is well with my soul'? Or do we get angry? Or hurt? Or resentful? Or defiant? Or . . . the range of our reactions could go on and on. But most of them aren't positive. So what made Horatio Spafford different? Why could he say that? Was he just putting on a brave face, pretending everything was okay, living in denial? Or was he somehow better than all of us?"

Dan shook his head. "Horatio Spafford could write these words because he knew God's goodness. And he didn't forget it in the middle of his troubles. He knew that in his goodness, God had willingly given up his own Son to save Spafford's girls from their sins. He knew what Paul tells us in 1 Corinthians 15:19: 'If only for this life we have hope in Christ, we are of all people most to be pitied.' His hope for his girls wasn't only for this life. He knew that God had prepared a home for them in heaven. And he knew that whatever hardships he faced in this world, he would be with them in heaven one day too."

Dan paused, looking thoughtful. "Just like Job, who even after troubles maybe worse than Spafford's, could still say, 'I know that my redeemer lives, and that in the end he will stand on the earth. And after my skin has been destroyed, yet in my flesh I will see God; I myself will see him with my own eyes—I, and not another. How my heart yearns within me!' You can hear it there, can't you? The truth of what Solomon says in Ecclesiastes: 'He has also set eternity in the human heart.' Our hearts long for something that lasts forever. He is that something."

James had to swallow against the painful rock that had lodged itself in his throat. Bethany set a hand on his forearm, and he realized he was probably crushing her other hand. He loosened his grip but didn't let go.

"It's easy to get amnesia about God's goodness, though, isn't it?" Dan paced to the far side of the church, but James's eyes followed him. "The Israelites sure did. Over and over again. God would bless them with all kinds of good things, but soon they'd forget that all those things came from him, and they'd turn to false gods or their own ideas, and they'd experience all kinds of hardships. And then, after a while—sometimes a long while—they'd snap out of their amnesia and remember God's goodness. It was a long list. He'd brought them out of Egypt, provided manna for them in the desert, defeated their enemies, and on and on. And when they finally remembered that, they'd turn back to God and it would be well with their souls. Until the next time they forgot about his goodness."

Dan laughed sadly. "It's a lesson they had to learn over and over again. It's a lesson *we* have to learn over and over again. And like I told my daughter Hope when I was teaching her to ride a bike, the best way to learn something is to practice." He took a breath, surveying the room. "You might feel silly doing this, but humor me. Close your eyes and think of five ways God has shown his goodness in your life. I'll wait."

He fell silent, and James glanced around. Next to him, Bethany had closed her eyes and seemed to be concentrating, one hand still in his, the other still on his arm. Next to her, Ruby wiggled but smiled over at him. Beyond her, several members of their group had either closed their eyes or were looking at their hands folded in their laps.

James sighed. He wasn't willing to play this game. All the goodness in the world could never make up for what God had taken from him. But in spite of himself, images came at him one after another: Sadie wrapping her sticky arms around his neck, his family at his side for her funeral, Emma smiling at him after her surgery, Ruby and Bethany sitting next to him right now—

"I'm sure you could continue to think of things all day," Dan interrupted James's thoughts. "But it might eventually get awkward for me to stand up here silently. Plus, here's one you maybe didn't put on your list: He remembers you. Even when you forget his goodness. Listen to his words—" Dan reached behind him and picked up a Bible off the podium. "'Can a mother forget the baby at her breast and have no compassion on the child she has borne? Though she may forget, I will not forget you! See, I have engraved you on the palms of my hands.'"

Dan set the Bible down and looked at the palms of his hands. He held them up. "That's pretty extreme. It'd be difficult to forget anything engraved on the palms of your hands. And someday we're going to see that love engraved on Jesus' hands in the shape of nail marks. We're going to be at his side—and he's going to remember us. He's going to call us by name. He's going to wipe every tear from our eyes and 'there will be no more death or mourning or crying or pain.' *Then* we won't be able to forget his goodness. Because we'll be living with him in it. Forever. *That's* why Horatio Spafford could say it was well with his soul. And that's why we can say it is well with our souls too. Amen."

As the sermon ended, Dan invited the congregation to join in singing "What a Friend We Have in Jesus."

"And in case you're interested in more hymn history," Dan said, "this one also came out of tragedy. Joseph Scriven's fiancée died the day before they were to be married. As you sing this hymn, notice that Scriven points to another aspect of God's goodness: He hears our prayers and carries our burdens."

Dan sat down and the music began, and James couldn't block out the words. It was a hymn he'd learned as a child. But the words seemed to hold new meaning now, as the congregation sang, "O what peace we often forfeit, O what needless pain we bear, All because we do not carry everything to God in prayer."

As the hymn continued, James ducked his head. He wasn't sure he remembered how to pray anymore. *I need* something, *Lord.* They were the only words he could find. Now he would have to wait and see if God remembered him.

By the time the service ended, James felt as if he'd been shaken and stirred and sifted. Not bodily, but in his heart. Maybe in his soul.

He was still trying to sort it all out as Bethany pulled her hand out of his. "If you don't want us to come along to the farm, I understand." She kept her voice low. "I can tell Ruby I have a headache or something."

James frowned, glancing at Ruby over Bethany's shoulder. "You don't want to come?"

Bethany shook her head. "No, I mean . . . Ruby forced the invite. And if you'd rather not . . . I know it's . . . After everything . . . And then . . ." She blew out a breath that stirred her hair. "I'm not explaining this very well."

James touched her arm. "I know what you're saying. And I think we should go."

Chapter 41

"Look how cute he is," Ruby squealed as they entered the barn at Ploughman Farms. "Isn't he cute, Mom?"

"He's the cutest." Bethany smiled at her daughter, trying to ignore the slight twinge at the base of her skull that signaled an oncoming headache. She was *not* going to ruin this day. Not when Ruby was so excited. Not when James seemed like a different man—lighthearted and hopeful. Not when her stomach sent itself into a spiral every time he looked at her like he was right now. Something was different today. She wasn't sure what it was, but she sure wasn't about to wreck it.

Mrs. Ploughman popped out of a door behind the calf's pen.

"What's that?" Ruby's eyes widened, and she pointed to the large bottle in the woman's hand.

"This is his bottle." Mrs. Ploughman held it out toward Ruby. "Do you want to feed him?"

"Yes." Ruby sprang forward and took the bottle. "How?"

Mrs. Ploughman laughed. "Just hold it out and he'll do the rest. He's a messy eater though. Here, Dad, it might help if you hold his head."

Bethany froze. Had she just called James "dad"? As in, she thought he was Ruby's dad?

James opened his mouth and Bethany assumed he was going to correct Mrs. Ploughman. But then he closed it and stepped forward, wrapping an arm over the calf's head and scratching its ears with his other hand.

"Thanks, Dad." Ruby grinned at James.

For heaven's sake. She had not just said that.

"Ruby Jane." Bethany used her most dire warning tone, but Ruby gave her an innocent look. Bethany rubbed her temple.

Poor James was probably ready to run out of here screaming.

But he said, "You're welcome."

Ruby brought the bottle to the calf's mouth, and the animal wrapped its tongue around it, sending milk splashing everywhere. Both Ruby and James laughed, readjusting as Mrs. Ploughman coached them through it. After a few minutes, they seemed to get the hang of it, and the calf guzzled down his milk, making a mess but seeming content.

As Bethany watched, an unexpected ache formed deep in her middle. Or maybe it wasn't an ache. More like a . . . what was the word Dan had used in church? Yearning. *For what?*

But she already knew the answer. She just couldn't let herself think it. Because it would never happen.

"Do you want to try?" James's question cut into her thoughts.

"Huh?" Bethany jumped. She hadn't voiced her thoughts out loud, had she?

He pointed to the calf.

"Oh. No. I'm good. You two make a good team."

She pulled out her phone to take a few pictures, then leaned against a post and closed her eyes. The twinge in her head had grown to a dull throb.

"Are you okay? You look pale."

Bethany opened her eyes to find James peering at her, his forehead creased into sweet wrinkles of concern. She blinked and looked around. Ruby was petting the calf's neck, and Mrs. Ploughman was gone. How long had she closed her eyes?

"Just a little headache." Her pulse throbbed against her forehead as she pushed herself upright.

"You should have said something. Come on, Ruby," James called over his shoulder. "Let's go tuck your mom in the truck and then you can help me load the hay. I need a supervisor to help me figure out how to stack it."

Ruby kissed the calf between the eyes, then skipped over to them. "That was so fun. Can we come along again next time?"

"I don't see why not." James gently turned Bethany toward the door and wrapped an arm around her lower back, as if afraid she would tip over.

"I'm okay. Really," she murmured.

But he didn't move his arm away, instead pulling her in closer. Bethany shut her eyes for a moment, letting the overwhelming feeling of safety overcome her common sense.

"Come back anytime," Mrs. Ploughman called from the far side of the barn. "You have such a nice family."

Bethany couldn't find the energy to correct the woman. James waved to her, and Ruby called, "Thanks. We will."

When they got to the truck, James opened her door and held her arm to help her in. "Close your eyes," he whispered as he shut the door quietly.

Her head was pounding too hard now to argue. She was vaguely aware of James's and Ruby's voices—first outside the truck and then in it, vaguely aware of movement, vaguely aware when they stopped and the engine cut out.

"Bethany." James's whisper cut through her fog. "We're home."

She dragged her eyes open and pain exploded in her forehead. She couldn't hold back a quiet moan.

"That bad, huh?" James brushed a hand over her forehead. "Should I take you to the emergency room?"

Bethany started to shake her head, but the throbbing was too intense. "No," she whispered. "Just need to lie down."

"Stay right there." He opened his door and jumped out and next thing she knew, he was on her side of the truck, reaching across her to unbuckle her seatbelt and then sliding an arm under her to lift her out of the truck.

"I can walk," she protested weakly.

"I've got you," James murmured, grunting a little as he started toward the house.

She should protest more, but she didn't have the energy, and his arms felt so strong against her back and his shirt smelled so good against her face.

"I'll open the door." Ruby ran ahead of them.

"My purse," Bethany mumbled. They'd need the keys.

"Ruby has it." James's chest moved as he spoke, and it was strangely comforting. He carried her inside and straight to her room, where he laid her on the bed.

"Oh," Bethany sighed as her head sank into the soft pillow. That was better already. She vaguely registered someone lifting her foot and easing her shoe off. "You don't have to—"

But he already had the second shoe off as well. "Can I get you anything?" James spoke softly, his voice drawing nearer her head. "Some medicine?"

"No thanks. I'll be fine in a minute."

"You're sure? I really think you should take some—"

"No." The protest came out louder than she intended and she winced at the extra jab to her forehead. But she refused to take any medications that weren't necessary for her survival.

James pulled the blankets up to her chin. "Just rest then. I'll take care of Ruby."

"Thank you." She wasn't sure if she spoke the words out loud or only in her head before everything else faded.

Chapter 42

"I won!" Ruby threw her hands in the air with a triumphant yell.

"Shh." James glanced down the hall toward Bethany's bedroom but then gave Ruby a fist bump. "Good job. I'm impressed. Not many people can beat me at checkers. Another game?" They'd already played six, not to mention the hour-long game of Monopoly they'd played before that. But James wasn't tired of it yet. Maybe he never would be.

Somehow, spending time with Ruby was like a balm for his heart, sliding into cracks he hadn't known were there, filling them with her laughter and her earnest expressions and her sheer joy.

"I'm hungry," Ruby announced. "When do you think Mom is going to wake up?"

"I'm not sure." He'd poked his head into Bethany's room a few times, just to make sure she was okay. She'd seemed to be sleeping peacefully. He hoped that meant her headache had gone away. It had cut at his heart to see her in so much pain. "Tell you what." James folded the checkerboard and stuck it into the box. "How about I make you something?"

Ruby squinted at him. "Can you cook?"

"Can I cook?" James chuckled. "Of course I can. Does making toast count as cooking?" He laughed at her wrinkled nose. "Just kidding. Let's go see what you have."

He followed Ruby into the kitchen, where Mrs. Whiskers was perched on top of the refrigerator.

"Mrs. Whiskers." Ruby giggled.

"At least she's not in the tree this time." James rummaged through the cupboards, refrigerator, and freezer, feeling oddly at home. After a quick inventory, he announced, "I can make eggs, spaghetti, hamburgers, or peanut butter and jelly."

Ruby made a face. "Not peanut butter and jelly."

"What kid doesn't like PBJ?"

"I like it." Ruby climbed onto a stool next to the counter. "But Mom gives it to me every day for school."

"So why don't you tell her you don't want it?"

Ruby gave him a look.

"You do tell her. She forgets?"

Ruby nodded.

James exhaled. "This is hard on you too, isn't it?"

Ruby lifted a shoulder. "It's not that bad. I just wish . . ."

James waited.

But Ruby hopped off the stool. "Let's have hamburgers."

"Hamburgers it is." He studied her as she washed her hands. It wasn't at all like her not to blurt out exactly what she was thinking. Should he press?

He passed her a towel. "What were you going to say before? What do you wish?"

She bit her lip, looking older than her ten years. "I wish my mom could stay like this."

"Sleeping?"

But Ruby didn't giggle like he'd expected. "No. Happy. Kind of . . . sparkly. Like she used to be."

"And why wouldn't she?"

"Because you're leaving," Ruby said simply.

"Because I'm— Oh." He opened the refrigerator and stuck his face in it. The ground beef was right in front of him, but he rummaged around to give himself a moment to figure out how to respond.

But finally, he had no choice but to come out. Mrs. Whiskers meowed indignantly as the door closed harder than he intended.

"Sorry," he muttered to the cat, who blinked at him with haughty eyes, then stood, stretched, and jumped elegantly to the floor. He set the meat on the counter and turned to Ruby. "I'm glad you think your mom is happy, but I'm sure it has nothing to do with me." Just like the fact that he felt happy for entire days at a time lately had nothing to do with Bethany. Or very little to do with her. Or— He swallowed as the realization hit him—almost everything to do with her.

"It does. But I know you can't stay."

"Yeah, my job is in Milwaukee, and—" And right now, going back to it held almost no appeal. Not when it meant he had to leave all this behind.

But he had to. Because otherwise he'd only risk losing it all in some much more painful way.

"I'm going to go start the grill." He didn't wait for a response but tore out the back door. The patio was small but tranquil, and James took a moment to breathe the fresh air, which still held a trace of warmth, though the sun was setting, staining the sky in shades of pink and red. A longing strong enough to steal back the breath he'd just taken crashed against his ribs.

What if this was what he wanted? Quiet nights at home. Surrounded by family.

Except Bethany and Ruby weren't family.

Yet.

The word refused to leave him alone, and he moved to start the grill so he'd have something else to think about. When he returned to the kitchen to get the meat, he found Ruby peeling carrots.

"Mom makes me have vegetables every night," she explained when James said he was impressed.

He laughed. "Your mom's a smart lady." He started forming the hamburger into patties.

"Yep." Ruby kept peeling. "Can I ask you something?"

Oh boy. This could be dangerous. But he couldn't refuse. "Go for it."

"Do you think God answers prayers?"

Wow. She couldn't have started with something easy? He was *so* not qualified to answer this question.

"Because I do," Ruby cut in. "When my mom was in her coma so long, I was afraid that maybe he didn't. But Pastor Dan told me God always answers our prayers. Just not always in the way we want him to."

"Hmm." James picked up the plate of meat, hoping the conversation was over.

"Did you pray for Sadie?" Ruby asked.

"Uh." James cleared his throat. "I did."

Ruby nodded, as if she'd already known the answer. "I'm sorry God didn't answer the way you wanted. But she's with Jesus now."

James turned to the door. "I have to get these on the grill."

Ruby set down her carrot and followed him out the door. "Would it be okay if I prayed for you?"

James opened the grill. "That depends. What are you going to pray for?"

"That you'll be happy when you think of Sadie being with Jesus."

James pressed his lips together. He didn't see how that could ever happen, but he wasn't sure there was a way to tell her that.

"And," Ruby continued. "That you make good hamburgers."

James laughed and ruffled her hair, the same way he'd always done to Sadie. "Now *that* you can pray for."

Bethany blinked at the dim room around her. Where was she?

When was she?

She brought a hand to her head, which felt heavy and groggy.

Had she been napping?

She felt for her phone on the nightstand, but it wasn't there. Sitting up gingerly, she searched the bed for it.

There. Next to her pillow.

She flicked it on to check the time. Seven o'clock.

She groaned. Ruby must be starving by now. She'd better get some dinner going.

She pushed her feet to the floor and stood slowly, testing her head. When there was no throbbing, she made her way to the bedroom door, calling that she'd have supper ready in half an hour. There was no answer, and when she inhaled to call again, she smelled something. Smoke.

"Ruby!" *Oh Lord, where is she?*

She raced to Ruby's bedroom, but it was empty. "Ruby!" Where was the smoke smell coming from?

She flew down the dark hallway toward the kitchen, where a light glowed. Had Ruby tried to cook something herself and started a fire?

"Ruby!" Bethany didn't know how she'd hear her daughter if she answered, the way her blood thumped in her ears.

There was no one in the kitchen either. And no fire.

Bethany stopped as she spotted two forms out on the dark patio. She made out faint wisps of smoke drifting up from the grill.

Her knees turned wobbly, and she leaned against the counter, forcing herself to take a few slow, deep breaths. Her heart had finally returned to near normal speed when the back door opened. Ruby walked through, followed by James carrying a plate of hamburgers. Her heart sped right back up at the way he smiled at her. "Feeling better?"

"Much. Thank you. You didn't have to do that." She gestured to the burgers.

"Yes I did. Ruby here questioned my cooking abilities, so I had to prove myself. You're sure you're feeling better? You still look pale." He stopped next to her, touching the back of his hand to her forehead.

She closed her eyes, letting herself lean into his hand. "I'm okay." She realized he probably wanted his hand back and stepped away. "I just woke up and smelled smoke, and I was afraid . . ."

"Oh wow. I'm sorry. I didn't even think of that."

She shook her head. "I should have realized it was the grill. It smells delicious."

"I think that's our cue." He gestured Bethany toward the table. "Dinner is served. Don't forget to bring your pièce de résistance, Ruby."

Ruby carried a bowl of haphazardly peeled and uncut carrots to the table. Bethany considered taking them and finishing the job, but Ruby looked so proud that Bethany couldn't bring herself to do it. A little carrot peel wouldn't hurt them.

Bethany pulled out a chair and sat. Ruby chose a chair on one side of her, James on the other. Her heart ballooned with contentment. This was what a family meal should be like. *Cooked by someone else?*

She giggled, and James gave her a funny look. "Something amusing?"

"No. Sorry. I just— It was really sweet of you to do this."

Was it her imagination, or was that a little flush under the scruff on his cheeks?

"It was Ruby's idea to make hamburgers. I was just the grill man." James passed the plate around and Ruby passed her carrots. Bethany made sure to take several.

Once they all had food, Ruby folded her hands in front of her. "I'll pray."

Bethany glanced at James. What if he didn't want—

But he already had his head bowed and eyes closed, a faint smile dusting his lips.

That was new. But welcome.

Bethany closed her own eyes as Ruby began to pray.

"Dear Jesus. Thank you for a fun day with James and Mom. Please help James when he misses his little girl."

Bethany sucked in a breath, her eyes popping open. "Ruby."

James kept his head bowed. His lips turned down, but he shook his head. "It's okay." Gravel roughed his voice, but he nodded for Ruby to go on.

Ruby looked to Bethany, who hesitated, but then reached to take James's hand and nodded too.

Ruby got up onto her knees on her chair so she could reach across to take James's other hand, then continued. "Help him be happy that she's with you, Jesus. And help him be happy that he's here with us right now and he'll see her again someday."

Ruby stopped, and Bethany slowly opened her eyes, not sure she was ready to meet James's gaze after that. How had her daughter so perfectly put her own heart into words?

"Oh," Ruby added, "and please let his hamburgers be good too. Amen."

James laughed, and it was the most wonderful sound Bethany had ever heard. "Thank you," he said to Ruby. "That was . . ." He cleared his throat and stared at his hamburger.

"That was lovely, Ruby," Bethany finished for him, and he sent her a grateful look. She smiled and let go of his hand. It felt good to help someone else find the words for once.

They were mostly silent as they ate, although every few minutes Ruby would start chattering about one topic or another. Bethany listened and responded as appropriate—but her eyes refused to leave James for long. And if she wasn't mistaken, he kept looking at her too.

"I have to get ready for bed," Ruby announced when her plate was clear.

Bethany raised an eyebrow. Ruby wasn't wrong. It was almost past her eight o'clock bedtime. But since when did she volunteer to go to bed? But Bethany would take the easy win. "I'll be there to tuck you in as soon as I get this cleaned up."

"You're going to tuck me in too, right James?" Ruby bounced out of the room, flinging the question over her shoulder.

"Ruby, I'm sure James—"

"Wouldn't miss it," James cut in.

"You don't have to," Bethany murmured as Ruby disappeared. She turned to grab a dishrag, but he was right there.

"It's all right." His smile was warm and gentle and only a little bit haunted. "It's been a long time since I've tucked anyone in, but I think I remember how."

"James, if it's too hard . . ." Her eyes caught on his, and she couldn't remember what she'd been about to say.

"Bethany." His whisper was hoarse, and his palm slid softly against her cheek.

Next thing she knew, she was on her tiptoes, and his lips were catching hers, and she was inhaling his scent of spice mixed with the burgers he'd grilled, and her hands were gripping his shoulders, and her head was spinning in the best way, and—

"Mom, James, I'm ready!"

Bethany broke away with a gasp. "Ruby." But she spun to find that she and James were still alone. Ruby must have called from her bedroom. *Thank you, Lord.*

"I— Um." She touched her lips, which were still tingling. "Sorry, I should—" She tipped her head toward the hallway. "I can tell Ruby you had to leave."

James reached for her, as if he was going to tuck her hair behind her ear, but then shoved his hands in his pockets instead. "Do you want me to leave?"

No. But *yes.* But *no.*

His smile wrapped her in tenderness, and she pressed a hand to her stomach. Why was this so confusing?

"Mom! James!" Ruby called again, poking her head into the kitchen this time. "Come on."

James gave Bethany a questioning look, but she couldn't move. He turned to Ruby. "Lead the way."

Chapter 43

James watched as Bethany hugged Ruby, then pulled the blankets up to her daughter's forehead.

"Mom," Ruby protested.

"What? Oh." Bethany pulled the blankets down and hugged Ruby, her movements flustered. "Sorry."

James would laugh at her, except he felt the same disconnected, dazed feeling after that kiss. He wasn't quite sure if he'd started it or Bethany had—all he knew was that he'd been more than disappointed when it had ended.

"Your turn, James." Ruby held out her arms to him.

James moved toward her bed, bending easily for her hug. She smelled of mint toothpaste and the same strawberry shampoo they'd used on Sadie's hair. Instead of tightening like it usually did, his chest eased at the memory. "Goodnight, Ruby."

"Goodnight, James."

He'd half-expected to hear the word "dad" from her lips, and he had to take a quick step back after he released her. He wasn't her dad.

But maybe—

He crashed into Bethany as he turned to leave the room, nearly sending her sailing onto the bed. He caught her at the last second.

Ruby giggled. "You guys look like you're dancing."

"Go to sleep, Ruby," Bethany said, not looking at him as she led the way out of the room.

James turned off the light, pulling the door closed behind him but leaving it open a crack out of habit. Sadie could never fall asleep with her door closed tight.

"That's perfect," Ruby called. "Goodnight."

James followed Bethany down the hall, the word *perfect* hanging on the edge of his thoughts.

When they reached the living room, Bethany stopped, glancing from him to the front door. "So. Um. Thanks for a great day. And thanks again for making supper."

Ah. That was his cue to leave, then. He should probably thank her for having enough sense to send him on his way. Because he wasn't certain he had that kind of sense right now.

"You're welcome." He couldn't think straight as his eyes fell on her kissable lips.

"Do you have to get going or . . . ?" Bethany tucked a strand of hair behind her ear. "I could make some coffee or lemonade or something."

"Yeah, okay." He didn't care that he sounded way too eager. He couldn't leave her right now. "How about lemonade?" His senses were still buzzing from that kiss, so adding caffeine to the mix would probably be a bad idea.

He followed her into the kitchen and got out two glasses while she mixed the lemonade. Neither of them said anything, and James needed to know if her mind was still on their kiss too.

Unless—

What if she had forgotten it, the way she'd forgotten kissing him in the stables?

But it wasn't like there was a good way to ask her.

"Should we sit outside?" Bethany smiled lightly and passed him a glass.

"Sure." He watched her movements, but she seemed calm and collected. Maybe he'd only imagined she was flustered when they'd tucked Ruby in. Or maybe she'd forgotten the kiss between then and now.

He followed her out to the small wicker love seat. It was the only piece of furniture out here, which left him no choice but to sit right next to her—or remain on his feet.

He chose to sit. And then wished he'd remained standing. Being this near her, with that peach scent floating to him on the breeze, he could barely keep himself from leaning closer.

He lifted his glass to his mouth and took a long drink. The tart lemonade burned slightly on its way down—but it was the best way to resist the urge to kiss her.

When he lowered his glass, she was staring at him. "Wow. You must have been thirsty."

He glanced down to find that his glass was nearly empty. Hers was still full.

"Would you like me to get you some more?" She set her glass on the deck and held out a hand for his.

"I'm good, thanks."

She tucked her hands into her lap and tilted her head back, exposing the long, delicate line of her neck.

James let out a breath.

"Is everything okay?" Bethany sat up. "If you don't want to stay . . ."

"I'm sorry about before," he blurted.

"Before?" Bethany's forehead wrinkled. "I don't . . ."

"For kissing you." There. Now it was in the open and he could see if she'd forgotten.

"Oh." It was impossible to read her expression in the dark. "I— It was— You don't need to apologize for that."

Okay. So did that mean she remembered it? If he wanted to know, he was going to have to come out and ask. "So you remember . . . ?"

She chuckled. "Of course I remember. But I thought I was the one who kissed you."

James's heart rocketed around his chest cavity as he laughed. "It's just . . . Last time you forgot. Not that I blame you. But—"

"James." Bethany's hand fell softly on his arm. "I didn't forget."

"Yes, you did. You forgot the whole conversation we had—"

"No, I didn't. We were in the stables and I yelled at you for not talking about Sadie and you yelled back at me and then I kissed you."

James stared at her. He very clearly remembered each of those details. But she hadn't seemed to. "Then why . . ."

She ducked her head. "I was embarrassed. You hadn't shown any sign you wanted me to kiss you and I just threw my lips on yours."

He laughed but then leaned closer. "If you're looking for a sign that I want you to kiss me . . ." He lifted both hands to her cheeks and brought his face toward hers.

Her laugh was low, and it only lasted a second before she closed the gap between them and brought her lips to his. He closed his eyes, letting his hands slide into her hair as her hands came to the back of his neck, tugging him closer. His mind searched for the perfect word for this, but the only thing it could land on was *something*.

He slowly pulled away and opened his eyes. Bethany looked at him quizzically, and he stroked his thumb over her cheek. He'd prayed in church this morning for *something*. Was this it? Bethany and Ruby?

"James?" Bethany asked tentatively.

"Sorry. I was just thinking."

"Me too." But instead of smiling as he was, she frowned. "I have to tell you something."

Chapter 44

Bethany forced herself to swallow. To breathe. But she couldn't make herself speak.

Once she told him this, she wouldn't be able to take it back—and she knew he would never forget it.

"Hey." His hand brushed over hers. "Whatever it is, you can tell me. Or you don't have to. It's up to you."

Oh, the compassion in his eyes. Bethany wanted to bury her face in his chest. It would be so much easier.

But he had to know this. Had to know who she really was.

Even if it destroyed *this*—whatever this was. She couldn't live in a lie. She had left that all behind.

"I'm a drug addict. I mean, I was. I've been sober for ten years, but . . ."

James's expression changed almost imperceptibly—a slight downturn in his lips, a slighter crease in his forehead. But he kept his hand on hers and squeezed her fingers. "I know."

"What? You . . . Have I told you this already?"

James laughed softly. "No. Cam mentioned it. I don't think he meant to," he rushed to add. "I think he was trying to protect you. Making sure I wouldn't hurt you after everything you've been through."

Bethany watched his thumb trace circles on the back of her hand. This wasn't the reaction she'd expected. She'd been prepared for him to get up and walk away.

But he didn't know all of it.

"Did he tell you that he was the one who first found me shooting up? On Thanksgiving?"

There it was. The flinch. "No." James's thumb stilled, but he kept his hand wrapped firmly around hers. "Bethany, you don't have to do this. It doesn't matter."

But she did have to. "I was in high school. I had surgery on my shoulder for a volleyball injury. The pain pills . . ." She hadn't realized how quickly she'd started to rely on them, to need them, to crave them. But when her prescription had run out, she'd easily found new ways to get her hands on more. And when she couldn't get pills, she'd found people who could get her what she needed easily enough.

"My parents got me into the best rehab program they could, even though it cost them a fortune. I did okay for a while. But I kept going back to the drugs. It was like they . . . owned me."

"That's what addiction does," James said. "You couldn't help—"

She shook her head. She hadn't gotten to the worst part yet. "I stole from them, James," she whispered. "I was out of rehab and they wanted to help me, so they gave me a job at my dad's landscaping business. And I . . . took it all. They had no idea until it was too late." She pulled her hand out of James's and wrapped her arms around her middle. Why couldn't she forget these memories, instead of all the new things she wanted to hold onto?

"They lost the business. And then my dad had a heart attack. He didn't make it."

James reached for her, tried to pull her close, but she pushed him away. She still wasn't done. "I promised myself I'd get cleaned up after that. But it was so . . . hard." It sounded lame. A lot of things were hard, but people did them anyway. "It was like . . ." She groped for words. "Like they consumed me. When I didn't have them, they were all I could think about. It was like I would die if I didn't get some." She swallowed, clearing her throat.

"My mom tried to help, let me live with her, but I pushed her away. She—" Bethany pressed her fingers to her burning eyes. Water pooled on her fingertips, and she pulled them away in surprise. Was she crying? She sniffled, but she had to see this through. "She had a stroke a few years after my dad died. I'd come home a few weeks before that because I needed some money. She talked me into staying. But I was strung out when she needed me." The tears built into a full-out sob. She had never talked about this before, never told anyone—not even Cam—where she'd been while Mom was lying helpless on the floor of their house, dying. While a repairman had discovered her body. "I didn't mean for them to—" She choked as a pair of strong arms circled her shoulders. She clutched at him. It had been so long since she'd cried, and the tears came so hard that she wasn't sure how she would ever breathe again.

James stroked her hair silently, his arm wrapped tightly around her back. She should pull away, let him flee, as he no doubt wanted to, but she couldn't let go. Finally her tears abated, and she lifted her head off his chest. His arms loosened, but he didn't let go completely. Still, Bethany knew he couldn't want to stay. He was just too nice to say so. "You can go if you want. I'm fine." She eased his arms off of her.

"What if I don't want to go?" he whispered.

"You don't?"

He shook his head, wiping the tears off her cheeks. "I don't think you understand how strong you are. You left that life."

"Because I got pregnant," she said. It wasn't like she'd had the strength to quit on her own. If it hadn't been for Ruby, she'd likely still be living like that today.

"Exactly." James leaned forward and pressed a kiss to her forehead. "You gave up something you thought you were going to die without for the sake of your daughter. That takes an incredible amount of strength. And courage. And selflessness."

"Stop." Those words didn't apply to her.

"And determination." He grinned. "And perseverance. And—"

She had to stop him somehow. So she launched herself forward and pressed her lips to his.

He chuckled as his arms came around her and he pulled her closer.

Satisfied that she'd silenced him, she pulled away after a moment.

"And bravery. And resil—"

She had no choice but to kiss him again.

Chapter 45

James hummed as he grabbed a protein bar out of the cupboard.

"Look how happy you are." Emma's eyes danced as she strolled into the room. "I wonder why. Or should I say I wonder who?"

James eyed her jeans and boots. "You'd better not be planning to work in the barn today."

"Relax. I'm just meeting a potential new rider. I promise I won't lift a thing." She held up three fingers.

"What's that supposed to be?"

She shrugged. "Some kind of scout signal or something?"

He laughed. How had his sister made it through all of this—with the prospect of starting chemo still looming—with her humor intact? Was it because she was like that Horatio guy Dan had talked about in his sermon yesterday—she didn't forget God's goodness?

"Anyway." Emma poked his side in the way that had made him jump since they were kids. "You got home late last night."

He snorted. "If you call eleven o'clock late." Though it had taken an extreme act of willpower to get up and leave rather than sit outside holding Bethany all night. He hoped his grin didn't look as goofy as it felt.

"So you and Bethany kissed, huh?"

"I— What? She told you?" When had they even spoken? It was only seven in the morning.

Emma laughed, clasping her hands together and pointing at him. "No. But you just did."

He made a face at her. "That's really mature."

"Seriously though." She laid a palm on his forearm. "I'm happy for you. It's good to see you smiling again. Does this mean you're staying?"

"Staying?" He'd be lying if he said he hadn't sat up all night thinking about it. But staying meant saying his future was here. With Bethany and Ruby. And what if that future was ripped away from him?

"You're staying?" Mom flew into the room, her face wreathed in a huge smile. "That's wonderful news."

"No." James held up a hand. "I'm not— I mean, I can't— I mean—" He couldn't make sense of his thoughts. "I don't know," he finally relented.

"What's not to know?" Emma asked. "You're in love with Bethany, right? And you love Ruby too. I can tell." She squinted at him, as if challenging him to deny it.

He shook his head. "I have to go." They'd realized as he was leaving Bethany's last night that her car was still in the church parking lot. He'd promised to come by to take Ruby to school and then drive Bethany to get her car. "I'll be back to take care of the horses shortly."

All the way to Bethany's house, he tried to get the *l-word* out of his head.

But the moment he pulled into the driveway and Ruby came bounding outside with her enthusiastic wave, Bethany trailing behind with a shy but joyous smile, the word hit him powerfully in the chest.

Still, that didn't mean he loved them. He *couldn't* love them. He wouldn't let himself love them.

He got slowly out of the truck.

"Good morning, James." Ruby skipped right to his side. "I like seeing you every day."

He ruffled her hair, unable to talk against the sudden well of emotion.

"Good morning." Bethany's voice was soft, and she only brushed her hand over his, as if she could sense his turmoil. He nodded, hoping his smile would speak for him since he couldn't get the words out.

Ruby chattered all the way to school, and James listened gratefully.

But the moment they dropped her off, a charged silence fell over the truck.

"The lake looks happy today," Bethany said as he turned onto Hope Street.

He glanced toward the waves, which seemed to be dancing in the sunlight. "Yeah. It does."

"Are you?"

"Am I what?"

"Happy?" The question in her voice made him reach for her hand and squeeze.

"Yeah. I am. Really happy. For the first time in a very long time."

She exhaled. "Oh good."

He pulled into the church parking lot and parked next to her car. She didn't reach for the door handle but instead turned toward him, looking troubled.

He slid her hair behind her ear. "What's wrong?"

"Hmm? Nothing." She leaned forward and brushed her lips lightly over his, but he caught her and pulled her close, deepening the kiss. The tightness in his lungs eased, like she was his oxygen.

But after a minute, she pulled back.

"What is it?" He took both of her hands in his.

But she pulled them away and ran a finger over her lips. "I'm sorry. I just— What is this? Between us?"

He thought of that l-word again. But it was so much more complicated than that. "I don't know," he finally whispered. "I'm not sure if I'm ready for . . . whatever comes next."

She nodded, as if that was the answer she'd expected. "Then I think," she said quietly, "that we probably shouldn't do this anymore." She touched her lips. "Until you know. I have to think about Ruby. She's so attached to you already, and if . . ." She trailed off and looked out the window, toward the church.

"Bethany." This was torture. He couldn't do this to her. Or to himself. "I'm . . ." He swallowed. "Sorry," he whispered.

She smiled gently. "It's all right."

Chapter 46

"How many more are there?" Ruby peered into the kiddie pool Bethany had spent the past hour filling with water balloons. Bethany squinted at the bags of uninflated balloons at her feet and sighed. "Lots." She was soaked through already by the dozens of balloons that had popped in the process.

"Cool." Ruby picked up a balloon and juggled it from hand to hand.

"Please put that down." Bethany cringed as Ruby missed and the balloon hit the ground, dousing her legs.

"Oops. Sorry." Ruby ducked her head.

Bethany sighed again. It felt like all she'd been doing for the past two days was sighing. "Why don't you go see if Uncle Cam needs help setting up the picnic tent?"

"Where's James? I thought he was going to help."

Bethany swallowed. "I'm sure something came up. But we have plenty of other helpers." Nearly all of her friends had shown up, along with lots of other parents from the school. A group of dads was diligently setting up the giant Jenga game. And Tiffany had looked more than a little impressed at all of Bethany's plans.

"But I miss James." Ruby pouted. "I haven't seen him since Monday."

"I know." Bethany missed him too. She kept hoping he'd suddenly appear, take her into his arms, and tell her he was ready for whatever came next. But that didn't seem likely to happen, and she needed to prepare her daughter for the probability that he wouldn't be in Hope Springs much longer. But not right now. "Go help Cam."

"Fine." Ruby sulked over toward Cam's tent.

The deepest sigh yet worked its way up from Bethany's core. She paused, stretching out a kink in her neck, letting the afternoon sun warm her face. She could be content like this. Just her and Ruby forever. She really could.

She only wished she hadn't let herself indulge those fantasies of family life. And that she hadn't let Ruby get caught up in them too.

She didn't blame James. After all he'd been through, she understood why he wanted to protect his heart. Too bad knowing that didn't make her own ache any less.

James didn't know how he'd ended up at the marina. He was supposed to be at the school, helping set up for tomorrow's field day. But he couldn't seem to get his truck to drive in that direction. So he'd been driving around aimlessly for the past hour. Until he'd arrived here. He pulled into a parking spot and shut off the vehicle.

Now what?

He gazed at the waves, choppy today, though the sun shone brightly on their frothy tips. What mood would Bethany say the lake was in?

Conflicted.

With a hard breath intended to beat back the questions that had been assaulting him for the past two days, he got out of the truck and strode toward the breakwater. He didn't expect that he'd find any answers here, but maybe, with the wide expanse of the lake stretching in front of him, he'd be able to breathe at last.

He didn't know what to say to Bethany. He understood why she wanted to know what *this* was before . . . whatever came next. But he didn't know what it was—what he wanted it to be. Sometimes—most of the time—he wanted it to be everything. He wanted to be with her and Ruby forever. But other times—when he was thinking rationally—he wanted to run screaming from all of this and wrap his heart back up in its Kevlar vest.

He reached the end of the breakwater and stared out over the expanse of the lake. But the longer he looked, the less empty it seemed. Gulls swooped low over the water, then wheeled toward the sky. Sailboats rode the waves, their masts pointing toward the heavens. James tipped his head skyward. "As the heavens are higher than the earth . . ." The verse Dan had shared in his sermon a few weeks ago surfaced in his mind. Was this part of God's plan? Bringing him here, to Hope Springs? And had God brought James here to heal him from something deeper than a bullet wound?

He closed his eyes. *I want to trust your ways, Lord. But I don't know how.*

Water doused his shoes, and he opened his eyes, taking a step backwards. Was that God's way of saying he was in control? Or was it just a wave?

He watched the water for another minute, but when no clarity came, he turned toward the parking lot. Standing here wasn't getting him anywhere.

Halfway there, two teenage boys stood perched on the rocks, fishing poles in hand. James slowed as he recognized them. "Catch anything?"

"Hey, man." Pete waved at him. "I thought that was you who barreled past us before, but you seemed like you were on a mission."

James laughed. "You could say that."

Chris eyed him but didn't speak. Nor did he tense like he was getting ready for a fight, which James took as an improvement.

"You want to join us?" Pete asked, gesturing toward an extra pole dangling between two rocks.

Chris watched him out of the corner of his eye, as if sizing up his answer.

"Nah, I should—"

Chris turned away, a defeated sneer on his lips, and James wondered how many people had said they didn't have time for this kid.

"Maybe a couple of casts." It wasn't like he'd figured out what to say to Bethany. Maybe a few minutes of fishing would help. He worked his way over the rocks and picked up the pole, casting the line easily out over the water.

"How are Bethany and Ruby?" Pete asked.

"They're—uh—good." He reeled the line back in slowly.

"Uh oh. Trouble in paradise?" Pete joked.

James shook his head. "Speaking of trouble, you guys staying out of it?"

When neither answered, James stared them down.

"Mostly," Pete muttered.

James stopped reeling. "What does that mean?"

"Shut up, Pete," Chris called. "It was nothing. It's all taken care of now."

"Yeah, with more community service," Pete muttered. "We still got thirty hours to do."

"You'd better do them, and then some." James sounded like his dad. "And then clean up your act. How many second chances do you think you're going to get?"

The crashing waves swept the words away, but James heard them echo in his head.

How many second chances was he going to get to have a family?

He finished pulling the line in and set the pole down. "I have to go."

"Chill, man. You don't gotta leave. We learned our lesson and all that." Chris seemed genuinely regretful.

"No. Sorry. I just realized—there's somewhere I have to be."

"Let me guess." Pete grinned at him. "It has to do with Bethany and Ruby."

"Actually." James scrambled up the rocks. "It does."

Chapter 47

Bethany sank into the couch, too tired to lift her aching feet onto the footstool.

The doorbell rang, and Bethany's heart catapulted right from her stomach to her throat. She forgot about her fatigue as she vaulted for the door.

It had to be James.

He'd never shown up to help with getting the field day ready, and her multiple calls to him had gone unanswered. Her brain insisted on sticking by what she'd said to Ruby—something must have come up. And now he must be here to apologize.

She yanked the door open. "Oh." Exhaustion submerged her. "Hi, April."

"Hi," the neighbor girl said cheerfully. "Can Ruby come bike with me?"

Bethany eyed the sky. The sun was sinking but hadn't set yet. "Sure. For a little while." Maybe that would give Bethany some time alone to figure out how to answer Ruby's constant questions about when they were going to see James again.

"Ruby," Bethany called toward the hallway. "Do you want to bike with April?"

Ruby popped out of her room, as energetic as ever even though she'd bounced from station to station, helping whoever needed it as they'd set up the field day. "If James comes over, tell him to wait for me. I want to talk to him."

Ah. Now Bethany remembered why her first thought when the doorbell rang had been of James. Ruby had been talking all the way home about how he'd probably come over to explain why he hadn't been able to help.

She considered telling her daughter not to get her hopes up, but she didn't have the energy to have that conversation right now. "Be home in half an hour. And watch for cars."

"Yes, Mom," Ruby said dutifully. Then she took off for the garage to get her bike. Bethany watched until Ruby and April pedaled down the street, making sure they used proper hand signals as they turned at the end of the block.

The little pit of worry that always opened in her stomach when Ruby was out of sight tried to grow, but she pushed it back. *I trust that she's in your hands, Lord.*

She plopped onto the couch and closed her eyes. But James hovered behind her eyelids, and the feel of his kisses floated over her lips.

The doorbell rang again, and her eyes sprang open. Had she fallen asleep? She glanced at the clock. No, she'd only sat down three minutes ago.

Limbs heavy, she pushed herself up from the couch. Was it really only 7:30? She could happily go to bed right now.

But her whole body sprang awake as she opened the door. "James."

"Bethany, I'm sorry. I should have been there. I was at the marina and I saw Pete and Chris and I realized I was being stupid and I do want a second chance and—" He cut off. "Am I making any sense?"

She laughed. "Not one bit. But that's okay. Do you want—"

"I want—" He stepped forward, his hands coming to her face. He leaned closer and she closed her eyes, letting herself anticipate the moment his lips would contact hers. Something soft brushed past her leg, and before she could register what it was, James had let go of her and dashed into the yard.

"Mrs. Whiskers," he shouted as the cat bolted for the street.

"Oh no." Bethany pressed her hands to her cheeks.

At the last second, the cat veered right, toward the tree. But James was in her path and managed to scoop her up. The cat fought for a second but then settled into James's arms.

"Well." James reached the door. "That didn't go quite like I expected."

"It seems like kids and cats have a way of changing our plans."

James tilted his head, cat still in his arms, a soft smile on his lips.

A flutter went through Bethany.

"They're not the only ones." James stepped closer and brought his lips to hers. Even with the cat between them, the kiss was everything Bethany had ever longed for. It went beyond the physical sensations, as if she could feel his heart and soul right through his lips.

When James pulled back, he was smiling a full-out, glorious smile. "Sorry. I just had to do that. Now maybe I can slow down and make some sense. If you don't mind if I come in?"

Bethany stepped back from the door, her mind too full of that kiss to find any words.

She swung the door shut behind him, but at the last second before it closed, James called, "Wait."

"Huh?" She turned to look at him over her shoulder, but he was already reaching past her to yank the door open wide.

Bethany followed his gaze to the girl on the bike. "That's April," she told James.

It took her a moment to realize that the girl was alone. "Where's Ruby?"

"There was a car," April gasped, swinging her leg off her bike. "Ruby's hurt."

Chapter 48

James burst out the door. "Where?" The word barked out of him.

The girl on the bike pointed. "Around the corner. She's—"

But he didn't have time to listen to the rest of her sentence. He turned around long enough to shove the cat at Bethany, then took off down the street. His hard footfalls drummed in his head, marking the rhythm of his prayers. *Not her, Lord. Not her.*

Sadie's image floated in front of him, merging with Ruby's.

Not her, Lord.

Why were his limbs encased in concrete? Why couldn't he run faster?

He wasn't going to get there in time. He wasn't going to be able to save her.

Finally, he rounded the corner. His eyes fell on a small form halfway down the block, sitting along the curb.

Sitting. Moving.

That meant...

Thank you, Lord. Thank you. His knees turned to melted butter but still he ran.

"Ruby," he called.

She looked up, tipping her head back so she could see him past her helmet. Tears shone on her cheeks, but she smiled as she spotted him. "I knew you'd come," she called.

He commanded his legs to slow as he drew closer, then crouched at her side, his momentum nearly toppling him into her. "What happened? What hurts?" He inspected her for abrasions. She had a pretty good scrape on her knee, but other than that, she looked okay.

"My arm." Ruby sniffled as tears speckled her cheeks again. "Where's my mom?"

"She's coming. She had to put Mrs. Whiskers inside." He should have taken care of the cat. Let Bethany run for Ruby. But he hadn't been able to wait. Not when he'd thought she might be...

James couldn't breathe normally, the adrenaline from the run, from finding her okay, still pumping through him. He took Ruby's arm, grimacing at the purple swelling already marring her wrist. "Looks like you might have broken it. Your friend said there was a car?" James scanned the street. If this was a hit and run . . .

"On the other side of the road. I got nervous and crashed into the curb and fell off. Is my bike okay?"

James unclasped her helmet and pulled it off. "I'll check in a minute. Did you hit your head?"

"I don't think so. My arm really hurts." Her tears fell faster, and James pulled her in for a hug, smoothing her hair. "I know, sweetie. It's going to be all right." The sound of footsteps drew his attention.

"She's okay," he called to Bethany, who kept running until she reached them and dropped to the ground, throwing her arms around them both. She didn't say a word, just held them until James eased back and let her hug her daughter.

He went to inspect the bike. The front wheel appeared a little off kilter, but it was nothing that couldn't be replaced.

Unlike Ruby.

A wave of nausea rolled over him, and he bent over, bracing his hands on his knees. What would he have done if . . .

"James?" Bethany called. "Do you think you could help me get her home?"

"Yeah. Of course." He straightened and drew in a painful breath. He moved toward them and scooped Ruby carefully into his arms.

Bethany righted the bike and walked it next to them.

When they reached the house, James waited for Bethany to grab her car keys, then tucked Ruby into the back seat for the ride to the emergency room.

"Call me and let me know how she is, okay?" he said over the seat to Bethany as he helped Ruby fasten her seatbelt.

"But you're coming along, aren't you?" Ruby asked.

James swallowed, his eyes going from Ruby to Bethany. Both wore the same hopeful, needful expression.

He let out a breath. "Of course I'm coming."

Bethany couldn't stop looking from Ruby—seated next to her in the doctor's exam room—to James, seated on the far side of the room.

Never had she been as scared as she had when April had said Ruby was hurt. Scared and frozen.

By the time her mind had caught up with what was happening, James had already been almost to the end of the block. He'd run toward Ruby as if . . . as if she were his own daughter.

There was a knock on the exam room door, and a second later, it squeaked open.

"I'm Dr. Kramer." A youngish looking woman stepped through the door. "Which one of you is Ruby?" She stopped in front of James. "I understand you hurt your arm."

"*I'm* Ruby." Ruby giggled, and Bethany smiled, but James's face didn't move. He hadn't cracked the hint of a smile since he'd carried Ruby home, and he'd barely said a word since then either. It was like Bethany could physically feel him transforming back into James the Gray. Her heart longed to hold him and tell him it was okay—Ruby was okay—because of him.

"That makes more sense," the doctor was saying to Ruby. "Just between you and me, he doesn't look much like a Ruby."

Ruby giggled again but then winced. "It really hurts."

Across the room, James's face tightened.

"I know, honey." The doctor moved closer to examine the wrist, and Bethany gripped her daughter's other hand. "Did you hurt your head at all?"

"Nope." Ruby sounded proud. "I was wearing a helmet."

"Good job." The doctor smiled at Ruby, then made some notes on her computer. "And good job teaching her to wear one, Mom and Dad."

Bethany's head jerked up in time to see James's jaw jump.

"Oh, we're— I mean, I'm—" The words twisted themselves into knots in her head.

"They're the best," Ruby cut in.

Bethany huffed out a breath. Her daughter knew very well that wasn't what she'd been trying to say.

The doctor turned from the computer. "I have a hunch we're looking at a broken bone, but we won't know for sure until we take some X-rays. Do you want Mom and Dad to come with you or wait here? It's just down the hall."

"I'll come." Bethany stood, but Ruby shook her head.

"I can do it myself."

"But—" For one thing, Ruby was Bethany's baby. And for another, Bethany wasn't sure she wanted to be left alone with James right now.

"Really, Mom," Ruby insisted. "I'll be fine."

"Don't worry." Dr. Kramer smiled. "I'll have her back to you in a jiffy."

"Okay," Bethany said feebly, retaking her seat.

The door closed behind Ruby and the doctor. Bethany glanced across the room to James, who seemed to be concentrating on the floor.

She sat silently, trying to organize her words before she spoke them out loud. But every time she thought she had them in order, she lost them. So she simply said, "Thank you."

James met her eyes, the torture in his own evident. "For what?" His voice was hoarse.

"For being there." Emotion thickened her voice and brought tears to her eyes. "I know it had to be . . . hard." So much more than hard, but it was the only word she could think of.

He nodded once, his teeth clenched as if he was determined not to say anything else.

She let him sit in silence for what felt like forever, but finally she couldn't take it anymore. "I think you were going to say something? At the house. Before . . ." She waved a hand around, as if that could take them all back in time. She tried to remember what he'd been talking about, but all she could remember was that it involved a kiss. A wonderful, amazing, heart-stirring kiss.

James shook his head without looking up. "I don't remember."

"Oh." She played with a broken fingernail.

Fortunately, Ruby and the doctor burst back into the room a few minutes later. And then the doctor was showing them the X-ray results—it was broken—and setting Ruby's arm and giving Bethany care instructions.

And then they were on their way home. Ruby made a few half-hearted attempts at conversation, but Bethany could tell she was exhausted and in pain and finally told her to just rest.

James didn't say a word the entire ride, and when Bethany turned the car off, he just sat, even after Bethany and Ruby had gotten out. Bethany was debating whether she should go around and open his door when he climbed out slowly, moving straight for his own truck.

"See you tomorrow, James," Ruby called, and he startled as if he'd forgotten they were there.

"Tomorrow?"

"The field day." Ruby grinned. "You're still going to be my partner in the three-legged race, right?"

James swiveled his head, as if judging how long it would take to make a getaway in his truck. "I'm not sure—"

"Ruby, you know the doctor said you have to be careful so you don't hurt your arm," Bethany jumped in.

"It's a three-*legged* race, Mom, not a three-armed race. And James will keep me safe, right James?"

"Uh. Safe." James gripped the door of his truck.

"See, Mom." Ruby sounded victorious, but Bethany saw the look on James's face as he climbed into his vehicle.

"We'll see," she mumbled, gently turning Ruby toward the house.

Chapter 49

James did one final scan of the room he'd lived in for the past two months. He'd gotten everything . . . except the blue plastic Easter egg from Ruby. He'd left it on purpose, intending to make a clean break from this place and all it held—all he'd almost lost. But something made him go back and grab it now. He stuffed it into a pouch in his duffel bag, then swept the bag over his shoulder and pounded down the stairs.

Emma, Mom, and William stood in a line across the kitchen—a human barricade of sorts. James grimaced. He'd told them an hour ago that he planned to leave, and though they'd tried to talk him out of it, he'd thought they understood.

Apparently not.

They advanced toward him as one, and he tensed. Couldn't they make this easier on him?

"I'm sorry." His voice cracked. "I know you don't—"

But then Mom was hugging him on one side and Emma on the other, and William was patting his shoulder. He let out a ragged breath and dropped a kiss on Mom's head, then Emma's. When they pulled back, he held out a hand to shake William's.

"You'll be all right?" He looked to Emma. He hated to leave when she was just starting her chemo, but he didn't see any other way. And Mom was going to stay until Emma's treatments were done. Plus he knew now that Emma's friends would be at her side even when he couldn't be.

"I'll be fine." Emma nudged him. "And I'll be here. You know you're welcome anytime."

James nodded, though he knew it would be a long time before his heart would be able to handle coming back. "Tell them I'm sorry," he whispered, then rushed out the door.

At the end of the driveway, he hesitated. It wasn't too late to change his mind. He could turn right, head into Hope Springs, and go to the field day with Bethany and Ruby, and then . . .

And then what?

Going would only make it harder to say goodbye.

So don't say it. Stay.

A car whizzed past the driveway, headed toward town. James gripped the wheel, easing his foot off the brake.

Everything you love is here.

The *l-word* hit him, sharper than a bullet. He punched at his chest, as if that could dislodge the feeling. Then he wrenched the wheel in the opposite direction, pressing his foot to the accelerator as he aimed his truck away from town.

Chapter 50

Bethany scanned the living room, wrinkling her nose in concentration.

She'd come in here for a reason—but what was it?

Her eyes fell on the trophy she and Ruby had won in the three-legged race at the field day, and she moved toward it, picking it up with a sigh. Ruby had been so crushed when James hadn't shown up—and so had Bethany, though she'd half-expected it.

He'd called the next day to explain, to apologize, and as much as she'd wanted to ask him to come back, not to give up, she couldn't. She'd seen the fear in his eyes when Ruby had gotten hurt—and she couldn't ask him to go through that again. That was why every time her fingers were tempted to tap on his name on her phone, she put it away.

With another sigh, she set the trophy down. It wouldn't do any good to dwell on what could have been—the family they could have become.

Keep busy. The words had served as her mantra over the past three weeks. She'd worked for Cam and Kayla. She'd helped out at the stables. She'd taken Ruby for ice cream. But all of it reminded her of James until it felt like she had started to get her short-term memory back—but all the memories were of him.

What she and Ruby needed to do was make some new memories. And she'd take plenty of pictures to make sure she didn't forget them.

"Ruby," she called, rushing down the hall toward her daughter's room. "Let's go to the beach."

Ruby looked up from her desk. "No thanks."

"Ruby." Bethany tried not to sound impatient. "I know you miss James, but we can't just sit here being sad. We need to do something fun, just the two of us."

"Okay. Then I know what I want to do."

Bethany smiled. She'd expected a harder fight. "And what's that?"

"I want to go see James."

"Oh." The syllable was barely a breath. How was she supposed to tell her daughter no? But there was no way she could say yes. "Ruby, sweetie, I don't think James wants to see us."

But Ruby shook her head, a stubborn glint in her eyes. "That doesn't mean he doesn't need us, Mom. Plus, we never got to tell him that we love him."

"What?" Bethany's eyes snapped to her daughter. "Who said—"

Ruby rolled her eyes. "It's obvious, Mom. Don't worry, I love him too. He's like . . . the dad I always wanted."

Oh no. How was Bethany supposed to hold it together, when her heart was being pulled in so many directions at once?

Protect Ruby. That was what she had to do. Protect Ruby.

No matter if her own heart was screaming that Ruby was right and she did love James.

"Ruby, I don't think James wants a family," she said gently. "Losing his daughter was very hard for him. He's too afraid of what would happen if he lost someone else."

"But Miss Emma says when you fall off the horse, you have to get back up and try again. Otherwise, you'll be afraid for the rest of your life, and no one can live like that."

Bethany blew out a frustrated breath. How did you tell a ten-year-old that life wasn't that easy?

"We have to at least ask him to come back," Ruby added before Bethany could respond. "I know he might say no." Ruby bounced past Bethany and out her bedroom door. "But maybe he'll say yes."

Bethany chewed her lip. She had to be the responsible one here. She had to keep Ruby from getting hurt. She had to . . .

What if Ruby was right?

"All right." Her heart took control of her tongue. "But before we go, I need two things from you."

Ruby nodded.

"First, you have to promise not to get your hopes up."

Ruby nodded again.

"And second, please use the bathroom before we go."

Ruby threw her arms around Bethany. "It's going to be good, Mom, you'll see."

"What'd I say about getting your hopes up?" But Bethany couldn't keep her own hopes from soaring right out the door, leading the way to James.

Chapter 51

James's feet dragged across the grass of the cemetery, the flowers in his hand weighing him down almost as much as his heart. Clouds had begun to roll in a few hours ago, building to an ominous gray mass that seemed to press him harder to the earth with every step.

He hadn't been to Sadie's grave since the funeral. But today was the six-year anniversary of her death, and as much as he'd told himself not to come, he'd felt something pulling him to it. He'd worked all day to ignore it, to push it to the background as he'd always done before. But it was too insistent, and he'd stopped to pick up the flowers, shooting the poor florist a death glare when she had asked the occasion for the bouquet.

He reached the row Sadie's grave was down, and his feet drew to a stop. He stared toward the end of the row, to the third headstone from the edge. The flowers fell from his hand.

He couldn't do this. He couldn't go down there and think about the fact that his little girl was buried under it. A sharp sob threatened to work its way up, but James stuffed it down, the force of the grief folding him in half.

He didn't know how long he stood there, hands braced on his knees, fighting against the waves and waves of memories that surfaced, mingled memories of Sadie and Melissa, of Ruby and Bethany, of laughing and crying, before a hand on his shoulder made him ratchet upright.

"James?" The woman's voice was tentative but familiar, and a fresh rush of pain washed over him.

"Melissa." He should have realized his ex-wife would be here today. His gaze snagged on Melissa's stomach. It bulged the same way it had when . . . "You're expecting?" Gravel filled his words.

She nodded, glancing over her shoulder toward a man who hovered a few rows away. Her new husband, James presumed. Or maybe not so new. They must have been married for two years now, he realized with a start. It still seemed wrong that time kept moving without Sadie.

"Emma didn't tell you?" she asked.

He shook his head dumbly.

"I called her a few weeks ago, but . . ." Melissa looked over her shoulder again, then back at him. "She said you met someone. She has a daughter?"

James sighed, running his hand over his head. He'd been trying so hard not to think about Bethany and Ruby. About the way he'd left them. About how much he missed them. About how badly he wanted to go back. "How do you do it?"

"Do what?" Melissa tipped her head to the side, the way she always had when she wanted to understand someone better. How had he never appreciated that about her?

He searched for words. What was it, exactly, that he didn't know how to do? "Keep going, I guess," he said. "Build a new family? Aren't you terrified something could happen to them too? I couldn't handle it if—" His voice cracked, and he stopped before he broke down.

Melissa smiled gently, rubbing a hand over her belly. "If I knew today that I was only going to get five years with this baby—or one year, or one month, or one day—I'd still want to have that time. I'd cherish it. Isn't that how you feel about . . ." She tilted her head, and he realized she was waiting for him to fill in a name.

"Bethany," he said reluctantly. "And her daughter Ruby." Saying their names made his heart heavy and light all at once. He sighed. He wouldn't have willingly given up a day with Sadie, even if he'd known how short her time would be.

But . . . "I can't just replace her, Melissa. I miss her so much." He pinched the bridge of his nose and blinked up toward the clouds.

"You're not replacing her." Melissa shuffled closer to him. "You'll see her again one day in heaven. But until then, while you're still here, you have to live. Loving Bethany and Ruby doesn't mean you love Sadie any less."

"It's my fault she's gone, Mel. You said it yourself. I don't deserve to love again. Or to be a father again."

A beat of silence followed the awful truth—and then a pair of arms wrapped tightly around him.

He stiffened. It had been a very long time since his ex-wife had hugged him.

"It's not your fault, James." Melissa's voice was thick. "I should have told you that a long time ago. I'm sorry I ever blamed you."

All the resolve, all the determination not to fall apart, seeped out of James, and a sob burst out of his chest, its echo ricocheting off the headstones around them. He gulped, trying to hold back the rest of his grief, but it was useless.

Melissa's arms tightened around him. "You were helping people, James. That's who you are. That doesn't make it your fault. You couldn't have known. You couldn't have done anything differently. You were there with her at the end, and I'm so glad you were." She kept whispering, kept holding him, until his grief was spent.

When he finally pulled away, he swiped at his face and cleared his throat. "I'm sorry. I didn't mean to fall apart like that."

Melissa wiped at his cheek. "I wish you would have fallen apart back when it happened."

Shaking his head, James worked to pull himself together. "I was being strong for you."

Melissa's head shake was adamant. "Maybe that's what you told yourself. But you were doing it for *you*. So you wouldn't have to feel it. And now you're running away from your feelings again."

"I—" James started to argue. But then he let Melissa's words sink in. She was right. He'd directed every ounce of his energy for the past six years to not feeling. To not letting anything hurt him. Until he'd met Bethany and Ruby, and the feeling had started to come back. "I'm sorry," he said instead.

"I know." Melissa bent to pick up his flowers, then wrapped her hand around his elbow. "Come on. Let's go put these on her grave. And then I think you have a call to make."

James sniffed and swallowed. Maybe. He was going to have to take this one step at a time.

Chapter 52

Bethany pulled her phone away from her ear and hung up. Again.

They shouldn't have come. It was her job to protect Ruby, and sitting on the porch of James's house for two hours wasn't the way to do it. She should have insisted they go to the beach instead of letting Ruby talk her into coming here. Stupid impulse control.

Except she knew she couldn't blame her impulse control issues this time. She'd thought it through. And she'd made a deliberate decision to come. She'd wanted so badly to believe that Ruby was right, that James just needed to see them, to hear that they loved him, and then everything would be perfect again.

But given the fact that she'd called him a dozen times since they'd gotten here and he hadn't once picked up, she had to admit that wasn't going to happen.

She turned her phone on again and searched for something nearby that she and Ruby could do. Maybe they could salvage the day before they headed home.

"You want to go to the zoo?"

Ruby shook her head, looking sullen.

"How about this? They have a botanical garden inside domes." She angled her phone so Ruby could see the pictures.

But Ruby barely looked at it.

"Oh, Rubes. I'm sorry. I shouldn't have brought you here."

Ruby's lip trembled, and a tear slid down her cheek. "I'm sorry."

"Oh, sweetie." Bethany wrapped her arms around her daughter. "You don't have anything to be sorry for. I shouldn't have let you think that James could maybe one day be your . . ."

Ruby sniffled and pulled away. "No. That's not it. Do you remember when my school had bring your mom to school day and you didn't come?"

Bethany tightened her arms around her daughter, closing her eyes. How was it that she didn't even remember letting her daughter down yet again?

"I'm sorry, I—"

But Ruby shook her head. "You couldn't have come because I didn't tell you about it on purpose. I didn't want you to come."

"Oh." Bethany kept her grip on her daughter as tears filled her own eyes. She couldn't blame Ruby. But that didn't make it hurt any less.

"I was worried," Ruby said. "Because you always forget things and what if you forgot something and then the kids made fun of you and—"

"Oh, Ruby." Bethany closed her eyes against the ache. She so wanted to be a normal mother for her daughter. To give her a normal life and a normal family. "It's not your job to protect me. It's my job to protect you."

Ruby sniffled. "You do, Mom. And next time I want you to come."

"All right then." Bethany wiped the tears off her daughter's cheeks. "Next time I'll be there. But you might have to do me a favor."

Ruby waited.

"Remind me." Bethany tapped her daughter's nose, and they both giggled.

"Look!" Ruby jumped to her feet and pointed to the street, where a pickup made its way slowly toward the house. "That's James's truck!"

Bethany stood too, grasping at the porch railing as a wave of dizziness she was pretty sure had nothing to do with vertigo almost knocked her off her feet. Her heart thundered so hard that she couldn't hear what Ruby said next, and her mouth dried, gluing her tongue to the back of her teeth. All the things she'd been thinking she'd say when she saw him leaked from her brain, leaving her with only one thought: she loved this man.

He eased the pickup into the driveway, his eyes not coming to them until he'd turned the truck off, and then Bethany saw the surprise on his face. Surprise and— Was that dismay?

Bethany's heart thudded harder as Ruby bolted toward the truck. She wanted to call out to stop her daughter, to keep her from getting hurt if James didn't want to see them.

But her words were trapped under a layer of hope. And Ruby was already to the truck, already throwing her arms around James.

James's arms immediately went around Ruby, but his eyes came to Bethany. They were red-rimmed and his face was drawn.

"I'm sorry." Bethany managed to find her voice as she stepped off the porch. She had to get over there and pull Ruby away from him. He clearly didn't want this. "Ruby, come here."

But James shook his head and lifted one arm from Ruby's back, holding it out to Bethany. She looked to it, then to his face, and he nodded, gesturing her forward.

With a sharp gasp, she let her feet rush for him and threw herself into his arms behind her daughter.

James didn't say a word, just wrapped his arm around her and inhaled, holding them both close.

Ruby was the first to wriggle away. Unwilling to lose the contact with James, Bethany snuggled into her daughter's spot.

"Where were you?" Ruby asked. "We were waiting *forever*."

"I'm sorry." James's voice sounded raw. "I went to the cemetery and then I just . . . drove around."

Bethany pulled back a fraction to study his face. "Are you okay?"

He nodded, but his body shook. "It's been six years. Today."

"Oh, James. I'm sorry. I didn't know. We shouldn't have come." But she held him as tightly as she could, rubbing her hand up and down his back.

He squeezed her so hard that her ribs hurt, but she didn't complain. After a few minutes, he loosened his grip but didn't pull away. "I'm glad you came."

"Me too," Ruby piped up. "When you guys are done hugging, Mom and I have to tell you something."

James's chuckle was quiet but so good to hear. He kept one arm wrapped around Bethany but turned to look at Ruby.

"Well," Ruby said boldly, and Bethany smiled, overwhelmed by how fortunate she was to parent this little creature. "We came here because—" Ruby broke off. "Um. Because we—"

She gave Bethany a helpless look.

And for once, Bethany didn't have to search for words. They were right there. "We came here to tell you we love you," she said to James.

"Yeah," Ruby jumped in. "And we know you're scared. And we know you might not come back to Hope Springs. But we thought you should know. And also we hope you do. Come back."

Bethany laughed at her daughter's boisterous return to speaking but grew serious as James cleared his throat.

"You came here to tell me that?" He looked from Ruby to Bethany and then back to Ruby, who nodded vigorously.

James tipped his head back, blinking up at the sky, and Bethany's heart nearly gave out. He was going to say it didn't matter. That he couldn't come back with them. And she was going to have to pick up the pieces for her daughter. And for herself.

Finally, James brought his eyes to hers. "I'm glad you came." He turned to Ruby. "Because I love you too." And then his eyes were on Bethany's, and he was pulling her tight to him. "Ruby," he called. "Close your eyes a second." He brought his face toward Bethany's. "I love you," he whispered, before his lips closed over hers.

"I'm not closing my eyes," Ruby called. They both laughed but didn't pull apart, until Ruby was there too, throwing her arms around them both.

Chapter 53

"Mom says she'll be ready in a second." Ruby bent to scoop up Mrs. Whiskers as the cat tried to make an escape out the door. "Want to see the bracelets I made with the kit you gave me for Christmas? They're so cool."

"Absolutely." James danced from foot to foot. "But first come outside for a second."

Ruby eyed him doubtfully, readjusting her hold on the cat, who was struggling to jump out of her arms. "It's cold out."

"I know." James's breath floated in front of his face. Though they'd only had a dusting of snow so far this winter—just in time for Christmas—the days had grown frigid as the New Year approached. "Just for a second. I have to ask you something." He was going to burst if he didn't ask her right now. But he couldn't risk Bethany overhearing.

"What?" Ruby seemed totally oblivious to the fact that he was trying to be sneaky.

"It's a secret."

Bingo.

Ruby's eyes lit up and she tossed the cat to the ground behind her, stepping out the door in her socks. "What secret?"

James reached behind her to pull the door closed. "Here." He took off his jacket and wrapped it around her, pulling the hood over her head. Ruby giggled as her whole face disappeared.

That was no good. James needed to see her reaction to his question. He slid the hood back enough that he could see her face. The sun was just setting, but there was still enough light that he could read her expression.

"What's the secret?" Ruby whispered, leaning toward him and looking around furtively, as if they were spies.

"I—" James swallowed. Was he really ready to do this? But he knew he was. His certainty had grown day by day for the past six months.

Ruby tilted her head at him. "Did you forget?"

James laughed. "No. I have to ask you something."

Ruby watched him expectantly.

"Remember when you said I'd make a good dad?" James rubbed his hands together against the cold. He hadn't expected a second chance to be a father.

Ruby nodded.

"Now that you know me better, do you still think that?" He held his breath as Ruby stared at him.

"No," she said slowly, and his heart flopped. "You wouldn't make a good dad. You would make the best dad." She giggled as if she'd told a great joke.

He let out a rough breath.

Ruby tilted her head at him. "Why?" Her eyes widened. "Wait. Do you mean . . ."

"I want to ask your mom to marry me. But that would mean—"

"You would be my dad!" Ruby threw her arms, clad in the puffy sleeves of his jacket, around him. "Are you going to ask her tonight? On New Year's Eve? That's so romantic."

James mock frowned. "If I'm going to be your dad, I don't want to hear any more from you about romance. You're too young." But he couldn't keep the huge smile from overtaking the frown.

"Do you have a ring?" she asked.

James pointed to the jacket she wore. "In the pocket."

"Can I see it?"

He glanced at the door. No sign of Bethany. "Sure."

Ruby reached her hand into the jacket pocket, withdrawing a velvety ring box. She eased it open to reveal the simple marquise cut diamond.

"Wow!" Ruby gaped at it. "It's so pretty. You have good taste for a guy."

James laughed. "Thanks. I think. Now put it away before your mom—"

The door opened behind them, and Ruby snapped the box closed and slid her hand into the pocket with a conspiratorial giggle.

"What are you two doing out here?"

"Nothing, Mom." Ruby squeaked past her and back into the house.

"Hmm." Bethany gave him a questioning look, and James pulled her in for a kiss.

"Happy New Year's Eve." He ran a hand down the sleeve of her soft blue sweater, incredibly grateful once again that he'd come back. That he hadn't let his fear keep him from experiencing this joy. "You look beautiful. As always."

"Thank you." Bethany dropped her eyes for a moment, then looked up at him with a smile. "So where are we going?"

"You'll see. Grab your coat. And a hat. And gloves."

Behind them, Ruby giggled, and Bethany glanced over her shoulder at her as she pulled on a thick white jacket. "What's going on with you?"

Ruby peered past her mom toward James, and he winked and held a finger to his lips.

"Nothing." Ruby giggled again. "I'm just excited to play with baby Evelyn. Plus Uncle Cam said I can stay up until ten." She passed Bethany her purse and nudged her toward the door.

"Ruby?" James looked at the jacket she was still wearing. "I think you're going to need to change into your own coat."

Ruby clapped a hand over her mouth. "Oh yeah. I almost forgot about the—"

James shot her a warning look, and she clapped a second hand over her mouth.

He rolled his eyes.

If he wasn't careful, Ruby was going to ask Bethany before he had a chance. Ruby wriggled out of the coat and passed it to him.

"You two are up to something." Bethany gave them each a mock suspicious look.

"I'm sure we don't know what you're talking about." James held the door open for Bethany, reaching behind to give her daughter—maybe soon his daughter—a fist bump.

Chapter 54

You have to tell him. The thought pounded against Bethany's brain again and again. First, she'd told herself that she'd wait until after they'd dropped Ruby off at Cam and Kayla's. But they'd dropped Ruby off twenty minutes ago, and still she hadn't found the courage. James hadn't said much either, but he'd probably had a long day at work.

Work. That was what they could talk about.

"How was work today?"

"There was a break-in at Mrs. Marzetti's."

Bethany gasped. "Is she all right?"

"Yep. Caught the burglar with his hand in the cookie jar. Literally."

"Someone broke in to steal her cookies?"

"A raccoon. I had to call the DNR. Took us an hour, but we got the little guy. I thought about giving him to Ruby as a pet but . . ."

"Don't you dare." But Bethany laughed with him.

This was so good. So right.

But she had to tell him—

"I think I've convinced Pete to be a mentor for the new fishing program too." He glanced toward her. "The one we're starting for at-risk kids."

"I remember." But she smiled. She appreciated his thoughtful way of reminding her of things she may have forgotten without making her feel foolish.

"I'm still working on Chris, but he's harder to get through to. Got into a fight at school last week."

Bethany nodded. She knew too well how hard it was to leave a lifestyle you'd grown accustomed to. But she trusted that James would get through to the kid eventually.

Silence fell for a moment, and Bethany knew she couldn't put it off any longer.

"We're here." He slowed the truck and turned into a driveway, smiling at her with such a look of anticipation that she swallowed her comment and directed her eyes out the window.

James eased the vehicle past an old farmhouse and parked in front of a large red barn with Christmas lights twinkling along its roofline.

"Is this the same place you took Ruby and me to?" It looked similar but not quite right—unless that was her memory playing tricks on her.

"Nope." James grinned at her. "Austin and Leah told me about this place. They have sleigh rides, and I thought since you can't ride a horse, it would be the next best—" He faltered. "You don't like it?"

"It's not that. It's—" No. She couldn't do this to him now. "It's just that there's not much snow."

James smiled mysteriously. "Don't worry about that." He opened his door, pulling a stocking cap over his ears as his breath curled around his face.

Bethany exhaled slowly as she watched him round the truck to open her door. She had to tell him. It wasn't fair not to. But what if it was too much for him? What if he ran again and didn't come back this time?

He reached her door and pulled it open, taking her hand to help her out. The moment her feet touched the ground, he pulled her to him in a crushing hug. "I love you," he murmured into her hat. "Do you know that?"

She bobbed her head against his jacket, tears pricking at her eyes. She did know that. And it only made this so much harder. James kissed her forehead and wrapped his hand around her mittened one. "Come on." He tugged her toward the barn.

As they stepped inside, Bethany gasped. It was a winter wonderland. A path of Christmas trees and fake snow and lights wound through the building, ending at large doors on the far side.

James opened them, and Bethany could only stare.

"It's . . ." She took a careful step outside and bent to touch the fluffy white powder that extended in a wide ribbon from the door into the woods in front of them. Sure enough, it was cold and powdery and melted in her hands. She looked at the ground on either side of the trail, where brown grass showed through the sparse dusting of snow they'd gotten before Christmas. "How in the world . . ."

An older woman chuckled as she came up next to them, pointing to a gray pipe that stood in the shadows at the side of the trail. "We make it. Because everyone needs a little Christmas magic." The sound of jingle bells floated on the wind, and the woman smiled. "And speaking of magic. Here comes your ride."

Bethany couldn't ignore the wave of excitement that rolled over her as she spotted the beautiful draft horses pulling the sleigh, and she wrapped her arm around James's.

He smiled and kissed the top of her hat. "So this was a good idea?"

"The best." She let herself forget everything else as she climbed into the sleigh and snuggled into the seat next to him. The warmth of his arm around her enveloped her in a cocoon where it felt like nothing could ever hurt her. Nothing from outside. And nothing from inside.

The driver urged the horses forward, and Bethany let herself marvel at the lantern-lined path that stretched in front of them, the stars that twinkled above them, the sleigh bells that jingled around them. If only this moment could last forever. If only she never had to tell him.

James shifted, unwrapping his arm from around her and sliding his hand into his coat pocket. "I have something for you."

"James. You just gave me a Christmas present. You can't give me anoth—" Her eyes fell on the hand he'd pulled out of his pocket. It held a small velvet jewelry box. She swallowed, telling herself it wasn't what she thought it was. It was probably a necklace. Or maybe a pair of earrings.

With his other hand, James reached for hers and pulled her mitten off.

She swallowed. It wasn't a necklace or earrings in that box.

"James. Wait." She gulped at the cold night air. *Lord, give me strength.* It wasn't fair to let him do this without telling him the truth.

"I— Wait?" Confusion wrinkled the part of his brow that peeked out from under his hat.

"There's something I have to tell you."

James wrapped his hand around hers but didn't put her mitten back on. "What is it?"

"I—" Oh, why did she have to do this?

"Bethany?" A quaver of fear shook his voice, and he slid closer to her. "What is it?"

"I had a doctor appointment yesterday." The steam from her words hung between them, blurring her view of him.

"And?" His grip on her hand tightened.

"And—" Bethany rocked forward as the sleigh drew to a halt, and James threw out his arm to steady her.

"Here we are." The driver hopped down from the sleigh and held out a hand to help Bethany down. "You two are in this gazebo." Bethany's eyes swept over the glass-enclosed gazebos that dotted the woods, soft lighting glowing from inside each, but then went right back to James. He had climbed out of the sleigh and stood a few feet from her. But he may as well have been miles away for the gulf she felt between them. His jaw was tight, his hands fisted at his sides—she wondered briefly where the ring had gone.

"Your server will be by with your food shortly." The driver climbed into the sleigh. "Enjoy your meal. I'll be back for your return ride." The bells jingled cheerfully as the horses trotted off.

Bethany stared after the sleigh, then gazed at the gazebos. Couples were already dining and laughing in a few of them, and one pair was dancing.

"Let's go inside." James's voice was hollow. He gestured her forward but didn't hold her hand.

The rush of warm air that surrounded them as they entered wasn't enough to chase away her chill.

James led her to the table and held out a chair for her, then sat down across from her.

Bethany fiddled with the zipper on her jacket but didn't take it off. As soon as he heard what she had to say, he might want to hop the next sleigh out of here.

"The doctor," he prompted.

She let out a breath. She could tell him everything was fine. That she had a clean bill of health. But he'd find out eventually. "It was a checkup. But she wanted to do a scan, just to make sure there weren't any new aneurysms."

James sucked in a breath so loud it made her jump, but he nodded for her to continue.

"She found something," Bethany whispered. "It's small and not an immediate danger, but she wants to do surgery to clip it. Just to be safe." She choked on her swallow as James's face crumpled. He shoved his chair back, pacing to the other side of the small space, his hand gripping the back of his neck.

When he didn't move, she took a breath, slid her chair back, and stood. "Do you want to leave?"

Chapter 55

James blinked, unseeing, at the blurred forest out the gazebo window.

How could this be happening? Again? Every time he loved someone.

"James?" Bethany's tentative voice cut through the fog of his thoughts, piercing him right to the heart.

He wanted to be with Bethany more than anything.

For however long they might have together.

The realization hit him so hard that he staggered backward, then spun and strode to her, sweeping her hands in his as he dropped to one knee.

"James." Bethany's eyes widened as she shook her head. "You don't have to—"

But he gently pulled her down so that she was sitting in the chair in front of him. "I want to." He nearly choked on his emotion but he wasn't going to let that stop him. "I want to marry you, Bethany. For better or worse. For richer or poorer. In sickness and health. I want to be with you through all of it."

"But what if . . ." She looked away.

James dropped his head to her knees, unable to breathe. What if . . .

He straightened and reached a hand up to her cheek. "I've spent the past six years regretting all the days I didn't have, when I should have been thanking God for the ones I did. I won't make that mistake again."

Bethany bit her lip, and he could see the uncertainty in her eyes.

"Do you remember the day we met?" he asked.

Bethany shook her head, her eyes falling.

"That's okay. I'll remember it for both of us. I had just gotten to Hope Springs, and I was feeling bitter and resentful and angry. And you were in line, looking all beautiful and flustered at the same time because you forgot your purse and you were trying to buy Ruby a birthday present."

Bethany winced, and he slid his hand into hers. "I know you hate when things like that happen. But look how God used it. You told me once that God puts people in our lives for a reason. I didn't understand that then. But I do now. He put you in my life for a reason. You showed me that it was possible to love again. And that he hadn't abandoned me. I love you, Bethany. And Ruby."

Bethany gasped. "Ruby! She—"

"Sends her blessing." James chuckled. "I asked her when I came to pick you up. That's what we were doing outside."

Bethany laughed, the sound filling James with hope.

He swallowed and gripped both of her hands tightly in one of his as he pulled the ring box back out of his pocket. "Bethany, I don't know how many days we have in this world. Only God knows when he'll call us home. But until then—" He had to stop to clear his throat. "Until then, I want to spend every day at your side. As your husband." He let go of her hands to open the ring box. "Will you marry me?"

Bethany looked from the ring to his eyes, biting her lip and giving him a thoughtful look. James's heart sank. "What is it? What are you unsure about?"

"Nothing." Her lips slid slowly into a smile. "I just wanted to make sure that I had my impulses under control before I answered."

"Okay." He nodded slowly. "I can wait."

"I think that's long enough." Her smile grew into a full-out laugh. "Yes, James. I will marry you." She bent and lowered her face to his, her lips catching his on a breath as his arms went around her.

"Oh wait." She drew back suddenly.

"What? What's wrong?" He grabbed her hands, but she pulled one away and reached into her jacket pocket for her phone.

"Nothing." She grinned. "I just don't want to forget this moment." She snapped a picture of him still on one knee.

He slid the ring onto her finger. "Trust me, I won't let you forget."

Epilogue

"It's snowing!" Ruby's gleeful cry rang through the house.

Bethany shot upright in bed, reaching for her notebook. She already knew what was written on today's date, but she wanted to verify it anyway.

There was only one item on her list: "Get married!"

With a silly laugh at herself, she sprang out of bed, then immediately clutched the dresser so she wouldn't tip over. Passing out wasn't the way she wanted to start her wedding day. She felt for the stitches on the back of her head where they'd cut a small incision for the successful surgery to clip her aneurysm last week. Fortunately, Kayla had offered to let Bethany borrow the veil from her wedding, so it would be hidden. And she was going to wear Leah's dress. And Grace's shoes.

Warmth went through Bethany as she thought of the friends who had surrounded her since she'd moved to Hope Springs. Who had made it possible for her to plan this wedding in only three weeks when Ruby had insisted that she couldn't wait until summer to be a family and James had heartily agreed. Who would be here with her on this new adventure.

She followed the sound of Ruby's voice to the living room window, gasping at the thick layer of white that covered everything. Windswept flakes whipped past the house, blowing into large drifts that blocked the driveway. It wasn't just snowing. It was a blizzard.

And from the looks of it, the plows hadn't made it through yet. Bethany glanced at the clock. They were supposed to be at the church in two hours. Hopefully the roads would be cleared by then. They'd planned a small wedding since it was such short notice, but at this rate, they'd be lucky if even she and James made it.

"We may have to sled to church," she muttered to Ruby.

"Really?" Her daughter's eyes widened, as if she was totally up for that.

But Bethany shook her head. "No, silly goose. I'm not going to sled in a wedding dress. Should we—"

She broke off as the lights flickered, the thrum of the furnace suddenly cutting out. With a groan, she reached for the light switch. Nothing.

"Now what, Mom?" Ruby asked, as if Bethany would have an answer.

Bethany ruffled her daughter's hair. "I have no idea. But we'll figure it out together. First things first, let's get some breakfast. How does cold cereal sound?"

Once she had Ruby settled, she picked up her phone to call James. But there was no answer.

She supposed she'd have to get ready as planned and pray the roads cleared by the time she had to leave.

She was just pouring Ruby a second bowl of cereal when the doorbell rang.

She blinked at Ruby. "Who on earth could have made it through that snow?"

As she pulled the front door open, a joyous laugh burst from her. "James." She stepped into his arms, looking over his shoulder at the crew he'd brought with him: his mom and William—who had gotten married a few months ago and moved back to Hope Springs—along with Emma and Cam and Kayla and baby Evelyn.

"Spencer and Tyler are picking up everyone else. They said they'd take trips if they need to." He brushed a kiss on her forehead, then stepped aside so the others could enter the house.

"I don't— What are—" Bethany tried to make sense of what was happening here. Other than the fact that her little house was soon going to be bursting at the seams.

"Did you think I was going to let a snowstorm keep me from marrying you today? Dan called me last night to say the heat was out in the church."

"Last night?" She blinked at him. "Why didn't you call me?"

James took her hand. "I didn't want you to worry. Everything's under control. We have a contingency plan."

"We do?" She didn't remember making one.

"We're getting married here." James grinned at her.

"Here?" Bethany looked around her small house. "But the power just went out."

"Nothing a little firewood and candles can't fix. We'll be nice and cozy." He kissed her lips gently, then gave her a nudge toward the hallway. "And besides, you're here. That's the most important part. Now go get ready. Unless you want to get married in that." He grinned at her flannel pajamas. "Which I'm totally fine with, by the way."

"Give me an hour."

"I'm not sure I can wait that long." He smiled at her, then turned toward the door.

"Wait. Where are you going?"

"To grab my tuxedo out of the truck. Can't get married in this thing." He patted the puffy sleeves of his ski jacket.

"Come on. Let's go get you ready." Emma pointed down the hall, pulling off her stocking cap to reveal the short layer of hair that had grown back since she'd finished her chemo and been declared cancer-free. "You too, Ruby."

"This is going to be the best day ever, Mom." Ruby skipped ahead of them.

Bethany swallowed, too overcome for a moment to answer. "Yes," she finally managed. "I think it will."

As she got ready, Bethany heard the sound of the door opening and more people filling the house with laughter. Her stomach looped in anticipation, and her hand shook so much that Kayla had to help with her makeup.

But an hour later, as promised, she emerged from her bedroom in her wedding dress and veil—she'd decided to forgo the shoes, since she was at home.

"Wait here," Kayla said as she wheeled down the hallway. "I'll tell them you're ready."

"You look pretty, Mom," Ruby whispered as they waited.

"Thank you, sweetheart. So do you."

Ruby beamed at her. "I'm glad you're my mom." She slipped her hand into Bethany's, and there was no way to hold it in anymore. Tears burst from Bethany in a gasp, and she bent to pull her daughter into a hug.

"I'm glad you're my daughter." She sniffled, trying to pull herself together as Kayla returned and gestured for them to come forward.

The voices drifting toward them quieted as she and Ruby followed Kayla toward the living room.

But the moment she reached the end of the hallway, Bethany burst into tears all over again, even as her lips stretched into what might have been the world's biggest smile. She beamed at the room through her blurry vision. Candles glowed on the mantle and the shabby little TV stand she'd picked up at a garage sale years ago, a fire roared in the fireplace, her friends were seated and standing on every available surface, and at the front of them all stood James, blinking and wiping at his own eyes as he waited for her.

This, she thought suddenly. This was the purpose she'd been searching for. The way she could be a woman God used. She'd been so convinced it had to be something big, something that would prove her worth. When really, she could see it in the faces of all the people gathered here. God had created her to be part of this family of believers. To serve him together with them.

From somewhere, strains of Canon in D filled the room, and Bethany's feet moved as if the music were pulling her forward. Ruby's hand was still in hers, and she tugged her daughter with her. She and James had already agreed that they wanted Ruby to be standing next to them as they said their vows.

As they reached James's side, he pulled each of them into a hug, then they all turned to Dan as the music stopped.

"I know this isn't what you had planned for this day," Dan started, and everyone chuckled. "But in a way, I think it's fitting. You both have been through a lot of things you didn't plan for. Hard things and good things. And God has been with you through them all. Even when you didn't realize it."

James reached for Bethany's hand as Dan invited them to recite the vows they'd written.

"Bethany—" James's voice cracked, and he cleared his throat with a rueful smile. "Sorry. I didn't expect— Well, you. I didn't expect you to come into my life. Or you." He turned to smile at Ruby, and Bethany's heart hummed. He was going to be a wonderful father to her daughter. "But I'm so glad you did. You helped show me the way back to faith. And that I could love again. I don't know what this life is going to hold for any of us. But I promise that whatever it holds, we will face it together. Because I will be with you through it all: sickness, health, lost cats, and crazy homework projects, good days and bad days. I want to live it all with you."

Bethany took a shaky breath and wiped her cheeks as James's eyes reflected the sincerity of his words.

"Bethany?" Dan looked to her expectantly.

"What?" She couldn't peel her gaze away from James.

"Your vows?" Dan prompted.

"My . . ." Her mind went completely blank as she turned to him. Had she written vows? She was pretty sure she had. But what had she done with them? "I'm sorry, I . . ."

"Here, Mom," Ruby whispered, passing Bethany a crumpled sheet of paper.

Bethany gave her a quizzical look, but Ruby nodded toward the paper. "Read it," she whispered.

Bethany unfolded the paper, staring down at her daughter's handwriting. *Sometimes my mom forgets things*, it began, and Bethany blinked again at her daughter.

"Out loud," Ruby whispered.

"Ruby—"

But Ruby looked so earnest that she couldn't refuse.

"Sometimes my mom forgets things," she began, licking her too-dry lips. "But there are three things I know she'll never forget. 1) Me." Bethany chuckled along with the rest of the group, reaching to give her daughter a hug before directing her eyes back to the paper. "2) God. And 3) You, James."

Bethany's hand shook as she looked up at James, whose face glowed with a tender smile in the candlelight.

She let the paper fall to her side. She would read the rest later. But right now, she had some words of her own she needed to say. "James." It came out as a whisper, and she tried again. She wanted everyone to hear this. "James, my life has been . . . a mess at times. And I don't even remember all of it. But I do remember that when I was a little girl, I used to dream about the kind of man I would marry. Someone who was patient and loving, who made me laugh, who would do anything for me. As I got older, I realized that kind of man didn't exist." She offered him a wobbly smile. "But then I met you. I might not remember the exact date we met or where or even what happened. But I do remember that it changed my life. And I know that sounds corny and maybe exaggerated, but it's true. Because until then, having someone at my side, someone to go through this crazy life with, to be a family with us, was only a dream. And now—" She smiled from him to Ruby. "Now it's real."

The rest of the service, as they exchanged rings and prayed and Dan said a blessing, passed in a blur, until the next thing Bethany knew, Dan was introducing them as Mr. and Mrs. James Wood and their friends were clapping and Ruby was throwing her arms around both of them.

"I was right. This is the best day ever!" Ruby declared.

Bethany nodded, her head pressed against James's chest.

"Okay, I brought food," Leah called. "I left it out in the car so it would stay cold. Who wants to help me get it?"

As their friends volunteered to help Leah get things set up, James grabbed his ski jacket and wrapped it around Bethany, then tugged her out the back door into the still-falling snow. The wind had calmed, leaving a peaceful hush over the backyard.

"James, what—"

But he pulled her into a kiss that stole her words, stole her thoughts, stole everything but the overwhelming joy that filled her from the inside out.

"Sorry." James pulled back, keeping his arms wrapped around her waist. "I just needed a minute alone with my wife."

Bethany giggled at her new title. "Thank you for this." She snuggled closer to his warmth. "It was perfect." But a slight shadow hovered in the back of her mind. "What if I forget it?"

James shook his head. "You won't. We made a video. You can watch it every day if you want."

"But—"

James silenced her with a kiss. "It doesn't matter if you remember this day. It's only a moment. We have forever ahead of us. I'll help you when you can't remember. You'll help me when I get scared about the future. And we'll figure it all out together. Deal?"

Bethany nodded, bringing her lips to his again. "You've got yourself a deal."

"Good." James's lips played over hers. "We should probably go back inside and get some food."

"I know. But first, there's something I have to do." She dug in the pocket of the jacket he'd wrapped around her, coming out with his phone.

He raised an eyebrow. "Who could you possibly need to call? Everyone we know is here."

She laughed, swiped at the screen, leaned back into him, and held the phone out at arm's length. "Say 'just married.'"

James wrapped an arm around her and pulled her in close as they recited the phrase together. Bethany snapped the picture, then studied their smiling image. "There." She tucked the phone back into the coat pocket. "The first memory of our life together."

"With many more to come." James nuzzled his face into her hair, then led her into the house.

Thanks for reading books 7-9 in the Hope Springs series! I hope you enjoyed becoming part of the big Hope Springs family as Grace and Levi, Cam and Kayla, and James and Bethany each found their happily ever after. Join the whole group in the final Hope Springs book, Not Until The End, as Emma finally gets her own chance to fall in love!

And be sure to sign up for my newsletter to get Ethan and Ariana's story, Not Until Christmas, as a free gift.

Visit https://www.valeriembodden.com/gift or use the QR code below to join.

More Books by Valerie M. Bodden

Hope Springs

Not Until Forever (Sophie & Spencer)
Not Until This Moment (Jared & Peyton)
Not Until You (Nate & Violet)
Not Until Us (Dan & Jade)
Not Until Christmas Morning (Leah & Austin)
Not Until This Day (Tyler & Isabel)
Not Until Someday (Grace & Levi)
Not Until Now (Cam & Kayla)
Not Until Then (Bethany & James)
Not Until The End (Emma & Owen)

River Falls

Pieces of Forever (Joseph & Ava)
Songs of Home (Lydia & Liam)
Memories of the Heart (Simeon & Abigail)
Whispers of Truth (Benjamin & Summer)

Promises of Mercy (Judah & Faith)
Hearts of Hope (Zeb & Victoria)

River Falls Christmas Romances

Christmas of Joy (Madison & Luke)

Love on Sanctuary Shores

Trusting His Promise (Beckett & Jo)

Want to know when my next book releases?

You can follow me on Amazon to be the first to know when my next book releases! Just visit amazon.com/author/valeriembodden and click the follow button.

Acknowledgements

First and above all, I thank my Heavenly Father, who gave me this gift of writing and has led me to this point in my life where I can use that gift to serve him daily. I certainly haven't done anything to earn or deserve this privilege—and I stand in awe every day of what he is doing with my books. I thank him for leading me to these stories of hope, love, and redemption. And most of all, I thank him for forgiving every last one of my sins through the blood of his Son, Jesus Christ. I pray that through my books, readers will be reminded that all their sins are forgiven in Jesus as well.

I thank God every day for the blessing of my family. For my husband, who not only sets an example of Christ's love for me every day but who is also my number one fan and strongest supporter—not to mention an incredible book cover designer. For our four children, who have taught me more about love and grace and trust and forgiveness than I'll ever be able to teach them. For my parents, who raised me in a Christian home, where I knew God's love from before I can even remember. For my sister, my in-laws, and my extended family, who have supported and encouraged me as I have worked to get this series into the world.

A heartfelt thank you also goes out to my amazing Advance Reader Team. If I named all the people who have contributed their thoughts and feedback on the three books in this volume, the list would go on for another two pages! So let me just say that I'm so grateful for all of you. It's been wonderful to get to know you and to consider you friends. Thank you for sharing your honest thoughts on my books, brainstorming with me when needed, and giving so generously of yourselves to encourage me.

One of the amazing and unexpected benefits of writing books in the digital age is that I have had an opportunity to connect with readers from around the world. Thank you for being one of them! I know this world is a busy place—and I thank you for choosing to spend some of your time with me and the characters of Hope Springs. I hope you've enjoyed their journey.

About the Author

Valerie M. Bodden has three great loves: Jesus, her family, and books. And chocolate (okay, four great loves). She is living out her happily ever after with her high-school-sweetheart-turned-husband and their four children. Her life wouldn't make a terribly exciting book, as it has a happy beginning and middle, and someday when she goes to her heavenly home, it will have a happy end.

She was born and raised in Wisconsin but recently moved with her family to Texas, where they're all getting used to the warm weather (she doesn't miss the snow even a little bit, though the rest of the family does) and saying y'all instead of you guys.

Valerie writes emotion-filled Christian fiction that weaves real-life problems, real-life people, and real-life faith. Her characters may (okay, will) experience some heartache along the way, but she will always give them a happy ending.

Feel free to stop by www.valeriembodden.com to say hi. She loves visitors! And while you're there, you can sign up for your free story.

Printed in Dunstable, United Kingdom